FROM THE MISSISSIPPI WESTWARD
TO THE PACIFIC COAST . . . .

WONDERFUL SHORT FICTION
THAT CONVEYS THE WESTERN EXPERIENCE

"Sleepwalkers" by Ursula K. LeGuin

The guests at Hannah's Hideaway, cabins set in the Northwest Woods, never guess the truth about the past of a quiet, hardworking maid named Ava.

"Winter of '19" ~~~~ ~oig

A brilliantly written tale of the ~~~~ ~ts the struggle of two sheep ranchers to save ~~~~ both the danger and the promise of life ~ ~~~~

"~~~~ ~y Tan

This story of a Ch~~~~ ~asts two generations, one the immigrant who strugg~~~~ ~merican, and one the American-born daughter who is s~ ~nt and yet so similar to her China-born parent.

AND 43 OTHER SUPERB, ORIGINAL STORIES THAT ARE
ON THE LEADING EDGE OF CONTEMPORARY
AMERICAN FICTION

DREAMERS AND DESPERADOES

Also by Craig Lesley:

RIVER SONG

WINTERKILL

TALKING LEAVES:
Contemporary Native American
Short Stories

DREAMERS
AND
DESPERADOES

CONTEMPORARY
SHORT FICTION
OF THE
AMERICAN WEST

CO-EDITED BY
CRAIG LESLEY
AND
KATHERYN STAVRAKIS

Craig Lesley
12-5-93

A LAUREL TRADE PAPERBACK
Published by
Dell Publishing
a division of
Bantam Doubleday Dell Publishing Group, Inc.
1540 Broadway
New York, New York 10036

ISBN: 0-440-50517-8

Printed in the United States of America

Published simultaneously in Canada

May 1993

10 9 8 7 6 5 4 3 2 1

BVG

CONTENTS

INTRODUCTION

When I was fourteen and working in the peppermint fields of central Oregon, I was run over by a mint chopper, a wicked farm implement —first cousin to a corn chopper. If you mention my name around Madras, most likely that's how people there still remember me. In those days a lot of transient workers came through towns following the harvests: wheat in Grass Valley and Moro, apples in Hood River and up into Washington, potatoes, alfalfa, and mint near my home.

Some were women but most were men with easy laughs and red-rimmed troubled eyes. Their hands were scarred and broken-knuck-led from fights and field-doctoring decrepit farm equipment. Their battered cars served as motel rooms and featured expired license plates from California, Montana, Texas. Nearly all were hardworking, honest, and reliable—unless they were drinking. Their troubles ran as deep as the creases in their faces—difficulties with the law, family— tales of old wounds and long-nursed grudges. "Long-suffering" was how my uncle summed it up, and I heard one worker named Reno put it this way when we were taking a coffee break in the shade of the chopper's boom: "If life doesn't deal you enough trouble, your family will."

The details of being run over by the chopper remain blurry, but I woke up praying, surrounded by a tight ring of these men who as-sured me I was going to make it and tried to kid me a little. Under-neath, though, they thought I was a goner, and their tense smiles indicated they'd seen these kinds of troubles before. One had been a medic in the service and did some minor patching until the ambu-lance arrived.

In those days the ambulance was run by volunteers, and two stayed with me in the back on the thirty-eight-mile run to Prineville, the nearest hospital then. I recognized one as a welder who umpired Babe Ruth baseball games. The week before, he had thrown me out for disputing a call. The second worked at the plywood mill and coached a rival team. But in my condition, neither recognized me, although my Babe Ruth baseball cap covered what was left of my right hand.

Three weeks after touch-and-go intensive care at the Prineville hospital, I could have visitors for a few minutes, and I was surprised when three of the field workers showed up bearing a large Motorola transistor radio. Their car had gone kaput, so they had hitchhiked to Prineville and it cost them a day's wages. The radio cost $39.50. These men made $1.25 an hour, $1.50 if they could operate equipment. I was amazed, remain amazed, at their generosity. Thirty-two years later, I still treasure that radio, even though I have no idea where those men have gone.

◆

Putting my way through college, I longshored in Alaska, worked at the Bunker Hill Lead and Zinc Company in Kellogg, Idaho, helped out my uncle Oscar Lange Junior at the Deschutes River Guide Service. Everywhere, I encountered hardworking, generous people who stood up to their troubles or laughed them away as long as they could. These included men and women, for my mother was a single parent raising my sister and me on a secretary's salary.

The West I know contains working people living a hardscrabble existence and trying to stay ahead of the bills and banks. Many are descendants of pioneers who headed out West to find a better life somehow. This was a diverse group of adventurers, minorities, criminals, religious zealots—the dreamers and the disinherited.

Only the Indians were here at first, and perhaps they feel the deepest sense of displacement. When I worked on *River Song*, I spent months with the Wanapum, Columbia River Indians who were trying to live the traditional way, make a living fishing for salmon. Most had shoestring operations, and each day was a challenge to keep their boats floating. Once, all the river and its tributaries were theirs. Now they cling to a few rocky sites and dream that the diminishing salmon runs will increase.

As we worked on this anthology, we intended to make certain that working people were represented in the stories. During the years I served as fiction editor for *Writers' Forum* at the University of Colorado at Colorado Springs, I wasn't seeing enough good stories about people who worked. Too many of the pieces that came in were about professionals suffering the angst of a midlife crisis. Their troubles consisted of cocktail parties, committee meetings, and a tawdry affair or two. We longed for stories about characters named Pinky who worked at the twenty-four-hour towing company and saved an accident victim with the Jaws-of-Life.

In this collection, working people are represented. Barbara Kingsolver's narrator in "Why I Am a Danger to the Public" is tough, funny, and *union*. A determined Hispanic laborer at the mine controlled by the Emerson Company, she is on strike for improved wages and working conditions. In striking, she is following her father's lead. Some of the other women in town are jealous of her, especially Vonda, whose father owned the local drugstore. As a child the narrator was not allowed to sit at the counter, And because her family could not afford them, she admired the dangling bracelets Vonda wore. This story chronicles the struggle between the haves and the have-nots in a small town, and the narrator emerges with strength and dignity.

Ursula K. LeGuin's motel maid Ava accommodates her schedule to meet the needs of the motel's guests. Each guest has a different view of Ava, and the motel owner claims, "She's reliable, she's honest, and she's permanent." As the story unfolds, the reader comes to realize that she's a survivor, having suffered horrible family tragedy. In reading this story, I thought again of Reno's words "If life doesn't deal you enough trouble, your family will." LeGuin describes Ava's "walking carefully, one foot in front of the other, no sudden movements." Clearly she is on a precarious tightrope.

Frequently, working people are without a safety net, one disaster away from abrupt change. In Richard Ford's "Optimists," the young narrator Frank has witnessed his father strike and accidentally kill another man. Reflecting on that incident, Frank observes, "The most important things of your life can change so suddenly, so unrecoverably, that you can forget even the most important of them and their connections, you are so taken up by the chanciness of all that's happened and by all that could and will happen next."

In Annick Smith's "It's Come to This," the narrator remembers her husband, Caleb, "alive one minute, dead the next." And she recalls how he uttered, "Oh dear," then fell to the maple floor, "in one motion, a giant tree cut down." Her life as a widow taking care of children and managing the ranch is a Spartan one, but she finds a second love after a rocky courtship with a gyppo logger. Under the harshest conditions, love appears, redeeming the characters from their difficult times. "Grief will come," Smith's character notes. "Choose love."

—◆—

Driving through the semi-arid high desert of the West, one sees weathered wooden gates along the backroads, marking the entrances to vast ranches. Usually, the ranches themselves are not visible from the highway, and one can see only the two dirt tracks winding to the distance. It's desolate country at first glance—sagebrush and scattered junipers, an occasional loping coyote. But there's beauty here, too, in the shadows and sunsets. The ranch's brand adorns the gate, and frequently it has another marker—a worn-out workboot nailed to a post, a testimony to hard work. In spring and summer these boots serve as vases, holding a variety of desert flowers that bloom after seasonal rains.

Unlikely love also blooms in these rugged landscapes. In William Kittredge's "Do You Hear Your Mother Talking?" romance grows between a millworker, Ruth, and her boyfriend tree faller. She is described as "wet and working too hard and determined to be as single as possible," having left behind an ex-husband and two kids. He had suffered severe mental problems and bears scars from trying to slice imaginary wires out of his forearms. Even so, they begin building a cedar shake house together, and the possibility of raising children lingers in their thoughts.

Lola, a survivor of an abused and neglected childhood, passes by a trucker's love so she can care for her alcoholic and dying mother in John Keeble's "I Could Love You (If I Wanted)." In spite of her wretched childhood and underachievement, Lola maintains a wellspring of love for her mother and children.

Corazón, a dreamy teenaged waitress at Dixie's Burgers in Kathleen Alcalá's "Sweetheart," falls victim to her fantasies after hearing a navy man describe foreign ports and mermaids. But her fantasies are not entirely unrequited, and she manages to capture a mysterious love. In Rudolfo Anaya's "Iliana of the Pleasure Dreams," a mismatched couple find love after visiting the village church where an image of Christ has appeared. Clearly one message of these stories is the redemptive and miraculous nature of love.

◆

In addition to love, humor keeps appearing in these stories, as an antidote to hardship. The Western sense of humor ranges from the logger's and horsebreaker's tall tales to the farmer's wry asides when it won't rain or refuses to quit. During the years I worked for the guide service, humor helped warm the damp chill and occupy those long stretches when the fish kept tight mouths. At the Bunker Hill Lead and Zinc Company, the obdurate workers softened the impossible conditions by spinning yarns of how they beat the company—or aimed to.

At *Writers' Forum* I quickly learned how rare and wonderful good funny stories are, and I planned to include some here that testify to Westerners' senses of humor.

Ron Carlson's "Bigfoot Stole My Wife" and "I Am Bigfoot" are a marvelous pair of yarns flashing as lurid headlines of supermarket tabloids. In the first, a beleaguered husband laments the loss of his wife to Bigfoot. Bigfoot responds in the second, pointing out that a lot of wives are unhappy, a condition he notices while cruising the vicinity of Orange Julius stands in shopping malls.

Karen Karbo provides a humorous perspective on the immigrant theme in "Death by Browsing." Her Russian émigrés have come to the U.S. not for religious freedom or to escape political oppression. They have fled the Soviet Union to find better shopping and to put together "a look" at department store markdown sales.

East meets West over a car deal in James Houston's "A Family Resemblance" as a college professor intends to sell his car to an Asian graduate student. They meet in a shopping mall parking lot, and when a paranoid woman believes they are members of a car theft ring, the fun ensues.

Willy Loman never got the kind of attention the title characters do in Carolyn See's "Whitney and Tracie." The girls are sales representatives for José Cuerva tequila, and they take full advantage of the opportunity to sell in Hawaii.

———

Every editor must enjoy introducing "new" writers. Perhaps nothing gives quite as much pleasure as discovering wonderful talent and making that work available to a wider audience. When I judged the King County (Seattle) fiction competition in 1989, I chose Charlotte Watson Sherman's manuscript as the winner. A copy of her new book *Killing Color* arrived while I was working on this Introduction, and I am delighted this collection includes her story "The Emerald City: Third & Pike."

Kathleen Alcalá won that same competition the following year, and her story "Sweetheart," from the collection *Mrs. Vargas and the Dead Naturalist*, is highlighted above. Greg Sarris's first published story, "How I Got to Be Queen," appeared in the Dell/Laurel anthology Kathy and I edited, *Talking Leaves: Contemporary Native American Short Fiction*. After publication, it was selected for television production by American Playhouse Theater. Mr. Sarris's new story, "Slaughterhouse," appears here.

Robert Stubblefield has won several fiction competitions in Oregon and received a fellowship to the Fishtrap Writers' Conference where I heard him read "Pragmatists." Sylvia Watanabe's wonderful "Talking to the Dead" is the title story of her collection published by Doubleday in 1992. Overall, this collection tries to balance the voices by including a variety of well-established and new writers. Of highest importance are the stories themselves, enduring landmarks in the Western landscape.

◆

Five years ago, I had a twenty-eight-year-old Cambodian student in my freshman composition class. Koh had been finishing his medical training in Cambodia when the civil war brought devastation to his family and country. Fleeing to the refugee camps with surviving family members, he assisted International Red Cross doctors with caring for the sick and wounded. His documents included two letters from them attesting to his abilities and compassion. Of course, his official school records had been destroyed.

The first narrative paper he wrote for my class listed the losses his family had suffered: parents dead, wife and one child dead, several siblings and cousins dead. My hand trembled as I read his faltering account. Yet his paper concluded: "Now we are in Oregon—my cousins, son, myself. Everything is OK now here."

After reading Koh's account and talking with him, I was reminded of my wife's family's flight from the Soviet Union and the Greek Civil War, the hardships they endured, the foothold they struggled to establish. And the contributions they eventually made to their community, where the mayor set aside a day in my father-in-law's honor.

Koh was determined to complete his medical training here, but when going to medical school proved far too expensive, he elected to become a nurse and now works in the Portland area.

Koh's story and many stories in this anthology indicate that the recent migration to the West comes from Asia, Mexico, and Central America as much as it does from other parts of this country. As these stories affirm, if some settlers have found disappointment and loss over the years, others continue to arrive with determination and high spirits. And surely the West is a better place, a richer and more diverse land, thanks to the hopes and contributions of Koh and the new immigrants similar to the characters described in these stories. As editors, our hope is that by coming to these stories, readers will take away a better sense of this landscape and its varied inhabitants, their failures and triumphs. Moreover, we believe that by reading these stories, people will understand the importance of their own stories. Stories and compassion for one another bind our community.

—*Craig Lesley*

My husband, Craig Lesley, is a native Oregonian, born in The Dalles, a small town on the banks of the Columbia River, where his grandfather was a typesetter for the local newspaper. In a morning's drive, we can visit The Dalles and see the bench where his grandfather used to sit, smoke his pipe, and tell stories until long after quitting time. The bench, shiny and smooth from long use, now stands in the office of a bookstore where people still remember Oscar Lange and his stories.

The bookstore has a very fine collection, and it may surprise a visitor to this small town to find that its owners are fluent in Russian and frequently travel abroad. But as you will find in this anthology, today's West is never exactly what one anticipates. Just when you think you've got it figured out, the unexpected occurs. There's always another discovery just around the bend.

My husband is native to a region of silver sage and high desert. He counts among his friends farmers and cowboys, Native American artists and storytellers. His uncle was a longtime guide on the Deschutes River. In eastern Oregon, towns cling to the vast landscape, seemingly in danger of blowing away with the stiff desert wind, like the giant tumbleweeds thrown against barbed-wire fences. Here one finds towns of eleven people, places with names such as Hardman and Gouge Eye. They were named by people who lived in the hardscrabble past of the region—people with no time for niceties.

I was born in Delaware, in the center of the East Coast hub, an area of rapidly disappearing farmland giving way to the relentless progress of cities and sprawling suburbs. My family's own westward migration goes back to the time they came to this country as refugees from Greece only a year before I was born. Earlier, they had fled the Ukraine, escaping the terrors of their homeland on foot, leaving behind most of what they owned. Like millions of others from all over the world, they carried their hopes westward.

When my husband and I filled out our marriage license, we were startled into thoughtfulness. Under "Father's Place of Birth" he had written "Monument, Oregon." Next to that I had filled in "Kiev, Ukraine." It seemed unlikely that we ever should have met, but that is precisely the point. Today, the vast diversity of our country is best exemplified in the West, a region still open to change and transition. Here people come to make their stand—people trying to live together, or just trying to live. In the contemporary West, chapters of American history are still being written.

Today's world is international. We live and work wherever we place our fax machines and computers. Boundaries of regions and even countries have disappeared. In this newly mobile age, the American West, long a mythic region in itself, has come under increasing scrutiny. Articles and books debate the once unsullied, magnificent lands and rivers. Historians write into new books the stories of people traditionally overlooked by history—Native Americans, African Americans, Latino people, people of Asian descent. The West as our land of traditional myth—of cowboys, of rugged individuality and great aspiration—has taken a beating in the popular and scholarly consciousness. As the place of last hope for so many people, both those who migrated here and those who only dreamed of doing so, the West has carried the burden of high expectations. That has made the disappointments experienced all the deeper.

And yet, fly across the country. If the day is clear, look beneath you at the white peaks of the Rockies stretching forever. Watch the Snake River curling its way through Hell's Canyon between Oregon and Idaho. Notice the great desert plains, empty of people even today. Take in the greatness of this landscape and feel, as so many others doubtless have, that your heart and mind must expand to exist within it.

The rutted grooves of the wagons that forged the Oregon Trail in the 1800s can still be seen today, preserved in the ancient ground of the high desert. The tracks are so clearly visible that one could believe they were made by dirt bikes only last week. Time compresses, and one is reminded of this country's youth and the brief American history that we all share. The grooves of the Oregon Trail lying in these tranquil desert grasses belie the vivid and often tumultuous past of the American West—the tragedy of the American Indian, the stories of immigrants, people whose own circumstances in this country or abroad were often so dire that they were willing to leave everything they knew and face unknown dangers, hardships, and disease.

As we read these stories by contemporary writers of the West, we were struck by a characteristic many of the people they write about share: These are *working* people making a go of a tough situation, often with humor and courage and insight. Their foes today are much changed from the time of the old West but are still formidable: alcoholism, bad jobs, or none at all. Their confusion and bewilderment are evident in such stories as Tess Gallagher's "Girls." Two elderly women, one of whom has lost her memory to a stroke, are struggling to re-create the past and make some sense of hard lives.

In these stories, there aren't many illusions. And yet the characters go on believing that America can work. Here is Nevada, a Guatemalan refugee whose mother was murdered for her politics in her native land, trying to break up a fight between a Basque sheepherder and a cowboy poet: "Stop. Stop this. . . . This is America. We are American people. We are all from—yes—different places. But this is our land. . . ."

Such a statement is jarring to the modern ear for its passion and simplicity and for its call to bring people together. In the contemporary United States we are far more accustomed to seeing diverse groups struggle against each other to attain their own ends. But for the people in these stories, such as Nevada, there is no choice. For them Thomas Wolfe's famous phrase "you can't go home again" carries a unique meaning. They cannot afford cynicism. Against all odds, they believe in America. They have to.

◆

Over the years we've had the pleasure of reading, and in some instances meeting, a number of writers who write about the West. When we started this project, we knew there was a great deal of talent, but we were still taken aback to find out just how much. The discovery confirmed our feeling that writers of the West are on the cutting edge of literature in this country, mining a deep vein of energy and vitality.

We purposely drew the boundaries broadly. The only geographical restriction you will find is that all the stories take place west of the Mississippi. This was our deliberate choice, because inclusiveness, an acceptance of diverse peoples and landscapes, best fits our vision of the West today, both as it is in reality and as it is seen in the imaginations of our best writers.

We have tried, by our choices, to give a new slant on the West and on what it means to be a Westerner and, by extension, an American. Writing illuminates the lives of people whose voices would not otherwise be heard, and it is our great pleasure to find writers who are able to do just that. When thinking of the West, how often do the lives of African Americans come to mind? Colleen McElroy gives us a vivid description of the dynamic but harsh life on the black side of the town in the 1950s in her story "The Woman Who Would Eat Flowers." She reminds us of the unsung black and Chinese laborers who were an integral part of the building of the cross-country railroad but who were never included in the celebratory photos when the work was completed.

And Percival Everett offers a different angle on contemporary ranch life as seen through the eyes of his protagonist, a compassionate African American cowboy, in "Cry About a Nickel."

◆

Years ago, when my brother and I were children visiting the Smithsonian Institution in Washington, D.C., we noticed three men standing at the top of the long steps, listening silently to a guide as they looked out over the city. They had long braids and were dressed in colorful clothing that seemed exotic to us, but more than that, they had a sad, self-contained manner that set them apart. With the curiosity of a youth, my brother ran up to the eldest and said, "Sir, what is your country?" The old man turned and gave us a long look before replying, "Son, Arizona is my country."

Today, the first Americans are finally taking their place in our history. Credit for this must go to Native American writers, both those who have become established literary names, and the many lesser known. We included both in our anthology *Talking Leaves*, devoted exclusively to Native American fiction, and we are proud to add their voices to this current collection of stories from the West.

As new generations of Asian Americans mature, thoughtful stories are being told about growing up Asian American, and the culture clashes that ensue, as in Amy Tan's "Double Face," an excerpt from her very successful *Joy Luck Club*. Jeanne Wakatsuki Houston's "The Rock Garden" sheds new light on the internment of Japanese American citizens during World War II. And readers are bound to discover a world new to them in Hawaiian writer Sylvia Watanabe's "Talking to the Dead."

There is a modern-day myth of the small-town West as a place where one can go to escape the troubles of the larger society. Mary Clearman Blew turns this myth on its ear with the story "The Snowies, the Judiths," which touches a deep chord in American society—random violence. In this instance, the shock comes from the particular place where the violence occurs—at a school in a small Montana town, the kind of place people move to to escape just that. The story is unnerving because it tells us something we suspected all along: The society we create will follow us, fax machines, computers, and all.

◆

When I was a child, the coastline of Delaware and Maryland consisted of long stretches of white sand dunes and beach grasses, as far as I could see. There was little else, and since we brought our own food and pumped water from the lighthouse, little else was needed. When development started, it all happened so quickly there was barely time to understand or reflect until it was too late—it seemed a foregone conclusion. Fifteen years ago I stood on a stretch of beach, as yet untouched, but surrounded by development on either side. I compelled myself to memorize what I saw, as in a photograph of the mind: white sand dunes and swaying beach grasses; the soft gray ocean behind.

Ocean City, Maryland, today is a disaster of development run amok. A nine-mile-long strip features motels, fast-food restaurants, and entertainment arcades. At its center is a row, miles long, of skyscrapers that block the sun from the beach. Due to overbuilding and razing of the sand dunes that naturally protect it, the fine white beach sand I remember from my childhood has been washed away. In a move to restore the beach for tourism, the city has dredged coarse brown sand from deeper offshore. Due to the artificial slant of the new beach, the waves break with such abrupt force that swimming is hazardous for all but the most hardy. Scientists warn that this new beach will last only five years at most. Then what? Will the whole process have to be repeated?

A few years ago I took my children to the Ocean City boardwalk, and as we strolled past the rides and concessions, we came upon a small sand dune enclosed in a picket fence. A sign read "Baby Sand Dune" and went on to describe what a sand dune was, and how it was formed by the interaction of waves and shore. All the other sand dunes were gone, covered with condominiums, flattened by dune buggies. I was struck by the absurdity of the situation: Here I was standing in front of an artificial sand dune, explaining to my children what it was. And I remembered that day fifteen years ago when I had seen this coming—that all I would have of the ocean shore, that miracle of nature, was the imprint that still lived in my memory.

The natural environment is an integral part of writing of the West, and the West is surely at the forefront of environmental battles today. Landscape appears in many forms in Western writing, whether as a main player in the action of the story, as in Ivan Doig's dramatic "Winter of '19," or as background that shapes people's perceptions and lives. In Greg Sarris's "Slaughterhouse," a boy and a girl, both Native American and both poverty-stricken, are about to kiss when he sees:

> Her eyes was open and holding that sun in little dots of light and if I hadn't closed my eyes just then and kept looking I would've seen the mountain range, everything in her eyes clear to the ocean and back.

Such is the power of the Western landscape that it comes to inhabit the heart and mind.

Here there is a sense of loss, and a warning. Rick DeMarinis describes an industrial pit in the Southwest, now a tourist attraction that "glows like iridescent pus," in his story "Paraiso: An Elegy." Molly Gloss offers a fresh and frightening vision in "Personal Silence," a futuristic story that paints an eerily familiar portrait of the coastal Northwest as it might look years from now if we continue on our current course with regard to the environment and war.

And Barry Lopez, long a champion of the environment, creates an untouched, fictional wilderness in "The Interior of North Dakota," and a character who expresses these depths of feeling:

> I look on these hills, writing by the light of the full moon this
> evening, and know that, though this land is not mine nor ever could
> be, that for what I have found here I would die.

Yet the complexities of environmental issues, so bitterly played out in
current politics, are not ignored. In "Heartwood," Rick Bass paints a
compassionate but unsentimental picture of a contemporary logging
community and how it is affected by renegades driving spikes into the
trees to injure the loggers at work.

These are stories for our time. They are tough, funny, tender,
suspenseful, and just plain good reading. And they are telling us
something important. From the Chesapeake Bay and the disappearing coastline of Ocean City, Maryland, to the great old growth forests
of the Pacific Northwest, we are all confronted with the same serious
challenges. How we face up to them will determine the course of our
world for years to come.

The West is still a land of possibility. Hope remains; and where
hope is slim, one still finds a dogged tenacity, a belief that things can
come right. Listen: Hear the voices of the people who populate the
fictional worlds in this collection. Work to make things come right.

—*Katheryn Stavrakis*

SWEETHEART

When people noticed Corazón, it was to say, "She certainly doesn't resemble her sister."

Corazón was tall and shy. At seventeen, she had never had a boyfriend, and felt that her overly romantic name, which meant "sweetheart," mocked her. With her height and frizzy hair, Corazón looked like a dark candle standing at the back of her senior class picture, her mournful gaze lost in the reflection of her glasses.

Corazón's younger sister was named Isabella, called Queenie. Where Corazón was shy, Queenie could captivate a group with her quick wit and flirtatious personality. If Queenie could have helped it, no one in San Antonio would have known that they were sisters at all.

Corazón worked in a place called Dixie's Burgers. When she graduated from school, no one asked if she had any further plans. Each day she walked to work with the hot Texas sky pressed down upon her, and tied on a butterscotch-colored apron before taking her place behind the counter.

That was the summer that Arturo and Tonia's son came home on leave. Art, Jr., served in the Merchant Marine. Although he was short, like his father, his life at sea gave him a self-confidence no job in San Antonio could have offered. Soon he had a following of neighborhood boys who gathered every time he stopped to tell one of his stories.

Art had been to Hong Kong and India, to the Philippines and Singapore, everywhere a ship could travel, and as he told about meeting Russian sailors and Japanese fishermen, he would hold his audience rapt with his level gray gaze. Even Corazón would pause while cleaning the counter as Art talked and the flies buzzed and steam condensed around the fluorescent lights on the ceiling.

"So then this good-looking Jap girl comes out and bows to you. She's wearing this kimono and these sandals that make it so she can hardly walk. You bow, and she hands you a flower. A girl gives a guy a flower. Then everyone bows again and sits on the floor and she serves you tea. That's all there is to it."

Corazón thought about the tea ceremony for a long time afterward. That night, she imagined herself handing a perfect flower, a chrysanthemum, to a man. She could not see his face, but he had fine, artistic hands. "Thank you," he said, and she fell asleep.

When Art came into Dixie's Burgers to tell his stories, Corazón tried to creep closer without being seen so she could hear. Not that he would have noticed. Every girl in the neighborhood was trying to get his attention, but Art and Queenie hit it off right away. Although her parents thought she was too young to have a *novio*, Queenie and Art spent a lot of time together, hanging around Dixie's and the riverfront.

Art mostly told stories about the good times he and his buddies had in different ports, but sometimes he talked about how hard life at sea was, and the mysterious things that could happen there. Corazón began to imagine herself as an invisible passenger on a ship like his, the U.S.S. *Adventurer,* free to move about the decks, walkways, and passages without being observed, watching the sailors do their jobs, and visiting strange and exotic ports with them.

After each time that Art came into Dixie's and told a story, Corazón would repeat it to herself while falling asleep that night. She could almost feel the gentle rise and fall of the ship under her as she dozed off. After a while, she was keeping an invisible journal and sending postcards to invisible relatives. She imagined herself dressed in a long, pale pink coat with a large-brimmed hat and a long trailing scarf around her neck. Corazón practiced to give her handwriting just the right flourish.

My dearest Hermalinda,

The weather is lovely in Kuala Lumpur. The monsoons have not yet begun, but the orchid forests are in full bloom. I do hope little Josie is over the chicken pox.

Yours faithfully,
Corazón

Art told a story about stopping in the Aleutian Islands, and Corazón stood on the deck in a fur wrap as the ship glided past huge, unfathomably blue glaciers. Eskimos came out to greet them in kayaks.

Later, after traveling through perilous seas, the ship docked briefly in Hawaii, and Corazón waved a fond farewell as the perfume from the many leis around her neck filled the air around her. She wrote,

My Dear Tia Rosauria,

The Pacific seas are endlessly blue. Dolphins follow us for miles, as though fascinated by this huge, floating city. We are headed for the South Pacific, where palm trees sway in balmy breezes.

Sorry to miss the garden party this year. Please convey my regrets to Uncle.

Fondly,
Corazón

Corazón's shipgoing alter ego had by now abandoned her flowing pink coat for the more practical bell-bottoms of the sailors, and even enjoyed their singing in the evenings. She wore a navy peacoat against the evening chill, and read her mail as eagerly as the young men who suffered from being so far from home. Sometimes she had a fiancé who played polo in Argentina, but when she tired of his endless chatter about horses, Corazón fancied a minor count in a small European country. They both remained vague, distant figures, and Corazón felt no compulsion to cut her voyage short and return to either of them. As she scrubbed down the metal counters at Dixie's, or sprayed stain remover on her greasy uniform before washing it, Corazón composed letters in her head to her two beaus, scarcely noticing the heat and grime that were constant parts of her life.

By early August, Art's leave was almost over. He and Queenie seemed to slip away more and more often, and Corazón suspected that her sister was sneaking out at night to see him. His appearances at Dixie's were less frequent, but his stories seemed to be taking a more fantastic turn. Corazón suspected that he had run out of real stories, and was starting to make things up just to please the hungry faces around him. She didn't mind. The more exotic his voyages, the more wonderful her own.

◆

One especially oppressive afternoon, when the dogs lay in the dust in any patch of shade, and the little old ladies didn't even bother to move their chairs outside, Art swung into Dixie's for a cold beer. He seemed unusually pensive, and took a plastic straw out of the dispenser to chew on. Five neighborhood boys soon filled the tables around him.

"Tell us about monsters," said Jorge. "Didn't you see any sea monsters out there?"

Art thought about this as he sprawled in his chair. "Yeah," he said, "I seen some pretty strange things. Not monsters, exactly. More like weird fish. Though not really fish." His eyes narrowed as he thought. "I guess they was mermaids."

A general sound of disbelief rose from the group.

"Aw, c'mon," said Jorge. "You didn't see no mermaids. There's no such thing!"

"Well," said Art. "I'll tell you exactly what happened, and you can make up your own minds. I'm not saying I did, and I'm not saying I didn't, but something strange was going on out there. I'm not the only one who saw it. A bunch of the guys did."

Corazón moved down the counter in order to hear better.

"We was way down in the Indian Ocean, near a bunch of islands called the Maldives. We was a little off course, though the navigator wouldn't admit it until we came right up to these islands he didn't know was there."

Art squirmed down in his seat as he talked, and seemed to be in a more serious mood than usual. His audience waited quietly, sipping their Cokes and wiping their sweaty hands on their jeans.

"There are coral reefs out there, so we decided to stop until we could figure out where we was. We dropped anchor in a bay between two islands, and you could hear the howler monkeys calling back and forth between the trees. The water was dead calm, and you could see clear to the bottom. We was all out on deck smoking and stuff, but outside of the howlers, it was real quiet, kind of eerie.

"Jim, Slim Jim, we call him, was bragging about his girlfriend, who's an Olympic swimmer or something, when one of the guys points in the water and says, 'Hey, Jim, there goes your girlfriend now!' We all started laughing, figuring it was some fat porpoise or even a cowfish, these really ugly things, but it was something I'd never seen before, real humanlike. It was circling the ship about a hundred yards away, and the light was getting dim, so it was hard to see. Kind of brown and shiny. We'd about decided it was a big sand shark, or some other reef fish, when there's this sharp whistle from near one of the islands. This thing we'd been watching raises up out of the water and lets out a really sharp whistle in return, like an answer. It looked just like a woman when it did that, with long hair and big boobs and everything."

Art sounded so serious at this point that the boys didn't even snicker. Corazón stood transfixed at the counter, not even pretending not to listen.

"Well, after that," said Art, still chewing on the straw, "we got out a spotlight and tried to see it better, but by then it was gone. The sun had gone down, and the captain refused permission for a small boat to go out. All we could do was wonder what the hell it was all about.

"The next day, we got our bearings and headed up to Sri Lanka. We had been south of where we were supposed to be, and the captain was pretty pissed. Anyway, we got an afternoon's leave in Sri Lanka, which is a big island near India, and some of us got to talking to some shipping clerks who spoke English. We described what we'd seen the night before. One of the Sri Lankans said there was legends about warrior mermaids in those waters. He said there are abandoned temples, and the mermaids are guardian spirits. They kill men who try to go ashore. The other Sri Lankans looked real uncomfortable, because they don't want us to think they're superstitious. They wouldn't let the other guy talk anymore, so we left."

Art sat quiet for a moment, then sat up and said, "That's it. That's my mermaid story. You guys don't believe it, suit yourselves."

"I don't believe it," said Manny. "You're just pulling our leg."

"I wouldn't do that," said Art, standing up. "I wouldn't do that."

He grabbed Manny by the leg and dragged him out of the chair kicking and hollering until the boss, Nelson, came out and told them to cut the rough stuff. Then they all went outside, leaving Corazón glued to the counter by her greasy rag until Nelson told her to get back to work. She hurried out to clean up their table and found a small, rough pebble where Art had sat. Without thinking, Corazón slipped it into her pocket before picking up the plastic cups and running her damp rag across the tabletop.

That night, Corazón dreamed again of the rise and fall of the waves. But this time she was in the waves, not on them. She felt her long green hair as it trailed about her neck and shoulders, and the little fish that moved under her hands and brushed her sides as she swam. When she rose out of the water on her tail, she could just glimpse a crumbling white temple through the trees of the island. A piercing whistle startled her awake, but was only the alarm clock saying it was time to get up.

Corazón stumbled to the bathroom, where she was disappointed by her short, lifeless hair and flat chest. No warrior mermaid wore glasses. Only a waitress at Dixie's in San Antonio. She threw down her glasses and got in the shower to disperse the night's dream.

Corazón stopped being a passenger on the ship, and scarcely listened to Art's stories when he came in now. As the end of his leave approached, he spent less time in Dixie's and probably more time with Queenie.

Corazón stopped writing to the aunt and uncle in San Francisco, and gave up on the polo player and the European playboy. She laid the imaginary pink dress and coat in a steamer trunk, and carefully wrapped the wide-brimmed hat in tissue paper before placing it in a leather hatbox. Then she shed her clothes and jumped overboard into the still, green waters of the lagoon. She found a copper spear lying on the white sand, green with age, and carried it as lightly as a cane. It fit her hand exactly.

"I'm going to have to let you go if you don't shape up," said Nelson. "You've been daydreaming an awful lot lately. There're plenty more would like your job if you don't."

Corazón promised to pay more attention. But the bright Texas sunlight hurt her eyes now, and she longed for the watery depths of sleep. She moved clumsily about the diner, thrashing at glasses as though they were always out of reach, dropping the plastic trays when she tried to stack them on the counter. Only at night did she move gracefully, the warm waters like a mantle across her shoulders, the whistling language ringing in her ears.

The day before his leave ended, Art stopped in at Dixie's to say good-bye to the boys. There was a lot of kidding around and punching, and Corazón went to the back room to get supplies and escape the noise. As she opened the swinging door from the back, Corazón heard one of the boys ask Art if he really had seen a mermaid.

"Yeah, a beaut," said Art, "a real sailor's dream. And you know what I'd do if I caught one?"

Here, Art suggested something that couldn't possibly be done to a mermaid, twisting his thumb low in the air before him as he said it. The boys giggled wickedly, if a little uncertainly, and Corazón sagged against the door, unable to go either out or back. She realized at that moment, as though she had been struck in the face, that Art had done this to her sister Queenie. All the blood rose to her head, then drained away. She dropped the plastic plates and paper napkins on the floor. Corazón turned dully when footsteps approached.

"What's the matter?" asked Nelson. "You look awful."

"I don't feel so good," she answered.

"Take the afternoon off," said Nelson. "This weather's getting to everyone. It's quiet anyway." She stooped to pick up the plates, but Nelson stopped her and motioned for her to leave. Corazón mechanically removed her apron and got her purse out of the closet. She didn't remember walking home.

Corazón skipped supper that evening. She went to bed early, saying that her head hurt.

"Well, what's wrong with *her?*" said Queenie sarcastically. She was on her way to meet Art, and pouted her lips in the hall mirror to make sure her lipstick was right.

That night, Corazón's bed was rocked by steep waves. She hung on desperately and gulped ragged breaths of air as each wave rose up and up before crashing down on her. The room tipped from side to side and the wind screamed as Corazón clung to the blankets and shut her eyes tightly.

Finally, Corazón could hold on no more, and was wrenched from the bed and thrown into the depths of the black sea. Her lungs burning, she gasped and her mouth filled with water. A searing pain tore her in two before she gasped one last time and her lungs burst.

The stormy sea quieted. Corazón drifted up, lifted on a stream of bubbles. She pitied the poor creature lying on the sea bottom, pale and spent, its hair in its eyes. She brushed back her own luxuriant green tendrils before darting off to join her sisters.

◆

They found Corazón the next morning lying on the floor, limp as a wrung-out washrag. A line of salt crusted her upper lip, and there was sand under her nails. A stroke, said the doctor, brought on by the heat and dehydration.

When her clenched fist was pried open, a rough, pink object fell out. Coral, shaped like a heart.

"That's Art's," said Queenie, and was suddenly silent.

Art had sailed that morning for Japan, and wasn't due to return for a long time.

Corazón opened her eyes just then and looked at her sister, unable to speak. Queenie, crying, left the room.

Corazón stayed in the hospital for several days, then home for many weeks, propped in a chair by the window. When her sister delivered a baby the following spring, Corazón moved into an apartment with her to help take care of the little girl. Jade, as they called her, had eyes the color of seawater, or of a Texas sky just before a storm.

Corazón gradually got well, but everyone agreed that she was different after that. She moved with a purposeful stride, and wheeled her sister's baby down the street like they were on parade. Sometimes she disappeared for days at a time, and people said that she was meeting a man in Galveston. Others said that she returned with the strong smell of seaweed on her, and a wild look in her copper eyes. But everyone agreed that she wore a pink stone at her throat, suspended on a thin gold chain, and shaped exactly like a human heart.

RUDOLFO A. ANAYA

ILIANA
OF THE PLEASURE
DREAMS

Iliana stirred in the summer night, then awakened from her dream. She moaned, a soft sigh, her soul returning from its dreams of pleasure. She opened her eyes, the night breeze stirred the curtains, the shadows created images on the bare adobe wall, an image of her dream which moved, then changed and was lost as the shadows moved away from dream into reality.

In the darkness of the night, smelling the sweet fragrance of the garden which wafted through the open door, lying quietly so as not to awaken Onofre her husband, she lay smiling and feeling the last wave of pleasure which had aroused her so pleasantly from her deep sleep. It was always like this, first the images, then the deep stirring which touched the depths in her, then the soft awakening, the coming to life.

In the summer Onofre liked to sleep with the doors and windows open, to feel the mountain coolness. Her aunts had never allowed Iliana to sleep in the moonlight. The light of the moon disturbs young girls, they had said.

Iliana smiled. Her aunts had given her a strict religious upbringing, and they had taught her how to care for a home, but they had never mentioned dreams of pleasure. Perhaps they did not know of the pleasure which came from the images in her dreams, the images which at first were vague, shadows in a place she did not recognize, fragments of faces, whispers. The images drew clearer, there was a quickening to her pulse, a faster tempo to her breathing, then the dream became clear and she was running across a field of alfalfa to be held by the man who appeared in her dreams. The man pressed close to her, sought her lips, caressed her, whispered words of love, and she was carried away into the spinning dream of pleasure. She had never seen the man's face, but always when she awakened she was sure he was standing in the garden, just outside the door, waiting for her.

Yes, the dream was so real, the flood of pleasure so deep and true, she knew the man in the dream was there, and the shadows of the garden were the shadows of her dreams.

She rose slowly, pushing away the damp sheet which released the sweet odor of her body. Tonight the man had reached out, taken her in his arms and kissed her lightly. The pleasure of his caress consumed her and carried her into a realm of exhilaration. When she awakened she felt she was falling gently back to earth, and her soul came together again, to awaken.

She walked to the window quietly, so as not to awaken her husband. She had never told him of her private world of dreams, and even when she confessed her dreams to the priest at Manzano she could not tell him everything. The dreams were for her, a private message, a disturbing pleasure she did not know how to share. Perhaps with the man in the dream she could share her secret, share the terrible longing which filled her and which erupted only in her dreams.

She leaned against the door and felt the cool breeze caress her perspiring body. Was he there, in the shadows of the garden, waiting for her? She peered into the dark. The shadows the moon created were as familiar as those she saw in her dreams. She wanted to cry out to understand the dream, to share the pleasure, but there was no one there. Only the soft shrill of the night crickets filled the garden. The cry of the grios foretold rain, the clouds would rise over the mountain, the thunder would rumble in the distant sky, and the dry spell of early summer would be broken.

Iliana sighed. She thought of her aunts. Tia Amalia and Tia Andrea. Why had they not explained the dreams of pleasure? They were women who had never married, but they had said marriage would be good for her. All of the girls in the village married by eighteen and settled down to take care of their families. Onofre was a good man, a farmer, a hard worker, he did not drink, he was a devout Catholic. He would provide a home, they said, she would raise his children.

The girls of the mountain valley said Onofre was handsome but very shy. He would have to wait many years and marry a widow, they said, and so they were surprised when Iliana married him. Iliana was the most beautiful girl in the valley. It was a marriage of convenience, the young women whispered to explain the match, and Iliana went to her marriage bed with no conception of what was expected of her. Onofre was gentle, but he did not kiss the nape of her neck or whisper the words of pleasure she heard in her dreams. She vaguely understood that the love of Onofre could be a thread to her secret dreams, but Onofre was abrupt, the thread snapped, the fire of her desire died.

She was unsure, hesitant, she grew timid. They ate in silence, they lived in silence. Like an animal that is careful of its master, she settled around the rhythms of his work day, being near when it was time to be close, staying in her distant world the rest of the time. He too felt the distance; he tried to speak but was afraid of his feelings. Sitting across the table from her he saw the beauty of her face, her hands, her throat and shoulders, and then he would look down, excuse himself, return to his work with which he tried to quench the desires he did not understand.

There is little pleasure on earth, the priest at the church said. We were not put on earth to take pleasure in our bodies. And so Onofre believed in his heart that a man should take pleasure in providing a home, in watching his fields grow, in the blessing of the summer rains which made the crops grow, in the increase of his flocks. Sex was the simple act of nature which he knew as a farmer. The animals came together, they reproduced, and the priest was right, it was not for pleasure. At night he felt the body of Iliana, the pleasure came to engulf him for a moment, to overwhelm him and suffocate him, then as always the thread severed, the flame died.

Iliana waited at the window until the breeze cooled her skin and she shivered. In the shadows of the garden she felt a presence, and for a moment she saw again the images of her dream, the contours of her body, the purple of alfalfa blossoms. A satisfaction in the night, a sensuous pleasure welled up from a depth of soul she only knew in her dreams. She sighed. This was her secret.

How long had it been in her soul, this secret of pleasure? She had felt it even in the church at Manzano where she went to confession and mass. She had gone to the church to confess to the priest, and the cool earth fragrance of the dark church and the sweetness of the votive candles had almost overwhelmed her. "Help me," she whispered to the priest, desiring to cleanse her soul of her secret even as the darkness of the confessional whispered the images of her dream. "I have sinned," she cried, but she could not tell him of the pleasures of her dreams. The priest, knowing the young girls of the village tended to be overdramatic in the stories of their love life, mumbled something about her innocence, made the sign of the cross absolving her, and sent her to her small penance.

Iliana walked home in deep despair. Along the irrigation ditch the tall cottonwood trees reminded her of strong, virile men, their roots digging into the dark soul of the earth, their branches creating images of arms and legs against the clear sky. She ran, away from the road, away from the neighboring fields; over the pine mountain she ran until exhausted she clutched at a tree, leaned against the huge trunk; trembling she listened to the pounding of her heart. The vanilla smell of the pine was like the fragrance of the man in her dreams. She felt the rough bark, like the rough hands of Onofre at night. She closed her eyes and clutched at the tree, holding tight to keep from flying into the images of her dream which swept around her.

Iliana remembered her visit to the church as she returned to her bed, softly so as not to awaken Onofre. She lay quietly and pulled the sheet to her chin. She closed her eyes, but she could not sleep. She remembered the images at the church and felt again how she was overcome when she pressed close to the tree. It was the same tonight in her dream, the immense pleasure which filled her with a desire so pure she felt she was dying and returning to God. Why?

She thought of her aunts, spinsters whose only occupation was to care for the church at Manzano. They swept, they sewed the cloths for the altar, they brought the flowers for mass, they made sure the candles were ready. They had given their lives to God, they did not speak of pleasure. What would they think if they knew of the dreams that came to Iliana?

Release me, Iliana cried. Free me. Leave me to my work and to my husband. He is a good man, leave me to him. Iliana's tears wet the sheet, and it was not until the early morning that she could sleep again.

"We can go this afternoon," Onofre said as they ate.

"Oh, yes," Iliana nodded. She was eager to go to the church at Manzano. Just that morning her aunts had come to visit her. They were filled with excitement.

"An apparition has appeared on the wall of the church," Tia Amalia said.

"The face of Christ," Tia Andrea said, and both bowed their heads and made the sign of the cross.

That is what the people of the mountain valleys were saying, that at sunset the dying light and the cracks in the mud painted the face of Christ on the adobe wall of the church. A woman on the way to rosary had seen the image, she ran to tell her comadre. Together they saw it, and their story spread like fire up and down the mountain. The following afternoon all the people of the village came and gathered in the light of dusk to see the face of Christ appear on the wall. Many claimed they saw the face, some said a man crippled by arthritis was cured and could walk when he saw the image.

"I see! I see!" the old man had shouted, and he stood and walked. The people believed they had experienced a miracle. "There!" each shouted in turn as the face of Christ appeared. The crown of thorns was clear, blood streamed down the sad and anguished face. The women fell to their knees. A miracle had come to the village of Manzano.

The priest came and took holy water and blessed the wall, and the old people understood that he had sanctified the miracle. The following evening people came from miles around, from the mountain villages and ranches they came to see the miracle. Those who saw the face of the savior cried aloud or whispered a private prayer, the women on their knees in the dust prayed rosary after rosary.

People from the nearby villages came, families came in their cars and trucks. The women came to pray, eager to see the image of Christ. Their men were more guarded, they stood away from the church wall and wondered if it was possible. The children played hide-and-seek as all waited for the precise moment of dusk when the image appeared.

The young men came in their customized cars and trucks, drinking beer, eager to look at the young women. Boys from the ranches around the village came on horseback, dressed in their Sunday shirts and just-pressed Levi's, they came to show off their horsemanship to the delight of the girls. A fiesta atmosphere developed, the people were glad for the opportunity to gather.

The men met in clusters and talked politics and rain and cattle. Occasionally one would kick at the ground with his boot, then steal an uncomfortable glance at his wife. The women also gathered in groups, to talk about their children, school, marriages and deaths, but mostly to talk about the miracle which had come to their village and to listen to the old women who remembered a prior apparition when they were young. A young woman, they said, years ago, before cars came to the mountains, had seen the image of the Virgin Mary appear, on a wall, and the praying lasted until the image disappeared.

"One never knows which is the work of the devil or the work of God," an old woman said. "One can only pray."

A strange tension developed between the men and the women who went to see the miracle. It was the women who organized the rosaries and the novenas. It was the women who prayed, kneeling on the bare ground for hours, the raw earth numbing their knees and legs. It was they who prayed for the image to appear, their gaze fixed on the church wall, their prayers rising into the evening sky where the nighthawks flew as the sun set red in the west.

The priest grew concerned, he tried to speak to the men, but they greeted him quietly, then looked down at the ground. They had no explanation to share. The priest turned to the women, they accepted him but did not need him. Finally he shut himself up in the church, to pray alone, unsure of the miracle, afraid of the tension in the air which had turned the people in a direction he did not understand. He could not understand the fervent prayer of the women, and he could not control it. The people of this valley in the Sangre de Cristo mountains, he had been warned, were different. Now he understood the warning. The image had come to the wall of the church and the people devoutly accepted it as a miracle. Why had he been sent to the church at Manzano? He belonged in the city, where the politics of the church were clear and understood. This transformation in his parishioners he did not understand. He opened the chest where he kept the altar wine and drank, wondering what it was he had seen in the lines and shadows when he looked at the wall. He couldn't remember, but he couldn't look again.

In the afternoon Onofre and Iliana drove over the ridge of the mountain to the church at Manzano. Onofre drove in silence, wondering what the visitation of the image meant. Iliana rode filled with a sense of excitement. Perhaps the image on the wall of the church was a sign for her, she would see her savior and he would absolve the pleasure dreams, all would be well.

Iliana smiled, closed her eyes and let herself drift as the rocking of the truck swayed her gently back and forth. Through the open window the aroma of the damp earth reached her nostrils. She smelled the pregnant, rich scent of the soil and the pine trees. She remembered the dapple horse she used to ride across the meadow from her Tia Amalia's house to her Tia Andrea.

When they arrived at Manzano, Iliana opened her eyes and saw the crowd of people around the church. Cars and trucks lined the dirt road. Together Onofre and Iliana walked toward the group by the church.

Onofre felt awkward when he walked in public with his wife. She was a young and beautiful woman. He did not often think of her beauty, except when they were with other people. Then he saw her as others might see her, and he marveled at her beauty.

"It's the Spanish blood of her mother which gives her her beauty," her aunts were fond of saying.

Her oval face reminded Onofre of a saint he had seen once in a painting, perhaps at the cathedral at Santa Fe. Her face, the dark eyelashes, the dark line of the eyebrows, the green eyes. She was exquisite, a woman so beautifully formed that people paused to watch her. Onofre felt the eyes of the young men on his wife as they walked, and he tried to shake away the feeling of self-consciousness as he walked beside her. He knew the men admired the beauty of his wife, and he had been kidded about being married to an angel.

Iliana was aware of her beauty, it was something she felt in her soul. Everything she did was filled with a sensuous pleasure in which she took delight, and as they walked toward the church she took pleasure in feeling the gaze of the men on her. But she cast down her eyes and did not look at them, understanding that she should not bring shame to her husband.

Instead she looked at the children who played around the church; the gathering had become a fiesta. Someone had brought an ice machine to sell flavored ice. Another person had set up a stand to sell rosaries and other religious items, and a farmer was selling green chile and corn from the bed of his truck. There were people Iliana did not recognize, people from as far away as Taos and Española.

As Iliana and Onofre passed, friends and neighbors greeted them, but when the young bachelors of the village saw her a tension filled the air. Her beauty was known in the mountain villages, and at eighteen she was more beautiful than ever. All of the young men had at one time or another dreamed of her, now they looked at her in awe, for underneath her angelic beauty lay a sensuality which almost frightened them.

"Onofre must be treating her right," one young man whispered to his friend. "She is blossoming."

How lucky Onofre is, they thought. He so plain and simple, and yet she is his. God is not fair, they dared to think as they tipped their cowboy hats when she passed. All were young and virile men of the mountains, handsome from their Spanish and Indian blood, and all were filled with desire when they saw Iliana.

They called Onofre a lucky man, but the truth was that each one of them had had a chance to court Iliana. Each one of them had seen her at school, they saw her at church on Sundays, and each day they saw her beauty grow. They could not touch her, even in the games they played as children, they dared not touch her. When they grew into young manhood a few of them sought her out, but one glance in her eyes told them that Iliana was a young woman filled with mystery. They turned away, unwilling to challenge the sensuous mystery they felt in her presence. They turned away and married the simple girls of the village, those in whom there was no challenge, no mystery to frighten and test them.

Now, as Iliana passed them, she felt the admiration of the young men of the mountains. She smiled and wondered as she stole a glance at their handsome faces if one of them was the man who appeared in her dreams.

Her aunts were there; indeed, they had been there all day, waiting for the setting of the sun, waiting for the image of Christ to appear. They saw Iliana and drew her forward.

"We're pleased you arrived," they said. "Come, *hija,* it's almost time." They pulled her away from Onofre, and he sighed with relief and stepped back into the crowd of men.

The women parted as the two aunts drew Iliana forward so she could have a good view of the church wall. Already candles were lighted, a rosary was being prayed. The singing of the Hail Marys fell softly on their ears, and the sweet scent of paraffin filled the air. The women drew close together, prayed; the crowd grew quiet as the sun set. The cracks of the old plaster on the wall appeared thick and textured as the sun touched the horizon of the juniper-covered hills to the west. If the image appeared, it would be only for a few minutes, then it would dissolve into the grey of the evening.

Iliana waited. She prayed. Pressed between her aunts and the women, she felt their fragrances mix with the wax smell of the candles. So it had been at the church, the distinctive aroma of women comingling with the sanctity of God. The hush of the crowd reminded her of the hush of the church, and she remembered images and scenes. She remembered the pleasure that came with her first blood, the dapple horse she rode from the house of one aunt to the other . . . the field of alfalfa with purple blossoms and the buzzing of the honey bees, the taste of the thick, white paste at school, the tartness of the first bite of an apple, the fragrance of fresh bread baked in the *horno* behind her tia Amalia's house, the day the enraged bull broke loose and tore down the *horno* until there was only a pile of dirt left, and the frightened women watching from their windows, cursing the bull, praying to God. She swayed back and forth on her knees, felt the roughness of the pebbles, heard the prayers of the women, felt the flood of disconnected images which dissolved into the smell of the mountain earth after a summer rain, the welcome smell of *piñon* wood burning in the fireplace and flavoring the air, the feeling of pleasure which these sights and sounds and memories wove into her soul. . . .

She closed her eyes, and pressed her hands to her bosom to still the pounding of her heart, to stop the rush of heat which moved up from the earth to her knees and thighs. Around her she heard the women praying as if in a dream. Beads of sweat wet her upper lip as the images came to tease her, she licked at the sweat and tasted it.

Then the crowd grew still, the magic hour had come. "Look," one of the aunts whispered. Iliana opened her eyes and looked up at the lines and shadows on the wall.

"You see!" the other aunt said.

Iliana, in revery, nodded, smiled. Yes, I see, she wanted to say aloud, her gaze fastened on the scene on the wall. She saw a figure, then two. Arms and legs in an image of love. Yes, it was the image of her dream. Iliana smiled and her body quivered with pleasure.

"Dear God," she cried, overwhelmed by the pleasure of the waves which rolled through her body. "Dear God," she cried, then Iliana fainted.

In her dream she walked on purple blossoms, and the sweet aroma rose like sweet wine and touched the clouds of summer. Red and mauve and the crimson of blood. In the darkness of the field the man waited by the dapple horse. The waves of pleasure dissipated, the thread broke before she reached the man.

Tia Amalia touched camphor to her nose and Tia Andrea patted her hand vigorously. Iliana awoke and saw the shadows of the women around her. Beyond the women Iliana caught a glimpse of the wall, dark now, the congealing of shadows and lines no longer held the secret she had seen.

"A miracle," her aunt whispered. "You saw the face of Christ, you are blessed."

"Blessed be the Lord Jesus Christ," the chorus of the women responded.

"When you fainted you smiled like an angel," her aunt said. "We knew you had seen the miracle."

"Yes," Iliana whispered, "I have seen the face of God." She struggled to rise, to free herself from the press of the women. On their knees they prayed, in the darkness, and when she rose they looked up at her as if she was part of the miracle.

"Onofre," she cried. She pulled away from the cluster of women, away from the ring of candles which danced and snapped in the rising wind of night. What had become of Onofre?

Onofre, who in his quiet way had gazed at the wall, now stood waiting in the dark. He stood alone, confused, unsure, not understanding the strange messages of his blood. He had looked at the wall, but he had not prayed to see the image of Christ, he had prayed that Iliana would understand his dreams of the warm earth he worked daily. He had seen the men leave, taking away the exhausted children, the limp bodies of the boys and girls who moaned in their dreams as they were carted home. Chairs and blankets were brought for the women, they would pray all night. The men would return to work the following day.

The wind rose in the dark night, it moaned on the pines of the mountain, it cried as it swept around the church and snapped at the candle light, creating shadows on the church wall. The women huddled in prayer. Iliana stumbled in the dark, wondering why she had seen the image of pleasure on the wall and not the face of Christ. Was it the devil tempting her? Or had the image on the wall been the answer she sought?

"Onofre!" she cried in the dark. The cold wind made her shiver. She found the truck, but Onofre was not there. In the dark she crossed the road, drawn by the dark, purple scent of alfalfa. She ran across the field, stumbling forward, feeling the weakness in the pit of her stomach give way to an inner resolution she had to follow. "Onofre!" she cried, feeling as if she had awakened from a dream into another dream, but this dream was one she could live in and understand.

In the middle of the field she saw the image of the man, the man who stood in the dark holding the neck of a horse, the dapple horse of her dreams. Heart pounding, she ran into the arms of Onofre. She felt his strong arms hold her, and she allowed herself to be held, to feel the strength of his body, his muscles hardened by work, his silence instilled by the mountains.

"I did not see the face of Christ," Iliana confessed.

"Nor I," Onofre said.

"What then?" Iliana asked.

"A dream," Onofre said, unsure of what she meant, sure of his answer.

"Have I done wrong by dreaming?" Iliana asked.

Onofre shook his head. "I remember the old people saying: life is a dream. . . ."

"And dreams are dreams," Iliana finished. "There is a meaning in my dreams, but I don't understand it. Do you understand your dreams, Onofre?"

"No," he smiled, the first time in a long time he had smiled at his young wife. Holding her in the dark in the middle of the field, the desire he felt was new, it was a desire rising from the trembling earth, through his legs into his thighs and sex and into the pounding of his heart.

"Sometimes at night I awaken and go to the open door," he said. "I look at the beauty of the night. I look at you lying so peaceful in the bed. You make soft sounds of contentment. I wish I could be the one who draws those sounds from you. Then you awaken, and I step into the shadows, so I won't frighten you. I watch as you go to the door to look at the garden. I know you have awakened from a beautiful dream because you are alive with beauty. At those times, you are all the beauty on earth."

"We need to share our dreams," Iliana said. Onofre nodded. They looked at each other and understood the secret of dreams was better shared.

"It is time to go home," Iliana said.

Yes, it was time to go home, to sleep, to unravel dreams. Arm in arm they walked across the field of alfalfa, walking together with much pleasure, stirring the purple blossoms of the night.

T wo boys, wild boys, in my, our valley—but it wasn't their fault. The valley itself was wild: How could they be otherwise? Victor was tall, massive, a man already—he helped his mother in the mercantile rather than going to school. His friend Percy didn't do much of anything. Percy's father, whose last name was Coward, was an alcoholic, and his mother did most of the chores around the house: the wood-splitting and baby-raising, the cooking, the egg-collecting. It was funny how we had already written Percy off, even though he had just turned fifteen.

Percy was short and pale, thin, and he bruised easily. He always seemed to be wiping his nose. One eye went slightly off course when he tried to focus on something. The cabin he lived in was back in the woods, with only propane lanterns for lighting, and so it was always a little dark in his house. His hair was never combed.

When Percy's father was cognizant enough to crawl down the Yaak River Road and make it into the bar, things were okay. But usually his father just stayed at home and drank. When life wasn't going well, he threw things at Percy: chunks of firewood, beer bottles, stones, cats. Mister Coward was a large man who had lost his leg in a logging accident almost eight years ago, when Percy was seven, and even then, Mister Coward had been a drinker. It just got worse after the accident.

What Percy and Victor began to do, when they turned fifteen, was to drive long, steel nails deep into the trunks of all the giant larch trees in the valley. A single larch tree, a hundred and fifty or two hundred feet tall, and as big around at the base as a small car, could be worth several thousand dollars to a logging crew. The valley used to be filled with them, a sea of giants, trees that had already been a hundred years old back when the big fire of 1910 came through, destroying everything but those giant larches; but now they were being logged out.

The way that I knew the boys were doing it—spiking the big larch trees—was that they kept their spikes in my hay barn; and they painted murals of their deeds inside the barn, with cans of spray paint, on the barn's old weathered wood walls.

I never spoke to the boys, not once—words did not pass between us. When we met we'd look long and hard at each other—centuries, and forests, of words between us—but we never ever spoke. Why did they choose my barn?

Because they could read my heart, I believe. They were devils, they were cold young men and already wild. Dirt and fright and wildness were in their own hearts. I'm pretty sure that they wanted me to join them.

I loved those trees. I loved wildness, too, but was frightened of it.

The boys met in my barn nearly every night, with a lantern, and painted their pictures—bright red and blue and yellow hieroglyphics of two figures in the forest, pounding spikes into glowing trees. The trees had strange yellow halos—and beneath the paintings the boys told roughly where the trees were: Vinal Ridge Road, Flatiron Mountain Road, Lower Fowler Creek.

I'd watch, from my cabin, their lantern-glow seeping through the chinks in my barn.

The next day, in the safety of daylight, I'd go down and look at the new murals, and I'd find myself sweating. The forests are so lovely up here: They demand nothing of anyone. So safe! Why do they have to cut the biggest, oldest trees? Why couldn't they leave the few, very few, remaining giants?

Then the kickbacks began. When loggers cut into the big spiked trees, the spinning saw blade would touch the spike and snap back with the recoil of a fired cannonball, slamming right back at the sawyer. It ruined the blade, of course, and was dangerous as hell. After only a few kickbacks, when it was clear that evil was at work, the men began to take precautions, testing trees with a metal detector before felling them—but even so, they were often forgetting the metal detector, or they would think, Surely this tree, so far off from anything, hasn't been tampered with: and then they would get hurt, sometimes badly.

No one except me knew who was spiking the trees. It seemed I should do something, something to stop it, but I didn't know what.

One man took four hundred stitches in his shoulder, out in the field, with string and a sewing needle, and almost died. Another had the saw hit his helmet and crack it in half, and they thought he was dead and had taken him home to get him ready for burial, were already building the warming fires to thaw the earth, when he woke up.

He said he felt better than he had in twenty years, that he felt like a kid again, and he spoke of seeing a great white light hovering over him the whole time: a white light that wanted him but would not have him.

I kept thinking one side would give in. I kept thinking the saw-yers would give up and stop cutting the giants.

Those boys—the loggers would have killed those boys.

The men were, I think, angry, but also strangely alive—feeling the edges of life is how I imagined it—and each day they went into the woods as if going off to war, and there was no doubt that if any of them ever saw who was doing it there would be one shot from a 30.06, one crisp shot on a winter morning, and the story would be over.

It was the women whom the spikes bothered the most. They'd play pinochle at the mercantile nearly every day, and get drunk and talk about the things they were going to do if they found out who it was: castrations, that sort of thing.

I'd dated—"slept with" is the better term, the more accurate words, for this valley—Victor's mother for a while, back when Victor must have been eleven or twelve. I remembered once when I'd been over there, staying the night, wide-assed naked on the bed—I re-member what I was doing with Carol clearly, what she was having done—when Victor came into the room, just opened the door and walked right in, and stood there.

Carol leapt up and ushered him out of the room, didn't even put a robe on or wrap a sheet around herself—just hustled him right back out the door.

Not long after that Carol and I got tired of one another's bodies and drifted apart.

◆

Sometimes the women would be playing cards at the mercantile when I went in for groceries. They played all day long in the winter—

the men out sawing, while I, the nature writer, the nature boy, hung around town, hung around the cabin—and the mercantile would be blue with smoke. The thing I liked about Carol, the way I remembered her, besides in bed, was how she held her cards, arranging them, and how she let her cigarette dangle from the corner of her mouth. I liked to watch all of the women play as I moved down the short aisles, selecting that day's canned goods: soup, beans, mixed fruits.

"I'll get him," Carol said one day to the other women—deciding to lay her cards down when she realized, belatedly, that she had won. Winning always seemed to surprise her, or any of them, and they'd stare at the cards for a few moments whenever they won, even after they had laid the last card down, as if not trusting their eyes, as if unsure of what they were seeing. "Whoever it is, I'll kill him," she said, and they all nodded.

The women started up a new hand then, and played, I'm sure, late into the afternoon, trying not to look at the clock, trying not to wonder if one of the men was down at that very moment. It was February, and hysteria seemed only a step away, as if they could walk right into it, comfortably, and settle in with no effort at all. They spoke carefully and slowly, trying to help each other, watching for signs.

I saw Carol's hands tremble that afternoon as she held her cards. The man she was sleeping with now was a logger. All of the men were. It was all or nothing.

◆━━

It was also in February, that year when Victor and Percy were fifteen, that they began riding the horses. Davey Prouder, who ran the saloon, was keeping the horses in my pasture in exchange for my free drinks at the saloon, since I didn't drink that much, and it was one of my jobs to feed them, and to keep the ice from clogging up on their hooves, and to exercise them, if I could. Buck was a sweet line-backed dun, but Fuel was a ferocious cutting horse from Oklahoma who was so mean they hadn't even been able to trailer him—instead, they'd had to ride him all the way up here, and it had taken three months.

But when Percy turned fifteen, he somehow got it into his mind to begin riding Fuel. He'd found out that he could ride him as long as it was dark and cold; and he rode after midnight, after he and Victor got in from spiking trees.

Percy, poor ugly Percy, would slip up on wild Fuel—all the cold stars at their brightest, and every sound magnified, every sound a shout—and Victor would climb up on Buck, the sweet horse, the tamer horse, and the two boys would ride around the pasture at a full gallop, riding the horses through the deep drifts and up through the woods behind my cabin, clinging to the wild, startled horses' necks and shutting their eyes, trying to keep from being popped by frozen branches. I'd watch from the window, still passive, and frightened, and amazed at their fury, their anger. I wanted to get back together with Carol, but she was pretty sweet on her new logger. Things were good between them—you could see that. Why did I want to ruin that? Something about the spikes, and all the trouble in the valley that year, made me want to make love to her again.

I would see Victor and Percy in the store, on weekends, and we'd exchange strange looks—glares, sometimes. Percy would be bruised or cut from where his father had hit him with things. No one liked it; everyone wished the old man would go ahead and die, or rot away, so that Percy and his mother and brothers and sisters could start over. And in April, that is what happened: Mr. Coward ruptured something, some kind of bleeding started going on inside him, filling him up with his own blood, bloating him horribly, until his face was black and he was shouting, and Mrs. Coward, hysterical, called the mercantile on the truck's radio.

The pain had to have been horrendous. We could hear his screams all over the valley, and one of the men finally had to pull him outside and shoot him, to put him out of his misery.

I helped bury Percy's father in the marsh, in the cemetery for loggers. It was full of tall, shady larches, centuries old, with fine filtered sunlight that came drifting down, so slowly, through the lacy fernlike leaves of the smaller trees, and the forest floor was covered with larch needles. Granite headstones crept up into the woods, dating back to the early 1800s, with names like "Piss Fir Jim" and "Windy Joe Doggs." A slight breeze was always stirring in that cemetery, and that magic, gold light was always there, with the sound of the river below, even at night. It was the most beautiful spot in the valley, a fine resting spot.

Mister Coward had been thirty-eight. Hardly any of the loggers made it to thirty-eight.

One day, on the mural wall inside my barn, there was a spray-painted picture of what had to be me and Carol, in her bed—me doing what I'd been doing that time three years before. It was as if the boys were daring me, challenging me to hurt them—to turn them in.

There's a life to live; fear and lust are in this life. I went over to Carol's one day when Joe, her logger, was out in the woods and there wasn't a pinochle game going. Victor was gone, too. Carol and I had a couple of beers. I got brave and told her I wanted to get back together again. It wasn't so hard. Carol said we should, but that she wanted to keep it a secret.

Used to be, I wouldn't be much on that action—being secret, seeing her like that. But I was changing like crazy with those boys in my barn. I felt like I was on fire. I felt like burning myself up, like hurting myself. "Okay," I said. "Sure. However you want it."

I'd hike over to her house and make love to her during the day. She stopped going to all of the pinochle games. I'd never known a woman with such fury, such unquenchable fury. It was such a strange valley, back when Victor and Percy were fifteen.

Just fury: Ten men couldn't have done her, and that's a fact. Joe's benign picture—her logger—stared at us from the crowded dresser as we rutted. Nature boy, I thought, and then I'd think, nature boy, you've lived too long, you've gotten too dirty. The world has defeated you, has claimed you. It controls you.

Ten men couldn't have done her. It was better than before. It was wild.

Sometimes she seemed to want me to take her to the edge of pain; and sometimes she would try to hurt me.

Sometimes I let her. I don't know why.

In May, Victor and Percy started getting into fights. Usually Victor won, quickly blackening one of Percy's eyes or bloodying his nose; but in June, Percy got the idea of jousting rather than just simply fistfighting.

At first they went at it up in the woods, chasing each other around on the horses with sawed-off poles, more swatting than any sort of jousting—the horses leaping the fallen logs in the trails, one rider taking his horse down the creek into the mist of the great larches, into the summer morning fog, then wheeling around and riding hard back out of the ferns and mist, the sun gold in the other's eyes, blinded, just a hard-riding dark shape coming at him fast and then the swat of the pole, knocking one of them off of the barebacked horse, and landing hard on the spongy, rotting carpet of larch needles and bog.

All that silence around them after that, and the sun so far above them, at the tops of the great trees, struggling to make it down to them. . . .

I would run up from behind the house, up into the woods, and would crouch down behind logs, following them, as they galloped and wheeled, and chased each other through the woods on horseback.

But slowly, through the early summer, the boys' swats turned to true jousts, and they would lift each other off the backs of the horses, catching the other rider under the armpit, or high up in the chest, driving them backward, even lifting them up, then, as the horse continued forward, suddenly riderless—and then there'd be that long, twisting fall for the defeated rider, back down into the moss and old, dark soil.

It had to be a familiar feeling for Percy. He would pick himself up, never any broken bones, not at that age, and would whistle for Fuel, who, I was beginning to see, was the better fighting horse. Percy would have sugar cubes in his pocket, stolen from Victor's store, I'd bet, and it was how he got Fuel to return, and he would slip them to him when Victor wasn't looking, would whisper things in Fuel's ear.

What I saw was this: Percy was letting Victor knock him off that horse. He was only pretending to lose.

I don't know why—even today, I can't figure it out. Perhaps losing, and pain, and stupidity are simply things that are in the blood.

◆

A man on one of the logging crews was killed by the kickback from a spiked larch. Everyone had known it would happen sooner or later, they had just not known to whom it would happen. I felt immensely guilty. But they would have killed Percy, and maybe Victor. Strung them up if they hadn't shot them.

I dreamed about the dead man's face. Sometimes, when I was behind Carol and bucking on her, her back would suddenly look like a man's, in the night—*that* man's—and I'd gasp and not be able to finish, not want to finish.

A number of men had seen the accident, and the death, and were starting to have nightmares about it. Some who hadn't seen it were having nightmares, too. The women didn't know what to do about this. None of their men had ever had nightmares before. These were strong men. But now they were going into the woods without joking, without joy. They were gaunter, less interested in their wives, their girlfriends, in hunting and drinking, in anything. The June sun climbed higher in the sky earlier, and stayed up above them all day, hanging, shining white and warm, but it did not seem like spring to them, did not seem like anything.

Another man caught a kickback on the top of his helmet two weeks later, and he lay there unconscious for two hours in the ferns by the spring creek as the men splashed water on his face, trying to revive him, and when he came to he spoke of seeing the same white light hovering just above him, just out of reach: seeming to want him but unable to take him—seeming sad, disappointed.

◆

The boys moved out into the meadow with their jousts. They began to use longer poles, too: heavy lodgepole, with pillows lashed to one end, like a boxing glove, and heavy steel garbage can lids for shields—and the horses were running stronger, faster, rich on the green June hays and grasses.

The women in the valley began to watch them in the early summer, bringing picnic lunches and ice chests, which they sat on as if they were chairs. They would play cards, set up umbrellas to protect themselves from the high sun in the thin mountain air—umbrellas and parasols—and they would pour each other glasses of white wine. At that time no one had been injured, had not even seen a kickback, in almost a month. It was rumored that all of the spiked trees had been cut down.

The women would place bets on the two boys, bets that increased as the afternoon lengthened, and the wine bottles became empty. Some of the men built bleachers for the wives to sit on, and out in the pasture, every half hour or so, after resting and watching the horses, the two boys would go at it.

Sometimes Victor won, but more often now Percy would win. I was glad to see that Percy seemed to have gotten hold of himself, that he was not letting Victor win on purpose, that he was no longer just giving himself over to abuse.

They were the town darlings. No one had ever seen anything like it before.

Part of the bets went to Percy and Victor. Percy bought his mother a battery-operated radio, a new dress, some perfume. Victor saved his money. Carol said he wanted to get out of the valley. I think Victor was nervous about the legacy he and Percy had already left, at fifteen, and knew that there were entire forests of spiked trees that had not yet had the first tree felled in them; next year's cuttings, and the year's after that, and the next. I don't think he understood what had gotten into him. It had been Percy's idea, I think, but Victor had gone along with it. Bad luck.

Victor gave me the most murderous looks, in town and at the jousting meets; and later in the summer, as I continued to see Carol, he began to spray-paint murals of my death on my barn wall—pictures of me being dismembered by two boys with chain saws.

I'd stand there in the barn, in the daytime, and I'd know that I should tell—that Victor was challenging me to tell, and that Percy was, too. At fifteen, these two boys were simply tired of living, such was the dirt and hardness and emptiness of their lives. But I was too far into it, a man had died, and it was too late; and still, too, I held out hope for victory, hope that the spikes would save the biggest trees. I'm not saying that what I did—or didn't do—was right. I'm just saying I did it. That's all. I got into a bad situation, is all—like the boys—and got swept along by it.

In August, Percy caught Victor in the neck with the pole, and everyone who saw it agreed it was an accident, pure and simple—everyone but me.

It was true that Percy hit Victor with the pole no differently than he had a hundred times before—and no differently than he had been hit by Victor a hundred times—but what I believe now was that it had been a fight to the death all along, that Percy had known from the beginning that one of them would be killed jousting, and that he had determined to himself that he would ride hard until it happened, and just leave it up to luck.

Victor died before he hit the ground; bounced twice. Did he see the white light? It took him. The horse, Buck, kept running, into the trees. I was sitting with Carol and Joe. Carol screamed and leapt up and looked out into the meadow at her son—and then, strangely, looked off at the runaway horse for a long time—two, three seconds —before looking back at her son; and then, finally, she hurried down the bleachers and ran out to the meadow to hold him, though it was too late for that.

We buried Victor where we buried everyone: Always, in this valley, it seems, we're burying people.

They were just kids, but I was a grown man. The valley was pretty, but somehow the goodness finally left it. The magic and beauty went out of it years ago, and that was that, an end of good luck. We did something wrong, somewhere—I don't know what. We might simply have held our breath wrong.

The Kootenai Indians who used to hunt up here believe that luck is like pine sap, like tar, that it's something you step into—and that it can be good or bad, but that once you've stepped into it you've got to wear all of it off of your moccasin, if it's bad, say, before you can have the chance to step into good luck. And vice versa. And I have to agree. My luck's still holding, up here in the woods. But I feel like I've used up an awful lot, being associated with those two boys. I feel like I'm getting really close to the bottom by now, really wearing it out.

I'm here to bear witness to luck. I fell away from Carol once again. Joe lost her, too—she became nothing in her sorrow, a living ghost. They've both drifted to other places on the earth—probably still living, but barely: passive, damned, I suppose. Percy's still angry. Perhaps there was a way his anger could have been softened, could even have been healed, but it did not happen; and even today, as a grown man roaming the valley, cutting trees for the Forest Service, drinking, driving wildly, and getting in wrecks, Percy is still alive, and that anger is still in him, I can see, with his heart wrapped around it, wrapped like wood around a deep spike, a spike that is hidden and that can never be gotten out.

Those great trees, silent in the high forest, some of them still loaded with spikes, from the year that Percy was fifteen, are still standing. And still a danger.

In the end, it all comes down to luck. We're here, and if we're lucky, we're alive. Remember this, and be grateful. And be frightened.

MARY CLEARMAN BLEW

THE SNOWIES,
THE JUDITHS

A knock came at the door, and all eyes rose from the lesson. Mrs. Trask, looking troubled at yet another distraction, laid her book face down on the rules regarding *ser* and *estar* and went to answer it. Her first try at opening the door, however, met resistance. Had the knocker forgotten that the classroom doors opened outward into the corridor, or had he changed his mind about delivering his message, or was he merely being funny?

The students snickered, and Mrs. Trask flushed. It was hard enough for a substitute teacher to contain their excess energy during tournament season, let alone pretend to teach a lesson, without pranksters in the hall. She wrenched hard at the knob just as its resistance gave way.

The door opened so violently that the students saw Mrs. Trask lurch and almost lose her footing. Then she was taking a fast step back into the classroom. Her feet, however, in her new high heeled shoes, were far from fast enough to balance the backward propulsion of her body. She landed on her back, her head bumping against the glazed oak floor. Her feet scrabbled frantically out of her shoes, as though in search of some small lost possession of great value, while her torso bucked and thrust in such a familiar and explicit way that some of the students laughed outright. But the most surprising thing about Mrs. Trask was the red flower that bloomed where her face had been, bloomed and pulsed and overflowed its petals on the oak.

Mary Dare in the back row had put her fingers in her ears to stop the vibrations. Now she took her hands away, because she knew what made ears ring the way hers were ringing. She recognized the whine and crack, too, that had run like lightning around the edges of the explosion. Impossible to mistake those sounds. Only last weekend her father had let her fire a round with the .44, and her first shot had ricocheted off sandstone and whined. What she did not recognize, never had heard before in her life, were the staccato pips and shrills and squeals—well, yes, they did remind her of waking suddenly at night to the yammer of coyote pups, a pack of fools as her father called them, rallying for the first time in their lives with thin immature yips that chilled her and yet drew her out of her warm sleep to imagine herself walking with them through the cutbanks in the dark —the sounds that were rising now outside the classroom door and down the corridor as more shots reverberated.

Mary Dare stood up, thinking to see and perhaps comprehend. Then Ryan Novotny tackled her, big Ryan who as a senior really shouldn't have been in the first-year Spanish class at all but sat beside Mary Dare so he could copy her answers. Mary Dare found herself lying on her back between two rows of desks, looking up at the fluorescent lights burning away.

"Ho*ly*, Ryan," she said.

"Get down! Get down!" Ryan was yelling. "You crazy bastards, get your heads down!"

Now Ryan was crawling up the aisle next to hers on his elbows and knees. His rear end in his 501's was higher than his shoulders, and Mary Dare wanted to laugh at the sight he made. Somebody in the front of the room was laughing. Or hiccoughing, one or the other.

Mary Dare rolled over on her belly, wishing she hadn't worn her good white cotton sweater and jeans. She crawled below the surfaces of desks, as Ryan had done, over trails of dust and forgotten pencils and past crouching people's feet in shoes she recognized but never had expected to see at eye level. She crawled until she reached Jennifer Petty and took her hand and felt Jennifer's fingers lock on to hers while Jennifer went on hiccoughing and snuffling. Mary Dare lay with something, she thought a Spanish book, digging into her shoulder and her fingers in Jennifer's slippery grip. She could see the dark underside of Jennifer's desk, wafered with petrified discs of gum, and the pilling red Dacron mountain that was Jennifer in her awful sweater from Bonanza, and the inside of Jennifer's fat white wrist so close to Mary Dare's face that Mary Dare barely could bring her eyes to focus on individual freckles. Not a hand Mary Dare normally would be holding. Jennifer was weird. Jennifer's fingers kept slipping almost out of hers, but at the last second Jennifer would grab on again, so tight that Mary Dare could see her own fingers turning as white as Jennifer's, with tiny red lines seeping out between them and crawling down her wrist into the sleeve of her sweater.

Mary Dare arched her back to ease it off the cutting edge of the book or whatever she was lying on and settled down to wait for Ryan. Nothing would happen until Ryan came back. Ryan would be her early warning system. Mary Dare reduced the disgusting underside of Jennifer's desk to a blur by focusing on the ceiling light and letting all thought escape her. Nothing ever had happened to her, nothing ever would again. Fighting this morning with Amy and her mother over the hair dryer or Amy's endless sappy Bon Jovi tapes, guarding her painfully acquired collection of cosmetics and her really nice sweaters, getting on the school bus this morning in the dark, looking forward to getting out of classes early for the basketball tournament—none of it existed. All was reduced to the pain in her back, and Jennifer's grip in hers, and the light endlessly burning.

A shadow grew over the mountain of Jennifer, thrusting its head between Mary Dare and the light. Mary Dare blinked, and the shadow took form as Ryan.

"I can't see nothing. It's crazy out there."

Mary Dare pulled back from the brink with regret. Lint stuck in Ryan's hair and rolls of dust tracked his sweater. She felt bored with the sight of him, then sick. She rolled up on her elbow, tentatively. The line of windows was too high for her on the floor to see anything of the world outside except the fading February daylight and the distant tips of the mountains, snow-capped. For a moment she almost could breathe the freezing clean air of escape, almost feel the snow on her ankles as she ran.

"Forget it," Ryan whispered. "Them windows don't open. The bastards must of thought they was building a fucking jail when they built this place."

"Could you see him?" came a whisper behind Mary Dare.

"No, shit, couldn't see anything. I couldn't get far. All those doors and halls. He bagged Zeidel, though. I could see that."

Mary Dare closed her eyes. Ten feet away, on the other side of their wall, was the main corridor leading to the school offices. Lined with lockers, interspersed with classroom doors. After the utility dark greens and high ceilings of the old high school, the new doors painted in blues and violets had zinged at her for about the first week of school before they subsided into a familiarity as invisible as the soles of her feet.

The corridor had taken back its substance now, though. She could feel it through the wall.

"Always knew it would happen," Ryan was complaining. "Always knew it, always knew they'd pen us up like this and then take shots at us—"

"You're *paranoid*, Ryan," Mary Dare said. But she understood what he meant. She too, always had known somehow that it would come to this: the closed room, the graying windows, herself and all her classmates huddled under their desks, none daring to raise their heads while they waited for the inevitable next act. It was as though she had dreamed a thousand times about every detail. The hardwood floor, the dark underside of the desk, her knees drawn up, her arms wrapped around her skull; dreamed so many times, become so familiar that she no longer saw nor felt nor was aware of it, until now, by daylight, she recognized it at once. It was the end she always had known was coming, *and now that it's here,* unexpectedly rose her innermost voice, *we might as well get on with it.*

"Hey! Ryan! Town-ass!"

"What?" hissed Ryan.

It was Tom Barnes. She could see the blue flowered sleeve of his cowboy shirt; she remembered he usually sat in front.

"Could you see Zeidel?"

"Hell, yes. He was down. I could tell it was him by his suit."

Tom reared up on his elbows. "Oh shit, your arm."

"Yeh, her arm. And she calls me paranoid. Just because they're out to get us doesn't mean—"

Now that she was reminded of it, Mary Dare remembered how warm and wet her wrist and forearm felt. She glanced along the line of her sleeve and saw the sodden dark cuff of her white sweater and her red glistening fingers locked in Jennifer's.

"I don't think it's me," said Mary Dare. "It must be Jennifer."

To roll out from under Jennifer's desk, she was going to have to let go of Jennifer's hand. Testing, Mary Dare relaxed her fingers and felt a flutter of protest.

"Don't cry," Ryan pleaded.

"I *wasn't,*" said Mary Dare. "Oh, you mean her."

Mary Dare dug the heels of her hightops into the floor and arched her back much as Mrs. Trask had done. By squirming on her shoulders and inching herself along with her heels, she got her head clear of Jennifer's desk and rolled over and sat up without quite pulling her fingers out of Jennifer's. She glanced around. Although the desks were more or less in their rows, even with books still open at the assignment, nothing seemed quite in its usual place or even in its usual shape or color.

"Get your head *down!*"

"Hell, he ain't after us," said Tom.

With her free hand Mary Dare probed the mess of red sweater and ploughed red flesh and found the pressure point in Jennifer's arm right where in health class they had said it would be. She bore down through the fat until she felt bone. The depth of her fingers brought Jennifer's eyes popping open.

"I'm sorry," Jennifer whimpered.

"What are you sorry about?" Mary Dare asked her, fascinated.

Jennifer's eyes met Mary Dare's. Mary Dare watched the tip of Jennifer's tongue run around her lips as though she were about to explain herself.

"What makes you so sure?" Ryan was arguing.

Tom Barnes squatted in the aisle in his blue flowered shirt with the pearl snap pockets and his cowboy boots with the genuine undershot heels that had to be specially ordered. "I seen him. He ain't after us."

"Who was he?" Mary Dare wanted to know.

Ryan glared at Tom. Mary Dare, caught between them, looked from one to the other. Ryan the town-ass, really massive, as the kids here still were saying, and little Tom, who wasn't embarrassed by wearing his team roping jacket to high school.

"Then how come she's laying here bleeding?" insisted Ryan.

"Hell, he was aiming at Trask, not us."

"You're being pretty fucking cool about it. For a goat roper. How come she's bleeding?"

He was glaring at Tom, as urgent as if his being called massive by everyone hung on Tom's answer. Mary Dare knew he had no idea that in Portland they wouldn't call him anything. Or Tom either, for that matter. They wouldn't know what to *do* with Tom in Portland. She never had heard of goat ropers until she moved back to Montana.

"Are you trying to tell me that ain't a fucking gunshot wound in her arm?"

"He just flung in a couple extra shots to keep us out of his way," said Tom. "He ain't after us. Petty probably just caught a ricochet."

Tom hunkered forward on his precious boot heels. Watching,

Mary Dare understood what he was doing, finally understood what her dad had meant when he caught her horse for the third time last weekend and then advised her to cowboy up. It was amazing. Tom Barnes had cowboyed up.

He studied Jennifer Petty's glistening face and the raw red crater in her arm where Mary Dare was pinching off the spurt of blood. "She ain't going to die of that," he said.

"Who *was* it?" Mary Dare persisted.

"I don't know his name, but he's a kid. I've seen him around."

"I know him," came a whisper from under another of the front desks. "I mean, I seen him around, too. I don't know his name, either."

"You're saying he's after them," said Ryan.

"Well, he got Trask," said Tom Barnes. "And you say he got Zeidel."

"I said Zeidel was down."

Ryan's face worked to contain the idea of being incidental. He was on the verge of tears, Mary Dare realized; she never had seen a boy's tears before, and she didn't want to look at Ryan's, so she shut her eyes.

"Wonder where he went," came from the whisperer.

"Or if he lost his nerve," said Tom.

Mary Dare heard Ryan snuffle hard against his arm. At least the cowboy was keeping his nerve. The floor was grinding into her hip. She remembered the pine floors in the old high school. Softwood boards, varnished a dark brown that wore away by the spring of every year, hollow as the palms of hands from receiving the feet of generations of students. Floors trodden by her uncles in turn, all of them probably wearing boots like Tom's with undershot heels, and then her dad in his turn. This year should have been Mary Dare's turn. One of the reasons her dad had wanted to move back from the West Coast was so that Mary Dare and Amy could ride a school bus down the gulch into the shelter of the mountains, the way he had, and go to the old high school with kids like Tom Barnes. Her dad had recited the names of the mountains, the Snowies, the Judiths, the North Moccasins, the South Moccasins, like charms against any counterarguments her mother could raise, like the fine strings program and the languages program for the girls at Santa Angela High School. Charms for safety, the Snowies, the Judiths, the North Moccasins, the South Moccasins. Snowcapped blue mounds that ringed the town and that had offered a haven even in the long-ago days before there was a town and the Blackfeet had ridden down from the north to hunt and raid the Crows. The Snowies, the Judiths, the North Moccasins, the South Moccasins, charms against this moment, which, she suddenly understood, her father, too, must have dreamed a thousand times.

But instead of haven there was the new high school with its low maze of corridors, built and paid for by a levy her parents and the parents of practically every ranch kid she knew had voted against. The old high school wasn't even there anymore. On the square block on Water Street was only an empty crater. Little kids had howled in glee when the wrecking ball had knocked its bricks to rubble, its soft floors to splinters. The charm had not worked, the moment had come when she and probably Amy had had to crouch under the futile shelter of their desks in spite of anything her parents or anyone's parents could have done to avert it, the only difference between the dream and waking reality being that another kid, apparently, had pulled the trigger.

And now Mary Dare opened her eyes and met the frozen, astonished eyes of a man in a dark brown uniform with his revolver out.

In the glazed moment in front of the revolver, Mary Dare could remember only the necessity of keeping her fingers down hard on Jennifer's arm until the very end. Then she saw the man's lips move and found with surprise that she could hear what he was saying; in fact, his tone seemed unnecessarily loud, even distorted by volume.

"Oh shit no," he was saying.

It's not me that's bleeding but still alive, it's Jennifer, she thought to answer, but she could not be sure he understood her or even heard her or, although his eyes were fixed on her, even saw her. The others were rising beside her, around her. She could sense their slow unfolding, arms releasing their holds, tentative white faces emerging from under desks. Faces she could name, Tom Barnes and Ryan and Valier and Shannon and Stephen and Michael S. and Tyler and Michael J. and Ashley and Amber, like faces out of the dream, drained of life, all sockets and bones. And then, as they silently rose together, staring across the gulf at the patrolman, he seemed to recognize them with a start. He reholstered his gun.

"We'll get you out of here," his voice boomed and ebbed. He looked from face to face, then wet his lips. "Don't worry, we'll get you out of here."

"I can't let go of Jennifer," whispered Mary Dare. She felt glued to her.

"Somebody say he got another one?"

A sheriff's deputy in a tan gabardine jacket and a gray Stetson stuck his head in the door. His gaze wandered over Mary Dare and he started to say something else. Then his gaze fell to the floor and riveted there. Other men crowded the doorway behind him, vanished, reappeared. More highway patrolmen in dark brown, city policemen in navy blue. Mary Dare saw how their eyes, too, fell first to the floor and then rose in slow surmise to her face and the other faces in the room.

Ryan nudged her, more himself. "Looks like they got all the fuzz in Montana here."

"Something here you'll have to walk by," said the patrolman. "But you don't have to look."

"I can't let go," said Mary Dare. She could feel her own pulse in her fingertips and, faintly, Jennifer's. As long as she held on to Jennifer, she could put off the walk back into the ordinary.

But men were everywhere, all the fuzz in Montana, shoving through the rows of desks, kneeling beside her, their voices thundering at Jennifer while their fingers replaced Mary Dare's in Jennifer's wound. A draught streamed over her warm sticky fingers. She was being lifted by her elbows, steadied on her feet. "You done fine, little girl. We'll take care of her now."

One of the navy blue policemen had brought in a plastic pouch of yellowish fluid and was holding it above his head. A tube dangled down from it. Noise seemed amplified; Mary Dare wanted to yell at Amy to turn down the tape. She saw Jennifer being lifted on a stretcher with a needle taped into the fat part of her arm. The policeman with the pouch and the tube followed her. Mary Dare took a step after her, as toward her last link with flesh and blood, but hands held her back and a voice flexed and roared like a distorted cassette tape over her head: "She'll be all right. Now we're gonna get you out of here."

The floor felt unstable under her, the way the ground felt after a long horseback ride. Mary Dare wobbled toward the door. She knew the others were following her in a shaky line, Valier and Shannon and Stephen and Michael S. and Tyler and Michael J. and Ashley and Amber and everybody. Police on both sides were guiding the line, not quite touching kids with their hands. The corridor ahead was hot with lights.

"A big step, now. We got a blanket down. But you don't have to look."

Mary Dare took the giant step and several baby steps and found herself in the throbbing corridor. She paused, getting her bearings by herself. She was standing in the main hall to the school offices amidst bright lights and confusion and unfamiliar smears on the floor. To her left was the north hall, to her locker, and she turned automatically in that direction. Then she stopped, fascinated. Band music was seeping through the barred doors of the gymnasium at the far end of the north hall.

Hands turned her, started her in the other direction, hovered around her as though she might dissipate through their fingers like smoke. "This way. We're taking you into the study hall for now."

"*Study* hall!" moaned someone behind her in the line.

But news somehow was in the air, crackling in fragments.

"I guess for a while they thought he was going to shoot up the *gym*."

"He's that kid that never comes to class. Somebody said they guessed he thought it was her fault he got a pink slip."

"Maybe he thought Mrs. Trask was her."

"Wonder what happened to Zeidel."

The patrolman heard that and answered. "Mr. Zeidel took a hit in the leg and, uh, one in the lower abdomen, and they're taking him by air ambulance to Great Falls. We think he heard the shots and ran up the hall and, uh, met the kid running out."

"Wonder if he got away," said Tom Barnes low in Mary Dare's ear, but the patrolman heard that, too.

"He ran out of the school and, uh, we don't have other information as yet."

Silenced, they filed through the double doors. Mary Dare took the first desk she came to; it wasn't where she usually sat. The others were taking desks at random around her, a small cluster in the huge hall. Through the west windows she could see the last red stain of daylight.

"Wonder how the game came out," somebody whispered.

Sounds in the room were getting back to normal. A desk lid creaked.

"In here, sir," said the patrolman at the door. Everyone looked up as a man in a dark suit and a tie came in and sat down on the corner of a desk opposite them. The man's eyes moved from face to face; he looked stricken at what he saw, but that, too, was beginning to seem normal.

"We won't be keeping you here long," he said. He nodded two or three times, promising. "Your parents are, most of them, the ones we got hold of or, uh, heard about it, are out there waiting. They're wanting to see you, and we won't be keeping you long, but there's just a few questions, just one or two—"

He paused, and his mouth worked rapidly. Was he going to cry? Mary Dare looked away just in time. The red stain in the windows was darkening into nightfall. It must be way past the time when the school buses left.

"Did any of you see him?"

They shook their heads. Somebody, Valier, jerked a furtive finger across his eyes.

A stray voice from the hall cut in, angry—"in the middle of Montana, for chrissake, shit like this ain't supposed to go on here—" and was cut off as the patrolman pulled the door closed.

"No."

"No."

"Mrs. Trask," said Tom Barnes. "We saw her keel over."

"Yes."

"Yes."

They all had seen that, they agreed, nodding. Ryan wore a slight smile. Tom Barnes was lazing back in his desk on his spine with one leg stuck out into the aisle and the other leg crossed over it. The teachers hated it when kids sat like that. As though in the white glare of a searchlight, Mary Dare saw the downy hair on the back of Tom's neck and the bleached blue flowers of his shirt and the fragile overwashed blue of his Levi's. He looked like love's fading dream, Mary Dare thought. She knew she must look worse.

The man in the dark suit massaged his eyes with his hands. Maybe they all really did look like fading dreams to him. "We know you saw that," he said. "And I'm so sorry. Please believe me. I'd give anything if you hadn't had to. But did you see him?" He was looking straight at Mary Dare.

"No," she said truthfully. "No."

He sighed and was silent. "All right," he said at last. "We might have to talk to some of you again. Just maybe. But we'll hope not. We'll hope he—"

His voice died away. They waited. Finally he sighed again and slid off the desk without explaining to them what it was he hoped for. "Anyway," he said, "I know some parents who are going to be awfully glad to see some kids."

"I wonder who won the game," said somebody else as they filed out of the study hall.

But that was one piece of news that hadn't floated down to them. Mary Dare thought the scrap of band music she had heard might have been the Libby Loggers' fight song, which might have meant Fort Maginnis was behind. She wondered if the kids had been scared to play basketball while policemen with shotguns guarded the exits of the gym, or if they had gotten used to it, or if they even had known about it.

In the adjacent classroom the faces of parents turned toward them like wet white blobs in overcoats and heavy jackets and snowy overshoes. "Oh shit," said Ryan, "the old man wouldn't—oh shit, he is here."

Mary Dare saw her mom and dad just before her mom grabbed her. She felt the crush of wool collar and a wet cheek in her neck.

"Told you she'd be all right," said her dad. He had on his good Stetson. Melted snow dripped from the brim.

Mary Dare's mother let her go, except for one tight handhold, and turned on Mary Dare's dad. "Can't you see?" she cried, picking up their argument. "She's my baby, she's fourteen, she's only fourteen, and now I'll never get her back."

"Linda," said Mary Dare's dad, and her mother stopped talking but went on crying quietly while her grip on Mary Dare's hand tightened.

"Hell, she's all right. These Montana kids grow up tough. You didn't see anything, did you, Mary Dare?"

"No," said Mary Dare. She barely could feel her fingers in her mother's grip.

They walked abreast through the double doors, her mother and father on either side of Mary Dare as though she might disappear in their hands. Someone brushed against them from behind, trying to get past the three of them in the archway; it was Tom Barnes, in a hurry, pulling on his satin team roping jacket as he went.

"You need a ride home, Tom?" called her father.

He glanced back. "No thanks, Doc. I got my truck."

"He's a good kid," said her dad. "Was he there, too?"

"Yes," said Mary Dare.

Across the dark half-filled parking lot waited a school bus hung with painted banners, dieseling. Kids in Libby Logger letter jackets burst out of the double doors behind Mary Dare and her mother and father and ran yipping across the parking lot toward the bus.

"Pack of fools," said her dad angrily.

"No," said Mary Dare. "No, they're not."

You're the pack of fools, she wanted to say, but she shivered instead. In the refraction of frost under the exit lights she still could see the outline of Tom Barnes, hunching into his inadequate jacket against the freezing bite of the air and walking rapidly through the tumuli of shoveled snow toward the north lot. The sharp sounds of his boot heels on the scraped sidewalk receded as his shape faded beyond the radius of the lights, but for a moment Mary Dare followed him in her mind and faded with him into transparency in the dark. Far out in the circle of the mountains their glowing outlines fell to ash.

The problem is credibility.

The problem, as I'm finding out over the last few weeks, is basic credibility. A lot of people look at me and say, sure Rick, Bigfoot stole your wife. It makes me sad to see it, the look of disbelief in each person's eye. Trudy's disappearance makes me sad, too, and I'm sick in my heart about where she may be and how he's treating her, what they do all day, if she's getting enough to eat. I believe he's being good to her—I mean I feel it—and I'm going to keep hoping to see her again, but it is my belief that I probably won't.

In the two and a half years we were married, I often had the feeling that I would come home from the track and something would be funny. Oh, she'd say things: *One of these days I'm not going to be here when you get home,* things like that, things like everybody says. How stupid of me not to see them as omens. When I'd get out of bed in the early afternoon, I'd stand right here at this sink and I could see her working in her garden in her cut-off Levi's and bikini top, weeding, planting, watering. I mean it was obvious. I was too busy thinking about the races, weighing the odds, checking the jockey roster to see what I now know: He was watching her, too. He'd probably been watching her all summer.

So, in a way it was my fault. But what could I have done? Bigfoot steals your wife. I mean: Even if you're home, it's going to be a mess. He's big and not well trained.

When I came home it was about eleven-thirty. The lights were on, which really wasn't anything new, but in the ordinary mess of the place, there was a little difference, signs of a struggle. There was a spilled Dr Pepper on the counter and the fridge was open. But there was something else, something that made me sick. The smell. The smell of Bigfoot. It was hideous. It was . . . the guy is not clean.

Half of Trudy's clothes are gone, not all of them, and there is no note. Well, I know what it is. It's just about midnight there in the kitchen, which smells like some part of hell. I close the fridge door. It's the saddest thing I've ever done. There's a picture of Trudy and me leaning against her Toyota taped to the fridge door. It was taken last summer. There's Trudy in her bikini top, her belly brown as a bean. She looks like a kid. She was a kid I guess, twenty-six. The two times she went to the track with me everybody looked at me like how'd I rate her. But she didn't really care for the races. She cared about her garden and Chinese cooking and Buster, her collie, who I guess Bigfoot stole, too. Or ate. Buster isn't in the picture, he was nagging my nephew Chuck, who took the photo. Anyway I close the fridge door and it's like part of my life closed. Bigfoot steals your wife and you're in for some changes.

You come home from the track having missed the Daily Double by a neck, and when you enter the home you are paying for and in which you and your wife and your wife's collie live, and your wife and her collie are gone as is some of her clothing, there is nothing to believe. Bigfoot stole her. It's a fact. What should I do, ignore it? Chuck came down and said something like well if Bigfoot stole her why'd they take the Celica? Christ, what a cynic! Have you ever read anything about Bigfoot not being able to drive? He'd be cramped in there, but I'm sure he could manage.

I don't really care if people believe me or not. Would that change anything? Would that bring Trudy back here? Pull the weeds in her garden?

As I think about it, no one believes anything anymore. Give me one example of someone *believing* one thing. I dare you. After that we get into this credibility thing. No one believes me. I myself can't believe all the suspicion and cynicism there is in today's world. Even at the races, some character next to me will poke over at my tip sheet and ask me if I believe that stuff. If I believe? What is there to believe? The horse's name? What he did the last time out? And I look back at this guy, too cheap to go two bucks on the program, and I say: It's history. It is historical fact here. Believe. Huh. Here's a fact: I believe everything.

Credibility.

When I was thirteen years old, my mother's trailer was washed away in the flooding waters of the Harley River and swept thirty-one miles, ending right side up and nearly dead level just outside Mercy, in fact in the old weed-eaten parking lot for the abandoned potash plant. I know this to be true because I was inside the trailer the whole time with my pal Nuggy Reinecker, who found the experience more life-changing than I did.

Now who's going to believe this story? I mean, besides me, because I was there. People are going to say, come on, thirty-one miles? Don't you mean thirty-one feet?

We had gone in out of the rain after school to check out a magazine that belonged to my mother's boyfriend. It was a copy of *Dude,* and there was a foldout page I will never forget of a girl lying on the beach on her back. It was a color photograph. The girl was a little pale, I mean, this was probably her first day out in the sun, and she had no clothing on. So it was good, but what made it great was that they had made her a little bathing suit out of sand. Somebody had spilled a little sand just right, here and there, and the sand was this incredible gold color, and it made her look so absolutely naked it wanted to put your eyes out.

Nuggy and I knew there was flood danger in Griggs; we'd had a flood every year almost and it had been raining for five days on and off, but when the trailer bucked the first time, we thought it was my mother come home to catch us in the dirty book. Nuggy shoved the magazine under the bed and I ran out to check the door. It only took me a second and I hollered back *Hey no sweat, no one's here,* but by the time I returned to see what other poses they'd had this beautiful woman commit, Nuggy already had his pants to his ankles and was involved in what we knew was a sin.

If it hadn't been the timing of the first wave with this act of his, Nuggy might have gone on to live what the rest of us call a normal life. But the Harley had crested and the head wave, which they estimated to be three feet minimum, unmoored the trailer with a push that knocked me over the sofa and threw Nuggy, already entangled in his trousers, clear across the bedroom.

I watched the village of Griggs as we sailed through. Some of the village, the Exxon Station, part of it at least, and the carwash, which folded up right away, tried to come along with us, and I saw the front of Painters' Mercantile, the old porch and signboard, on and off all day.

You can believe this: it was not a smooth ride. We'd rip along for ten seconds, dropping and growling over rocks, and rumbling over tree stumps, and then wham! the front end of the trailer would lodge against a rock or something that could stop it, and whoa! We'd wheel around sharp as a carnival ride, worse really, because the furniture would be thrown against the far side and us with it, sometimes we'd end up in a chair and sometimes the chair would sit on us. My mother had about four thousand knickknacks in five big box shelves, and they gave us trouble for the first two or three miles, flying by like artillery, left, right, some small glass snail hits you in the face, later in the back, but that stuff all finally settled in the foot and then two feet of water which we took on.

We only slowed down once and it was the worst. In the railroad flats I thought we had stopped and I let go of the door I was hugging and tried to stand up and then swish, another rush sent us right along. We rammed along all day it seemed, but when we finally washed up in Mercy and the sheriff's cousin pulled open the door and got swept back to his car by water and quite a few of those knickknacks, just over an hour had passed. We had averaged, they figured later, about thirty-two miles an hour, reaching speeds of up to fifty at Lime Falls and the Willows. I was okay and walked out bruised and well washed, but when the sheriff's cousin pulled Nuggy out, he looked genuinely hurt.

"For godsakes," I remember the sheriff's cousin saying, "The damn flood knocked this boy's pants off!" But Nuggy wasn't talking. In fact, he never hardly talked to me again in the two years he stayed at the Regional School. I heard later, and I believe it, that he joined the monastery over in Malcolm County.

My mother, because she didn't have the funds to haul our rig back to Griggs, worried for a while, but then the mayor arranged to let us stay out where we were. So after my long ride in a trailer down the flooded Harley River with my friend Nuggy Reinecker, I grew up in a parking lot outside of Mercy, and to tell you the truth, it wasn't too bad, even though our trailer never did smell straight again.

Now you can believe all that. People are always saying: Don't believe everything you read, or everything you hear. And I'm here to tell you. Believe it. Everything. Everything you read. Everything you hear. Believe your eyes. Your ears. Believe the small hairs on the back of your neck. Believe all of history, and all of the versions of history, and all the predictions for the future. Believe every weather forecast.

Believe in God, the afterlife, unicorns, showers on Tuesday. Everything has happened. Everything is possible.

I come home from the track to find the cupboard bare. Trudy is not home. The place smells funny: hairy. It's a fact and I know it as a fact: Bigfoot has been in my house.

Bigfoot stole *my* wife.

She's gone.

Believe it.

I gotta believe it.

I AM
BIGFOOT

That's fine. I'm ready.

I am Bigfoot. The Bigfoot. You've been hearing about me for some time now, seeing artists' renderings, and perhaps a phony photograph or two. I should say right here that an artist's rendering is one thing, but some trumped-up photograph is entirely another. The one that really makes me sick purports to show me standing in a stream in northern California. Let me tell you something: Bigfoot never gets his feet wet. And I've only been to northern California once, long enough to check out Redding and Eureka, both too quiet for the kind of guy I am.

Anyway, all week long, people (the people I contacted) have been wondering why I finally have gone public. A couple thought it was because I was angry at that last headline, remember: "Jackie O. Slays Bigfoot." No, I'm not angry. You can't go around and correct everybody who slanders you. (Hey, I'm not dead, and I only saw Jacqueline Onassis once, at about four hundred yards. She was on a horse.) And as for libel, what should I do, go up to Rockefeller Center and hire a lawyer? Please. Spare me. You can quote me on this: Bigfoot is not interested in legal action.

◆

"Then, why?" they say. "Why climb out of the woods and go through the trouble of 'meeting the press,' so to speak? (Well, first of all, I don't live in the woods *year round,* which is a popular misconception of my life-style. Sure, I like the woods, but I need action, too. I've had some of my happiest times in the median of the Baltimore Belt route, the orchards of Arizona and Florida, and I spent nearly five years in the corn country just outside St. Louis. So, it's not just the woods, okay?)

◆

Why I came forward at this time concerns the truest thing I ever read about myself in the papers. The headline read "Bigfoot Stole My Wife," and it was right on the money. But beneath it was the real story: "Anguished Husband's Cry." Now I read the article, every word. Twice. It was poorly written, but it was all true. I stole the guy's wife. She wasn't the first and she wasn't the last. But when I went back and read that "anguished husband," it got me a little. I've been, as you probably have read, in all fifty states and eleven foreign countries. (I have never been to Tibet, in case you're wondering. That is some other guy, maybe the same one who was crossing that stream in northern California.) *And,* in each place I've been, there's a woman. Come on, who is surprised by that? I don't always steal them; in fact, I never *steal* them, but I do *call them away,* and they come with me. I know my powers and I use my powers. And when I call a woman, she comes.

◆

So, Here I Am. It's kind of a confession, I guess; kind of a warning. I've been around; I've been all over the world (except Tibet! I don't know if that guy is interested in women or not). And I've seen thousands of women standing at their kitchen windows, their stare in the mid-afternoon goes a thousand miles; I've seen thousands of women, dressed to the nines, strolling the cosmetic counters in Saks and I. Magnin, wondering why their lives aren't like movies; thousands of women shuffling in the soft twilight of malls, headed for the Orange Julius stand, not really there, just biding time until things get lovely.

And things get lovely when I call. I cannot count them all, I cannot list the things these women are doing while their husbands are out there in another world, but one by one I'm meeting them on my terms. I am Bigfoot. I am not from Tibet. I go from village to town to city to village. At present, I am watching your wife. That's why I am here tonight. To tell you, fairly, man to man, I suppose, I am watching your wife, and I know for a fact that when I call, she'll come.

PARAISO:
AN ELEGY

art is dead. Cancer got him. He died well. What I mean is, he died pretty much as he lived, without fear or dread, and he died without the sort of high-torque pain or mind-gumming drugs that would have blunted his ability to find interest in the process of dying. We still talk about him in the present tense. "Hart has presence of mind," we say, and "Hart can't tolerate French movies," and "Hart likes his beer freezer-cold." His gray stare, somewhat quizzical due to the tumors thriving near the occipital region of his brain, asks you to be honest: Never say what you don't mean. If in doubt, remember, silence is incorruptible. You can spend half a day with Hart and maybe trade three opinions. But he likes his jokes. He likes the sharp observation that punctures the gassy balloons of hypocrisy, pomp, and self-importance. As a photographer and poet, that's what he's about. And so he can get you in trouble. He's a little guy with a proud chest. His camera bag, always slung on his shoulder, makes him list ten degrees to port. It makes him walk with a limp.

It began with an omen. We were in Juárez, Christmas 1988, fending off a gang of seasonal pickpockets who had moved into the border town from somewhere in the interior. They circled us like a half-dozen bantamweight boxers, nodding and shrugging, feinting in and dancing back, bumping us, confusing us with large, friendly smiles. Hart pulled out his little Zeiss and started to spend film while our wives, Rocky and Joyce, dealt with the footloose thieves. These wives are tough, friendly women from the bedrock towns of Butte and Anaconda, Montana, respectively. When a quick brown hand slipped into the throat of Rocky's purse, she slapped it away, brisk as a frontier schoolmarm, and my tall, strong-jawed Joyce yanked her purse clear with enough force to start a chain saw. The thieves tap-danced away from the white-knuckled determination of these good-looking *güeras,* with no hard feelings, no need to get righteous. The phrase *No me chinguen, pendejos* was ready on my lips, and I whispered it in rehearsal since I am fluent with set phrases only. And Joyce, who *is* fluent, hissed, "Don't you *ever* say that in this town unless you want to take your gringo whizzer back across the bridge in segments."

Joyce works in a Juárez industrial park, teaching idiomatic, rust-belt American to executives of the *maquiladora* industry who need to travel north. Her company assembles computer components for GM and pays its workers an average of five dollars a day, which is a full dollar above the Mexican minimum wage. Joyce gets eighteen dollars an hour because she insists on being paid what the job's worth, having come from Anaconda, a town so unionized you can't pour tar on your leaky shed without getting hard stares from the organized roofers. It troubles her that the Tarahumara Indian beggar women on Avenida Diez y Seis de Septiembre can make twice as much on a good day as a worker in a *maquiladora.* That's why she didn't get hysterical over the pickpockets. Their mostly seasonal earnings are on a puny scale compared to what the foreign-owned *maquiladoras* siphon into their profit margins. If anyone was close to hysteria it was me (the gringo instinct to protect and prevail knocking at my heart), not the iron-willed women from Montana. My fists were balled up, and my mind was knotted, too, with such off-the-subject irrelevancies as my honor, my male pride. *¡Lárguense a la chingada!* I felt like saying, but I also knew that if I did, things would get serious in a hurry because these thieves from Chihuahua or wherever have a more commanding sense of honor than I do. We gringos might have a more commanding sense of *fair play,* but honor is too abstract to touch off instantaneous grass fires in our blood. It applies to flag and parents and, at one time, to a young man's conduct in the vicinity of decent girls, but it has never functioned as a duty, uncompromising as the survival instinct, to oneself.

And if I did get lucky and scatter them with a few wild punches, then what? The streets were dense with locals who do not think the world of these pale, camera-toting, wisecracking, uninhibited laughers from a thousand miles north of the Río Bravo. And when a nearby *tránsito*—a black-and-tan-uniformed traffic cop, the local version of the *guardia civil*—strolled by to see what was what, speaking the same street Spanish as the purse-snatchers, whose story did I

think would be heard? Who did I think would go to jail? This was
before Hart's diagnosis, when we were all planning a succession of
trips starting with the thrill-a-minute train ride from Ciudad Chihuahua to Creel and on to the Barranca de Cobre, and later in the year,
to Puebla and Vera Cruz. *"Que le vaya bien,"* Joyce called to the
retreating pickpockets. And a smiling thief replied, his Spanish
courtly and dignified, "And may it also go equally well for you, lady."
Rocky, a former parachute journalist who now teaches Bullshit De-
tection 101, rolled her black Irish eyes and muttered, "Jesus. Joyce
must be campaigning for sainthood. The Bleeding Virgin of the Cut-
purse. They wanted to take your MasterCard, honey, not test your
Spanish."

We stopped in the Kentucky Club on Avenida Juárez for a round
of self-congratulatory margaritas, then crossed back into Texas, purses
and wallets intact. We felt generally upbeat. But in the river, on the
north bank, we saw a decapitated mule. We hung over the rail, staring
at the mud-colored carcass bloating in the silty river, as if this had
been the planned high point and ultimate purpose of our tour. Hart
said, "Omen, troops." We looked at him. This was one of those moments in life when things get too slippery to catch in a net of words.
We looked at each other. An innocence rising up from childhood
struck us dumb as Hart attached a long lens to his Zeiss and photographed the headless mule.

2

Joyce and I are on this trip with Hart and Rocky, looking for
something in the desert. A kind of comradely spitefulness has made
us rowdy and solemnly amused by turns. I guess it is Death we are
spiting, though no one comes out and says so. We like each other
because we know we are misfits who have found our niche in the
friendly halls of universities.

We are Western by chance, and remain so by choice. We love
cars and rock and roll more than we love fine art and baroque music.
We wear this preference on our pearl-buttoned sleeves. We've been
antsy from birth: The verb "to go" was the first one we learned to
conjugate. We've got Cowboy Junkies in the tape deck and a six-pack
of Lone Star balanced on the console between the seats. Drinking

and driving is a Western birthright. This is Texas, where it's legal to
have opened containers in a moving car. This law (known affection-
ately as the Bubba Law) may be repealed soon, but we're not in a
mood to worry about it: The lab report on the biopsies is in and now
we all know the worst. Hart has six months, if he's lucky—six months,
that is, if the tumors crowding his vertebrae don't break in and van-
dalize the spinal cord tomorrow or the next day.

Hart has the perfect vehicle for this type of travel. A 1972 Chevy
Blazer with the big 350 long-block V-8 throbbing under the hood.
The Blazer is a two-ton intimidator. Hart is not into intimidation, but
the slender Celicas, Maximas, and Integras that pull into our slip-
stream don't know that. They tend to keep their distance from the
big, rust-brown, generously dented Chevy. Hart and I sit up front,
Rocky and Joyce sit in back—a Western arrangement not meant to
signify the relative status of the sexes. A traveler from New Haven,
say, might look into the Blazer and see Hart and me up front in straw
hats with beer cans on the dash, and the women eating coffee chews
in back, perhaps catch a strain of the Cowboy Junkie's visionary wailing, and think *highway buckaroos and the little women, tsk, tsk.* This
is unfair to the Yankees, of course. You might find the same arrangement in a dented Blazer in New Haven. Only in New Haven, I suspect, the highway buckaroo remark might be justified. Two couples
riding this way back there *would* be making a statement, whether
they wanted to or not. Turning ourselves into an illustrated idea is the
last thing in the world the four of us would do.

We're heading in our roundabout way for Tucson, normally a
five-hour trek from El Paso, where we live. The sandstorms have
raised cubic miles of desert, turning it into coastal fog. Our running
lights are on and we've slowed to forty and the wind is making the big
Blazer rock and roll. Hart is feeling the strain, having just undergone
his first series of radiation treatments, which he found entertaining.
("Star Wars, troops. They levitate you into the center of a big dome
where smart machines that know your body better than you do sniff
out and then zap the intruders.") I have offered to drive, but no one
drives the Blazer except Hart. He loves this truck as a settler might
have loved his big-bore buffalo gun, his horse, or his quarter section
of homestead bottomland. And so it's decided: We'll turn off at exit
331, get on U.S. 666, and head for my widowed mother's adobe
hacienda in Paraiso, Arizona, where Death has left his stain and dull
gloom not long ago.

It is late afternoon when we pull into her driveway, and Mom—Sada—is already in her cups. She's been working all morning on *Storm over the Dragoons,* a six-by-three-foot oil painting, and now is drinking ruby port to unwind. Painting has helped fill in the gaps left by the removal of Lenny Burbek, her husband for the last twenty-six years. Cancer got him, too.

Sada pours wine for us at her kitchen table. The house smells of oil paint, even though her studio is out in the attached garage. "Hart, you look fer shit," she says. Sada, at eighty-two, has dispensed with all the social delicacies.

"Fer shit is an improvement over yesterday," Hart says, holding the cup of ruby port but not drinking. The road beers have already given him grief. Alcohol, mixed with the tumor-poisoning chemicals circulating in his system, make him sick. He's got a tumor in his liver, too, and his liver won't forgive and forget. Hart puts the wine down and takes a picture of Sada. She is a mask of fierce wrinkles and looks more like an old Navajo or Apache squaw than the immigrant Scandinavian that she is. Hart has this theory: The land eventually has its way with us. Live in this desert long enough and sun, wind, sand, and thirsty air will eventually give a native shape to your clay, just as thirty years in Oslo will fade, elasticize, and plump up the austere skin of an Apache. The land works us like a craftsman works maple or oak. Ultimately, the tools and strategies of the craftsman overcome the proud immutability of any hardwood. The land owns us, not vice versa, the current triumph of the capitalist zeitgeist notwithstanding. This is Hart's pet idea. The land owns us and we had better treat it with the proper deference. You can see it in his prints. It is often the text and always the subtext of his poems. "We all need a pet idea," Hart says, "even if it's a stupid one. Even a stupid idea, pursued long enough with enough dedication, so that all its dead ends are discovered, will lead you to the same place as a nifty one." We don't ask Hart what or where that place is. We act like we know, and maybe we almost do. "Besides," Hart says, "*ideas* are ultimately wrong anyway."

Sada fixes her favorite dish that night, linguini with clam sauce, along with big prawns from Puerto Peñasco, down on the Sea of Cortez. Tyrell Lofton, Sada's boyfriend, eats with us. Tyrell is a West Virginia mountain man bent on turning his piece of Paraiso into mountaineer country. He's planted black walnut trees, tulip trees, and a variety of conifers, and has a fecund greenhouse that produces several tons of winter tomatoes. He dreams of building a small still—

a genetic mandate. And his house, made of scrap wood, has been half built for twenty years. He's a lean, hard-knuckled seventy-five-year-old widower who also has the weathered Apache look. As we eat, I can tell Hart is planning photography sessions with Tyrell and Sada, for no one we know proves his pet idea better than these two.

After dinner, Sada begins to fidget around. She wants to go dancing. "Have you kids been to the Duck Inn?" she asks coyly. The Duck Inn is a little geezer saloon that caters to the population of Paraiso. "They've got a terrific little band there. The ex-sheriff of Tombstone owns the place. He's also the bandleader."

Sada was a dancer in the Ziegfeld Follies and there is no quit in her. Her bottle-blond hair is startling above her brown, massively grooved, big-cheeked, purse-leather face. "I think we'll pass, Mom," I say.

She scoffs. "Don't be an old fart, sonny, you're not even fifty yet. Come on, we'll have a few laughs."

Tyrell, who always has a twinkle in his faded blue eyes, says, "Goodness me, I don't think they ever had *four* professors in the Duck Inn all at once." Tyrell is quick to spot the potential fun in a given situation, but his remarks are never mean or sour. According to Tyrell, it's okay to take the light view of humanity, since only trees have honest-to-God dignity. It's his pet idea.

"Hart doesn't feel up to it," I say.

"The hell I don't," Hart says, his face drawn, his jaw tight enough to reflect light.

And so we all walk to the bar, surrounded by black night and the thousand unblinking stars of this high desert. Hart amazes me, plodding along, one painful step after another, Rocky hanging on his arm. What amazes me is his placid indifference to the Big Change coming his way, his refusal to let it become the major dramatic event of the season. And then I think of his pet idea, and how the desert might shape a body for pain, too. The Apaches took pain in stride, even sought it out as a measuring stick of their individual worth. The deserts of the Near East have produced prophetic pain-seekers for thousands of years. Jesus, destined for pain, did not pile up annuities or build Alpine retreats to hide himself from it. Blood and sand are the primary colors of the desert. The agonies of crucifixion are storming in Hart's bones and guts, but he won't let us in on this internal secret. I am reminded of Sada's third and last husband, Lenny (another de facto Apache), settling into his easy chair gingerly, as if some wickedness had turned his burly, ex-ironworker's frame into crystal stemware. Lenny and his pal from down the street, also dying of cancer, would sit in their bathrobes and watch the Playboy channel for hours at a time, sampling each other's painkillers. There they were —two old men, all the vigor of their lives sucked into the unappeasable black hole of cancer—denying the sex-hating Intruder by watching the rosy, pile-driving rumps of fornicating youths hour after hour, snacking on chips and *queso,* washing down opiates and tranks with beer, giving a thin cheer now and then to the gymnastic skills of the actors. Lenny died in bed pushing himself up to a sitting position while insisting that he felt much, *much* better.

Paraiso is not exactly a retirement village, though most of the residents are retired. There are a few younger people who commute the ninety miles to Tucson to work. They live here because real estate costs half as much and because the air is about as clean as late-twentieth-century American air can get. A few of these people are in the Duck Inn, dancing and carrying on. Sada knows them all and shouts their names. She backs her straight shots of vodka with draft beer and she has a what-the-hell look in her eyes. Soon she is up on her feet, dancing alone among the younger folk, holding her peasant skirts up over her old hardscrabble knees and yelling, "Yippee, son of a bitch, yippee!" while her carpet slippers flap. Then Tyrell leaps up, his wide pale eyes almost glassy, and does a solo mountaineer buckdance which no one challenges. Rocky is laughing her choppy, nicotine-stained laugh, and Hart, though he's got a white-knuckled grip on his untouched mug of beer, is smiling. Joyce nudges me under the table, whispering, "Hope you feel strong. You and Tyrell are going to have to carry Sada home." And the fiddlers chop down feverishly into their fiddles as if everything now depended on this crazed music.

Later that night, as the coyotes howl and the screech owls make their eerie electronic screams, Joyce and I hear Rocky crying softly through the wall that separates our bedrooms, and under the crying, Hart's laboring snores. Unable to sleep, I get up and prowl the house. It is 3:00 A.M., the hour of the wolf, dead center of night when all of us are naked in our small separate selves. At this hour all the technological wonders and powers of America seem like a feeble dream: the optimistic cities of glass and steel, the superhighways, the elaborate networks of instant communication, and the medical colossus that, for all its precise weapons and collective strategic genius, cannot discourage the barbarous imperialism of a wretched horde of mindless tumors.

The garage light is on. Sada is up, too, working on her big landscape. She doesn't hear me come in, and I watch her drag a broad, paint-fat brush across the base of the Dragoons, the range of mountains where Cochise and his band of righteous Chiricahua warriors held off the U.S. Army for ten years. The mountains are blue-black under the angry flex of muscular storm clouds. All the rage of Sada's eighty-two years is in this canvas, which, the longer I look at it, seems more like a thunderous shout than a painting. "Some painting, Ma," I say.

She whirls around, her leaky Apache eyes burning with a warrior's need to run a spear into the dark gut of the beast.

"It's all I can do now," she says.

3

As we head south toward Douglas and Agua Prieta, I am thinking of the strange girl who lives across the street from Sada. She is sixteen and suffering the pain of boredom and the deeper pain of her own oddness, which will isolate her more than geography ever could. Joyce and Rocky found her lying in the middle of the street, her hair chopped close to her scalp, as if by a hunting knife. Thunderclouds sat on the Dragoons. Joyce thought at first that the girl had been run over, but she was only waiting. I am waiting for something to happen to me, is what she said. Joyce and Rocky left her there, spread-eagled in the road, as the tall clouds moved closer and God's original voice began to rumble with its old no-nonsense authority. Red-tailed hawks lofty as archangels swept down out of the dark sky, choosing among opportunities. Joyce and Rocky decided: Maybe the odd girl was right and was playing her aces now, while she still had them. Maybe we are all waiting for something to happen to us—death or life—but for the girl lying in the street the issue was unclouded by career, marriage, property, and all the other trump cards that must be deferred to before we can clear the slate and move on.

Hart's Blazer pitches and yaws over a rough highway that will take us into the mountains. We have turned onto a narrow, shoulderless road that cuts west into the southern foothills of the Dragoons, as we head now for Bisbee instead of Douglas and Agua Prieta. "I've always wanted to see the Lavender Pit," Hart says.

Traveling by whim is touring at its best.

The old houses of Bisbee cling to the sides of the mountains, prayerfully as exhausted climbers. And the streets, angled like derailed trains, work their way up to the highest ledge of dwellings. We walk these steep streets, finding level ground in a doorway now and then to catch our breath. Hart's been taking painkillers and tends to stagger against the unexpectedly oblique tugs of gravity that have made the older buildings lean into each other like amiable drunks. He stops now and then to photograph the odd geometry of a ruined hotel, the grit-pocked face of an old miner, the bands of Japanese tourists who photograph everything in their path as if making a visual record of what will one day be all theirs. The four of us often agree that World War Two is still being fought, that the atomic bombings of Japan merely forced a change in weaponry. After Hiroshima and Nagasaki, the tide turned, and now Japanese samurai in three-piece suits, portfolios in hand, are succeeding where Tojo's fanatic armies failed. Choice Hawaiian beachfront and Rockefeller Center are theirs, the great evergreen forests of Oregon are theirs, and lately, giant cattle ranches in Montana. "I could settle down here," Rocky says. "In one of those shacks on the side of the mountain. This place is like Butte, without Butte's winters."

Rocky prides herself for being realistic. She knows we all understand that she is imagining her life without Hart. The terms are hard, but they always have been. We are alone, we have nothing to sustain us but a few pet ideas fueled by a dram of courage. The rest is a pipe dream. Not that pipe dreams are not necessary, we've just got to know the differences. This is Rocky's pet idea, and it's one that she's earned. Ten years ago she survived the removal, from her brain, of a benign plum-sized tumor that made her trade her career in parachute journalism for an academic one.

We are required to be brave. Another pet idea. Also Rocky's.

The Lavender Pit is really two pits, big enough to drop a pair of medium-size cities into. On the way out of Bisbee, after getting half-drunk in the Copper Queen Hotel (Hart managing this with a carefully sipped double shot of mescal), we stop with the tourists to gape at this man-made Grand Canyon. Rocky, who has seen her town, Butte, more or less consumed by such a pit, says, "Sucks, don't it?" to a tourist lady from Arkansas. The tourist lady smiles stiffly and turns her camera on her husband and daughter, who backstep dutifully toward the Cyclone fence that guards the lip of the pit and the thousand-foot drop beyond. The red gouge in the earth looks like a fresh wound, the god-size tumor removed, the lake of blood vacuumed out. A lifeless pond at the bottom of the pit glows like iridescent pus. Oh yes, the planet here is dead. It is deader than the moon, because it was once alive.

"I'm losing my buzz, campers," Rocky says. "Let's clear the fuck out." The lady with the camera gives Rocky a murderous look, protecting the innocence of her child. Rocky grins good-naturedly. "Too late for Miss Manners, hon," she says cryptically, swinging her arm out to indicate the pit, the precarious town, the silent witness of the elderly mountains.

4

We skip Tucson and head back, but the Blazer heats up outside of Deming, New Mexico. We were headed for Palomas, the little Mexican town where General Pershing launched his failed attempt to bring a taste of gringo justice to Pancho Villa, but are now stalled in a gas station where two head-scratching mechanics decide the problem is in the fan clutch and that it will take about an hour and a hundred dollars to fix it. It's hot, over a hundred degrees, and we sit inside the crankcase smell of the garage drinking lukewarm Cokes and watching a TV that seems to have only one color: puce. One of the advertising industry's truly horrifying commercials comes on: "Your marriage will never end. Your children will never grow old. Your pets will never die." It's an ad for a video camcorder, showing a family watching their dead past captured and preserved forever. Whatever unhappiness lies ahead, it cannot touch these moments of joy. Mom kissing Dad in the kitchen; Junior chasing a ball; Rover begging for table scraps—immortal, immutable. Old age, sickness, alienation, divorce: all our little hells defeated by videotape. Paradise secure in a cassette, the grim episodes edited out.

We step back into the heat and stroll up the desert road. To the east, the gray humps of the Florida Mountains wobble in the corrugated air. A man, ragged and barefoot, approaches us. He's so far beyond the liberal dream of salvage and social recycling that he almost seems happy. His weak hair and crosshatched sunburned skin make him look sixty but his clear blue eyes put him closer to thirty. He is hashed with small cuts, as if he's been climbing through barbed-wire fences all morning. Hart greets him with the head-on nod of equals. Hart and the ragged man are down to common denominators, and they recognize this in each other. The man asks for a cigarette and Hart gives him one, then lights it for him. As the rest of us stroll on, Hart reaches into his camera bag. When Hart has his camera ready, the man begins to shift his weight from left foot to right and back again. The asphalt road is burning hot and I assume the man is moving oddly because his bare feet are giving him trouble, but then he raises his stick-figure arms as if they were big sunny wings and begins to turn in half-circles, first one way, then the other, his cigarette held delicately in his fingertips. He lifts his face up to the sky to let God see him better, and chants a broken-throated nonsense. It's an Indian dance, or his idea of one. "He didn't want any money," Hart says when he rejoins us. "He said all he needs now is smokes. He gave me permission to take his picture, but only while he was doing his atonement dance."

We continue our stroll; the man, who doesn't need an audience, continues his dance. The sun has baked curiosity out of our thoughts. Curiosity is a luxury of the temperate zone. When a shoeless man in a parched land tells you he's doing an atonement dance, you more or less have to accept him at his word. Besides, there's enough to atone for to keep half of humanity dancing shoeless in the desert for a century while the other half lights cigarettes for them.

A few months later I will think of this moment while looking at Hart's photographs matted and framed on our apartment walls, and it will seem as if all of us are moving to the drumbeat of some privately realized dance—the ducking pickpockets with large incongruous smiles under their stony eyes; Sada and Tyrell holding hands shyly but glaring like unyielding Apaches from their mountain stronghold, determined to make their stand; Rocky tugging defiantly on her cigarette as she fixes something at infinity with wide-open eyes that won't blink; even the headless mule floating near the concrete bank of the Río Grande like an offering to the indifferent northern gods. And Joyce and me, caught looking at each other with slightly shocked expressions, as if on that very day, before the small white church in Palomas, we grasped for the first time that love is possible only because it must end.

—for Zena Beth McGlashan

Winter was with us now. The snow that whitened the foothills at the start of October repeated within forty-eight hours, this time piling itself shin-deep all across the Two Medicine country. We did the last of autumn chores in December circumstances.

That first sizable snowstorm, and for that matter the three or four that followed it by the first week in November, proved to be just the thin edge of the wedge of the winter of 1919. On the fifteenth of November, thirty inches of snow fell on us. Lacelike flakes in a perfect silence dropped on Scotch Heaven that day as if the clouds suddenly were crumbling, every last shred of them tumbling down in a slow thick cascade. From the windows Adair and I watched everything outside change, become absurdly fattened in fresh white outline; our woodpile took on the smooth disguise of a snow-colored haystack. It was equally beautiful and dismaying, that floury tier on everything, for we knew it lay poised, simply waiting for wind the way a handful of dandelion seeds in a boy's hand awaits the first flying puff from him. That day I did something I had done only a few times in all my years on the Scotch Heaven homestead: I tied together lariats and strung them like a rope railing between the house and the barn, to grasp my way along so as not to get lost if a blizzard blinded the distance between while I was out at the chores.

The very next day I needed that rope. Blowing snow shrouded the world, or at least our polar corner of it. The sheep had to be fed, somehow, and so in all the clothes I could pile on I went out to make my way along the line to the barn, harnessed the workhorses Sugar and Duke, and prayed for a lull.

When a lessening of the blizzard finally came, Rob came with it, a plaster man on a plaster horse. He had followed fencelines down from Breed Butte to the North Fork, then guided himself up the creek by its wall of willows and trees. Even now I have to hand it to the damn man. Here he was, blue as a pigeon from the chill of riding in that snow-throwing wind, yet as soon as he could make his mouth operate he was demanding that we plunge out there and provide hay to the sheep.

"Put some of Adair's coffee in you first," I stipulated, "then we'll get at it."

"I don't need—" he began croakily.

"Coffee," I reiterated. "I'm not going to pack you around today like a block of ice." When Adair had thawed him, back out we went into the white wind, steering the horses and hay sled along the creek the way Rob had done, then we grimly managed to half-fling half-sail a load of hay onto the sled rack, and next battled our way to my sheep shed, where the sheep were sheltering themselves. By the time we got there they were awful to hear—a bleated chorus of hunger and fear rending the air. Not until we pitched the hay off to them did they put those fifteen hundred woolly throats to work on something besides telling us their agony.

That alarming day was the sample, the tailor's swatch, of our new season. The drought of that summer, the snow and wind of that winter: the two great weathers of 1919. Through the rest of November and December, days were either frigid or blowy and too often both. By New Year's, Rob and I were meeting the mark of that giant winter each day on our route to the sheep's feedground. At a place where my meadow made a bit of a dip, snow drifted and hardened and drifted some more and hardened again and on and on until there was a mound eight or ten feet deep and broad as a low hill there. "Big as the goddamn bridge across the Firth of Forth," Rob called it with permissible exaggeration in this case. This and other snow bridges built by the furrowing blizzards we could go right over with the horses and hay sled without breaking through, they were so thickly frozen. *Here winter plies his craft,/soldering the years with ice.* Yes, and history can say the seam between 1919 and 1920 was triple thickness.

Thank heaven, or at least my winning cut of the cards, that we had bought twice as much hay as Rob wanted to, which still was not as much as I wanted to. Even so, every way I could calculate it now— and the worried look on Rob said his sums were coming out the same as mine—we were going to be scratching for hay in a few months if this harsh weather kept up.

It kept up.

◆

Near the end of January I made a provisioning trip into town. Every house, shed, barn I passed, along the North Fork and the main creek, was white-wigged with snow. Gros Ventre's main street was a rutted trench between snowpiles, and no one was out who didn't have dire reason to be. All the more unexpected, then, when I stomped the white from my boots and went into the mercantile, and the person in a chair by the stove was Toussaint Rennie.

"What, is it springtime on the Two Medicine?" I husked out to him, my voice stiff from the cold of my ride. "Because if it is, send some down to us."

"Angus, were you out for air?" he asked in return, and gave a chuckle.

"I thought I was demented to come just a dozen miles in this weather. So what does that make you?"

"Do you know, Angus, this is that '86 winter back again."

I suddenly found myself at that supper of so long ago, when Rob and I journeyed north to look at the grass beyond the Two Medicine River. Before we were brothers-in-law, partners in sheep, enemies; before any of the snip and snap between us. We had wagoned into Toussaint Rennie's place for the night and as Toussaint sauced the meal for us with his talk of the Two Medicine country, I was the one to ask him of the winter everyone told of in this Montana. *"The winter of '86, Toussaint. What was that like up here?"*

"That winter. That winter, we ate with the axe."

Rob made as if to clear an ear with his finger. "You did which?"

"We ate with the axe. No deer, no elk. No weather to hunt them in. I went out, find a cow if I can. Look for a hump under the snow. Do you know, a lot of snowdrifts look like a cow carcass?"

Rob was incredulous. "Toussaint, man, you mean you'd go out and find a dead cow to eat?"

"Any I found was dead," Toussaint vouched. "Chop her up, bring home as much as the horse can carry. West wind, all that winter. Everything drifted east. You had to guess. Whether the horse could break snow far enough to find a cow." Toussaint seemed entertained

by the memory. "That winter was long. Those cattlemen found out. I had work all summer, driving wagon for the cowhide skinners. That was what was left in this country by spring. More cowhides than cows."

"A once-in-a-lifetime winter," Rob summarized, "and I'm glad enough I wasn't here to see it. Now we know to have hay and sheds, anyway. It's hard luck that somebody else had to pay for that lesson, but life wasn't built even, was it."

"That '86 winter went around a corner of the mountains and waited to circle back on us, Angus," the broad figure planted by the warm stove was saying now. "Here it is."

"As good a theory as I've heard lately," I admitted ruefully. "Just how are your livestock faring, up there on the reservation?"

Toussaint's face altered. There was no chuckle behind what he said this time. "They are deadstock now."

◄◆►

February was identical to the frigid misery of January. At the very start of the last of its four white weeks, there came the day when Rob and I found fifteen fresh carcasses of ewes, dead of weakness and the constant cold. No, not right. Dead, most of all, of hunger.

Terrible as the winter had been, then, March was going to be worse. Scan the remaining hay twenty times and do its arithmetic every one of those times and the conclusion was ever the same. By the first of March, the hay would be gone. One week from today, the rest of the sheep would begin to starve.

A glance at Rob, as we drove the sled past the gray bumps of dead sheep, told me that his conclusion was the same as mine, with even more desperation added. He caught my gaze at him, and the day's words started.

"Don't work me over with your eyes, man. How in hell was I supposed to know that the biggest winter since snow got invented was on its way?"

"Tell it to the sheep, Rob. Then they'd have at least that to chew on."

"All it'd take is one good chinook. A couple of days of that, and enough of this snow would go so that the sheep could paw down and graze a bit. That'd let us stretch the hay and we'd come out of this winter as rosy as virgins. So just put away that gravedigger look of yours, for Christ's sake. We're not done for yet. A chinook will show up. It has to."

You're now going to guile the weather, are you, Rob? Cite Barclay logic to it and scratch its icy ears, and it'll bounce to attention like a fetching dog to go bring you your chinook? That would be like you, Rob, to think that life and its weather are your private pets. Despite the warning he had given me, I told him all this with my eyes, too.

◆

The end of that feeding day, if it could be called so, I was barning the workhorses when a tall collection of coat, cap, scarf, mittens and the rest came into the yard atop a horse with the Long Cross brand. If I couldn't identify Varick in the bundle, I at least knew his saddlehorse. I gave a wave and he rode through the deep snow of the yard to join me inside the barn's shelter.

"How you doing?" asked my son when he had unwrapped sufficiently to let it out.

"A bit threadbare, to say the truth. Winter seems to be a whole hell of a lot longer than it ever used to be, not to mention deeper."

"I notice the sheep are looking a little lean." Lean didn't begin to say it, Varick. They were getting to resemble greyhounds. "You got enough hay to get through on, you think?"

"Rob and I were just discussing that." I scanned the white ridges, the white banks of the North Fork, the white roof of the sheep shed. Another week of this supreme snow sitting everywhere on us and we had might as well hire the coyotes to put the sheep out of their hungry misery. "Neither of us thinks we do have anywhere near enough, no."

Varick was plainly unsurprised. He said, part question and part not, "What about that Dakota spinach they've got at Valier?" Trainloads of what was being called hay, although it was merely slewgrass and other wiry trash, were being brought in from North Dakota to Valier and other rail points and sold at astounding prices.

"What about it?" I nodded to the east, across more than thirty miles. "It's in Valier and we're here."

"I could get loose from Noon Creek for a couple days to help you haul," offered Varick. "Even bring my own hay sled. Can't beat that for a deal, now can you?"

I said nothing, while trying to think how to tell him his generosity was futile, Rob and I were so far beyond help.

Eyeing me carefully, Varick persisted: "If you and Unk and me each take a sled to Valier, we can haul back a hell of a bunch of hay, Dad."

I stared east again, to the white length of Scotch Heaven, the white miles beyond that to the railroad cars of hay in Valier. Why try, even? A sled journey of that sort, in a winter of this sort. *There is so much of this country, Angus.* That quiet mountaintop declaration of Adair's. *People keep having to stretch themselves out of shape trying to cope with so much. This Montana sets its own terms and tells you, do them or else.*

Or else. There in the snow of the valley where Rob and I had just pitched to them half the hay they ought to have had, the sheep were a single gray floe of wool in the universal whiteness. I remembered their bleating, the blizzard day we were late with the feeding; the awful hymn of their fear. Could I stand to hear that, day after day when the hay was gone?

Finally I gave Varick all the answer I had. "All right, I'm one vote for trying it. But we'll need to talk to Rob."

"He'll be for it. Dead sheep are lost dollars to him. He'll be for it, Dad."

◆

In the winter-hazed sky, the dim sun itself seemed to be trying to find a clearer look at our puzzling procession. A square-ended craft with a figurehead of two straining horses was there in the white no-where, plowing on a snow sea. Then an identical apparition behind it, and a third ghost boat in the wake of that.

Three long sleds with hay racks on them, Varick at the reins of the first, myself the next driver, Rob at the tail of this sled-runner voyage toward Valier, our convoy crept across the white land. But if slowly, we moved steadily. The big horses walked through the snow as if they were polar creatures. Copenhagen and Woodrow, my pair was named. Even American horses had the mix of two lands. Horse alloys, strong there in the dark harness in front of me.

We stopped at the Double W fenceline, half the way between Gros Ventre and Valier, to eat from the bundle of lunch Adair had fixed us. Rob and I stomped some warmth into ourselves while Varick cut the barbed wire strands so we could get the sleds through. Of the four-wire fence, only the top two strands were showing above the snow. While Varick was at that, I gazed around at the prairie. Cold and silence, stillness and snow. Once upon a time there were two young men, new to Montana, who thought they were seeing snow. *This is just a April skift,* was the freight wagon driver's assessment to us. That April and its light white coverlet sounded like high summer to me now. That flurry that had taken the mountains and the wheel tracks from our long-ago trek into the Two country was a pinch of salt compared to this. And Rob and I of then, how did we compare with what we are now? The journeys we had made together, across thirty years. Steamship and railroad and horse and foot and every kind of wheel. And by ash sled runners, enmity accompanying us. What, were we different Rob and different Angus, all the time before? Else how did the enmity manage to come between us? In all likelihood I am not the best judge of myself. But I can tell you, from trudging through the days of this winter beside the unspeaking figure known as Rob Barclay, that this was not the Rob who would throw back his head and cockily call up to the hazed sun, *Can't you get the stove going up there?*

Onward from the fence, the marks of our sled runners falling away into the winter plain behind us. Silence and cold, snow and stillness. The murmurs within myself the only human sound. Adair asking, when Varick and I went into the house with his offer to make this hay trip: *Do both of you utterly have to go?* Reluctant *yeah* from her son, equally involuntary *yes* from her husband. From her: *Then I have to count on each of you to bring the other one back, don't I.* Toussaint, when I arranged for him to feed the sheep while we were gone, saying only: *This winter. You have to watch out for it, Angus.* And myself, here on this first ground I ever went across on horseback, scouting for a homestead site. Did I choose rightly, the high valley of Scotch Heaven over this prairie? That farmhouse there on the chalky horizon. If I had chosen that spot those years ago, I would right now be in there drinking hot coffee and watching hay-hungry sheepmen ply past on their skeleton ships. No, not that simple. In the past summer of drought and grasshoppers and deflated prices, that farm, too, was bitter acres. The year 1919 had shown that farming could be a desperate way of life, too. Maybe everything was, one time or another.

It was dusk when we came around the frozen length of Valier's lake and began to pass the stray houses of the outskirts. Valier did not have as much accumulation of winter as Scotch Heaven or Gros Ventre, but it still had about as much as a town can stand. The young trees planted along the residential streets looked like long sticks stuck in to measure the snowfall. The downtown streets had drifts graceful as sand dunes. Stores peeked over the snowbanks. Pathways had been shoveled like a chain of canals, and at the eastern edge of town we could see the highest white dike of all, where the railroad track had been plowed.

Along the cornices of the three-story hotel where we went for the night, thick icicles hung like winter's laundry. When we three numb things had managed to unharness the teams at the stable and at last could think of tending to ourselves, Varick gave his sum of our journey from Scotch Heaven: "That could've been a whole hell of a lot worse."

And Rob gave his. "Once we get those sleds heavy with hay, it will be."

◆

At morning, the depot agent greeted us with: "I been keeping your hay cool for you out in the icebox."

When no hint of amusement showed on any of the three of us, he sobered radically and said: "I'll show you the boxcar. We can settle up after you're loaded."

We passed a dozen empty boxcars, huge husks without their cargo, and came to a final one with a stubbly barricade of hay behind its slatted side. The agent broke ice from its door with a blacksmith hammer, then used a pinch bar to pry the grudging door open. "All yours," he stated, and hustled back inside the warmth of the depot.

The railroad car was stacked full of large bales like shaggy crates. Rob thrust a mitten under his armpit, pulled out his hand, and thrust it into a bale. The handful he pulled out was brown crackly swampgrass, which only in a winter of this sort would qualify as hay at all. "Awful stuff," Rob proclaimed.

"The woollies won't think it's as awful as starving," I told him. "Let's load and go." The weather was ever over our shoulder, and this was a lead-colored day that showed no intention of brightening. First thing of morning, I had taken a look out the hotel window to the west for the mountains and they were there, white-toothed as if they had sawed up through the snow prairie. As long as the mountains stayed unclouded we had what we needed from the weather today, neutrality.

Our work was harsh, laboring the bales from their stacks in the boxcar to the sleds alongside, as if we were hauling hundreds of loaded trunks down out of an attic. Oftener and oftener, Rob and I had to stop for breath. The smoke of our breathing clouded between us, two aging engines of work. To say the truth, without Varick's limber young strength I do not know how we ever would have loaded those three hay sleds.

When the last bale was aboard, even Varick looked close to spent, but he said only, "I guess that's them." A marker in our journey, that final bale; with it, the easy half of our hay task was over. Now to haul these loads, and ourselves, all the miles to Gros Ventre before nightfall, and on to Scotch Heaven the next day. Rob and I headed for the depot with our checkbooks to pay an outlandish price for this godawful hay that was the only hay there was, and then we would have to get ourselves gone, out onto the prairie of winter.

◄━━━

We had our own tracks of yesterday to follow on the white plain west of Valier, smooth grooves of the sled runners and twin rough channels chopped by the horses' hooves. The horses strained steadily as they pulled our hay loads. With every step they were rescuing us a little more, drawing us nearer to Scotch Heaven and out of this width of winter.

All was silence except for the rhythm of the horses' labor, muscle against harness, hooves against snow. Existence crept no faster than our sleds, as if time had slowed to look gravely at itself, to ponder what way to go next, at what pace. I know I had thoughts—you can't not—but the lull we were traveling in held me. Keeping the team's leather reins wrapped in my mittened hands was the only occupation that counted in the world just then.

The change in the day began soon after we were beyond Valier's outlying farms and homesteads, where our tracks of yesterday went on into the prairie of the Double W range. At first the mountains only seemed oddly dimmed, as if dusk somehow had wandered into midday. I tried to believe it as a trick of light, all the while knowing the real likelihood.

In front of me I could see Varick letting only his hands and arms drive the team, the rest of him attentive to those dimming mountains. Behind me Rob undoubtedly was performing the same.

So the three of us simultaneously watched the mountains be taken by the murk. As if a gray stain was spreading down from the sky, the mountains gradually became more and more obscure, until they simply were absorbed out of sight. We had to hope that the weather covering the western horizon was only fog or fallow cloud and not true storm. We had to hope that mightily.

The wind, too, began faintly enough. Simply a sift along the top of the snow, soft little whiffs of white dust down there. I turtled deeper into the collar of my sheepskin coat in anticipation of the first gust to swoosh up onto the sled at me. But a windless minute passed, then another, although there were constant banners of snow weaving past the horses' hooves. I could see Varick and his sled clear as anything; but he and it seemed suspended in a landscape that was casually moving from under them. A ground blizzard. Gentle enough, so far. A breeze brooming whatever loose snow it could find, oddly tidy in its way. Another tease from the weather, but as long as the wind stayed down there at knee-high we were out of harm.

I believed we were nearly to our halfway mark, the Double W fence, yet it seemed an age before Varick's sled at last halted. I knew we were going to feed our teams, and for that matter ourselves, at this midpoint. But when Rob and I slogged up to Varick, we found he had more than replenishment on his mind.

"I don't know what you two think," he began, "but I figure we better just give up on the notion of going back the same route we came by."

Rob gave a grimace, which could have been either at Varick's words or at the sandwich frozen to the consistency of sawdust which he had just taken first bite of. "And do what instead?" he asked skeptically.

"Follow this fence," Varick proposed with a nod of his head toward it, "to where it hits the creek." Half a fence, really, in this deep winter; only the top portions of the fenceposts were above the snow, a midget line of march north and south from our cluster of hay sleds and horses. "Once we get to the creek," Varick was postulating, "we can follow that on into Gros Ventre easy enough."

"Man, that'd take twice as long," Rob objected. "And that's twice as much effort for these horses, not to mention us."

Varick gave me a moment's look, then a longer gaze at Rob. "Yeah, but at least this fence tells us where the hell we are," he answered. He inclined his head to the prairie the other side of the fence, where the wind's steady little sift had made our yesterday's tracks look softened. "It won't need a hell of a lot more of this to cover those tracks."

"Even if it does, Varick, we know that country," Rob persisted. "Christ, man, the hills are right out there in plain sight." The benchlands north of Noon Creek and the Double W were like distant surf above the flow of the blown snow.

"We won't know an inch of it in a genuine blizzard," Varick insisted. "If this starts really storming and we get to going in circles out there, we'll end up like the fillyloo bird."

Rob stared at him. "The which?"

"The fillyloo bird, Unk. That's the one that's got a wing shorter than the other, so that it keeps flying in littler and littler circles until it disappears up its own rear end."

Rob gave a short harsh laugh, but credit him, it was a laugh. I chortled as if I was filled with feathers. Were we all going giddy, the cold stiffening our brains? Would they find us here in the springtime, with ice grins on our faces?

"All right, all right," Rob was conceding, as much to the notion of the fillyloo bird as to Varick. If I had been the one to broach the fence route to him, Rob would have sniffed and snorted at it until we grew roots. But here he was, grudging but giving the words to Varick. "Lead on to your damn creek."

We began to follow the Double W fenceline south. The low stuttered pattern of the fenceposts could be seen ahead for maybe a quarter of a mile at a time, before fading into the ground blizzard. Occasionally there was a hump, or more often a series of them, next to the barbed wire—carcasses of Double W cattle that had drifted with the wind until the fence thwarted them. I wondered if Wampus Cat Williamson in his California money vault gave a damn.

A tiny cloud caught on my eyelash. I squinted to get rid of it and it melted coldly into my eye.

I blinked, and there were other snowflakes now, sliding across the air softly.

The stillness of their descent lasted only a few moments, before the first gust of wind hit and sent them spinning.

Quickly it was snowing so hard there seemed to be more white in the air than there was space between the flakes. In front of me Varick's sled was a squarish smudge.

The wind drove into us. No longer was it lazing along the ground. From the howl of it, this blizzard was blowing as high as the stars.

The horses labored. Varick and I and Rob got off and walked on the lee side of our hay sleds, to lessen the load for the teams and to be down out of the wind and churning whatever warmth we could into ourselves. I had on socks and socks and socks, and even so my feet felt the cold. This was severe travel, and before long the ghostly sled in front of me halted, and Varick was emerging from the volleys of wind and snow to see how we were faring. Rob promptly materialized from behind. A gather seemed needed by all three of us.

The wind quibbled around our boots even in the shelter of my hay sled. There we huddled, with our flap caps tied down tight over our ears and scarves across our faces up to our eyes. Bedouins of the blizzard. One by one we pulled down our scarves and scrutinized each other for frostbite.

"We're doing about as good as we can, seems to me," Varick assessed after our inspection of each other. In the howl of the wind, each word had to be a sentence. "I can only see a fencepost or two at a time in this," Varick told us, "but that'll do. Unk, how's it going with you, back there?"

"Winterish," was all Rob replied.

"How about you, Dad—are you all right?"

That question of Varick's was many in one. I ached with cold, the rust of weariness was in every muscle I used, I knew how tiny we three dots of men, horses and hay were in the expanse of this winter-swollen land. But I took only the part of the question that Varick maybe had not even known he was asking: Was I afraid? The answer, surprise to myself: I was not. Certainly not afraid for myself, for I could make myself outlast the cold and snow as long as Rob Barclay could. If one of us broke, then the other might begin to cave. But our stubbornnesses would carry each other far. We would not give one another the satisfaction of dying craven, would we, Rob.

"I'm good enough," I answered my son. "Let's go see more snow."

◆

Trudge and try not to think about how much more trudging needed be done. Here was existence scoured down as far as it could go. Just the flecked sky, filled with fat snowflakes and spiteful wind; and us, six horse creatures and three human. Hoofprints of our horses, sliced path of our sled runners, our bootprints, wrote commotion into the snow. Yet a hundred yards behind Rob you would not be able to find a trace that we had ever been there. Maybe winter was trying to blow itself out in this one day. Maybe so, maybe no. It had been trying something since October. I felt pity for Woodrow, the horse of my team who was getting the wind full against his side. But he simply turned his head and persevered with his work.

I pounded my arm against my side and trudged. The wind whirled the air full of white flakes again. *Old mad winter/with snow hair flying.* This must be what mesmerism is, every particle of existence streaming to you and dreamily past. A white blanket for your mind. A storm such as this blew in all the way from legendary times, other winters great in their fury. The winter of '83. *The Starvation Winter, these Blackfeet call that, and by Jesus they did starve, poor bastards them, by the hundreds. Pure gruesome, what they went through.* Gruesome was the apt word for such winters, yes. The winter of '86, Toussaint's telling of it. *That winter. That winter, we ate with the axe.* And Rob saying, *A once-in-a-lifetime winter.* It depended on the size of the lifetime, didn't it.

The wind blowing, the snow flowing. Try to pound another arm's worth of warmth into myself and keep trudging. Every so often Varick, tall bundle of dimness ahead in the blowing snow, turned to look for me. I did the same for Rob. Rob. Rob who was all but vanished back there. Say he did vanish. Say he stumbled, sprawled in the miring snow, could not get up in time before I missed him, next time I glanced back. Say Rob did vanish into the blizzard, what would I feel? Truth now, Angus: what? As I tried to find honest reply in myself, a side of my mind said at least that would end it once and all, if Rob faltered back there in the snow and Varick and I could not find him, the poisoned time that had come between us—this entangled struggle between McCaskill and Barclay—would at last be ended. Or would it.

Whether it was decision or just habit, I kept watching behind me periodically to Rob. The team he had were big matched grays, and against the storm dusk they faded startlingly, so that at a glance there simply seemed to be harness standing in the air back there, blinders and collars and straps as if the wind had dressed itself in them. And ever, beside the floating sets of harness, the bulky figure of Rob.

We were stopped again. Varick came slogging to me like a man wading surf, and reported in a half shout that the fenceline had gone out of sight under a snowdrift that filled a coulee. We would need to veer down and around the pit of snow, then angle back up once we were past it to find the fenceline where it emerged from the coulee.

"If we've got to, we've got to," I assented to Varick, and while he returned to his sled I beckoned for Rob to come up and hear the situation. He looked as far from happy as a man could be, but he had to agree that the detour was all there was to do.

The horses must have wondered why they had to turn a corner here at the middle of nothingness, but they obediently veered left and floundered down the short slope.

Now the problem was up. The slope on the other side of the coulee was steep and angling, the top of it lost in the swirling snow, so that as the horses strained they seemed to be climbing a stormcloud. This was the cruelest work yet, the team plunging a few steps at a time and then gathering themselves for the next lunge, all the while the loaded sled dragging backward on them. It hurt even to watch such raw effort. I sang out every encouragement I could, but the task was entirely the horses'.

Up and up, in those awful surges, until at last the snow began to level out. The horses' sides still heaved from the exertions of getting us here, but I breathed easier now that we were atop the brow of the coulee and our way ahead to the fenceline would be less demanding.

Varick had halted us yet again. What this time?

One more time I waved Rob up to us as Varick trudged back from the lead sled.

"This don't feel right to me," Varick reported. He was squinting apprehensively. "I haven't found that fenceline yet and we ought've been back to it by now."

"We must not have come far enough to hit it yet, is all," Rob said impatiently, speaking what was in my mind, too.

Varick shook his head. "We've come pretty damn far. No, that fence ought to be here by now. But it isn't."

"Then where to Christ is it?" demanded Rob belligerently into the concealing storm. Our faces said that each of the three of us was morally certain we had come the right way after veering around the coulee. Hop with that first leg of logic and the second was inevitable:

We ought to have come to the fence again. But no fence, logical or any other kind, was in evidence.

For a long moment we peered into the windblown snow, our breath smoking in front of our faces like separate small storms. Without that fence we were travelers with nowhere to go. Nowhere in life, that is. Bewilderment fought with reasoning, and I tried to clear my numb mind of everything except fence thoughts. Not even a blizzard could blow away a line of stoutly set posts and four lines of wire. Could it?

"There's just one other place I can think of for that fence to be," Varick suggested as if he hated to bring up the idea. "The sonofabitch might be under us."

With his overshoe he scuffed aside the day's powdery freshfall to show us the old hardened snow beneath. Rob and I stared down. Oh sweet Christ and every dimpled disciple. A snow bridge, was this? If it was, if we were huddled there on a giant drift where the snow had built and cemented itself onto the brow of the coulee all winter, fenceposts and barbed wire could be buried below us, right enough. Anything short of a steeple could be buried down there, if this truly was a snow bridge. And if we were overshooting the fenceline down there under the winter crust, we next were going to be on the blind plain, in danger of circling ourselves to death.

"Damn it," Rob seemed downright affronted by our predicament, "who ever saw snow like this?"

Varick had no time for that. Rapidly he said, "We can't just stand around here cussing the goddamn situation. What I'd better do is go out here a little way"—indicating to the left of us, what ought to be the southward slope of the long hump of drift we were on, if we were —"and take a look around for where the fence comes out of this."

His words scared my own into the air. "Not without a rope on you, you won't."

"Yeah, I'm afraid you're right about that," Varick agreed. The three of us peered to the route he proposed to take. Visibility came and went but it was never more than a few dozen strides' worth. I repeated that Varick was not moving one step into the blizzard without a rescue rope to follow back to us, even though we all knew the cumbersome minutes it would cost us to undo the ropes that were lashing the hay to the sled racks, knot them together, affix them around his waist—"It won't take time at all," I uttered unconvincingly.

Hateful as the task was, stiff-fingered and wind-harassed as we were, we got the ropes untied from each of our hay loads. Next, the reverse of that untying chore. "Rob, you're the one with the canny hands," I tried on him. He gave me a look, then with a grunt began knotting the several ropes together to make a single lifeline for Varick. One end of the line I tied firmly around Varick's waist while Rob was doing the splice knots, then we anchored the other end to Varick's hay rack.

"Let's try it," Varick said, and off he plunged into the blizzard. Rob and I, silent pillars side by side, lost sight of him before he had managed to take twenty effortful steps.

With my son out there in the oblivion of winter, each moment ached in me. But I could think of no other precaution we might have done. If Varick didn't come back within a reasonable time, Rob and I could follow the rope into the blizzard and fetch him. I would do it by myself if I had to. It might take every morsel of energy left in me, but I would get Varick back out of that swirling snow if I had to.

The rope went taut.

It stayed that way a long moment, as if Varick was dangling straight down from it instead of out across a plain of snow. Then the line alternately slackened and straightened, as Varick pulled himself back to us hand over hand.

His face, strained and wincing, told us before his words did. "I didn't make it to the fence. Ran out of rope."

Rob swore feelingly; I tried to think. We needed more rope, more line of life, to explore again into that snow world, and we did not have more rope. We just had ourselves, the three of us.

"Varick," I began. "Can you stand another try at it?"

"Floundering around out there isn't really anything I want to make a career of," he admitted, breathing as if he'd been in a race. "But yeah, I can do it again if I have to."

"Then this time I'll go out with you, for however far he can still see me." I jerked my head to indicate Rob. "You give us a yell when we're just about out of sight, Rob. Then you go out beyond me, Varick, while I hold the rope for you. What do you think? It would gain us that much distance"—I nodded to the edge of visibility out there—"for looking, at least."

"That sounds as good as any," Varick assented. Rob only bobbed his head once; we McCaskills could take it for yes if we wanted.

Varick and I set out, the wind sending scythes of snow at us. The cold sawed at us through every seam in our clothing. Quickly we were up to our knees in a fresh drift. Varick broke the way and I thrashed after him. A drift atop a drift, this latest dune of snow would be. And other layers beneath that as we slogged. October snow, November on top of that. And December atop that, and January, and February . . . How many tiers of this winter could there be? This wasn't a winter, it was geologic ages of snow. It was a storm planet building itself layer by layer. It was—

Abruptly I stopped, and reaching a hand ahead to Varick's shoulder, brought him to a halt, too. When he turned, the apprehension in my manner made words unnecessary.

We looked back. Nothingness. The white void of snow, the blizzard erasing all difference between earth and sky. No glimpse of Rob. No sound in the air but the wind.

We stood like listening statues, our tracks already gone into the swirling snow we had come out of. Again, yet, no voice from the safety of there.

The bastard.

The utter betraying triple-slippery unforgiving bastard Rob had let us come too far. I ought to have killed him with my own hands, the day we fought there on Breed Butte, the day it all began. He was letting the blizzard eat us. Letting Varick and me vanish like two sparks into the whirl of this snow. Letting us—

Then sounds that were not quite the wind's.

. . . *arrr* . . .

. . . *ough* . . .

The blizzard swirled in a new way, and the wraith figure of Rob was there, waving both arms over his head.

"Far enough," his voice faintly carried to us. "Far enough."

Varick's heavy breathing was close to mine. "He always was one to press the luck, wasn't he," my son uttered. "Particularly when it's somebody else's."

We breathed together, marking the sight and sound of Rob into our senses, then turned ahead to squint for any sign of the fenceline. None.

"You ready to go fishing?" asked Varick, and away he plunged again, the rope around his waist and in my mittened hands.

Through my weariness I concentrated on the hemp in my hands. *To see a world in a grain of sand* . . . Would grains of snow do? By the dozens and hundreds they fell and fell, their whiteness coating my sleeves and mittens. . . . *Hold infinity in the palm of your hand.* . . . Would mittened palms be deft enough for that? I had to force my cold claw of a hand to keep making a fist around the moving line of rope. The rope paying out through my grip already had taken Varick from sight, into the snow cyclone. Thoughts swarmed to fill his absence. What if he stumbled out there, jerking the rope out of my stiff hands? Hold, Angus. Find a way to hold. I fumbled the end of the rope around my waist, clutching it tightly belted around me with my right hand while the left hand encircled the strand going out to Varick. If he fell I would fall, too, but nothing would make me let go of this rope. I would be Varick's anchor. Such as I was, I would be that much. A splice knot caught in my grip an instant before I let it belly out and away. The knots. Rob's knots. Lord of mercy, why hadn't I done them myself? What if he hadn't tied them firmly, what if just one began to slip loose? No. No, I could trust Rob's hands even if I couldn't trust him.

Only a few feet of rope left. If Varick did not find the fenceline now, we never would. My heart thundered in me, as if the enormity of clothing around it was making it echo. A quiver of chill went through me each time the wind clasped around my body. If we couldn't go on we would need to try to hide ourselves in caves of the hay, try to wait out the blizzard. But if this cold and wind went on through the night, our chances were slim. More likely they were none. If any one of us could live through, let it be Var—

Tugs on the rope, like something heavy quivering at the end of the hempen line. Or something floundering after it had fallen.

"Varick!" I shouted as loud as I could. The wind took my words. I might as well have been yelling into a bale of that Dakota hay.

The tugs continued. I swallowed, held firm, clutching the jerking rope around me. I resisted a hundred impulses to plunge forward and help Varick in his struggle. I resisted another hundred to whirl around in search of Rob, to see whether he still was there as our guidemark. The distance back to him and the hay sleds was the same as it ever had been, I had to recite to my bolting instincts, only the snow was in motion, not the white distance stretching itself, as it gave every appearance of. Motion of another wild sort at the invisible end of this rope, the tugs continuing in a ragged rhythm that I hoped had to be—

Varick suddenly coming hand over hand, materializing out of the whirl. A struggling upright slab of whiteness amid the coiling swirl of whiteness.

He saved his breath until he was back to me, my arms helping to hold him up.

"It's there!" he panted. "The fenceline. It comes out of the drift about there"—carefully pointing an angle to our left, although everything in me would have guessed it had to be to our right. "The sleds are actually on the other side of the sonofabitch. We about went too far, Dad."

Fixing ourselves on the figure whose waves and shouts came and went through the blowing flakes, we fought snow with our feet until we were back beside Rob. Varick saved him the burden of asking. "We got ourselves a fence again, Unk."

Laboriously we retied the ropes across the hay loads, as well as men in our condition could. Then Varick turned his team to the left—they were glad enough to, suffering in the wind as they had been—and I reined Woodrow and Copenhagen around to follow them, and Rob and his grays swung in behind us. Once our procession was down off the mound of snow, the tops of fenceposts appeared and then the topmost single strand of barbwire, the three strands beneath it in the accumulated white depth. This white iron winter, with a brutal web in it. That single top strand, though. That was our tether to the creek, to survival. I had never known until then that I could be joyously glad to see barbed bramble.

Now how far to the creek? We had to keep going, following the line of fence, no matter what distance it was. There was no knowing the hour of the day, either. The storm had made it all dusk. The complicated effort of trying to fumble out my pocket watch for a look, I couldn't even consider. Slog was all we needed to know, really. But how far?

Another laborious half-mile, mile. Who knew? This day's distances had nothing to do with numbers.

Then thin shadows stood in the snowy air.

Trees, willows of the creek. Dim frieze that hung on the white wall of weather. But as much guidance as if it was all the direction posts on earth, every one of them pointing us to Gros Ventre and safety.

A person is never too weary to feel victory. Blearily exultant, I stood and watched while Varick halted his sled and began to slog back to meet Rob and me. Now that we had the creek, consultation wasn't really needed anymore. But maybe he simply had to share success with us, maybe—then as I squinted at the treeline of the creek, something moved in the bottom corner of my vision, there where the fence cornered into the creek.

I blinked and the something still moved, slowly, barely. A lower clot of forms beneath the willow shadows: Double W cattle, white with the snow coated onto them, caught there in the fence corner.

"The two of you go ahead and take your sleds across the creek, why not?" my son said as nonchalantly as if our day of struggle was already years into the past. "I'll snip the fence for these cows and give them a shove out into the brush, then catch up with you."

"Man, why bother?" Rob spoke bitterly. He still wore that bleak look, as if being prodded along by the point of an invisible bayonet. "They're goddamn Williamson's."

"That isn't their fault," Varick gave him back. "Head on across, you two. I won't be long."

I made my tired arms and tired legs climb atop the hay on the sled, then rattled the reins to start Copenhagen and Woodrow on their last few plodded miles to town, miles with the guarantee of the creek beside us. When we had crossed the narrow creek and made our turn toward Gros Ventre, Rob and his gray team copying behind us, I could hear faintly above the wind the grateful moans of the cattle Varick was freeing from the blizzard.

◆

In the morning, our procession from Gros Ventre west toward home was a slow glide through white peace. New snow had freshened everything, and without the wind the country sat plump and calm.

As we passed the knob ridge at the mouth of the North Fork valley, branchloads in the tops of its pine trees were dislodging and falling onto the lower branches, sending up snow like white dust. The all-but-silent plummets of snow in the pines and the sounds of our teams and sleds were the only things to be heard in Scotch Heaven. The lone soul anywhere here in the center of the valley was George Frew, feeding his sheep beside the creek. George's wave to us was slow and thoughtful, as if he was wondering whether he, too, would soon be making such a journey as we had.

And now we were around the final turn of the valley to my homestead, mine and Adair's, and there on their feedground beside the

North Fork were the sheep in their gray gather, and the broad bundled figure of Toussaint distributing dabs of hay. For a long minute he
watched our tiny fleet of bale-laden sleds, Varick in the lead, next me,
Rob at the tail. Then Toussaint gripped his pitchfork in the middle of
the handle, hoisted it above his head and solemnly held it there as if
making sure we could see what it was, as if showing us it was not an
axe.

DAVID JAMES DUNCAN

◆

SCIENCE MEETS PROPHECY

Gather an athletic millworker, a patriarchal matriarch, four testosteroneous teenaged boys and a tautology of first-grade girls under the roof of one rickety, four-bedroomed, one-and-a-half-bathroomed house and what you'd get, if that house were ruled by an ordinary mortal, would be abject chaos. Fortunately for us, our home had always been governed by our mother, and Mama's greatest gift, in fact her life's vocation, was her ability to comprehend, integrate and orchestrate the 2,920 days (365 × 8) of the Collective Chance Family Year into a manageable series of events. With the possible exception of the ever-popular "Shuttup!" the piece of advice most frequently and profitably slung round our house had always been "Ask Mama!" She was a maestro at conducting her family. The kitchen was her podium, an immense wall calendar her score, and a piercing I-will-brook-no-nonsense voice the combination baton/scepter/cattle prod with which she set the tempo and integrated our multitudinous entrances and exits. Only she could tell you at all times which of her seven charges was where, doing what, returning home when, at which time she'd soon have them accomplishing such and such a task or keeping such and such an appointment. More importantly, only she could comprehend and wield the bewildering hierarchy of domestic values that made quick decisions possible and quashed most interfamilial conflicts before they could fester into feuds. What—to cite a historic example of these values—is the more important promise for a seventeen-year-old boy to keep: the one to take his seven-year-old sisters on their first-ever ice-skating excursion or the conflicting one to chauffeur his transportationless grandmother clear across town and back for the year-end bash of the West Vancouver Women's "Great Decisions" group? Don't ask me. Ask Mama.

So when—the morning after the Psalm War—Mama abruptly stopped conducting Everett, Peter and me and instead began to wage a kind of Cold War against us, it was not just a passing disaster: it was the instantaneous unraveling of our family as we knew it. For what she called "Christian reasons," Mama stopped advising, stopped solving domestic koans, stopped helping the three of us in any way. And when Papa saw it happening and tried to reason her out of it, she went from intractable to irrational to hysterical to abusive, and finally just set her Bible in her lap and turned to stone.

I remember seeing a TV news clip, one night that year, of the famous UN Assembly during which Nikita Khrushchev fell silent, slipped off his shoe, and proceeded to bang it steadily against a microphoned table throughout the testimonies of every delegate whose opinion on the Cuban Missile Crisis differed from his own. It was an unforgettable performance. World War III was the thinly veiled topic, the fate of all humanity was at stake—and there sat the Russian Premier, for hours on end, banging away with his shoe. In terms of diplomatic skills, in terms of a willingness or ability to alter his course or sidestep a crisis, Khrushchev's mind and his foot had become perfect equals: if his brain had been in his sock and his foot on his shoulders, no opportunity for meaningful negotiation would have been lost.

And so it was, beginning the day after the Psalm War, with my mother. Except in her case the mind-substitute was not her shoe, but her Bible. Beginning the morning after the blowup, she no longer spoke her mind to Everett, Peter or me at all: she just flipped herself open now and then and rattled off a few blazing Letters of the Law. She had become as infallible as scripture. And as predictable. And as inflexible, deaf and blind. She had carried Christian literalism to its logical extreme: she'd become a holy inanimate object.

◆

Shortly after the Psalm War, Bet and Freddy invented a game called "Famous Scientists." It was not a coincidence. The new game had nothing whatever to do with church, sports, prayers, pitching or any of the other family obsessions. In fact it was not so much a game as an all-out surrender to a way of life the rest of us were too religious, too athletic, too complicated or just too busy to comprehend— and that was the way they wanted it.

Famous Scientists, in Bet and Freddy's eight-year-old view, were an elite handful of absentminded, charmingly disheveled, Margaret Mead or Louis Leakey-like personages who at some point in their earthly careers had simply said "Forget it!" to pedestrian jobs, lives and ways of thinking, and began to spend long, scintillating days working one ingenious experiment after another. It was a naïve definition, certainly. But the beauty of it—and the marked advantage over more sophisticated definitions—was that it obliterated the usual gap between theory and action. Famous Science had nothing to do with things like knowing the difference between lepidopterology and otorhinolaryngology or Andy Celsius and Gabe Fahrenheit. All Famous Science had to do with was saying "Let's be Famous Scientists!" to someone who could be depended upon to say "Okay!," and then to behave and experiment accordingly.

During Mama's most Bible-headed periods the twins sometimes remained in Famous Science Mode for days at a time, and as the years passed it became crucial for my brothers and me to recognize this mode, because our Scientists were increasingly attracted to the field of experimental psychology, and their "lab rats" of choice were their ever-credulous brothers. It can be more than a minor annoyance to find that the innocuous chat you've just had with a seemingly airheaded, bubble-gum-smacking, preadolescent girl was in fact a prefabricated, carefully calculated quiz designed to lay bare the most inane foible of your personality. It can also be troubling to find that every cross-grained, self-damning sentence you just blabbed without thinking has been immortalized in one of Famous Science's increasingly nefarious lab notebooks.

But the psychological dismemberment of male siblings was a later twist. Most of the early Famous Science research tended to be either in no recognizable field of science or else in three or four fields intrepidly bulldozed together. Take, for example, a little experiment known to its progenitors as "Centrifuging Flickers":

A red-shafted flicker is a lovely mottled woodpecker with warpainted cheeks, auburn pinions and, when fleeing, a rump as startlingly white as any Caucasian skinny-dipper's. They were so common in Camas that, during hard winter rains, six or eight of them would frequently come to roost in the warmth and dryness of our second-story eaves—and hearing, just inches from our heads as we lay in bed, the talons of a sleeping woodpecker tightening their grip on the siding was a stirring experience. Unfortunately, the flicker's sole method of expressing gratitude for a warm night's sleep was even more stirring: it came smack at the rosy crack of dawn, and consisted of a beak-on-siding applause that sounded, from the sleeper's side of the siding, about like machine-gun fire sounds from the point-blank side of the machine gun. Mill-town people cherish their sleep. After all, come morning it's time to go work at the mill. For this reason a lot of starling-brained Camas residents used to deal with their red-shafted machine-gun problems by leaning out their windows and blasting away with retaliatory BB, pellet or even shotgun fire. I'm proud to say that the Chance family resorted to more enlightened measures: we just unleashed our Famous Scientists on them.

"Centrifuging" was a concept the twins had gleaned from Famous Science's most formidable new ally and supporter, Marion Becker Chance. While buttering a homemade scone for each of them in her apartment one morning, this fanatical pacifist and devoted birdwatcher unwittingly mentioned that a centrifuge was any rapidly rotating apparatus that used centrifugal force to separate substances of different densities—for instance butterfat from milk. That her increasingly scientific hence increasingly adorable granddaughters would take this innocuous bit of information, add a flashlight, a stepladder and a smelt-dipper's net with a twelve-foot handle to it, and proceed to apply it to one of her favorite woodpeckers was unthinkable. But, as anyone who's ever seen a mushroom cloud, a cooling tower or an aerosol can of cheese spread can tell you, the unthinkable is often the very thing the Famous Scientist comes up with.

Centrifuging flickers was a straightforward process: waiting till well after sunset, when the roosting flickers had gone into their rainy-night torpor, our two Scientists donned raincoats (the birds only came during downpours), snuck out under the eaves, flashlighted a prospective victim, set up and climbed the ladder, and caught a stupefied flicker in the smelt net. After "tagging" the bird's ankle with a piece of adhesive-tape labeled "CENTRIFUGED 2-25-'65" (or whatever the date), they would fold it gently but tightly back into the smelt net, turn on Papa's shedball spotlights, start giggling with anticipation, march out into the middle of the backyard, grab the very end of the net's twelve-foot handle in their four little hands, and proceed to centrifuge their captive's brains out by twirling round and round, fast as they could go, while the experiment's greatest fan (guess who?) sat howling and loon-laughing his appreciation from an upstairs window.

We're not sure whether the Scientists ever actually separated, say, a flicker's blood from its lymphatic fluids or its gizzard juice from its stones, but we *are* sure that not one of the tagged-and-processed birds that wobbled off into the night ever showed its Caucasoid rump in our eaves again. One good centrifuging lasted a lifetime.

◆

"The Hump of Energy" was a Famous Science experiment as tedious to outside observers as "Centrifuging Flickers" was interesting, but it remained a great favorite on sultry summer afternoons. To work this meager wonder the two Scientists would simply take time out from running through the sprinkler, disconnect the garden hose, stretch it straight out across the lawn, then give one end of it a violent, four-handed snap. The Ω-shaped hump that proceeded to fly from their hands down the length of the hose gave the experiment its name. They would do this six or eight times, scrutinizing the Ω with a look of far greater interest than they possibly could have felt. Then they'd reconnect the sprinkler, sprawl belly-down in the grass beneath the spray, and while the sun baked them hot and the sprinkler bathed them cool they would proceed to speculate—at unbelievable length—upon the possible "meanings" of the hump.

The charm of the experiment completely eluded my brothers and me. All that talk about a wiggle in a hose seemed more like an affliction, an attack of logorrhea maybe, than a scientific experiment.

◆

But one scorching-hot day during Famous Science's inaugural summer, the "Hump of Energy" caught no less a thinker than Peter by surprise. Having just mowed a humongous lawn a few blocks up the street, he'd returned home dripping with sweat. And since, in those days, Peter's feelings about having sweat on his body were akin to most people's feelings about having feces on theirs, when he saw the sprinkler whirring and my sisters lolling beneath it, he took a short sprint, did his patented headfirst base-thieving slide across the soft, sopped grass, and came to a tidy halt right between them just in time to hear Beatrice say, "If a hose could reach from here clear to Spokane, do you think there could be a man strong enough to jerk it hard enough to make the Hump travel all the way?"

The twins were fortunate: if Everett had been the one to overhear this sentence, he'd have taken the words "hump," "hard," "hose," "jerk" and "all the way" and more or less robbed the twins' ears of their virginity. But Peter was a gentleman: all he did was groan. And when the twins ignored him, this pleased him. He liked it that the Scientists, while engaged in speculation, paid no heed to the banal protestations of the laity.

"I don't know about Spokane," Freddy hesitantly replied. "I mean, I don't know how far a hump of energy could travel down a hose, because if some muscleman or machine or something jerked it *really* hard, I guess the hose might just break."

"I never thought of that," said Bet.

I didn't either, Peter thought.

"But I do think," Freddy continued, "there might be all sorts of humps of all sorts of energy that go traveling all sorts of directions people can't see. For instance when a person gets mad at some-body . . ." (Her words came quicker now, and her breathing had become audible.) "Like when you get *really* mad and maybe slap somebody or jerk their arm or something, like Mama does to us sometimes, I think an invisible hump of energy might go flying all the way up their arm and right into their skeleton or insides or whatever —a hump of mean, witchy energy—and I think it might fly round and round in there like a witch on a broomstick flies round the sky, and go right on hurting invisible parts of the person you don't even know you're hurting, because you can't see all the ways their insides are connected to the mean thing you did to their outside. And from then on, maybe that hump of mean energy sits inside the hurt person like a coiled-up hose or a rattlesnake, just *waiting* in there. And someday, when that person touches somebody else, maybe even *way* in the future, that rattlesnake energy might come humping up out of them by accident and hurt that next person too, even though they didn't mean to, and even though the person didn't deserve it." She paused for a moment. Then, with feeling, concluded, "I think it happens. I really think it does."

"I think it does too," Peter said.

He felt Bet's scowl, knew that he was trespassing on Scientific turf, but finished his thought anyway. "I think what you said can happen, *does* happen. But every witch who ever lived was once just a person like you or me, that's what I think anyway, till somewhere, sometime, they got hit by a big, mean hump of nasty energy them-selves, and it shot inside them just like Freddy said, and crashed and smashed around, wrecking things in there, so that a witch was created. The thing is, though, I don't think that first big jolt is ever the poor witch's fault."

Bet thought about this, and finally nodded cautiously. Freddy said nothing. The sprinkler hissed like a Halloween cat. "Another thing," Peter said, "is that *everybody* gets jolted. You, me, before we die we'll *all* get nailed, lots of times. But that doesn't mean we'll all get turned into witches. You can't avoid getting zapped, but you *can* avoid passing the mean energy on. That's the interesting thing about witches, the challenge of them—learning not to hit back, or hit somebody else, when they zap you. You can just bury the zap, for instance, like the gods buried the Titans in the center of the earth. Or you can be like a river when a forest fire hits it—*phshhhhhhhhhhhhh!* Just drown it, drown all the heat and let it wash away . . ."

Bet was scowling again, but Freddy just lay still, watching his face. "And the great thing," he said, "the reason you can lay a river in the path of any sort of wildfire is that there's not just rivers inside us, there's a *world* in there." Seeing Bet's scowl deepening, he added, "Not because I say so. Christ says so. And Krishna. But I feel it sometimes too. I've felt how there's a world, and rivers, and high mountains, whole *ranges* of mountains, in there. And there are lakes in those mountains—beautiful, pure, deep blue lakes. *Thousands* of them. Enough to wash away all the dirt and trouble and witchiness on earth."

Bet's scowl was gone now, because her mind had eased down into a place where hiss of sprinkler, splash of drops and babbling of brother were all just soothing sensations. But Freddy was still watching Peter's face, and still listening when he said, "But to believe in them! To believe enough to *remember* them. *That's* where we blow it! Mountain lakes? In *me?* Naw! Jesus we believe in, long as He stays out of sight. But the things He said, things like *The kingdom of heaven is within you,* we believe only by dreaming up a heaven as stupid and boring as our churches. Something truly heavenly, something with mountains higher than St. Helens or Hood and lakes purer and deeper than any on earth—we never look for such things inside us. So when the humps of witchiness come at us, we've got nowhere to go, and just get hurt, or get mad, or pass them on and hurt somebody else. But if you want to stop the witchiness, if you want to put out the fires, you *can* do it. You can do it if you just remember to crawl, *right while you're burning,* to drag yourself if that's what it takes, clear up into those mountains inside you, and on down into those cool, pure lakes."

Bet was half asleep by now, and Peter was gazing at the spray as if into a blaze, when, quite suddenly and quite loudly, Freddy burst into tears. *"What!"* Bet shouted, jumping clear to her feet. "Is it a bee-sting? What *is* it?"

"I'm sorry," Freddy sobbed, hiding her face. "I'm sorry. But . . . but I'm just so *glad!*"

"Glad?" Bet was flummoxed. "About a bee-sting? About *what?*"

"The mountains!" Freddy whispered, eyes closed, tears streaming. "The lakes."

◆

For a believer in the empirical method and an acerbic critic of religious hocus-pocus of all kinds, Marion Becker Chance was surprisingly fond of making prophetic statements. Her prophecies were invariably dire. She made them only in the privacy of her apartment. Her "chosen people" were invariably her grandchildren. Her purpose, however, was far more pragmatic than that of the usual doom prophet: all Grandawma really wanted out of a prophesy was to scare our pants off. Having personally experienced, as an inmate in an ancient British parochial school, how much quieter and better behaved a quailing, apprehensive child is than a happy one, she would do her prophetic best, whenever our boisterousness threatened her china or fragile furniture, to create an atmosphere conducive to the dread of untold evil and impending disaster.

Unfortunately for her possessions, we were onto her. Though she used her irony-armored voice, hawklike face, red-rimmed eyes, innate pessimism, disastrous past and palsying to considerable effect, we knew all along that she was no prophet. She was just an overgrown Famous Scientist in disguise.

Her favorite doom prophecy was a surprisingly anemic specimen. It went something like this: "The one thing, perhaps the *only* thing you can all be certain of, is that your lives are going to be very different, and probably very much darker, than you'll ever dream or expect as children."

"That's great news, Gran!" was Everett's famous reply to this. "I was expecting I'd turn out exactly like you!"

Poor Grandawma. Another common doom, this one foretold for

the twins as soon as they grew old enough to act the least bit giddy around little boys, went like this: "You think you'll grow up to marry a handsome prince, don't you? Well, let me tell you something, young lady. You shall, you shall. And *that's* when you'll find out that the fairy tale has it backwards. A few kisses, a few years—that's all it takes to turn the handsomest prince on earth into a big, ugly frog."

Freddy's best response to this came when she was seven—and already a discerning student of her big brothers' vernacular. She said, "You mean like Charles de Gaulle?" Bet's most interesting reply to the same prophecy had come a year or two earlier. It went, "I'll *never* kiss a boy! Not even a prince. But if I do, I hope he turns into a cute little doggy." We were difficult kids to scare.

In 1965, however—in the midst of a religious Cold War that *had* begun to scare us—Grandawma finally made a prophecy that had the desired effect. It was that same anemic one she'd made a dozen times at least to my brothers and me—about our lives being doomed to turn out differently than we expected. This time, though, she found a way of giving it some real oomph: not sixty seconds after she said it, she died.

◆

It was a bright, sunny spring morning. The twins had spent the night on the hide-a-bed couch in Grandawma's livingroom. Their joint plan for the day was a bus trip down to Portland to visit the city zoo and the Oregon Museum of Science and Industry—the Famous Scientists' Medina and Mecca. Grandawma's health had been fine. In fact she'd been on a roll, bustling on foot around the school basements, libraries and junk stores of Camas, begging or buying old microscopes and chemistry sets, butterfly nets and lab notebooks, fossils, gyroscopes, geodes, atomic charts, Indian artifacts and anything else she could think of to enhance and prolong the twins' science phase. The three of them were seated together at her little oak breakfast table, eating oatmeal and drinking orange juice and tea, when it happened. Freddy had just idly recited the Quaker Oats motto aloud: *"Nothing Is Better for Thee Than Me."* But Bet—whose mouth had been full of the same tepid bite of the stuff for two or three minutes—took vehement exception: "That's a lie!" she blurted, dribbling milk down her chin. *"Tons* of things are better for thee than *oat*meal!"

"It's an exaggeration, certainly," Grandawma said. "But you'll not leave this table till you finish what's in your bowl. And if you speak again with your mouth full, I'll double your helping."

"It's the Right Thing to Do," Freddy read from the box.

Bet sighed, rolled her eyes, and started lapping milk from the bowl with her tongue.

"Stop that at once!" Grandawma snapped.

"I'm a kitty cat," Bet said gloomily.

"Perhaps you were. But now you're human."

"Whooo saaaaays?" she meowed.

"Your sister and I, and this nice Quaker gentleman on the box," Grandawma replied patiently. "We are going on a scientific expedition today, and cats are infamously inept scientists. Just look at the way they dissect mice and frogs."

"I like *playing* Famous Scientist," Bet said, unscientifically slapping her spoon against the gluey mush in her bowl, "but I don't want to *be* a scientist. Not when I grow up."

Grandawma scowled, both at the statement and at the slapping. Bet looked to be in a state of rapid devolution. If the trend continued, she might lapse clear back into one of her *Irwin* moods! It would be the ruin of the day. Marion Becker Chance narrowed her eyes and sniffed loudly. The time had definitely come to brew up a little behavior-altering apprehension: "You may well grow up to become a gargoyle, or a harridan, or a guttersnipe!" she snapped. "We can't possibly know—and thank goodness not! What most of us become as adults would *terrify* us as children."

It was working better than usual: Bet had already stopped slapping her spoon, sat up straight, and was betraying no feline qualities whatever as she peeped, "Why?"

But Grandawma decided she'd best rub it all the way in. "I don't quite know," she said, unleashing the palsy now, and glowering far off into a hideous future. Then out she came with it: "I only know that the one thing, perhaps the *only* thing we can always be certain of, is that our lives will turn out very differently, and very much more darkly, than most of us ever dream as children."

It may have been a bit cruel, but it was also an unusually effective piece of behavioral engineering: the two girls stopped eating and reading and stared morosely down into their bowls, their hands neatly folded, their rambunctious little mouths closed, their comportment perfect. The room was silent, but for the tidy ⁓⁓⁓⁓⁓⁓ing of the electric wall clock. Marion took a grimly satisfied sip of tea, placed her cup in its saucer with a dainty clink, and was about to broach the subject of the Natural Science Exhibit they'd be studying at OMSI that day when, for the first and last time in her life, her behavior modification technique backfired and became a genuine act of prophecy:

First she looked up at the ceiling and said, *"Oh!"*

It was her last word. She said it softly, but with such hushed enthusiasm, perhaps even delight, that the twins immediately looked up at the ceiling too. But there was nothing there but plaster.

Next Grandawma closed her eyes, opened her mouth, and slowly began to bow her head—another thing they'd never seen her do. Bet later said, with a somewhat wooden air of piousness, that it looked as though she'd been bowing her head to pray. But Freddy said not. Freddy said she bowed so slowly that it was more like an OMSI exhibit they'd once seen on the laws of kinetics. To me this seems the likelier explanation, since when the center of gravity passed the meridian the bowing head became a falling head that didn't slow or alter course till Grandawma's brow smacked the front rim of her cereal bowl, the milk and oatmeal splashed up onto her neat gray bun, and the bowl stayed balanced, like a little cap, right there on top of her head. The twins gaped at her, saying nothing. Grandawma gaped down at the floor, also saying nothing. Her arms were folded neatly in her lap; her rambunctious old mouth was closed; except for the food on the floor and the bowl on her head, her comportment was perfect. The room was silent, but for the tidy ⬝⬝⬝⬝⬝⬝⬝⬝ing of the clock. She'd even stopped palsying.

Then—quite suddenly—she bounced, as if she'd had a single violent hiccup.

It was her final movement. Peter later theorized that this bounce had been caused by the soul's departure from her body. Everett, however, ruthlessly maintained that it was only the soul *attempting* to leave her body, and that since she'd never believed in it the poor thing was so weak and malnourished that rather than fly away it could only "hop, then croak—like one of those prince-cum-frogs in that backasswards fairy tale she was always trying to scare the twins with."

Either way, when our grandmother, or the top half of her body, came down from the bounce, the forehead missed the bowl, hit the edge of the table, slid on past the table when the neck bent back, and flopped neatly down between her knees; meanwhile her arms slid out of her lap, her hands swished down her sides, and her free-falling knuckles hit the hardwood floor with a rattlingly eerie clunk which both girls recognized at once as the sound of utter finality.

From opposite ends of the table, they leaned down and peered at her. She didn't move. She didn't make a peep. Nor did she breathe. "Are you all right, Gran?" asked Beatrice.

"She might be all right," Freddy said. "But she sure is dead."

"She just fainted," Bet said doubtfully. "Huh, Gran."

"She never faints. Anyhow, it's not stuffy."

Bet began thinking this over. Meanwhile Freddy slid out of her chair, seated herself, cross-legged, on the floor beneath the table, and took advantage of this unique opportunity to study her first nonliving human without motherly or brotherly interference. "Don't leave me up here!" Bet cried. And grabbing her little black lab notebook, she too moved down to the floor.

"It *does* look like fainting," Freddy admitted, studying Grand-awma's head-between-knees posture. "I mean, that's just how Peter used to sit so he wouldn't faint in church, back before he started *not* sitting that way, so he *would* faint, so he'd get to leave."

Bet nodded.

"Maybe dying *feels* like fainting," Freddy theorized.

"I hope so," Bet murmured. But she was not up to the usual scientific banter.

"Didn't look like it hurt much."

"No," Bet said—and for a moment it looked as though she might manage to jot some of these observations down. But then she half gasped, hugged her notebook to her chest, turned to Freddy, and said, "They turn *cold* . . . don't they?"

Winifred nodded.

"How long do you suppose it takes?"

Freddy thought about it. "Maybe about as long," she said finally, "as for a hot bowl of oatmeal to cool down."

It was the wrong metaphor: Bet put on an extremely grave expression, turned to her sister, and said, "You mean as long as it takes to cool down on the table? Or on your head?" Then she burst into hysterics.

"Don't!" Freddy said.

Which made Bet laugh harder.

"It's not funny."

But Beatrice was beside herself. "Did you see the mush go flying?" she howled. "Did you see the bowl on her *bun?* Ha ha ha! Dove right in and tried for that last bite! Hahahahahaha! You can get down now, Gran, that's a good girl! *Nothing was better for thee than he!*"

Freddy never smiled or said a word, but Bet was still trying, through a hemorrhoidal kind of squeezing, to glean a little more escapist hilarity out of the idea—when they both suddenly heard the dripping, turned, and saw the urine, raining down through the wicker chair seat, pooling on the floor beneath. Bet let out a last staccato bark. Then, in a small, very surprised voice, she said, "Gran? Are *you* doing that?"

The body didn't move. The urine kept dripping. Bet began to quiver.

"I think," Freddy whispered, "I think they—bodies, I mean— they just do that."

Bet turned away, and for a long time they were silent. Then, in the same surprised, minuscule voice, Bet said, "I *loved* her, Freddy. I loved her a lot." And though she never sniffled, never sobbed, just held her head rigid and sat there shivering, tears began streaming down her cheeks.

For a long time Freddy couldn't speak. She just watched the spilled milk swirl along the borders of the other pool. Finally, though, she said, "I loved her too, Bet. And . . . and if we really loved her, I . . . we . . . I think we've got to love her still."

Bet drew her knees up and clenched them hard to try and slow the shivering. "What do you mean?" she asked.

"I mean"—Freddy shook her head—"I mean she wouldn't want this. I mean we, I . . . I think I've got to clean her up before we let an ambulance or anybody find her."

Hearing this, Bet just hid her face between her knees and curled up like a foetus. But she heard Freddy sigh after a bit, then crawl out from under the table, cross the kitchen, and unbutton the never-before-used pink terry-cloth hand towels from the oven handle; heard her fetch sponges and soap from beneath or beside the sink, fill a saucepan with water, return to the table; heard her wipe the surface clean, draw a breath that sounded as trembly as her own, move to the floor, hesitate, then slowly continue cleaning.

When Freddy returned to the sink Bet finally peeked, saw the floor was spotless, saw a pile of clean rags lying beneath the wicker. She heard Freddy dump and rinse the saucepan, run fresh water, wring her towels and sponges, and they were soothing, these sounds: it could have been 'Dawma or Mama just cleaning as usual. But when

Freddy recrossed the kitchen, took a stand by the chair, and Bet realized what must come next, she hid her face and curled up even more tightly than before. Then all but the one sound stopped:

This stasis went on so long and Bet had curled so tightly and deeply down into herself that when she finally heard a loud sniff she believed, for an instant, that it had come from Grandawma, and that she was about to get scolded for being under the table. But when the sniff was followed by a sob, then by the broken breathing that accompanies silent weeping, Bet knew it was her sister, knew that her strength had finally come to an end, and knew that no one was going to help them, that no one was coming to soothe them, that the situation was not going to change unless she herself somehow managed to change it.

She tried the easy route first: scrinching up into an even tighter ball, she whimpered, "Dear Jesus. *Help!*"

The result was instantaneous: Freddy's sobs became uncontrollable, half the water in her saucepan spilled onto the floor, and she gasped, *"Bet!"*

"Phooey!" Bet said with a sudden strength born, I guess, of exasperation with her fear and helplessness. But even the crudest of prayers has a way of making things difficult to interpret. Take this odd (given the context) utterance, "Phooey!" It appears that Bet either said it to Christ because she felt He wasn't helping her, or to no one because she was frustrated. But who's to say her prayer hadn't invoked Him so fast that both the exasperation and the phooey came from the Christ in Bet as He moved the frightened child in her gently aside, in order to help?

I don't know. I suspect only fools understand prayer. All I know is that after uttering hers, Bet said "Phooey!" then unfolded herself, crawled almost angrily out from under the table, stood up across the chair from her undone twin, tried to picture Peter's inner mountains and lakes, failed utterly, tried to smile at Freddy, failed utterly, but finally reached, nevertheless, for the towel in the saucepan. All I know is that, after wringing it out with weak, trembling hands, she began, ever so gently, to cleanse the bowed head, the withered neck, the steel-gray hair. All I know is that this somehow enabled Freddy to start helping too, and that when the ambulance and Mama arrived a half hour or so later, our grandmother was lying on the floor neatly wrapped in a blanket, dignified, dry and spotless.

PERCIVAL EVERETT

CRY ABOUT A NICKEL

Clouds hung like webs in the firs and a fine mist wet the air. Black-berry thickets sprawled wide and high, most of the berries withered past picking. Back home, on an autumn morning like this, we might be sharpening knives and boiling water to butcher a hog. But here I was in the wet Cascades. I pulled my pickup to the side of the road and got out. I looked down the steep slope at the Clackamas River tumbling at a good clip over and around rocks. I made my way down a path to the bank and found it littered with fishermen, shoulder to shoulder, casting lures and dragging them past a great many large fish just sitting in a pool as if parked in a lot. Being sincerely ignorant I figured I was running little risk of sounding so when I asked the man nearest me—

"What kind of fish are those?"

The man let his eyes find me slowly and his smile was a few beats behind. "Why, they're steelhead."

"They don't seem to be very interested," I said.

The man turned back to his line and said nothing.

I watched a bit longer, then climbed back to the road. In South Carolina fishing was done quietly, in private, for creatures hidden from view. At least a man could say, "Aw, there ain't no fish here." But this seemed like premeditated self-humiliation.

A boy at the house told me I'd find his father in one of the stables. I wandered into the near one, didn't see him, but I caught a mare nosing around her hock. I found a halter on a nail outside her stall and put it on her, tied her head up.

"What're you doing there?" a man yelled at me.

"She was nosin' around her hock and I saw it was capped and had ointment on it. I raised her head up so she wouldn't burn her nose."

"What do you know about capped hocks? Who are you?"

"Are you Mr. Davis?"

"Yeah. I'm waitin'."

"Name's Cooper. I heard you had a job open."

"What do you know about horses?"

"I know enough to tie a horse's head up when I'm trying to blister her."

"Where're you from?"

"Carolina."

"North?"

"No, the good one."

Davis rubbed his jaw and studied the mare. "We don't get many blacks around here."

"The horse said the same thing."

"Five hundred a month. readubIncludes a two-room trailer and utilities."

◀━━━━━◆

Davis had twenty-three horses, most pretty good, and a lot of land. He rented rides to hunters and to anybody who just wanted to get wet in the woods.

The first thing was to clean out the medicine chest. The box was full of all sorts of old salves and liniments and I just had to say aloud to myself, "Pathetic."

Davis had stepped into the tack room without me noticing. "What's pathetic?" he asked.

I sat there on the floor, thinking oh no, but I couldn't back off. "All this stuff," I said. "Better to have nothing than all this useless trash."

He didn't like this. "What's wrong with it?"

I looked in the box. "Well, sir, I appreciate the fact that this thermometer is fairly clean, but better to have a roll of string in the chest than keep this crap-crusted one on all the time. This is ugly."

"So, you've got a weak stomach."

I shook my head. "You've got ointments in here twenty years old. Why don't you grab the good stuff for me. Where's the colic relief? You've got three bottles of Bluestone and they're all empty."

He didn't look directly at me, just sort of flipped me a glance. "Fix it," he said and left.

—

There were no crossties, so I had to set up some for grooming. I was currycombing a tall stallion when Davis's son came into the stable.

"Hey, Joe," the kid said.

"Charlie."

"Mind if I help?"

I looked at the teenager. It was really a question. As a boy, I would have been required to work the place. "I don't know," I said. "Your father might think I'm not earning my pay. Don't you have other chores?"

"No."

I didn't understand this at all. I looked around. "I tell you what. You comb out the hindquarters on Nib here and then dandy-brush his head. I'm gonna shovel out his stall real quick."

The boy took the comb, stood behind the horse, and began stroking.

"No," I said and I pulled him away. "Stand up here next to the shoulder, put your arm over his back, and do it like that. So he won't kick the tar out of you."

Charlie laughed nervously and began working again. I shoveled at the stall and watched him. He was a nice boy. I couldn't tell if he was bright or not, he was so nervous. I stopped and listened to the rain on the roof.

"Does it ever stop raining?" I asked.

"One day last year."

I laughed, but he just stared at me. Then I thought he wasn't joking. "You're not saying—" Before I finished he was smiling.

"How'd you learn about horses?" he asked.

"Grew up with 'em. You don't spend much time with the animals?"

"Not really."

"People say that horses are stupid." I fanned some hay out of my face. "And they're right, you know. But at least it's something you can count on."

Then Davis showed up. "Charles."

The boy snapped to attention away from the horse and, glancing at the currycomb in his hand, threw it down. "I asked Joe if I could help, Daddy."

"Get in the house."

The boy ran from the stable.

"He's a good boy," I said.

Davis picked up the comb and studied it. "I'd appreciate it if from now on you just sent him back to the house."

"All right." I leaned the pitchfork against the wall and moved to take the horse from the crossties. "He's got a bunch of chores in there to take care of, does he? Homework and stuff?"

"Yeah."

Davis looked around at the stable and at the horses, at the stallion in front of him. "The other stables look this good?"

"Gettin' there."

◆

It was a full-time job, all right, and I went to bed sore every night. Finally, I took a weekend off and drove the hour to Portland. I got a hotel room downtown on Saturday and tried to figure out what I was going to do all day. I went to the zoo and a movie, ate at a restaurant, watched bizarrely made-up kids at Pioneer Square, saw another movie, shot pool at a tavern, and went to bed. I dreamed about women. You work ranches and you talk about women and you talk about going to town to get yourself a woman, but you end up watching movies in dark rooms and shooting pool with men.

After a big breakfast at the hotel restaurant, I headed back to the ranch. The weather in Portland had been nice and, to my surprise, the sun was out all during my drive home. I parked by my trailer. Charlie was splitting wood over beside the house. Seeing him doing this made me feel good. I went inside and stowed my gear. There was a knock.

"Come," I said.

Davis came in. He had a bottle with him and a couple of glasses. "How was your trip?"

"Oh, it was a trip."

"Mind if I sit?"

I nodded that he was welcome and watched him fill the glasses. "You like bourbon?"

"You bet."

"Here you go." He handed the drink over.

I took it and sat with him at the table. He knocked his back and I followed suit. He poured another round.

He cleared his throat and focused on me. He had already had a few. "You're all right, Cooper." He leaned back. "Naw, I mean it." He sipped from his glass. "You want to hear how I lost my wife?"

I didn't say anything. I just looked at him.

"Killed herself."

I had a headache.

"Know what she died of?"

"A sudden?"

He frowned off my joke. "She took pills. She was an alcoholic and a diabetic and a Catholic. All three, any one of which is fatal alone."

"I'm sorry," I said.

He drank more. "They said she was manic, too." He looked out the window at the sky, which was growing overcast. "Charles is a good boy."

"He's quiet."

"That's my fault, I guess."

"That's not a problem."

"He's small, you know."

I just looked at him.

"I don't have a lot of patience. I don't have a lot of friends either. I guess the two go together."

"I reckon."

"Tell me something, Cooper. What do you think of a man who can't talk to his kid?"

I swirled my whiskey in the glass and held his eyes.

"I've got a temper. A bad one."

I nodded.

"You want to hear what happened at Charlie's school last year?"

"To tell the truth, no, I don't."

Davis pulled a pack of cigarettes from his shirt pocket and fumbled his way through lighting one, blew out a cloud of blue smoke and coughed. He stood and went to the window, watched as his son split wood. "Look at him. He could do that all day. He's small, though."

I polished off my drink.

"You think I'm crazy."

I shook my head. "No, I don't."

"Well, I ain't crazy. He ain't right." He was hot and I was beginning to think he *was* touched. "Don't tell me how to run things!"

"Sure thing."

I didn't know what he was talking about.

He snatched up his bottle and walked out.

I fell on my bunk and looked at the ceiling. I wanted to pack up and leave, but I needed the job and I wasn't the sort to leave a man in a lurch. He had a mare ready to drop and a couple of horses with thrush real bad. I didn't like what I had seen in Davis's eyes. He was slow-boiling and soon there wouldn't be anything left to scorch but the pot.

I fixed some grits and scrambled eggs and sausages and sat down to dinner by myself. An evening rain came and went and I could see the fuzzy glow of the moon behind the clouds. I felt bad for little Charlie. Funny, I hadn't thought of him as small before, but he was. I felt sorry for him and I didn't know why. I wasn't about to get involved, though. My mother had a number of hobbies, but raising fools wasn't one of them.

◆

A couple of days later, four fellows rented horses and went into the hills for elk. I knew when they rode out that all they were going to get up there was drunk. They didn't deserve the weather that day. It was almost hot when they came back. I was trimming hooves. Charlie was in the stable with the pregnant mare.

"Woowee," said one man, "what a day."

"That was fun," said another, groaning and trying to work a kink out of his back as he climbed down. "That was more fun than huntin' coons."

They all dismounted and I took the horses. They'd ridden the animals hard right up to the end and they were sweating like crazy.

I called Charlie over. "Take these horses out and walk 'em around, get 'em cool." As he stepped away, I yelled for him to loosen the girths. His dad had let up a little and he was freer to hang about and help.

The men lined up along the fence and watched Charlie in the corral.

"Ain't he pretty?" I heard one of the men say. I thought he was talking about a horse, but another spoke up.

"Hey, I heard about that locker-room business," he said.

"Oh, this was the boy?"

"Yeah."

I stepped out and saw that Charlie was ignoring them pretty good. They said a few more things and I got fed up, started toward them.

"Looks like we got the nigger riled," one said.

I stopped at the crack of a rifle shot. Davis was out of his house and just yards from the corral.

"You boys paid?" Davis asked.

The leader, more or less, put his hands up and laughed a little. "Yeah, we paid."

"Then get along."

"Okay, Davis. We'll get along. Nice boy you got there." The man chuckled again. They got into their car and left.

Davis watched them roll away. "Charles," he said. "Go on inside."

I caught Davis by the arm. "Hey, just let him forget about it."

He pulled away, didn't even look at me.

I watched him disappear into the house. Things were becoming a little more clear. More reason to ignore it. My motto: Avoid shit.

It was raining real good when I came back from the grocery store. As I swept around the yard I saw Charlie standing by the tree behind the house. I parked at the trailer, got out of my truck, and went inside for lunch. I finished my coffee and shivered against the chill in the air. Outside, I found it warmer than in the trailer. I started to go check the horses when I noticed that Charlie was still standing by that tree. I went to him. At twenty yards I could see that he was tied to it.

"What's the story?" I asked, looking around.

The boy just cried and I was pretty damn close to it myself. Rain dripped from his hair and ran down his face.

"Your father do this?" I was looking at the house, but I knew Charlie was nodding. "Why? Did he say why?" I was hesitant about untying him. I thought Davis had flipped and might be waiting at a window to blow my head off. I shouted as I reached for the rope. "Davis! I'm untying the boy! Okay!" I undid the knots and led the kid back to the house.

Davis was sitting in a chair in front of the fireplace. He looked really spaced out. "Hey, Davis, you all right?"

He said nothing.

"I brought Charlie inside here."

"I heard you." He leaned forward and poked at the burning logs. "He wouldn't tell me who they were."

"He's a strong boy," I said.

"You could call it that." He sat back again. "Earl Pryor has a mare ready, wants to breed her with Nib. Be over tomorrow."

"I'll have him ready. What time?"

"Said eight-thirty. Maybe I should have Charlie watch."

"For the love of God, Davis, stop and think. Listen to yourself. Charlie's a good kid who got beat up—think of it like that. It's none of my business, but—"

Davis cut me off. He stood and faced me. "You're right. It's none of your business and you don't know what the hell you're talking about."

"Charlie didn't do anything."

"Pack up, drifter."

I looked at him for a second, but I'd heard him right. "Okay. Fine. But listen up, you're gonna drive that boy away and for no good reason."

But he wasn't listening. He was at his desk. "I'm paying you for this month and next. Fair enough?"

I looked across the room at Charlie. He had settled on the sofa and was looking out the window. Davis waved the check in front of me. I wanted to tell him what he could do with his goddamn money, but I didn't. I didn't look at his face. I just took the check, went to the trailer, and started packing.

I kept waiting for a knock on the door; Charlie coming to say goodbye or Davis coming to tell me to have that stallion ready in the morning. But there was no knock. I climbed into my pickup and drove away.

ll of this that I am about to tell happened when I was only fifteen years old, in 1959, the year my parents were divorced, the year when my father killed a man and went to prison for it, the year I left home and school, told a lie about my age to fool the Army, and then did not come back. The year, in other words, when life changed for all of us and forever—ended, really, in a way none of us could ever have imagined in our most brilliant dreams of life.

My father was named Roy Brinson, and he worked on the Great Northern Railway, in Great Falls, Montana. He was a switch-engine fireman, and when he could not hold that job on the seniority list, he worked the extra board as a hostler, or as a hostler's helper, shunting engines through the yard, onto and off the freight trains that went south and east. He was thirty-seven or thirty-eight years old in 1959, a small, young-appearing man, with dark blue eyes. The railroad was a job he liked, because it paid high wages and the work was not hard, and because you could take off days when you wanted to, or even months, and have no one to ask you questions. It was a union shop, and there were people who looked out for you when your back was turned. "It's a workingman's paradise," my father would say, and then laugh.

My mother did not work then, though she *had* worked—at waitressing and in the bars in town—and she had liked working. My father thought, though, that Great Falls was coming to be a rougher town than it had been when he grew up there, a town going downhill, like its name, and that my mother should be at home more, because I was at an age when trouble came easily. We lived in a rented two-story house on Edith Street, close to the freight yards and the Missouri River, a house where from my window at night I could hear the engines as they sat throbbing, could see their lights move along the dark rails. My mother was at home most of her time, reading or watching television or cooking meals, though sometimes she would go out to movies in the afternoon, or would go to the YWCA and swim in the indoor pool. Where she was from—in Havre, Montana, much farther north—there was never such a thing as a pool indoors, and she thought that to swim in the winter, with snow on the ground and the wind howling, was the greatest luxury. And she would come home late in the afternoon, with her brown hair wet and her face flushed, and in high spirits, saying she felt freer.

The night that I want to tell about happened in November. It was not then a good time for railroads—not in Montana especially—and for firemen not at all, anywhere. It was the featherbed time, and everyone knew, including my father, that they would—all of them— eventually lose their jobs, though no one knew exactly when, or who would go first, or, clearly, what the future would be. My father had been hired out ten years, and had worked on coal-burners and oil-burners out of Forsythe, Montana, on the Sheridan spur. But he was still young in the job and low on the list, and he felt that when the cut came young heads would go first. "They'll do something for us, but it might not be enough," he said, and I had heard him say that other times—in the kitchen, with my mother, or out in front, working on his motorcycle, or with me, fishing the whitefish flats up the Missouri. But I do not know if he truly thought that or in fact had any reason to think it. He was an optimist. Both of them were optimists, I think.

I know that by the end of summer in that year he had stopped taking days off to fish, had stopped going out along the coulee rims to spot deer. He worked more then and was gone more, and he talked more about work when he was home: about what the union said on this subject and that, about court cases in Washington, D.C., a place I knew nothing of, and about injuries and illnesses to men he knew that threatened their livelihoods, and by association with them, threatened his own—threatened, he must've felt, our whole life.

Because my mother swam at the YWCA, she had met people there and made friends. One was a large woman named Esther, who came home with her once and drank coffee in the kitchen and talked about her boyfriend and laughed out loud for a long time, but who I never saw again. And another was a woman named Penny Mitchell whose husband, Boyd, worked for the Red Cross in Great Falls and had an office upstairs in the building with the YWCA, and who my mother would sometimes play canasta with on the nights my father worked late. They would set up a card table in the living room, the three of them, and drink and eat sandwiches until midnight. And I would lie in bed with my radio tuned low to the Calgary station, listening to a hockey match beamed out over the great empty prairie, and could hear the cards snap and laughter downstairs, and later I would hear footsteps leaving, hear the door shut, the dishes rattle in the sink, cabinets close. And in a while the door to my room would open and the light would fall inside, and my mother would set a chair back in. I could see her silhouette. She would always say, "Go back to sleep, Frank." And then the door would shut again, and I would almost always go to sleep in a minute.

◆

It was on a night that Penny and Boyd Mitchell were in our house that trouble came about. My father had been working his regular bid-in job on the switch engine, plus a helper's job off the extra board—a practice that was illegal by the railroad's rules, but ignored by the union, who could see bad times coming and knew there would be nothing to help it when they came, and so would let men work if they wanted to. I was in the kitchen, eating a sandwich alone at the table, and my mother was in the living room playing cards with Penny and Boyd Mitchell. They were drinking vodka and eating the other sandwiches my mother had made, when I heard my father's motorcycle outside in the dark. It was eight o'clock at night, and I knew he was not expected home until midnight.

"Roy's home," I heard my mother say. "I hear Roy. That's wonderful." I heard chairs scrape and glasses tap.

"Maybe he'll want to play," Penny Mitchell said. "We can play four-hands."

I went to the kitchen door and stood looking through the dining room at the front. I don't think I knew something was wrong, but I think I knew something was unusual, something I would want to know about firsthand.

My mother was standing beside the card table when my father came inside. She was smiling. But I have never seen a look on a man's face that was like the look on my father's face at that moment. He looked wild. His eyes were wild. His whole face was. It was cold outside, and the wind was coming up, and he had ridden home from the train yard in only his flannel shirt. His face was red, and his hair was strewn around his bare head, and I remember his fists were clenched white, as if there was no blood in them at all.

"My God," my mother said. "What is it, Roy? You look crazy." She turned and looked for me, and I knew she was thinking that this was something I might not need to see. But she didn't say anything. She just looked back at my father, stepped toward him and touched his hand, where he must've been coldest. Penny and Boyd Mitchell sat at the card table, looking up. Boyd Mitchell was smiling for some reason.

"Something awful happened," my father said. He reached and took a corduroy jacket off the coat nail and put it on, right in the living room, then sat down on the couch and hugged his arms. His face seemed to get redder then. He was wearing black steel-toe boots, the boots he wore every day, and I stared at them and felt how cold he must be, even in his own house. I did not come any closer.

"Roy, what is it?" my mother said, and she sat down beside him on the couch and held his hand in both of hers.

My father looked at Boyd Mitchell and at his wife, as if he hadn't known they were in the room until then. He did not know them very well, and I thought he might tell them to get out, but he didn't.

"I saw a man be killed tonight," he said to my mother, then shook his head and looked down. He said, "We were pushing into that old hump yard on Ninth Avenue. A cut of coal cars. It wasn't even an hour ago. I was looking out my side, the way you do when you push out a curve. And I could see this one open boxcar in the cut, which isn't unusual. Only this guy was in it and was trying to get off, sitting in the door, scooting. I guess he was a hobo. Those cars had come in from Glasgow tonight. And just the second he started to go off, the whole cut buckled up. It's a thing that'll happen. But he lost his balance just when he hit the gravel, and he fell backwards underneath. I looked right at him. And one set of trucks rolled right over his foot." My father looked at my mother then. "It hit his foot," he said.

"My God," my mother said and looked down at her lap.

My father squinted. "But then he moved, he sort of bucked himself like he was trying to get away. He didn't yell, and I could see his face. I'll never forget that. He didn't look scared, he just looked like a man doing something that was hard for him to do. He looked like he was concentrating on something. But when he bucked he pushed back, and the other trucks caught his hand." My father looked at his own hands then, and made fists out of them and squeezed them.

"What did you do?" my mother said. She looked terrified.

"I yelled out. And Sherman stopped pushing. But it wasn't that fast."

"Did you do anything then?" Boyd Mitchell said.

"I got down," my father said, "and I went up there. But here's a man cut in three pieces in front of me. What can you do? You can't do very much. I squatted down and touched his good hand. And it was like ice. His eyes were open and roaming all up in the sky."

"Did he say anything?" my mother said.

"He said, 'Where am I today?' And I said to him, 'It's all right, bud, you're in Montana. You'll be all right.' Though, my God, he wasn't. I took my jacket off and put it over him. I didn't want him to see what had happened."

"You should've put tourniquets on," Boyd Mitchell said gruffly. "That could've helped. That could've saved his life."

My father looked at Boyd Mitchell then as if he had forgotten he was there and was surprised that he spoke. "I don't know about that," my father said. "I don't know anything about those things. He was already dead. A boxcar had run over him. He was breathing, but he was already dead to me."

"That's only for a licensed doctor to decide," Boyd Mitchell said. "You're morally obligated to do all you can." And I could tell from his tone of voice that he did not like my father. He hardly knew him, but he did not like him. I had no idea why. Boyd Mitchell was a big, husky, red-faced man with curly hair—handsome in a way, but with a big belly—and I knew only that he worked for the Red Cross, and that my mother was a friend of his wife's, and maybe of his, and that they played cards when my father was gone.

My father looked at my mother in a way I knew was angry. "Why have you got these people over here now, Dorothy? They don't have any business here."

"Maybe that's right," Penny Mitchell said, and she put down her hand of cards and stood up at the table. My mother looked around the room as though an odd noise had occurred inside of it and she couldn't find the source.

"Somebody definitely should've done something," Boyd Mitchell said, and he leaned forward on the table toward my father. "That's all there is to say." He was shaking his head *no*. "That man didn't have to die." Boyd Mitchell clasped his big hands on top of his playing cards and stared at my father. "The unions'll cover this up, too, I guess, won't they? That's what happens in these things."

My father stood up then, and his face looked wide, though it looked young, still. He looked like a young man who had been scolded and wasn't sure how he should act. "You get out of here," he said in a loud voice. "My God. What a thing to say. I don't even know you."

"I know you, though," Boyd Mitchell said angrily. "You're another featherbedder. You aren't good to do anything. You can't even help a dying man. You're bad for this country, and you won't last."

"Boyd, my goodness," Penny Mitchell said. "Don't say that. Don't say that to him."

Boyd Mitchell glared up at his wife. "I'll say anything I want to," he said. "And he'll listen, because he's helpless. He can't do anything."

"Stand up," my father said. "Just stand up on your feet." His fists were clenched again.

"All right, I will," Boyd Mitchell said. He glanced up at his wife. And I realized that Boyd Mitchell was drunk, and it was possible that he did not even know what he was saying, or what had happened, and that words just got loose from him this way, and anybody who knew him knew it. Only my father didn't. He only knew what had been said.

Boyd Mitchell stood up and put his hands in his pockets. He was much taller than my father. He had on a white Western shirt and whipcords and cowboy boots and was wearing a big silver wristwatch. "All right," he said. "Now I'm standing up. What's supposed to happen?" He weaved a little. I saw that.

And my father hit Boyd Mitchell then, hit him from across the card table—hit him with his right hand, square into the chest, not a lunging blow, just a hard, hitting blow that threw my father off balance and made him make a *chuffing* sound with his mouth. Boyd Mitchell groaned, "Oh," and fell down immediately, his big, thick, heavy body hitting the floor already doubled over. And the sound of him hitting the floor in our house was like no sound I had ever heard before. It was the sound of a man's body hitting a floor, and it was only that. In my life I have heard it other places, in hotel rooms and in bars, and it is one you do not want to hear.

You can hit a man in a lot of ways, I know that, and I knew that then, because my father had told me. You can hit a man to insult him, or you can hit a man to bloody him, or to knock him down, or lay him out. Or you can hit a man to kill him. Hit him that hard. And that is how my father hit Boyd Mitchell—as hard as he could, in the chest and not in the face, the way someone might think who didn't know about it.

"Oh, my God," Penny Mitchell said. Boyd Mitchell was lying on his side in front of the TV, and she had gotten down on her knees beside him. "Boyd," she said. "Are you hurt? Oh, look at this. Stay where you are, Boyd. Stay on the floor."

"Now then. All right," my father said. "Now. All right." He was standing against the wall, over to the side of where he had been when he hit Boyd Mitchell from across the card table. Light was bright in the room, and my father's eyes were wide and touring around. He seemed out of breath and both his fists were clenched, and I could feel his heart beating in my own chest. "All right, now, you son of a bitch," my father said, and loudly. I don't think he was even talking to Boyd Mitchell. He was just saying words that came out of him.

"Roy," my mother said calmly. "Boyd's hurt now. He's hurt." She was just looking down at Boyd Mitchell. I don't think she knew what to do.

"Oh, no," Penny Mitchell said in an excited voice. "Look up, Boyd. Look up at Penny. You've been hurt." She had her hands flat on Boyd Mitchell's chest, and her skinny shoulders close to him. She wasn't crying, but I think she was hysterical and couldn't cry.

All this had taken only five minutes, maybe even less time. I had never even left the kitchen door. And for that reason I walked out into the room where my father and mother were, and where Boyd and Penny Mitchell were both of them on the floor. I looked down at Boyd Mitchell, at his face. I wanted to see what had happened to him. His eyes had cast back up into their sockets. His mouth was open, and I could see his big pink tongue inside. He was breathing heavy breaths, and his fingers—the fingers on both his hands—were moving, moving in the way a man would move them if he was nervous or anxious about something. I think he was dead then, and I think even Penny Mitchell knew he was dead, because she was saying, "Oh, please, please, please, Boyd."

That is when my mother called the police, and I think it is when my father opened the front door and stepped out into the night.

◆

All that happened next is what you would expect to happen. Boyd Mitchell's chest quit breathing in a minute, and he turned pale and cold and began to look dead right on our living-room floor. He made a noise in his throat once, and Penny Mitchell cried out, and my mother got down on her knees and held Penny's shoulders while she cried. Then my mother made Penny get up and go into the bedroom —hers and my father's—and lie on the bed. Then she and I sat in the brightly lit living room, with Boyd Mitchell dead on the floor, and simply looked at each other—maybe for ten minutes, maybe for twenty. I don't know what my mother could've been thinking during that time, because she did not say. She did not ask about my father. She did not tell me to leave the room. Maybe she thought about the rest of her life then and what that might be like after tonight. Or maybe she thought this: that people can do the worst things they are capable of doing and in the end the world comes back to normal. Possibly, she was just waiting for something normal to begin to happen again. That would make sense, given her particular character.

Though what I thought myself, sitting in that room with Boyd Mitchell dead, I remember very well, because I have thought it other times, and to a degree I began to date my real life from that moment and that thought. It is this: that situations have possibilities in them, and we have only to be present to be involved. Tonight was a very bad one. But how were we to know it would turn out this way until it was too late and we had all been changed forever? I realized, though, that trouble, real trouble, was something to be avoided, inasmuch as once it has passed by, you have only yourself to answer to, even if, as I was, you are the cause of nothing.

In a little while the police arrived to our house. First one and then two more cars with their red lights turning in the street. Lights were on in the neighbors' houses—people came out and stood in the cold in their front yards watching, people I didn't know and who didn't know us. "It's a circus now," my mother said to me when we looked through the window. "We'll have to move somewhere else. They won't let us alone."

An ambulance came, and Boyd Mitchell was taken away on a stretcher, under a sheet. Penny Mitchell came out of the bedroom and went with them, though she did not say anything to my mother, or to anybody, just got in a police car and left into the dark.

Two policemen came inside, and one asked my mother some questions in the living room, while the other one asked me questions in the kitchen. He wanted to know what I had seen, and I told him. I said Boyd Mitchell had cursed at my father for some reason I didn't know, then had stood up and tried to hit him, and that my father had pushed Boyd, and that was all. He asked me if my father was a violent man, and I said no. He asked if my father had a girlfriend, and I said no. He asked if my mother and father had ever fought, and I said no. He asked me if I loved my mother and father, and I said I did. And then that was all.

I went out into the living room then, and my mother was there, and when the police left we stood at the front door, and there was my father outside, standing by the open door of a police car. He had on handcuffs. And for some reason he wasn't wearing a shirt or his corduroy jacket but was bare-chested in the cold night, holding his shirt behind him. His hair looked wet to me. I heard a policeman say, "Roy, you're going to catch cold," and then my father say, "I wish I was a long way from here right now. China maybe." He smiled at the policeman. I don't think he ever saw us watching, or if he did, he didn't want to admit it. And neither of us did anything, because the police had him, and when that is the case, there is nothing you can do to help.

———◆———

All this happened by ten o'clock. At midnight my mother and I drove down to the city jail and got my father out. I stayed in the car while my mother went in—sat and watched the high windows of the jail, which were behind wire mesh and bars. Yellow lights were on there, and I could hear voices and see figures move past the lights, and twice someone called out, "Hello, hello. Marie, are you with me?" And then it was quiet, except for the cars that drove slowly past ours.

On the ride home, my mother drove and my father sat and stared out at the big electrical stacks by the river, and the lights of houses on the other side, in Black Eagle. He had on a checked shirt someone inside had given him, and his hair was neatly combed. No one said anything, but I did not understand why the police would put anyone in jail because he had killed a man and in two hours let him out again. It was a mystery to me, even though I wanted him to be out and for our life to resume, and even though I did not see any way it could and, in fact, knew it never would.

Inside our house, all the lights were burning when we got back. It was one o'clock and there were still lights in some neighbors' houses. I could see a man at the window across the street, both his hands to the glass, watching out, watching us.

My mother went into the kitchen, and I could hear her running water for coffee and taking down cups. My father stood in the middle of the living room and looked around, looking at the chairs, at the card table with cards still on it, at the open doorways to the other rooms. It was as if he had forgotten his own house and now saw it again and didn't like it.

"I don't feel I know what he had against me," my father said. He said this to me, but he said it to anyone, too. "You'd think you'd know what a man had against you, wouldn't you, Frank?"

"Yes," I said. "I would." We were both just standing together, my father and I, in the lighted room there. We were not about to do anything.

"I want us to be happy here now," my father said. "I want us to enjoy life. I don't hold anything against anybody. Do you believe that?"

"I believe that," I said. My father looked at me with his dark blue eyes and frowned. And for the first time I wished my father had not done what he did but had gone about things differently. I saw him as a man who made mistakes, as a man who could hurt people, ruin lives, risk their happiness. A man who did not understand enough. He was like a gambler, though I did not even know what it meant to be a gambler then.

"It's such a quickly changing time now," my father said. My mother, who had come into the kitchen doorway, stood looking at us. She had on a flowered pink apron, and was standing where I had stood earlier that night. She was looking at my father and at me as if we were one person. "Don't you think it is, Dorothy?" he said. "All this turmoil. Everything just flying by. Look what's happened here."

My mother seemed very certain about things then, very precise. "You should've controlled yourself more," she said. "That's all."

"I know that," my father said. "I'm sorry. I lost control over my mind. I didn't expect to ruin things, but now I think I have. It was all wrong." My father picked up the vodka bottle, unscrewed the cap and took a big swallow, then put the bottle back down. He had seen two men killed tonight. Who could've blamed him?

"When I was in jail tonight," he said, staring at a picture on the wall, a picture by the door to the hallway. He was just talking again. "There was a man in the cell with me. And I've never been in jail before, not even when I was a kid. But this man said to me tonight, 'I can tell you've never been in jail before just by the way you stand up straight. Other people don't stand that way. They stoop. You don't belong in jail. You stand up too straight.' " My father looked back at the vodka bottle as if he wanted to drink more out of it, but he only looked at it. "Bad things happen," he said, and he let his open hands tap against his legs like clappers against a bell. "Maybe he was in love with you, Dorothy," he said. "Maybe that's what the trouble was."

And what I did then was stare at the picture on the wall, the picture my father had been staring at, a picture I had seen every day. Probably I had seen it a thousand times. It was two people with a baby on a beach. A man and a woman sitting in the sand with an ocean behind. They were smiling at the camera, wearing bathing suits. In all the times I had seen it I'd thought that it was a picture in which I was the baby, and the two people were my parents. But I realized as I stood there, that it was not me at all; it was my father who was the child in the picture, and the parents there were his parents—two people I'd never known, and who were dead—and the picture was so much older than I had thought it was. I wondered why I hadn't known that before, hadn't understood it for myself, hadn't always known it. Not even that it mattered. What mattered was, I felt, that my father had fallen down now, as much as the man he had watched fall beneath the train just hours before. And I was as helpless to do anything as he had been. I wanted to tell him that I loved him, but for some reason I did not.

———◆———

Later in the night I lay in my bed with the radio playing, listening to news that was far away, in Calgary and in Saskatoon, and even farther, in Regina and Winnipeg—cold, dark cities I knew I would never see in my life. My window was raised above the sill, and for a long time I had sat and looked out, hearing my parents talk softly down below, hearing their footsteps, hearing my father's steel-toed boots strike the floor, and then their bedsprings squeeze and then be quiet. From out across the sliding river I could hear trucks—stock trucks and grain trucks heading toward Idaho, or down toward Helena, or into the train yards where my father hostled engines. The neighborhood houses were dark again. My father's motorcycle sat in the yard, and out in the night air I felt I could hear even the falls themselves, could hear every sound of them, sounds that found me and whirled and filled my room—could even feel them, cold and wintry, so that warmth seemed like a possibility I would never know again.

After a time my mother came in my room. The light fell on my bed, and she set a chair inside. I could see that she was looking at me. She closed the door, came and turned off my radio, then took her chair to the window, closed it, and sat so that I could see her face silhouetted against the streetlight. She lit a cigarette and did not look at me, still cold under the covers of my bed.

"How do you feel, Frank?" she said, smoking her cigarette.

"I feel all right," I said.

"Do you think your house is a terrible house now?"

"No," I said.

"I hope not," my mother said. "Don't feel it is. Don't hold anything against anyone. Poor Boyd. He's gone."

"Why do you think that happened?" I said, though I didn't think she would answer, and wondered if I even wanted to know.

My mother blew smoke against the window glass, then sat and breathed. "He must've seen something in your father he just hated. I don't know what it was. Who knows? Maybe your father felt the same way." She shook her head and looked out into the streetlamp light. "I remember once," she said. "I was still in Havre, in the thirties. We were living in a motel my father part-owned out Highway Two, and my mother was around then, but wasn't having any of us. My father had this big woman named Judy Belknap as his girlfriend. She was an Assiniboin. Just some squaw. But we used to go on nature tours when he couldn't put up with me anymore. She'd take me. Way up above the Milk River. All this stuff she knew about, animals and plants and ferns—she'd tell me all that. And once we were sitting watching some gadwall ducks on the ice where a creek had made a little turn-out. It was getting colder, just like now. And Judy just all at once stood up and clapped. Just clapped her hands. And all these ducks got up, all except for one that stayed on the ice, where its feet were frozen, I guess. It didn't even try to fly. It just sat. And Judy said to me, 'It's just a coincidence, Dottie. It's wildlife. Some always get left back.' And that seemed to leave her satisfied for some reason. We walked back to the car after that. So," my mother said. "Maybe that's what this is. Just a coincidence."

She raised the window again, dropped her cigarette out, blew the last smoke from her throat, and said, "Go to sleep, Frank. You'll be all right. We'll all survive this. Be an optimist."

When I was asleep that night, I dreamed. And what I dreamed was of a plane crashing, a bomber, dropping out of the frozen sky, bouncing as it hit the icy river, sliding and turning on the ice, its wings like knives, and coming into our house where we were sleeping, leveling everything. And when I sat up in bed I could hear a dog in the yard, its collar jingling, and I could hear my father crying, "Boo-hoo-hoo, boo-hoo-hoo"—like that, quietly—though afterward I could never be sure if I had heard him crying in just that way, or if all of it was a dream, a dream I wished I had never had.

The most important things of your life can change so suddenly, so unrecoverably, that you can forget even the most important of them and their connections, you are so taken up by the chanciness of all that's happened and by all that could and will happen next. I now no longer remember the exact year of my father's birth, or how old he was when I last saw him, or even when that last time took place. When you're young, these things seem unforgettable and at the heart of everything. But they slide away and are gone when you are not so young.

My father went to Deer Lodge Prison and stayed five months for killing Boyd Mitchell by accident, for using too much force to hit him. In Montana you cannot simply kill a man in your living room and walk off free from it, and what I remember is that my father pleaded no contest, the same as guilty.

My mother and I lived in our house for the months he was gone. But when he came out and went back on the railroad as a switchman the two of them argued about things, about her wanting us to go someplace else to live—California or Seattle were mentioned. And then they separated, and she moved out. And after that I moved out by joining the Army and adding years to my age, which was sixteen.

I know about my father only that after a time he began to live a life he himself would never have believed. He fell off the railroad, divorced my mother, who would now and then resurface in his life. Drinking was involved in that, and gambling, embezzling money, even carrying a pistol is what I heard. I was apart from all of it. And when you are the age I was then, and loose on the world and alone, you can get along better than at almost any other time, because it's a novelty, and you can act for what you want, and you can think that being alone will not last forever. All I know of my father, finally, is that he was once in Laramie, Wyoming, and not in good shape, and then he simply disappeared from view.

A month ago I saw my mother. I was buying groceries at a drive-in store by the interstate in Anaconda, Montana, not far from Deer Lodge itself, where my father had been. It had been fifteen years, I think, since I had seen her, though I am forty-three years old now, and possibly it was longer. But when I saw her I walked across the store to where she was and I said, "Hello, Dorothy. It's Frank."

She looked at me and smiled and said, "Oh, Frank. How are you? I haven't seen you in a long time. I'm glad to see you now, though." She was dressed in blue jeans and boots and a Western shirt, and she looked like a woman who could be sixty years old. Her hair was tied back and she looked pretty, though I think she had been drinking. It was ten o'clock in the morning.

There was a man standing near her, holding a basket of groceries, and she turned to him and said, "Dick, come here and meet my son, Frank. We haven't seen each other in a long time. This is Dick Spivey, Frank."

I shook hands with Dick Spivey, who was a man younger than my mother but older than me—a tall, thin-faced man with coarse blue-black hair—and who was wearing Western boots like hers. "Let me say a word to Frank, Dick," my mother said, and she put her hand on Dick's wrist and squeezed it and smiled at him. And he walked up toward the checkout to pay for his groceries.

"So. What are you doing now, Frank?" my mother asked, and put her hand on my wrist the way she had on Dick Spivey's, but held it there. "These years," she said.

"I've been down in Rock Springs, on the coal boom," I said. "I'll probably go back down there."

"And I guess you're married, too."

"I was," I said. "But not right now."

"That's fine," she said. "You look fine." She smiled at me. "You'll never get anything fixed just right. That's your mother's word. Your father and I had a marriage made in Havre—that was our joke about us. We used to laugh about it. You didn't know that, of course. You were too young. A lot of it was just wrong."

"It's a long time ago," I said. "I don't know about that."

"I remember those times very well," my mother said. "They were happy enough times. I guess something *was* in the air, wasn't there? Your father was so jumpy. And Boyd got so mad, just all of a sudden. There was some hopelessness to it, I suppose. All that union business. We were the last to understand any of it, of course. We were trying to be decent people."

"That's right," I said. And I believed that was true of them.

"I still like to swim," my mother said. She ran her fingers back through her hair as if it were wet. She smiled at me again. "It still makes me feel freer."

"Good," I said. "I'm happy to hear that."

"Do you ever see your dad?"

"No," I said. "I never do."

"I don't either," my mother said. "You just reminded me of him." She looked at Dick Spivey, who was standing at the front window, holding a sack of groceries, looking out at the parking lot. It was March, and some small bits of snow were falling onto the cars in the lot. He didn't seem in any hurry. "Maybe I didn't appreciate your father enough," she said. "Who knows? Maybe we weren't even made for each other. Losing your love is the worst thing, and that's what we did." I didn't answer her, but I knew what she meant, and that it was true. "I wish we knew each other better, Frank," my mother said to me. She looked down, and I think she may have blushed. "We have our deep feelings, though, don't we? Both of us."

"Yes," I said. "We do."

"So. I'm going out now," my mother said. "Frank." She squeezed my wrist, and walked away through the checkout and into the parking lot, with Dick Spivey carrying their groceries beside her.

But when I had bought my own groceries and paid, and gone out to my car and started up, I saw Dick Spivey's green Chevrolet drive back into the lot and stop, and watched my mother get out and hurry across the snow to where I was, so that for a moment we faced each other through the open window.

"Did you ever think," my mother said, snow freezing in her hair.

"Did you ever think back then that I was in love with Boyd Mitchell? Anything like that? Did you ever?"

"No," I said. "I didn't."

"No, well, I wasn't," she said. "Boyd was in love with Penny. I was in love with Roy. That's how things were. I want you to know it. You have to believe that. Do you?"

"Yes," I said. "I believe you."

And she bent down and kissed my cheek through the open window and touched my face with both her hands, held me for a moment that seemed like a long time before she turned away, finally, and left me there alone.

TESS GALLAGHER

◆

GIRLS

da had invited herself along on the four-hour drive to Corvallis with her daughter, Billie, for one reason: she intended to see if her girlhood friend, Esther Cox, was still living. When Billie had let drop she was going to Corvallis, Ada had decided. "I'm coming, too," she said. Billie frowned, but she didn't say no.

"Should I wear my red coat or my black coat?" she'd asked Billie. "Why don't I pack a few sandwiches." Billie had told her to wear the red coat and said not to bother about sandwiches; she didn't like to eat and drive. Ada packed sandwiches anyway.

◆

Billie had on the leather gloves she used when she drove her Mercedes. When she wasn't smoking cigarettes, she was fiddling with the radio, trying to find a station. Finally, she settled on some flute music. This sounded fine to Ada. "Keep it there, honey," she said.

"Esther was like a sister to me, an older sister," Ada said. "I don't know anyone I was closer to. We did the cooking and housekeeping for two cousins who owned mansions next door to one another—the Conants was their name. Esther and I saw each other every day. We even spent our evenings together. It was like that for nearly four years." Ada leaned back in her seat and stole a look at the speedometer: 75 miles an hour.

"It's like a soap opera," Billie said. "I can't keep the names straight or who did what when." She brought her eyes up to the rearview mirror as if she were afraid someone was going to overtake her.

Ada wished she could make her stories interesting for Billie and make it clear who the people were and how they had fit into her life. But it was a big effort and sometimes it drove her to silence. "Never mind," she'd say. "Those people are dead and gone. I don't know why I brought them up." But Esther was different. Esther was important.

Billie pushed in the lighter and took a cigarette from the pack on the dash. "What are you going to talk to this person about after all these years?" she said.

Ada considered this for a minute. "One thing I want to know is what happened to Florita White and Georgie Ganz," Ada said. "They worked up the street from us and they were from Mansfield, where Esther and I were from. We were all farm girls trying to make a go of it in the city." Ada remembered a story about Florita. Florita, who was unmarried, had been living with a man, something just not done in those days. When she washed and dried her panties she said she always put a towel over them on the line so Basil, her man, couldn't see them. But that was all Ada could remember Florita saying. There had to be more to the story, but Ada couldn't remember. She was glad she hadn't said anything to Billie.

"You might just end up staring at each other," Billie said.

"Don't you worry," Ada said. "We'll have plenty to say." That was the trouble with Billie, Ada thought. Since she'd gone into business, if you weren't *talking* business you weren't talking. Billie owned thirty llamas—ugly creatures, Ada thought. She could smell the llama wool Billie had brought along in the back seat for the demonstration she planned to give. Ada had already heard Billie's spiel on llamas. There were a lot of advantages to llamas, according to Billie. For one thing, llamas always did their job in the same place. For another, someone wanting to go into the back country could break a llama in two hours to lead and carry a load. Ada was half inclined to think Billie cared more about llamas than she did about people. But then Billie had never gotten much out of people, and she *had* made it on llamas.

"Esther worked like a mule to raise three children," Ada said.

"Why are you telling me about this woman?" Billie said, as if she'd suddenly been accused of something. She lit another cigarette and turned on her signal light. Then she moved over into the passing lane. The car sped effortlessly down the freeway.

Ada straightened herself in the seat and took out a handkerchief to fan the smoke away from her face. What could she say? That she had never had a friend like Esther in all the years since? Billie would say something like: *If she was so important then why haven't you seen her in forty-three years?* That was true enough, too; Ada couldn't explain it. She tried to stop the conversation right where it was.

"Anyway, I doubt if she's still living," Ada said, trying to sound unconcerned. But even as she said this Ada wanted more than ever to find Esther Cox alive. How had they lost track? She'd last heard from Esther after Ada's youngest son had been killed in a car crash twenty years ago. Twenty years. Then she thought of one more thing about Esther, and she said it.

"The last time I saw Esther she made fudge for me," Ada said. "You'll see, Billie. She'll whip up a batch this time, too. She always made good fudge." She caught Billie looking at her, maybe wondering for a moment who her mother had been and what fudge had to do with anything. But Ada didn't care. She was remembering how she and Esther had bobbed each other's hair one night, and then gone to the town square to stroll and admire themselves in the store windows.

◆

In the hotel room, Ada hunted up the phone book.

"Mother, take off your coat and stay awhile," Billie said as she sat down in a chair and put her feet up on the bed.

Ada was going through the *C*'s, her heart rushing with hope and dread as she skimmed the columns of names. "She's here! My God, Esther's in the book." She got up and then sat back down on the bed. "Esther. She's in the book!"

"Why don't you call her and get it over with," Billie said. She was flossing her teeth, still wearing her gloves.

"You dial it," Ada said. "I'm shaking too much."

Billie dropped the floss into a waste basket and pulled off her gloves. Then she took Ada's place on the bed next to the phone and dialed the number her mother read to her. Someone answered and Billie asked to speak to Esther Cox. Ada braced herself. Maybe Esther was dead after all. She kept her eyes on Billie's face, looking for signs. Finally Billie began to speak into the phone. "Esther? Esther Cox?" she said. "There's someone here who wants to talk to you." Billie handed Ada the phone and Ada sat on the bed next to her daughter.

"Honey?" Ada said. "Esther? This is Ada Gilman."

"Do I know you?" said the voice on the other end of the line.

Ada was stunned for a moment. It *had* been a very long time, yes. Ada's children were grown. Her husband was dead. Her hair had turned white. "We used to work in Springfield, Missouri, when we were girls," Ada said. "I came to see you after my first baby was born, in 1943." She waited a moment and when Esther still did not say anything, Ada felt a stab of panic. "Is this Esther Cox?" she asked.

"Yes it is," the voice said. Then it said, "Why don't you come over, why don't you? I'm sorry I can't remember you right off. Maybe if I saw you."

"I'll be right over, honey," Ada said. But as she gave the phone to Billie she felt her excitement swerving toward disappointment. There had been no warm welcome—no recognition, really, at all. Ada felt as if something had been stolen from her. She listened dully as Billie took down directions to Esther's house. When Billie hung up, Ada made a show of good spirits.

"I'll help you carry things in from the car," she said. She could see Billie wasn't happy about having to drive her anywhere just yet. After all, they'd just gotten out of the car.

Billie shook her head. She was checking her schedule with one hand and reaching for her cigarettes with the other. "We don't have much time. We'll have to go right now."

◆

The street they turned onto had campers parked in the front yards, and boats on trailers were drawn up beside the carports. Dogs began to bark and pull on their chains as they drove down the street.

"Chartreuse. What kind of a color is that to paint a house?" Billie said. They pulled up in front of the house and she turned off the ignition. They didn't say anything for a minute. Then Billie said, "Maybe I should wait in the car."

The house had a dirty canvas over the garage opening, and an accumulation of junk reached from the porch onto the lawn. There were sheets instead of curtains hung across some of the windows. A pickup truck sat in the driveway with its rear axles on blocks. Esther's picture window looked out onto this. Ada stared at the house, wondering what had brought her friend to such a desperate-looking place.

"She'll want to see how you turned out," Ada told Billie. "You can't stay in the car." She was nearly floored by Billie's suggestion. She was trying to keep up her good spirits, but she was shocked and afraid of what she might find inside.

They walked up to the front door. Ada rang the bell and, in a minute, when no one answered, she rang the bell again. Then the door opened and an old, small woman wearing pink slacks and a green sweater looked out.

"I was lying down, girls. Come in, come in," the woman said. Despite the woman's age and appearance, Ada knew it was Esther. She wanted to hug her, but she didn't know if she should. Esther had barely looked at her when she let them in. This was an awful situation, Ada thought. To have come this far and then to be greeted as if she were just anyone. As if she were a stranger.

A rust-colored couch faced the picture window. Esther sat down on it and patted the place beside her. "Sit down here and tell me where I knew you," she said. "Who did you say you were again?"

"God, woman, don't you know me?" Ada said, bending down and taking Esther's hand in hers. She was standing in front of the couch. "I can't believe it. Esther, it's me. It's Ada." She held her face before the woman and waited. Why wouldn't Esther embrace her? Why was she just sitting there? Esther simply stared at her.

"Kid, I wished I did, but I just don't remember you," Esther said. "I don't have a glimmer." She looked down, seemingly ashamed and bewildered by some failure she couldn't account for.

Billie hovered near the door as if she might have to leave for the car at any moment. Ada dropped the woman's hand and sat down next to her on the couch. She felt as if she had tumbled over a cliff and that there was nothing left now but to fall. How could she have been so insignificant as to have been forgotten? she wondered. She was angry and hurt and she wished Billie *had* stayed in the car and not been witness to this humiliation.

"I had a stroke," Esther said and looked at Ada. There was such apology in her voice that Ada immediately felt ashamed of herself for her thoughts. "It happened better than a year ago," she said. Then she said, "I don't know everything, but I still know a lot." She laughed, as if she'd had to laugh at herself often lately. There was an awkward silence as Ada tried to take this in. Strokes happened often enough at their age so she shouldn't be surprised at this turn of events. Still, it was something she hadn't considered; she felt better and worse at the same time.

"Is this your girl? Sit down, honey," Esther said and indicated a chair by the window stacked with magazines and newspapers. "Push that stuff onto the floor and sit down."

"This is my baby," Ada said, trying to show some enthusiasm. "This is Billie."

Billie let loose a tight smile in Esther's direction and cleared a place to sit. Then she took off her gloves and put them on the window sill next to a candle holder. She crossed her legs, lit a cigarette and gazed out the window in the direction of her Mercedes. "We can't stay too long," she said.

"Billie's giving a talk on business," Ada explained, leaving out just what kind of business it was. "She was coming to Corvallis, so I rode along. I wanted to see you."

"I raise llamas," Billie said, and turned back into the room to see what effect this would have.

"That's nice. That's real nice," Esther said. But Ada doubted she knew a llama from a goat.

"Now don't tell me you can't remember the Conants—those cousins in Springfield we worked for," Ada said.

"Oh, I surely do remember them," Esther said. She was wearing glasses that she held to her face by tilting her head up. From time to time she pushed the bridge of the glasses with her finger. "I've still got a letter in my scrapbook. A recommendation from Mrs. Conant."

"Then you must remember Coley Starber and how we loaned him Mrs. Leslie Conant's sterling silver," Ada said, her hopes rising, as if she'd located the scent and now meant to follow it until she discovered herself lodged in Esther's mind. Billie had picked up a magazine and was leafing through it. From time to time she pursed her lips and let out a stream of smoke.

"Coley," Esther said and stared a moment. "Oh, yes, I remember when he gave the silver back. I counted it to see if it was all there. But, honey, I don't remember you." She shook her head helplessly. "I'm sorry. No telling what else I've forgot."

Ada wondered how it could be that she was missing in Esther's memory when Coley Starber, someone incidental to their lives, had been remembered. It didn't seem fair.

"Mom said you were going to make some fudge," Billie said, holding the magazine under the long ash of her cigarette. "Mom's got a sweet tooth."

"Use that candle holder," Esther told Billie, and Billie flicked the ash into the frosted candle holder.

Ada glared at Billie. She shouldn't have mentioned the fudge. Esther was looking at Ada with a bemused, interested air. "I told Billie how we used to make fudge every chance we got," Ada said.

"And what did we do with all this fudge?" Esther asked.

"We ate it," Ada said.

"We ate it!" Esther said and clapped her hands together. "We *ate* all the fudge." Esther repeated the words to Billie as if she were letting her in on a secret. But Billie was staring at Esther's ankles. Ada looked down and saw that Esther was in her stocking feet, and that the legs themselves were swollen and painful-looking where the pantleg had worked up while Esther sat on the couch.

"What's making you swell up like that?" Billie said. Ada knew Billie was capable of saying anything, but she never thought she'd hear her say a thing like this. Such behavior was the result of business, she felt sure.

"I had an operation," Esther said, as if Billie hadn't said anything at all out of line. Esther glanced toward a doorway that led to the back of the house. Then she raised up her sweater and pulled down the waistband of her slacks to show a long violet-looking scar which ran vertically up her abdomen. "I healed good though, didn't I?" she said. Esther lowered her sweater, then clasped her hands in her lap.

Before Ada had time to take this in, she heard a thumping sound from the hallway. A man appeared in the doorway of the living room. His legs bowed at an odd angle and he used a cane. The longer Ada looked at him, the more things she found wrong. One of his eyes seemed fixed on something not in this room, or in any other, for that matter. He took a few more steps and extended his hand. Ada reached out to him. The man's hand didn't have much squeeze to it. Billie stood up and inclined her head. She was holding her cigarette in front of her with one hand and had picked up her purse with the other so as not to have to shake hands. Ada didn't blame her. The man was a fright.

"I'm Jason," the man said. "I've had two operations on my legs, so I'm not able to get around very easy. Sit down," he said to Billie. Jason leaned forward against his cane and braced himself. She saw that Jason's interest had settled on Billie. Good, Ada thought. Billie considered herself a woman of the world. Surely she could handle this.

Ada turned to Esther and began to inquire after each of her other children, while she searched for a way to bring things back to that time in Springfield. Esther asked Ada to hand down a photograph album from a shelf behind the couch, and they began to go over the pictures.

"This arthritis hit me when I was forty," Jason said to Billie.

"I guess you take drugs for the pain," Billie said. "I hear they've got some good drugs now."

Ada looked down at the album in her lap. In the album there were children and babies and couples. Some of the couples had children next to them. Ada stared at the photos. Many of the faces were young, then you turned a page and the same faces were old. Esther seemed to remember everyone in the album. But she still didn't remember Ada. She was talking to Ada as to a friend, but Ada felt as if the ghost of her old self hovered in her mind waiting for a sign from Esther so that she could step forward again and be recognized.

"But that wouldn't interest you," Esther was saying as she flipped a page. Suddenly she shut the book and gazed intently at Ada.

"I don't know who you are," Esther said. "But I like you. Why don't you stay the night?" Ada looked over at Billie, who'd heard the invitation.

"Go ahead, Mother," Billie said, a little too eagerly. "I can come for you tomorrow around two o'clock, after the luncheon."

Ada looked at Jason, who was staring out the picture window toward the Mercedes. Maybe she should just give up on getting Esther to remember her and go back to the hotel and watch TV. But the moment she thought this, something unyielding rose up in her. She was determined to discover some moment when her image would suddenly appear before Esther from that lost time. Only then could they be together again as the friends they had once been, and that was what she had come for.

"You'll have to bring my things in from the car," Ada said at last.

"I wish I could help," Jason said to Billie, "but I can't. Fact is, I got to go and lay down again," he said to the room at large. Then he turned and moved slowly down the hallway. Billie opened the door and went out to the car. In a minute she came back with Ada's overnight bag.

"Have a nice time, Mom," she said. "I mean that." She set the bag inside the door. "I'll see you tomorrow." Ada knew she was glad to be heading back to the world of buying and selling, of tax shelters and the multiple uses of the llama. In a minute she heard Billie start up the Mercedes and heard it leave the drive.

The room seemed sparsely furnished now that she and Esther were alone. She could see a table leg just inside the door of a room that was probably the dining room. On the far wall was a large picture of an autumn landscape done in gold and brown.

"Look around, why don't you," Esther said, and raised herself off the couch. "It's a miracle, but I own this house."

They walked into the kitchen. The counter space was taken up with canned goods, stacks of dishes of every kind, and things Ada wouldn't expect to find in a kitchen—things like gallon cans of paint. It was as if someone were afraid they wouldn't be able to get to a store and had laid in extra supplies of everything.

"I do the cooking," Esther said. "Everything's frozen but some wieners. Are wieners okay?"

"Oh, yes," Ada said. "But I'm not hungry just yet."

"I'm not either," Esther said. "I was just thinking ahead because I've got to put these feet up. Come back to the bedroom with me."

Ada thought this an odd suggestion, but she followed Esther down the hallway to a room with a rumpled bed and a chrome kitchen chair near the foot of the bed. There was a dresser with some medicine containers on it. Ada helped Esther get settled on the bed. She took one of the pillows and placed it under Esther's legs at the ankles. She was glad she could do this for her. But then she didn't know what to do next, or what to say. She wanted the past and not this person for whom she was just an interesting stranger. Ada sat down in the chair and looked at Esther.

"Whatever became of Georgie Ganz and Florita White?" she asked Esther, because she had to say something.

"Ada—that's your name, isn't it? Ada, I don't know who you're talking about," Esther said. "I wish I did, but I don't."

"That's all right," Ada said. She brightened a little. It made her feel better that Georgie and Florita had also been forgotten. A shadow cast by the house next door had fallen into the room. Ada thought the sun must be going down. She felt she ought to be doing something, changing the course of events for her friend in some small but important way.

"Let me rub your feet," Ada said suddenly and raised herself from the chair. "Okay?" She moved over to the bed and began to massage Esther's feet.

"That feels good, honey," Esther said. "I haven't had anybody do that for me in years."

"Reminds me of that almond cream we used to rub on each other's feet after we'd served at a party all night," Ada said. The feet seemed feverish to her fingers. She saw that the veins were enlarged and angry-looking as she eased her hands over an ankle and up onto the leg.

After a little while, Esther said, "Honey, why don't you lie down with me on the bed. That way we can really talk."

At first Ada couldn't comprehend what Esther had said to her. She said she didn't mind rubbing Esther's feet. She said she wasn't tired enough to lie down. But Esther insisted.

"We can talk better that way," Esther said. "Come lay down beside me."

Ada realized she still had on her coat. She took it off and put it over the back of the chair. Then she took off her shoes and went to lie down next to Esther.

"Now this is better, isn't it?" Esther said, when Ada was settled. She patted Ada's hand. "I can close my eyes now and rest." In a minute, she closed her eyes. And then they began to talk.

"Do you know about that preacher who was sweet on me back in Mansfield?" Esther asked. Ada thought for a minute and then remembered and said she did. "I didn't tell that to too many, I feel sure," Esther said. This admission caused Ada to feel for a moment that her friend knew she was someone special. There was that, at least. Ada realized she'd been holding her breath. She relaxed a little and felt a current of satisfaction, something just short of recognition, pass between them.

"I must have told you all my secrets," Esther said quietly, her eyes still closed.

"You did!" Ada said, rising up a little. "We used to tell each other everything."

"Everything," Esther said, as if she were sinking into a place of agreement where remembering and forgetting didn't matter. Then there was a loud noise from the hall, and the sound of male voices at the door. Finally the front door closed, and Esther put her arm across Ada's arm and sighed.

"Good. He's gone," Esther said. "I wait all day for them to come and take him away. His friends, so called. He'll come home drunk, and he won't have a dime. They've all got nothing better to do."

"That must be an awful worry," Ada said. "It must be a heartache."

"Heartache?" Esther said, and then she made a weary sound. "You don't know the start of it, honey. 'You need me, Mom,' he says to me, 'and I need you.' I told him if he stopped drinking I'd will him my house so he'd always have a place to live. But he won't stop. I know he won't. He can't.

"You know what he did?" Esther asked and raised up a little on her pillow. "He just looked at me when I said that about willing him the house. I don't think he'd realized until then that I wasn't always going to be here," Esther said. "Poor fellow, he can't help himself. But girl, he'd drink it up if I left it to him."

Ada felt that the past had drifted away, and she couldn't think how to get back to that carefree time in Springfield. "It's a shame," she murmured. And then she thought of something to tell Esther that she hadn't admitted to anyone. "My husband nearly drank us out of house and home, too. He would have if I hadn't fought him tooth and nail. It's been five years since he died. Five peaceful years." She was relieved to hear herself admit this, but somehow ashamed, too.

"Well, I haven't made it to the peaceful part yet," Esther said. "Jason has always lived with me. He'll never leave me. Where could he go?"

"He doesn't abuse you, does he?" Ada said. *Abuse* was a word she'd heard on the television and radio a lot these days, and it seemed all-purpose enough not to offend Esther.

"If you mean does he hit me, no he doesn't," Esther said. "But I sorrow over him. I do."

Ada had done her share of sorrowing, too. She closed her eyes and let her hand rest on Esther's arm. Neither of them said anything for a while. The house was still. She caught the faint medicinal smell of ointment and rubbing alcohol. She wished she could say something to ease what Esther had to bear, but she couldn't think of anything that didn't sound like what Billie might call "sappy."

"What's going to become of Jason?" Ada said finally. But when she asked this she was really thinking of herself and of her friend.

"I'm not going to know," Esther said. "Memory's going to fall entirely away from me when I die, and I'm going to be spared that." She seemed, Ada thought, to be actually looking forward to death and the shutting down of all memory. Ada was startled by this admission.

Esther got up from the bed. "Don't mind me, honey. You stay comfortable. I have to go to the bathroom. It's these water pills."

After Esther left the room Ada raised up in bed as if she had awakened from the labyrinth of a strange dream. What was she doing here, she wondered, on this woman's bed in a city far from her own home? What business of hers was this woman's troubles? In Springfield, Esther had always told Ada how pretty she was and what beautiful hair she had, how nicely it took a wave. They had tried on each other's clothes and shared letters from home. But this was something else. This was the future and she had come here alone. There was no one to whom she could turn and say without the least vanity, "I was pretty, wasn't I?" She sat on the side of the bed and waited for the moment to pass. But it was like an echo that wouldn't stop calling her. Then she heard from outside the house the merry, untroubled laughter of some girls. It must be dark out by now, she thought. It must be night. She got up from the bed, went to the window and pulled back the sheet that served as a curtain. A car was pulling away from the house next door. The lights brushed the room as it moved past. In a moment, she went back to the bed and lay down again.

◄—

For supper Esther gave her wieners, and green beans fixed the way they'd had them back home, with bacon drippings. Then she took her to the spare room, which was next to Jason's room. They had to move some boxes off the bed. Esther fluffed up the pillows and put down an extra blanket. Then she moved over to the doorway.

"If you need anything, if you have any bad dreams, you just call me, honey," she said. "Sometimes I dream I'm wearing a dress but it's on backwards and I'm coming downstairs, and there's a whole room full of people looking up at me," she said. "I'm glad you're here. I am. Good night. Good night, Ada."

"Good night, Esther," Ada said. But Esther went on standing there in the doorway.

Ada looked at her and wished she could dream them both back to a calm summer night in Springfield. She would open her window and call across the alley to friend, "You awake?" and Esther would hear her and come to the screen and they would say wild and hopeless things like, "Why don't we go to California and try out for the movies?" Crazy things like that. But Ada didn't remind Esther of this. She lay there alone in their past and looked at Esther, at her old face and her old hands coming out of the sleeves of her robe, and she wanted to yell at her to get out, shut the door, don't come back! She hadn't come here to strike up a friendship with this old scarecrow of a woman. But then Esther did something. She came over to the bed and pulled the covers over Ada's shoulders and patted her cheek.

"There now, dear," she said. "I'm just down the hall if you need me." And then she turned and went out of the room.

◄◆►

Sometime before daylight Ada heard a scraping sound in the hall. Then something fell loudly to the floor. But in a while the scraping sound started again and someone entered the room next to hers and shut the door. It was Jason, she supposed. Jason had come home, and he was drunk and only a few feet away. She had seen her own husband like this plenty of times, had felt herself forgotten, obliterated, time after time. She lay there rigid and felt the weight of the covers against her throat. Suddenly, it was as if she were suffocating. She felt her mouth open and a name came out of it. "Esther! Esther!" she cried. And in a few moments her door opened and her friend came in and leaned over her.

"What is it, honey?" Esther said, and turned the lamp on next to the bed.

"I'm afraid," Ada said, and she put out her hand and took hold of Esther's sleeve. "Don't leave," she said. Esther waited a minute. Then she turned off the light and got into bed beside Ada. Ada turned on her side, facing the wall, and Esther's arm went around her shoulder.

◄◆►

The next day Billie came to the house a little early. Ada had just finished helping Esther wash her hair.

"I want you to take some pictures of us," Ada said to Billie. "Esther and me." She dug into her purse and took out the Kodak she'd carried for just this purpose. Billie seemed in a hurry to get on the road now that the conference was over.

"I was a real hit last night," Billie said to Ada as if she'd missed seeing her daughter at her best. Little tufts of llama wool clung to Billie's suit jacket as she took the camera from Ada and tried to figure out where the lens was and how to snap the picture. Ada felt sure she hadn't missed anything, but she understood Billie's wanting her to know she'd done well at something. That made sense to her now.

"Let's go out in the yard," Billie said.

"My hair's still wet," Esther said. She was standing in front of a mirror near the kitchen rubbing her hair with a towel, but the hair sprang out in tight spirals all over her head.

"You look all right," Ada said. "You look fine, honey."

"You'd say anything to make a girl feel good," Esther said.

"No, I wouldn't," Ada said. She stood behind Esther and, looking in the mirror, dabbed her own nose with powder. They could be two young women readying themselves to go out, Ada thought. They might meet some young men while they were out, and they might not. In any case, they'd take each other's arm and stroll until dusk. Someone—Ada didn't know who—might pass and admire them.

Billie had them stand in front of the picture window. They put their arms around each other. Esther was shorter and leaned her head onto Ada's shoulder. She even smiled. Ada had the sensation that the picture had already been taken somewhere in her past. She was sure it had.

"Did you get it?" Ada said as Billie advanced the film and moved closer for another shot.

"I'm just covering myself," Billie said, squatting down on the lawn and aiming the camera like a professional. "You'll kill me if these don't turn out." She snapped a few more shots from the driveway, then handed the camera back to her mother.

Ada followed her friend into the house to collect her belongings and say goodbye. Esther wrapped a towel around her head while Ada gathered her coat, purse, and overnight bag.

"Honey, I'm so sorry I never remembered you," Esther said.

Ada believed Esther when she said this. *Sorry* was the word a person had to use when there was no way to change a situation. Still, she wished they could have changed it.

"I remembered *you*, that's the main thing," Ada said. But a miserable feeling came over her, and it was all she could do to speak. Somehow the kindness and intimacy they'd shared as girls had lived on in them. But Esther, no matter how much she might want to, couldn't remember Ada, and give it back to her, except as a stranger.

"God, kid, I hate to see you go," Esther said. Her eyes filled. It seemed to Ada that they might both be wiped from the face of the earth by this parting. They embraced and clung to each other a moment. Ada patted Esther's thin back and then moved hurriedly toward the door.

—

"Tell me all about your night," Billie said as Ada slid into the passenger's seat. But Ada knew this was really the last thing on Billie's mind. And anyhow, it all seemed so far from anything Ada had ever experienced that she didn't know where to begin.

"Honey, I just want to be still for a while," Ada said. She didn't care whether Billie smoked or how fast she drove. She knew that eventually she would tell Billie how she had tried to make Esther remember her, and how she had failed. But the important things— the way Esther had come to her when she'd called out, and how, earlier, they'd lain side by side—this would be hers. She wouldn't say anything to Billy about these things. She couldn't. She doubted she ever would. She looked out at the countryside that flew past the window in a green blur. It went on and on, a wall of forest that crowded the edge of the roadway. Then there was a gap in the color and she found herself looking at downed trees and stumps where an entire hillside of forest had been cut away. Her hand went to her face as if she had been slapped. But then she saw it was green again, and she let her hand drop to her lap.

PERSONAL
SILENCE

T here was a little finger of land, a peninsula, that stuck up from the corner of Washington State pointing straight north at Vancouver Island. On the state map it was small enough it had no name. Jay found an old Clallam County map in a used-book store in Olympia and on the county map the name was printed the long way, marching northward up the finger's reach: Naniamuk. There was a clear bubble near the tip, like a fingernail, and that was named, too: Mizzle. He liked the way the finger pointed at Vancouver Island. Now he liked the name the town had. He bought a chart of the strait between Mizzle and Port Renfrew and a used book on small-boat building, and when he left Olympia he went up the county roads to Naniamuk and followed the peninsula's one paved road all the way out to its dead end at Mizzle.

It was a three-week walk. His leg had been broken and badly healed a couple of years ago when he had been arrested in Colombia. He could walk long-strided, leaning into the straps of the pack, arms pumping loosely, hands unfisted, and he imagined anyone watching him would have had a hard time telling, but if he did more than eight or ten miles in a day he got gimpy and that led to blisters. So he had learned not to push it. He camped in a logged-over state park one night, bummed a couple of nights in barns and garages, slept other nights just off the road, in whatever grass and stunted trees grew at the edge of the right-of-way.

The last day, halfway along the Naniamuk peninsula, he left the road and hiked west to the beach, through the low pines and grassy dunes and coils of rusted razorwire, and set his tent on the sand at the edge of the grass. It was a featureless beach, wide and flat, stretching toward no visible headlands. There were few driftlogs, and at the tide line just broken clamshells, dead kelp, garbage, wreckage. No tide-pools, no offshore stacks, no agates. The surf broke far out and got muddy as it rolled in. When the sun went down behind the overcast, the brown combers blackened and vanished without luminescence.

The daylight that rose up slowly the next morning was gray and damp, standing at the edge of rain. He wore his rubber-bottom shoes tramping in the wet grass along the edge of the road to Mizzle. The peninsula put him in mind of the midcoast of Chile, the valleys between Talca and Puerto Montt—flat and low-lying, the rain-beaten grass pocked with little lakes and bogs. There was not the great poverty of the Chilean valleys, but if there had been prosperity up here once, it was gone. The big beachfront houses were boarded up, empty. The rich had moved in from the coasts. Houses still lived in were dwarfish, clinker-built, with small windows oddly placed. People were growing cranberries in the bogs and raising bunches of blond, stupid-faced cattle on the wet pasturage.

At the town limit of Mizzle a big, quaintly painted signboard stood up beside the road. WELCOME TO MIZZLE! MOST WEST-ERLY TOWN IN THE CONTIGUOUS UNITED STATES OF AMERICA! Jay stood at the shoulder of the road and sketched the sign in his notebook for its odd phrasing, its fanciful enthusiasm.

The town was more than he had thought, and less. There had been three or four motels—one still ran a neon vacancy sign. An RV park had a couple of trailers standing in it. The downtown was a short row of gift shops and ice cream stores, mostly boarded shut. There was a town park—a square of unmown lawn with an unpainted ga-zebo set on it. Tourists had got here ahead of him and had gone again.

He walked out to where the road dead-ended at the tip of the peninsula. It was unmarked, unexceptional. The paving petered out and a graveled road kept on a little way through weeds and hillocks of dirt. Where the graveled road ended, people had been dumping gar-bage. He stood up on one of the hillocks and looked to the land's end across the dump. There was no beach, just a strip of tidal mud. The salt water of the strait lay flat and gray as sheet metal. The crossing was forty-three nautical miles—there was no seeing Vancouver Is-land.

He went back along the road through the downtown, looking up the short cross-streets for the truer town: the hardware store, the grocery, the lumber yard. An AG market had a computerized check-out that was broken, perhaps had been broken for months or years—a clunky mechanical cash register sat on top of the scanner, a long list of out-of-stock goods was taped across the LED display.

Jay bought a carton of cottage cheese and stood outside eating it with the spoon that folded out of his Swiss Army knife. He read from a free tourist leaflet that had been stacked up in a wire rack at the front of the store. The paper of the top copy was yellowed, puckered. On the first inside page was a peninsula map of grand scale naming all the shallow lakes, the graveled roads, the minor capes and inlets. There was a key of symbols: Bird scratchings were the nesting grounds of the snowy plover, squiggly ovoids were privately held oyster beds, a stylized anchor marked a public boat launch and a private anchorage on the eastern, the protected shoreline. Offshore there, on the white paper of the strait, stood a nonspecific fish, a crab, a gaff-rigged daysailer, and off the oceanside, a long-necked razor clam and a kite. He could guess the boat launch was shut down: Recreational boating and fishing had been banned in the strait and in Puget Sound for years. There was little likelihood any oysters had been grown in a while, nor kites flown, clams dug.

Bud's Country Store sold bathtubs and plastic pipe, clamming guns, Coleman lanterns, two-by-fours, and plywood, marine supplies, teapots, towels, rubber boots. What they didn't have they would order, though it was understood delivery might be uncertain. He bought a weekly paper printed seventy miles away in Port Angeles, a day-old copy of the Seattle daily, and a canister of butane, and walked up the road again to the trailer park. *Four Pines RV Village* was painted on a driftwood log mounted high on posts to make a gateway. If there had been pines, they'd been cut down. Behind the arch was a weedy lawn striped with whitish oystershell driveways. Stubby posts held out electrical outlets, water couplings, waste water hoses. Some of them were dismantled. There was a gunnite building with two steamed-up windows: a shower house, maybe, or a Laundromat, or both. The trailer next to the building was a single-wide with a tip-out and a roofed wooden porch. *Office* was painted on the front of it in a black childish print across the fiberglass. There was one other trailer parked along the fence, somebody's permanent home, an old round-back with its tires hidden behind rusted aluminum skirting.

Jay dug out a form letter and held it against his notebook while he wrote across the bottom, "I'd just like to pitch a tent, stay out of your way, and pay when I use the shower. Thanks." He looked at what he had written, added exclamation points, went up to the porch and knocked, waiting awkwardly with the letter in his hand. The girl who opened the door was thin and pale, she had a small face, small features. She looked at him without looking in his eyes. Maybe she was eleven or twelve years old.

He smiled. This was always a moment he hated, doubly so if it was a child—he would need to do it twice. He held out the letter, held out his smile with it. Her eyes jumped to his face and then back to the letter with a look that was difficult to pin down—confusion or astonishment, and then something like preoccupation, as if she had lost sight of him standing there. It was common to get a quick shake of the head, a closed door. He didn't know what the girl's look meant. He kept smiling gently. Several women at different times had told him he had a sweet smile. That was the word they all had used— "sweet." He usually tried to imagine they meant peaceable, without threat.

After a difficult silence, the girl may have remembered him standing there. She finally put out her hand for the letter. He hated waiting while she read it. He looked across the trailer park to a straggly line of Scotch broom on the other side of the fence. In a minute she held out the paper to him again without looking in his face. "You have to ask my dad." Her voice was small, low.

He didn't take the letter back yet. He raised his eyebrows in a questioning way. Often it was easier from this point. She would be watching him for those kinds of nonverbal language. He was "keeping a personal silence," he had written in the letter.

"Over in the shower house," she said. She had fine brown hair that hung straight down to her shoulders, and straight bangs she hid behind. Jay glanced toward the gunnite building with deliberate, self-conscious hesitation, then made a helpless gesture. The girl may have looked at him from behind her scrim of bangs. "I can ask him," she said, murmuring.

Her little rump was flat, in corduroy pants too big for her. She had kept his letter, and she swung it fluttering in her hand as he followed her to the shower house. A man knelt on the concrete floor, hunched up at the feet of the hot water tank. His pants rode low, baring some of the shallow crack of his buttocks. He looked tall, heavy-boned, though there wasn't much weight on him now, if there ever had been.

"Dad," the girl said.

He had pulled apart the thick fiberglass blanket around the

heater, to get at the thermostat. His head was shoved inside big loose wings of the blanketing. "What?" he said, without bringing his head out.

"He wants to put up a tent," she said. "Here, read this." She shook Jay's letter.

He rocked back on his hips and his heels and rubbed his scalp with a big hand. There were bits of fiberglass, like mica chips, in his hair. "Shit," he said loudly, addressing the hot water heater. Then he stood slowly, hitching up his pants above the crack. He was very tall, six and a half feet or better, bony-faced. He looked at the girl. "What?" he said.

She pushed the letter at him silently. Jay smiled, made a slight, apologetic grimace when the man's eyes finally came around to him. It was always a hard thing trying to tell by people's faces whether they'd help him out or not. This one looked him over briefly, silently, then took the letter and looked at it without much attention. He kept picking fiberglass out of his hair and his skin, and afterward looking under his fingernails for traces of it. "I read about this in *Time*," he said at one point, but it was just recognition, not approval, and he didn't look at Jay when he said it. He kept reading the letter and scrubbing at the bits of fiberglass. It wasn't clear if he had spoken to Jay or to the girl.

Finally he looked at Jay. "You're walking around the world, huh." It evidently wasn't a question, so Jay stood there and waited. "I don't see what good will come of it—except after you're killed you might get on the night news." He had a look at his mouth, smugness, or bitterness. Jay smiled again, shrugging.

The man looked at him. Finally he said, "You know anything about water heaters? If you can fix it, I'd let you have a couple of dollars for the shower meter. Yes? No?"

Jay looked at the heater. It was propane-fired. He shook his head, tried to look apologetic. It wasn't quite a lie. He didn't want to spend the rest of the day fiddling with it for one hot shower.

"Shit," the man said mildly. He hitched at his pants with the knuckles of both hands. Jay's letter was still in one fist and he looked down at it inattentively when the paper made a faint crackly noise against his hip. "Here," he said, holding the sheet out. Jay had fifty or sixty clean copies of it in a plastic Ziploc in his backpack. He went through a lot of them when he was on the move. He took the rumpled piece of paper, folded it, pushed it down in a front pocket.

"I had bums come in after dark and use my water," the man said. He waited as if that was something Jay might want to respond to. Jay waited, too.

"Well, keep off to the edge by the fence," the man warned him. "You can put up a tent for free, I guess, it's not like we're crowded, but leave the trailer spaces clear anyway. I got locks on the utilities now, so you pay me if you want water, or need to take a crap, and don't take one in the bushes or I'll have to kick you out of here."

Jay nodded. He stuck out his hand and after a very brief moment the man shook it. The man's hand was prickly, damp.

"You show him, Mare," he said to the girl. He tapped her shoulder with his fingertips lightly, but his eyes were on Jay.

Jay followed the young girl, Mare, across the trailer park, across the wet grass and broken-shell driveways to a low fence of two-by-fours and wire that marked the property line. The grass was mowed beside the fence but left to sprout in clumps along the wire and around the wooden uprights. There was not much space between the fence and the last row of driveways. If anybody ever parked a motor home in the driveway behind him, he'd have the exhaust pipe in his vestibule. The girl put her hands in her corduroy pockets and stubbed the grass with the toe of her shoe. "Here?" she asked him. He nodded and swung his pack down onto the grass.

Mare watched him make his camp. She didn't try to help him. She was comfortably silent. When he had everything ordered, he looked at her and smiled briefly and sat down on his little sitz pad on the grass. He took out his notebook, but he didn't work on the journal. He pulled around a clean page and began a list of the materials he would need for beginning the boat. He wrote down substitutes when he could think of them, in case he had trouble getting his first choice. He planned to cross the strait to Vancouver Island and then sail east and north through the Gulf Islands and the Strait of Georgia, across the Queen Charlotte Strait and then up through the inland passage to Alaska. He hadn't figured out, yet, how he would get across the Bering Strait to Siberia—whether he would try to sail across in this boat he would build, or if he'd barter it up there to get some other craft, or a ride. It might take him all winter to build the skipjack, all summer to sail it stop and go up the western coast of Canada and Alaska, and then he would need to wait for summer again before crossing the Bering Strait. He'd have time to find out what he wanted to do before he got to it.

The girl after a while approached him silently and squatted down on her heels so she could see what he was writing. She didn't ask him about the list. She read it over and then looked off toward her family's trailer. She kept crouching there beside him, balancing lightly.

"Do you think it's helping yet?" she asked in a minute. She whispered it, looking at him sideward through her long bangs.

He raised his eyebrows questioningly.

"They're still fighting," she murmured. "Aren't they?"

◆

His mother had written to the Oklahoma draft board pleading Jay's only-child status, but by then the so-called Third World's War was taking a few thousand American lives a day and they weren't exempting anyone. Within a few weeks of his eighteenth birthday, they sent him to the Israeli front.

The tour of duty was four years at first, then extended to six. He thought they would extend it again, but after six years few of them were alive anyway, and they sent him home on a C31 full of cremation canisters. He sat on the toilet in the tail of the plane and swallowed all the pills he had, three at a time, until they were gone. The illegal-drug infrastructure had come overseas with the war and eventually he had learned he could sleep and not dream if he took Nembutal, which was easy to get. Gradually after that he had begun to take Dexamyl to wake up from the Nembutal, Librium to smooth the jitters out of the Dexamyl, Percodan to get high, Demerol when he needed to come down quickly from the high, Dexamyl again if the Demerol took him down too far. He thought he would be dead by the time the plane landed, but his body remained inexplicably, persistently resistant to death. He wound up in a Delayed Stress Syndrome Inpatient Rehab Center, which was housed in a prison. He was thirty years old when the funding for the DSS Centers was dropped in favor of research that might lead to a Stealth aircraft carrier. Jay was freed to walk and hitchhike from the prison in Idaho to his mother's house in Tulsa. She had been dead for years, but he stood on the curb in front of the house and waited for something to happen, a memory or a sentiment, to connect him to his childhood and adolescence. Nothing came. He had been someone else for a long time.

He was still standing on the curb there after dark when a man came out of the house behind him. The man had a flashlight but he didn't click it on. He came over to where Jay stood.

"You should get inside," he said to Jay. "They'll be coming around pretty soon, checking." He spoke quietly. He might have meant a curfew. Tulsa had been fired on a few times by planes flying up to or back from the Kansas missile silos, out of bases in Haiti— crazy terrorists of the crazy Jorge Ruiz government. Probably there was a permanent brownout and a curfew here.

Jay said, "Okay," but he didn't move. He didn't know where he would go anyway. He was cold and needing sleep. There was an appeal in the possibility of arrest.

The man looked at him in the darkness. "You can come inside my house," he said, after he had looked at Jay.

He had a couch in a small room at the front of his house, and Jay slept on it without taking off his clothes. In the daylight the next morning he lay on the couch and looked out the window to his mother's house across the street.

The man who had taken him in was a Quaker named Bob Settleman. He had a son who was on an aircraft carrier in the Indian Ocean, and a daughter who was in a federal prison serving a ten-year sentence for failure to report. Jay went with him to a First Day Meeting. There was nothing much to it. People sat silently. After a while an old woman stood and said something about the droughts and cold weather perhaps reflecting God's unhappiness with the state of the world. But that was the only time anyone mentioned God. Three other people rose to speak. One said he was tired of being the only person who remembered to shut the blackout screens in the Meeting Room before they locked up. Then, after a long silence, a woman stood and expressed her fear that an entire generation had been desensitized to violence, by decades of daily video coverage of the war. She spoke gently, in a trembling voice, just a few plain sentences. It didn't seem to matter a great deal, the words she spoke. While she was speaking, Jay felt something come into the room. The woman's voice, some quality in it, seemed to charge the air with its manifest, exquisitely painful truth. After she had finished, there was another long silence. Then Bob Settleman stood slowly and told about watching Jay standing on the curb after dark. He seemed to be relating it intangibly to what had been said about the war. "I could see he was in some need," Bob said, gesturing urgently. Jay looked at his hands. He thought he should be embarrassed, but nothing like that arose in him.

He could still feel the palpable trembling of the woman's voice—in the air, in his bones.

Afterward, walking away from the Meeting House, Bob looked at his feet and said, as if it were an apology, "It's been a long time since I've been at a Meeting that was Gathered into the Light like that. I guess I got swept up in it."

Jay didn't look at him. After a while he said, "It's okay." He didn't ask anything. He felt he knew, without asking, what Gathered into the Light meant.

He stayed in Tulsa, warehousing for a laundry products distributor. He kept going to the First Day Meetings with Bob. He found it was true, Meetings were rarely Gathered. But he liked the long silences anyway, and the unpredictability of the messages people felt compelled to share. For a long time, he didn't speak himself. He listened without hearing any voice whispering inside him. But finally he did hear one. When he stood, he felt the long silence Gathering, until the trembling words he spoke came out on the air as Truth.

"If somebody could walk far enough, they'd have to come to the end of the war, eventually."

◆

He had, by now, an established web of support: a New York Catholic priest who banked his receipts from the journal subscriptions, kept his accounts, filed his taxes, wired him expense money when he asked for it; a Canadian rare-seeds collective willing to receive his mail, sort it, bundle it up, and send it to him whenever he supplied them with an address; a Massachusetts Monthly Meeting of Friends whose members had the work of typing from the handwritten pages he sent them, printing, collating, stapling, mailing the 10,000 copies of his sometimes monthly writings. He had a paid subscription list of 1,651, a nonpaid "mailing list" of 8,274. Some of those were churches, environmental groups, cooperatives, many were couples, so the real count of persons who supported him was greater by a factor of three or four, maybe. Many of them were people he had met, walking. He hadn't walked, yet, in the Eastern Hemisphere. If he lived long enough to finish what he had started, he thought he could hope for a total list as high as 50,000 or 60,000 names. A Chilean who had been a delegate at the failed peace conferences in Surinam had kept a year-long public silence as a protest of Jay's arrest and bad treatment in Colombia. And he knew of one other world-peace walker he had inspired, a Cuban Nobel chemist who had been the one primarily featured in *Time*. He wasn't fooled into believing it was an important circle of influence. He had to view it in the context of the world. Casualties were notoriously underreported, but at least as many people were killed in a given day, directly and indirectly by the war, as made up his optimistic future list of subscribers. It may have been he kept at it because he had been doing it too long now to stop. It was what he did, who he was. It had been a long time since he had felt the certainty and clarity of a Meeting that was Gathered into the Light.

◆

On the Naniamuk peninsula, he scouted out a few broken-down sheds, and garages with overgrown driveways, and passed entreating notes to the owners. He needed a roof. He expected rain in this part of the world about every day.

One woman had a son dead in India and another son who had been listed AWOL or MIA in the interior of Brazil for two years. She asked Jay if he had walked across Brazil yet. *Yes,* he wrote quickly, *eight months there.* She didn't ask him anything else—nothing about the land or the weather or the fighting. She showed him old photos of both her sons without asking if he had seen the lost one among the refugees in the cities and villages he had walked through. She lent him the use of her dilapidated garage, and the few cheap tools he found in disarray inside it.

The girl, Mare, came unexpectedly after a couple of days and watched him lofting the deck and hull bottom panels onto plywood. It had been raining a little. She stood under her own umbrella awhile, without coming in close enough to shelter under the garage roof. But gradually she came in near him and studied what he was doing. A look rose in her face—distractedness, as before on the porch of her trailer, and then fear, or something like grief. He didn't know what to make of these looks of hers.

"You're building a boat," she said, low-voiced.

He stopped working a minute and looked at the two pieces of plywood he had laid end to end. He was marking and lining them with a straight edge and a piece of curving batten. He had gone across the Florida Strait in a homemade plywood skipjack, had sailed it around the coast of Cuba to Haiti, Puerto Rico, Jamaica, and then across the channel to Yucatán. And later he had built a punt to cross the mouths of the Amazon. A Cuban refugee, a fisherman, had helped him build the Caribbean boat, and the punt had been a simple thing, hardly more than a raft. This was the first time he had tried to build a skipjack without help, but he had learned he could do about anything if he had time enough to make mistakes, undo them, set them right. He nodded, yes, he was building a boat.

"There are mines in the strait," Mare said, dropping her low voice down.

He smiled slightly, giving her a face that belittled the problem. He had seen mines in the Yucatán Channel, too, and in the strait off Florida. His boat had slid by them, ridden over them. They were triggered for the heavy warships and the armored oil tankers.

He went on working. Mare watched him seriously, without saying anything else. He thought she would leave when she saw how slow the boatmaking went, but she stayed on in the garage, handing him tools and helping him to brace the batten against the nails when he lofted the deck piece. At dusk she walked with him up the streets to the Four Pines. There was a fine rain falling still, and she held her umbrella high up so he could get under it if he hunched a little.

In the morning she was waiting for him, sitting on the porch of her trailer when he tramped across the wet grass toward the street. Since Colombia, he had had a difficulty with waking early. He had to depend on his bladder, usually, to force him out of the sleeping bag, then he was slow to feel really awake, his mouth and eyes thick, heavy, until he had washed his face, eaten something, walked a while. He saw it was something like that with the girl. She sat hunkered up on the top step, resting her chin on her knees, clasping her arms about her thin legs. Under her eyes, the tender skin was puffy, dark. Her hair stuck out uncombed. She didn't speak to him. She came stiffly down from the porch and fell in beside him, with her eyes fixed on the rubber toe caps of her shoes. She had a brown lunch sack clutched in one hand, and the other hand sunk in the pocket of her corduroys.

They walked down the paved road and then the graveled streets to where the boat garage was. Their walking made a quiet scratching sound. There was no one else out. Jay thought he could hear the surf beating on the ocean side of the peninsula, but maybe not. He heard a dim, continuous susurration. They were half a mile from the beach.

Maybe what he heard was wind moving in the trees and the grass, or the whisperings of the snowy plover, nesting in the brush above the tidal flats, on the strait side of the peninsula.

He had not padlocked the garage—a prybar would have got anybody in through the small side door in a couple of minutes. He pulled up the rollaway front door, let the light in on the tools, the sheets of plywood. Mare put her lunch down on a sawhorse and stood looking at the lofted pieces, the hull bottom and deck panels drawn on the plywood. He would make those cuts today. He manhandled one of the sheets up off the floor onto the sawhorses. Mare took hold of one end silently. It occurred to him, he could have gotten the panels cut out without her, but it would be easier with her there to hold the big sheets of wood steady under the saw.

He cut the deck panel slowly with hand tools—a brace and bit to make an entry for the keyhole saw, a ripsaw for the long outer cuts. When he was most of the way along the straight finish of the starboard side, on an impulse he gave the saw over to Mare and came around to the other side to hold the sheet down for her. She looked at him once shyly from behind her long bangs and then stood at his place before the wood, holding the saw in both hands. She hadn't drawn a saw in her life, he could tell that, but she'd been watching him. She pushed the saw into the cut he had started and drew it up slow and wobbly. She was holding her mouth out in a tight, flat line, all concentration. He had to smile, watching her.

They ate lunch sitting on the sawhorses at the front of the garage. Jay had carried a carton of yogurt in the pocket of his coat, and he ate the yogurt slowly, with his spoon. Mare offered him part of her peanut butter sandwich, and quartered pieces of a yellow apple. He shook his head, shrugging, smiling thinly. She considered his face, and then looked away.

"I get these little dreams," she said in a minute, low-voiced, with apple in her mouth.

He had a facial expression he relied on a good deal, a questioning look. *What? Say again? Explain.* She glanced swiftly sideward at his look and then down at her fingers gathered in her lap. "They're not dreams, I guess. I'm not asleep. I just get them all of a sudden. I see something that's happened, or something that hasn't happened yet. Things remind me." She looked at him again cautiously through her bangs. "When I saw you on the porch, when you gave me the letter, I remembered somebody else who gave me a letter before. I think it was a long time ago."

He shook his head, took the notepad from his shirt pocket and wrote a couple of lines about déjà vu. He would have written more but she was reading while he wrote and he felt her stiffening, looking away.

"I know what that is," she said, lowering her face. "It isn't that. Everybody gets that."

He waited silently. There wouldn't have been anything to say anyway. She picked at the corduroy on the front of her pant legs. After a while she said, whispering, "I remember things that happened to other people, but they were me. I think I might be dreaming other people's lives, or the dreams are what I did before, when I was alive a different time, or when I'll be somebody else, later on." Her fingernails kept picking at the cord. "I guess you don't get dreams like that." Her eyes came up to him. "Nobody else does, I guess." She looked away. "I do, though. I get them a lot. I just don't tell anymore." Her mouth was small, drawn up. She looked toward him again. "I can tell you, though."

Before she had finished telling him, he had thought of an epilepsy, *le petit absentia,* maybe it was called. He had seen it once in a witch-child in Haiti, a girl who fell into a brief, staring trance a hundred times a day. A neurologist had written to him, naming it from the description he had read in Jay's journal. He could write to the neurologist, ask if this was *le petit* again. Maybe there was a simple way to tell, a test, or a couple of things to look for. Of course, maybe it wasn't that. It might only be a fancy, something she'd invented, an attention-getter. But her look made him sympathetic. He pushed her bangs back, kissed her smooth brow solemnly. *It's okay,* he said by his kiss, by his hand lightly on her bangs. *I won't tell.*

◆

There hadn't been a long Labor Day weekend for years. It was one of the minor observances scratched from the calendar by the exigencies of war. But people who were tied in with the school calendar still observed the first weekend of September as a sort of holiday, a last hurrah before the opening Monday of the school year. Some of them still came to the beach.

The weather by good luck was fair, the abiding peninsula winds balmy, sunlit, so there were a couple of small trailers and a few tents in the RV park, and a no-vacancy sign at the motel Saturday morning by the time the fog was burned off.

Jay spent both days on the lawn in front of the town's gazebo, behind a stack of old journals and a big posterboard display he had pasted up, with an outsized rewording of his form letter, and clippings from newspapers and from *Time*. He put out a hat on the grass in front of him, with a couple of seed dollars in it. His personal style of buskering was diffident, self-conscious. He kept his attention mostly on his notebook, in his lap. He sketched from memory the archway at the front of the RV park, the humpbacked old trailer, the girl, Mare's, thin face. He made notes to do with the boat, and fiddled with an op-ed piece he would send to *Time*, trying to follow up on the little publicity they'd given the Cuban chemist. The op-ed would go in his October journal, whether *Time* took it or not, and the sketches would show up there, too, in the margins of his daybook entries, or on the cover. He printed other people's writings, too, things that came in his mail—poetry, letters, meeting notices, back-page news items pertaining to peace issues, casualty and armament statistics sent at rare intervals by an anonymous letter writer with a Washington, D.C., postmark—but most of the pages were his own work. On bureaucratic forms he entered *Journalist* as his occupation without feeling he was misrepresenting anything. He liked to write. His writing had gotten gradually better since he had been doing the journal—sometimes he thought it was not from the practice at writing, but the practice at silence.

Rarely somebody stooped to pick up a journal, or put money in his hat, or both. Those people he tried to make eye contact with, smiling gently by way of inviting them in. He wouldn't get any serious readers, serious talkers, probably, on a holiday weekend in a beach town, but you never knew. He was careful not to look at the others, the bypassers, but he kept track of them peripherally. He had been arrested quite a few times, assaulted a few. And since Colombia, he suffered from a chronic fear.

Mare came and sat with him on Sunday. He didn't mind having her there. She was comfortable with his silence; she seemed naturally silent herself much of the time. She read from old copies of his journal and shared the best parts with him as if he hadn't been the writer, the editor, holding a page out for him silently and waiting, watching, while he read to the end. Then her marginalia were terse, absolute: "Ick." "I'm glad." "She shouldn't have gone." "I'd never do that."

After quite a while, she had him read what he had written about a town in the Guatemala highlands where he had spent a couple of months, and then she said, in a changed way, timid, earnest, "I lived there before. But I was a different person."

He had not gotten around to writing anyone about the epilepsy after he'd lost that first strong feeling of its possibility. His silence invited squirrels, he knew that, though it made him tired, unhappy, thinking of it. He was tired now, suddenly, and annoyed with her. He shook his head, let her see a flat, skeptical smile.

"Mare!"

The father came across the shaggy grass, moving swiftly, his arms swinging in a stiff way, elbows akimbo. Jay stood up warily.

"I'm locked out of the damn house," the man said, not looking at Jay. "Where's your key?"

Mare got up from the grass, dug around in her pockets, and brought out a key with a fluorescent pink plastic keeper. He closed his fingers on it, made a vague gesture with the fist. "I about made up my mind to bust a window," he said. "I was looking for you." He was annoyed.

Mare put her hands in her pockets, looked at her feet. "I'm helping him stop the war," she said, murmuring.

The man's eyes went to Jay and then the posterboard sign, the hat, the stacked-up journals. His face kept hold of that look of annoyance, but took on something else, too; maybe it was just surprise. "He's putting up signs and hustling for money, is what it looks like he's doing," he said, big and arrogant. For a while longer he stood there looking at the sign as if he were reading it. Maybe he was. He had a manner of standing—shifting his weight from foot to foot and hitching at his pants every so often with the knuckles of his hands.

"I got a kidney shot out, in North Africa," he said suddenly. "But there's not much fighting there anymore, that front's moved south or somewhere. I don't know who's got that ground now. They can keep it, whoever." He had a long hooked nose, bony ridges below his eyes, a wide, lipless mouth. Strong features. Jay could see nothing of him in Mare's small pale face. It wasn't evident, how they were with each other. Jay saw her now watching her dad through her bangs, with something like the shyness she had with everyone else.

"Don't be down here all day," her dad said to her, gesturing again with the fist he had closed around the house key. He looked at Jay but didn't say anything else. He shifted his weight one more time and then walked off long-strided, swinging his long arms. He was tall enough; some of the tourists looked at him covertly after he'd passed them. Mare watched him, too. Then she looked at Jay, a ducking, sideward look. He thought she was embarrassed by her dad. He shrugged. *It's okay.* But that wasn't it. She said, pulling in her thin shoulders timidly, "There is a lake there named Negro because the water is so dark." She had remained focused on his disbelief, waiting to say this small proving thing about Guatemala. And it was true enough to shake him a little. There was a Lago Negro in about every country below the U.S. border, he remembered that in a minute. But there was a long startled moment before that, when he only saw the little black lake in the highlands, in Guatemala, and Mare, dark-faced, in a dugout boat paddling away from the weedy shore.

◆

He had the store rip four long stringers out of a clear fir board, and then he kerfed the stringers every three inches along their lengths. With the school year started he didn't have Mare to hold the long pieces across the sawhorses. He got the cuts done slowly, single-handed, bracing the bouncy long wood with his knee.

Mare's dad came up the road early in the day. Jay thought he wasn't looking for the garage. There was a flooded cranberry field on the other side of the road and he was watching the people getting in the crop from it. There were two men and three women wading slowly up and down in green rubber hip waders, stripping off the berries by hand into big plastic buckets. Mare's dad, walking along the road, watched them. But when he came even with the garage he turned suddenly and walked up the driveway. Jay stopped what he was doing and waited, holding the saw. Mare's dad stood just inside the rollaway door, shifting his weight, knuckling his hips.

"I heard you were building a boat," he said, looking at the wood, not at Jay. "You never said how long you wanted to camp, but I didn't figure it would be long enough to build a boat." Jay thought he knew where this was headed. He'd been hustled along plenty of times before this. But it didn't go that way. The man looked at him. "In that letter you showed, I figured you meant you could talk if you wanted to." He sounded annoyed, as he had been on Labor Day weekend with Mare. "Now I heard your tongue was cut off," he said, lifting his chin, reproachful.

Jay kept standing there holding the saw, waiting. He hadn't been asked anything. The man dropped his eyes. He turned partway from Jay and looked over his shoulder toward the cranberry bog, the people working there. There was a long, stiff silence.

"She's a weird kid," he said suddenly. "You figured that out by now, I guess." His voice was loud; he may not have had soft speaking in him anywhere. "I'd have her to a psychiatrist, but I can't afford it." He hitched at his pants with the backs of both hands. "I guess she likes you because you don't say anything. She can tell you whatever she wants and you're not gonna tell her she's nuts." He looked at Jay. "You think she's nuts?" His face had a sorrowful aspect now, his brows drawn up in a heavy pleat above the bridge of his nose.

Jay looked at the saw. He tested the row of teeth against the tips of his fingers and kept from looking at the man. He realized he didn't know his name, first or last, or if he had a wife. Where was Mare's mother?

The man blew out a puffing breath through his lips. "I guess she is," he said unhappily. Jay ducked his head, shrugged. *I don't know.* He had been writing about Mare lately—pages that would probably show up in the journal, in the October mailing. He had spent a lot of time wondering about her, and then writing it down. This was something new to wonder about. He had thought her dad was someone else, not this big, sorrowful man looking for reassurance from a stranger who camped in his park.

A figure of jets passed over them suddenly, flying inland from the ocean. There were six. They flew low, dragging a screaming roar, a shudder, through the air. Mare's dad didn't look up.

"She used to tell people these damn dreams of hers all the time," the man said after the noise was past. "I know I never broke her of it, she just got sly who she tells them to. She never tells me anymore." He stood there silently looking at the cranberry pickers. "The last one she told me," he said in his heavy, unquiet voice, "was how she'd be killed dead when she was twelve years old." He looked over at Jay. "She didn't tell you that yet," he said when he saw Jay's face. He smiled in a bitter way. "She was about eight, I guess, when she told me that one." He thought about it and then he added, "She's twelve now. She was twelve in June." He made a vague gesture with both hands, a sort of open-palms shrugging. Then he pushed his hands down in his back pockets. He kept them there while he shifted his weight in that manner he had, almost a rocking back and forth.

Watching him, Jay wondered suddenly if Mare might not put herself in the path of something deadly, to make sure this dream was a true one—a proof for her dad. He wondered if her dad had thought of that.

"I don't know where she gets her ideas," the man said, making a pained face, "if it's from TV or books or what, but she told me when she got killed it'd be written up, and in the long run it'd help get the war ended. Before that, she never had noticed we were even in a war." He looked at Jay wildly. "Maybe I'm nuts, too, but here you are, peace-peddling in our backyard, and when I saw you with those magazines you write, I started to wonder what was going on. I started to wonder if this is a damn different world than I've been believing all my life." His voice had begun to rise so by the last few words he sounded plaintive, teary. Jay had given up believing in God the year he was eighteen. He didn't know what it was that Gathered a Meeting into the Light, but he didn't think it was God. It occurred to him, he couldn't have told Mare's dad where the borders were of the world he, Jay, believed in.

"I don't have a reason for telling you this," the man said after a silence. He had brought his voice down again so he sounded just agitated, defensive. "Except I guess I wondered if I was nuts, and I figured I'd ask somebody who couldn't answer." His mouth spread out flat in a humorless grin. He took his hands out of his pockets, hitched up his pants. "I thought about kicking you on down the road, but I guess it wouldn't matter. If it isn't you, it'll be somebody else. And"—his eyes jumped away from Jay—"I was afraid she might quick do something to get herself killed, if she knew you were packing up." He waited, looking off across the road. Then he looked at Jay. "I've been worrying, lately, that she'll get killed, all right, one way or the other, either it'll come true on its own or she'll make it."

They stood together in silence in the dim garage, looking at the cutout pieces of Jay's boat. He had the deck and hull bottom pieces, the bulkheads, the transom, the knee braces cut out. You could see the shape of the boat in some of them, in the curving lines of the cuts.

"I guess you couldn't taste anything without a tongue," the man said after a while. He looked at Jay. "I'd miss that more than the talking." He knuckled his hips and walked off toward the road. All his height was in his legs. He walked fast with a loose, sloping gait on those long legs.

━◄━

In the afternoon Jay took a clam shovel out of the garage and walked down to the beach. The sand was black and oily from an offshore spill or a sinking. There wasn't any debris on the low tide, just the oil. Maybe on the high tide there would be wreckage, or oil-fouled birds. He walked along the edge of the surf on the wet, black sand, looking for clam sign. There wasn't much. He dug a few holes without finding anything. He hadn't expected to. Almost at dusk he saw somebody walking toward him from way down the beach. Gradually it became Mare. She didn't greet him. She turned alongside him silently and walked with him, studying the sand. She carried a denim knapsack that pulled her shoulders down: blocky shapes of books, a lunch box. She hadn't been home yet. If she had gone to the garage and not found him there, she didn't say so.

He touched the blade of the shovel to the sand every little while, looking in the pressure circle for the stipple of clams. He didn't look at Mare. Something, maybe it was a clam sign, irised in the black sheen on the sand. He dug a fast hole straight down, slinging the wet mud sideways. Mare crouched out of the way, watching the hole. "I see it!" She dropped on the sand and pushed her arm in the muddy hole, brought it out again reflexively. Blood sprang along the cut of the razor shell, bright red. She held her hands together in her lap while her face brought up a look, a slow unfolding of surprise and fear. Jay reached for her, clasping both her hands between his palms, and in a moment she saw him again. "It cut me," she said, and started to cry. The tears maybe weren't about her hand.

He washed out the cut in a puddle of salt water. He didn't have anything to wrap around it. He picked up the clam shovel in one hand and held on to her cut hand with the other. They started back along the beach. He could feel her pulse in the tips of his fingers. *What did you dream?* he wanted to say.

It had begun to be dark. There was no line dividing the sky from the sea, just a griseous smear and below it the cream-colored lines of surf. Ahead of them Jay watched something rolling in the shallow water. It came up on the beach and then rode out again. The tide was rising. Every little while the surf brought the thing in again. It was pale, a drift log, it rolled heavily in the shallow combers. Then it wasn't a log. Jay let down the shovel and Mare's hand and waded out to it. The water was cold, dark. He took the body by its wrist and dragged it up on the sand. It had been chewed on, or shattered. The legs were gone, and the eyes, the nose. He couldn't tell if it was a man or a woman. He dragged it way up on the beach, on the dry sand, above the high-tide line. Mare stood where she was and watched him.

He got the clam shovel and went back to the body and began to dig a hole beside it. The sand was silky, some of it slipped down and tried to fill the grave as he dug. In the darkness, maybe he was shoveling out the same hole over and over. The shovel handle was sticky, from Mare's blood on his palms. When he looked behind him, he saw Mare sitting on the sand, huddled with her thin knees pulled up, waiting. She held her hurt hand with the other one, cradled.

When he had buried the legless body, he walked back to her and she stood up and he took her hand again and they went on along the beach in the darkness. He was cold. His wet shoes and his jeans grated with sand. The cut on Mare's hand felt sticky, hot, where he clasped his palm against it. She said, in a whisper, "I dreamed this, once." He couldn't see her face. He looked out but he couldn't see the water, only hear it in the black air, a ceaseless, numbing murmur. He remembered the look that had come in her face when she had first seen his boat-building. *There are mines in the strait.* He wondered if that was when she had dreamed this moment, this white body rolling up on the sand.

He imagined Mare dead. It wasn't hard. He didn't know what kind of a death she could have that would end the war, but he didn't have any trouble seeing her dead. He had seen a lot of dead or dying children, written about them. He didn't know why imagining Mare's thin body, legless, buried in sand, brought up in his mouth the remembered salt taste of tears, or blood, or the sea.

"I know," he said, though what came out was shapeless, ill-made, a sound like *Ah woe.* Mare didn't look at him. But in a while she leaned in to him in the darkness and whispered against his cheek. "It's okay," she said, holding on to his hand. "I won't tell."

He had sent off the pages of his October journal already, and Mare was in them, and Lago Negro, and the father standing shifting his feet, not looking up as the jets screamed over him. It occurred to

Jay suddenly, it would not matter much, the manner of her dying. She had dreamed her own death and he had written it down, and when she was dead he would write that, and her death would charge the air with its manifest, exquisitely painful truth.

NEBRASKA

The town is Americus, Covenant, Denmark, Grange, Hooray, Jerusalem, Sweetwater—one of the lesser-known moons of the Platte, conceived in sickness and misery by European pioneers who took the path of least resistance and put down roots in an emptiness like the one they kept secret in their youth. In Swedish and Danish and German and Polish, in anxiety and fury and God's providence, they chopped at the Great Plains with spades, creating green sod houses that crumbled and collapsed in the rain and disappeared in the first persuasive snow and were so low the grown-ups stooped to go inside; and yet were places of ownership and a hard kind of happiness, the places their occupants gravely stood before on those plenary occasions when photographs were taken.

And then the Union Pacific stopped by, just a camp of white campaign tents and a boy playing his Harpoon at night, and then a supply store, a depot, a pine water tank, stockyards, and the mean prosperity of the twentieth century. The trains strolling into town to shed a boxcar in the depot sideyard, or crying past at sixty miles per hour, possibly interrupting a girl in her high-wire act, her arms looping up when she tips to one side, the railtop as slippery as a silver spoon. And then the yellow and red locomotive rises up from the heat shimmer over a mile away, the August noonday warping the sight of it, but cinders tapping away from the spikes and the iron rails already vibrating up inside the girl's shoes. She steps down to the roadbed and then into high weeds as the Union Pacific pulls Wyoming coal and Georgia-Pacific lumber and snowplow blades and aslant Japanese pickup trucks through the open countryside and on to Omaha. And when it passes by, a worker she knows is opposite her, like a pedestrian at a stoplight, the sun not letting up, the plainsong of grasshoppers going on and on between them until the worker says, "Hot."

Twice the Union Pacific tracks cross over the sidewinding Democrat, the water slow as an oxcart, green as silage, croplands to the east, yards and houses to the west, a green ceiling of leaves in some places, whirlpools showing up in it like spinning plates that lose speed and disappear. In winter and a week or more of just above zero, high-school couples walk the gray ice, kicking up snow as quiet words are passed between them, opinions are mildly compromised, sorrows are apportioned. And Emil Jedlicka unslings his blue-stocked .22 and slogs through high brown weeds and snow, hunting ring-necked pheasant, sidelong rabbits, and—always suddenly—quail, as his little brother Orin sprints across the Democrat in order to slide like an otter.

July in town is a gray highway and a Ford hay truck spraying by, the hay sailing like a yellow ribbon caught in the mouth of a prancing dog, and Billy Awalt up there on the camel's hump, eighteen years old and sweaty and dirty, peppered and dappled with hay dust, a lump of chew like an extra thumb under his lower lip, his blue eyes happening on a Dairy Queen and a pretty girl licking a pale trickle of ice cream from the cone. And Billy slaps his heart and cries, "Oh! I am pierced!"

And late October is orange on the ground and blue overhead and grain silos stacked up like white poker chips, and a high silver water tower belittled one night by the sloppy tattoo of one year's class at George W. Norris High. And below the silos and water tower are stripped treetops, their gray limbs still lifted up in alleluia, their yellow leaves crowding along yard fences and sheeping along the sidewalks and alleys under the shepherding wind.

Or January and a heavy snow partitioning the landscape, whiting out the highways and woods and cattle lots until there are only open spaces and steamed-up windowpanes, and a Nordstrom boy limping pitifully in the hard plaster of his clothes, the snow as deep as his hips when the boy tips over and cannot get up until a little Schumacher girl sitting by the stoop window, a spoon in her mouth, a bowl of Cheerios in her lap, says in plain voice, "There's a boy," and her mother looks out to the sidewalk.

Houses are big and white and two stories high, each a cousin to the next, with pigeon roosts in the attic gables, green storm windows on the upper floor, and a green screened porch, some as pillowed and couched as parlors or made into sleeping rooms for the boy whose next step will be the Navy and days spent on a ship with his hometown's own population, on gray water that rises up and is allayed like a geography of cornfields, sugar beets, soybeans, wheat, that stays there and says, in its own way, "Stay." Houses are turned away from the land and toward whatever is not always, sitting across from each other like dressed-up children at a party in daylight, their parents looking on with hopes and fond expectations. Overgrown elm and sycamore trees poach the sunlight from the lawns and keep petticoats of snow around them into April. In the deep lots out back are wire clotheslines with flapping white sheets pinned to them, property lines are hedged with sour green and purple grapes, or with rabbit wire and gardens of peonies, roses, gladiola, irises, marigolds, pansies. Fruit trees are so closely planted that they cannot sway without knitting. The apples and cherries drop and sweetly decompose until they're only slight brown bumps in the yards, but the pears stay up in the wind, drooping under the pecks of birds, withering down like peppers until their sorrow is justly noticed and they one day disappear.

Aligned against an alley of blue shale rock is a garage whose doors slash weeds and scrape up pebbles as an old man pokily swings them open, teetering with his last weak push. And then Victor Johnson rummages inside, being cautious about his gray sweater and high-topped shoes, looking over paint cans, junked electric motors, grass rakes and garden rakes and a pitchfork and sickles, gray doors and ladders piled overhead in the rafters, and an old windup Victrola and heavy platter records from the twenties, on one of them a soprano singing "I'm a Lonesome Melody." Under a green tarpaulin is a wooden movie projector he painted silver and big cans of tan celluloid, much of it orange and green with age, but one strip of it preserved: of an Army pilot in jodhpurs hopping from one biplane onto another's upper wing. Country people who'd paid to see the movie had been spellbound by the slight dip of the wings at the pilot's jump, the slap of his leather jacket, and how his hair strayed wild and was promptly sleeked back by the wind. But looking at the strip now, pulling a ribbon of it up to a windowpane and letting it unspool to the ground, Victor can make out only twenty frames of the leap, and then snapshot after snapshot of an Army pilot clinging to the biplane's wing. And yet Victor stays with it, as though that scene of one man staying alive were what he'd paid his nickel for.

Main Street is just a block away. Pickup trucks stop in it so their drivers can angle out over their brown left arms and speak about crops or praise the weather or make up sentences whose only real point is their lack of complication. And then a cattle truck comes up and they mosey along with a touch of their cap bills or a slap of the door metal. High-school girls in skin-tight jeans stay in one place on weekends, and jacked-up cars cruise past, rowdy farmboys overlapping inside, pulling over now and then in order to give the girls cigarettes and sips of pop and grief about their lipstick. And when the cars peel out, the girls say how a particular boy measured up or they swap gossip about Donna Moriarity and the scope she permitted Randy when he came back from boot camp.

Everyone is famous in this town. And everyone is necessary. Townspeople go to the Vaughn Grocery Store for the daily news, and to the Home Restaurant for history class, especially at evensong, when the old people eat graveled pot roast and lemon meringue pie and calmly sip coffee from cups they tip to their mouths with both hands. The Kiwanis Club meets here on Tuesday nights, and hopes are made public, petty sins are tidily dispatched, the proceeds from the gumball machines are tallied up and poured into the upkeep of a playground. Yutesler's Hardware has picnic items and kitchen appliances in its one window, in the manner of those prosperous men who would prefer to be known for their hobbies. And there is one crisp, white, Protestant church with a steeple, of the sort pictured on calendars; and the Immaculate Conception Catholic Church, grayly holding the town at bay like a Gothic wolfhound. And there is an insurance agency, a county coroner and justice of the peace, a secondhand shop, a handsome chiropractor named Koch who coaches the Pony League baseball team, a post office approached on unpainted wood steps outside of a cheap mobile home, the Nighthawk tavern where there's Falstaff tap beer, a green pool table, a poster recording the Cornhuskers scores, a crazy man patiently tolerated, a gray-haired woman with an unmoored eye, a boy in spectacles thick as paperweights, a carpenter missing one index finger, a plump waitress whose day job is in a basement beauty shop, an old woman who creeps up to the side door at eight in order to purchase one shot glass of whiskey.

And yet passing by, and paying attention, an outsider is only aware of what isn't, that there's no bookshop, no picture show, no pharmacy or dry cleaners, no cocktail parties, extreme opinions, jewelry or piano stores, motels, hotels, hospital, political headquarters, philosophical theories about Being and the Soul.

High importance is only attached to practicalities, and so there is the Batchelor Funeral Home, where a proud old gentleman is on display in a dark brown suit, his yellow fingernails finally clean, his smeared eyeglasses in his coat pocket, a grandchild on tiptoes by the casket, peering at the lips that will not move, the sparrow chest that will not rise. And there's Tommy Seymour's for Sinclair gasoline and mechanical repairs, a green balloon dinosaur bobbing from a string over the cash register, old tires piled beneath the cottonwood, For Sale in the sideyard a Case tractor, a John Deere reaper, a hay mower, a red manure spreader, and a rusty grain conveyor, green weeds overcoming them, standing up inside them, trying slyly and little by little to inherit machinery for the earth.

And beyond that are woods, a slope of pasture, six empty cattle pens, a driveway made of limestone pebbles, and the house where Alice Sorensen pages through a child's *World Book Encyclopedia,* stopping at the descriptions of California, Capetown, Ceylon, Colorado, Copenhagen, Corpus Christi, Costa Rica, Cyprus.

Widow Dworak has been watering the lawn in an open raincoat and apron, but at nine she walks the green hose around to the spigot and screws down the nozzle so that the spray is a misty crystal bowl softly baptizing the ivy. She says, "How about some camomile tea?" And she says, "Yum. Oh, boy. That hits the spot." And bends to shut the water off.

The Union Pacific night train rolls through town just after ten o'clock, when a sixty-year-old man named Adolf Schooley is a boy again in bed, and when the huge weight of forty or fifty cars jostles his upstairs room like a motor he'd put a quarter in. And over the sighing industry of the train, he can hear the train saying *Nebraska, Nebraska, Nebraska, Nebraska.* And he cannot sleep.

Mrs. Antoinette Heft is at the Home Restaurant, placing frozen meat patties on waxed paper, pausing at times to clamp her fingers under her arms and press the sting from them. She stops when the Union Pacific passes, then picks a cigarette out of a pack of Kools and smokes it on the back porch, smelling air as crisp as Oxydol, looking up at stars the Pawnee Indians looked at, hearing the low harmonica of big rigs on the highway, in the town she knows like the palm of her hand, in the country she knows by heart.

FRIENDS AND FORTUNES

W here I live, people do things outdoors. Out in the open air, they do what wealthier and more private people hide inside their homes. Young couples neck beside the broken lilac bushes or in old cars parked along the street. Women knead bread on their steps, and sometimes collapse in a fury of weeping on the sidewalk. Boys break windows in the broad daylight.

We are accustomed to displays, so when Mr. Wrenn across the street has the DT's in front of his house, conversations continue. *What will be, will be, and life goes on,* as my mother is fond of saying. The men who are at home go over to convince Mr. Wrenn that the frogs are not really there. If that tack fails, they kill off the frogs or snakes with imaginary machetes or guns. While they are destroying the terrors that crawl out of the mind, the rest of us talk. We visit while the men lift their arms and swing, aiming at the earth, saying there are no more alligators anywhere.

"Lovely day, isn't it?" someone says. "Did you hear the Beelah girl ran off with the Gypsy fellow? The one with long fingernails?"

I lean against the tree on the other side of my mother, like we are holding up the dry elm. "She didn't have fingernails at all," I say. "She is a chewer. Everyone knows that. She even buys hot stuff to put on them to break her out of the habit." My mother jabs me with her elbow.

"Him. He's got long fingernails. He's fancy as a rooster up for the fair." It is Mrs. Bell speaking. She is wearing a pink cardigan buttoned only at the top and her stomach protrudes from the triangular opening.

Mr. Wrenn grows quiet and the men sit beside him on his small front porch, a slab of cement. This day it is my father who is sitting with him. Father has been sick with his heart and he looks pale. Even sick, he is better than a telephone or a newspaper. He's right in the action. He knows everything that happens in the neighborhood. When June Kim, the Korean woman who used to live next door, stabbed her enormous husband in his massive stomach, my father was the first to know. He, in fact, surveyed the damage before driving the large, balding man to the hospital. And he is the first man on the scene of any accident. When a Buick drove through Sylvia Smith's bedroom wall, my father was the first man there, catching Mrs. Smith in her nightgown, her pale chubby hands trying to cover up the rollers in her hair.

He was also the one to speak through the police megaphone to Mr. Douglas, who held his wife and kids hostage with a machine gun. "Hey, Doug." My dad called him that for short, like he calls Mr. Smith by the name of Smitty. "Hey, Doug," he yelled. "Don't make it any harder on yourself." And so on about how Marge Douglas wouldn't really leave him this time even though Mrs. Martinez had given her spells and charms to help her get away. "Doug. You are a logical man. You know you don't believe in any of that magic crap."

Women sat on the curb, their legs spread like crickets, their dresses great flowered hammocks pushed down between their open thighs. The police did little. They were only interested in how Mr. Douglas got a machine gun and the ammo. They don't really care who shoots each other out here. They don't even answer calls from our neighborhood at night.

I remember the women talking from the curb. "Maybe the crazy loon will shoot himself. I'm going to give Marge some of my grocery money to get away."

"Shoot. You know she won't ever leave that bastard."

"Watch your language. The kids'll hear you."

The women seem to know everything. They know why Mr. Wrenn drinks so much and they are pretty good to him. I like to be with the women. They know, for instance, when a man with a gun will really use it. They can feel it in the air. Maybe the direction of the wind or the vacuum heat of summer. They know Marge is more afraid to leave her husband now than she ever was, that she will instead find ways to get the kids away into early marriages, lives of being orderlies at the hospital, and then she will settle down to old age with Tom Douglas, who will become slow and feeble and stupidly sweet. The women know, and have said, that Douglas will be one of those men who spend hours folding handkerchiefs into the shapes of birds and the shapes of women's pointed brassieres, hours tending the few eggplants that will grow in his small plot of garden and when no one even likes eggplant. Children will like him. The women know that. They also know that children will dislike the bitter and grumpy Marge when she is aged and wrinkled and full of anger from living beside Tom, who will tell the same stories day and night as if she's never heard them, her scrubbing and sweeping, him story-telling about his wonderful life.

The wide-hipped women know just about everything, including how many books of green stamps it takes to get a bathroom scale or an electric mixer, and they talk about what they will get while my dad returns from Mr. Wrenn's.

But even with all their knowing, the people who are new to the block are still a mystery to the women. The Peñalba family moved into the house next door when June Kim and her husband moved out. The Peñalbas don't do much of their living outside. They seldom come out at all except when the mother and daughter go to church. Then the two females walk solemnly down the street in black old-fashioned looking dresses and black veils on their heads. They walk like a procession, the daughter trailing along behind the mother.

The daughter, Nora, is my age. She speaks with an accent and looks older than us Indian girls in the neighborhood. Her flesh has a gray light around it, like the grayness around the sick. Her house has the odor of burning. There is something feverish about it. Maybe it is the new shabbiness around it, or the way light hits some of the windows now that it is spring. The house is like the great eye of a tornado that the crows have disappeared into.

The streets are brown in the morning light. All the tiny houses fit closely together in the early shadows. They are painted. Some are green, some pink or gold. Occasionally there is a dark brown house as if the tenant wished to make the house invisible, or like a house of the forest. I hear people singing sometimes in the bathrooms, or fighting in the kitchens. I like the sounds.

Last night it rained and now the streets have water rushing in the gutters, climbing the curbs. The water passes over some broken yellow dishes and old leaves that look lovely in the gutter, like something rich and exquisite, like gold in Venice in the history books. I stop to look. There is an earthworm drowning in the water and it is very thin and pale. I take it out and place it on a patch of earth.

Nora Peñalba is suddenly standing beside me, come as silently from the black hole of her house as the quiet air that surrounds it. She is not wearing black. She has changed into a brightly flowered, low-cut dress that makes her look much older and more knowing than anyone else in El Grande County.

Steam is rising off the street in the first sunlight and it surrounds her like fog around a new crop of tulips. Nora has very loose hips. When she walks, it is indecent the way her skirt swings from side to side, her thighs apart and natural, but I like the way she walks and I practice it alone in front of the mirror. She has black curly hair with red highlights. She is lovely, but whenever I look close I notice that grayness, and a secret.

Now she comes outside occasionally at night, but we seldom speak. We walk together to school. She goes with me because the tiny blond social worker who wears expensive gray dresses has visited Mrs. Peñalba and told her that she is breaking the law if her children do not attend school. Mrs. Peñalba hunches over and looks at the floor. Nora translates between Señora Peñalba and Frau Betty, as my father calls her. To the tiny blonde with white nail polish and lipstick, Nora says things like, "Mama says we attend schools. We do not go against none of the legals." She has looked up the words in her dictionary in the presence of Frau Betty. She says such things as, "Yes, we are not citizens. We have been them a long while."

Her English is better than mine and I do not understand why she cannot speak with the little blonde. I imagine it is because she is afraid of her, as we are all afraid of the people from the country. But Nora reads the newspapers, unlike the rest of us, although she does not bother much with school. She understands, though, when I talk about nothing but boys and how I am going to fix hair for a living when I am done with school. She understands my eyes following the two GI's that moved in down the street and that play loud music. She understands when I dress up and sit outside at night looking off in the direction of that house, but she is silent and holds an anger in her blood. "Like a spitfire," my mother says.

"I don't understand," Nora has told me, "why in the North of America you girls do not hold hands and walk the street together. I think we aren't friends."

"Oh, yes, we are friends," I tell her. "We are the best of friends. But the people here don't like that kind of touching."

"No, then we are not friends."

Maybe we aren't. She is so burning and deep. Somewhere in my stomach I feel that we can never be close. And also, my mother does not like her. As Nora and I walk to school, I hear my mother's voice in the back of my mind. "She is sneaky, that girl," my mom says to Sylvia Smith across the street. But Sylvia changes the subject. Sylvia says, "I tell him I will even kiss his ass. In fact, I have done it." I listen and make a silent vow to never get married. I can see up Sylvia's skirt, which is much too short for a woman her size, see her white ragged underpants.

"Besides," my mother says, "there is something wrong with them, something not right in their house." That's the way they talk, two distinct conversations.

"I would do anything for him. That man. And then he runs off and leaves me all week with his retarded son." Mikey. That is the son's name. And my mother, behind Sylvia's back, says Mikey is retarded because of the way they beat him, and beat him in full view of the neighborhood, right out in front of the house. I feel sorry for Mikey and for his sister, too. Their dad eats steak for supper when he is home and the kids must sit in the other room and have only a bowl of cereal. But Sylvia, herself, is a good woman who goes to confession to tell how poor a wife she is, and she does her penance.

"They put their garbage in the back yard," my mother says. "On the ground. And there are flies all over the place. The old woman doesn't even bother to brush the flies away from her face. She hardly moves at all. She just sits with flies all around her."

"Yes," says Sylvia, shocked into my mother's conversation. "And almost all of their windows are broken and they don't seem to give a darn."

"And with all those flies," Mom says, and then changes her tune. "But that isn't their fault. The local boys asked for protection money and broke their windows to get it."

"Those damn boys. I wish they'd all fall into hell. Where do they get off terrorizing the neighborhood and making us pay them not to wreck our places?"

Today I have some money to see Mrs. Martinez about my future. I walk to her house, making notes in my mind of all I want to ask her. I want to ask her if I will be a beauty operator, if I will get a date with that tall boy in class, Mike Nava. I want to ask if I'll have children or go to someplace exciting. There are small lizards near her house. I frighten them from the sun and they go into hiding beneath the foundation and under the shingles. Mrs. Martinez lets me in.

"Are you happy?" asks Mrs. Martinez. She is robust and wears long gold earrings.

I am surprised. I have seen her three times and she has never asked me about happiness. I have nothing to say. I haven't thought about whether I am happy or not. I had a conversation with Deborah, a girl who used to live a few blocks over. Deborah claimed to have once lived down a street from Marilyn Monroe. I remember saying to Debbie that all I wanted was a nice man and he didn't need to have money because that wasn't the key to happiness. Love was everything, I said. Deborah said she wanted the money and could toss away love because it never lasted anyway, like her mom and dad, for example. In fact, she said she had done away with love already because all the fellows from families around here would never amount to a hill of beans, let alone a house with a swimming pool or a big yard with white plaster statues of swans. She told me about a woman she once knew who even had the cloth for her bedspread imported from Germany, ancient and rich cloth. I didn't believe her. That was last year. I was younger. Then I never believed anyone lived much differently than we did. Now I look at the houses on television and I see what those people live like and it is better than here, even if they don't have much going on outside at all.

Mrs. Martinez heats water for the tea. While it is simmering, she takes out the cards and places them on the green card table where I am sitting. She prepares the tea leaves in the blue china cup. I look at her clean white stucco walls trimmed with enamel red and wonder if she got the money for the red paint from Mrs. Douglas, who will never leave her husband.

I drink the tea and Mrs. Martinez looks into the leaves. She says that she sees a dog and a star. I am going to be a star in the world like that very bright one, the morning one, Venus, she says, shining early in the morning when the others have faded. She tells me I will live long, like that star. She asks me if I once had a dog that died. I did, but I don't ever give her too much information about my life because then she will be able to figure me out and my money will be wasted with her.

Mrs. Martinez doesn't even put her hand to her forehead when she says, "No, you won't date that tall boy. You will not have many dates at all because you are going to be following that star alone."

Then it is time to look at my palm. It is upturned and a very lovely rich color. I like the lines on it. They are like fish nets cast out upon some river or sea. I have many lines and my palm is almost as cracked as my mom's geographic tongue. Mrs. Martinez touches each fissure and she tells me that I must be patient for three years and that I have a friend who will teach me all about life.

When Mrs. Martinez is finished, I give her two dollars. She looks deep into my eyes like she is reading my soul and she tells me, earnestly, that I have hope and I must find a way to get an education and must study hard at school.

I don't like the solemnity of it, but when I leave I feel lighter and happier. I can tell that my future is full of excitement. When I walk by the preacher's house I remember how I used to get saved every Friday just for something to do, go into the back room with the man and the other children and kneel at the bed and say I believed and beg forgiveness for my sinful thoughts. Now I feel as light and relieved as I did when I used to get saved.

◆

At home, at night, I am sitting on the bed and staring at the gray tile floors. I am not happy. I wonder what has gone wrong with my life. I can think of no living reason on God's green earth for my despair. There is something greatly wrong in the world and something wrong in myself. But I do not know what it is. It's the first time I have thought about happiness and now I know that I have none. Damn Mrs. Martinez, I think, and then feel afraid that, all the way up the street, she will read my thoughts and curse me. I brush the words out of the air before me like they are stolen smoke from a cigarette.

I can hear my mother in her bedroom closing a drawer. I call her and she comes. My father is sitting in the living room in his favorite chair eating peanuts and I imagine his animal warmth and the smell of his shirt. But it is my mother I want.

"What is it?" she asks, and I look up at her with sad eyes. She is wearing her blue robe and a blue hairnet. "What is it? What's wrong?"

"Are you happy?" I ask.

"What kind of question is that?"

"I'm not a happy person."

"Nonsense, Sarah Bernhardt. Of course you are. What's there to be unhappy about?"

I can see that she has never thought about it either, and now it is an even deeper and more troublesome question to me. I wonder if anyone asks themselves if they are happy. Mrs. Martinez has probably ruined my entire life.

My mother says, "It is probably time for your period and so you feel blue." But when she leaves I look in the mirror and see, as if for the first time, my face. It is very pale although I am an Indian and I think perhaps that is what is wrong with me. My eyes are very dark and lonely and they are mysterious in a way I have never noticed, as if Nora's presence were haunting me from the inside out. I put orange lipstick on my hair to see if a tint or a rinse would make me happy but it doesn't look good. I wipe it out with a Kleenex. And then I lift back the covers of my small bed and crawl inside. I stay awake until long after the folks are in bed and I listen to them talking and do not feel comforted.

◆

I think, this morning, that if I wear a yellow dress I will feel happy. As I put on my slip, I look out the window, pull the curtain back to check the weather. Nora and her mother are returning from early Mass, dressed like funeral mourners, in black. Nora's younger brother follows them and he is wearing a white shirt. They look tragic and beautiful on the street, walking in the spring light, in the diffuse air that is charged with electric sparks of pollen. Nora's youth is hidden in the black cloth.

I dress and eat some toast and wear a rhinestone barrette in my hair. I leave the house early and go sit on the curb, careful not to dirty my daffodil-colored dress. Nora comes out early also, dressed in red. She sits beside me. It is too early for school but we sit in the sunlight like new flowers.

"Oh, Nora," I say. "I am not happy."

She looks at me with her great nocturnal eyes and says nothing.

"I don't even know when this sadness began."

"Maybe I'll tell you something happy. About the rain in Nicaragua."

"You're from Mexico?"

"No. It is more south than Mexico. And it rains. Warm rain.

There are green and blue seas and rain forests of rosewood and balsa and cedar. With vines. In them live tiny, tiny monkeys and birds you call parrots with big eyebrows. It is like a paradise of the Bible, the garden called Eden. In the night you hear the monkeys chattering about their boyfriends and the big cats roaring in the jungle out there like this, Grr." She looks fierce. I lean back laughing. "Raar," she yells again, with her hands open like claws. "And sometimes the earth quakes to tell us we have been bad. It roars, too."

I try to see it, but I don't. I feel badly that she is giving me some vision of her world and I can't form it in my mind. I wonder what shyness has kept me from asking her about life.

"What color are the houses?" I ask her.

"They are, oh, they are house-colored." She laughs. It is a funny joke. And then she hisses, "Pah!" More a burst of air than a real word. "Of course you are unhappy, being so poor for North Americans." She gestured about in a wide circle and her hand's motion opened my eyes like a camera. For the first time I saw it, the two of us like bright flowers growing out of bulbs, blooming one time only before the winter, surrounded by the oil rags beside cars that did not run, beside the sea-green shards of Coca-Cola bottles that the boys had broken at night, and beer cans, the old yellowed newspapers stuck in fences and trees, saw a few children outside crying, two little boys hitting the earth with sticks that were also used as rifles for playing soldier. I do not think she means it, that we are poor. I think she is making fun of my unhappiness, and I want to be away from her. My body feels tense. I think of Linda at school who announces each week who she loves and I want to be with Linda, want to hear her tell me this week, as she does, "I am in love." I want to see the dreamy look on Linda's innocent face when she tells me she is in love with Rudolph Nureyev and I laugh at the foreign name and laugh even harder when she tells me he is a ballet dancer, laugh until she brings out the magazine picture of him all glorious and almost naked in that stretchy cloth you can see right through.

"It was Mrs. Martinez that caused it," I tell Nora. "When I went to have my fortune, she asked me if I was happy." Some hammering begins in the distance. It is rhythmic.

"I have tried to think when it first began." Nora is silent now and listening to me. "I think it began when the boys on the street were killing the lizards, were throwing them against the walls of houses and breaking them and the lizards would scream like people. And I know

I am unhappy when Mr. Smith beats up his son, Mikey. And it all makes me sad." I feel about to cry.

Nora is quiet a long time and I know she is thinking of something. Then she says, "I think sometimes they are born bad. Men. I wonder, too, what makes them kill things. My own father, he was a good man and a leader of the people. He hated killings. There were so many killings the whole land was made of bullets and he always said we could rise up."

"What?" I think she is lying. A leader whose family is penniless and living right here in El Grande, next door to us?

"Yes. He was fighting against the government because they were cruel. You know, everywhere in the hot sun there were bodies. My father wanted us to rise up. He got men together to battle the predators." She speaks so slowly now, and words I don't know and have never heard. I try to read the truth on her face. I don't know why she would lie to me. I am her friend.

"How do you speak of the deaths? They hung his head on a pole. When I saw it I began to scream but some old woman put her hand over my face and ran with me away from there."

I don't know how she can say such a thing. She is worse than our history teacher who has scared me half to death of the Communists by telling how they will come and cut my brother in half in front of me and will make me choose between my mother and father and then kill them both. It all puts my nerves on edge.

"And they came and took my brothers. I adored my brothers. They were young." She is so matter-of-fact, as if she is saying nothing.

"Stop it." I put my hands over my ears. My face is burning. My dress is moist and my palms are wet. "Stop it. That's a lie. Shut your lying mouth." I stand up and I want to hit her with stones.

Nora stands up, too. Breaking as her windows had broken. Her face is pale beneath her rouge and lipstick. She is in a rage, her entire body taut. "No," she screams. "It's true."

Something in her is falling away. It is also falling away in me. "It isn't true! It isn't. Let me alone!"

And she is hitting me in the face and grabbing my hair to pull it. I pull at her dress and we are twisting together on the curb, like flowers in a horrid wind. The people going to work around us are watching and pointing. She hits me again and again and I bend over to protect myself and then grab her to stop the blows while she breaks and screams. She stumbles away and falls, weeping, weeping all the rose colors of makeup over her chest. She falls and then she begins to run away while the children are shouting into the street and the gang of boys are cheering. I don't really hear them, just see Nora racing over the broken glass. Time stops. I have not believed and time stops. I have been pale and American, Gringa, as she calls me now, the screaming girl breaking as the windows of her house have broken, the girl who ran at me in a frenzy hitting me and me with nothing to do but hit her, to hold her and hit her back. As she runs away now, her fingers spread over her face, she is breathing in loud gasps and then she vanishes into the house, her footsteps gone and the door slamming behind her, and the wailing breaking the solitude of that house.

I t wasn't a bad-looking car, a 1984 Citation with AM/FM, air conditioning, automatic transmission. Baby blue. Not my first choice for
getting around, but my mother had enjoyed it. I started out thinking I could get thirty-three or thirty-four hundred, which seemed
to be a fair price at the time, according to the classifieds. I was
prepared to take less. I had to get rid of it. I wasn't planning to drive
it, and storing it was not an option.

After the ad came out half a dozen people called. Three stopped
by the house to look at the car, among them Harold Wang, a medical
student from Shanghai. He drove it around the block and haggled in a
preliminary way, then said he wanted his cousin's opinion. For reasons too trivial to go into—let's say it was mutually convenient—we
agreed to meet a second time in a parking lot at the edge of Santa
Monica, behind a Safeway on a long boulevard of malls and discount
stores.

I had decided I would let Harold have the car for thirty-two, or
even a bit less, if he could come up with the money right away and
not keep me waiting. I liked the way he had presented himself. He
was 26 or 27, a clean-cut fellow—dark slacks, sport shirt—in his second year at UCLA and obviously under a lot of pressure, as graduate
students always are. He had brought along his young wife and their
new baby and a couple of people who stayed in another car while we
talked. One of them was his father. They were all from mainland
China. Though the father did not open his mouth the whole time, I
could tell he had coached the son on how to shop for a car in the
United States. The son was in a way performing for the father, trying
to be shrewd and manly in these negotiations. I liked the family unity,
since this was the way I had grown up, among relatives who had come

west during the thirties, new to this coast and sticking together while they made their way.

I also figured Harold had access to the necessary cash. I had only seen the father from a distance, but he had a prosperous look about him. At our second meeting, as a matter of fact, I was certain Harold carried an envelope full of bills in his coat pocket. He was as ready to buy as I was to sell. Or almost as ready.

The cousin he brought along was younger by four or five years, a small and careful fellow, also from mainland China. He wore running shoes and sunglasses and an acid-washed jacket, blue denim streaked with white. He could not speak much English but he knew something about cars. He tapped around on the doors and fenders searching for bondo patches underneath the paint. He examined the spare tire and the muffler and the door latches and the seals around the windows. He opened the hood and listened to the engine and held his hand at the end of the exhaust pipe to feel the engine's pulse. He tried the brakes and the horn and the lights and the radio. Finally the hood was shut, the engine was silent. It was just a matter of reaching an understanding.

Harold had offered me twenty-nine hundred. I told him my absolute bottom price was thirty-one. Anything lower and I would be losing money, I said. We both knew he wanted the car and we knew what the final price would be. Yet Harold was procrastinating. It wasn't the money, really. I didn't feel that. It was a matter of trust. We had not yet crossed some final threshold of trust.

I had the feeling that he needed to be reassured about my opinion of the car, or about my loyalty to this transaction. Or perhaps he needed to be reassured about me. I was after all an unknown quantity, not simply a fellow with a car for sale, but a foreigner, the mysterious other. If I were in Shanghai trying to bargain in Chinese with someone I did not know, for something in this price range, I would surely feel the same. I wondered if they had classified ads in China, and I wondered if it would be the first time Harold had thought of handing over this much cold cash to an American.

Standing in the Safeway lot at 3 P.M. on a sunny, blue-sky afternoon, we had reached this curious impasse when a woman came toward us, pushing a shopping cart between the diagonal rows of cars. She looked to be in her late 50s, and she wore a neck brace that made her back too erect. She had short red hair and the kind of white skin that turns to flame when anything unexpected occurs.

Between the rows she stopped, with a tight and cautious smile. "That's my car," she said.

A Dodge two-door was parked in the next slot, eight or ten years old. We had all inadvertently gathered next to it.

"We just happen to be standing here," I said. "They're looking at my mother's Chevrolet."

"Your mother's?"

"By chance," I said.

"What are you talking about?"

Her hand held the cart as if its push bar were the guard rail at a drop-off cliff.

"I mean, it's by chance I'm parked next to you."

"I just don't know what to expect anymore."

She was speaking to me but looking hard at Harold, whose sallow and scholarly face had turned severe as he pondered his cash flow.

"Sorry," I said for the three of us.

"It's been broken into so many times I've lost count. They chip the glass, they ruin the doors. My life has been threatened. I'm a teacher. But do you think that makes any difference? Right outside the classroom I have had things happen."

"I know the feeling," I said.

We moved well away from the Dodge, giving her plenty of room. Harold was now consulting in Chinese with the cousin, who kept looking at his watch. Harold explained to me that a brother had dropped them off and would soon return. Time was becoming a factor. His jaw muscles were pumping. He had to make a decision. He stared at me, then he stared at his cousin's wrist, as if the watch held the answer to the riddle of this moment.

Our tense reverie was broken by a long, grinding scrape, then the clunk of thick metal. About 30 feet from where we stood, the woman had jumped a circular divider. Her Dodge now straddled it. Inside the car she twisted and turned, as if pursued. She lurched into reverse, scraping the underside again. When the front tires met the divider, she shifted into low. The car lurched forward, and the rear tires hit the island, which was the height of sidewalk curbing. She was stuck.

She opened the door and called out to anyone within earshot. "What did I do? What did I do?"

This was a huge parking lot that merged with other huge lots, all filled with diagonal rows of empty vehicles. There was no one else around.

"You went over that divider," I said.

"Oh, my God! Did I ruin the car?"

"Just a scrape," I said. "When your wheels fell, the body hit."

"I didn't see it! I didn't see it! With the three of you so close I thought I ought to get out of here."

She was outside the car, next to the open door, her face red with accusation and alarm.

When Harold asked if the Dodge had front- or rear-wheel drive, her brimming eyes went wide.

He held his hands low in front of him to make a lifting motion. "Then we will know where to lift," he said.

She did not seem to hear this. Or perhaps she did not believe he would understand her reply. She spoke to me. Her eyes were aimed at me, as if I were Harold's interpreter.

"It's too heavy to lift," she said. "It's a very heavy car. Can't you see that?"

The cousin had his hands on an invisible steering wheel, telling her with sign language and broken English to cramp it tightly, then inch the car back and forth. He was moving toward her grille, while Harold approached the trunk, ready to organize a lift. They were both talking, signalling. The woman's eyes leaped wildly from one to the other, then looked at me across the roof, asking me to translate their cryptic messages. Her eyes said she was prepared for the worst.

I guess I wanted to put her mind at ease. I dropped down on all fours to peer at black tire scuffs on the concrete curbing and at her car's crusted underbelly, searching for dents and hanging parts. I thought about my Levi's, which were recently washed. I thought about my life and the ludicrous indignity of this scene: All I wanted to do was get rid of a car for a reasonable price and there I was on the asphalt squinting at this unknown woman's oil pan and tie rods and grimy axle.

"Is it ruined?" she cried. "What if it won't drive? I can't take this car back to the shop. I couldn't face taking it back."

"It's O.K.," I said. "I really don't see anything here. Just get in and do what that fellow says."

She looked at the cousin, who pantomimed another tight turn of the wheel. Above the brace her neck and cheeks seemed to fill with blood that could not escape.

Still on my hands and knees I said, "Cramp it hard to the right, then back up as far as you can."

"This car has been trashed so many ways. It's been to the shop for everything. I never find out who does it. The police aren't any help."

I ducked again to examine the muffler, the rusty tubing. "I don't think anything has happened. Really. Just get in and give the wheel a try."

By the time she slid onto the front seat I was around on her side of the car, standing at an angle that happened to block the sun. I must have looked ominous to her. She froze, staring straight ahead. By a freak of timing, Harold's brother appeared just then. He pulled his Toyota pickup into the slot she had vacated, hopped out and looked around, but said nothing, evidently grasping the situation.

Unfortunately, he, too, wore sunglasses and an acid-washed denim jacket. As he moved toward the front of her car, joining the cousin, the glasses and the jackets had the look of a uniform they both shared.

In all three of these fellows you could see the family resemblance now, narrow faces with black hair angled across high foreheads, and all equally somber as they waited to see what the woman would do—while she waited to see what we were going to do. I could imagine what was running through her mind: We were some kind of transpacific shopping-mall gang working our way down the California coast, and now we had her surrounded, the cousin and the brother in front, Harold behind, me looming on the driver's side. She was trapped and outnumbered. She was babbling.

"I hear something in the steering wheel. Do you hear it? When I turn the wheel like this? My God! It *is* something. What did I do?"

"You didn't do anything," I said. "It's going to be O.K. Try cranking it hard to the right."

With the car in reverse she gripped the wheel and tried a tight turn. The effort squeezed her face with pain. She could not make the move. Her eyes, when she turned to me, were full of terror and defeat.

I hunkered next to the window. "Is it your arm? Your neck?"

Her shoulders slumped. Her tears began to fall.

"What happened?" I said.

"It was whiplash," she said. "Somebody braked in front of me. I never saw who. I didn't hit them but I got thrown around. It's the second time it happened. Do you know what it's like to be completely out of control? And to realize that nothing you have ever planned for yourself is going to work out? I think I am having a nervous breakdown. I don't even know what I'm doing here. I never come to this part of town."

The way color rose into her face had been reminding me of someone. Now I saw that her sense for the pointless anarchy of this moment reminded me of me, while in coloring she resembled my mother. I felt my own tears welling. I almost reached through the open window to touch her arm. Perhaps I should have. I had seen my mother in a similar state of mind, after she'd been sideswiped in heavy traffic. For weeks she had had the highway jitters and the late-life jitters, and being a widow had not helped matters much. From where I hunkered I could see this woman was on her own. Her manner told me that, and the single sack of groceries and something about the interior of the Dodge, the way the seats were strewn with paperwork, bits of clothing and Kleenex and receipts, the back seat, as well as the passenger side. This was how my mother's car had looked before I cleaned it up to sell, a car no one rode in but her.

"Would you like me to try it?" I said.

She couldn't answer.

"Scoot over," I said.

"Oh, no. No. Please. I'll get out."

As if she had to choose between the car and her life, she surrendered the wheel. I slid in. With my eyes on Harold hand-signalling in the rearview, I cramped it and inched backward until the tires touched concrete. In low I cramped it the other way and watched the cousin and the brother in their matching jackets waving and winding their hands in the air, with their eyes on the front tires, calling out one-word instructions.

"More! More! Stop! Stop! O.K.! O.K.!"

It took five moves in each direction, and for those couple of minutes we were allies, liberating the Dodge. When the front wheels finally cleared the divider, their three faces opened in sudden grins.

The woman was grinning, too, a wild grin. She was giddy, on the edge of crazy laughter. She had been prepared, I think, to see me disappear with her car. In the driver's seat again she only wanted to flee. She shifted fast and the car lurched again.

"What am I doing here?" she called out the window. "None of this makes any sense. I never shop at Safeway!"

We watched her swing a wide U-turn into the next aisle, speeding for the exit lane. Harold said nothing about this episode. Neither did I. It was hard to know what to say. Yet there was no doubt that she had brought us closer together. Her panic had cleared the way. I knew he was ready now to make another offer.

I was thinking Harold would be getting the car for a decent price, one to make his father proud. And I was thinking again about my mother, who had started life in rural Oklahoma and in some ways never left. She would have panicked at the sight of any three or four men standing around in a parking lot for no apparent reason. If she had come upon an Anglo in Levi's and three young men from China outside Safeway, well, it would have made her dizzy; the foreign faces would have been enough to push her sense of peril to the limit.

"I can pay three thousand," Harold said at last. "But no more. I do not have more than that."

I waited a moment, as if weighing this proposal. "To sell the car for that amount, I would have to have it all in cash."

He nodded and reached inside his coat for the bulging envelope.

While the cousin and the brother observed from the back seat, we sat in front, where I filled out a notice of sale and passed it to him along with the pink slip and a tire warranty from Sears, and a battery warranty. He counted out thirty one-hundred-dollar bills and asked me to count them. Then we shook hands.

The brother and the cousin left first in the pickup, followed by Harold in the Citation, hunched forward, nervous with responsibility. I had expected the money to bring more satisfaction than it did. Watching him leave, I felt abandoned. I stood there on the asphalt while the car turned right at the intersection and the flow of traffic carried it away.

The boulevard sounds receded with that car, as if an invisible screen had closed behind it. In this strange stillness, as the tail light winked its final wink and the baby-blue trunk disappeared, I wondered why I had kept to myself the collision that once mangled her rear fender. I wondered why the cousin had not noticed the repair, and if he had, why he hadn't mentioned it, thinking then of the many things we never mention. My mother's passing, for example. I had not mentioned that to Harold, either. She had lived a long life, so it came as no surprise, but it wasn't something I was ready to talk to anyone about.

The afternoon breeze fell away. Alone among the rows I found myself inside a tent of silence. An awful yearning gripped me, and then the fear that can stop you in your tracks, the fear of what is not yet known, which will sometimes take in everything imaginable. I couldn't tell you how long it held me there, how long I stood watching the long parade of silent cars.

ROCK
GARDEN

arly morning was Reiko's favorite time. Above white-peaked
Mount Whitney, the cloudless sky sparkled and crisp air cooled
the desert flatland. Alone, she could sit on the tree stump outside
the barracks door and watch people begin their day.

Her family's cubicle faced the latrines, giving her a grandstand
view of neighbors clattering past in homemade wooden/*geta* slippers
as they formed lines outside the two buildings—one for men, another
for women. Like colored rags of a kite's tail, the queue of robes and
kimonos snaked through the block's center. Yawning and clutching tin
basins that held their toiletries, the neighbors seemed not to notice
the lone spectator.

Since coming to the internment camp a year earlier, Reiko had
learned to entertain herself. The elders had talked about starting a
school, but so far, the only classes were those run by Miss Honda and
Myrtle Fujino, old maids from Block 22. Shy and soft-spoken, the
thirtyish spinsters volunteered their services, which actually
amounted to caretaking, since neither was a teacher. They taught the
girls sewing. Not knowing what to do with boys, they made them saw
wood, or sent them out to the firebreaks, which were open, sandy
acres between the barrack block compounds. For hours boys roamed
in the sand, looking for arrowheads left from the days when Paiute
Indians flourished in these high desert valleys.

Reiko hated sewing. She never had handled needles and thread,
and kept pricking her fingers while stitching rag dolls made out of old
clothes. What was supposed to be Raggedy Ann's white shirt face
looked more like a mangled fist, lumps and bloody smears disfiguring
it.

People-watching in the morning was much more interesting than sewing. It was Reiko's new game. She imagined herself a queen seated on a throne while the throngs passed in review. A wise and dignified queen. When Potato ran by in his Boy Scout uniform, twirling a dead rattlesnake like a lasso, she remained unruffled. Nor did she flinch when he came back and dangled the limp snake in front of her face.

Potato was the block idiot. Fat and tall, he always wore his Boy Scout uniform, swollen torso and haunches bursting at the khaki seams. He was twenty but had the mind of someone Reiko's age. She was ten. He was her court jester, and when she grew tired of the sinewy rope swaying in her face, she waved him away imperiously. With a final flick of the snake, he stuck his tongue at her and lumbered out of sight.

One morning someone joined her. Old man Morita, who lived two barracks away, was sitting outside his door, whittling wood. She figured he was people-watching, too. In the year they had been neighbors she never had spoken with him. Morita-san was deaf. The block people said the din of his wife's nagging had caused him to lose his hearing. Reiko believed it. She had heard Lady Morita's high-pitched rumbling while waiting in line at the mess hall. It was no wonder they called her Thunder-mouth. Her loud words crashed and gushed like white water storming over river rocks.

After a week of sitting, Reiko finally caught Morita-san looking her way. She waved. He smiled, creasing his walnut-brown face into tiny folds. Even from a distance, she could see his eyes were merry, and those eyes filled her with sadness. Both grandfathers were dead, and she hadn't seen her father for more than a year, ever since the FBI took him away to prison in North Dakota. The only male in the family was Ivan, who was fourteen. Seeing Morita-san's smiling eyes reminded Reiko how much she missed her father.

The next morning she waved at the old man and called cheerfully, "Good morning, Morita-san." Showing off she knew some Japanese, she added, "*O-hai-yo-gozai-mas.* Good morning." Then she remembered he probably couldn't read lips from a distance.

Morita-san beckoned. She scampered over to his perching place, which was a large square boulder, probably retrieved from one of the creeks. Sitting on the rock and framed by closed double wooden doors, he looked like pictures she had seen of her ancestors in Japan. He wore a dark blue kimono belted low on his belly and was barefoot.

"You like meditate in morning?"

It was the first time Reiko heard his voice. She had wondered if deaf people could speak, and it surprised her he spoke pidgin English, just like Ba-chan, her grandmother.

"What's meditate?" She spoke the new word slowly.

"Like pray," he said. His warm eyes crinkled. He dropped the long limb he was carving and bowed his forehead against his clasped hands. She'd seen Ba-chan doing the same thing before the Buddha statue in their room.

"Oh, to Buddha, you mean?"

"So, so," he answered. "I pray Indian spirit, too."

This fascinated Reiko. People said the internment camp was built over old Indian burial grounds. That's why there were so many arrowheads. The countless stories of Indian ghost sightings terrified her and she never walked in the firebreaks alone or went to the latrine at night except with Mama. In a way, she wished she weren't afraid, because she would like to see a ghost.

"Have you ever seen an Indian spirit?" she asked.

"All time. I see many. They talk me."

"Really? What do they say?" She wondered if he read their lips.

"They happy Japanese people here in desert. Say we come from same tribe across ocean."

He stood up, leaning on the cane he was whittling, and motioned for her to follow. Standing next to him, she was startled to see he was her height. They rounded the barrack corner past tall bamboo plants that extended in a row to the next barrack, screening from view the space between. She had often wondered what was behind that feathery wall.

Reiko knew she was entering a special place, maybe even a holy place. In her view, Morita-san already had changed from a deaf old henpecked man to a wizard.

Hidden behind the bamboo was a brilliant white lake of tiny pebbles. Kidney-shaped and smoothly raked, it was about four feet wide and seven long. At one end, five huge stones formed an altarlike platform. One flat stone held dried bones, rocks, feathers, and gnarled driftwood. Two covered urns stood in the middle.

She watched while the old man knelt before the altar, eyes closed, lips moving. He stood up and shuffled over to a moss-covered rock. With a tin cup, he drew water from a bucket and ladled it over the green velvet mound, chanting strange sounds.

"I teach you meditate," he said.

"*Arigato.* Thank you." She spoke another one of the few Japanese words she knew. She still didn't know what "meditate" was, but if it meant getting to know Morita-san, she would try it.

"Tomorrow morning. Same time," he said and patted the top of her head.

For some reason she decided not to tell anyone. Not that anyone would be interested. Since coming to camp, her brother and sister went their own way, making friends and eating in another block mess hall away from the family. Ba-chan was suspicious of everything and probably would claim that Morita-san's deafness was a punishment from the gods.

"Bad karma," she could hear her grandmother say. "He do something bad in past life."

The first few days he never spoke a word. He sat cross-legged, ignoring her. But she guessed that was the way he began things, remembering how he didn't acknowledge her when they people-watched earlier.

On the sixth morning, just as she was about to decide not to come anymore, things changed. He had set up a low table, a smooth, flat slab of driftwood, and motioned for her to sit down across from him.

"Close eyes," he said.

She obeyed. Her eyelids quivered, eager to lift so she could see what he was doing, but she kept them closed. A breeze blew above her head, like someone had waved a fan.

"*Namu-amida-butsu* . . . Crazee Horse-su . . . Geroneee-mo. *Namu-amida-butsu* . . . Crazee Horse-su . . . Geroneee-mo," he chanted. Over and over he singsonged the Buddhist mantra and Indian names until Reiko was lulled into a dreamy state.

She imagined braves on horses galloping across the open firebreak. She heard drumming—sharp, staccato beats that cracked like firecrackers. Racing back and forth across the desert, the horses' manes fluttered like torn flags, and orange smoke trailed from dilated nostrils. They flew to the desert's edge but stopped suddenly, rearing up and neighing. Something prevented them from passing over to green pastureland. It was barbed wire!

Her eyes snapped open. The old man was beating two smooth stones together. Clack-clack-clack.

"So, so. You see something?"

"Am I supposed to?"

"What you see?"

Reiko liked this game. "I saw Indians. They were riding horses with smoke coming out of their noses. They were trying to get out of camp."

"Hah! Hah!" Morita-san laughed loudly. "Very good. You good meditate."

"Is that all I do? Just imagine things?" It wasn't much different from making up stories about people, except she had never seen these Indians before.

He brought one of the urns to the table and from it retrieved a large obsidian arrowhead. It was glittering, black, and perfectly shaped.

"For you," he said.

She gasped, too pleased to speak.

"This magic. Make wish come true."

"Thank you, Morita-san. *Arigato.*" She couldn't wait to show it to Ivan.

From that day on, Reiko practically lived at the old man's sanctuary. After breakfast, instead of going to recreation classes, she sat with him before the shrine, "meditating," and helped garden his rocks. She learned to chant while pouring water over the moss stone, which looked to her like a turtle, asleep with head drawn inside its shell. Once she thought she saw it move.

He taught her to rake the white pebbles with rusty prongs, to carve flowing lines that undulated through the frozen sea.

"Rock, water, plant, wood all same. You, me, rock same." He pointed at Reiko and then some stones. "Everything same, same."

It amazed Reiko how his garden reflected this. He had watered a boulder until it became alive with moss. It wouldn't surprise her if it did turn into a turtle someday and crawl away. And the lake of pebbles seemed to surge and roll, making her seasick if she stared too long.

Sometimes he performed rituals. After burning orange peels in a tin can, he sprinkled ashes on the altar and drew symbols . . . circles, diamonds, squares, calligraphy. They rarely talked, mostly meditating, which she saw as another form of people-watching, except she made up the people, too. When she told him what she saw in her mind, he would cackle and laugh very hard, slapping a hand against his sinewy thigh.

One day he took her outside the camp. People had begun to venture beyond the barbed-wire fence since the soldiers in the guard towers had left. Reiko was glad they were gone. She was afraid of guns. One of the soldiers had shot Daryl Izumi, who was only fifteen and just looking for arrowheads. She stayed far away from the high wooden towers, thinking of them as castle turrets bordering a wide desert moat.

About a half mile out, a clump of elder trees rose from the barren landscape. Inside the oasis, a creek gurgled over shiny white pebbles, the same as Morita-san's rock lake.

"We walk on path," he said, and splashed into the creek.

Reiko was baffled, but followed anyway, having learned to accept his strange way of seeing things.

As they waded in the creek/path, he picked up pebbles and driftwood, depositing them in a sack tied around his waist. It was almost as if he were plucking fruit from a watery garden.

Then one morning she found Morita-san dressed in shirt and baggy trousers and boots. He was tinkering with a bamboo fishing pole. She wondered if he planned on fishing in the pebbled lake, not doubting for one moment he could pull up a wriggling trout from its raked depths.

"I go fishing up mountain." He pointed west to the sheer wall of the high Sierra Nevada.

"But that's so far away. Are we allowed to go that far?"

Reiko knew it was at least ten miles to the base of the mountain.

"Me old man. I go fishing."

Just then, Lady Morita flung open the door and began jabbering. Morita-san continued working on his pole, as if she weren't there. Thunder rolled from her mouth. Finally she stomped back into the cubicle.

Reiko walked with him to the edge of camp.

"Can I go with you, Morita-san?" She felt nervous about his going alone.

"No," he said bluntly, then patted the top of her head, smiling. "I come back tonight."

He shuffled past the barbed wire. "I catch many fish!" he shouted, waving to her as he trudged through the sagebrush. She watched him weave around tumbleweed and boulders until he became a small spider, the bamboo pole an antenna scanning the desert. She imagined his path turning into a creek glittering with brilliant stones that led up to Mount Whitney.

He didn't return that night or the next day. By the third day, Mr.

Kato, the block manager, called a meeting, and the men voted to form a search party. Lady Morita was screaming and hysterical, afraid the administration would find out her husband had violated the boundary. It was a mess . . . with neighbors arguing about ways to keep her from having a nervous breakdown.

Reiko wasn't worried. She knew Morita-san could take care of himself. The gossip made her angry, though. Someone said he had committed suicide, driven to it by his thunder-mouth wife. Someone else said he drove himself crazy meditating. She even heard he had hiked over the mountains to Fresno, where he was passing as Chinese.

After a week, she, too, became anxious. Very early in the morning, when the sky was gray and still sprinkled with stars, she stole over to the sanctuary. She sat in front of the shrine, cross-legged, the large arrowhead in her hand, and began to chant. She tried to emulate Morita-san.

"*Namu-amida-butsu* . . . Crazee Horse-su . . . Geroneee-mo. *Namu-amida-butsu* . . . Crazee Horse-su . . . Geroneee-mo." She made her voice quiver, sucking in her belly, surprising herself with strange guttural sounds. She lost track of time.

The urgent swishing of leaves . . . and then a horse's neigh broke her reverie. Across the rock lake, several warriors approached, leading horses. When they arrived at the pool's edge, the pebbles turned to water. As the horses drank, their frothy flanks heaved. They had been riding hard. Suddenly a figure materialized. It was Morita-san! Standing with the braves as if he belonged there! Her heart raced. She wanted to open her eyes, to shout and swim across the pool!

But a whirlwind suddenly spun up from the center. It grew wider and wider, churning waves and shaking leaves, whirling through the garden. Encircling Morita-san and the Indians, it lifted them high over the barracks. Morita-san was smiling, waving to her with his bamboo pole. She stood up to wave back, and was just about to open her eyes when the figures became iridescent, enveloped in golden light.

"Morita-san!" she cried.

◀━━▶

The search for the old man continued. After another week, it was called off. By then, Reiko had resigned herself to his permanent disappearance, even to the thought of death.

She returned to people-watching, no longer caring to meditate. And soon the much-talked-about school finally began, a real school like the one she had attended in Santa Monica before the war. Her life became full—with studies and new friends. Ivan began lessons at the judo pavilion, where Reiko spent many warm hours at dusk watching him flip and fall, grunting unintelligible commands.

Years later, in the last month before the camp closed, some Caucasian hunters hiking in the mountains reported sighting human bones at the bottom of a narrow ravine. It was assumed the remains were those of Morita-san. Reiko didn't feel too sad. Her old mentor had taught all things were one—flesh, rocks, plants, water. "Same, same," he had said. And so his bones, strewn about in the deep crevice, were resting comfortably, slowly returning to mountain granite and later, desert sand, while his ghost would roam the barbed-wire firebreaks forever with the Indians, his tribesmen, chanting and laughing as they galloped in the clear black night.

THE FLOWER GIRLS

The Meeting

This is the story of Cherry and Rose—two little girls who were almost sisters. They were almost twins, actually, because although they came from different families, they were both born on the very same day in very same city of Portland, Oregon.

They met in the first grade on the very first day of school. They sat in the front row, right next to each other. They both had on pink dresses and white shoes. They even had their hair combed the same way—parted right down the middle. When the teacher saw them, she said, "Well, well, well—so you're Cherry, and you're Rose. Looks like we have a couple of real flower blossoms here. Why, I'll just call you my Flower Girls—and you can help me right now by passing out these pencils to the class. Come on, Flower Girls—let's go!"

Naturally, Cherry and Rose became best friends. From the very first day, they did everything together. They did very well in school, they ate lunch together, and during recess they jumped rope, played jacks, and played hopscotch together. They were good at things by themselves, but together they were even better.

After School

Now, in those days, everyone walked home after school. The kids all lived close to school, but they went in different directions. Cherry went one way and Rose went another. But one day, when school was over, Cherry said to Rose, "Rose, why don't you ask your mother if you could come over to my house to play tomorrow? I live just down over there and around the corner. We could have lots of fun, and I'll walk you home for dinner. Okay?" "Okay!" said Rose.

So the next day, Rose went home with Cherry. As they got close, Cherry said, "I bet you can't guess where I live." Rose said, "Over there?" Cherry said, "No, silly—that's a newspaper office. Guess again." Rose said, "Over there?" Cherry said, "No, silly—that's the fish store. Guess again." Rose said, "Over there?" Cherry said, "No, silly—that's the *manju-ya*. You only get one more guess."

Then Rose said, "Well, how about that place?" "Right!" said Cherry. "But what does that sign say?" said Rose. "Don't be silly," said Cherry. "That sign says 'Sakura Tofu Company.'" "But what does that mean?" said Rose. "Don't be silly," said Cherry. "That means 'Cherry Blossom Tofu Company.'" "But what is a 'tofu'?" said Rose. "Don't be silly," said Cherry. "A tofu is a tofu, don't you know?" "But where do you live?" said Rose. "Don't be silly," said Cherry. "We live in back of the store. Come on! My mom is waiting!"

Sure enough, Cherry's mom was waiting for them. A little bell tinkled when they went into the store. Cherry's mom said, "My, oh, my—don't you Flower Girls look pretty today! Cherry, here's ten cents for you and Rose to spend. Why don't you show your friend around?" "Okay!" said Cherry. "Let's go!"

Sno-Kones and *Manju*

The girls had a great time that afternoon. It was a nice, warm day, and they walked around the busy neighborhood, looking in stores and saying hello to people. After a while, Rose said, "Cherry, what are we going to do with the ten cents?" Cherry said, "Come on—I'll show you!"

They went into the place called the *manju-ya*. There were many good things to eat on the shelves—everything looked so pretty and colorful, and everything smelled so good and tasty. Rose said, "Boy, oh, boy—I've never seen anything like this! What are we going to get?" Cherry said, "I'll show you."

When the man came out from the back, Cherry said, "We'll have two Sno-Kones, please—with rainbow flavors." The man went over to the Sno-Kone machine, put in a big, shiny piece of ice, and cranked the ice around and around. He made snow, scooped the snow into paper cones, and poured all the flavors of the rainbow on top of the snow. The girls watched with wide-open eyes and licked their lips.

Cherry gave the man ten cents, and they got their cones. Then the man said, "Just a minute." He got a small paper bag and put in some of the prettiest *manju* for them to take home, free. Naturally, the girls said, "Thank you, very much!"

They had to eat the Sno-Kones pretty fast, because it was a hot day, but if they ate it too fast, it hurt their heads. So they walked down the sidewalk very slowly, being careful to eat with good manners, not to slurp too much, and not to spill anything on their dresses. Rose bumped into an old lady coming out of the fish store, but since nothing was spilled, they all laughed.

At the street corner, though, as they were finishing their Sno-Kones, tipping them upside down, Rose looked at Cherry and started to laugh. "What's the matter?" said Cherry. "You should look at your mouth!" said Rose. "You should look at *your* mouth!" said Cherry. And both girls went and looked into a mirror in the window of the beauty shop. They laughed when they saw their colorful mouths. They laughed some more when they saw some old ladies inside with curlers on their heads. The old ladies were laughing at them.

On the way to Rose's house, they stopped in the park and sat on a bench. Rose said, "I hope that Sno-Kone won't spoil my supper. Now why don't we try some of that stuff in the bag?" Cherry said, "Sure." They shared bites of one that was very soft and white, with something sweet and red inside. Cherry said, "Why don't you take the rest home to your mother?" "Okay!" said Rose.

Shaving the Ice

Rose had a lot to tell her mother that night, about her best friend's neighborhood, and, before long, Rose was visiting Cherry almost every day after school. They played in Rose's neighborhood, too, doing what they called the "regular things"—like going to the grocery store, going to the butcher shop, and walking by the noisy factory full of big machines and boxes—but they both agreed that Cherry's neighborhood was much more interesting, so they played there most of the time.

At school their teacher said, "My, oh, my—you Flower Girls are almost like a secret club, always talking about things like *manju* and tofu. Can you girls explain some of that to me and the class?" Rose said, "*Manju* is *manju* and tofu is tofu, but eating a Sno-Kone is like eating Mount Hood!" Everybody laughed. Then Rose said, "And after eating a Sno-Kone, you look like a clown because your mouth is all orange and purple and red!" Everybody laughed. Everybody wanted to try eating a Sno-Kone. Then the teacher said, "Class, a Sno-Kone is just shaved ice." That made the class laugh even more, because who ever heard of 'shaving the ice'?" One boy put his hand up and said, "Teacher, my daddy shaves his face every morning, but I didn't know that the ice had to shave!" Everybody laughed again.

Learning Names

As the year went by, all the children learned to read and write and count at school. But the Flower Girls also learned how to count in Japanese, from Cherry's mother, and they could point to their fingers and say *ichi, ni, san, shi* just like that. Then Cherry's mother taught the Flower Girls how to write their names in Japanese. It took practice, over and over, because it was almost like drawing a picture, but when they learned how to do it right, their names looked very fancy, very beautiful, and the Flower Girls felt very special when they showed the kids at school. The other kids tried to write their names in Japanese, too, and made a lot of funny marks on paper. The teacher couldn't write her name either.

Cherry's mother was like a teacher at home, but a fun teacher, and she would always explain things to the girls as they went with her to make deliveries. They would walk down the sidewalks carrying packages of tofu, and when Cherry's mother got paid, the girls would also say *"Arigato."* That always made the customers smile.

Sometimes the girls would play with dolls in the kitchen in back of the tofu store, and Cherry's mother would always teach them interesting things, such as how to make cinnamon toast without burning the toast or spilling the cinnamon, or how to blow soap bubbles without making too much of a mess, or how to make glue and clean up afterward, or how to answer the phone even though your mouth is full of peanut butter, or how to fold and cut newspapers into snowflakes and birds.

One day, Cherry's mother told the girls that Japanese names had very interesting meanings in Japanese, such as "rice field" and "pine forest" and "mountain river" and "rocky seashore." She said that everybody's name means something, and that names such as "Portland" and "Multnomah" and "Oregon" mean something, too. And the same for "Columbia" and "Willamette" and "Roosevelt" and "Studebaker" and "Chevrolet" and "Ford.

"How about 'Burnside'?" asked Rose. "Yes," said Cherry's mother, "that must mean something, too." "How about 'Atkinson School'?" asked Cherry. "Yes, that must mean something, too," said Cherry's mother. "And the same for 'Atlantic' and 'Pacific' and 'Blitz Weinhard' and 'Jantzen Beach' and 'Washington Park' and 'Meier and Frank.' " "How about 'Nabisco'?" said Cherry. "Yes," said Cherry's mother, "that just means 'National Biscuit Company.' 'Na-Bis-Co'—you get it?" "Sure we do!" said the Flower Girls.

More Places and Names

Actually, Cherry's neighborhood had so many people, places, and names that the girls couldn't remember everything. There were places upstairs, there were places downstairs; there were places in front, there were places out back. There were barbershops, beauty shops, bathhouses, laundries, fish markets, dry goods stores ("What's 'dry goods'?" asked the girls), grocery stores, stores full of appliances, shoe repair shops, auto repair shops, many restaurants, very many hotels, one newspaper office called the *Oh Shu,* one newspaper office called the *Nippo,* another newspaper office called the *Ka Shu,* doctors' offices, dentists' offices, and pharmacies ("What's a 'pharmacy'?" asked the girls).

Sometimes the Flower Girls would just walk around, saying names like songs. *"Oh Shu* and *Nippo* and *Ka Shu*—Step right up and get your latest news!" At other times they would play a game to see if they remembered all the churches. "Portland Buddhist Church"— that was easy. It was also called "Bu-kyo-kai." Then there was "Japanese Methodist Church"—that was easy. But how about "Ken-jyo-ji," "Kon-ko-kyu," "Minori-nakai," "Nichiren," and "Sei-cho"—those were not as easy. So the girls would have to count them all on their fingers, like a test, and they would always pass.

One time, Cherry's mother said, "Girls, listen to the names of these clubs: 'Fukuoka-kenjinkai,' 'Hiroshima-kenjinkai,' 'Okayama-kenjinkai,' 'Wakayama-kenjinkai,' and 'Nippon-kenjinkai.' Do you think you can remember all that?" And the girls said, "Sure! We'll try! Say those again! You can't trick us!" And Cherry's mother said, "Well, *go-men-na-sai*, Flower Girls!"

The Dog Named Cat

One day, when Rose got home, she told her mother, "Mother, did you know that Cherry has a new puppy? It's brown and very soft and furry, but guess what she named it?" Her mother couldn't guess, so Rose said, "Cherry wanted a kitten instead, but since she's allergic to cats, she named her puppy Nekko. And Nekko means 'cat.' So she has a dog named cat. Do you get it, huh? Do you get it? Isn't that funny? Don't you think that's funny? She has a dog and a cat at the same time!" And then, after a while, Rose said, "Mother, can I get a dog or a cat?"

Another day, Rose came home and said, "Mother, did you know that I was a '*hakujin*'? That's just what I am. And Cherry is a '*nihonjin.*' That's what she is. That's all. But we're both Americans. Isn't that interesting? And Cherry's mother says that we're *both* her Flower Girls."

Another time, Rose said, "Mother, did you know that where Cherry lives is called 'Shi-ta Machi'? That means 'bottom town' or 'under' or 'below.' Isn't that interesting? Cherry's mother says that's because they live down by the river."

The Creature in the River

The teacher read a story to the class about the man in the moon. After it was over, Cherry raised her hand and told the class, "My mother says there is not a man in the moon but instead there are two rabbits with their hammers pounding rice." Some kids said that wasn't true, but Cherry said that when the moon was full, they should go outside and *see* those rabbits that her mother showed her.

Cherry also said, "My mother says that the *kappa* is a creature who lives in the Willamette River. When you go down by the river, you can see his tracks. Kappa lives in the river, swimming under the boats and bridges, but he walks around on land at night. He likes to dump over garbage cans and play tricks on people." One boy asked if the *kappa* likes to hurt people. Cherry said, "No, because he likes kids, but not even the police can catch him." Another boy asked Cherry if she had seen the *kappa.* Cherry said, "No, because I can't stay up at night. But one time I heard him. And in the morning, the garbage can was turned over." One boy said that he had seen the *kappa* late at night and that the *kappa* was big and hairy like a monster. Cherry said, "No, that's not the *kappa,* because the *kappa* is small, like a first-grader. Besides, he has a shell, like a turtle." One girl asked if the *kappa* wore any clothes. Cherry said, "No." Everybody laughed. Then Cherry said, "But you have to look out, because the *kappa* is very strong." Then one boy said, "If the kappa ever came to my house, me and my dad would beat him up, just like that!" Another boy said, "I would shoot him with a gun! Boom!" And Cherry said, "Nobody could ever shoot or catch the *kappa,* because he's too fast. He could jump right into the river and swim right back to Japan. Or, if he wanted to, he could put on some clothes and walk around in a disguise, like a man." One girl raised her hand and asked, "But why does he tip over garbage cans? Does he eat garbage?" Cherry said, "No, he just does that for fun." One boy said, "But if he wears a disguise, how does he hide his face?" Cherry said, "He wears a big, black hat. Besides, he could change his face to look like a man. And he wears a big overcoat to cover his shell." Rose said, "One time, me and Cherry found a big overcoat in the alley. We didn't touch it. We ran home! The next day, it was gone!" Everybody was quiet.

The Celebrations

One day, after New Year's, Cherry told Rose that there was going to be a Girls' Day celebration in Shi-ta Machi and that there would be many beautiful dolls on display but not to play with. Then there was also going to be a Boys' Day, when everybody would go on a picnic to a place called Montevilla, out in the country, to fly kites and play games, and that Rose could come with them. Then Cherry said that they could both dance in the Cherry Blossom Festival, too, but they would have to practice dancing after school. "Oh, that will be fun," said Rose. "Yes," said Cherry, "and we also get to wear special clothes."

Rose couldn't wait to get home to tell her mother. On the way home, she sang her own cherry blossom song. *"Sakura, sakura,"* she sang as she skipped along. *"Sakura, sakura . . ."*

The Flower Girls had a lot of fun at those special celebrations, and everybody said, "My, you Flower Girls are so beautiful!" And one day, in the summer, Rose came home and told her mother, "Mother —guess what? Our teacher says we get to be in the Rose Parade! Isn't that great? We get to ride on a float! And Cherry says she's going to ride on the Shi-ta Machi float! Her float is going to have roses, too, but it is also going to have lots of fruits and vegetables on it, like strawberries and radishes and onions! Oh, I can't wait! Won't that be neat?"

In the Second Grade

So the Flower Girls rode in the Rose Parade, and they had a lot of fun playing together all that summer. Then, when school started again, they were both in the same class in the second grade, and they even sat in the same front seats, right next to each other. On the first day, the new teacher said, "Well, well, well—looks like we have the Flower Girls together again. Now, Flower Girls, will you help me pass out these brand-new books?"

School was so much fun, as usual, but one day, after Thanksgiving, when the class was going to start practicing on a Christmas play about Santa Claus and all the good little children, the teacher said, "Class, as you all know, America is having a war against Japan. But let's be good boys and girls and put on the best Christmas play we can. Okay?" And all the kids said, "Okay!"

But that day, at recess, there were fights among the older kids in the playground, and a lot of kids got called "Jap!" Then a sixth-grade girl came up to Rose and Cherry and said, "You guys aren't supposed to play together because she's a *Jap* and *you're enemies!"* And Rose said, "No, we're not! *We're friends!"* And the older girl said, "No, you're not! You're enemies! You're having a war! Ha, ha, ha—you're having a war-ar! You're having a war-ar! Boo-hoo-hoo! Enemies, enemies, enemies! Ha, ha, ha—you're having a war-ar!"

Just Because

The Christmas play was canceled, and it was not a very happy Christmas for anybody. The Flower Girls did not visit each other anymore, and one day, after New Year's, Cherry said to Rose, "We're not going to have a Girls' Day or a Boys' Day or a Cherry Blossom Festival this year." And Rose said, "Why not? How come?" And Cherry said, "Just because. Because we're having a war."

Then, on a fine, spring morning, the teacher said, "Class, as you know, some of you kids are going to be moving away soon, so this week let's all have a real nice good-bye party, okay?" Nobody knew what to say.

At recess, Rose said, "Cherry, where are you going?" Cherry said, "I don't know." Rose said, "What do you mean you don't know? How come you don't know?" "Because I don't know, stupid!" said Cherry. "All I know is that we're going down the river." "But how come you're going down the river?" said Rose. "Because we're going down the river, stupid!" said Cherry. "Because we're going to war." "But how come you're going to war?" said Rose. "Because we're Japs, stupid!" said Cherry. "But how are you going?" said Rose. "I know— maybe you get to float on a boat! Maybe you get to float on a float!" "Don't be stupid, stupid!" said Cherry. "I bet you wouldn't want to go." "Yes, I would!" said Rose. "That's because you're stupid, stupid!" said Cherry. "I'm not stupid!" said Rose. "Yes you are!" said Cherry. "You're stupid, stupid, stupid!"

The next day, Cherry said to Rose, "Rose, my mother wants to know if you could take care of Nekko for us." "Why?" said Rose. "Because we can't take her with us, stupid!" said Cherry. "Why not? How come?" said Rose. "Just because!" said Cherry. "Just because!"

The Letters

On a warm, beautiful summer day, the mailman brought a letter to Rose. The letter said:

Dear Rose,

How are you? I am fine. How is Nekko? This place stinks. P U
GARBAGE. Are you my friend? I can see Portland.

> Your friend,
> Cherry

With the help of her mother, Rose wrote a letter back to Cherry.
The letter said:

Dear Cherry,

How are you? I am fine. Nekko got ran over. She went to
heaven. I am your friend. You are in the map of Portland.

> Your friend,
> Rose

More Letters

On a lovely fall day, with a warm wind blowing, Cherry sat up in
a bed and wrote a letter. The letter said:

Dear Rose,

How are you? I am fine. I am in the third grade. Who is your
teacher? My teacher is American. We live in Idaho. I went to the
hospital. This is my picture of you and Nekko. She is eating a
manju. You are eating a Sno-Kone. This is my picture of you in
the Rose Parade. The float is beautiful. You are my friend.

> Your friend,
> Cherry

The letter was never answered.

No One Knows

No one knows what happened to Cherry. No one knows what
happened to Rose. Shi-ta Machi is no more. The buildings are still
there, with different stores and businesses in them, but the Shi-ta

Machi people did not return to Shi-ta Machi. Shi-ta Machi is no more.

There are still Shi-ta Machi people, though, living in all parts of the city, and if you want to see Shi-ta Machi, you have to look deep into the eyes of the Shi-ta Machi people. You have to look deep into the eyes, under the surface, you have to look deep below the surface of the shining eyes, you have to look deep down to the bottom of the eyes of the Shi-ta Machi people, and you will see Shi-ta Machi shining in their eyes. You will see the shining streets, the sidewalks full of people. You will see children like Cherry and Rose, playing after school.

You will see the tofu store, you will see the *manju-ya* (you can even smell the sweet *manju,* you can even hear the *manju* man shaving the ice, you can even taste the Sno-Kone, oh, so cold, with all the flavors of the rainbow), you can walk down the sidewalks past all the stores and offices, and when you stop at the corner, you can look into the window of the beauty shop and see your face in the mirror.

Then, in the blink of an eye, Shi-ta Machi will be gone. Shi-ta Machi is no more.

The Song of Cherry and Rose

There is a beautiful park in the hills of Portland. It is full of trees and lawns, with many places to sit and play and walk and run. In one part of the park is a Japanese garden, full of beautiful plants and rocks, with a beautiful pond. In the Japanese garden, a very special cherry tree grows.

In the same part of the park, there is a beautiful rose garden. There are roses with all the colors of the rainbow, and in that garden grows a very special rose.

When the park is quiet, you can walk through the Japanese garden, and you can hear the wind blow. When the park is quiet, you can walk through the rose garden, and you can hear the wind blow.

The song you hear is the song of Cherry and Rose.

It is a beautiful song of friendship, of being best friends together, of going to school together, of playing together, of growing up together. It is a beautiful song of being the Flower Girls, of being sisters. It is a beautiful song of becoming women together, of always being sisters.

The song you hear is the song of Cherry and Rose.

The Continuing Story

On a fine summer day, a family was on a picnic in the park. After lunch, the little girl said, "Mother, I'm going for a little walk through the rose garden. Okay?"

The little girl went walking through all the beautiful roses. Everything smelled like roses, felt like roses, everything was colored like roses. When the little girl was right in the middle of the rose garden, right when she was sniffing a big red rose, she looked up and saw another little girl doing the same thing.

Both girls said "Hi!" at the same time. One girl said, "My name is Cherry. What's your name?" The other girl said, "My name is Rose." And Cherry said, "Do you want to walk over to the Japanese garden?" And Rose said, "Okay. I'll ask my mother." And Cherry said, "Okay. I'll ask my mother." And Rose said, "Okay. I'll meet you back here. Okay?" And Cherry said, "Okay. I'll meet you back here."

And off they went.

◆

Pronunciation of Japanese is very simple and consistent, very much like Spanish.

Tofu is a soft cake made from soybeans.

Manju is a variety of confections often made from rice.

Ichi, ni, san, shi are one, two, three, four.

Arigato means thank you.

Go-men-na-sai means excuse me.

Cherry was first sent to the Portland Assembly Center, otherwise known as the Multnomah County Exposition Center, adjoining the Portland Union Stock Yards.

Cherry was next sent to the Minidoka Relocation Center, in southern Idaho.

Shi-ta Machi was located north of Burnside, in the area down toward the river.

For further reference:

Zaigaku Kodachi and Jan Heikkala, trans., "Portland Assembly Center: Diary of Saku Tonita," ed. Janet Cormach, *Oregon Historical Quarterly* (Summer 1980).

Barbara Yasui, "The Nikkei in Oregon, 1834–1940," *Oregon Historical Quarterly* (September 1975).

KAREN KARBO

◆

DEATH BY
BROWSING

Bella Bogoga

Last Saturday my husband, Yuz, collapsed in front of the Bullock's Wilshire department store in Los Angeles, California.

Forever I will see him falling against the palm tree, sliding down, down, his golf shirt bunching up under his arms, his poor bald head so sunburnt, his scattered few hairs stiff from sunscreen oil. I think of those frail hairs and cry.

I left him in the palm's stingy shade to rest and went for help. On my return, I found strangers buzzing over him, wondering about lawsuits and who should touch him. A man in a khaki safari shirt said, "The Russians! Such a beleaguered race!" This happened on the four-month anniversary of our departure from Moscow.

◆

More difficult than deciding the fate of Yuz's ashes is writing to my friend Lidia Nikolaevna about his death. For the moment, I keep his urn in a shoebox in the closet (former home of an adorable pair of moss-green pumps) and spend the warm winter evenings on my shoebox-sized balcony, ripping up letter after letter to Lidia. Finally, afraid she might hear of it through friends of friends of the nitwits I work with at Slavic Languages Department, I manage to write:

2 February

Greetings, Cookie!

I have some horrible sad news. First, I could not find that black-and-white Norma Kamali T-shirt dress you asked me about in your last letter. Also, dear Yuz died three weeks ago Sunday.

Los Angeles is perfect except the air and it caused him to

suffer a heart attack while shopping on Wilshire Boulevard. The man on the news that morning had said, "Beware. Third-stage smog alert. Breathe only when necessary." But they always say that, and you have to live, right? I did not realize it was eight miles to walk to Bullock's Half-Year Sale, and who could have known the bad state of Yuz's heart? Months before, he had modern hospital tests which said he was okay. The emergency ward doctors felt that decades of vodka tormenting his system were probably to blame.

It is no secret that my love for Yuz expired long ago, but he was my husband, and the people at the university allowed me time away to heal. It was fantastic. Every day I spent visiting my friend Cricket, darling salesgirl of Trendsetter Sportswear at fancy downtown department store. You would love her, Lidichka! She is Miss Au Courant, straight from *Vogue*. With her tiny waist and saucy hairstyle, she reminds me of you, only she is dark-eyed like an Armenian. She admires greatly my style of dressing and often asks my opinion on how to put together a Look. She says I have natural gifts for fashion and should be In Retail (as salesgirl or clothes buyer) instead of teaching Russian to college students.

I would appreciate if you kept the situation of Yuz to yourself, as all those nasty black-market girls, Irina especially, who tries to pass her cheap Polish lipstick off for Revlon, will be delighted to hear of my misfortune.

All my love,
Bella

16 March

Bellinka *doushka:*

I am *crushed* to hear what California has done to our sweet Yuz! I think of you stranded there with no one and nothing and I weep, Bella Semyonovna, weep. Masha—you remember, the gymnast who bought the HAWAII towel from you last spring?—she just returned from a gymnastics exhibition in San Jose, California, and said there is a mass murderer going around Los Angeles. So what else is news, I thought!

I couldn't help but tell Irina about Yuz. She *was* upset and not nasty at all. Those girls love and miss you, Bellinka. (They have me for all their high-fashion needs, but who to get sunglasses from now that you're gone?) Please keep well and keep your door locked. Mass murderers especially prefer women alone, you know. When you think about it, could you check for the Norma Kamali in blue and white?

> Kisses,
> Lidia

I answer this by folding it in thirds and placing it under the short leg of the kitchen table to stop the wobble. *What California has done to our sweet Yuz!* I can just see Lidia's eyes glittering with pity. What a relief! Life in emigration *is* worse than Soviet Union.

The fact is, she is Miss Jealous.

◆

Last summer, back in Soviet Union, when we did our rounds on Kalinin Prospekt, Lidia selling the sharpest illegal shoes in Moscow, me moving vacation apparel from a Samsonite briefcase I found on the metro, we debated our favorite topic: how we would live in the West. If I said I wanted to work in a clothes boutique, Lidia wanted to own one. If I wanted to be a *Vogue* photographer, Lidia would be the model I photographed. If I, exasperated, said I wanted to own *Vogue*, Lidia hiked up a lovely shell-pink nostril in disdain. "You're so *ambitious*, Bella. I'd rather live a simple life, having many children."

All this time, I never told her that Yuz, with his modest dream of picking lemons off his own tree in California, had changed our last name from Bogoga to Bogogowicz and was petitioning for emigration papers with a yarmulke on his head, fashioned from the cup of one of my black-market bathing suit tops.

The day the papers came through, I found Lidia on Kalinin Prospekt seducing a pigeon-toed clerical worker with a pair of Avia aerobics shoes. "Lidia, listen: Yuz has gotten—you won't believe it—we are leaving for United States."

She slowly turned. Her light-eyed gaze crashed down on me. "America, oi. When *I* emigrate, I'm going to Paris."

◆

One day I come across Yuz's glasses under the nightstand. Without tears I suffered his cremation and a visit to the Foundling Home for the Children of Estonia, Westside Branch, where I donated his few clothes. But the glasses, the glasses, Yuz's most needed thing. I try to throw them away under the sink, then throw them off the balcony, which overlooks a Dumpster in the apartment building's parking lot. But I end by crawling through the garbage to retrieve them. I kiss them and place them in the shoebox, beside his urn. I realize it is time to bury him.

My fellow teaching assistants, all well-meaning émigré ladies with the fashion sense of potato farmers, suggest trying "Crypts" in yellow pages, or calling a little-known Russian actor/pilot who makes his living distributing ashes over the Pacific.

"What about Children of Estonia?" asks Valeria, dressed in black wool so old it's beginning to turn green.

Valeria, Marina, and I are in the office of the Slavic Languages Department, standing before Mr. Coffee pot, waiting for him to finish brewing our morning cup.

"Heavens to Bessie, no," I say. "They already have enough of him, all his nice slacks."

"Well, they were most helpful in finding me lawyer—a lawyer— for my divorce proceedings," says Valeria.

"Maybe under a lemon tree," I say suddenly. "Yes! To honor dream that brings him to this marvelous land."

"So marvelous," says the imperious Marina, "that if you attempted to bury the urn in a lemon orchard they would lock you away in prison. There are laws forbidding it, Bella."

"I will buy my own tree, then."

"I can just see it," says Marina, sipping on her coffee, winking at Valeria through the steam, "growing right in the middle of your lovely apartment."

I go to a discount nursery and find a potted tree still too young for fruit. I squeeze it onto the balcony. Inside of a week, the sun turns the leaves brown. In the evening, while I wait for news to be over and television to begin, I snap off the crisp, dead curls and miss the good side of Lidia Nikolaevna, which believes, on principle, that crazy ideas are the best kind.

◀◆▶

I go to Trendsetter Sportswear, not to bother Cricket but to see if she has suggestions on a nice gift. I have never answered Lidia's condolence letter, and rather than apologize, I will find some luscious department store item to give to Jim Spaniel to take to Moscow to give to Lidia. Jim Spaniel is an assistant professor in the department, who takes, every summer, some Russian majors to Soviet Union. He is no big hunk, Jim, and his hairline has tiptoed back at least an inch in the few months I have known him, but he appreciates a good conversation and does not tease me about my fashion awareness.

On this day, one of Cricket's co-workers sees me before I even get off the escalator. She is tall and wrinkled, a permanent frown embedded in her saddle face. I wave to her, but she just looks back down at the rack of blouses she is straightening.

"Cricket has gone to lunch," she calls out.

"All right. I will just browse, then."

Cricket never comes, and I wander downstairs, where I find *the* item: soft caramel in color, soft as a baby's earlobe to touch, it is the most fantastic handbag I have ever seen. Unfortunately, it is hanging off the shoulder of a teenage girl with the haircut of an army officer. Mother, she calls, come here. She replaces the bag on top of a pile of other bags, all marked down from full price, her paw resting on the flap, staking it out for her own. But I *must* have it. I can just see it swinging down Kalinin Prospekt on Lidia's delicate shoulder. I can just see Irina and the rest of the black-market girls purring and stroking it like a talisman. Oh, to live in Los Angeles like Bella, they'll say.

The handbag will be trickier to capture when Mother gets involved. I reach deep into the pile until cool leather nudges my armpit. I root around until I find a strap, then pull. The teenager screeches as an avalanche of navy-blue, bone, and dove-gray handbags cascades down on her feet.

The salesgirl comes and asks would I like the handbag cash or charge.

◆

During the summer, I do not have to teach and am free to spend my days in the cool concrete wombs of my favorite department stores. I often stop downtown to visit Cricket but am always interrupting her at something: waiting on customers, clearing out dressing rooms, cleaning mirrors.

At home, I have managed to fit a stool on the balcony next to the lemon tree, and in the evenings I sit and work on my clippings file. With some money left from Yuz, I purchased subscriptions to *Elle, Glamour, Mademoiselle*, of course *Vogue*, and others, and I keep a file of valuable articles on, to give example, "Plaids: The Ultimate Mix and Match Challenge." I do not sit outside on Tuesdays, however, the evening before garbage pickup, because the Dumpster flies are too bothersome.

Sometimes I imagine Jim Spaniel and Lidia, together in Moscow at that very moment. I imagine him presenting her with the handbag, shyly, because he is undone by her pale, cat beauty, and Lidia saying oh-oh-oh, taking the bag to her breast, stroking it, inhaling the odor of real leather.

In early August, Jim Spaniel calls and invites me out to take a beer. In honor of his return, I wear my new melon-colored cotton twill skirt with royal-purple top-stitching, which I had been saving for the first day of class. With my bolero jacket and new lace-up gladiator sandals, I plan on being a sight for eyes sore from looking at frumpy Russian women all summer.

◆

Of course, I say it's wonderful. I tell him he is the luckiest boy in the world. He smiles idiotically and tears his cocktail napkin into strips. He is thinner than I remember and, unlike every other person in Los Angeles, hasn't a hint of suntan. In fact, his skin is the color of mushrooms, no doubt from making love all day in the bad air of Lidia's stuffy apartment.

"She's a great lady," he breathes.

"Oh, yes, Cookie, she is fantastic. She is my dearest friend. And so beautiful, really like an American beauty!"

"Oh, no, she's typically Slavic. That's what makes her so unique."

"Yes, Cookie, unique as the two hundred fifty million other Russians in the world. When is the wedding?"

He tells me a date. He says it will be in Moscow.

On my way home on the bus—that lovelorn imbecile doesn't even offer me a ride—I get off two stops early and buy some plant food and a half gallon of rum raisin ice cream.

When I was able, finally, to ask about the handbag, he looked blank at me for a minute, as though he'd forgotten. "Oh, right," he said. "She enjoyed it very much."

"Did she love it?"

"Sure. You know how excited she gets. The smallest thing sends her into orbit."

19 August

Dear Lidichka:

What fantastic news I hear from your fiancé, a certain Mr. Jim Spaniel. Jim is my favorite person in the Slavic Department, and we are great friends. As soon as he returned from Moscow he called me, and we Did the Town, celebrating your happy news. When, Lidichka, are you coming to Los Angeles? It is a fabulous town. I will mention you to Cricket (she is a darling, offering me such compliments when I emerge from my dressing room, whirling and twirling like a dancer from the Kirov), but she may not immediately be able to see us. Retail is a very competitive business, and she has a very busy and erratic schedule. Not to be disappointed, you'll have me and my Los Angeles expertise. Oh, I nearly forgot, did you enjoy the handbag? Just a trifle from yours truly.

All my love,
Bella

Jim Spaniel insists on meeting Lidia at the airport alone. I try to arrange for champagne and a telegram singer, but he says absolutely not. I think he is envious of my panache.

Several days after her arrival, Lidia and I finally rendezvous at Santa Monica Mall. We cover each other's faces with kisses. Mascara tears of joy dribble out from under Lidia's sunglasses.

"Are you sure you want to go shopping?" I say. "It looks like you've already been." I had expected her in her drab Moscow best; instead she is wearing a gorgeous red-and-white-striped sundress of Irish linen, cinched at the waist with a wide red leather belt.

"A present from Jim. Luckily, he is sturdier than Yuz. We must have been to every store in the city."

"And you purchased at full price?"

She shrugs. "Jim makes big money. He can afford nice things for his wife."

"He doesn't make so much money."

"Well, he must make more than you, Bellinka, and you're doing so well yourself. And look, you're wearing that fantastic dress! I almost didn't remember. You know, something like that would *sag* on me, but you fill it out so nicely." She shakes her head. Her butter-yellow curls erupt in a brand-new perm.

Stupidly, I chose for this special reunion a sentimental favorite, the polyester green-and-orange plaid A-line with contrasting yoke and pockets. I wanted Lidia to feel at ease, not intimidated by my new American Look.

"It was the only thing ironed," I say.

"And those *shoes*." Suddenly she drops to her knees. She strokes the tips of my moss-green pumps, like a jeweler feasting on a rare stone. Shoppers entering the store stare down at her. She is almost knocked over by a reckless mother and a baby stroller. But she sees none of it. She also does not see that this old, honest gesture has saved me from pulling the belt from this fantastic dress which I fill out so nicely and strangling her.

"A friend of Irina's was looking for a shoe just like this," she whispers, "but it was impossible to find. My one order I could never fill."

"Cookie! Please! There are shoes like this all over city! These were marked down at Bullock's. Nobody wanted green, apparently."

"I can see why," she says, standing and rubbing at two round bruises of dirt on the bottom of her dress.

◆

In the mornings, she comes to work with Jim Spaniel, wearing each day some breathtaking new ensemble. The department secretary calls her the Russian Grace Kelly. To pass the time, she eavesdrops on the secretary's phone conversations or flips through dusty copies of *Soviet Life*. I have offered to give her my already read copies of *Vogue*, *Glamour*, etc., but she refuses them, then goes out and buys the exact ones I've offered. She says she can't do the help-yourself quizzes with my answers always staring her in the face.

On weekends, when Jim Spaniel is doing lesson plans or watching football, we go shopping.

As we sit one Sunday in afternoon beach traffic, silent and bored as mannequins, Lidia pokes into the bag on the seat between us. We are driving in Jim Spaniel's convertible car and playing his cassette tape deck. "Returning these, Bellinka? Too small?" She pulls out some blue jeans and checks the tag. "Fourteen. I guess not."

"They fit perfect. The waist is even too big. I buy them downtown for thirty-three dollars and return them in Beverly Hills, where they are forty-five dollars."

"They can't be the same blue jean."

"They are."

"You are sure?"

"Every store in the city carries them—they are a popular brand."

"And the style is the same?"

"Lidichka, I have been doing this for months."

"Well, I've never heard about it."

In the store, at the department of Misses Casual Fashions, I get around the question of a receipt by telling the salesgirl, a freckled darling of no more than seventeen, that I bought the blue jeans on the same day I discovered I was pregnant with twins. "So you can understand how I would misplace it."

"Je-sus, twins!" exclaims the girl, ringing open the cash register.

"Yes, I was thinking perhaps of calling them Bella and Lidia if they are girls."

"We had twins in my high school. You won't believe *their* names. Raoul and Bertha Controla. Bertha Controla. Could you like die?"

◆

"This is Lidia's kind of game," I tell Jim Spaniel one afternoon over tamales. He has invited me to lunch to discuss what Lidia has told him is her new career.

"Buying blouses on sale at one store and selling them back to another one at full price?"

"She also does shoes and lingerie," I say.

"Terrific. This all happens to be completely illegal. Does she know she can go to jail?" In a short-sleeved blue-striped shirt, his pale face corrugated with worry, Jim looks like an inmate himself. He says he has lost sleep during the past three weeks. In the morning he gives Lidia fifty dollars, and in the evening, when he comes home, she has hundreds of dollars' worth of clothing piled on the sofa. "I understand what she's going through," he says, reaching for a napkin to shred. "I'm no stranger to the problems of Soviet émigrés. The difficulties of adjusting to a new culture, dealing with Western decadence, the sudden availability of goods. I even realize that she misses her black-market involvement. But she can't behave this way. She's here now. This is L.A., not some Tashkent bazaar."

"I don't know. To me it seems she has gotten back in her personality the kick and sparkle she had in Moscow."

"You want kick and sparkle? This keeps up, I'll show her some kick and sparkle."

I tell Jim Spaniel I will talk to her. Instead I borrow his car one day after school and take her to the garment district downtown.

——

These big warehouses have no air conditioning, and every outlet reeks of perfumed sweat and frying hamburgers from the snack bar. I prefer my stores tranquil: soothing music, thick carpeting, private dressing rooms. Lidia, however, was born for such a rough-and-tumble consumer workout as this. In one and a half hours, she emerges from Bob's Discount House of Polyester lugging four sweaters, a leather vest, five poly-blend blouses, and ten pairs of leather sandals from Milan. Her face is as radiant as a young mother bringing home her firstborn.

"Now where?" she chirps as I steer the car from the parking lot. She leans down and helps her toes swiggle into a new sandal and buckles it. The buckle comes off in her hand. She shrugs and drops it out the window.

I suggest lunch. There are good burgers at Cassell's, greasy piroshki at Gorky's.

"Uff, it's too hot. How can you even think about food? I want to meet your friend Cricket. She works around here, doesn't she?"

"She is busy. She can't always talk."

"Let's go anyway. We can buy some Godiva chocolate."

As we enter Trendsetter Sportswear, I see Cricket standing behind the counter, folding bright cotton sweaters and talking on the phone. Her head is bent, the receiver clamped to her shoulder with the aid of her small, pointed chin. She is listening, and while she waits for her turn to talk, she mouths the words to a rock-and-roll song coming from a television mounted near the ceiling. The television portrays three singing boys in black leather driving motorcycles around Greek ruins.

Lidia stops halfway to the counter, diverted by some lovely cranberry-colored silk blouses. She flips through the rack wildly. "Bellinka," she says, "these blouses!"

Cricket looks up, startled. I wave to her. Despite the music and Lidia's chatter, I am close enough to hear her whisper into the receiver: "Oh, God, Molly, you won't believe who's here. The Russian pest."

I pretend to watch the boys on television. They hurl one of the motorcycles over a cliff. They sing: "You're a one-woman torture chamber, got my heart on the rack."

Cricket gets off the telephone. She knows I hear, so she becomes official. "If you ladies would like me to start a dressing room for you today, just let me know."

"I would like to return this blouse," says Lidia. As she approaches the counter, she pulls one of her cheap outlet blouses from her handbag. "See?"

"I can't do that," says Cricket.

"My receipt, I had it as bookmark in book which I returned to library."

"You didn't get that here. It's from Bob's Discount House of Polyester."

"No, is from here."

"I'm sorry, but I can't take anything back without a receipt."

"But I just explained about receipt. The book was overdue."

"Lidia, please," I finally say. "This is Cricket. You shouldn't give her a bad time."

"So this is our Cricket! I am Lidia Nikolaevna, Bella's friend from Moscow."

Cricket picks up the sweaters she was folding and hugs them to her chest. "Please leave. I can't help you."

"Then perhaps the question is how can I help you? At home I have lovely Calvin Klein blue jeans that look just your size. And a gorgeous pink sweater, hand-knitted from People's Republic of China. Hand-knitted, Cricketchka! Imagine how luxurious! It would look stunning on you, emphasize the nice figure. Make the boyfriend swoon. If you make a refund on this blouse, I fix you up with an entire outfit. You be czarina of the high school. Cricketchka. Crinketinka."

Cricket puts the sweaters down. Her eyes are averted, her shoulders stiff with discomfort and fear. She picks up the telephone and dials the department of security.

◆

Two weeks later, the lemon tree looks better. I have learned the trick of not too much sunlight, not too much shade, not too much water, not too much dry. One night, I decide it's time to distribute Yuz's ashes. I retrieve his shoebox from the bottom of my closet. It is late, past the late movie, and I jump when the doorbell rings. It's Lidia. She has suitcases. She comes inside without saying hello and asks, "Can I come live with you?"

"If you do not mind some of Yuz's things still around."

"*Spasiba*, Bellinka." She stares down at the shoebox in my hand. She tilts her head to read the end of the box. "The moss-green pumps. My favorite."

"They are good shoes. Faithful. Come, I'll show you where to put your things."

I don't ask what happened with Jim Spaniel. After he came and straightened us out with the department store security officer, he stopped bringing Lidia to work with him. I assume he also displayed to her the threatened kick and sparkle.

I show her how to use the washing machine in the basement and make a space on the balcony for another chair. During the day she watches the television. During the night she sets the alarm so she can get up and talk long distance to Moscow. I never get around to Yuz's ashes. The shoebox sits on the kitchen counter under a stack of magazines.

One day I come home from the Bullock's Thanksgiving Pre-Sale, to find a note:

Bella *doushka:*

My friend Arkady—you know, at *Pravda?*—he has pulled some strings and managed to get me back. I tried to call at the office but they said you were in class all day. I had to do it standby, so there was no time. Thank you for the past few weeks at your apartment. I hope you don't mind, I took those nice moss-green shoes. My lady who was looking for them will be ecstatic!

Love,
Lidia

I fold the note, then rip it in two. I sit down at the table, push back a cuticle with my thumbnail, pick some fuzz from the carpet. Strange. I notice that I am wearing my nice moss-green shoes.

Suddenly I see her, marching down Kalinin Prospekt. She

searches out the old customer, pulls her into an empty street and, touching her lips to an ear already raw from Moscow cold, whispers, "This is *nothing* compared to the other shoes of Los Angeles," or, "Look, just for you!" then finally, slowly, lifts the lid off the box, only to discover that instead of pumps, she has in her possession an urn in basic black and a pair of Soviet spectacles.

Poor Yuz, I think. All that effort to emigrate.

From my balcony, I can dispose of the lemon tree. I make a little ceremony of it, then drop it into the Dumpster, where it lands with a *thook*.

JOHN KEEBLE

I COULD
LOVE YOU
(IF I WANTED)

ola had decided to move out of the apartment that nestled in the shadow of the hospital tower where her mother lay dying. A real estate salesman came and drove her and her two little girls out to see a rental house in the country. He said the owners had installed a new roof and paid five hundred dollars to have the interior cleaned. The salesman was gaunt and skeletal. He wore a red vinyl coat and a blue ball cap that matched the color of the big blue Toronado which he steered with his fingertips. His name was Bob. When Lola caught him stealing looks at her, she gazed back evenly in order to thwart his interest. He glanced at her again, and then quickly away, which permitted her to inspect him. He had sallow skin, a mustache as thin as a pencil line, and a patch of stubble on the side of his jaw that he'd missed with his razor.

They drove through the trees and came out into the long evening light of autumn, then turned onto a lane that led to an old farmhouse. Bob told her that the place had stood empty for a year. They'd stripped out the carpeting, he said. But there was a new space heater in the living room and a fresh coat of sealant in the basement. When Lola got out of the car, she had to step around a jackhammer that had been left to rust on the ground. Bob came up beside her, lit a cigarette, and brushed her arm lightly as they started toward the house.

Lola looked at the wreckage: besides the jackhammer, the corrugated steel sections blowing away from the walls of the huge hay barn up on the rise to the left, an acetylene welder leaning against a tree, and in a ring like battlements around the house the hulks of cars and scores upon scores of abandoned tools. Her daughters, Yvette and

Nikki, scrambled over the fire-scorched foundation of a milking parlor. The house had weathered, silvery siding. Its new galvanized roof reflected the sky. The narrow, two-story building looked light, as if it were about to float away. Behind it were wheat fields. To the right, the ground sloped into a pasture where a dozen Holstein cows grazed. Their black-and-white coats glistened.

An iron fence encircled the house. Bob opened the gate and when Lola passed through, he leaned toward her and said, "We'll put in a new water heater, too." His coat squeaked in the cold. He blew out a cloud of cigarette smoke. The sweet odor filled Lola's nostrils. Inside the fence and up against the house, the flower beds were choked with weeds. The sinking sun glanced against the windows of the house, turning them into mirrors. Lola saw herself in one—black coat and hood, blonde hair, cream-colored face—and it seemed as if she were glimpsing a stranger.

Bob said that if she took the place he'd be pleased to come by to make sure everything was right. "I bet," Lola said acidly. She had never met this man before, but believed she knew him absolutely. At her words, his body rocked back, and she thought it remarkable . . . a man so thin his bones almost chimed against each other, so unlike her own Louis, who brimmed with life. Her daughters shrieked with mock fright as they swung inside the fence and ran toward her. Lola placed her hand on a wobbly banister, stepped up to the door, and peered inside through the window. She saw a dark plank floor and pale walls flooded with angular light, and to one side another doorway leading to an obscure room.

Lola turned back and said, "Two-fifty a month is too much. Look at this place."

"The inside is fine. You haven't even seen it," Bob said.

"I'd give you two-fifty if I had the rights of salvage to all the crap that's lying around. Then you'd get it cleaned up. It's going to snow. If you leave it, what's good will be ruined, and you'll have to pay somebody to haul it all out."

◆

To Lola's surprise, her proposal was accepted. She returned to her apartment, then walked to the hospital. She left the girls in the waiting room and went to see her mother. The old woman, Wanda, wanted out of bed, but her sickness had moved into her legs. They swelled and bled. She had hot and cold flashes. She had cancer in her liver. She wanted to have a tea party. She wanted to go out drinking. "Talk to me," she said. Lola began reading aloud from the *National Enquirer,* something about Kenny Rogers and his hundreds of women, and then the one about the lady who gave birth to a salamander. "The sky's the limit with these things," Lola interjected.

"Shut up," Wanda said.

Wanda forgot who was at her bedside, and yet she began to moan when Lola prepared to leave. Despite her resolution not to judge her mother and to hold her old outrage in abeyance, Lola was angry. Her mother twisted the sheet in her hands and contorted her ashen face. She said she wanted to take a drive, then she imagined that she was in a car, traveling with a man. "Let's go to Reno," she said to the imaginary man. To Lola, she said, "Me and Johnny have to go to Reno to gamble. It's Johnny Carson, you know. It's his last year, too. Excuse us." When she tried to climb out of bed, Lola pressed her back into the mattress and was amazed at how light her mother was, like a leaf. Wanda stared at Lola with her opaque eyes, and said, "Who are you?"

"You don't know? You don't know who I am?" Lola said.

It was a two-person room, divided by a white curtain. The high-pitched voice of the other old woman in the room spoke up from behind the curtain. "Yes, she does. Deep down truly she knows. You keep coming, honey. A mother needs a daughter."

◆

The next day, Lola rented a U-Haul trailer. Her friend, Fanny Blue, who lived on the same block, helped her carry her things to the street. Fanny was heavyset, kind, and a cousin of Louis'. She worked in a gift and secondhand shop owned by Louis' brother, Sam. Lola had worked in Sam's shop, too, before she got a better job at the department store. That was how she'd first met Fanny, and then Louis, and through Fanny she'd found this apartment close to the hospital for the sake of her mother's treatments. For a time, her mother had lived here with her. That was over. Two weeks ago, Lola lost her department store job. Fanny had said that Sam would hire her back, but Lola declined. Now, Fanny wanted to come along to help unload the trailer, but Lola lied, saying she would have help there.

"Of course. You have Louis," Fanny said hopefully. "Is he back in town?"

They stood at the rear of the trailer. Fanny had a low center of gravity and the smile on her face seemed connected by a stem to the bottom of her belly. She seemed to grow heavier and heavier, as if to counterbalance Lola's lie, then her expression grew sad. Lola felt sad, too, because to refuse Fanny's help was to insult her, because to lie to accomplish this was a yet deeper insult. Lola felt trapped. It seemed as if the earth were tipping under the sheer weight of Fanny's generous nature, and yet Lola couldn't bring herself to say that all she wanted in the world just now was to be alone with her daughters, to get away to some place where she didn't have to look at the hospital tower every time she stood at her kitchen sink, not even to see Louis unless she chose to.

She grasped the handle that latched the trailer door and listened as the girls chanted from the front seat of her old Chrysler, which was hitched to the trailer, "We love our Mama. We love our Mama. Let's go. Let's go."

Lola stared at the sidewalk where someone had spray-painted a swastika. "I have to change my life, Fanny."

"Listen," Fanny said. "When someone you love dies, their presence changes form. But they're still with you. You'll be all right." Fanny's face was broad, brown, and soft as flour. She had three red ribbons tied into her black hair.

Lola wondered why what Fanny said alarmed rather than reassured her. "I'll come by," she said. "Right away. You'll see." Her eyes welled with tears because Fanny was her friend and she was still lying to her.

She moved quickly to her car, started it, and drove out of the valley. In the distance the mountains stood against the sky. The trailer made her old Chrysler handle like a boat. Nikki and Yvette became still as waiting spiders. Lola headed west. They crossed the river and entered the woods, then the road wound through the mound country. Soon, Lola turned onto the gravel lane and parked next to her new house. The girls leaped out of the car and ran in ever-widening circles, farther and farther away until their delighted shouts sounded like the cries of crows.

Lola unloaded everything herself—boxes, kitchen table, easy chair. She pulled her mattresses out of the trailer and dragged them through the gate, up to the porch, and inside. She did the same with her sofa, dragged it to the porch, then shifted from one end to the other in order to jockey it up the steps. When she had it close to the door she threw herself down on it, lay back, and stared upwards. The sun turned the sky above the horizon a metallic lemon color. Otherwise, the sky was slate-blue. Small, puffy clouds floated by. A flock of geese passed beneath the clouds. They made a racket with their honking. She watched and thought about how they must have been talking among themselves, that what she heard might actually be a contentious conversation over the next, best place to stop and eat, although from the ground the flock looked like a single, serrated V.

Nikki and Yvette had gone into the house. Their running footsteps reverberated in the rooms. The moldy odor of the ancient, flowered wallpaper wafted through the screen door. The footsteps of her daughters talked to her as if they were played upon a drum. This is how it should be, Lola thought as she listened to her daughters and the dwindling racket of the geese heading south.

◆

People had always said Lola was smart. Back in high school, her counselor had asked why she got A's one semester and F's the next. Lola couldn't answer. The counselor told her she should think of college. "Look," he'd said in exasperation. "Your test scores are awfully high. What is it?"

It was the lack of hope. Her mother was a drinker. As a girl, Lola had lived in one place after another with one man after another moving in for a year, a few months, or sometimes for a week or two. She had grown exhausted, seeking the father she'd never known in these men, and seeking him not just for herself, but also to be the ballast, the counterweight to the wildly listing life of her mother. Sometimes, Lola had to care for her mother as if her mother were the child, taking her cure of orange juice, toast, and long, heavy sleeps.

A year after high school Lola was married. A year later she was divorced. In three years she had Yvette out of wedlock, and then Nicole. The fathers of the girls had also dropped off the edge of the earth. Her mother came to visit, once, from her home a hundred miles to the north. Not yet ill, her mother announced that it had only taken one baby to teach her how to get an abortion. Stunned at first, and speechless, Lola was just now beginning to understand that it was a falsehood, a profound lie by which her mother's life had been governed. Lola required her daughters, although she had Louis, too, in his way, floating at the far edge of a whirlpool that turned slowly around her, but it was the girls she held close in the powerful eye of the vortex.

Lola was good with numbers. People at the department store said they'd never seen anybody learn the computer so fast. She'd been assigned to train new workers, but then she was fired for absenteeism. It was because attending to her children and her mother became too much to manage. Lola told that to her supervisor, not to gain sympathy, but because it was the truth. The supervisor, a well-kept woman with many sharp edges—tailored suit, crisp blouse, sharp chin, plucked eyebrows, and glasses with rectangular frames—said, "Maybe we can hire you back when you get your life in order."

"Whose order?" Lola said. "Where do you keep it?"

The supervisor's eyebrows went up. "I beg your pardon."

Lola liked numbers. She liked the certainty of numbers, the way they became a part of a day, as domestic as teaspoons, hours, and miles to go. She also felt drawn to the flimsiness of the world of numbers, the chaos at its heart. She saw numbers in her dreams, phosphorescent, flooding from the mouths of the people in her life.

◀━━

She returned the trailer to town that evening, went by McDonald's, then drove to the Saddle Inn to meet Louis. He was a trucker. She saw his rig, the Lodestar tractor and his grain trailer, pulled up at the edge of the road. Lola parked near the front door where Nikki and Yvette could watch the lighted Hamm's beer sign in which a yellow canoe dropped again and again over a blue waterfall. The night had turned cold. She let the girls open the McDonald's bag with its load of hamburgers and French fries, then dumped a heap of blankets over them and gave them strict instructions not to move, not to argue, not to unlock the doors for anybody. "Count the canoe," she told them. "How many times it goes over."

They began immediately: "One. Two."

Inside, she found Louis in a booth against the wall. When she slid in opposite him, he filled a glass from a pitcher of beer, pushed it toward her, and said, "I'm surprised you came. Who do you think you are? The Queen of England?"

"I'm here," she said.

He had black hair and a dark, pockmarked face that looked like it was carved out of wood. He smiled. He often smiled, but his face could change expressions behind the smile. It was as if there was a river running behind the mask of wood. He wore a leather vest with big silver buttons and under it a plaid shirt that was open over his smooth chest. To one side, his gray Stetson rested upside down on its crown. His eyes held points of light.

"I'm moving," she said.

"I'll help you."

"I have moved," she said.

He gazed at her. "I got a new run that gives me three days off a week. We could go up to the hot springs."

"Mama's back in the hospital," she said.

Louis made a silvery sound in his throat.

Lola took a sip of beer and looked away. From the beam above the bar hung old lanterns, bridles, harnesses, and dangerous-looking tools, shears, prods, hooks, branding irons, and hunks of chain attached to metal hasps. Behind the back bar was a gun display. Four men in cowboy hats sat at the bar. A man and woman were next to each other in a booth near the door. The woman was closest to the wall, but Lola could see that the man had his hand on her leg. An image of her mother flashed into her mind—the tall woman flat as a board under the sheets with the ravaged face like a tattered flower sticking out the top.

Louis placed five twenty dollar bills on the table and looked expectantly at her. "Maybe we need some fun."

She stared at the bills. It was more than she had to get to her next unemployment check. Louis made good money. He was thirty-eight, married, and his wife, Rose, kept the books for the hauling operation. Between Louis and Rose there was a complicated equation into which she—Lola—had somehow been entered. She supposed that Louis' play money was allowed to leak out in order to keep the relationship from hemorrhaging. For two years Lola had lived for Louis' arrivals, for the hardness of his body. She liked to submit to him. She had grown attached to the sadness that swept through her when he left, the way her other problems passed away as she dwelled upon the trouble he always brought, the way the trouble made her life stop and hang as if between heartbeats, the way it pushed her through that hiatus into the jungle of herself, deep into the thick of the dark, absolute wild.

The bench creaked as Louis leaned back. Lola sat poised, touching her arms lightly to the table. He squinted at her and slowly tapped his glass with a fingernail. They sat that way, eyeing each other, until Lola finally said, "I need to be alone."

Louis made the silvery sound again, deep in his throat. It was a sound like heavy coins shifting in a purse. Lola looked down at her hands, stretched out to touch her glass. She looked up at an old axletree nailed to the wall, then at the jewel-studded saddle that hung over the jukebox and wondered how much it was worth. Louis leaned forward on his elbows. "You think you do. But you don't. Not now."

"You don't know what I think."

"People in pain shouldn't be alone."

"Who are you to talk about pain?"

"It ain't natural to be alone like that when you're in pain. It ain't safe, either."

"You cause me pain."

"Look," he said softly. "Sometimes, it's damn hard to tell whose pain is rightfully whose. What do you want?"

"Nothing."

He smiled. "Everybody wants something." Behind the smile the waters churned.

"I could . . ." she began, then stopped.

"Could what?" When she didn't answer, he said, "Besides, I know where you're moving to. It's the Bodines' old place. Fanny saw the realtor's sign on the car that picked you up. I called the office. I want to help."

Lola's teeth felt huge inside her mouth. It was how she'd felt as a girl when her mother left her with the produce man who beat her with his pale, clean hands that smelled of lettuce. She remembered the produce man telling her again and again to do what she was told. The tavern jumped in her vision. The hooks, prods, and chains grew distinct. She looked at the woman in the booth by the door. The woman had a narrow face. Her head was thrown back and her mouth was open like a pit. Her partner was turned toward her, crouched like a leopard. Finally, Lola gazed fixedly at the broad backs of the four men at the bar. They were utterly still, heavy as iron on their stools.

Louis touched her hand. "Let me help." In his mouth, a gold tooth glimmered and his eyes glinted like shards of glass. It was as if light came from behind the dark beautiful mask.

"No," she said. Louis had never hurt her, and yet she knew that if she stayed here she would give in and travel back through the shadows to the jungle. At the same time she wanted to touch the softness of Louis' skin between the scars on his face, to feel the smoothness of his chest, the fine hairs on his belly, to stroke the earth-color of his body, to feel his callused hands holding her, to make her pain pivot upon his dark flesh. She was filled with desire. Suddenly, she stood. Her legs shook wildly. "Don't you see that I could love you?" she said.

"Easy," he said, looking up at her.

"I could love you, if I wanted to." Her voice broke. It seemed as if something within her were about to explode.

"Easy, honey," he said. His eyes glittered.

She lurched away. She glimpsed him sliding out of the booth behind her. She stumbled through the tavern doorway to her car. She looked back and saw Louis silhouetted in the doorway. The light from within shone around his head and body and between his legs. Lola put the key into the lock, opened her car door, and slid in. The two small faces in the front seat tipped up toward her like plates.

"Ten million!" Yvette announced.

"It's Louis. Look!" Nikki cried. She sat up straight and waved frantically.

The next day, Lola drove into the city to visit her mother.

"It's Rodney," her mother said.

"Rodney?"

"Hi, sweetie," said the old woman behind the curtain.

"Dangerfield, you idiot," her mother said, wheezing with laughter. It sounded as if she were choking.

"Mama, please, no," Lola said.

"Get it?" her mother said. "The fields of danger. What happened to him? Where'd he go? My Rodney." She stopped and rolled her eyes slowly from one side to the other, then said, "We're having our drugs. We're taking our drugs." Slowly, her mother reached over to her tray and lifted a glass of water. The glass trembled in her hand. "Drugs," she said. "More drugs. They've got us drugged. Trapped in our drugs. We want our drugs. We like our drugs." She dumped the water onto her face. "Drugs!" she shouted hoarsely.

A nurse hurried in.

"More drugs," Lola's mother moaned.

"You've had your medicine," the nurse said.

"We want more. The pain is killing us." Lola's mother began to laugh again. "Get it? Killing us. Me and Rodney. He's clawing his way back." She gazed at Lola. "What do you want, you little whore?"

The voice of the old lady behind the curtain piped up: "She doesn't mean it. She's not herself. She needs you."

Lola was filled with despair. A doctor came and took her out into the hall. He was a young man hardly older than Lola herself. Lola understood that in the medical profession the young were allowed to cut their teeth on welfare cases. He had a smooth, fleshy face and probably drove a BMW. He said her mother was fading quickly, that the best they could do now was ease the pain, that perhaps if her condition stabilized she might go home with Lola. The hospice people could visit to help, he said.

Home!—Lola thought. It's my home!

But for now, the doctor said, it would not be wise to move her mother. Until that very moment, Lola hadn't believed that her mother would actually die.

It began to snow as she drove through the city. Darkness fell. The city had on its Christmas lights, the tiny white lights on the trees that bordered the streets. Snowflakes danced in light and swirled against the buildings. On the open road outside the city, the snowflakes raced by the windshield. Lola and the girls pretended they were in a spaceship and that the snowflakes were stars. The girls lost themselves in the phantasm.

Lola thought about the infinity of stars. She'd read that this universe was connected to another by a pipe, that the two universes were mirrors of each other, and that at any moment one might rush into the other. Only gravity kept everything just barely arranged. Infinity was chaos. She wondered how things would be if people just did away with it, if there were no infinity but only the known piling up higher and higher like wheat. Maybe infinity was nothing more than a bad turn taken after a pretty good idea, like the bomb. She wondered if the way her mother's life kept rushing into her own would end after the death.

◆

Lola did not want to bring her mother to her house, but that night she cleaned as if it were foreordained. It was doom she felt, made out of the old contradiction: the necessity that she care, and her resistance to that compulsion. There were tack marks around the edge of the hardwood floor in the living room. The kitchen linoleum had tears in it. Dirt was still caked to the kickspace under the counters and in the corners of the windowsills. Everywhere she looked she found dirt, and sometimes even bits of what she thought was dung. She scrubbed the crevices with a brush and washed the floors with bleach. She soaked the stovetop parts in the sink. Fumes filled the rooms. She played a Dead Kennedys tape on her stereo, and then The Cure. The girls followed her about, filled with wonder at the fury of her energy. Angrily, Lola told them to go play, but immediately called them back, knelt, and hugged them, bringing her head down between their heads. "I'm sorry," she said. "It's not your fault."

She turned off the stereo, pushed the couch to the center of the living room floor, set up the TV for the girls to watch, and resumed her work. In the corners of cupboards, she found remnants of the previous occupants: a bowl, two dishes, a can of cayenne, cutlery, a shoebox full of jewelry. She gave the box to the girls. She cleaned her bedroom for her mother, she who might or might not come, who Lola did not want here. She stacked her own boxes of things tightly against a wall. If necessary, she could sleep on the couch. High on a shelf in the closet she found a carton. When she opened the flaps, the smell of mothballs assaulted her nose.

She found a woman's sealskin coat within, wrapped tightly in oilcloth. She laid it on the bed, unfolded it, and tried it on. The crimson lining slid along her arms. The coat reached her knees. It had thick shoulder pads in the old style. The collar felt luxurious against her neck. The black fur shone. When she stroked it, the fur coursed deeply between her fingers. She hugged herself in the coat and threw her head back. If she took it to Louis' brother, Sam, he could get at least two hundred for it. She walked to the living room and modeled it for Nikki and Yvette.

"Look at that thing," Yvette said.

"It's animal fur," Lola said. "Seal."

Nikki said, "They do tricks. They swim like nobody's business."

"It keeps them warm in the cold ocean," Lola said as she sat between the girls.

The girls touched the coat and pressed their faces into it. Lola liked the way their elbows and knees poked at her as they squirmed. The girls went to sleep against her, under her arms. Their birthdates fell in such a way that they would both start kindergarten next year. Lola liked to think of them being bound up with each other forever as if they were twins. She reached out with her foot and poked off the TV, and sat that way for a long time, as warm as toast. Outside, the snow fell steadily. She could hear the wind in the trees and the snow hissing against the eaves. It's a storm—she thought. Thank God!

◆

It snowed all night and continued into the next day. By morning, everything was white outside. The fields were white. The roofs were white. The limbs of the trees sagged under the white weight. Lola had dressed the girls in their snowsuits and sent them out to play, then went out herself. She loaded the jackhammer in a wheelbarrow she'd found. The jackhammer lay there, a pig of a thing with its hydraulic hosing coiled on top of it. Laboriously, she pushed it up the slope to store in a dry corner of the hay barn. Nikki and Yvette followed her, pulling plastic sleds.

Lola unloaded the jackhammer in a corner where she already had a small cache of things—a set of socket wrenches, screwdrivers, battery charger, an electric drill, a power saw, a portable air compressor she'd dragged up on its broken wheels . . . She'd wiped them down with oil and laid them out in a line on a tarp. It pleased her to see them, bright against the green canvas, the consequence of a deal cut on a whim. She intended to make money.

She tipped the jackhammer out of the wheelbarrow and laid it on the tarp next to the compressor, then rolled the wheelbarrow back to the bay of the hay barn and watched Yvette and Nikki hurtle down the slope. Their sleds careened away from each other, returned, bumped and crossed paths. They skidded on yesterday's ice and plowed through today's snow, out of control. At the bottom, the sleds crashed and the girls tumbled off. Afraid for them, Lola leaned forward, but then she heard their laughter. Beyond them, beyond the house, lay the white hayfield from which the cows had been withdrawn. A sheet of snow abruptly slid off the steel roof of the house and a small flock of finches that had been searching for seed on the ground fluttered into the air. Off to the side, she heard a truck laboring. The girls scrambled to their feet and ran toward the lane.

A gray flatbed with an orange snowblade appeared and stopped. The girls danced at its side. The door swung open and Louis stepped down, holding a shiny, aluminum case. The girls led him toward the house. She heard their excited voices rising and falling and Louis's low voice, punctuating theirs. They were telling him about the house. The three passed through the iron gate and out of view. Lola heard the front door open and shut. For a moment, Lola didn't move, then she walked down, went inside, and found Louis and the girls sitting on the living room couch. They stopped talking when she entered.

"Thank you," Lola said. "For plowing, I mean. But I have chains." She had a sinking feeling. Although the chains would do for today's wet snow, she'd need to find a way to have the road plowed in the future.

Louis grinned. "I knew that name was familiar. Bodine. The old fart. He had a fire." He gestured over his shoulder. "Did you see the shit lying around out there?"

"I can give you some coffee," Lola said. She realized that if she told Louis about her salvage deal, he would want to help. And he could help. With his trucks, he'd make it easy. He would take it over. If she kept it secret and he hung around, he'd start poking through the equipment for himself and take it over that way. She knew him. She looked at her watch and said, "Then I have to go."

"Sure."

Lola walked into the kitchen.

Louis followed and said, "It was the wood chips the old guy used to bed down his cows. That's how I knew him, delivering wood chips a few years ago."

Lola poured the coffee and set it on the kitchen table. The girls came in and she poured juice for them. The four of them sat down. Louis set his case on the floor, took off his Stetson, and carefully perched it on the table. "You got to watch those chips," he said. "They rot. You get rot, then fire. Sometimes people don't care what the hell happens."

When he pulled the snaps of his leather coat apart, Lola smelled the whiskey in his sweat. He said he'd heard that once the fire started, the old man had turned his cows loose, then started throwing tools out the barn door. He kept going back into the flames to throw out more tools. "He lost his parlor, burned clean down to the stubs, but saved the tools and then left them. I guess he never touched the tools again except what he needed for the boat."

"Boat?" Lola said.

"Boat?" Louis said, mimicking her. Yvette and Nikki squirmed in their chairs and looked up happily at Louis, whom they liked because he made them laugh. Lola stared at her hands.

"An old logging tug," Louis said. "He sold off his herd, bought the boat and refitted it. He called and asked if I would haul it over to Seattle for him, but I couldn't. His old lady'd died and it broke him up. I heard he was planning to spend the rest of his life in his boat, fishing and floating wherever he wanted." Nikki reached out and put her small hand on top of Louis's weathered one. Louis got a faraway look in his eyes. "Claude," he said softly. "That's it. Claude Bodine."

Lola looked out a kitchen window at the snow. She thought about a man who loved his wife with such steadiness that when he lost her, he left everything to rust and rot and set out for the high seas. She pictured such a man . . . his silver hair tufting out from beneath a seaman's hat and a craggy, resolute face set against the wind and spray, the eyes gazing past the roiling waves into the distance. "So?" she said.

Louis cocked his head like a crow. "Why did you move here?"

"I like the country."

"There's picnics for that."

"It's cheaper than the apartment."

"What're you going to do when your unemployment runs out?"

"Get work. Maybe go to school."

He squinted at her. "From here?"

"Look, my mother might be dead now," Lola said. "If I had a phone they might have called by now to tell me she's dead. If she's not, I may bring her here."

Nikki and Yvette had fallen still. They gazed at their mother, then at Louis when he spoke.

"That's crazy."

"Maybe," Lola said. "But the next time I go in, she may be dead. Maybe today. Don't you see?"

"Sure," Louis said. He reached down for his aluminum case and set it on the table. He unsnapped the latches and opened the case. It was stuffed with clothes. From the bottom, he pulled out a binder and set it on the table in front of Lola. "There."

"I can't have you here."

He flipped open the binder. She looked down at a page that was filled with numbers, written in a neat, round hand in black ink. "I'm out of my place," he said. "Rose said I could take my clothes, my truck, whatever I wanted, but if I took the titles and books she was through with me. That was the line, and I crossed it."

"You cross the line with her all the time," Lola said.

"Not this line. Look, I got my car over at Fanny's place. My rig's at Sam's. What is it? You want me to beg? Shit!"

They stared at each other. The mask of his face was as shiny as polished wood in the hard white light of the kitchen. He raised his arms and set his elbows on the table and cocked his head to one side again. He looked like a big crow, rustling as it adjusted its wings. He scrutinized her sideways and closely. His eyes sparked with the rapacious intelligence of a crow, looking to see what could be taken. Lola had read that crows were smarter than dogs. If they were that smart —she thought—and since the root of their intelligence was finally unknown, no one understood just how smart they really were. Louis was suddenly a complete mystery to her. A week ago, Lola would have taken him in and been glad for it. Even now, she felt the old trigger of her wildness about to be pulled. If it were pulled, she might accept him. She could feel his energy, electric and full, swelling across the table. She stayed as she was, rapt in her sense of being watched, waiting to hear if the trigger in her cocked back. It did not. For her, his mystery transformed into a void. "No," she said. "I can't."

His expression didn't change.

"Please Mama," Yvette said.

"No. Go home, Louis. Keep what you have."

◆

Lola drove to town. The packed snow squeaked under her tires. At the hospital, she led Nikki and Yvette into the elevator. The girls' eyes widened and they smiled as the elevator shot up the tower. Lola situated them in the waiting area, went to her mother's room, and found her curled up on her side, moaning, "There. There. Yes." Her mother writhed and moaned, "There. There. You're wonderful." A nurse was in the room. The other elderly lady lay in her bed over by the window, her form silhouetted behind the curtain. "Touch me there. Yes, there," her mother said. "There," she said. "Everywhere."

The nurse had thick eyebrows and a dark, downy mustache. Her eyes were set wide apart. She had acne scars on her cheeks. She was perhaps the homeliest woman Lola had ever seen, but Lola envied her, her job, her white dress, white shoes, and white hose. The nurse smiled. She had a husky, sweet, melodious voice. "Wanda must have been a player in her day," she said.

Lola thought: Wanda was a waitress, a barmaid, and not a stupid woman, but she changed the sheets in motels, too, stood in the lines and served countless men. All she ever wanted was to be a player. She's my mother, for God's sake! Lola looked around the room with its cream walls and steel fixtures. "Can I take her out of here?" she asked.

Her mother went on moaning: "There. Touch me there."

The nurse said, "No. Not yet."

"Will I be able to?"

"She's not doing well. The doctor will soon be up to talk to you."

Lola moved to the bed and placed her hand on her mother's shoulder. The old woman stank of medicine and decay. The nurse slipped out of the room. Lola thought that along with Johnny Carson, Rodney Dangerfield, and whoever else, Tony Bennett, maybe, or Joe DiMaggio, it might be any one of the actual men her mother dreamt of: the lumberman, logger, the lineman, the produce man with the decontaminated hands, the hardware salesman. . . . From each of these, her many fathers, Lola learned a fear, and the fears had become a gauntlet through which she had to repeatedly run.

She looked into her mother's haggard face and wondered if all the men had entered together to make one complicated male creature in her mother's mind, like a griffin. The long, ravaged body was outlined like a ledge beneath the sheet. Lola thought: I need this woman to be here just this once. Slowly, her mother turned her head and looked up at Lola. Her lips moved, forming the words: "Touch me."

Lola thought: I want to take you home, you and your many men. We could be together for a while in the wrecked house. You could make as much noise as you want and have a few drinks and take a drive and carouse and fall out of your bed. What the hell. We could turn up the music.

"Touch me here," her mother whispered in her ragged voice.

Lola thought: She's lost in her need, her life distilled to the one relentless desire.

"Touch me," her mother whispered.

Lola held her mother's arms.

"Touch me."

Lola touched her cheek to her mother's head. She thought of things she could do if her mother came home with her, a mental list: she needed a dresser, another bed, a tray for her mother to eat from. Wheelchair. Flowers to place in the window against the light. She spoke into her mother's ear, "I could love you there."

"Touch me."

From the other side of the room, the other old woman spoke out in her squeaky voice: "If you ask me, she's lucky to have a beautiful daughter like you."

"Touch me."

"I love you, Mama," Lola said. She thought her voice might be mistaken for the voice of the desired, composite one and so enter her mother's crazed interior. She considered herself in there, spinning along the wild routes. The trigger in her clicked and she felt as free as a goddess, breathing in the corrupt breath of the dead. "If I can, I'll take you home."

BARBARA KINGSOLVER

WHY I AM
A DANGER TO
THE PUBLIC

*B*ueno, if I get backed into a corner I can just about raise up the dead. I'll fight, sure. But I am no lady wrestler. If you could see me you would know this thing is a *joke*—Tony, my oldest, is already taller than me, and he's only eleven. So why are they so scared of me I have to be in jail? I'll tell you.

Number one, this strike. There has never been one that turned so many old friends *chingándose,* not here in Bolton. And you can't get away from it because Ellington don't just run the mine, they own our houses, the water we drink and the dirt in our shoes and pretty much the state of New Mexico as I understand it. So if something is breathing, it's on one side or the other. And in a town like this that matters because everybody you know some way, you go to the same church or they used to baby-sit your kids, something. Nobody is a stranger.

My sister went down to Las Cruces, New Mexico, and got a job down there, but me, no. I stayed here and got married to Junior Morales. Junior was my one big mistake. But I like Bolton. From far away Bolton looks like some kind of all-colored junk that got swept up off the street after a big old party and stuffed down in the canyon. Our houses are all exactly alike, company houses, but people paint them yellow, purple, colors you wouldn't think a house could be. If you go down to the Big Dipper and come walking home *loca* you still know which one is yours. The copper mine is at the top of the canyon and the streets run straight uphill; some of them you can't drive up, you got to walk. There's steps. Oliver P. Snapp, that used to be the mailman for the west side, died of a heart attack one time right out there in his blue shorts. So the new mailman refuses to deliver to those houses; they have to pick up their mail at the P.O.

Now, this business with me and Vonda Fangham, I can't even tell you what got it started. I never had one thing in the world against her, no more than anybody else did. But this was around the fourth or fifth week so everybody knew by then who was striking and who was crossing. It don't take long to tell rats from cheese, and every night there was a big old fight in the Big Dipper. Somebody punching out his brother or his best friend. All that and no paycheck, can you imagine?

So it was a Saturday and there was just me and Corvallis Smith up at the picket line, setting in front of the picket shack passing the time of day. Corvallis is *un tipo*, he is real tall and lifts weights and wears his hair in those corn rows that hang down in the back with little pieces of aluminum foil on the ends. But good-looking in a certain way. I went out with Corvallis one time just so people would have something to talk about, and sure enough, they had me getting ready to have brown and black polka-dotted babies. All you got to do to get pregnant around here is have two beers with somebody in the Dipper, so watch out.

"What do you hear from Junior?" he says. That's a joke; every-body says it, including my friends. See, when Manuela wasn't hardly even born one minute and Tony still in diapers, Junior says, "Vicki, I can't find a corner to piss in around this town." He said there was jobs in Tucson and he would send a whole lot of money. Ha-ha. That's how I got started up at Ellington. I was not going to support my kids in no little short skirt down at the Frosty King. That was eight years ago. I got started on the track gang, laying down rails for the cars that go into the pit, and now I am a crane operator. See, when Junior left I went up the hill and made such a rackus they had to hire me up there, hire me or shoot me, one.

"Oh, I hear from him about the same as I hear from Oliver P. Snapp," I say to Corvallis. That's the rest of the joke.

It was a real slow morning. Cecil Smoot was supposed to be on the picket shift with us but he wasn't there yet. Cecil will show up late when the Angel Gabriel calls the Judgment, saying he had to give his Datsun a lube job.

"Well, looka here," says Corvallis. "Here come the ladies." There is this club called Wives of Working Men, just started since the strike. Meaning Wives of Scabs. About six of them was coming up the hill all cram-packed into Vonda Fangham's daddy's air-condition Lincoln. She pulls the car right up next to where mine is at. My car is a Buick older than both my two kids put together. It gets me where I have to go.

They set and look at us for one or two minutes. Out in that hot sun, sticking to our T-shirts, and me in my work boots—I can't see no point in treating it like a damn tea party—and Corvallis, he's an eyeful anyway. All of a sudden the windows on the Lincoln all slide down. It has those electric windows.

"Isn't this a ni-i-ce day," says one of them, Doreen Carter. Doreen visited her sister in Laurel, Mississippi, for three weeks one time and now she has an accent. "Bein' payday an' all," she says. Her husband is the minister of Saint's Grace, which is scab headquarters. I quit going. I was raised up to believe in God and the union, but listen, if it comes to pushing or shoving I know which one of the two is going to keep tires on the car.

"Well, yes, it is a real nice day," another one of them says. They're all fanning theirselves with something paper. I look, and Corvallis looks. They're fanning theirselves with their husbands' paychecks.

I haven't had a paycheck since July. My son couldn't go to Morse with his baseball team Friday night because they had to have three dollars for supper at McDonald's. Three damn dollars.

The windows start to go back up and they're getting ready to drive off, and I say, "Vonda Fangham, *vete al infierno.*"

The windows whoosh back down.

"What did you say?" Vonda wants to know.

"I said, I'm surprised to see you in there with the scab ladies. I didn't know you had went and got married to a yellow-spine scab just so somebody would let you in their club."

Well, Corvallis laughs at that. But Vonda just gives me this look. She has a little sharp nose and yellow hair and teeth too big to fit behind her lips. For some reason she was a big deal in high school, and it's not her personality, either. She was the queen of everything. Cheerleaders, drama club, every school play they ever had, I think.

I stare at her right back, ready to make a day out of it if I have to. The heat is rising up off that big blue hood like it's a lake all set to boil over.

"What I said was, Vonda Fangham, you can go to hell."

"I can't hear a word you're saying," she says. "Trash can't talk."

"This trash can go to bed at night and know I haven't cheated nobody out of a living. You want to see trash, *chica*, you ought to come up here at the shift change and see what kind of shit rolls over that picket line."

Well, that shit I was talking about was their husbands, so up go the windows and off they fly. Vonda just about goes in the ditch trying to get that big car turned around.

To tell you the truth I knew Vonda was engaged to get married to Tommy Jones, a scab. People said, Well, at least now Vonda will be just Vonda Jones. That name Fangham is *feo*, and the family has this whole certain way of showing off. Her dad's store, Fangham Drugs, has the biggest sign in town, as if he has to advertise. As if somebody would forget it was there and drive fifty-one miles over the mountains to Morse to go to another drugstore.

I couldn't care less about Tommy and Vonda getting engaged, I was just hurt when he crossed the line. Tommy was a real good man, I used to think. He was not ashamed like most good-looking guys are to act decent every once in a while. Me and him started out on the same track crew and he saved my butt one time covering the extra weight for me when I sprang my wrist. And he never acted like I owed him for it. Some guys, they would try to put the moves on me out by the slag pile. Shit, that was hell. And then I would be downtown in the drugstore and Carol Finch or somebody would go *huh-hmm*, clear her throat and roll her eyes, like, "Over here is what you want," looking at the condoms. Just because I'm up there with their husbands all day I am supposed to be screwing around. In all that mud, just think about it, in our steel toe boots that weigh around ten pounds, and our hard hats. And then the guys gave me shit, too, when I started training as a crane operator, saying a woman don't have no business taking up the good-paying jobs. You figure it out.

Tommy was different. He was a lone ranger. He didn't grow up here or have family, and in Bolton you can move in here and live for about fifty years and people still call you that fellow from El Paso, or wherever it was you come from. They say that's why he went in, that he was afraid if he lost his job he would lose Vonda, too. But we all had something to lose.

◆

That same day I come home and found Manuela and Tony in the closet. Like poor little kitties in there setting on the shoes. Tony was okay pretty much but Manuela was crying, screaming. I thought she would dig her eyes out.

Tony kept going, "They was up here looking for you!"

"Who was?" I asked him.

"Scab men," he said. "Clifford Owens and Mr. Alphonso and them police from out of town. The ones with the guns."

"The State Police?" I said. I couldn't believe it. "The State Police was up here? What did they want?"

"They wanted to know where you was at." Tony almost started to cry. "Mama, I didn't tell them."

"He didn't," Manuela said.

"Well, I was just up at the damn picket shack. Anybody could have found me if they wanted to." I could have swore I saw Owens's car go right by the picket shack, anyway.

"They kept on saying where was you at, and we didn't tell them. We said you hadn't done nothing."

"Well, you're right, I haven't done nothing. Why didn't you go over to Uncle Manny's? He's supposed to be watching you guys."

"We was scared to go outside!" Manuela screamed. She was jumping from one foot to the other and hugging herself. "They said they'd get us!"

"Tony, did they say that? Did they threaten you?"

"They said stay away from the picket rallies," Tony said. "The one with the gun said he seen us and took all our pitchers. He said, your mama's got too big a mouth for her own good."

At the last picket rally I was up on Lalo Ruiz's shoulders with a bull horn. I've had almost every office in my local, and sergeant-at-arms twice because the guys say I have no toleration for BS. They got one of those big old trophies down at the union hall that says on it "MEN OF COPPER," and one time Lalo says, "Vicki ain't no Man of Copper, she's a damn stick of *mesquite.* She might break but she sure as hell won't bend."

Well, I want my kids to know what this is about. When school starts, if some kid makes fun of their last-year's blue jeans and calls them trash I want them to hold their heads up. I take them to picket rallies so they'll know that. No law says you can't set up on nobody with a bull horn. They might have took my picture, though. I wouldn't be surprised.

"All I ever done was defend my union," I told the kids. "Even cops have to follow the laws, and it isn't no crime to defend your union. Your grandpapa done it and his papa and now me."

Well, my grandpapa one time got put on a railroad car like a cow, for being a Wobbly and a Mexican. My kids have heard that story a million times. He got dumped out in the desert someplace with no water or even a cloth for his head, and it took him two months to get back. All that time my granny and Tía Sonia thought he was dead.

I hugged Tony and Manuela and then we went and locked the door. I had to pull up on it while they jimmied the latch because that damn door had not been locked one time in seven years.

———

What we thought about when we wanted to feel better was: What a God-awful mess they got up there in the mine. Most of those scabs was out-of-towners and didn't have no idea what end of the gun to shoot. I heard it took them about one month to figure out how to start the equipment. Before the walkout there was some parts switched around between my crane and a locomotive, but we didn't have to do that because the scabs tied up the cat's back legs all by theirselves. Laying pieces of track backwards, running the conveyors too fast, I hate to think what else.

We even heard that one foreman, Willie Bunford, quit because of all the jackasses on the machinery, that he feared for his life. Willie Bunford used to be my foreman. He made fun of how I said his name, "Wee-lee!" so I called him Mr. Bunford. So I have an accent, so what? When I was first starting on the crane he said, "You aren't going to get PG now, are you, Miss Morales, after I wasted four weeks training you as an operator? I know how you Mexican gals love to have babies." I said, "Mr. Bunford, as far as this job goes you can consider me a man." So I had to stick to that. I couldn't call up and say I'm staying in bed today because of my monthly. Then what does he do but lay off two weeks with so-call whiplash from a car accident on Top Street when I saw the whole story: Winnie Hask backing into his car in front of the Big Dipper and him not in it. If a man can get whiplash from his car getting bashed in while he is drinking beer across the street, well, that's a new one.

So I didn't cry for no Willie Bunford. At least he had the sense to get out of there. None of those scabs knew how to run the oxygen machine, so we were waiting for the whole damn place to blow up. I said to the guys, Let's go sit on Bolt Mountain with some beer and watch the fireworks.

———————◆———————

The first eviction I heard about was the Frank Mickliffs, up the street from me, and then Joe Gomez on Alameda. Ellington wanted to clear out some company houses for the new hires, but how they decided who to throw out we didn't know. Then Janie Marley found out from her friend that baby-sits for the sister-in-law of a scab that company men were driving scab wives around town letting them pick out whatever house they wanted. Like they're going shopping and we're the peaches getting squeezed.

Friday of that same week I was out on my front porch thinking about a cold beer, just thinking, though, because of no cash, and here come an Ellington car. They slowed way, way down when they went by, then on up Church Street going about fifteen and then they come back. It was Vonda in there. She nodded her head at my house and the guy put something down on paper. They made a damn picture show out of it.

Oh, I was furious. I have been living in that house almost the whole time I worked for Ellington and it's all the home my kids ever had. It's a real good house. It's yellow. I have a big front porch where you can see just about everything, all of Bolton, and a railing so the kids won't fall over in the gulch, and a big yard. I keep it up nice, and my brother Manny being right next door helps out. I have this mother duck with her babies all lined up that the kids bought me at Fangham's for Mother's Day, and I planted marigolds in a circle around them. No way on this earth was I turning my house over to a scab.

The first thing I did was march over to Manny's house and knock on the door and walk in. "Manny," I say to him, "I don't want you mowing my yard anymore unless you feel like doing a favor for Miss Vonda." Manny is just pulling the pop top off a Coke and his mouth goes open at the same time; he just stares.

"Oh, no," he says.

"Oh, yes."

I went back over to my yard and Manny come hopping out putting on his shoes, to see what I'm going to do, I guess. He's my little brother but Mama always says "*Madre Santa,* Manuel, keep an eye on Vicki!" Well, what I was going to do was my own damn business. I pulled up the ducks, they have those metal things that poke in the ground, and then I pulled up the marigolds and threw them out on the sidewalk. If I had to get the neighbor kids to help make my house the ugliest one, I was ready to do it.

Well. The next morning I was standing in the kitchen drinking coffee, and Manny come through the door with this funny look on his face and says, "The tooth fairy has been to see you."

What in the world. I ran outside and there was *pink* petunias planted right in the circle where I already pulled up the marigolds. To think Vonda could sneak into my yard like a common thief and do a thing like that.

"Get the kids," I said. I went out and started pulling out petunias. I hate pink. And I hate how they smelled, they had these sticky roots. Manny woke up the kids and they come out and helped.

"This is fun, Mom," Tony said. He wiped his cheek and a line of dirt ran across like a scar. They were in their pajamas.

"Son, we're doing it for the union," I said. We threw them out on the sidewalk with the marigolds, to dry up and die.

After that I was scared to look out the window in the morning. God knows what Vonda might put in my yard, more flowers or one of those ugly pink flamingos they sell at Fangham's yard and garden department. I wouldn't put nothing past Vonda.

◆━━

Whatever happened, we thought when the strike was over we would have our jobs. You could put up with high water and heck, thinking of that. It's like having a baby, you just grit your teeth and keep your eyes on the prize. But then Ellington started sending out termination notices saying, You will have no job to come back to whatsoever. They would fire you for any excuse, mainly strike-related misconduct, which means nothing, you looked cross-eyed at a policeman or whatever. People got scared.

The national office of the union was no help; they said, To hell with it, boys, take the pay cut and go on back. I had a fit at the union meeting. I told them it's not the pay cut, it's what all else they would take if we give in. "Ellington would not have hired me in two million years if it wasn't for the union raising a rackus about all people are created equal," I said. "Or half of you either because they don't like cunts or coloreds." I'm not that big of a person but I was standing up in front, and when I cussed, they shut up. "If my papa had been a chickenshit like you guys, I would be down at the Frosty King tonight in a little short skirt," I said. "You bunch of no-goods would be on welfare and your kids pushing drugs to pay the rent." Some of the guys laughed, but some didn't.

Men get pissed off in this certain way, though, where they have to tear something up. Lalo said, "Well, hell, let's drive a truck over the plant gate and shut the damn mine down." And there they go, off and running, making plans to do it. Corvallis had a baseball cap on backwards and was sitting back with his arms crossed like, Honey, don't look at me. I could have killed him.

"Great, you guys, you do something cute like that and we're dead ducks," I said. "We don't have to do but one thing, wait it out."

"Till when?" Lalo wanted to know. "Till hell freezes?" He is kind of a short guy with about twelve tattoos on each arm.

"Till they get fed up with the scabs pissing around and want to get the mine running. If it comes down to busting heads, no way. Do you hear me? They'll have the National Guards in here."

I knew I was right. The Boots in this town, the cops, they're on Ellington payroll. I've seen strikes before. When I was ten years old I saw a cop get a Mexican man down on the ground and kick his face till blood ran out of his ear. You would think I was the only one in that room that was born and raised in Bolton.

◆

Ellington was trying to get back up to full production. They had them working twelve-hour shifts and seven-day weeks like Abraham Lincoln had never freed the slaves. We started hearing about people getting hurt, but just rumors; it wasn't going to run in the paper. Ellington owns the paper.

The first I knew about it really was when Vonda come right to my house. I was running the vacuum cleaner and had the radio turned up all the way so I didn't hear her drive up. I just heard a knock on the door, and when I opened it: Vonda. Her skin looked like a flour tortilla. "What in the world," I said.

Her bracelets were going clack-clack-clack, she was shaking so hard. "I never thought I'd be coming to you," she said, like I was Dear Abby. "But something's happened to Tommy."

"Oh," I said. I had heard some real awful things: that a guy was pulled into a smelter furnace, and another guy got his legs run over on the tracks. I could picture Tommy either way, no legs or burnt up. We stood there a long time. Vonda looked like she might pass out. "Okay, come in," I told her. "Set down there and I'll get you a drink of water. Water is all we got around here." I stepped over the vacuum cleaner on the way to the kitchen. I wasn't going to put it away.

When I come back she was looking around the room all nervous, breathing like a bird. I turned down the radio.

"How are the kids?" she wanted to know, of all things.

"The kids are fine. Tell me what happened to Tommy."

"Something serious to do with his foot, that's all I know. Either cut off or half cut off, they won't tell me." She pulled this little hanky out of her purse and blew her nose. "They sent him to Morse in the helicopter ambulance, but they won't say what hospital because I'm not next of kin here. He doesn't have any next of kin here, I *told* them that. I informed them I was the fiancée." She blew her nose again. "All they'll tell me is they don't want him in the Bolton hospital. I can't understand why."

"Because they don't want nobody to know about it," I told her. "They're covering up all the accidents."

"Well, why would they want to do that?"

"Vonda, excuse me please, but don't be stupid. They want to do that so we won't know how close we are to winning the strike."

Vonda took a little sip of water. She had on a yellow sun dress and her arms looked so skinny, like just bones with freckles. "Well, I know what you think of me," she finally said, "but for Tommy's sake maybe you can get the union to do something. Have an investigation so he'll at least get his compensation pay. I know you have a lot of influence on the union."

"I don't know if I do or not," I told her. I puffed my breath out and leaned my head back on the sofa. I pulled the bandana off my head and rubbed my hair in a circle. It's so easy to know what's right and so hard to do it.

"Vonda," I said, "I thought a lot of Tommy before all this shit. He helped me one time when I needed it real bad." She looked at me. She probably hated thinking of me and him being friends. "I'm sure Tommy knows he done the wrong thing," I said. "But it gets me how you people treat us like kitchen trash and then come running to the union as soon as you need help."

She picked up her glass and brushed at the water on the coffee table. I forgot napkins. "Yes, I see that now, and I'll try to make up for my mistake," she said.

Give me a break, Vonda, was what I was thinking. "Well, we'll see," I said. "There is a meeting coming up and I'll see what I can do. If you show up on the picket line tomorrow."

Vonda looked like she swallowed one of her ice cubes. She went over to the TV and picked up the kids' pictures one at a time, Manuela, then Tony. Put them back down. Went over to the *armario* built by my grandpapa.

"What a nice little statue," she said.

"That's St. Joseph. Saint of people that work with their hands."

She turned around and looked at me. "I'm sorry about the house. I won't take your house. It wouldn't be right."

"I'm glad you feel that way, because I wasn't moving."

"Oh," she said.

"Vonda, I can remember when me and you were little girls and your daddy was already running the drugstore. You used to set up on a stool behind the counter and run the soda-water machine. You had a charm bracelet with everything in the world on it, poodle dogs and hearts and a real little pill box that opened."

Vonda smiled. "I don't have the foggiest idea what ever happened to that bracelet. Would you like it for your girl?"

I stared at her. "But you don't remember me, do you?"

"Well, I remember a whole lot of people coming in the store. You in particular, I guess not."

"I guess not," I said. "People my color was not allowed to go in there and set at the soda fountain. We had to get paper cups and take our drinks outside. Remember that? I used to think and *think* about why that was. I thought our germs must be so nasty they wouldn't wash off the glasses."

"Well, things have changed, haven't they?" Vonda said.

"Yeah." I put my feet up on the coffee table. It's my damn table. "Things changed because the UTU and the Machinists and my papa's union the Boilermakers took this whole fucking company town to court in 1973, that's why. This house right here was for whites only. And if there wasn't no union forcing Ellington to abide by the law, it still would be."

She was kind of looking out the window. She probably was thinking about what she was going to cook for supper.

"You think it wouldn't? You think Ellington would build a nice house for everybody if they could still put half of us in those falling-down shacks down by the river like I grew up in?"

"Well, you've been very kind to hear me out," she said. "I'll do what you want, tomorrow. Right now I'd better be on my way."

I went out on the porch and watched her go down the sidewalk—click click, on her little spike heels. Her ankles wobbled.

"Vonda," I yelled out after her, "don't wear high heels on the line tomorrow. For safety's sake."

She never turned around.

◆

Next day the guys were making bets on Vonda showing up or not. The odds were not real good in her favor. I had to laugh, but myself I really thought she would. It was a huge picket line for the morning shift change. The Women's Auxiliary thought it would boost up the morale, which needed a kick in the butt or somebody would be busting down the plant gate. Corvallis told me that some guys had a meeting after the real meeting and planned it out. But I knew that if I kept showing up at the union meetings and standing on the table and jumping and hollering, they wouldn't do it. Sometimes guys will listen to a woman.

The sun was just coming up over the canyon and already it was a hot day. Cicada bugs buzzing in the *paloverdes* like damn rattlesnakes. Me and Janie Marley were talking about our kids; she has a boy one size down from Tony and we trade clothes around. All of a sudden Janie grabs my elbow and says, "Look who's here." It was Vonda getting out of the Lincoln. Not in high heels, either. She had on a tennis outfit and plastic sunglasses and a baseball bat slung over her shoulder. She stopped a little ways from the line and was looking around, waiting for the Virgin Mary to come down, I guess, and save her. Nobody was collecting any bets.

"Come on, Vonda," I said. I took her by the arm and stood her between me and Janie. "I'm glad you made it." But she wasn't talking, just looking around a lot.

After a while I said, "We're not supposed to have bats up here. I know a guy that got his termination papers for carrying a crescent wrench in his back pocket. He had forgot it was even in there." I looked at Vonda to see if she was paying attention. "It was Rusty Cochran," I said, "you know him. He's up at your dad's every other day for a prescription. They had that baby with the hole in his heart."

But Vonda held on to the bat like it was the last man in the world and she got him. "I'm only doing this for Tommy," she says.

"Well, so what?" I said. "I'm doing it for my kids. So they can eat."

She kept squinting her eyes down the highway.

A bunch of people started yelling, "Here come the ladies!" Some of the women from the Auxiliary were even saying it. And here come trouble. They were in Doreen's car, waving signs out the windows: "We Support Our Working Men" and other shit not worth repeating. Doreen was driving. She jerked right dead to a stop, right in front of us. She looked at Vonda and you would think she had broke both her hinges the way her mouth was hanging open, and Vonda looked back at Doreen, and the rest of us couldn't wait to see what was next.

Doreen took a U-turn and almost ran over Cecil Smoot, and they beat it back to town like bats out of hell. Ten minutes later here come her car back up the hill again. Only this time her husband, Milton, was driving, and three other men from Saint's Grace was all in there besides Doreen. Two of them are cops.

"I don't know what they're up to but we don't need you getting in trouble," I told Vonda. I took the bat away from her and put it over my shoulder. She looked real white, and I patted her arm and said, "Don't worry." I can't believe I did that, now. Looking back.

They pulled up in front of us again but they didn't get out, just all five of them stared and then they drove off, like whatever they come for they got.

—

That was yesterday. Last night I was washing the dishes and somebody come to the house. The kids were watching TV. I heard Tony slide the dead bolt over and then he yelled, "Mom, it's the Boot."

Before I can even put down a plate and get into the living room Larry Trevizo has pushed right by him into the house. I come out wiping my hands and see him there holding up his badge.

"Chief of Police, ma'am," he says, just like that, like I don't know who the hell he is. Like we didn't go through every grade of school together and go see *Suddenly Last Summer* one time in high school.

He says, "Mrs. Morales, I'm serving you with injunction papers."

"Oh, is that a fact," I say. "And may I ask what for?"

Tony already turned off the TV and is standing by me with his arms crossed, the meanest-looking damn eleven-year-old you ever hope to see in your life. All I can think of is the guys in the meeting, how they get so they just want to bust something in.

"Yes, you may ask what for," Larry says, and starts to read, not looking any of us in the eye: "For being a danger to the public. Inciting a riot. Strike-related misconduct." And then real low he says something about Vonda Fangham and a baseball bat.

"What was that last thing?"

He clears his throat. "And for kidnapping Vonda Fangham and threatening her with a baseball bat. We got the affidavits."

"*Pa'fuera!*" I tell Larry Trevizo. I ordered him out of my house right then, told him if he wanted to see somebody get hurt with a baseball bat he could hang around my living room and find out. I trusted myself but not Tony. Larry got out of there.

The injunction papers said I was not to be in any public gathering of more than five people or I would be arrested. And what do you know, a squad of Boots was already lined up by the picket shack at the crack of dawn this morning with their hands on their sticks, just waiting. They knew I would be up there, I see that. They knew I would do just exactly all the right things. Like the guys say, Vicki might break but she don't bend.

They cuffed me and took me up to the jailhouse, which is in back of the Ellington main office, and took off my belt and my earrings so I wouldn't kill myself or escape. "With an earring?" I said. I was laughing. I could see this old rotten building through the office window; it used to be something or other but now there's chickens living in it. You could dig out of there with an earring, for sure. I said, "What's that over there, the Mexican jail? You better put me in there!"

I thought they would just book me and let me go like they did some other ones, before this. But no, I have to stay put. Five hundred thousand bond. I don't think this whole town could come up with that, not if they signed over every pink, purple, and blue house in Bolton.

It didn't hit me till right then about the guys wanting to tear into the plant. What they might do.

"Look, I got to get out by tonight," I told the cops. I don't know their names, it was some State Police I have never seen, seem like they just come up out of nowhere. I was getting edgy. "I have a union meeting and it's real important. Believe me, you don't want me to miss it."

They smiled. And then I got that terrible feeling you get when you see somebody has been looking you in the eye and smiling and setting a trap, and there you are in it like a damn rat.

What is going to happen I don't know. I'm keeping my ears open. I found out my kids are driving Manny to distraction—Tony told his social-studies class he would rather have a jailbird than a scab mom, and they sent him home with a note that he was causing a dangerous disturbance in class.

I also learned that Tommy Jones was not in any accident. He got called off his shift one day and was took to Morse in a helicopter with no explanation. They put him up at Howard Johnson's over there for five days, his meals and everything, just told him not to call nobody, and today he's back at work. They say he is all in one piece.

Well, I am too.

WILLIAM KITTREDGE

DO YOU HEAR YOUR MOTHER TALKING?

They offered me work in the mill when the woods closed down, but we had enough money and I hate the cold and ringing of the night shift, everything wet and the saws howling. So I stayed home with Ruth.

This is one of those company towns, here in southern Alaska but elsewhere, too, that the logging industry builds on its second-growth hillsides. You can stand at our big window and not see anything but the dripping roofs of green frame houses below us in the brush and piles of split wood covered with plastic tarps and old swing sets and wrecked cars, most of them without glass or tires, which are bright and washed in the rain, and stained with rust; and you can watch the rain dimple the puddles showing black and wet on the black asphalt, and you can wonder.

The place where Ruth parked her De Soto was empty, and I figured she must have gone down to be at the Mercantile when it opened. My Chevy four-by-four was on blocks in the shed behind the house. I thought about spending the afternoon getting it ready to ship south again.

It surprises me even now. I let the idea go through my mind with the taste of the coffee. I had wondered when I would come to feel that way. It just came to my head. I could feel myself leaving.

It was a dream in which Ruth was staying behind forever. For a long moment I couldn't even get myself to see her face, or understand how I had come to this yellow-painted kitchen. The idea of leaving just fell into me like a visitor. I blew my breath on the window and rubbed my initials in the steamy place.

It was light as it was going to get. The coffee was heavy and sweet, so I poured another cup and lit up another cigarette. Some days nothing moves. You can look out at the evening and see the fog that was there in the morning feathering off into the canyon where the river cuts toward the ocean.

What saved it was Ruth's old De Soto. She had the headlights glowing. Ruth drives slow and careful.

Outside you could hear the water in the river. I stood on the porch, holding the coffee cup, and watched her park.

Ruth took a paper sack in her arms and stepped around the puddles until she was beside me. Her hair was wet on her forehead and the shoulders of her cloth coat were soaked. She grinned and shoved the sack at me, and I thought then I wasn't going anywhere.

During the winter Ruth can look blotchy and strange. Some nights she will go alone to a movie and come back after I am sleeping. But she was smiling now, and I could read myself, and I had to smile.

"Turn off the headlights," I said, and I took her sack.

Ruth ran back through the rain and stuck her head inside the car door and fumbled at the switch. Her skirt was pulled high and it stuck to the backs of her legs, and I could see the dark net of veins behind her knees.

The summer we met, Ruth was deep brown from the sun and her legs looked like something out of pictures. She was working nights as a cocktail waitress in Brownie's, where I'd seen her lots of times, and sleeping away her days on the beach. I caught her there early one morning and spoke only a few words to her that first time. I'd woken her, not so much to start something with her as interested in why these runaway women act like they do. You see them in the mill, dirty and wet and working too hard and determined to be single as possible.

She told me she could always sleep if she was listening to the ocean, and she smiled and didn't look unhappy with me at all. Her hair was long and yellow and she was hard and tight enough, even after two kids, but she was a little too easy.

That was the first thing they told me about her: that she had two kids living with her first husband. But she was eager and not bad. She never talks of her other life and has never hinted at going to see those kids.

She slammed the car door and came back.

"I got bacon and eggs and juice," she said, taking the sack. "I'm going to cook a regular breakfast."

◆

The fields smelled of fire. You could imagine little runs of fire burning behind the combines. My father would shred the heads of the ripe barley between his callused hands, and blow away the chaff and bite down on the kernels, chewing like they were something to eat. I would lie on my back, hidden down in the barley, breathing the smell of burning while the stalks rattled in the breezes.

All I could see was the sky. Ruth might have been with me, listening and quiet. That would have been a fine childhood thing, me and Ruth.

Ruth smiles when she looks away to the window where the rain runs in streaks. You have to wonder who she sees in her reflection, and what she sees in me and her.

◆

We live on a big cedar-forest island at the edge of the Japan Current, where it never snows. Everything comes in by boat or float-plane. Ruth and I do not tell each other much of what we came from, letting it go at the fact that we are lucky, and here.

The first morning, after we woke up in her bed, she came along to spend the day with me. Before noon we were down in Brownie's, which is a dark old barn built of cedar planking and shakes. No one knows who it was named for. Big smoky windows look out to the street, if you want to look.

All winter while it rains people gather to sit around a barrel stove welded together from sections of culvert, looking at the little isinglass window in the door, where you can see in at the fire. The shadows run up the walls and over our faces.

"We can give them something to talk about," Ruth said that first morning. I should have told her I was proud to walk in with her.

That was October, and I was already done felling timber for another winter. The low clouds hung down into the fog coming off the seawater. That afternoon we sat outside Brownie's under the veranda, on the wood bench where everybody has carved their initials. We had our cans of beer and we were out of the rain as we watched two nuns go along with their tiny steps on the boardwalk. You could see the trouble they had taken to make themselves precious in the world.

"They think it's something," Ruth said.

I'll give myself some credit. Right then I knew this wasn't just some woman from the night before.

◄►

The dark red bedsheets are part of Ruth. She changes them every day. She says winter is under water enough without damp sheets.

The rain was flushing through the galvanized gutter above the window. Ruth would be in close beside the oil stove and reading. I could see her, wrapped in one of the Hudson Bay blankets I bought in Victoria. She keeps a pile of magazines on the floor beside the new platform rocker that was supposed to be mine after we moved in together.

Turned out I like to sit at the kitchen table, under the bare bulb. Ruth wanted to put a shade on the bulb, but I said no. There is a big window in the kitchen. I can see out into the canyon through the mirror of my face on the inside of the window and imagine the runs of salmon and the old Tlingit fishermen in their round cedar hats.

◄►

My father and my mother were sleeping, and I stood in the doorway and watched them sleep in the square of moonlight from the window. I walked away beside the shadows of the long row of poplar trees that ran between the irrigation ditch and the road from the house. Over on the highway at daybreak, while the sprinklers turned their arcs over the alfalfa, I hooked a ride on the back of a stake-body truck. The last thing I saw was the trees along the high irrigation ditch; I can still see them clear as yesterday. My father was just like me. But Ruth is nothing like my mother. I wonder what a kid would remember from this place we live in Alaska.

◄►

The cardboard patches Ruth nailed over the knotholes are already turning green. At least we didn't buy the house. I was right about that: This wasn't the house we wanted. We want to build a house of cedar logs.

Ruth always keeps a big jug of orange juice in the refrigerator. It burns away the taste of my cigarettes. That first night, in one of the cabins by the beach, where she was living by herself, saying she had come north only for the summer, while I was still living in the logging-camp barracks, Ruth said she had grown up learning to sleep naked. I can almost taste the feel of her.

My boots sat over by the wall, ready and oiled for the day when I can go back into the timber. You have to wonder what there is to like about felling those virgin-growth cedar trees, and what kind of man would stay with timber-felling long as I have. The cedars are the most beautiful trees in the world.

I work alone, which is dangerous, but I want silence when I shut down the saw. The red-grained back wedge comes falling out, and I shut down my long-bladed Stihl, and I sit there letting the quiet settle in. The sawdust smells like some proper medicine. Right then I have enough of everything.

The first-growth trees fall true as angels, with the whoosh of their needles through the air, and they are dead. Like the natives, I have learned to tell the trees I am sorry, but not so sorry I won't cut another in the afternoon. You kill to fill your belly, and then you tell them it was necessary. You have to smile at such things.

It is my best life, out in the woods, and this winter there have been times I ache for it as I sit through the rainy afternoon in Brownie's and listen to the talk of fish. I wonder if felling trees is true work. But I forget such worries as Ruth and I walk downhill through the dripping early darkness to the movie house, and we are saying hello to everybody and Ruth is excited like a girl.

◆

"I walked in the rain," Ruth said. "After you went to sleep I walked in the rain." Then she said, "You got to tell me what was wrong with you," and she ran her cool fingers down the long scar on my inner arm.

Each step of it had seemed right at the time. I can see the pale tender skin along my inner arm separating as the blade traces toward the wrist, my flesh parting along the length of my wound in a perfect clean way, and the tough white sheath and the deeper seeping meat before it is all drowned in blood.

I am telling you about craziness. I lay in those beds and I thought

I heard my mother's voice and never slept until I came to believe there was some tiny thing wired into my arm, and electrical circuits flashing along with their messages, right at the core of my arm like a little machine, and all of it a trick. Then I could sleep, because I knew someone could cut it out with a surgeon's blade.

The idea got me in trouble. I found out about doctors, and I went into the office of the best doctor in Klamath Falls, I asked him to cut the wiring out of my arm, and the crazy part was cutting on myself when he refused.

It seemed like a good idea to think my troubles could be solved by the touch of what they call micro cutters. It was the kind of thing you come to believe like babies believe the things they learn before they are born. It was like knowing which way is up. But the trouble with me is over. I sit in our kitchen and read hunting magazines, and I imagine stalking water birds like they were my friends.

I am telling you about craziness, but I wouldn't tell Ruth. "We all been born with too much time on our hands." That is what I said.

◆

We have nights to think about our earliest memories. In mine there is a red dog resting in the dust beside a stunted little lawn juniper and the crumbling concrete walkway. There is a thunderstorm breaking.

That was out front of the apartment building where we lived when I was a little child in the farmhand town of Malin, on the northern fringes of the potato land that drops toward Tule Lake and California. My mother walked me on the sidewalks, in and out of the stores, and to the barbershop, where they smiled when I climbed up to the board across the arms of the chair.

That red dog barked in the night, but usually he was sleeping and wrinkled in the dust. What I see are heavy drops of rain. I can still count them as they puff into the dust. I can close my eyes and call up those raindrops striking each by each.

Like my mother would say, "Each thing in its place." I can hear her voice clear as my own.

My father had his 200 acres of barley-farming property out south of the Klamath Falls airfield. He was hiring winos to herd his few hundred head of turkeys, and he always had my mother. I would ride out with him in the gray pickup truck, gone to check on the well-being of his turkeys, and then home to my mother.

Him and my mother, in those good years after the war, they called themselves the free world. But they were playing it like a joke, at parties, with other men and women.

Men would come to the kitchen while my father was gone, and my mother would pour whiskey. They would sit at the kitchen table with their whiskey in a tumbler, and my mother would laugh and stand beside them, and those men would hug her around the waist and smile at me while they did it.

"You better go outside," my mother would tell me, and she would already be untying her apron.

"We was late with our lives," my father told me, "me and your mother, so we just stayed with our playground." He told me there was too much room for running with your mind when he was growing up in Tule Lake during the Great Depression. He said he went crazy during those years, and that I should be careful if I got my imagination from him.

My father told me this when I was thirteen, maybe as a way to explain his lifetime. That was the first time I left, wishing I could hear my mother say good-bye.

◆

"If you won't answer me," Ruth said. Then: "I was only going to tell you what happened." She was at the stove, tending the eggs and bacon.

"You were feeling bad," I said, "and you had a few beers and you walked in the rain and felt better. Like nobody ever did."

"I drove down to the ocean," Ruth said, "and walked on the beach. Before daylight." Her back was to me. She was turning the eggs. "It was nothing but that and I felt better."

Ruth colors her hair golden, and it had been running with seawater when she'd come walking up from the summer ocean. She shook her head, and I knew her face would taste of salt. Right there was the first time she reminded me of my mother. My mother was young, and her bare arms were red in the summer rain. The drops stood in her dark hair as she was laughing in the yellow light under the thunder.

◆

It was just before the Fourth of July and hot and clear and still when I came north. The low fog was banked far out over the ocean. After some drinking, I would see the gray summer tide coming cold over the sand and think about the Lombardy poplar trees you could see for twenty miles over the fields of alfalfa on the right sunny day around Tule Lake. If you imagined them clear enough, those trees would come closer until their leaves were real, like they could be touched.

Crazy is really a place you could learn to stay. You could learn to live there forever. It was a reason for drinking. I never imagined myself into somewhere else when I was drinking; it was only afterward.

Down in Victoria I bought myself a whole set of Alaska clothes as if that would turn me into an Alaska man, got me a barbershop shave, and rode the Alaska ferry north. It wasn't the right way to travel into such a place, but it was easy and at hand, and it was the season for seeing seabirds and whales and all the fish.

The days were warm and sunlit, and you could smell the evergreen trees over the diesel exhaust as we came to dock in midafternoon. I walked out over the sandy flats to the ocean, a wind was coming off the fog on the horizon, and I found a stone fireplace where fish had been cooked. The sand was littered with red berry boxes, and there were torn newspapers in the brush.

By nightfall I was sitting on the bench outside Brownie's, listening to some men talk about the salmon run and lumbering. The inside of Brownie's looked as hammered out as a cave. I thought of the mills where I'd worked, the howl of saws and wet sawdust, and I wondered if I had come to another wrong place.

Give it a summer, I thought. There was nobody to notify. I had my clothes folded into a canvas duffel bag and a half dozen thousand-dollar bills. My chain saw could earn me $150 on a good day. Only a fool does things without money.

◆

"We ought to be married," Ruth said. She was washing the few breakfast dishes and stacking them on the open-faced shelves above the sink. She went on placing the dishes carefully atop one another, then dried her hands and went to stand before the oil stove. "I could have another baby," she said. "It's not too late. That could be my calling." She smiled like that was going to be funny.

I got up and walked away from her and went into the bedroom. After closing the door, I sat on the bed. *That could be my calling*. I couldn't hear a thing from the other room, not even Ruth moving around. After a while I pulled my worn old black suitcase from under the bed. With the suitcase open, the next move was easy. Ruth could come and stand in the doorway and watch while I packed.

"I'll take a little money to travel on," I would say.

She would look down a moment, and her face would show no sign of anything, and I would think it was going to be easy to get out of here with no trouble. "Watch me," I would say. "I'm gone."

When the suitcase was packed I would head past her into the other room, pull on my slicker and leather cap, and go out to the shed where my four-by-four was up on blocks. It would be dry inside, with the rainwater splattering from the cedar leaves and the dirt like dust mixed with pine needles.

There is a pint of whiskey hidden under the driver's seat. Two long swallows and I would think about laughing, and sit in the dirt with my back against the wall and whistle *ring-dang-do, now what is that?*

My mother beat my ass for that song and washed my mouth in the irrigation ditch. It's a song I think about when I want to remember my mother and the way she laughed and hugged me as we sat on the grass with water coming from her hair in little streams. Now, that is not crazy, thoughts of the water streaming through the little redwood weir in that irrigation ditch and my mother knowing some joke I didn't understand.

Ruth came and sat beside me and my black suitcase on the bed, her elbows on her knees and her head down and her hair hanging forward like she was a wrecked woman with nothing to do but study her hands while some man made up his mind about her life.

"My mother told me a joke about times like this," I said.

Ruth didn't answer.

"My mother told me everything you got is like a china cup," I said. "Because it never came from China, and you always got to worry if it's going to break."

"Some joke," Ruth said, and her face was an old woman's face when she looked up at me.

Not that she was crying. Her eyes had just gone old, and the strength in her flesh had lost some of its hold on her bones. Her lower lip fell down and showed her teeth, stained by so many cigarettes. I could see the years to come, both of us old in some house where she looked like my mother and the radio was always playing in the other room.

◆

But at the Klamath Falls hospital a nurse unlocked the door and I walked into my mother's care, a man thirty-four years old and unable to even trust his own brain.

My mother's hands were cold. What could I tell her? That I had lived too long watching my father turn hermit in the house he built on the corner of his property out by the airfield where the Air Force pilots flew jet planes every hour or so like a clock? Could I tell her jet airplanes will make you crazy for answers to everything?

She showed me an old photograph of my father: a young man with just the tip of his tongue between his white teeth, his hands deep in his pockets and the brim of his city-man hat snapped down over one eye, like the picture-taking was going to stop everything for all time at this moment in his schoolyard. Behind him you can see the painted sign: TURKEYS. "He was the best man they ever had," my mother said. "Now he's made you crazy."

You could take the same picture of me, deep in my forest beside some fallen cedar tree, and you might think, *Who the hell does he think he is?* We've all seen pictures of men who are dead now, with their long saws crossed in front of some great stumpage and their sleeves rolled up over their elbows.

My mother puckered her soft mouth as she eyed me and didn't talk anymore, as if her tongue had locked and she had lost her speech. Then she shook her head. "I'll tell you the joke," she said. "This is the joke of it." She looked around at the house where she was making her stand; expensive hardwood furniture and a mantel decorated with half a hundred engraved stock-show trophies. Silver spires with imitation silver Angus bulls on the top.

She didn't look like anything was a joke.

"Things changed," she said. "Things will change." She was trying to make it sound like a hopeful notion. I imagine the first lie, and a time when they came to know there was nobody to trust. I imagine them coming to want every goddamn thing they could get their hands on. It's simple. You are going to die, so you better get in on the money and the screwing.

One afternoon she took off in a Lincoln Continental with a heavy-built man called Cutty. "Cutty had this house left over from the time he was married," she told me. "Your father wouldn't even take me to bed. Cutty knew better, right from the start."

She took off those frameless eyeglasses and cleaned them. There was a box of Kleenex on every table in that house. I picked up one of those trophies with the little silver Angus bulls on top, and I thought, like a child, *So this is the way to be rich.*

The fall-of-the-year sunlight percolated into my mother's house through layers of gauzy curtains, and she never went outside. Twice a week there was a cleaning lady, and every day there was a boy delivering things. My mother just cooked me meals and waited for me to make my peace.

Maybe it is true about my mother and Cutty, maybe they are still a great love. Over the years Cutty worked himself up from auctioneer to purebred cattle breeder. He was always sending flowers from Bakersfield or some show town.

◆

For nine years I worked my summers in the Oregon woods and spent winters with my father in his house. Afternoons in winter I would drive over to the local tavern and shoot some pool, then come home to stir up some tuna and noodles for the microwave oven. Nobody, my father or me, ever really cleaned up the kitchen, and more and more I started to feel tuned to the trembling of those microwaves, all the time closer to discovering I had been wired for other people's ideas.

Just a quarter mile south of my father's house there's a barroom built from a Quonset hut back in World War II, with gas pumps out front. My father was always eager for a walk down to the bar and some drinking and talk first thing in the morning. It's just that you can learn to live in some of those stories. But that is enough about craziness. It's a place you swim like deep in the black ocean with strange fish. You might never want to come up. It's a country where I could go visit and find a home.

◆

Ruth refolded each thing I owned, her hands trembling as she filled my suitcase. The unshaded overhead light was on bright in our bedroom, and she moved like an underwater creature. "Fine," Ruth said. "Just goddamn fine."

Her face was flushed with that fallen look you might imagine as secret to animals, her eyes glazed like stones and this way and that quick as lizards. I remember my mother late in the night when she was drunk in our kitchen, where the windows were thick with ice. I would come awake from hearing her laugh and ease from the bedroom, where the people's coats were piled on the other bed, and she wouldn't even see me with those eyes.

"Just fucking wonderful," Ruth said. "You pitiful son of a bitch." I didn't know if she meant me or herself.

Ruth unfolded my stiff canvas Carhartt timber-felling pants with the red suspenders, the cuffs jagged and the knees slick with pitch, and she stepped into them and pulled them up and hooked the suspenders over her shoulders, her dress wadded up inside, and she stood there like a circus girl. "How do you think?" she said. "You think I could work in the woods?"

"You ought to have a baby," she said then. "You ought to lie down on your back and come split apart and smell your own blood in the room. But you never can. What can you do?"

◆

This is what I could do. I could lace my boots. I could get the blocks out from under my Chevy and spend the afternoon cleaning the plugs until she idled like your perfect sewing machine. It would be twilight and the white Alaskan ferryboat would be rolling in the long ocean troughs as I stood at the rail with a pint of whiskey in my hand and watched the cedar-tree mountains turn to night under the snowy mountains beyond to the east. I could go anywhere in America.

But Ruth was smiling, and it wasn't her sweetheart smile. "You better get me," she said, and she dropped those suspenders and stepped out of my canvas Carhartt pants.

"You know what I can do?" she said. "I am going to lie down and come unseamed for a baby."

You wonder what the difference is between me and women, and if women really like to think there is some hidden thing inside them that is growing and will one day be someone else, some hidden thing telling them what to do. There was Ruth at thirty-nine years old, with her babies behind her, too old for what she said she wanted, standing there with her hands open and willing to look at the possibility of dying for some baby.

You think of the old explorers. You have to know there was a time when they smelled their land from out to sea and the clouds blew away, and it came to them that this coastline they had found was a seashore where nobody exactly like them was ever given a chance to walk before.

"I'm going to say, 'Baby,' " Ruth said, " 'do you hear your mother talking? Baby, are you listening?' "

Me and Ruth were there in the glare off the glass. I could see us, and I had to wonder what our children would see if they were watching and looking for hints about who they should come to be. Ruth looked mottled white like the blood was gone out of her. "Either that," she said, "or you can get the hell out of here."

Those old explorers must have studied their mountains, trying to think this was what they had always wanted, this place they didn't know about. You try to control the shaking of your hands, and you want to say, All right, this will be all right, this is what I'll take, I'll stay here.

"We'll split some shakes," I said. Teetering around the room, picking up my stuff and storing it back into where it belonged, refolding those stiff canvas Carhartt pants along the seams, carefully as they could be folded, I felt like a child on a slippery floor, and Ruth eyed my moves like all of a sudden she wasn't quite sure what she wanted after all. Ruth could see I wasn't going anywhere, and the rest was up to her. There was no one thing to say, and I still cannot name the good fortune I saw except as things to do.

"You coming with me?" I said. In this country they roof their houses with shakes split from pure cedar. We went out that afternoon and bought a straight-grain cedar-tree log and had it hauled to us. Ruth wouldn't hardly look at me or say anything, but she went along.

◆

That night Ruth slept in her chair with her magazines. By late the next day we had built a canopy of clear plastic to keep our work dry from the rain, and we started splitting the shakes, side by side. We will build a house where our things to do can be thick with time on our hands.

People will watch us build, and we will be the ones who know the secret. We'll watch strangers on the sand flats. We'll know they envy us our house built of cedar logs. We will live with one garden that grows nothing but red and yellow flowers, and we'll have another garden with cabbages. Our dogs and our cats will sleep on the beds, and me and Ruth will carve faces into the cedar-log walls, and those faces will smile back at us in our dreams and be our friends and warn us of trouble, looking back at us like we were the world, and watching what we do like we watch the seabirds picking on the rocks at low tide.

There will be cabins with covered walkways to the house. My father could live in one, and my mother could come visit, and Ruth and I and my father and mother could all go down to the movie house and over to Brownie's after the show.

Your mind is sometimes full of little animals and you have to trick them with things to see. We will live in our house like the old people lived in their houses. Maybe we will come to know what it is like to lie awake in the night while our children listen for our talking and laughing as we listen for theirs.

DAVID KRANES

NEVADA DREAMS

Nevada wakes up before her alarm in her half-trailer which sits atilt on a rock shelf in the Spanish Springs Valley at the foot of the Virginia Mountains, and she smells the Basco's blood. It is not her friend, the Basco, himself, of course—his blood—it's the lamb he slaughtered for Easter last night. The Basco lives in the trailer's other half—there with his wools and vegetable dyes and loom and hates being called the Basco; he says his name is yes-of-course Basque, but Emmett. Emmett Laxalt. Still, people don't always get called what they want. Which Nevada knows. And knows, as well, that such with-holding can be good, can keep a person's pride from running in herds like the mustangs Wild Horse Annie has struggled to save. So it's sometimes good, sometimes bad: to not call a person by his name; Nevada chooses good.

The Basco is a fine man though, a fine weaver and caretaker—both of his sheep and of Nevada herself, who he found living in an abandoned lavender Thunderbird. Fine enough, as well, not to worry about what he's called. But Nevada wishes nevertheless that the blood hadn't found its way through their common wall, especially with the snow falling. She's probably breathed the blood all night without knowledge and may well carry it to work, making change at the Comstock. Still, the Basco has been good in his pledge to cook them Easter dinner. He's outside, even now, so early, moving stones to line his firepit. A flame leaps up: he has set a match to the cedar; it's his way of saying good morning. The cedar tinder will enflame the logs which will make the coals to roast the lamb. They are not lovers, though both know the Basco has had that in his head. They share halves of this twin trailer out of need, out of circumstance. So he is good, the Basco—Nevada having said *no* and *no* again, twice, during the last year—to nevertheless care for her and try to make this Easter Day close and proper. Because there are other men, other places Nevada dreams of and hopes for. There are other lives she imagines.

Nevada is not *of* this place. She was not born but came here: to this Reno, this valley, these hills, this nearly bottomless lake. And her name has been only briefly Nevada. Before, it was two names—Iona and Gallegos, Iona Gallegos, the first before the second and both from the country of Guatemala. But on her way moving north in bursts and angles—hiding, working, taking flight, her English poor—when people asked *What'syourname?* she thought herself asked *Where'reyougoing?* and answered (because she'd heard of jobs with no green cards) *Nevada.* So, sixteen-seventeen-eighteen, then—working fields, cleaning a thousand overnight rooms—that became her name: she simply stopped being Iona Gallegos, daughter of the singing Elena Gallegos, and started being Nevada.

And she has been Nevada, now, for nearly a dozen years and in this trailer for six. Still, she remembers herself before. She remembers Iona Gallegos—the child, the emerging woman and daughter of her singing mother, Elena. And remembers their small home outside Puerto Barrios. She remembers being daughter of her father too, though he was nearby so seldom—appearing only with other men, all with guns. And there would be a meal—pig, lamb somehow suddenly instead of roots, beans, fried bread. And they would all eat, the men, like filthy ghosts, growling and laughing and making jokes with Elena Gallegos, her singing mother. But then they would all be gone in the morning. And Nevada remembers the Caribbean too, where she and her mother occasionally swam, there in the Gulf of Honduras. And she remembers the sounds of planes. And guns. And men's voices traveling to them over speakers—like but not like the Comstock's: "Mechanic to slot 273, please! Mechanic to slot 273!"—more, really, like dark birds with huge wings trying to fly, the wings ripping in the air; sounds, tearing and terrible and impossible to sing away.

And finally, what Nevada remembers about where she first lived near Puerto Barrios, were the men who came and began asking her singing mother, Elena, questions. About her father. And how they seemed nice at first and made jokes (one gave her a paper bird). But when her mother refused to answer and only sang—louder and louder—the men grew angrier and struck. Then Nevada remembers how sure she'd been something terrible would happen. And how it had.

Or . . . had it? It's, now sometimes, so hard to know. Yet Nevada remembers night. She remembers the men pulling her mother, still singing, outside. Starting the engine of their truck. Stringing small wires with clamps from under the hood (Nevada obscured in the bordering trees): how they revved the truck—her mother, singing all the more: proudly and sweetly over the growling truck—and how the men set their clamps to her mother's tongue. And Nevada remembers what seemed then to be a miracle: the sound of her mother's voice, her mother's tongue, like a bulb, lit in her mouth. And then it all going black. The night. The scene. Her mother's mouth and then whole face, black like burnt neon. And then one of the men saying: *Esta muerta,* another disconnecting the wires and clamps, the three climbing back into the truck and driving away.

And finally, Nevada remembers remembering her mother's words: *Corre. Corre hacia el norte. Si algro pasa . . . corre hacia el norte.* ("Run. Run north. If anything happens . . . run north"), and so, fifteen only that night but doing that: running. North. *What'syourname?/Where'reyougoing?/ . . . Nevada.*

And so: yes; in part it's a terrible place Nevada's come from and that visits her still sometimes, slipping behind her eyes, refusing disregard. And perhaps her life, making change, riding her trail bike to and from, being a woman nearly alone except for the Basco in these weed-and-stone-colored hills—perhaps all of this might appear without grace and to hold no future. But Nevada dreams! Of course, partly it is herself: the dreaming. But partly, as well, it is this land she's come to, filled, from first conquests, with its immense permission. Dreams! And she has seen huge birds, blue, blue birds, work their wings over the green bays of Pyramid Lake and a Vietnamese woman win over a million dollars on a MegaBucks. And every day, almost, she dreams her mother's tongue—all song, all light. So— dreaming, seeing—Nevada knows, for instance, that in America there are cowboys who speak the poetry of their sometimes-in-the-icy-wind working lives into microphones. She has heard them! In this very state! And they're real. And even the Basco tells stories. And she has seen him, his shirt like a silk flower on the ground, lift a cut ponderosa log over his head nearly a hundred times. So: if one good-then-better thing becomes possible, Nevada believes yet-the-next-better thing might as well, and so she practices what she practices: gratitude, patience and hope. She has told the Basco that. It has become a joke, but a true one, between them. And when she refused the last time to come with the Basco to his bed, he fixed his jaw briefly. There were hooks in his eyes that might have scared Nevada. He pressed his lips with a sadness even Nevada could see—but then said, "Well . . . gratitude, patience, hope . . . no problem. I've got time."

◆

When Nevada hauls her Yamaha bike out from her half-trailer to set off for the Comstock, the Basco says, "Good morning, my dear," and sweeps a hat down through the nearly five o'clock dark, parting the ash-dry snow and scattering it.

"Good morning," Nevada says and walks her bike over to what's become a full fire in the pit. Its sprockets make a low chatter.

"Beautiful scarf!" the Basco says. He winks. It was a gift, one he wove. Wove especially. After the second time she said no.

Nevada smiles. She sees the lamb, covered by a small tarpaulin, and can taste, suddenly on the roof of her mouth and behind her nose, its now-oiled spices and blood. "Nice fire," she says. She sees the Basco grinding leaves in a stoneware bowl. "What are those?" she asks.

"Herbs," he says. "More herbs."

She asks: "Which?"

He tells her: "Secret."

"Of course," Nevada says and smiles.

"You know what?" the Basco says—proud and suddenly grinning.

"What?" Nevada says.

"Someone . . . going to give you big tip today," he says.

"Good," Nevada says. "Good; we need it. We need all the tips I can get."

"We?" the Basco teases.

Nevada starts her bike. "Just us?" she asks; "Two? All that lamb?" She calls her questions over the Yamaha's drone.

The Basco shrugs.

"So maybe . . . maybe I'll invite my—I don't know—boy-friend," Nevada says then realizes she's pushed her playfulness too far. "Just kidding," she says.

"Of course," the Basco says and rocks back on his heels from the flame of his fire.

Then Nevada begins—along the packed trail which will take her

two miles to Nevada 445. The Basco's wine-and-gold and here-and-
there turquoise scarf beats the wind behind her.

◆

Reno's lights announce themselves halfway, and she's at the rear
of the Comstock a good ten minutes before morning shift, which
starts at six. She locks her bike, goes in, hangs her down vest and scarf
in her locker, retrieves her jacket and is on the floor fully three minutes before the hour. The slots are busy for a Sunday morning. But
it's Easter. By seven, an off-duty fry cook from Fitzgerald's hits a
quarter progressive for over four thousand and gives Nevada a hundred: You gave me the dollars that I used! he says. She smiles; the
Basco's already a prophet; it seems a good day.

At nine-thirty, she breaks for breakfast and sits eating hot seven-
grain cereal in the coffee shop with her friend, the dealer, Arnelle
who tells Nevada she did too much cocaine the night before. "Any
much is too much," Nevada says.

"Any much is too much!" Arnelle repeats; she coughs a laugh.
"That's good! I have to remember that." Then Arnelle tells Nevada
Arnelle's father has threatened to come in from Albuquerque: "I'm
on pins and needles," Arnelle says.

Often Nevada can only guess at things which Arnelle says—what
they mean. But she likes her friend; she likes her laugh; it sounds like
the beach waves pulling back across shells and pebbles on the Gulf of
Honduras. She likes Arnelle's fleshiness as well and frosted hair.
Arnelle's helped Nevada write her application to move from change
to dealing. Sometimes, when they break, Arnelle gives lessons with a
single deck, assuring Nevada she's a natural; it's just time. What Nevada likes most about Arnelle is that she's encouraging.

Back on the floor, Nevada gets another twenty dollars; it's a
woman whose Joker's Wild has just unloaded two hundred coins. And
then, circulating, Nevada sees a man with a yellow mustache taking
his turn at the dice table. And Nevada knows the man because she's
seen him—eyes like trout holding water behind a rock—seen him in
Elko being glad over a microphone. The man's a cowboy from near
Dixie Valley. And poet. She remembers him saying:

> I know what fills my heart
> and know what hurts.

> *I sew the buttons on*
> *my own work shirts.*

and remembers, as well, him singing about his sheepdog, a dog, Nevada recalls, named Tall, who—the Cowboy-Poet sang—could filet bones from German browns caught in the Humboldt Salt Marsh outlets.

Nevada moves nearly beside the Cowboy, the Poet, who has just made an eight and had the table cheer and feels, partly, that it's her admiration which has brought him luck: her wishing him all that she can wish, having loved his voice and words so much in Elko.

His name is Wayne McCloud. She remembers and says, without planning, "Wayne McCloud" openly. And, with her saying, Wayne McCloud turns and studies her and grins, his yellow mustache taking a turn, as on an axle, just above his lip; his body gently pressing a Stetson between himself and the dice table, leaning soft, Nevada thinks, as though one of the two—hat or cowboy—were a woman. Her words, his name, still trail lightly in the air. Like the smell of bacon. Like cigarette smoke. Wayne McCloud.

"In the flesh!" he says. "In the flesh . . . and winning!" He laughs.

And Nevada remembers his laugh, his gladness in Elko when he didn't mean to but then said *oops* over the microphone and how it tripped chills between her shoulders.

"You stay there!" Wayne McCloud instructs, and he turns back, lifts the dice, rolls an eleven. The table cheers. Wayne McCloud raises his fist over his head. He shouts, "Let it ride!" Eight other players shout back, "Let it ride!" and with their shout, Wayne McCloud circles an arm out and into the air which he clearly expects Nevada to step under, so that he can pull her close.

Which she does. And he does. Then rolls a seven and the entire table applauds. He sings a line—no guitar—*Some days it's all where you are,* and Nevada remembers the line and song. She's so nervous she can barely breathe. Wayne McCloud squeezes her; he calls her Peach.

For the next fifteen minutes, Wayne McCloud wins money and more money. Nevada says she should be on the floor, but Wayne says, Not a chance, and DeGrazzi, the pit boss, nods to her, no problem; you're fine, so Nevada relaxes. Then, when Wayne McCloud finishes winning, and after he's given her two black chips, Nevada reveals that she's seen him, once, in Elko. She says, You said this . . . you sang that, and she remembers specific verses such that Wayne McCloud lights up and says, "Well, I'll be a gelding's dick!" Then apologizes. His shame makes a kind of candle; it has light in it. So Nevada invites him after work, up to Spanish Springs Valley for an Easter dinner.

Wayne McCloud smiles. His smile smiles, somehow. He studies her, looking for . . . she can't tell what: something. "You've got it!" he says finally then, "Say: you're a pretty woman. You married?"

And now Nevada blushes. "No . . . no." She repeats the word curiously. Then, because she feels she must, she tells Wayne McCloud that it won't be just them; they won't be alone. Her friend, the Basco Emmett, will be there.

"Who?" Wayne McCloud asks.

"Emmett," Nevada says, "my friend, Emmett. He's the one cooking the lamb."

"Sounds like a winner," Wayne McCloud says—though he seems uncertain.

"How's Tall?" Nevada asks, remembering Wayne's wonderful brown trout poem. "Your dog, Tall?" It makes her feel good to ask the question.

But Wayne McCloud only shivers—blown by some blast of snow. The trout behind the rock pools in his eyes move laterally. He doesn't answer at first, and Nevada knows memory pictures are in his head: she has had them in hers. It's okay, she wants to say; it doesn't matter, but Wayne cuts in: "He's mostly stupid. He's mostly stupid these days. He got kicked in the head."

"Cow?" Nevada manages.

"No. No . . . stupid sheepherder," Wayne McCloud says. And his words seem to set them both thinking . . . but then they agree on a time—two-thirty—to meet back at this very table, and they move separate ways.

◆

So now Nevada has three hundred and twenty dollars and works with the knowledge she will be having Easter dinner with Wayne McCloud, the Cowboy-Poet. *America* . . . then *Nevada,* Nevada thinks: Men with trout in their eyes say poems into microphones . . . and you can meet them . . . and share bread. She has paid attention; she has seen and heard; she has dreamed and there is proof—again, Nevada feels: again—that dreams come true.

◆

So she works the floor: gives change—gives quarters, dimes, gives nickels. She fills in for her friend, Anita, on the Aurora Carousel, handing out trays of dollars. A blond girl in a rabbit skin coat and leather skirt wins two thousand for three blue sevens and gives Nevada another hundred. Nevada has never had this kind of day. When Anita gets back, Nevada tries giving the hundred to her, but Anita says no; split, and so they do. And when it's done, Nevada takes her own five minutes to walk outside because she's sure it will have stopped snowing, that the streets will be warm. And she's right: the sun's nearly overhead like ripe fruit, and the day, in fact, has that taste: gingerroot, plantain, lemon rind.

◆

When she meets Wayne McCloud, he is very drunk, so drunk it frightens her. His words don't light up like her mother's tongue but spill like sludge oil. She wonders if she should say no, even lie: say the lamb caught fire, burned up, is only bone, bone only. But Wayne McCloud—standing there in his soft-leather coat, his guitar in a canvas jacket slung over his shoulder—seems incredibly sad; he seems a sad poet and there should be sad poets too, or sad poet days: not every poem, not every song needs to make you wish and hope and smile.

So Nevada says nothing. But how should they get back? That's a question. Wayne McCloud has a Ford pickup, but he's drunk and knows it—"I couldn't drive a calf with the dry heaves!" he says. And then he asks—as though Nevada might have the answer—"Why am I drunk? Why did I do this?"

"I can't tell," Nevada says.

"Is it a secret?" Wayne McCloud asks. He's serious.

Nevada shrugs.

"I hate myself when I do this," Wayne McCloud confesses. "It's a stupid choice. Stupid, stupid choice. It's not me. Just . . . some kind of dumb version of . . . something . . . sometimes me." And then Wayne McCloud asks: "Do you know what I'm saying?"

"I might," Nevada says.

"I'm very angry at myself," Wayne McCloud says.

Nevada nods.

"I *did* keep my money though," he says. "That's good."

Nevada agrees.

Wayne McCloud gives Nevada his bulging soft-leather coat. "It's cold," he says. "You're a twig. Just a starter. Just a little thing. You'll freeze to death!"

Nevada wants to say: If I'd have frozen, I'd have frozen to death long before today. But she says nothing and accepts the coat, in the pockets of which, she can feel, are bottles.

But how will they get there? Wayne McCloud has his pickup but Nevada has no license. Applying, she's been told, might get her deported. So Wayne McCloud climbs onto the back of Nevada's Yamaha, and when he does the wheels seem only half as far from the ground. Still, the bike moves; the bike goes forward—puttering, belching—Wayne McCloud laughing now like three birds all in the air at the same time, his guitar thumping like an oil-drum—and they move along.

◆

It's not the best ride. Wayne falls off twice—once rolling almost under the tires of a semi heading south toward Sparks and making Nevada scream—then slyly rolling back just in time and scrambling to his feet: "Had you going there—didn't I?!" Nevada's heart pumps and hammers. She feels angry.

She nods *yes* and says: "Don't," and then "don't" again. Her words surprise her. They feel new. They feel good and bad at the same time. She thinks of Wayne McCloud's skin and what she knows will be road burn. It hurts. "Don't do that . . . or you can't come," she says.

And Wayne apologizes. If fact, he cries: "Why do I do this?" And when he cries, he shakes so that he can't stay on the back of Nevada's bike, so they have to wait, on the shoulder of Nevada 445, until his crying's done.

◆

But they manage and make it finally. On the approach, Nevada sees her dear, patient friend, Emmett the Basco, at the crest of the hill just above the trailer, and she knows he's been on the lookout and worried. Worrying *nos* and trying to weave them into *please-yeses*. Nevada waves. The Basco's mittened hand, bone colored in the air, speaks, and the word spoken is uncertainty. He's a good man. Nevada's late. He has seen another person behind her on the Yamaha. She wonders now whether she has made a choice which might not be the right one.

◆

Still, when Nevada and Wayne McCloud pull up, the Basco has run down on his snowshoes and is waiting with a broad smile. Nevada makes introductions. She calls the Basco "my friend, Emmett," and she can tell the Basco likes that. The Cowboy-Poet and the Basco shake. "Smells damn fine!" Wayne McCloud says; "somethin' here!" Then he surprises Nevada, suddenly reaching into the pockets of the long soft-leather coat he's bestowed and producing a bottle of Jack Daniel's black from one and of Irish Mist from the other: "We don't have to drink these," he says. "But they're my contribution. In fact: don't let me have any," he says; "I've had enough!"

It's well past four; the valley, almost all shadows, no visible sun— except a small flame at the top of the bare ridgetop trees. The Basco has a separate fire blazing for warmth. He's set one of his own woven pieces—black, gold, silver—over the outside table. There's a large cut-glass vase with piñon and yew boughs arranged—cones and berries. "You'd make any woman ashamed of being a woman," Nevada tells him. She hopes her words to be nice, especially, but they freeze in the air, somehow, like a bad announcement and no one seems to know what to do.

"Are you ashamed of being a woman . . . living here with me?" the Basco asks finally. Again: sincerity freezes midair.

Wayne McCloud moves over near the Basco's loom and unzips the case of his guitar, starts tuning. The Basco undoes the screwcap on Wayne McCloud's gift bottle of whiskey. He pours some into glasses, hands the glasses around. "To Our Lord," he proposes. Wayne McCloud regards his glass, uncertain. He studies the Basco, runs his tongue past his lips. They all drink, repeating, "To Our Lord"/"To Our Lord." It is Thanksgiving and Easter and a moment outside of time. Framed, the three look like figures in a painting.

Nevada asks, before they eat, if Wayne might say a poem and he does. It seems, momentarily, to sober him. He says one about an old rancher with just a single eye whose best friend is his three-legged dog; the poem's called "Stumbling Toward Love," and Wayne McCloud's own voice cracks and nearly breaks. He stands chest-forward and, under his milkblack silk cowboy shirt, seems to have Nevada's singing mother, Elena Gallegos' small breasts. The vision makes Nevada unsteady and, when that happens, she looks over to see the Basco running his hand, back and forth, over the wood shuttle of his loom.

They take seats. The Basco has placed Nevada beside himself, himself across from Wayne McCloud. The valley is dark now, the foothills barely marked against the night. There's a glow from the firepit, almost as if it comes from a deep underground—from another, a farther world. The Basco attempts a joke: he says one day, the whole state will be lit from beneath—like what they see: dig a hole, he says, the earth will shine frightening lights into the sky. He says all the lakes will be like green neon. His words twist Nevada's memory to a chill. There's an uncertain laughter, the Basco laughing more than the other two.

"He means the testing," Nevada explains to the Cowboy-Poet, but her mind moves back and forth like a white-tailed deer in a clearing.

"And the dump sites," the Basco says. "They going to make a new volcano out of Yucca Mountain."

This time no one laughs. There's too much truth. Wayne McCloud can't keep himself from staring, it seems, at the Basco. Caught doing it, he takes his hat off, takes his hair in a fist, resets his hat and fills everyone's whiskey glass.

Nevada wants both men to be friends. She smiles first at one then the other. She thinks: turn the conversation to sheep because they are in the hills and it's a subject. She remembers, only after she's introduced it, that Wayne McCloud's dog, Tall, has been kicked by a sheepherder in the head. Wayne McCloud drains his glass and recites an off-color poem entitled "Muttonshit." "Which is not to say," he tries, drunk again and ungainly in his recovery, "which is not to say, of course . . . that this is not an absolutely delicious dinner. Dead sheep . . . cooked . . . are wonderful. What's the green vegetable?"

The Basco says it's a kind of marsh grass.

"Marsh gas?" the Cowboy-Poet tries. He apologizes for his bad joke. "That's a stupid pun," he says: "Stupid . . . stupid pun. Don't let me drink anymore."

The Basco empties then fills his own whiskey glass. Wayne McCloud watches him. Nevada tries turning the conversation to trout. She thinks maybe it will prompt Wayne McCloud to think of Tall before his headkicking and remember when he was so clever, and she knows how the Basco loves fish. Fishing.

The two men end up shouting at one another: the Basco only fishes with lures and flies; he calls the Poet a "meathead" and "butcher" for using salmon eggs.

"I eat all the fish I catch," Wayne McCloud says then gestures toward their meal." "Who's the butcher?" he says.

"Please," Nevada says.

"You're a Basque—aren't you!" Wayne McCloud says. "You're one of . . ."

"He's an American," Nevada says. Her voice surprises her.

"I'm a Basque!" Emmett the Basco says: "Basque! Basco!" He leaps from the table, breaks into song, moves his feet; by firelight. They are being treated to a traditional dance.

Wayne McCloud observes. There's admiration: no doubt—Nevada can see; it's in his eyes—but then a craziness sweeps in and Wayne shouts: "You know—if sheep didn't spend all their stupid time pissing in the water, there'd be enough trout for everybody and they'd grow bigger."

Nevada asks both men: please . . . please, don't argue, then asks if either has been to the Mustang Ranch. She hates her question. She hates thinking of women, women like herself, doing what they do there in those trailers (she's seen; she's driven past), those rooms. Still, this *is* the place it is; it is its own state, and Nevada ventures that both men being single—it might be a common ground. So she asks. And both men stop. And look at her. And then they look at each other. There's silence.

"He doesn't need to . . . doesn't need the Mustang—he's got his sheep," Wayne McCloud finally offers. His words move, grumbling, in his mustache.

"And you've got your three-legged dog," the Basco roars.

Wayne McCloud's eyes flare.

"I wish we could all laugh!" Nevada says.

But there's new silence . . . which gets worse—so bad the tamarack branches snapping in the pitfire sound like ground strafing.

Finally the Basco barks a laugh, which opens up, like a hole, in the silence again . . . and then the silence opens to the Basco's question, straight across the table: "Wayne?"

Nevada knows—hearing the one word, the name—*Wayne?*—knows trouble.

"Wayne . . . ?" the Basco goes on, "I just cur'ous . . . how you getting back tonight?"

"He can stay," Nevada says quickly.

"Where?" the Basco asks.

"Here," Nevada says.

"No." The Basco speaks without margin.

"You have room," Nevada says.

"No," the Basco says. "No. No room."

"Well. . . ."

"No," the Basco repeats.

"No what?" Nevada finds herself angry; the Basco's not being who he can be.

"No: not with you," the Basco says.

"Well. . . ." Nevada feels her words sputter like bacon fat. "Well—not for you to say," she manages.

"Oh?" the Basco says. He laughs. "Oh—well, I say *yes*. Okay? I say yes . . . 'cause I won't lets him."

"Hey . . ." Wayne McCloud holds his hands out; the wind, a partner to his dance. "Hey . . . if the lady says: come to my bed. . . ."

"That's not what I . . ." Nevada begins.

"Funny: sounded like. . . ."

"You can use my couch," Nevada says.

"No bed; no couch!" the Basco says. "He use your couch . . . I come in . . . throw him out."

The Cowboy grabs the Jack Daniel's and skips the glass. The neck of the bottle pops in his mouth on the hit like a cork. Whiskey sprays up his nose. *"Throw me out!* Oh, yeah; hey: *Throw me out!"* he mocks. "You couldn't throw shit with a chainsaw!"

"Gentlemens . . . gentlemens . . . !" Nevada tries.

"Couldn't throw . . . ? No but you . . . you could—I heard you!" The Basco coughs. The night air, swept from the snow and rocks, has the chewed edges of scrap iron, and it's hit and circled his throat.

Suddenly both men are up and moving and away from the table.

The Basco's got a big and curved shearing knife in his glove, which keeps winking in the firelight. Wayne McCloud's fist is around the neck of the Irish Mist bottle. "You're a dead man!" he tells the Basco.

Nevada imagines the word *stop*. It's in her brain—*stop*—nearly in her mouth. But at first it's so small it's not even a ground squirrel a mile away. And the men—the Basco leading—flare on.

"Then my ghost . . . my ghost gonna feed you balls to my sheep!" the Basco says. "All fried up like scones!"

Wayne McCloud hooks a wide arc with his bottle.

The Basco's blade slices a diagonal down.

"Stop!" Nevada gets the word out—announces it, proclaims it. And both men stop. Then she says again—tears now, urgency—looking first to her friend, the Basco, then to Wayne McCloud: "Stop. Stop this. This is Easter."

And Nevada cries. Outright. Yet speaks. "Stop. Stop this. This is Easter. Our Lord died. Our Lord gave up his life. But lives. Lives, and we blessed Him, blessed His name. Before we shared our Easter dinner. 'To Our Lord.' I never told you, Basco, but my mother . . ." Nevada can't go on, can't speak, she is crying so hard. But both men wait because they see her need and feel her power and she recovers. "My mother . . . my mother died singing a song," Nevada says. "Her tongue lit up in her mouth . . . like the moon. And I saw her. And I see her. Every day, every night . . . in the sky of my life. My mother gave up her life for me . . . so that I might live. This is America. We are American people. We are all from—yes—different places. But this is our land. And this is our food." She gestures—to the nearby, to the close—where they have all been together. "Look! Look: our table. Our food. Are we strangers? Have we not shared this lamb? This delicious lemon rice, this bread—these things? No one will be without a bed. No one will be without a bed tonight. No one will be without a friend."

And like other moments before—Nevada's words knit up a picture in the air—the patience of them, the gratitude, their hope. And the moment is a stopped moment—like one by the painter Goya or by El Greco.

And both men set down what they have picked up ruthlessly and in anger: the Basco his knife into a sheath on a hanging belt. The Cowboy-Poet, the Irish Mist bottle which he immediately uncorks and hands on to Nevada, who pauses at first then lifts it and drinks, handing it on to the Basco, who drinks in turn and hands the bottle back to Wayne McCloud.

Then the Basco wanders to his loom. His fingers play and he moves its shuttle, as though weaving the flinty air, the dim crescent moon. And Wayne McCloud, the Cowboy-Poet, moves himself aside and looks up, up and out over the ridges of hills, and he begins speaking a poem: "It's called 'Branding In Winter,' " he says, really to himself; his words are quiet.

And Nevada, between them, begins to sing. Near where the Basco had arranged it that morning and begun the flame and where the earth is still opened in its light, Nevada squares herself against the stars and becomes the child of her mother. From the dull, childish landscape, it rises up. Nevada sings.

When they were children, both my grandmothers had their feet bound; thereafter they had to learn to balance their feelings very carefully. *The pain, too, will pass,* Renoir said in 1903. Renoir was to become a friend of my mother, Katherine, who was not yet born at the time he first said these words; but he repeated every word in 1910 when she was two and they became friends. This time he was, however, not referring to the pain which accompanied Katherine's mother's bound feet when she was a child, but instead anticipated the alienation that Katherine was to feel later from the Tai Chung community for not binding her feet. Strangers sitting on the stoops of their houses and shops all over the city would point to her outsized feet and untethered walk and whisper comments along under their breath.

◆

At five Katherine said to Renoir, *I will never drop an egg from the high beam.*

◆

Later she went to school abroad and met her husband shortly after he had publicly cut his cue in a Berkeley demonstration.

◆

Then the magical happened in 1944 in Chungking: overnight Katherine disappeared from our lives, followed by absolute silence. In the first forty-three years after her disappearance, not a whisper was said in the family about Katherine or her disappearance, at least not within my listening.

◆

But now the children and the other children are beginning to dissent. First there was the memory that would not go away. Then there was the garrulous word *Renoir,* eventually hatching question. Then the whispers ripped the shaded heart. Soon the nights were humming with telephone conversations. We made contact with the secretary of immigration, the archivist of birth records, the alumni minister; we pored over maps and old driving records; we interviewed postal carriers, tricksters, insurance chancellors, and even tried to get into the Mormon Redemption Center. We looked up every taxonomy and geography, and collected everything tangible from both sides of the Pacific.

◆

We are here for the duration, carefully balanced between address and rumor, carefully watching those who are siphoning from our pain, allowing us to go on. In the early morning our children will thrust from our thighs and float away from us, like chilled stars.

ABSENCES

I n the early spring of 1944 the Yangtze River wreaked its annual havoc on the inhabitants living along its shores. I had turned five, and remember crossing the river with my parents at the height of its flood.

No. In 1944 I crossed the Yangtze River with my parents. It seemed to me as a five-year-old that most of the world had sunk under the turbulent, heavy water. There as flotsam, the branches and logs and pieces of lumber, a dead chicken, bloated goat, carried a sucking dark smell that the wind and brown current would not dissipate.

◆

Everything has shifted just a little since, probably including more of what wasn't there than what was.

◆

From the first tense of my memory life, I have only two or three impressions of my father. This was one of them. He seldom told by example and even less by word. He was away most of the time, but he was to tell me four years later when I had just finished practicing the piano, he said *Don't follow in the steps of Turgenev.*

So this one I remember, though not in this order. The Yangtze starts somewhere in the Tibetan Highlands and meanders some 3,500 miles before it empties into the East China Sea at Shanghai. Until dams and levees were constructed to control the river's annual spring flood, much of the lowlands was threatened every year. But this was 1944, years before the completion of the flood-control project.

The water was muddy that spring, that is to say, I remember the color of the water.

◆

Shouting at another boat that had turned over upstream from ours, our boatman steered to scavenge the planks drifting downriver from the fast-sinking sampan. From the opposite end of ours, my father stood up dangerously with an oar and threatened to knock him overboard unless he helped with the drowning victims of the overturned boat. It had taken courage for me to get into that little boat in that swift water in the first place; then I cried and shivered and held on to my mother's hand for comfort, and kept an anxious eye on the diminishing closest shore. But the voices of my father's and the boatman's—shouting, cursing, threatening—made the crest of the opposite shore tilt ever so steeper as the two of them pitched back and forth, both boats sweeping downriver out of control.

◆

High above the Yangtze that summer, we lived in a house on a plateau to the south of the river. It was the last summer that my brother Will lived at home, the last summer that our father had a garden for his tomatoes. It was also the year before the end of the war.

◆

If what happened imperfectly there on that river included my holding on to my mother, Katherine's, hand for the crossing, I have no image of her face, not even from earlier photographs. I held on to her same hand again a year later when she and I flew from Chungking to Shanghai in a stuffed C-47 cargo plane with makeshift wooden seats roped alongside its inside wall.

◆

It was also a summer that involved a strange funeral procession that left me stranded by the gates of the house. Was it my mother's, and it was someone else's hand that I held on to during the flight to Shanghai? Did Katherine disappear that summer, or the next?

◆

Now when I am alone playing a piece on the piano, I sometimes hear the pitch shifting ever so slightly above the noise of that summer. Under my eyelids I can still see the pagodas perched high in the distance above the gorge of the rampaging river in my sleep, the tiny monks sequestered from the roily din below.

ALEX KUO

CICADAS

This happened in 1944, probably well into the August of summer, at least several months after the Yangtze had receded. The war must have started turning around for Chiang Kai-shek; daily, past the heavy wooden gates of our villa, endless columns of Kuomintang troops were marching towards the coast on the road parallel to the river. Breaking the monotonous clanging of their mess kits was the occasional low whirring hum of a staff car with its unit chevron, or a truck, its canvas flap concealing what was inside. But mostly there were hundreds and hundreds of soldiers moving at the same speed as the vehicles, their uniform the exact ordinary color as the road dust they stirred. Some of them didn't have rifles, and I remember my brother Will say that some of the others did not have ammunition. One or two of these faces would always be turned up toward where I was watching them from the top of the steps in front of the gates. My mother told me I had to keep the gates closed. I was five that summer, and lowered the bar on the gates as I was told.

That was also the summer I learned about cicadas and departures of another kind. Will had a highly prized bamboo stick of at least twelve or fifteen feet long, and he taught me how to catch cicadas with it. First he would show me by example, then he would stand behind me and help me as I was tested before I was on my own.

We would first slowly twist the upper tip of the stick around spiderwebs that were found in crevices around the house and the wall that surrounded it until the tip was darkened and crested with the sticky cobweb. When he was helping, there were four hands on that stick turning it in unison, and I remember feeling a sense of purposefulness in that exactitude. Occasionally he would ask me to let go of the stick so that he could reach higher under the roof's edges.

Finding the cicadas was easy. We would stand still and listen. It seemed in that summer the steady stridulation of a high-pitched resonance was always in the air. Even today when every other noise is down in my life, my inner ear would echo that continuous sound, the electrical strike of cicadas at first hearing. We would listen for breaks in that sound, a short but sustained grinding note repeated again and again, and follow it to the small, darkish lumps on tree branches silhouetted against the clear skies of Chungking.

The delicate movement of approaching the cicadas from below and behind was the most difficult technique to learn. It had to be done slowly, so the insect would not be frightened off, but not too slowly to allow its escape. I now suspect the truthfulness of this part of Will's instruction as much as his report about the soldiers' ammunition supply. Once enough strength was mustered to control the quivering of the stick's tip fifteen feet up and contact made, the cicada was doomed.

What I don't remember now is what we did with the cicadas afterwards. I imagine that Will probably had a little stickcage for them, or a matchbox, in which he kept alive our collection with daily ablutions of water. We would lift it once in a while, shake it, expecting to stimulate ethereal song from the captured cicadas. This was the summer of my earliest recollection, held captive until now in these unspoken and inescapable images. This was also the summer in which Will, being married at the time, had accidentally slipped into the bed of a servant one night and was henceforth banished forever into a cage of his own making.

ALEX KUO

GROWING
TOMATOES

In 1944, when I was very young, my family lived in a huge house outside Chungking, just a stone's throw from the river that flooded every spring. We had goats, ducks, geese that chased after me, and a vegetable garden. I remember my father gathering giant tomatoes from his garden and juicing them into a large porcelain bowl on the square dining room table. I still remember the glassfuls tasting dank and dark. To this day I still cannot stand its rawness, but drink it camouflaged in a Bloody Mary.

Since I've moved to Idaho and live in my own house, I've been raising vegetable gardens in the backyard every season. Among the corn, squashes, eggplant, spinach and beet I've always saved room for a few tomato plants, even though I never eat them but give them away to friends at harvest time.

In the middle of the summer I would sometimes walk out of the house and listen to these plants grow, often flicking tiny black aphids from off their stems and leaves. In these moments the tangy odor of their leaves draws childhood recollections of a father dead nineteen years, images of his hands immersed in the white bowl of tomato juice from his garden, his saying *Drink it, drink it, it's only good for you, it's vitamin C.*

Tonight, at exactly my father's age in 1944 and nearly five thousand miles and fifty years from my past, I wake to hear the tomato leaves brushing gently against the back door of my house in the breeze, and soon after, the fruit bursting like blood in the burgeoning quarter moon.

URSULA K. LeGUIN

◆

SLEEPWALKERS

John Felburne

I told the maid not to come to clean the cabin before four o'clock, when I go running. I explained that I'm a night person and write late and sleep in, mornings. Somehow it came out that I'm writing a play. She said, "A stage play?" I said yes, and she said, "I saw one of those once." What a wonderful line. It was some high school production, it turned out, some musical. I told her mine was a rather different kind of play, but she didn't ask about it. And actually there would be no way to explain to that sort of woman what I write about. Her life experience is so incredibly limited. Living out here, cleaning rooms, going home, and watching TV—*Jeopardy* probably. I thought of trying to put her in my characters notebook and got as far as "Ava: the Maid," and then there was nothing to write. It would be like trying to describe a glass of water. She's what people who say "nice" mean when they say, "She's nice." She'd be completely impossible in a play, because she never does or says anything but what everybody else does and says. She talks in clichés. She *is* a cliché. Forty or so, middle-sized, heavy around the hips, pale, not very good complexion, blondish—half the white women in America look like that. Pressed out of a mold, made with a cookie cutter. I run for an hour, hour and a half, while she's cleaning the cabin, and I was thinking, she'd never do anything like running, probably doesn't do any exercise at all. People like that don't take any control over their lives. People like her in a town like this live a mass-produced existence, stereotypes, getting their ideas from the TV. Sleepwalkers. That would make a good title, "Sleepwalkers." But how could you write meaningfully about a person who's totally predictable? Even the sex would be boring.

There's a woman in the creekside cabin this week. When I jog down to the beach, afternoons, she watches me. I asked Ava about her. She said she's Mrs. McAn, comes every summer for a month. Ava said, "She's very nice," of course. McAn has rather good legs. But old.

Katharine McAn

If I had an air gun I could hide on my deck and pop that young man one on the buttock when he comes pumping past in his little purple stretchies. He eyes me.

I saw Virginia Herne in Hambleton's today. Told her the place was turning into a goddamn writers' colony, with her collecting all these Pulitzers or whatever they are, and that young man in the shingled cabin sitting at his computer till four in the morning. It's so quiet at the Hideaway that I can hear the thing clicking and peeping all night. "Maybe he's a very diligent accountant," Virginia said. "Not in shiny purple stretch shorts," I said. She said, "Oh, that's John" Somebody, "yes, he's had a play produced, in the East somewhere, he told me." I said, "What's he doing here, sitting at your feet?" and she said, "No, he told me he needed to escape the pressures of culture, so he's spending a summer in the West." Virginia looks very well. She has that dark, sidelong flash in her eye. A dangerous woman, mild as milk. "How's Ava?" she asked. Ava house-sat her place up on Breton Head last summer when she and Jaye were traveling, and she takes an interest in her, though she doesn't know the story Ava told me. I said Ava was doing all right.

I think she is, in fact. She still walks carefully, though. Maybe that's what Virginia saw. Ava walks like a *tai ji* walker, like a woman on a high wire. One foot directly in front of the other, and never any sudden movements.

I had tea ready when she knocked, my first morning here. We sat at the table in the kitchen nook, just like the other summers, and talked. Mostly about Jason. He's in tenth grade now, plays baseball, skateboards, surfboards, crazy to get one of those windsail things and go up to Hood River—"Guess the ocean isn't enough for him," Ava said. Her voice is without color, speaking of him. My guess is that the boy is like his father, physically at least, and that troubles or repels her, though she clings to him loyally, cleaves to him. And there might be a jealousy of him as the survivor: *Why you, and not her?* I don't know what Jason knows or feels about all that. The little I've seen of him when he comes by here, he seems a sweet boy, caught up in these sports boys spend themselves on, I suppose because at least they involve doing something well.

Ava and I always have to reagree on what work she's to do when I'm here. She claims if she doesn't vacuum twice a week and take out the trash, Mr. Shoto will "get after" her. I doubt he would, but it's her job and her conscience. So she's to do that, and look in every day or so to see if I need anything. Or to have a cup of tea with me. She likes Earl Grey.

Ken Shoto

She's reliable. I told Deb at breakfast, you don't know how lucky we are. The Brinnesis have to hire anything they can pick up, high school girls that don't know how to make a bed and won't learn, ethnics that can't talk the language and move on just when you've got them trained. After all, who wants a job cleaning motel rooms? Only somebody who hasn't enough education or self-respect to find something better. Ava wouldn't have kept at it if I treated her the way the Brinnesis treat their maids, either. I knew right away we were in luck with this one. She knows how to clean and she'll work for a dollar over minimum wage. So why shouldn't I treat her like one of us? After four years? If she wants to clean one cabin at seven in the morning and another one at four in the afternoon, that's her business. She works it out with the customers. I don't interfere. I don't push her. "Get off Ava's case, Deb," I told her this morning. "She's reliable, she's honest, and she's permanent—she's got that boy in the high school here. What more do you want? I tell you, she takes half the load off my back!"

"I suppose you think *I* ought to be running after her supervising her," Deb says. God, she can drive me crazy sometimes. What did she say that for? I wasn't blaming her for anything.

"She doesn't need supervising," I said.

"So you think," Deb said.

"Well, what's she done wrong?"

"Done? Oh, nothing. She couldn't do anything wrong!"

I don't know why she has to talk like that. She couldn't be jealous, not of Ava, my God. Ava's all right looking, got all her parts, but hell, she doesn't let you see her that way. Some women just don't. They just don't give the signals. I can't even think about thinking about her that way. Can't Deb see that? So what the hell does she have against Ava? I always thought she liked her OK.

"She's sneaky," is all she'd say. "Creepy."

I told her, "Aw, come on, Deb. She's quiet. Maybe not extra bright. I don't know. She isn't talkative. Some people aren't."

"I'd like to have a woman around who could say more than two words. Stuck in the woods out here."

"Seems like you spend all day in town anyhow," I said, not meaning it to be a criticism. It's just the fact. And why shouldn't she? I didn't take on this place to work my wife to death, or tie her down to it. I manage it and keep it up, and Ava Evans cleans the cabins, and Deb's free to do just what she wants to do. That's how I meant it to be. But it's like it's not enough, or she doesn't believe it, or something. "Well," she said, "if *I* had any responsibility, I wonder if you'd find *me* reliable." It is terrible how she cuts herself down. I wish I knew how to stop her from cutting herself down.

Deb Shoto

It's the demon that speaks. Ken doesn't know how it got into me. How can I tell him? If I tell him, it will kill me from inside.

But it knows that woman Ava. She looks so mild and quiet, *yes Mrs. Shoto, sure Mrs. Shoto*, pussyfooting it around here with her buckets and mops and brooms and wastebaskets. She's hiding. I know when a woman is hiding. The demon knows it. It found me. It'll find her.

There isn't any use trying to get away. I have thought I ought to tell her that. Once they put the demon inside you, it never goes away. It's instead of being pregnant.

She has that son, so it must have happened to her later, it must have been her husband.

I wouldn't have married Ken if I'd known it was in me. But it only began speaking last year. When I had the cysts and the doctor thought they were cancer. Then I knew they had been put inside me. Then when they weren't cancerous, and Ken was so happy, it began moving inside me where they had been, and then it began saying things to me, and now it says things in my voice. Ken knows it's there, but he doesn't know how it got there. Ken knows so much, he knows how to live, he lives for me, he is my life. But I can't talk to him. I can't say anything before it comes into my mouth just like my own tongue and says things. And what it says hurts Ken. But I don't know what to do. So he leaves, with his heavy walk and his mouth pulled down, and goes to his work. He works all the time, but he's getting fat. He shouldn't eat so much cholesterol. But he says he always has. I don't know what to do.

I need to talk to somebody. It doesn't talk to women, so I can. I wish I could talk to Mrs. McAn. But she's snobbish. College people are snobbish. She talks so quick, and her eyebrows move. Nobody like that would understand. She'd think I was crazy. I'm not crazy. There is a demon in me. I didn't put it there.

I could talk to the girl in the A-frame cabin. But she is so young. And they drive away every day in their pickup truck. And they are college people, too.

There is a woman comes into Hambleton's, a grandmother. Mrs. Inman. She looks kind. I wish I could talk to her.

Linsey Hartz

The people here in Hannah's Hideaway are so weird, I can't believe them. The Shotos. Wow. He's really sweet, but he goes around this place all day digging in the little channel he's cut from the creek to run through the grounds, a sort of toy creek, and weeding, and pruning, and raking, and the other afternoon when we came home he was picking up spruce needles off the path, like a housewife would pick threads off a carpet. And there's the little bridges over the little toy creek, and the rocks along the edges of the little paths between the cabins. He rearranges the rocks every day. Getting them lined up even, getting the sizes matched.

Mrs. Shoto watches him out her kitchen window. Or she gets in her car and drives one quarter mile into town and shops for five hours and comes back with a quart of milk. With her tight, sour mouth closed. She hates to smile. Smiling is a big production for her, she works hard at it, probably has to rest for an hour afterwards.

Then there's Mrs. McAn, who comes every summer and knows

everybody and goes to bed at 9 P.M. and gets up at 5 A.M. and does Chinese exercises on her porch and meditates on her roof. She gets onto the roof from the roof of her deck. She gets onto the roof of the deck from the window of the cabin.

And then there's Mr. Preppie, who goes to bed at 5 A.M. and gets up at 3 P.M. and doesn't mingle with the aborigines. He communicates only with his computer, and his modems, no doubt, and probably he has a fax in there. He runs on the beach every day at four, when the most people are on the beach, so that they can all see his purple spandex and his muscley legs and his hundred-and-forty-dollar running shoes.

And then there's me and George going off every day to secretly map where the Forest Service and the lumber companies are secretly cutting old growth stands illegally in the Coast Range so that we can write an article about it that nobody will publish even secretly.

Three obsessive-compulsives, one egomaniac, and two paranoids.

The only normal person at Hannah's Hideaway is the maid, Ava. She just comes and says "Hi," and "Do you need towels?" and she vacuums while we're out logger-stalking, and generally acts like a regular human being. I asked her if she was from around here. She said she'd lived here several years. Her son's in the high school. "It's a nice town," she said. There's something very clear about her face, something pure and innocent, like water. This is the kind of person we paranoids would be saving the forests for, if we were. Anyhow, thank goodness there are still some people who aren't totally fucked up.

Katharine McAn

I asked Ava if she thought she'd stay on here at the Hideaway. She said she guessed so.

"You could get a better job," I said.

"Yeah, I guess so," she said.

"Pleasanter work."

"Mr. Shoto is a really nice man."

"But Mrs. Shoto—"

"She's all right," Ava said earnestly. "She can be hard on him sometimes, but she never takes it out on me. I think she's a really nice person, but—"

"But?"

She made a slow, dignified gesture with her open hand: I don't know, who knows, it's not her fault, we're all in the same boat. "I get on OK with her," she said.

"You get on OK with anybody. You could get a better job, Ava."

"I got no skills, Mrs. McAn. I was brought up to be a wife. Where I lived in Utah, women are wifes." She pronounced it with the *f*, wifes. "So I know how to do this kind of job, cleaning and stuff. Anyhow."

I felt I had been disrespectful of her work. "I guess I just wish you could get better pay," I said.

"I'm going to ask Mr. Shoto for a raise at Thanksgiving," she said, her eyes bright. Obviously it was a long-thought-out plan. "He'll give it to me." Her smile is brief, never lingering on her mouth.

"Do you want Jason to go on to college?"

"If he wants to," she said vaguely. The idea troubled her. She winced away from it. Any idea of leaving Klatsand, of even Jason's going out into a larger world, scares her, probably will always scare her.

"There's no danger, Ava," I said very gently. It is painful to me to see her fear, and I always try to avoid pain. I want her to realize that she is free.

"I know," she said with a quick, deep breath, and again the wincing movement.

"Nobody's after you. They never were. It was a suicide. You showed me the clipping."

"I burned that," she said.

LOCAL MAN SHOOTS, KILLS DAUGHTER, SELF

She had showed the newspaper clipping to me summer before last. I could see it in my mind's eye with extreme clarity.

"It was the most natural thing in the world for you to move away. It wasn't 'suspicious.' You don't have to hide, Ava. There's nothing to hide from."

"I know," she said.

She believes I know what I'm talking about. She accepts what I say, she believes me as well as she can. And I believe her. All she told me I accepted as the truth. How do I know it's true? Simply on her word, and a newspaper clipping that might have been nothing but the seed of a fantasy? Certainly I have never known any truth in my life like it.

Weeding the vegetable garden behind their house in Indo, Utah, she heard a shot, and came in the back door and through the kitchen to the front room. Her husband was sitting in his armchair. Their twelve-year-old daughter Dawn was lying on the rug in front of the TV set. Ava stood in the doorway and asked a question, she doesn't remember what she asked, "What happened?" or "What's wrong?" Her husband said, "I punished her. She has polluted me." Ava went to her daughter and saw that she was naked and that her head had been beaten in and that she had been shot in the chest. The shotgun was on the coffee table. She picked it up. The stock was slimy. "I guess I was afraid of him," she said to me. "I don't know why I picked it up. Then he said, 'Put that down.' And I backed off towards the front door with it, and he got up. I cocked it, but he came towards me. I shot him. He fell down forwards, practically onto me. I put the gun down on the floor near his head, just inside the door. I went out and went down the road. I knew Jason would be coming home from baseball practice and I wanted to keep him out of the house. I met him on the road, and we went to Mrs."—she halted herself, as if her neighbor's name must not be spoken—"to a neighbor's house, and they called the police and the ambulance." She recited the story quietly. "They all thought it was a murder and suicide. I didn't say anything."

"Of course not," I murmured, dry of tongue.

"I did shoot him," she said, looking up at me, as if to make certain that I understood. I nodded.

She never told me his name, or their married name. Evans was her middle name, she said.

Immediately after the double funeral, she asked a neighbor to drive her and Jason to the nearest town where there was an Amtrak station. She had taken all the cash her husband had kept buried in the cellar under their stockpile of supplies in case of nuclear war or a Communist takeover. She bought two coach seats on the next train west. It went to Portland. At first sight she knew Portland was "too big," she said. There was a Coast Counties bus waiting at the Greyhound station down the street from the train station. She asked the driver, "Where does this bus go?" and he named off the little coast towns on his loop. "I picked the one that sounded fartherest," she said.

She and ten-year-old Jason arrived in Klatsand as the summer evening was growing dark. The White Gull Motel was full, and Mrs. Brinnesi sent her to Hannah's Hideaway.

"Mrs. Shoto was nice," Ava said. "She didn't say anything about us coming in on foot or anything. It was dark when we got here. I couldn't believe it was a motel. I couldn't see anything but the trees, like a forest. She just said, 'Well, that young man looks worn out,' and she put us in the A-frame, it was the only one empty. She helped me with the rollabed for Jason. She was really nice." She wanted to linger on these details of finding haven. "And next morning I went to the office and asked if they knew anyplace where I could find work, and Mr. Shoto said they needed a full-time maid. It was like they were waiting for me," she said in her earnest way, looking up at me.

Don't question the Providence that offers shelter. Was it also Providence that put the gun in her hand? Or in his?

She and Jason have a little apartment, an add-on to the Hanningers' house on Clark Street. I imagine that she keeps a photograph of her daughter Dawn in her room. A framed five-by-seven school picture, a smiling seventh-grader. Maybe not. I should not imagine anything about Ava Evans. This is not ground for imagination. I should not imagine the child's corpse on the rug between the coffee table and the TV set. I should not have to imagine it. Ava should not have to remember it. Why do I want her to get a better job, nicer work, higher wages—what am I talking about? The pursuit of happiness?

"I have to go clean Mr. Felburne's cabin," she said. "The tea was delicious."

"Now? But you're off at three, aren't you?"

"Oh, he keeps funny hours. He asked me not to come and clean till after four."

"So you have to wait around here an hour? The nerve!" I said. Indignation, the great middle-class luxury. "So he can go *running*? I'd tell him to go jump in the creek!" Would I? If I was the maid?

She thanked me again for the tea. "I really enjoy talking with you," she said. And she went down the neatly raked path that winds between the cabins, among the dark old spruce trees, walking carefully, one foot in front of the other. No sudden movements.

CRAIG LESLEY

MINT

M ost people start brushing their teeth or pop one of those red-and-white-striped mint candies into their mouths without thinking much about what went into the flavoring. Well, there's peppermint oil, of course, but other things, too: lots of sweat, boot grease, sheep and goose shit. (The farmers turn them loose in the fields to eat the quack grass.) And there are odd items such as a pitchfork and lunch bucket or two. After three weeks of working mint harvest, the crew gets a little crazy, and someone tosses things through the chopper blades, just to see what comes out. All you get from a lunch bucket is metal filings. A pitchfork produces filings and shavings.

I know pitchforks because I used to be a stomper, and a pitchfork was my tool-of-trade. The stomper rides in the back of a mint truck, a special kind of dump truck, and stomps the mint stems and leaves after they have been run through the chopper. It's important to spread the mint around evenly and pack it down tight. The corners are tricky, because you have to duck around the chopper's boom. During the first few hours each day, your sinuses run constantly because of the menthol; your eyes sting, too, even behind the safety goggles.

The stomper, truck driver, and chopper driver make a team. Right away, the stomper works out signals with the chopper driver. He relays them to the truck driver, who pulls the truck up a little or drops back, snugs closer to the chopper or gives it some room, so the chopped mint coming through the boom piles in different parts of the truckbed, saving the stomper a lot of pitchforking.

Hank Stone was my favorite truck driver the summer I'm talking about, the summer of the accident. Everyone in Madras loved Hank, because he had starred at forward for the White Buffalos. People still

remember those twenty-two second-half points in the state champi-
onship against Coquille. Hank was working mint harvest for pin
money, even though he had a full-ride scholarship to Oregon State
starting that fall.

Grady Price was one of the drifters who followed the harvests.
Originally from Modesto, or so he said, and his old Buick Roadmaster
had California plates. He looked like a lot of men that pass through—
about forty, field clothes and coveralls, large lumpy hands that come
from working with machinery. But he drove that old Fox chopper as
if he came out of the womb clutching a steering wheel, keeping it
lined right on the windrows of mowed mint and hardly ever jumping
a corrugation. And those old Foxes were cranky, too, not like your
new Cases or Massey Fergusons. Grady claimed that nothing held
them together but baling wire and cussing, and we used a lot of both
that summer.

Stomping in the truckbed, I watched Grady hunched over the
chopper's wheel, his dark suspenders making an X across his back. On
windy days, he'd tug his stained gray cap lower and tuck his head
down like a turtle. I never knew how he caught all my hand signals—
he hardly ever looked back—but some days it went so smoothly, I
quit using the pitchfork and just stomped and grinned, the mint flakes
sticking in my teeth. Grady tagged me with the nickname "Boots"
when he saw how stained my boots got from the green mint.

The three of us usually ate lunch together, resting in the shade of
the chopper. Grady brought corned beef sandwiches with the meat
sliced thick as two of his fingers. When he had finished eating, he
wiped the crumbs from his pants and started telling stories about
other harvests or California. I knew most of them weren't true, but I
enjoyed them anyway, because they helped pass the time.

"We're lucky to be working day shift," Grady said one day about a
week into harvest.

"Too cold at night," Hank agreed.

"*You* could turn on the truck heater," Grady said. "But it's cold
for a chopper jockey. And Boots would freeze in the truckbed with
the damp mint pouring in." He paused a moment. "Damn dangerous,
too."

Hank winked at me, our signal that one of Grady's stories was
coming.

"Over to Nyssa," Grady said, "one wino stomper got to nipping
on the jug one night, just to warm up, but he fell asleep in the back of

the truck and got buried under the mint. The driver figured that wino had taken off to town, so he and the chopper man stomped that load down best they could, threw a tarp over it, and ran it into the still. Cooked that old bastard right up with the mint."

"I'll bet that warmed him some," Hank said, grinning and pulling on his black-and-orange OSU cap.

Grady scowled at him. "More than he reckoned. The next day the straw boss had us boys go through the dumped mint slugs real careful-like with pitchforks, until we found him. He was puckered up like your pecker, and all shrunk down to mummy size."

"No kidding," Hank said. "You see him yourself?"

"It's good as gospel," Grady said. "They wound up burying him in a child's casket."

Out of earshot, Hank started calling Grady "Baloney Joe," but I figured he was just a lonely guy shooting the breeze to impress a couple of kids.

And when Grady learned I was hitching to work, he offered me rides. He was staying close by at the Juniper Motel, so it wasn't any real trouble, and I liked the way he kept that old Buick Roadmaster. "Mint condition," he used to say and chuckle at his little joke.

He'd come by just after five so we'd have time to make a quick stop at Maw's Bakery before heading out to the fields. Mr. Maw would let us in the back door, and we'd stuff ourselves with jelly rolls and doughnuts, washing them down with coffee. While we ate, Mr. Maw would keep working, standing at the big fryer turning the doughnuts with a wooden spoon, or rolling out bread dough on a long table, the flour up to his elbows. The bakery smelled like fresh dough and cinnamon, and I tried to remember those smells later, when I was knee-deep in chopped mint, my nose running steadily.

Sometimes before we'd go, Grady walked around the bakery looking at the mixers, tapping the stainless steel bowls with his forefingers. He'd peer through the large oven's little window at the baking bread and nod. "Nice place," he'd say to Mr. Maw. "Very nice." And Mr. Maw would smile and touch two fingers to his baker's hat as a kind of agreement.

On Friday nights, I'd scrub and scrub to get the mint smell off, then head to the teen dances on the second floor of the VFW hall. Hank was always there, too, wearing a red shirt with silver threads through it and a double-buckled white belt about as thin as a shoelace. He danced with all the popular girls, even Sandy Swanson, whose parents had the only swimming pool in town. Things came easy like that for Hank.

One night I left the stag line early and started home when I saw Grady's Buick parked outside the Recreation Tavern. He was inside shooting pool. Maybe it was the light, or the way he held his face as he concentrated on the shots, but he looked different—weary and somehow sad. I've seen that look on other men, now that I'm older, but back then I didn't know what it meant. Still, I felt awkward, as if I was intruding on something personal, so I just slipped away before Grady saw me.

The next morning Grady was late and we didn't stop at Maw's. "I guess I had a wonderful time," he said. "I woke up broke and remember getting so damn drunk, I was eating matches thinking they were bar pretzels."

It was no party time when we got to the field either. The thick mint was damp with night dew and the chopper blades were dull, so the mint kept clogging the chopper's throat. Grady disengaged the chopper a few times, climbed off, and went around in front, kicking at the slugs of mint and pulling away the tangled stems. "Damn night crew must have run the ditch bank to screw up these blades so bad," he mumbled.

I scrambled out of the truckbed to help out with the pitchfork.

"Work harder, you guys," Hank yelled from the truck window. "Assholes and elbows. That's all I want to see."

"Thinks he's too good to get out and help," Grady said.

"Only room for two, anyway," I said.

We had to take a long lunch break so Grady could pull the chopper blades and sharpen them on the grinder in the machine shop. Grady concentrated on those blades, the sparks flying off the grinder, and he got that same look, even behind the safety goggles. I thought maybe he was sick from the drinking. When he finished sharpening, Grady switched off the grinder and sat down on the work bench. "Let's take five," he said.

He didn't say anything else at first—just took off the safety goggles and held them by the elastic band, spinning them slowly. "Mr. Maw has got a nice place," he said after a while. "A man needs that. A long time back, my wife and I had a nice place, too, there just outside Modesto. Combination wrecking yard and cafe."

"Sounds okay," I said. I was a little surprised to hear him mention a wife, since he hadn't before.

"It was fine," he said. "Amyx was real good with the customers."

"Funny name," I said.

"Her father counted on a boy real bad and felt he'd been crossed by God, so he tagged that X behind Amy. Always bothered her some —like a bad birthmark."

"Probably not much to a name," I said.

"She didn't let on, but I knew. Back then, we worked hard trying to get started. I was building up the wrecking business, bought my own tow truck. She was cooking a special barbeque sauce for the cafe trade—even had the name picked out—Modesto Red. People in California like things hot because of the Mexican influence. She tried all sorts of special ingredients to doctor that sauce. Maybe she even put in some mint leaves."

"You can keep it then," I said.

"Things went along, and we found out she was pregnant. Damn, we got busy then, getting everything ready. I put the tow truck on twenty-four-hour call. She kept cooking sauce, wanting to get it just right, and dreaming about the baby. She wanted to pay back her daddy and wished on it being a boy."

"Was it?"

He took off his gray cap, wiped his forehead, then replaced the cap. "Yes," he said, so quiet I hardly heard him. "But something happened during the delivery and the cord twisted around his neck."

I couldn't think of anything to say; maybe he didn't want me to, so we just sat there a while longer. Then Grady shrugged his shoulders. "Amyx took it hard. I started working more and more with the wrecking yard—getting out my grief. But sometimes I'd come back from a tow or road repair and find the cafe locked, her sitting in the corner booth, drinking coffee and tracing little circles on the Formica table. One day, all I came back to was a note and empty closets. After that, I sold the truck and bought that Buick. Been following harvests now for fifteen years."

By September, we were all pretty tired of mint and working twelve hours on, twelve hours off. I was getting anxious because high school was about ready to start up, and I hadn't done half the things over the summer I'd promised myself. Grady said he was going on to Hood River for the apples, just as soon as mint harvest was over. And Hank was already packing for OSU. Sometimes he'd bring a basketball out of his car at lunch and show off his dribbling. "After Labor Day, you can wave bye-bye to the Kid," Hank told us.

He was grinning at me one morning when I took my pitchfork and started climbing in the truckbed. "You might be looking at a bonus, Boots, just for sticking through the harvest," Hank said. "You're senior stomper now, because Perkins got fired last night for running two geese through the chopper."

"The hell he did," I said.

"The hell he didn't," Hank said. "They were sleeping on the ditch bank with their heads tucked under their wings, and he grabbed them and tossed them into the chopper before they could even squawk. Crazy bastard!"

"Not much left of those geese, I suppose."

"A puff of feathers and a fine red spray," Hank said. "But some-day, an old fart in Portland will unscrew his Pepsodent and have it honk at him."

The wind kicked up that morning, bringing the smell of rain, and I had to stomp harder to keep some farmer's profit from blowing across Jefferson County. The straw boss came out to bitch about the blowing mint, but Grady took my side and told him to put two stompers in back if he wanted a better job. At lunch, Grady muttered about the clutch slipping, but when the straw boss asked him if it would hold through shift, Grady said he thought so.

We tried to sit out of the wind while we ate lunch, but the mint flakes kept blowing around and we had to pick them off our food. Grady finished his corned beef sandwich and said, "The wind and the way that mint's blowing remind me of a story. I'd finished wheat harvest over at Jordan Valley one time and was coming towards Burns at night, when the wind kicked up like this, only harder. Every so often, I'd see something green flutter across the headlights. That was strange, because it's desert there, no trees.

"But there's a long straight stretch of road with a bad curve at the end, and getting closer to that curve, I saw more and more green things swirl past. I slowed down, and just beyond the curve was a brand new station wagon—flipped over—the lights shining at a cock-eyed angle.

"The back hatch had popped open and those green things were blowing everywhere. The ground was like a goddam golf course. When I got out of the car, I could see what they were—sheets of Green Stamps. Even the license plate said 'S&H.' So I started picking them up—good as money, I figured. Planned to get a coffee pot and fishing pole.

"Suddenly, I heard a groan—scared me 'most to death—and then I saw a man about a hundred feet from the car. It was the stamp salesman, all right. He was busted up pretty bad, but even so, he had crawled all around trying to save those stamps. He was clutching sheets in both hands and lying on a bunch more, trying to keep them from blowing away. As I carried him to the car, he kept muttering, 'The stamps, the stamps. I'm responsible.' "

Grady paused. "Can you beat that? At death's door and trying to save those damn stamps." Even Hank was quiet, as Grady finished the story.

"When I unloaded him at the hospital, I realized I hadn't saved any stamps at all, but maybe it's just as well. I never figured to profit from anyone's bad luck. I hope that guy made it, but I never knew. I looked at the papers when I got to my next job just out of Bend, but there wasn't anything about it."

That afternoon, it rained, little squalls that dampened the mint and caused it to choke the chopper, even though the blades were still sharp. Grady and I kept working out the slugs. I broke them apart with my pitchfork; he kicked and pulled at the tangled stems. Every so often, he'd glance up at the gray sky and mutter, "Piss some more."

I thought it might rain hard enough to get the mint real wet; then we'd have to shut down until it dried. But it rained by fits and spurts the whole afternoon, and we kept fighting the wind.

Just before the end of shift, I was finishing stomping a loaded truck so the driver could run it to the still. Grady and Hank had started loading another truck, and I planned on leaving that load for the night stomper, so I took my own sweet time finishing up. At the rate they were going, the truck would only be half full by quitting time. As I was tying down the flapping tarp to cover the load, I saw that old Fox lumber to a stop at the far end of the field and Grady climb off.

I smiled a little, because I had the pitchfork, and I knew it would take Grady a while to clear the slug from the chopper's throat. I finished tying the tarp, and the truck left for the still. Then I started walking slowly across the field toward the chopper. "Quitting time," I wished.

The chopper lurched forward and then stopped. I took a few more steps before I saw Hank jump out of the truck. He was yelling and waving his cap. I started running, because it hit me suddenly that Grady hadn't been driving the chopper when it jerked ahead.

Stumbling across corrugations, I ran as if in a dream, weighted by my boots and fatigue. I saw others running, too, and the straw boss's pickup bumping across corrugations toward the yellow farmhouse north of the field. Once, I tripped on my pitchfork and fell onto the hard earth, my wind gone. When I could breathe again, I scrambled up, dropping the pitchfork and running harder.

By the time I reached the cluster of men, someone had already looped his belt around Grady's right thigh and twisted it tight for a tourniquet. I stared at the stump, sliced clean as a steak in a butcher's case, the bone showing white.

Hank put his OSU cap over the stump. "We don't need him seeing that and going into deeper shock," he said.

I hunkered by Grady's head and started praying under my breath. After a while, he opened his eyes and tried to sit up, but Hank held him down. "Just take it easy," he said. "Everything's going to be okay."

Grady tried to kid at first. "Call damage control," he said. "What's the estimate?"

"Broken leg," Hank said.

Grady's smile got real tight then and he shook his head. "It's bad, huh?"

"Your right leg's gone," I said, and didn't look at Hank.

"That was my favorite," Grady said. After that, he kept very quiet, and I counted the minutes until we heard sirens. When they got close, and the ambulance was bouncing across the field, Grady handed me his car keys. "Bring that Buick up to the hospital," he said. "Just in case I want to take a spin."

After the ambulance left, Hank did a funny thing, and I was always glad he took me along. He climbed into the truck and nodded at me, so I jumped in beside him.

Hank drove to the end of the field and onto the blacktop, but instead of turning toward Highway 26 and the mint still, we went toward the Deschutes Canyon. We hit gravel and then found a place where Hank could back that truck right up to the rimrock. Then we dumped out that half load of mint and whatever was left of Grady's leg.

"Let the bastards dock us," Hank said. But we both knew they wouldn't. That evening, driving the Buick into town, I gagged when I passed the still and smelled the cooking mint.

They gave Grady a good hospital room. One window looked off toward Mt. Jefferson and you could see Grizzly Butte from the other. A lot of people sent flowers, too, considering he was a migrant. Both crews chipped in to buy Grady a nice radio, in case he got tired of watching TV. Hank and I gave it to him in person.

Grady pretended to give us hell for not bringing his boot. "That was a brand-new pair—practically," he protested. "What good is one boot?"

We all laughed at that, and when we told Grady about dumping the half load over the canyon, he laughed so hard he choked.

I parked the Buick right outside Grady's window and honked a couple of times so he'd know. Quail ran across the hospital lawn and rustled in the junipers, and I realized hunting season was coming up. I told Grady I knew some good places to road-hunt, where he wouldn't have to do any walking, but he said he'd given up hunting.

After school started, I still got up to see Grady a couple of times a week, taking him magazines, jelly rolls, that sort of thing. Hank had gone to Corvallis by then, so I guess I was the only regular visitor. But when I came for one visit, Grady waved a get-well card and handed it to me.

"Amyx," I said, reading the signature. There was no return address, but it was cancelled in Modesto.

"Maybe I should look her up," he said. "Time to quit running."

I was puzzled by his laugh, until I got the joke. "Running." Then I laughed, too.

The Buick was gone one Sunday when I went to visit. A woman at the front desk told me Grady had checked out. His forwarding address was General Delivery, Modesto.

I found the orderly who had wheelchaired Grady out to the Buick. "How could you just let him drive off like that?" I said. "For Christ's sakes! He's only got one leg."

"Look," the orderly said. "My job is to get him to the lot."

◆

A lot of years have passed by now, of course, but I never heard from Grady, even though I wrote several times and sent a Christmas card to Modesto. I don't see many of those old Buicks anymore, but when I do, I pull up real close, just to see who's driving. Grady and Amyx might have fixed up their place or gotten another. I'd like to think so. And maybe Grady will read this and get in touch. Stranger things have happened.

You've read about Hank's career at Oregon State, and he's still a legend around here, even though he got hurt playing pro ball. Now he sells real estate in Denver, flies his own plane back for the reunions. I mentioned Grady to him a couple of times, but he just shook his head.

I never worked another harvest, but after high school, I sold implements at the county coöp, mostly the new Massey Fergusons. Whenever I demonstrated a chopper, I'd tell about Grady and point out the new safety devices. Maybe that talk helped a sale or two, but most of those farmers are right-minded old boys who know that nothing's foolproof when it comes to machinery. But I felt I had to tell the story anyway. I don't believe Grady would mind.

There's something else I almost never tell, although I might tell Grady, if he were here. I used to wonder about my part in the accident, thinking that if I'd run right over to help out with the pitchfork, maybe Grady wouldn't have lost his leg. But then my arm could have been in there when the chopper kicked on. I've pretty much quit worrying about it, and I almost never dream of those old Foxes anymore.

Still, even now when August comes around, and I smell the cooking mint, I get to feeling restless and empty. Some nights I drive out to where Hank and I dumped the half load. I sit there with the motor running quietly, the headlights shining across the darkness of the canyon. I put on the radio and twist the dial until I get Modesto, coming in like next door. Then after a while, I tuck my right leg up on the front seat and practice driving with just my left. I tear down those country backroads, past the mint fields—black at night—until just before dawn, when the first farmhouse lights wink on.

◆

THE INTERIOR OF NORTH DAKOTA

The Bergdorf Hills rise unobtrusively in south-central North Dakota east of the badlands, and were not fully described until 1923, in a book by the youngest son of a prominent New York family, Meyer Bergdorf, who went west at the age of twenty, exasperated by the wealth and insouciance of his parents.

Bergdorf disembarked the Great Northern Railroad at Bismarck in May 1918. He took three disheveled Lakota into his employ, outfitted them, and rode south into the basin of the Heart River. He told the Indians he only wanted to look into that country, that he wasn't searching for anything specific. Indeed, he had intended to get off the train in Fargo, but gazing from the train door at Fargo's streets and stores, he'd been so put off by the town's earnestness he'd returned to his seat.

The Lakota Bergdorf elected to travel with—the whole party drew smirks of bemusement from the stablemen and shop clerks who fitted them out—took Bergdorf initially for an impulsive and presumptuous man, common features to them of white culture. But they were intrigued by the diversion he offered. When they saw that he could ride and, once they were clear of Bismarck, that Bergdorf rode alertly, studying the ground as if gleaning it, when they found he wasn't an incessant talker, they were pulled in by his determination. The alcoholic daze in which he'd found them began to fall away, like rotten and sour clothing.

At dusk on the first day they camped in country vaguely familiar to the Lakota. By the second day, moving always at Bergdorf's scrutinizing pace, they'd crossed to the south bank of the Heart and followed the river into a landscape none of them knew. Bergdorf studied the woody draws and stared at the grassy swales with their clusters of wild roses. The trail sign in the short grama grass showed nothing of the passage of horses or cattle. It was now only that of wild creatures. The eldest Indian, a man in his fifties called Weasel Confused by Sparrows, said they should cleanse themselves before they went any farther. They should build a sweat lodge the next morning.

Weasel Confused and the others, a man about forty named Five-Handed Horse and a younger man called Wind That Comes at Night, remained aloof with Bergdorf but each had come to a similar conclusion—that the young man was possessed. They thought he was headed to a specific place. Five-Handed, heavyset and with short hair, remembered a story he'd heard when he was young, about some low hills that now lay to the south of them. It was a holy place, like the Black Hills, where he and the other two had grown up. But, he told Bergdorf, these were very much smaller and treeless hills. And they were sacred to the Crow. (The Crow, the three Indians reflected privately, had once been their traditional enemies. Now, with all that shattered, it almost made no difference. If that was where this white man was headed, they would go.)

The next morning they built a sweat lodge close to the river, a willow frame covered tightly with wool blankets. Weasel Confused said he couldn't remember all the proper prayers or what their sequence was. But he assured Bergdorf that the purification would put life into them, no matter. When Bergdorf asked how well he knew the rite, Weasel Confused said, "I am using all the knowledge I have."

Bergdorf appreciated the rising sense of gravity in his companions and the emergence of their enthusiasm. He had asked them to accompany him—he'd found them sleeping in the city's park—partly as a show of contempt for the burghers of Bismarck but also because he wasn't entirely confident of his own skills. He assumed that these three swarthy men—Night Wind wearing rimless dark glasses and a fedora, all of them dressed in rumpled trousers and mismatched suit coats—knew the country. They knew it, he found out later, no better than he did. They had arrived only two days before, on the train from Dickinson.

Late in the afternoon, after they'd sweated, Five-Handed Horse approached Bergdorf and extended his hand wordlessly. Bergdorf, slicing bacon for dinner, knew instantly what he wanted. He handed Five-Handed the Colt .38/40 and three cartridges. A few hours later he and Night Wind came back with a mule deer, a small doe.

The next morning, Bergdorf records, the four of them worked

quietly at personal chores in the warming light. Bergdorf, whose nearly chronic disaffection had begun to abate, wrote and drew in a pasteboard journal. Five-Handed, having restitched the split uppers of his two-toned wing tip shoes, was helping Weasel Confused cut and dry the deer's flesh. Night Wind, a heavily pockmarked man with delicate hands, was painting his horse's face, a row of yellow bars down the muzzle and white circles around the eyes.

They left long before noon and rode the rest of the day south before they entered the low hills that Five-Handed could remember no name for. Bergdorf then and there named them the Four-Man Hills; but in a journal entry a few days later he says that naming them at all was a mistake. He meant to follow Weasel Confused's advice and inquire among the Crow as to their name.

The four of them spent a week there. The Lakota, in Bergdorf's estimation, rose visibly to a level of splendid awareness, of hawklike and wolverinelike behavior, economical and deliberate in their activities. Bergdorf, wandering the hills, sometimes astride his Appaloosa mare, sometimes on foot, focused his obvious pleasure on flowers. Though he knew almost nothing of botany, he examined several dozen species closely enough to draw them in their entirety. The drawings are clumsy, with no variation in the thickness of his line or the pressure of his pencil, but they are evocative and charming—a young man's self-conscious act of respect.

Just as they had not discussed the hills as a destination, so they did not later discuss their departure, but only rose one morning after a week and left. (In reading Bergdorf's journal, one is compelled by the short, enigmatic entry of his fifth day in the hills to believe that something unusual took place here, a kind of epiphany for Bergdorf, certainly, but of a sort he could not at first imagine, or which he didn't care to try to explain. Perhaps it wasn't obvious to him. But some realization of self-worth, an infusion of joy, seems to have reached him. The entries that follow on the return trail to Bismarck, where the journal abruptly ends, are marked by an attitude of profound courtesy and a prepossessing tone not present in the earlier entries.)

The riders, ranging far out to both sides of their original trail, returned to Bismarck in three days. Bergdorf alone no longer determined their route. They rode easily together, following each other by turns, a rhythm determined by the roll of the land and their combined idiosyncrasies. A day out of town, Bergdorf took certain of his possessions—a heavy overcoat, some packaged food, an extra pair of trousers—and set them in a neat pile on the gray-white trunk of a fallen cottonwood. Night Wind lay his rimless dark glasses alongside.

In Bismarck, Bergdorf sold the horses back to their original owner. He gave each of his three companions twenty dollars and some store-bought items—shoes, a small traveling bag for each one, a saddle blanket for each man. He got them rooms in the Centennial Hotel and treated them to dinner in the dining room. Bergdorf had by now the same dark patina of the trail the other three had had when they'd met. People glared at them while they ate. One or two, Bergdorf writes, murmured in disgust.

Bergdorf could not sleep that night. He dressed and went down to the livery stable where their horses were corraled—his Appaloosa, Weasel Confused's strawberry roan, the sorrel gelding that Five-Handed had ridden, and the two paints, Night Wind's and the pack animal. They nickered at his presence, and then bore off slowly into the far dimness of the corral.

The Lakota were gone in the morning. They took the night train to Dickinson, the station agent told him.

Bergdorf boarded the train east that morning. A week later he enlisted in the American army. On August 1, 1918, he was shot dead north of the Marne River in the Meunière wood. His eldest sister, Isabel, succeeded in having his journal published by a small press in Connecticut, in 1923. In a brief introduction she writes that her brother returned to New York from North Dakota burning with a sense of purpose and "marvelously poised." (It was she who petitioned the U.S. Board on Geographic Names to call the Bergdorf Hills after her brother.)

◆

During the American Depression of the 1930s, much of the settled land to the south and west of Bismarck was deserted. Ranching operations established along the Heart River as recently as the twenties went out of business. Large sections of Morton and northern Grant counties were acquired by banks in Bismarck, Fargo, and Minneapolis in default of loans. After the Second World War, most of these several hundred square miles of abandoned land were absorbed in the already huge holdings of ranches and farms on the surrounding shortgrass prairie. With so many documents involved, however, some parcels were unintentionally deeded to two different owners, some foreclosed land was assigned but never deeded, and some parcels were deliberately sold twice, by itinerant land operators.

In May 1958, a records clerk in the state archives in Bismarck began to sort through this confusion and legerdemain—a private preoccupation. Partway through she realized that a section of nearly twenty square miles in the drainage of the Heart River, including the Bergdorf Hills, was mostly without clear title and also unoccupied. The counties involved had not taken any notice because the taxes on the undeeded land had always been paid—since 1937 the aggregate of land had been apportioned in the tax parcels of twelve different ranching families. The ranches in question had not put stock on the sections because their fence lines followed the boundary lines described in their original deeds.

The clerk, a divorced woman without children named Lenore Crandall, traveled on her own, bit by bit, all across the undeeded land. She finally determined that the Bergdorf Hills themselves, about ten square miles, had never been occupied, and that little of even the deeded land along the south bank of the Heart River was being ranched. In 1963 Crandall bought a house near the Bergdorf Hills and moved there, fifty miles from Bismarck. She continued to work for the state. She explored widely around her home and in later years she painted, mostly images from her childhood in Chicago, though in her last years she began to paint the landscape of the Bergdorf Hills. Her journals of exploration are painstaking in their detail and striking in the range of subjects that held her attention, from the germination of grasses to the hunting behavior of swift foxes.

In the spring of 1977 I met Lenore Crandall while looking for work around Bismarck. I'd heard that a man was hiring in Almont, a small town to the east, and had gone there but found no one hiring and no work. I'd started out along the road south away from Almont with the idea of finding work in Rapid City, but also because the country in that direction, at that time of year, was beautiful. I am a decent-looking man, dress neatly, and am not alarming or offensive in my manner, so do not anticipate trouble in getting rides. It was Lenore Crandall who pulled over for me.

She lived about ten miles south of Almont, on the Heart River. In those few miles we had an amiable conversation, the sort of conversation you can have when no one has any pressing plan of action, no clear object of desire. She asked me if I would like to stay for dinner, and overnight. It was not the last time I was to be startled by her. I said yes. I remember most acutely, I think, her integrity with a stranger. And her generosity. In the morning I went on my way, promising to write when I settled somewhere for the winter.

I kept up my correspondence, and before she passed away in 1983, at the age of seventy, I managed to visit her twice at her home. Her attraction for me lay in that peculiar tension some people are able to affect by maintaining intimacy in their conversation while actually revealing little of their private lives. The last time I saw her, I brought her a present, a copy of Meyer Bergdorf's book I'd found in Salt Lake City. I picked it up initially out of curiosity, but finished it excited by a sense of coincidence. Lenore read it through that same night. The following morning she seemed both pensive and ebullient. She told me, then, for the first time, about the Bergdorf Hills, about their disposition and how she'd discovered them.

I had never heard such a story, and as much as I respected her, I was skeptical. There was always a part of Lenore that was slightly out of reach. It wasn't that she was unapproachable but that part of her was unattainable, as when a person doesn't have words or experience enough to grasp a particular frame of mind. She read to me all that morning from her journals. As I listened to her descriptions I saw that unattainable part of her more clearly than I ever had before. She described how she reached the Bergdorf Hills by following a path, hidden from the road, down the Heart River, before turning south at a certain spot. It wasn't until she said this that I realized I had never seen the Bergdorf Hills. They were not visible from her home. You could barely make them out from the road.

Lenore's gratitude for a copy of Bergdorf's book was extreme. I thought, after all that had passed between us that morning, the significance of what she had revealed, that she would invite me to walk with her into the hills. But she did not.

I learned of her passing several months after she died. A letter from probate court reached me in Omaha and I came back up to North Dakota. She'd left me a small amount of money and, to my surprise, the house with its few acres on the Heart River. I slowly realized that Lenore had made me aware of a certain aspect of my own isolation, and I was very grateful to her.

One morning, feeling somewhat apprehensive and also a little doubtful, I walked east along the Heart, down to the spot that Lenore had described. I then headed south toward the Bergdorf Hills. I'd not gone very far before I felt I could go no farther. The character of the land had changed distinctly in less than a mile. It had risen up gleaming, like a painting stripped of grime, the prairie colors richer, the air more prismatic. The smell of sun-warmed grasses and brush had become dense and fresh. I was still eager to go on, but in the face of this intensification I felt like an interloper. What was here, the undisturbed brilliance, belonged, it seemed, to Meyer Bergdorf and his Lakota friends, to the unheard-from Crow, and to Lenore.

That afternoon I withdrew because it was so obvious to me that I was unprepared. I was also afraid. The vividness of the land was intimidating, almost overwhelming. It had in every detail the penetrating aura, the immediacy, the insistence of a creature viewed through ground glass. The intertwining of wild rose thickets, the wind rushing the broad leaves of summer cottonwoods, and the calls of meadowlarks, a sound like running water, held me up. I turned on my trail and walked back to the river. I knew that I would return, but it would be with a desire clearer and deeper than what I then possessed. I had little doubt now that these hills would open out on a landscape of "unreasonable extent," as Lenore had indicated, and that if I were patient I might come to see aspects of the hills that were also bewildering and terrifying.

◆

That night I sat at Lenore's dining table reading her journals, all that was left of her personal effects. The Chicago paintings had been sold. The canvases she'd painted in the Bergdorf Hills, which I'd seen and now knew were full of disguise, had been taken from their frames and destroyed. She had asked that I read and destroy her journals. I considered her request wrongheaded, an act of selfishness. I understood, though she had not been explicit, that she wanted me to care for the Bergdorf Hills after she was gone. It might be years before they were entered, but she thought it would probably not be long before computers discovered the patchwork of deeds, the errant tax structure. Legal ownership of the hills would be settled on someone. By that very act, she believed, parceled and possessed, their vividness would pale, their pungency and resonance fade. They would become another almost indistinguishable part of the prairie. Against that eventuality, or at least until then, she had suggested to me—always indirectly, but with a passion that in other women is sexual—that I stay on.

So my plans are very simple. I'll finish reading her journals. I'll try to imagine as I read, though it runs against her wishes, whether there might not be some way to preserve the ecstatic and wondrous tone of her work, the reverie with which she writes of the Bergdorf Hills; whether by calling the hills by some other name, by giving them a different geography, I can't see to the publication of the journals. For she wrote not only of the charm and beauty of the land but also of its darkness, about the panic of being lost in it, its resolute indifference, of how lean and hard it had made her, of how profound an order had come to her core through all her foot travel, her night sleeps, in these inconspicuous hills.

I will finish the journals then, and think on that. And then, one day, I will walk off into that country to see it for myself. I'll imagine the Crow there, and their traditional enemies the Lakota. I will travel, I am certain now, with a companion, another person with whom it will be possible to speak and to imagine. Then if the hills should indeed disappear, if they should be realized in some other way, there will, at least, be our stories to preserve the memory of travel there.

I will step off into that country with the possibility of fathoming, perhaps, what made Lenore, on that last night I saw her, rise and wander off into the dusky light along the Heart River like an anguished bear. And I will know, perhaps, what Bergdorf meant when he wrote, "In all my travels I have never known a country so sweet, so redolent with the earth's perfume, nor air so full of light. When I think on my companions, different from me and whom I barely know, I sense the same resolve in them to strip away the horror of what we have accepted. I look on these hills, writing by the light of the full moon this evening, and know that, though this land is not mine nor ever could be, that for what I have found here I would die. These hills, their deer and badgers, their calling coyotes, the azure, red, and yellow species of birds, have lifted me out of myself. My anger is diminished, my loneliness gone."

COLLEEN McELROY

◆

THE WOMAN
WHO WOULD
EAT FLOWERS

Cora Kay waited until the old woman moved the broom a whisper away from her big toe before she yelled, "Don't be sweeping my feet! That broom mess my feet up from where I was going."

Kei-Shee mumbled something that probably sounded like "Shadedown," or "Chinatown," to most folks in the Flats, but Cora Kay's ear had been trained to understand a few Chinese phrases, and she knew when she'd heard one of those curses Kei-Shee muttered whenever she had the chance. That chance didn't happen very often, because it wasn't very often that Wu Yeung Lee allowed his mother to come out of the kitchen. In this respect, he was a good son, and she, obedient as any old-world Chinese woman, never entered the front part of Wu Fong's Eatery without her son's permission. In fact, through three generations of Chinese owners, none of the black folks in the Flats had seen any of the Chinese women waiting tables in Wu Fong's. Retired railroad men told stories about how their fathers had not seen old man Wu Fong's wife in the front of the restaurant when Wu Fong himself ran the place. Only men had waited tables until 1946, when Wu Fong's grandson, Wu Yeung Lee, hired Cora Ivory. Cora Kay had made the front of the eatery her domain, and as she sat there, watching Yeung Lee's mother sweep the floor with a heavy straw broom, Cora Kay Ivory exercised her reign over this kingdom.

"You can just swallow that spit," she told the old woman. "You think I don't know what *shyä-dan* means? I ain't no lazy chicken, or whatever it is you be saying under your breath. And I ain't gone sit here and let you sweep me into my grave with that broom neither."

The old woman looked up and grinned, her one ragged tooth hanging like a loose nail from the top of her mouth.

"You know what I'm talking bout, don't you?" Cora Kay shouted.

Kei-Shee began swinging the broom back and forth as if she were swaying to music. She moved closer to Cora Kay, swaying and grinning, the boom hissing against the wooden floor like the swish of a ball gown. Even though Kei-Shee had no ball gowns to remember, she remembered the brothel in San Francisco where she'd been trapped until, at eighteen, Yeung Lee's father had found her. And if she thought about the music of Chinatown streets, its nightlife similar to the stingy row of cafés and jook joints on either side of Wu Fong's Eatery, she could not stop her memories.

But Cora Kay's knowledge of street life was too recent, so she did not move. There was nothing in Kei-Shee's muttered oaths that would have made Cora Kay budge. Moving would not enter her mind until the wall clock reached 4:00 P.M., which was when she was officially bound to begin waiting tables. Even then, nothing moved Cora Kay if she didn't want to move—a trait she kept intact until she encountered a skinny little hobo named Clarence Henry, but that was yet to be. At the time, Cora Kay was about the business of polishing her nails, and the notion of pulling her body from its slumped position was no more a part of this ritual than sweeping floors was a part of waiting tables.

Cora Kay watched Kei-Shee and cast a few oaths of her own. "You can grin all you want to, old lady, but if you come near me with that broom, I'm gone make you a picture up on that wall, you hear me?"

Kei-Shee made the sound of a broom singing to itself—"*Säu, säu*"—her eyes glittering as she moved closer to Cora Kay's feet.

"Don't be sweeping my feet," Cora Kay warned her again.

The old woman did a little hop step and turned within inches of Cora Kay. The broom went back and forth, back and forth, and on its third swing, the one that most certainly would have made contact with its target, Cora Kay picked up a soy bowl of salt and flung it across the room—not at the old lady, but not away from her either.

The kitchen doors slammed open. Yeung Lee stood there, his machete knife already slick with a coating of duck grease. He glared first at his mother posed stock-still in the center of the floor, the broom frozen midway in its downswing, then at Cora Kay, languishing in the third booth from the door. Neither woman acknowledged him until Yeung Lee yelled, *"Mü-chin! Hwêi-chyu!"*

The old woman nodded to her son and began shuffling toward the kitchen, dragging the broom behind her. When she reached the door, she turned and said, *"Dzäi-djän."*

Cora Kay stuck out her tongue. "So long yourself, you old bat."

Then she turned her frown on Yeung Lee. Although his lip curled once, he said nothing. But in the space of that look, the two of them wrestled with what little understanding they had growing between them.

After a few moments, Yeung Lee marched back to the kitchen, cursing as he entered. Cora Kay returned to the task of lacquering her nails. Seconds later, Yeung Lee's daughter, Tea Rose, resumed the sweeping her grandmother had abandoned. In the doorway, Kei-Shee waited to see what went on between her granddaughter and Cora Kay. She could have saved herself the trouble. Both girls set their expressions to appear as if they were alone in the room.

Tea Rose melted into the broom, its sweeping consuming all of her attention. She was a plump girl, about as old as Cora Kay, with a round face sharpened by the pinched set of her mouth and downcast eyes. The way Tea Rose walked, like her speech, belonged to Kei-Shee, not the Flats, yet when she was out of Kei-Shee's sight, Tea Rose could be as much a part of the Strip as Cora Kay. The day Cora Kay had moved into the spare room in the crook of the upstairs hallway, Tea Rose had stood just outside the door. At first, Cora Kay did not realize the girl was there. Then she'd seen a shadow, a movement like a falling leaf, or a cockroach hovering on the other side of the doorjamb. Cora Kay hated roaches, so she'd waited to squash the bug, the shoe in her hand raised at just the right level to make contact before the thing sensed danger. Nothing else moved, and as Cora Kay was about to relax, Tea Rose spoke. "You come live here?" Tea Rose had asked. "Your mama come live here?"

"I ain't saying nothing till you out from behind that door," Cora Kay had told her. But the girl had sidled down the hall. Cora Kay had not had a chance to talk to her again until the girl was cleaning the hallway.

Without breaking her rhythm of wiping down the walls with a damp rag, Tea Rose had asked, "What name you have for papers?"

Cora Kay had told her. The rag had slapped the wall once, twice, before Tea Rose had tried repeating the name. "Don't like that," she'd said finally. "That name only one you speak?" Cora Kay had shrugged. The rag had slapped-slapped, louder this time.

"My mama calls me Cinnamon," Cora Kay had said. "It's cause of my coloring. But she the onliest one I allow to call me that."

Tea Rose had begun to rinse the rag. "*Sên-nà-mên,*" she'd said, moving to a new section of the wall. "Don't like that," she'd said, and once more slammed the rag into action. "I call you Hoisin. Like Chinese spice. Hoisin same brown-red, like you. I say Hoisin." The rag had echoed the name as Tea Rose worked her way down the hall.

"Chile's always cleaning," Cora Kay told herself. *"Moving like one of them church folk who seen the spirit and can't speak up right."*

Not speaking up was hardly one of Cora Kay's faults. Even the act of blow-drying her newly applied nail polish was a form of speech, each puff a challenge to whatever thoughts anyone might harbor about assigning her to sweep the floor. Cora Kay blew two puffs of air on each nail, then extended her hands to gaze upon the perfection of her rust-brown fingers, their coral-red tips the same shade of polish Tea Rose would secretly spread on her toenails later that night. Cora Kay repeated the blow-drying process until each fingernail received some ten puffs of air, but as Yeung Lee had found out by the end of the first week of her employment, she'd still spend the next several hours of work avoiding any direct contact between fingertips and dishes of food. Some nights, her fear of ruining her nails drove her into making Tea Rose place the orders on a tray, then forcing the customers to pluck their own food from tray to table.

Now, as Tea Rose swept, Kei-Shee lurked in the doorway and clicked her tongue in disapproval of both girls. The old woman hunkered there until the minute hand made its usual little jump-click sixty seconds before the hour; then she turned back to the kitchen. Just as the clock pinged its first count of four, Cora Kay pulled herself away from the booth. Strolling toward the front door, she dropped the bottle of nail polish into Tea Rose's cupped hand. Tea Rose closed her fingers over the gift, flicked her pile of dust under the nearest booth, and scuttled into the kitchen without once looking at Cora Kay, who had already reached for the CLOSED/OPEN sign stuck in a corner of the front window. On the fourth chime of the hour, she flipped the sign, announcing Wu Fong's was ready for business. Then Cora Kay Ivory turned her back on all who entered.

—◆—

Turning her back was how Cora Kay had learned to deal with the narrow little world of the Flats, and in the execution of that act, she fit right into the pattern of Wu Fong's Eatery. Wu Yeung Lee and his family had become masters at being both a party to, yet outside of, the crumbling district of tar-paper shacks, tenements, and factories, interrupted by a sprinkling of bars, jook joints, and cheap stores that spread across the flatlands into a neighborhood of sorts—all of it belted together by the skinny street known as the Strip.

Yeung Lee, like his grandfather, Wu Fong, managed a thriving business for black folks who the law said couldn't eat in the same place as white folks. Everyone knew they'd all get the same service at Wu Fong's, regardless of their color. Like most of those who lived in that part of town, Yeung Lee and his family had earned their living from the railroad at one time or another. In the 1800s, when the railroad was being built, Yeung Lee's grandfather, one of the few Mandarin Chinese to come west, had been a cook for the Chinese workers the railroad company had refused to feed, as it had done so willingly for their white coworkers. Then the company bosses had ordered Wu Fong to cook for the bucket brigade of black men hauling stones from Cobbler's Creek, so he'd fed them as well. And when the railroad finally had finished laying the east–west track across the country—the occasion for that famous picture of the hookup of tracks at the California-Nevada border—publicity did not include any of the Chinese or black workers who'd labored for the companies. Company policy had split those men into racial groups as clearly as the tracks had split the land.

Cora Kay didn't know it, but her grandfather had worked those yards most of his sixty-one years of life, and he had been one of the men fed by Wu Fong. Cora Kay's father had died following an accident in the yards. After that, Cora Kay and her mother had lived in one of the shanties at the edge of the tracks, where hoboes had been setting up camp since the Great Depression.

In those days, black men headed north the way geese traveled the migratory patterns into Canada, but unlike the geese, those men had no intention of returning to the breeding grounds south of the Mason-Dixon. The whistle of a southbound train would finally urge Clarence Henry to leave the sharecropper farm his father worked and jump a northbound freight near the Louisiana-Arkansas border. Other men left home in the rickety wooden Jim Crow part of the train, the only part colored people were allowed to ride. And others traveled as best they could, grabbing a passing train like the wind grabbed the sound clacking in its wheels. For the women living in the shanties, those men often represented their tickets out of town. When Cora Kay was sixteen, her mother had given her a choice.

"Cinnamon, ain't nothing here for us," she'd said. "Ain't no needa staying here listening to them trains come and go when we could be the ones doing the going. I got a man wants us to come along to Chi-town. Come with me, Cinnamon. Come with me, baby girl."

But Cora Kay had chosen Wu Fong's—"a steady job where I ain't grabbing holt of no freight car and cooking beans on no tin plate."

"Ain't nothing for you here," her mother had repeated.

"I don't know what's here and what ain't," Cora Kay had told her, "but I don't aim to leave 'fore I find out."

"Well, you ain't gone find out working for that Chinaman. These white folks ain't gone do nothing but give that Chinaman a hard way to go and a short time to get there. They don't even let them men bring they wives over here. That's how come there ain't nothing but that old woman and that chile working in that Chinaman's restaurant."

In the end, the absence of Cora Kay's mother gave her something in common with Tea Rose, whose mother had been forced to stay behind when Yeung Lee returned to the States following his obligatory trip to China to find a bride. Under immigration laws that made it nearly impossible for a Chinese worker to bring his wife into the country, Yeung Lee had returned with his child. But if the truth be known, he had listed six-year-old Tea Rose as male and given her the name Hêu-hwêi, or Sorrow.

Like Cora Kay, Tea Rose had grown up in the sorrow of the Strip, with its gambling men and hoboes, railroad families and Christians. When she was younger, Tea Rose had fled to the eatery's roof to escape school and the taunts of children singing: *"Chink, Chink. Chinaman, eat dead rats. Chew them up like ginger snaps."* From the roof, Tea Rose could watch the orange clay hillside for the first sign of smoke from inbound trains that, her father once told her, might be the one bringing her mother from China. Until her father hired Cora Kay, that view of the train yards had sustained Tea Rose.

"What you looking at that mud hole for?" Cora Kay had asked.

"My mother come sometime this track," Tea Rose had answered.

"Don't hold your breath," Cora Kay told her.

But when Tea Rose's father sent the two of them to gather day lilies, chrysanthemums, and sweet flower grasses growing in the meadow near the Hodiman Road shantytown, both girls would stare into windows of trains that were slowing down to make the approach to the station. Those outings made Cora Kay pull on the memories of her mother's cooking, and she would include coltsfoot and fireweed in the bundles of herbs she and Tea Rose gathered. Although Cora Kay had brought a large box of ground cinnamon in an effort to teach Yeung Lee and his family how to say her nickname, that box remained untouched on the pantry shelf. But Yeung Lee used the selection of wild herbs she'd picked in the meadow to spice his soups and stews, and in doing so added another reason to the list of those he'd concocted to rationalize hiring Cora Kay.

Still, folks on the Strip claimed they never understood the whys and wherefores of how Cora Kay came to work at Wu Fong's Eatery, even though everyone knew that, in 1946, Cora Kay had been the first black woman in town employed to work right out front in a business that was not owned by someone who was black.

"She young, but she sho know how to take care of herself," Dee Streeter said. "I 'spect that come from being raised in shantytown."

Dee was sitting in a booth with LuRaye Turner and Patsy Granger. At least once a week, on those nights when they couldn't bring themselves to go home and cook in a second kitchen after a day full of kitchens out in the Belmont District, the women stopped by Wu Fong's for takeout. They sat in the front booth next to Sister Vernida Garrison, the Ladies' Aid president, or Hattie Lou Pritchard, the doctor's wife, both of whom regularly brought Yeung Lee some of their Christian literature to heal the heathen ways they were sure infected the place, along with cockroaches and rats. Aside from spearheading a drive to get the city to tear down the shanties, these family women were among the first customers in the eatery, and quite often they took it upon themselves to try "talking some sense into Cora Kay."

"Chile, that Chinaman's got you waiting tables every night. Go to school so you can get a good job," Sister Garrison would tell her.

Cora Kay would flick Sister Garrison's order of pork fried rice off the edge of her hip so quickly, rice skittered away from the plate and danced toward the end of the table before bouncing into the woman's ample lap. Cora Kay had no patience with these women. It was their children who'd run her home from school.

"Your mama's like the railroad track," they'd chant. *"She been laid from one end to end."* They had teased her about living in the shanties the same way they picked on Tea Rose about being Chinese. So when Cora Kay reached the service window, she'd let Tea Rose know the church ladies had descended by writing the Chinese symbols for "religion up come" in the patina of grease covering the counter. In one way or another, those women paid for their cruel children.

"Lord, it's a sin and a shame that chile's mama up and left her by herself," Doc Pritchard's wife mumbled, her back teeth grinding sour against the extra dash of Szechwan vinegar Cora Kay had sprinkled on her order of Heavenly Greens. "That chile ain't got but one nerve and no manners," the doctor's wife added.

"But that Chinaman do give her a place to stay," Patsy Granger muttered. "Out in Belmont, that white woman didn't even want to give me a room to myself. Said I had to share it with the wet nurse." Then Patsy took another sip of tea and complained about how it was so strong, "it burns clear through your throat like red-eye likker."

"May be a job, but Cora Kay do smell like food all the time," Sister Garrison said. "Garlic and onion. Trashy smells."

"Beats some other smells," the women grunted, all of them inching toward the first twinges of heartburn they'd suffer from that hefty dollop of Mongolian fire oil Tea Rose put in their pepper rice.

"That Chinaman don't seem to mind them smells," LuRaye noted, a hint of the devil in her eyes as she burped sweet-and-sour chicken.

The other women said, "Um-hum," and "I hear that," and stared at Cora Kay sauntering between tables, her youth almost hidden under a shabby dress that was permanently stained with the grease of fowl, pork, and fish. Then they turned their attention to the service window, where they could see Kei-Shee and Tea Rose, and behind them, Yeung Lee chopping onions, chicken, and strips of pork on the butcher's block, his nostrils flaring with anticipation of the cut—the thunk of his machete knife and the gleam in his eyes as sure and definite as anger. That view prompted all sorts of comments about just what might be going on in those rooms at the top of the stairs. Though the women were unwilling to admit it, more than one of them had examined that six-foot-tall Chinaman with more than food on her mind. They all had noticed how Yeung Lee's eyebrows grew together over the bridge of his nose, like frayed bird wings—"wild like the night owls up in the woods," some said—and how his hair was black as light trapped in the deepest part of a well.

Cora Kay could have told them how Yeung Lee's eyes changed from liquid darkness to smoke, and how his voice was ribbed with silk when he looked up from the storage shed behind the restaurant and called to her while she stood in her bedroom window, the moonlight fashioning her rough cotton shift into a shapely garment. Cora Kay could have told them this if she were of a mind to speak to them. As it was, she simply watched them load their dinner plates with questions.

"You see them eyes?" they whispered. "Them eyes cut right through you," they told each other when they felt him stare at their hips as they slid out of a booth. And more than one woman had tried to provoke a smile that raised the dimples on either side of Yeung Lee's Fu Manchu mustache and goatee. Their dreams were always cut short by Cora Kay's presentation of the bill.

◆

But if the women were curious about what went on in the back rooms of the eatery, the men were outright baffled. It was a known fact that Wu Yeung Lee's daughter, Tea Rose, was old enough to wait those tables herself, so why would Yeung Lee hire Cora Kay to tempt them? "Is you blind?" men like Butler Sykes would cackle. "Take yourself a look at Cora Ivory, then ask why that Chinaman wants her round him."

And his railroad buddies, Maroon-Willie Evans, Lip Wooten, Whitaker Yarrow, and the other men who ran the road, would nod their heads. Running the road meant having to sit on their feelings and memories of home until the train pulled in, and they wanted a little something in their pockets once they left that train behind them. Men like Butler Sykes came home for a layover ready to see his woman and ready for a scam. But like most of the married men, Butler didn't let go of the road just because the train had pulled into the station. Unless his wife caught him, he spent the first hours of his layover with the unmarried men, combing the Strip, and later coaxing his friends into a little game in the room in back of his wife's funeral home. The problem was the funeral home game usually involved high stakes, and although gambling and women were almost second nature to railroad men, most of them didn't want to lose their entire paycheck on one game.

Necessity had taught the men to be careful about separating home and the railroad. When they dressed for work—checking shoes for rundown heels, double-checking facial hair, or checking for the hint of manly scents that had to be removed before the head conductor finished his white-glove inspection—they'd had to shed all memories of home. To carry that memory past the threshold of the trains was dangerous. One racist remark too many, and home could grab a man's throat and rip it open—"Just come tumbling out fore you can snatch it back," Whitaker Yarrow would say.

Maroon-Willie, chowing down at Wu Fong's, would praise Yeung Lee's cooking as he remembered serving under a vicious captain in the merchant marine, and how, midvoyage, he had abandoned ship to escape the captain's wrath, thereby earning the name Maroon. "You sho get your money's worth at the Chinaman's," he'd say. "Ain't like in the merchants when you be eating green chicken gizzards, or throwing up food done spoilt past rotten. They oughta have that Chinaman cooking on them boats. Make the boss cap'n eat that other slop himself."

"Food's good, but Cora Kay's got an attitude," Butler said.

"Still, it be betta than some offa places," Lip Wooten told him. Lip had been running the road so long—some said before A. Philip Randolph started the Brotherhood of Sleeping Car Porters—that he'd grown gray-haired and bent-back. The other members of the union protected him because he'd lost his strength, and the use of half of his mouth when he was hit in the face with a blackjack during a railroad strike before the war. They took up the slack when he doubled under the leadweight of a suitcase, or caught flak from white conductors who mimicked his thick-lipped speech.

"We'all ain't jus a membah of the Brothahhood," Lip added. "The Brothahhood be like fam-bily, but we'all still gots ta beg fuh food on that train. So longs ah git mah food heah-ah, don' mattuh how Cora Ivory be actin'. See, ah 'members time when we'all pullup to sa-town an they say: Don serv niggahs back heah-ah."

"Yeah, they say that in Chicago," Maroon-Willie nodded. "They say: Don't serve niggers here."

Whitaker laughed and said, "Well, Maroon, you and Lip shoulda told 'em: That's OK . . . we don't eat 'em neither."

Everyone howled at that inside joke, but the laughter died quickly when Whitaker added, "I still don't see why ain't no Chinawomen waiting tables."

"What's that Chinaman saying?" Butler would ask when Cora Kay served their food while Tea Rose peeked out at them from the kitchen. "He saying it be all right to have colored women working they butts off whilst he hides his own women in that back room?"

"Ah 'spect Cora inna puttin' out fuh the Chinee-man," Lip muttered.

"You just mad cause she ain't putting out for you," Maroon said.

"Ah don' need it. Mah woman waitin' fuh me at home heah-ah."

"Now Lip, where else that ugly woman gone be?" Whitaker asked.

"Don't be funning at Lip. All of y'all mad 'cause Cora Kay don't pay none of you no attention," Butler reminded the men.

And they'd look at the hip-riding tightness of Cora Kay's soiled dress as she leaned over to pick up a tray of dishes from a table. And they dreamed of train stops where fancy women catered to them.

While churchgoers and family folk were among the first round of customers at the eatery, the railroad men and the rest of the night trade took over the place after dark, when flickering neon lit up the Strip from the Flame Bar's dancing lights at one end, down to the Glass Bar's Seagram's sign blinking at the opposite end. From that time till an hour or so past midnight, Wu Fong's Eatery belonged to the night crowd. And every night, those folks found Yeung Lee at his chopping block, the machete's blade hissing toward its target with unerring accuracy. Every night, while Cora Kay sidled from table to table, her skin most often as oily as the plates she piled on the counter over the sink, Tea Rose sat in the back room, filling orders and folding dough for fortune cookies while her grandmother listened to radio tales of the Shadow, the Green Hornet, and the Fat Man. Between episodes, Kei-Shee washed dishes, stirred fresh noodles into the ever-present pot of broth, and checked the bin of rice. At times she muttered some oath to rid the room of spirits, or to warn Yeung Lee of trouble. And even before Clarence Henry showed up, there was plenty of trouble on the Strip that could touch Wu Fong's.

Not that any owner of Wu Fong's had been unfamiliar with trouble. Police cruised through the restaurant from time to time, and it was not uncommon for a family of church folks to watch several tables of gambling men scramble for the side exit, or rush for the pantry in back of the kitchen, where the dim outline of a door was barely visible under a grease-stained bamboo curtain. The old man, Wu Fong himself, had installed the door. He remembered the days of the tong gangs back in China and had neither encouraged nor obstructed this New World version of gangsters. That was one reason the restaurant had survived. Soon after opening his business, Wu Fong had hung up a scroll painting of a Chinese farm with a grass-writing motto:

> In a land where no rice grows, the man with full baskets
> Is the cold wind biting the beggar's coat.

During his gambling days, Wu Fong's baskets were full, and for the white men, gambling with the same odds against the wind, that presented a problem. Gambling was a thin vein that ran through all the railroad men and gold miners, so at first Wu Fong had tried his hand at a bit of back-room gambling behind the restaurant's kitchen. His luck with cards doubled his income. "Hit good *pü-kê-pái*," he'd said. "*Dä-djïr-pái*." Wu Fong's luck had almost cost him his life.

One day the cops had raided a game and not only destroyed the back room but most of the restaurant as well. From that point on, Wu Fong confined his card playing to close friends, and when he did not have outside players, he used his family. And so it was that Yeung Lee inherited his grandfather's card luck, a skill he'd passed to Tea Rose. And it was Tea Rose who perfected Cora Kay's beginner's luck, and later, Clarence Henry's fool's luck.

"Hoisin play low win lump money," Tea Rose would tell Cora Kay.

They'd practice on Sunday afternoons, when the restaurant closed at ten to accommodate the sensibilities of their Christian neighbors. At first, Tea Rose would come to Cora Kay's room. Later, when Yeung Lee became more comfortable around Cora Kay, he joined their games. He'd move the cards in a fast shuffle that spread them in an even pattern across the table, like the Chinese fan he'd brought from the old country, the one he'd given to Cora Kay a month after she'd come to work for him. He'd move the cards with the same speed as he moved that machete knife.

Between games, he'd offer a trick, closing his eyes and saying, "You think one card. I tell you number written that card."

No matter what Cora Kay did, Yeung Lee picked the right card every time. "We oughta sit in on a real game," Cora Kay told him.

"No, no. I not allowed go play some *pü-kê-pái* card here."

"We could make some big money," Cora Kay reminded him.

For a moment his eyes blinked with interest, but finally he said, "Make lump money downstairs," and folded the deck.

"Make lump money downstairs," Tea Rose echoed.

That stubbornness persisted until Tea Rose saw Clarence Henry. In fact, it was Tea Rose who spotted Clarence when he first came in the restaurant. Because she and her grandmother had a clear view of the comings and goings of both the restaurant and the street, they acted as lookouts. The old woman, Kei-Shee, sat on a stool that was high enough to be in direct line with the front door from the kitchen service window. If the old woman signaled the approach of the police with *"Um cha hwêi-lai!,"* Cora Kay would quickly hide the cash box under the bin of fortune cookies, while Tea Rose helped her father open the door for the gamblers to scoot through. All of that was just a simple courtesy. Usually the law was after bigger fish, big-time gamblers such as the district boss, John Gionio, who ate at Wu Fong's on a regular basis. The cops really didn't bother to harass the Chinaman, who, after all, was legally forbidden to give testimony in court by reason of a dusty 1800s edict.

"I no emancipated! *Dzêu-chyu!*" Yeung Lee would shout when the cops burst through the door. And when the flurry died down, he'd feed them dishes of noodles and rice, and after a decent interval of delay bow them back to their patrol cars.

But despite the traffic of Gionio and other up-and-coming hoodlums, the regular trade pretty much remained the same, and the service at Wu Fong's was dependable. Yeung Lee's generous bowls of sticky rice, the thin noodles in their broth of chicken feet and ginger, the pungent oxtail stew, or roast duck garnished with turnip roots, broccoli, and the leaves of sweet mustard and dandelion kept folks coming back. Until Clarence Henry showed up, folks took it for granted that Tea Rose would be confined to the back room while Cora Kay waited tables out front.

Although the railroad men boasted of seeing better-looking women, all of them agreed that with her single braid of kinky rust-colored hair, thick ankles, and skin dusted a silk brown tinged with the light of an October's sunset, Cora Kay Ivory certainly wasn't an ugly woman. Her long legs and wide hips earned her the nickname

"High Pockets," and the men followed the sway of her ass while she waited tables. But none got close enough to do more than watch. The fact was that like any woman who kept herself a mystery, the men couldn't stay away from Cora Kay. So until Clarence Henry tumbled out of that freight car and got himself a room at the Proctor Hotel, where the unmarried railroad men stayed on their layovers, all they could do was keep a close watch on Cora Kay.

They should have watched Tea Rose. Clarence Henry did.

◆━

The fate that brought Clarence Henry into Wu Fong's Eatery was as straight as the railroad tracks that brought him into town. Everyone knew Wu Fong's was one place where it didn't matter if a man was running the road on a job, or running to get away from where he'd been. Clarence Henry was running when he hit town. Butler Sykes had spotted Clarence when he and Maroon-Willie were standing in the doorway of the train when it slowed down to make the bend where the tracks spread away from the main line near the shanties. Seeing Clarence made Butler elbow Maroon-Willie, and Maroon-Willie inched away from the door to pass the word along so other Brotherhood members could watch out for Clarence once the train was in the yards. That was when Butler swears he saw Cora Kay Ivory romping in a field of wildflowers with somebody wearing a small brocade hat.

"With a tassel on top like the Chinaman's," Maroon-Willie said.

"No, it were sho Cora Kay, and she were a sight," Butler said when the other men questioned him. "Had on one of them long dresses, like the women be wearing when they go to the dances. 'Cept it was broad daylight, and them weeds and flowers so tall, she couldn't hardly move. And somebody else was with her—though I couldn't rightly tell who."

"Well, I sho caught me a glimpse of something in the field cross from the processing plant. And that Chinaman's car was parked up by tree over near Hodiman Road," Maroon-Willie added.

"You mean that DeSoto?" Whitaker asked. Butler nodded, but Whitaker shook his head. "Naw, naw . . . can't be."

"Ah heah-ah them Chinee-mans shooes it off like a pistol," Lip said. "Heard that myself," Maroon added. And all the men looked at Yeung Lee with a new bit of understanding glued to their eyes.

Cora Kay and Yeung Lee would have laughed to know the rumors about them were as thick as the egg-drop soup Yeung Lee served at the restaurant every Saturday night, but Maroon-Willie and Butler had to admit they never had a clear view of whatever was going on in the field, because that was the same moment Butler saw Clarence Henry push himself out of a boxcar, limbs thin as a praying mantis's, and climb the ladder to the roof.

Clarence had left that car intent on scrambling across the flatlands toward the town's black section, but when Butler spotted him slipping two steps ahead of the yard bulls, he'd set Clarence on a straight line into the Black Belt. Of all the railroad men, Butler had more pull than most, not only because his wife, Aleeda Grace, owned the colored funeral home, but also because he was the spokesman for the local Brotherhood union. Butler's layover hadn't ended before he'd found Clarence a job working from 5:00 A.M. to midnight at the boxers' gym. There Clarence cleaned up the resin and sweat of would-be prizefighters, white boys who had hopes of knocking the spit out of some black kid who wanted to be a champ like Jack Johnson and Joe Louis. But Clarence wasn't interested in fighting.

"It just be a job," he told Butler and the others when they came back to town that next weekend, and picked him up at the Proctor Hotel. "That job do for now, but I got me some plans."

They watched him straighten his square knot, then pull a loose thread into the inside seam of his shirt. It didn't take much for them to figure out where Clarence had bought his duds. Almost all of the men who lived in the Flats had bought swank clothes from Hoffmeyer's Pawnshop at one time or another. Those clothes helped them lose the leather-tight grins they'd learned to click into place when they boarded the trains, or shined shoes downtown by the courthouse, or chauffered cars in the Belmont District—or like Clarence, stacked towels at the gym. In his one-button rolled-lapel suit, with peg-legged trousers and jacket nipped at the waist, he was, as Butler said, a dollar short and twenty years too late.

"Slick, you just be sure that itching you got don't bring you a one-way ride out of town," Butler said.

Clarence kept smiling. "I come in on that train, so I can go out the same way." Then with a hairbrush in each hand, he plastered strands of hair against his skull, his hands moving so rapidly, the brushes crackled against kinky hair as if they were copying the sound of train wheels.

"Listen to the man," Maroon-Willie snickered. "He don't know he can leave this town riding in a pine box steada the boxcar."

"And don't think that train gone be waiting for your black butt neither," Butler warned.

"That train wouldn't get nowhere if it wasn't for a colored man named Elijah McCoy," Clarence said.

Lip slapped his knee and hooted. "Thazz right. He the one be invent-ah fuh them steam fits. Call 'em The-Real-Mc-Coy, they do. Then come long them other cullard boys. Them call Winn and Woods, an' they make 'em bettah even fore Mc-Coy."

"How you know so much?" Whitaker asked. He was really asking Clarence Henry, but for once, Lip Wooten had answers and he wasn't about to be outdone.

"Ah be readin' aftah y'all be talkin'," Lip said. "Sa'more cullard boys invent-ah fuh the rail, too. Burr an' Jackson an' Purvis an'—"

Clarence interrupted him. "Man, I ain't got no time to be standing here whilst you list all them cats. Less you got somebody inventing fast cards, there's a game out there with my name on it. And in case anybody ask, you can tell 'em my name is Lucky. As the song goes, *I guess I'm just a lucky so-and-so.*" With that, he strutted out of the room and left them to close the door behind him.

As they headed for Wu Fong's, Whitaker told Butler, "You gone help one poor boy too many one of these days."

"Aw, he ain't doing nothing but blowing off steam," Butler said.

"I don't know," Whitaker muttered. "I seen boys acting half that bad jump up in your face asking for death."

With as much traveling as Whitaker had done on the railroad, he had reason to be suspicious of drifters like Clarence Henry. But who was to say why Kei-Shee never trusted Clarence? Perhaps she remembered San Francisco and the gold miners. Perhaps she remembered the gamblers who frequented the brothel where she had worked off the price of her ticket from China until Yeung Lee's father had brought her to town as his bride. Perhaps she was tired from arguing with Yeung Lee about finding a husband for Tea Rose. Len Poo Yen, the laundryman's son, had been killed in the war two years before, and only the month before, Kei-Shee had urged Yeung Lee to put more money aside for a trip to China, or at least to the West Coast, where young Chinese bachelors dreamed of finding a bride who already lived in the land of the Gold Mountain. Perhaps she'd run out of names. Perhaps. At any rate, she was the one who over-heard Tea Rose mutter, *"Shên-yan-sê-dê."*

◆

Kei-Shee had turned to see just what patch of black skin had caught her granddaughter's eye and made her lose all of her senses by speaking without permission. The minute she saw Clarence Henry, she muttered, *"Hêi-fon Kwei!"* with such a vengeance, Cora Kay al-most dropped the stack of dirty dishes she was putting on the counter, and for once gave all of her attention to the restaurant.

Cora Kay saw several of the men from the cattle yards, high on their weekly pay and eating as much as they could before they had the rest boxed up as take-home for the family. She knew Kei-Shee would not have used them to mutter an oath about "foreign-black-devils." The old woman called working men *"häu-kàn rên"*—good-look-men. Cora Kay saw them sitting near Sister Garrison and Doc Pritchard's wife, who were downing their usual Saturday night help-ing of shrimp fried rice. She was sick of throwing Christian pamphlets in the trash after they left, but it would be too much to hope the old woman was referring to them as "foreign devils." Other than one or two kids picking up takeout for their mamas, she only saw Maroon-Willie, Whitaker, and the usual crew of railroad men fitting them-selves in a booth. True, they were loud and would try to cheat her every chance they got, but Aleeda Sykes let the Chinese use her funeral home if one of them died. And none of the other men would have made the old woman spit out the words "black devil." Then Cora Kay saw Clarence Henry—"six shades blacker than night," her mother would have said.

When she turned back to Tea Rose, she knew by the look in the girl's eyes that she'd spotted Kei-Shee's *"Hêi-fon Kwei."*

Clarence was a bit thin for her taste, his face a little too broad and his eyes somewhat shifty, but when he smiled, the chip in his front tooth made him look young and old at the same time. It made Cora Kay remember a time when she was a little girl before the WWII, and a man who used to visit her mother. He had given her candies, and promised her a trip to the circus when he came back that next spring. But the war had started, and he'd never returned. Still, she recalled his laughter and how he'd told her he'd broken his tooth riding in a rodeo in some town out in Oklahoma where all the folks were black.

"Don't be telling that chile all that devilment," her mother had said. "Whoever heard of such a thing? A town with no white folks in it and all the black ones riding horses like in them cowboy movies."

But the man had insisted there was such a town, and he'd gone off to find it, taking with him the devilment in his smile.

Cora Kay leaned across the service counter to signal Tea Rose, and once again Kei-Shee muttered, *"Hêi-fon Kwei!"*

"Shut up, snaggletooth. I ain't studying 'bout you," Cora Kay whispered in case Yeung Lee looked up from his chores of splitting celery root or cracking a duck's back with one stroke of his knife. "Old woman, why you always got to be flapping your lips?" Cora Kay hissed. "Why you always got to be taking a look-see at what I do? Look-see, *djäu*. Humph! You think I'm seeing something? Think I'm looking at something to talk about?"

Then, satisfied that she'd given Tea Rose as many clues as she dared, Cora Kay started to worm her way between tables and booths, ignoring customers who signaled her as she aimed for Clarence Henry. Kei-Shee grumbled as she watched Cora Kay's progress. Had it not been for the old woman's mutterings, Yeung Lee would not have looked up from his chopping block. When he saw his daughter was also staring at something in the front of the restaurant, Yeung Lee went to the service window. And that was how, in the early spring of 1946, trouble came between Clarence Henry and Wu Yeung Lee.

By the time Yeung Lee came to the service window, Clarence had started talking to Cora Kay, who was standing in the aisle. He'd had to turn around to talk to her, and in turning, he saw Tea Rose staring at him, her round face perfect in its moon-shaped wonder. Of course, he also saw Yeung Lee—it was hard to miss the big Chinaman —but Clarence Henry believed in luck, so he'd continued staring at Tea Rose. At the same time, Yeung Lee saw the target of his daughter's admiring glances was also the face that held Cora Kay's attention.

It was doubtful whether Yeung Lee tried dividing his anger equally between Cora Kay and Tea Rose, or whether he was aware of how tightly he gripped the knife's handle, or that he'd begun to shift his weight so that his next step would lead him out of the kitchen. But none of it mattered, because at that moment Clarence Henry's luck held true. Just as Yeung Lee reached the kitchen door, machete in hand, the police burst through the front door on one of their routine raids of joints along the Strip.

The regular customers had practice at timing their scramble, but without knowing where the rear exit was, Clarence tried running toward the front door. Immediately he was turned back by the onslaught of cops. At one point, Maroon-Willie tried to reach him, but Clarence vaulted across tables to the other side of the restaurant. There the church ladies beat him back with their purses, and the cops would have tagged him if Tea Rose hadn't snatched him into the kitchen. Yeung Lee already had the pantry door open, but Tea Rose took Clarence through the alley to the storage shed, where she locked him in as tightly as her father had locked in the burlap-covered bales of rice and tea that freight trains brought him from the West Coast.

And while her father cleared the air, shouting, "Here not allowed Tong! Here not allowed suckee *yä-pyän!* Not allowed card men! Here belong only honest man!," Tea Rose let the confusion help folks forget she'd neatly placed Clarence Henry in the storage shed.

The whole business might have gone unnoticed if Yeung Lee hadn't been suspicious already. But he was, and long after the cops had left, he watched the two girls. So Tea Rose had to wait until the eatery had closed and Yeung Lee and his mother were snoring in unison before she was able to release Clarence from the storage shed.

"Where you going?" Cora Kay whispered. Tea Rose was at the end of the hall when she stopped her. "Make water," Tea Rose said, as if Cora Kay suddenly couldn't remember where the chamber pots were.

"What brand of truth you giving me?" Cora Kay asked. Tea Rose's eyes were like a night breeze flowing past her, a splinter of light caught in the cinders of coal piled at the edge of shantytown. "What you up to, girl?"

Tea Rose said, "I make someone belong-safe when cops come *chyu-djêu.*"

For once, Cora Kay was impatient with the spiderweb of Chinese woven into English. "Where is he?" she hissed. "Where is he?"

Tea Rose bowed her head and moved away in what Cora Kay called her cockroach steps. Still, Cora had to walk fast to keep up with the girl, and Tea Rose, in her usual determination, never looked around to see how far away Cora Kay was.

When Tea Rose opened the shed, Clarence was a deeper shadow

huddled in a corner, and sleeping as if darkness were a solution to his problems. Tea Rose waited until Cora Kay closed the door before she lit the lantern; then they both watched Clarence rub sleep from his eyes. For a moment the three of them inspected each other. Tea Rose drank in images of Clarence as if he were a vision she'd seen those nights on the roof where, if she looked at it long enough, the sky's darkness became as thick as flesh. And Cora Kay stretched out toward something her mother told her about how a man smells when he awakens, the softness in back of his neck, the pillow of his shoulder. At the same time, she fought to see Clarence for what he was—his razor-boned frame too loose and slippery to stay in one place.

As the two women stood in the ring of light, what Clarence saw was Cora Kay's red-brown skin—not just the patch of cinnamon the railroad men had dreamed when she served their food off her hip in the same way some women carried babies, but something that made Yeung Lee remember a tapestry where dragon fire licked the edges of the ocean. But no sight had pleased Clarence more than Tea Rose. Her hair, purple-black, softened and darkened a face so pale he'd seen her clearly even before she'd held up the lantern. Clarence shuddered the way he had when he heard a train's mournful whistle. Already he was touching her—the soft skin behind her knees, the small of her back, the inside of her thighs where the rush of smells would fill his head and leave him drowning.

"You gone get us killed," Cora Kay said to both of them. "Yeung Lee gone come out here and chop us all to little pieces the way he chops up them ducks. Y'all must be crazy. I'm outta here." She moved toward the door, but Tea Rose stayed where she was. "You hear me, girl?" Cora Kay asked her. "Your daddy don't play. Specially with the likes of that," she added, nodding toward Clarence Henry.

But Tea Rose was well past reason. "What name you call?" she asked Clarence. "What place you live? What place belong your wife?"

As Cora Kay left the shed, she rightly assumed she had trouble on her hands.

◆━━◆

It wasn't long before Tea Rose and Clarence were meeting in secret on a regular basis. In fact, the two of them were more at ease with the mess they were creating than their friends were. As long as Tea Rose knew when Clarence was going to meet her, she easily assumed her expressionless pose behind the service window. Cora Kay, on the other hand, had to act as if Clarence were a piece of woodwork when he came into Wu Fong's with the railroad men.

"Well, Slick, she sho got your number fast," Whitaker told Clarence when Cora Kay barely stayed long enough to finish taking their order.

"Um-hum," Maroon-Willie added. "Come on strong the first time she seen you, now turning you cold as a tombstone."

"Hey, y'all know this cat's the best thing she seen since Wonder Bread." Butler laughed.

"Yeah, the butt enda bread," Lip said.

The others laughed, but Clarence said nothing. Like Cora Kay, he was relieved that the jokes reached Yeung Lee. After a while, the Chinaman stopped staring at him each time he came into the restaurant, so Clarence figured he was home free. But he didn't have to make excuses for the noises Yeung Lee heard drifting into the upstairs windows long after closing hours, when being with Cora Kay made his eyes glint black as the stones at the bottom of the creek.

When Yeung Lee heard laughter, Cora Kay would hold him closer and say, "It's them foxes. They useta come right up to the door when I lived in shantytown." And when the shed door creaked against a rock Tea Rose hadn't kicked out of its path, Cora Kay said, "It's them trains. Must be breaking in a new yard crew. Some ain't good for nothing."

After a while, Cora Kay began to look more strained than Tea Rose. Yeung Lee told her, "I no send you for flower-pick. You tired out work maybe."

"We need some place not for work," Tea Rose said. And after she'd gained her father's permission to return to the meadow, she told Clarence almost the same thing.

"We need some place invite me, hun?"

Cora Kay moved away from them. It wasn't that she wanted to leave them alone, but she simply did not want to hear Clarence Henry's answer. More than once, they'd said too much around her. And once, when they'd been in the meadow, she'd seen them sink into the tall grass. She'd wandered away to look at the shadows of Indian Hills, visible on the horizon some thirty miles south of town and tinted pink by the sun, like the clumps of pale agates she used to find at the edge of Cobbler's Creek. The creek was like a bright silver guardrail guiding the way toward the valley. She'd searched the valley for a while, then turned back to where she'd last seen Clarence and Tea Rose. At first the meadow had seemed empty. Then she'd spotted a slight depression in the grass. And with her hand shielding her eyes, she could see the two of them pillowed by wood violets and chicory bending under the weight of their bodies. A sparrow rustled the branches of a sycamore, and the flash of light was trapped in the movement of Tea Rose's arm curling toward Clarence Henry. If the wind blew just right, the grass spread back to its raw side and Cora Kay could clearly see them both: the smooth slant of Clarence Henry's back, humped marble-black, like the rocks the railroad had used to shore up the trestle, and Tea Rose's legs, bent in that crooked way women assumed when they opened their bodies for birth or love. And the two of them moving, pulsing like snakes, or the very grass itself, flower petals falling in the wake of a breeze.

Later, she wished she'd had the sense to turn away, because it was at that point that, somehow, Cora Kay began to feel responsible for the conspiracy that hummed between those two. And it didn't take long for her part in the act to come due.

"Hoisin, you make card men say yes for lump money game?" Tea Rose asked her. "Henry C. good card man," she said, reversing his name, Chinese fashion.

"Humph. Good for nothing," Cora Kay snorted.

"No. Make lump money. Big game when Fù-chin fall sleeping."

"Your daddy don't sleep that sound, and the onliest thing Clarence gone buy you a space in the graveyard," Cora Kay told her.

But in the end, she found herself setting up the game. *I'm running a fool,* she told herself, but she'd seen Clarence Henry double-shuffle cards, his long fingers tapered like ribbons, so graceful they seemed to flow into the act until cards and hands moved as one. Clarence had told them more than one story of how some redneck card player had been tempted to break those fingers just to erase their image from his memory. Cora Kay had to admit Clarence could move cards almost as well as Yeung Lee, but she still had her doubts about setting him up with the big-time gambling men.

"Takes more than the nerve of a brass monkey to shine in that game," Cora Kay told Clarence.

"Do I look like I'm short on nerve?" Clarence asked. "Besides, what I don't know, my woman know."

Cora Kay's eyes went from Clarence to Tea Rose. Tea Rose grinned. "Man, I think you musta hit your head when you fell off that train," Cora Kay said. "You think they gone let some Chinawoman come to a game with you?"

"Um-hum. And be glad for the gamble." Clarence laughed. His instinct always told him when to push for a bet and when to fold. Now it told him to bet. "You just tell 'em Tea Rose be ready. Can't be my doing, else they back off. You just pass the word at Wu Fong's."

"Hoisin, I have *shïng-yün,* much luck. We make lump money," Tea Rose said. "Invite you come big house."

"Not me," Cora Kay said. "I ain't going nowhere. Not to that game or some house you think you gone get. I'll do this and no more."

So the next time Cora Kay served the table of railroad men, she let Tea Rose's little firecracker drop. Clarence Henry's luck seemed to be spreading itself around, because not only were the railroaders there, but also John Gionio and a few big-time gamblers were in the next booth. Cora Kay said it loud enough for both groups to listen. For a second, all conversation came to a halt.

"Maybe y'all didn't hear me right," she said. "Maybe I oughta be serving you them fortune cookies early."

Gionio bathed her in one of his pale dog's-head grins. "If there's some other gentlemen interested, then you can bring us a couple dozen thousand-year-old eggs. They gonna need that much luck."

Cora Kay looked at the booth full of railroad men. Clarence didn't signal until Butler and Whitaker nodded. Maroon shrugged, but Lip looked confused, so Cora Kay figured he was out. No matter. She already had enough players. "Thousand-year-old eggs," she said, as if she were writing down a regular order. "I guess we can get 'em to you a little after midnight."

"But you make sure that Chinawoman washes the grease off the money 'fore she hands it over," Gionio said, then patted Cora Kay's hip as if he were stroking a horse's flank.

Cora Kay smacked him with her pencil, and the sound of the wood whacking across Gionio's knuckles was almost as sharp as the crack of Yeung Lee's machete on his chopping block.

Gionio laughed and leaned away from the booth to catch Butler's eye. "I'll take that colored dame for my table," he said.

"You take what you get," Clarence snapped.

Butler hunched Clarence. "Don't pay no 'tention to him, Mr. Gionio. He just selling buffalo chips."

Later, when they had left the restaurant and were walking toward the funeral parlor, Butler had a few choice words for Clarence. "Man, why you want to front-off somebody?" Butler asked him. "Ain't you got no better sense than to rile that white man? Watch your mouth. You asking for trouble."

"Trouble be my name, asking be my game," Clarence said.

"Well, Sporting Life, you best be asking for the right cards tonight," Whitaker told him.

Maroon said, "Um-hum," wagging his head.

But Clarence just threw back his head and laughed, showing a row of sharp, even teeth. Whitaker sighed. Like most black folks, he remembered how death could as easily knock at his door in the form of a posse as it could creep up behind someone caught in the wrong place by accident or forgetfulness. All night, he kept his eyes peeled for trouble.

Trouble didn't come until late in the game. By all rights, Clarence and Tea Rose should have bought themselves out of the play at least an hour before Gionio started chomping on his losing streak. Perhaps it was knowing the pile of winnings in front of them meant they'd passed the point of no return, or perhaps it was the thick air that left them groggy and overconfident. Certainly the back room of the funeral parlor carried that smell peculiar to any house of the dead. As night crept toward dawn, the scent grew heavier—even with the blue smoke of tobacco and whiskey fumes, even with the card players' body odors in a neighborhood where the usual odors rising from cattle pens could reduce folks to lizards scurrying for a place among the rocks, and spitting words at each other when they couldn't find their real targets. Gionio was losing, and he needed a target.

"Leda got some fresh blood in here?" Gionio asked Butler.

"I don't be asking my wife who she burying," Butler said.

Gionio looked at the cards in his hand. "Whatever she's burying turned rancid 'fore it died." He looked around for a response.

Everyone intently studied their cards. Whitaker worried the end of a cigar, and Butler rubbed the stubble of his beard, while the dealer, Hugh Spalding, Gionio's cut-buddy who controlled the city's water rights, sliced his forehead into a frown that was deep enough to fold skin over skin. Only Clarence seemed at ease—Clarence and Tea Rose, who was sitting right behind him. Tea Rose was wearing flowers in her hair, and each time she leaned forward to gaze at Clarence's hand, the petals quivered. Tea Rose's usual grease-stained smock had been replaced by a shantung dress, slit up both sides and so tight it seemed to dance across her hips of its own accord, music or not.

Gionio tried to imagine her naked and spread under him. When she leaned forward and coached Clarence to ask for three cards, Gionio heard her whispered signal of *"Yäu-sän-gê"* as "Y'all singing." Tea Rose felt him staring and looked up. Gionio could only see half of her eyes under their slanted lids. He didn't like anything hidden, especially something Chinese. "Maybe we oughta tell Leda to get another coffin ready," he said. "Something's turning rotten sure as I'm sitting here."

Nobody responded. Hugh Spalding dealt against each player's discard. Butler called and raised the ante. Everyone threw in money except Whitaker, who folded. The play should have gone smoothly, except Clarence hadn't been listening to Gionio's lament. Whitaker said, "Take it easy, man," but Clarence raised the bet again before he called in the hand. Butler shook his head, Hugh folded, and Maroon-Willie looked around the room as if he were searching for a pool of water to throw himself into. That left Gionio and Clarence in a face-off. Like the motto on Wu Fong's grass-writing scroll, Gionio's look was colder than the wind biting a beggar's coat.

He said, "Lay them cards out careful, boy."

"Any way you want 'em," Clarence said. "Read 'em and weep."

Gionio pushed back from the table. "I don't weep for no niggers. And don't think you gone get rich off me, boy. I'll be here when they done buried your black ass six feet under in a pauper's grave."

It's anyone's guess as to whether John Gionio ever looked at Clarence Henry's winning hand. It would be a shame to think that big-dog spread of aces high, nine low mixed suit, went unnoticed. But none of the players had time to attend to cards right at that moment.

Gionio came up from the chair with his gun drawn. The table spilled onto Hugh's lap, and Maroon raced Whitaker to the floor. It was probably Butler's alarmed cry of "John!" that stopped Gionio, who wasn't averse to killing but had long since hired others to do his dirty work. So he looked at his gun. For Clarence, that hesitancy was another bit of luck. He and Tea Rose wasted no time leaving the room. One scoop, and the money was in his hat. Two steps, and Tea Rose snatched him through the door. Three steps, and before Butler could finish saying, "Ga'damn black mothah . . ." they were in the alley.

As Clarence well knew, running was an art only survivors lived

long enough to brag about. Between his knowledge of the streets and
Tea Rose's history of clearing the restaurant during a raid, they were
halfway to Wu Fong's before Gionio could call his boys. But both of
them knew how small they'd carved that lead. They needed help. Tea
Rose sprinkled Cora Kay's window with pebbles four times before
Cora Kay lifted the sash. When she saw Tea Rose's panicky look and
the hatful of money Clarence was showing her, Cora grabbed her
clothes and sneaked past Yeung Lee. By the time she reached the
back door, by the time they told her Gionio was following them, she
knew they would get nowhere on foot. And Yeung Lee's DeSoto was
so conveniently parked by the storage shed.

Clarence's years of running had not put him in a place where he
could have learned to drive, but once behind the wheel of the car, he
had no recourse but to pretend he knew how. It had seemed so easy
when he'd watched other men doing it. He fiddled with the gears,
and keeping both feet on brake and clutch, waited for something to
happen.

Cora Kay stared at him as if he'd ordered some odd combination
of food, like sweet-and-sour ribs sprinkled with fried shrimp. She
tried to be patient. "Put it in gear, Clarence. Move your feet, man!"

By some accident, Clarence popped the clutch and stomped the
accelerator. The DeSoto lurched forward, stopped, lurched, stopped.

"Hit that stick again!" Cora Kay said.

He snatched it back and the gears screamed so loudly, Tea Rose
slid to the floor, certain her father would wake up right at that moment and find them. She needn't have worried. Yeung Lee didn't
wake up until Clarence had ground the gears for the third time, and
Yeung Lee didn't reach the window until the car had rolled into the
Mission Road intersection. They might have heard him shouting if
Clarence hadn't been snatching the gears again.

Cora Kay leaned over to see what his feet were doing. Her head
was so close to his crotch, Clarence almost unraveled. He slammed
his foot against the accelerator once more then, in an effort to hide
his rapidly growing erection, lifted his leg from the clutch, and the car
shot across the intersection as if it had been blown from one of the
cannons circus stuntmen used to propel a body into the air. That
move slammed Cora Kay into the dash and nearly took off the top of
her head. She moaned and sat up. The bundle of sage Yeung Lee had
hung from the rearview mirror quivered.

Cora Kay managed to say, "Jesus, you bout killed me."

And Tea Rose shouted, *"Hwêi-lai! Hwêi-chyu!"* Those were the first words she'd spoken since they'd climbed into the DeSoto.

Clarence yelled, "Shit!," but he had definitely passed the danger of his erection. Now he was sweating.

"What you saying, Tea Rose?" Clarence asked.

"She saying, 'Go back,' " Cora Kay told him.

"I got to get turned round," Clarence said. But the car hit the first set of train tracks and galloped from track to track before it died midway on the inbound line. He tried the motor again. The DeSoto protested. Tea Rose bounced up and down as if her backseat action would start the engine. Cora Kay wanted to wallop the girl.

"Why the hell am I here?" Cora Kay said to no one in particular.

She could smell the whiffs of sweet-sour cow manure, and the moldy yeast of grain elevators and old warehouses. On the other side of the tracks, she saw the beginning of the narrow streets that led to shantytown, where the road curved downhill toward the back side of the train yards. This wasn't her idea of coming home again, but then, none of it had ever been her idea. She turned to say something to this effect to Clarence when some lights reflected in the back window caught her eye. Cora Kay blinked. There were all sorts of visions she might have imagined seeing, but none of them involved Yeung Lee waving his machete and running down the road in front of several oncoming cars, motors churning on a low growl.

Clarence moaned. Tea Rose yelled, *"Fù-chin! Fù-chin!"* as if none of them could have recognized her father.

"Shit! And Gionio's behind him! That does it!" Cora Kay shouted. "That's it! See what y'all done done? First the car. Then them damn gamblers chasing you. Now you got Yeung Lee ready to kill us. What else could—" she began. And as if it had been waiting for that question, an inbound train's whistle screamed twice.

Clarence yelled, "Shit fucka-roony!" and leaped out of the seat. Where his feet had clumsily sought brake pedal and clutch, they easily found ground level and headed up the tracks without missing a step.

Cora Kay screamed and pulled at the door latch. For want of a quick escape route, Tea Rose merely screamed, a long, protracted sound like nails scratching glass, a sound that bypassed all of her language problems. Once more, a train answered, this one on the outbound track. Now all of them abandoned the car. Cora Kay panted and looked both ways. Town was out of the question, and going up the tracks would merely put her in the station. Clarence had already doubled back, and was diving into the car to retrieve his hatful of money. "Leave the damn money!" Cora Kay shouted at him. But he stuffed some in his pockets, then threw the hat at Cora Kay. Without looking at how much it contained, she plopped it on her head. Clarence took off again, this time up the outbound train tracks.

Cora Kay turned to Tea Rose. "C'mon!" she yelled, trying to grab the girl to get her moving. "This way!" Cora Kay shouted. And she heard Yeung Lee shout something, too. He was closer, close enough for her to see his hair streaming, like the tail of a stallion in full flight from the headlights of the cars behind him. And his machete blade picked up the glare of the car lights. He yelled again. This time Cora Kay clearly heard him shout, *"Djì-nyü!"* She vaguely wondered just who he was calling a whore, but the approaching train whistles told her it didn't matter. The cars behind Yeung Lee added their horns to the noise. Cora Kay snatched at Tea Rose again. "Move it!" she yelled, and started running. Out of the corner of her eye, she saw Clarence had turned back one more time. Tea Rose was already running toward him when Cora Kay hurled herself into the row of jimsonweed, skunk cabbage, and foxglove growing at the edge of the tracks.

Cora Kay cut diagonally across the tracks and slipped into the underbrush separating the railroad yards from shantytown. The ground was wet, and she slid down the embankment, past someone's outhouse. Behind her, the shouts of men grew louder, and the trains were rumbling nearer. When she entered a rut between the shanties, she heard gunshots, then a long crunch as first one train, then the other, chewed Yeung Lee's DeSoto. Cora Kay's headlong plunge took her right into the arms of Sister Vernida Garrison and her little band of Ladies' Aid volunteers on their nightly shantytown mission. Sister Garrison didn't know whether it was man or a woman falling into her arms—the hat askew on a hard, lumpy head, the face covered with stinking mud, and the dusty prickles of poisonous plants clinging to the arms that enfolded her.

"Lord help me! I been kissed by the evil eye!" she screamed.

Folks say Vernida Garrison was never quite the same after Cora Kay Ivory plowed into her that night. Certainly Yeung Lee was never the same. Only the food was dependable—and Yeung Lee's anger as his machete sliced the air, and he muttered about the black-foreign-devil who wrecked his car and took his love away from him. Folks who ate at the Chinaman's waited to see if Tea Rose and that badass Clarence Henry ever returned to the Flats. Like Yeung Lee, they were disappointed. No one saw Tea Rose after that night, but folks on the Strip frequented Cinnamon's Bar, and if they were real nice she'd speak a few words of Chinese while she poured their drinks.

VALERIE MINER

DROPPING
ANCHOR

The sailor leaves his ship, picks up an oar, and walks inland. He cannot stop until someone asks, "What's that you're carrying?" Then he can rest.

—*The Odyssey*

G rey. Brown. Beige. The colour of this high desert eludes her. The mountains are rocky ladders to a flat, pale sky. Macro arrowheads. Otherwise, scrub stretches for miles to the horizon. This reminds Patricia of travelling in the South. Perhaps because of the bus. She hasn't taken a long bus journey for fifteen years.

A Black woman across the aisle places a yellow-flowered pillow next to herself so she doesn't have to share the seat when they make the next stop at Murdoch. Patricia had heard the woman tell the young Chicano soldier behind them that she is travelling from New Orleans to visit her sister in Los Angeles. She needs the space to stretch. Who could argue?

A day-and-a-half in this bus, muses Patricia, who has less than four hours to ride from the El Paso airport to Murdoch, New Mexico. She glances at the blond sailor sleeping next to her, head jiggling against the window frame, snoring beer breath in and out. Now she watches his fog on the cold window, almost clearing when he inhales, then returning the net of moisture over the glass. Outside the window it is white: snow on the cactus, on the telephone poles, on the road ahead.

Patricia closes her eyes and tries to imagine what her father will look like. Instead, Mother's face appears, objecting to this visit. Patricia argues back that he is more her father than Mother's ex-husband. Her father. Patricia reflects that she was sixteen when he left the family and she has hardly seen him in twenty years. Oh, they have had the obligatory dinners and brunches when they happened to be in the same port. Three years ago in New York. Five years ago in London. Once in San Francisco. But these infrequent, indigestible meals were ritualized encounters. *She has always been better at observing rituals than at participating in them. Even as a devout child, she found the Eucharist stuck to the roof of her mouth.* Sometimes she wonders if Dad sent a stand-in to the dinners and brunches. Any number of people could have imitated that Boston Irish accent and affected the racial epithets. She wonders again why her father, a merchant seaman all his life, has retired to the desert to raise chickens.

The sailor shifts, disturbing her reverie, and she opens her eyes. Snow falls steadily as they approach a town. She consults her watch— almost two o'clock. Yes, "The Rotary Club Welcomes You to Murdoch, New Mexico. Population: 1,376. Elevation: 4,095 feet." Patricia never thought her father would get this far above sea level before he died. She had spent years praying for his death. Now he is seventy years old. He is a hoary, fat old man waving to her from the door of the small Greyhound station.

Patricia is the only passenger to disembark at Murdoch. Do the others know something she doesn't? She resists the impulse to turn and wave to the woman with the pillow; the friendliest gesture she can make is to hustle off this bus so that they can get on to Los Angeles.

Dad waves again as she emerges. He stays inside the station until the driver disengages her bag from the storage compartment. Then her father waddles towards her, pulling a poodle. A standard grey poodle, she notices, like the one they had when she was little.

"Hi there," he says.

"Hi." She smiles and pecks his cheek. 4711. Even in the frozen desert, he wears 4711 cologne.

"You like him?" His accent is stronger. Until now, he might have been any retired rancher. Now she knows he is her father, displaced from Newton, Massachusetts, and from Dun Laohaire before.

"Cute," she manages.

"Guards against the spics," he says.

Testing her already, or does he always talk like this? She realizes she can swallow the bait. He would love a fight. But it's only sport to him.

"I call him Fritzie. Got two more at home. They couldn't all come to welcome you. So I brought Fritzie. He's the quietest."

"Nice to meet you, Fritzie." She scratches the dog's neck and he rubs himself against her long, quilted coat.

"Better get you in the car," he says, "before you freeze. Crazy weather for New Year's. I said come for New Year's because it's usually hot."

"Weather doesn't matter," she shrugs. "I'm here to see you." It comes out naturally enough because it is the truth. She *has* come to see him. Now and then. She has come to be kind to him. She has come because he may die soon—how can he survive with all that weight?—and she would feel guilty if she hadn't come. Still, she is taken aback by her statement, so intimate and direct.

He walks up to a small, green Datsun truck. She is mildly surprised that it isn't a big, old Pontiac they could sail down the highway. However, he is a chicken rancher now.

"Mind if Fritzie rides with us? It's a little cold for him in the back."

"Not at all." She holds one bag on her lap, pushes her suitcase on the floor in front of her and draws the dog closer. The truck smells of country. She checks herself in the rearview mirror: a tall, redheaded woman looking a little younger than usual.

"Sorry I couldn't pick you up at the El Paso airport," he grunts, getting behind the wheel. She feels the truck lower a foot towards the ground. "But those roads were slick and I don't have chains. I knew you'd make it fine, though. Once, I took a bus down the Jersey Turnpike in weather like this and we made it fine. Who would have thought—chains in the desert?"

"It *was* fine. Really. I thought about the years I spent on buses, doing organizing at those mills in the South."

"Unions." He clears his throat of phlegm and pulls onto the highway. Fritzie barks frantically. "I still can't believe you threw away your college education to become a union organizer."

She stares ahead into the thick fog and prays they will make it safely to the ranchero. Suddenly she is overwhelmed with memories of Dad, lit up like a tree and swerving all over the road to Somerville on the way to spend Christmas at Grandma's. But the strongest thing she has smelled today is 4711.

"Didn't hear from Art at Christmas."

"Oh." She reminds herself that she has promised not to get involved in the feud between Dad and her older brother. "How about Henry? Did Henry call?"

"Your little brother always calls." His voice loses its edge. "Henry's doing great. Made assistant manager of the dealership last month."

"Yes." She smiles at the thought of her gregarious baby brother.

"Say, seriously now, how's your work? Your job going OK?"

He's trying, she thinks. The last time they met he didn't ask a thing about her.

"Fine." She nods. "We're working on a new contract. Management seems flexible. We'll see." She wished she could be forthcoming; wishes she could trust him more.

"The dentist liked your book." He clears his throat again. "He's a reader, that guy. He was impressed that I had a daughter who wrote a book. So was I." He looks at her.

Patricia is glad the weather is so cold; perhaps her blush will disappear quickly. It's a modest publication; more a handbook, really. She remembers a wonderful trip they once took together, just the two of them up the coast. "Tell me about the chickens," she says.

"Well, I got bantams and Rhode Island Reds . . . you'll see. Best this year are the pheasants. And I've got one terrific peacock."

"Peacock?"

"Yeah, a gorgeous male, wait till I show you."

She knows his place before he turns up the driveway. The flag-pole is an exclamation point in front of the house of Walt Lester, American citizen, who hated all the ports he visited and couldn't wait to retire at home. The front yard is filled with pastel gravel. She sees her father's wife, Dagmar, standing in the living-room window.

"Home, Fritzie, whadya say, boy? Glad to be home?"

The dog presses his nose on the windshield, yapping wildly.

A chorus of higher- and lower-pitched barks greet him. As soon as her father cuts the motor, Dagmar releases the other poodles from the front door.

"OK, OK, now," he shouts. "Down, boy. Down, girl. That's it, that's a good dog."

Patricia sits in the car, amused and touched by the chaos. Why is she taking it so good-naturedly? He used to drive her nuts.

"It's all right." Her father looks over, "They won't bite."

"Oh, I'm not worried about that," she begins defensively and hops out of the car.

"Welcome, Patricia," the tall blond woman says. She begins to hug her and then remembers the cup of cocoa in her hand. "To warm you up, after the trip."

"Yes, thanks." Patricia nods, accepting the cocoa. Should she stand here and drink it? Won't Dagmar freeze if she stays outside in her slippers?

"That's it; that's it." Her father is still talking to the dogs.

Patricia sips the cocoa. "Delicious. Perhaps we should get in the house?" She shifts her shoulder bag and reaches for the suitcase.

Dagmar claims it. "This way, yes, what was I thinking about, serving you on the ice-cold driveway?"

They leave him outside with the dogs. She shivers at the familiar sensation of being abandoned. She remembers, as a little girl, waving goodbye at the side of a big, white roaring ship. Why the panic? He's just gone to quell the dogs.

"Sit," Dagmar instructs, "I'll show you the guest room in a minute. But relax here on the couch. You can see two mountain ranges when it's clear. He's been talking about your visit for months. And he gave your book to the dentist two weeks ago so as to talk with you about it. We're not much on reading."

Patricia looks out the big picture window at the heavy mist sweeping down the street. The barking has grown fainter and she guesses her father has gone to check on the chickens.

"I've taken to watercolours myself." She bobs the marshmallow up and down in her cocoa. "I did oils for a while, but the texture wasn't right for the desert. Too rough. You have to look close to see things here. Sometimes in the middle of nothingness, miles of nothingness, there will be a small gem—literally a gem, or a flower—you know and oils are just not delicate enough for that. I don't suppose you paint. You must be too busy."

Patricia wishes she could excuse herself to lie down for a few moments. "I don't have the talent for painting, for creative things like that."

"Don't be modest, an educated girl like yourself." Dagmar turns. "Oh, now, dear, brace yourself for an invasion."

He walks in, followed by three huge poodles. "Behave," he warns them. "Come meet Patricia and behave, you hear me?"

He introduces Schooner, Taffy and Fritzie again.

"Sometimes he gets mixed up," Dagmar laughs, "calls them your names, 'Art, Patricia and Henry.' Can you believe it?"

Patricia smiles thinly and gulps the cocoa.

"Oh, here, let me get a refill. And some cookies. Your father has been baking all week."

He always did this before he went to sea, Patricia remembers. The house would rise with delicious aromas as he canned peaches and tomatoes and made sauces for Mother to serve when he was away. Then he would disappear. For three months. Six months. "It's his job," Mother would explain. "He doesn't like it any better than we do." Patricia knew she should trust her parents; she knew she was exaggerating her fears. But even when he got a shore job, he would be gone for weeks loading cargo. Then one day, what she had always suspected happened: he left for good.

The dogs continue to bark. Dagmar continues to talk. Patricia and her father exchange stale items of family news. The sky outside grows dark and, finally, Dagmar beckons Patricia to her room at the back of the house.

"It's my room, actually, I can't sleep with your father's snoring. Sounds like a bull elephant, you know."

Patricia thinks how Mother would be happy to hear the old buzz saw at night. Surprised by the reflex to defend Mother after all these years, she declares, "Very cosy. I like the colours." She glances surreptitiously at the silver crucifix knotted with palm leaves and hanging over the bed. She has forgotten that Dad persuaded Dagmar to convert to Catholicism. He had talked his way into an annulment and remarriage, protecting his immortal soul. Our father. It's all coming back.

"I'm glad you like it. I sent to Santa Fe for the curtain fabric. . . ."

That night, as Patricia brushes her teeth, she reads a prayer tacked to the mirror. "Please God, help me remember that silence is golden. When I open my mouth to speak, let me breathe in the glory of your universe. . . ." She has been judging Dagmar too harshly. So she stole Dad from Mother twenty years ago; surely she's had second thoughts. Besides, Mother is probably better off alone. She's more independent, more outgoing than she ever was when Dad was around.

Patricia climbs into the warm bed and considers the first day. She is confused by the great affection she feels for him. Of course, he is still bombastic and single-minded. But she keeps having glimpses of him in the past—driving her to a basketball game; winning double pinochle with her against Mother and Henry. They had some good times when he was in port and sober. She reads for a while, then slips down beneath the rustling comforter and fresh yellow-flowered sheets. Yellow flowers. She thinks of the woman on the bus and wonders how many hours she has to go before Los Angeles.

◆

The noises start before light. Roosters. High, shrieking whistles. Dogs barking. Patricia puts the pillow over her head and falls back to sleep. Sun creeps into the room and the back door bangs. Dad going out to feed the chickens. Six o'clock. He always hit the deck early. She draws down the shade and crawls under the pillow again. She dreams she is at Olduvai Gorge.

The barking wakens her. Eight o'clock, well, she doesn't want to be a slouch. Tentatively she sticks one foot out of the warm covers and pulls it back. She reaches over and raises the shade to find the street still socked in with fog. Yawning, she gets up; rushes into her clothes.

"You didn't have to get all dressed," Dagmar greets her in the kitchen. "I'm not usually decent until nine or ten. Your father, sometimes, he wakes the rooster."

He walks in, brushing his hands. Patricia is filled with fondness. His gesture reminds her of a past moment she cannot quite place.

"Ready for a real breakfast?" he asks.

"Starving." Then she remembers how much he piled on her plate the previous night. "Medium starving."

"Your father is such a cook," Dagmar sighs. "Especially this season. When we had Father Bailey over for spaghetti and meatballs, he spent the whole day preparing. I tell him, 'Walt, relax, you don't have to sustain people for the next ten years; it's only one meal.' But he loves it. Loves it. I just wish he would love to wash the dishes."

"Thought we could go visit Admiral Dirk, the breeder, while Dagmar's at the picture framer's today. I mean, we could all drive to town and you and me could check out the new birds."

"Now, Walt, remember, you yourself said we didn't have room. . . ."

"All right. All right. Doesn't do an old man harm to browse."

Patricia remembers her mother's warning that his backyard tomato patch would take over Massachusetts.

"Well, Patricia will be with you. I'm sure that will keep you sensible."

Mother had said this when he went up to Portland to load cargo. Patricia read while he was at work. Then he took her out to dinner and introduced her to that nice woman, Dagmar, who was staying at the same hotel.

In the truck, Dagmar makes Patricia promise that she will drag him away from the birds by ten o'clock, complaining about how he had to extend the pens twice that autumn after shopping sprees. Patricia tenses, resentful of Dagmar's intimacy with him. What does she expect? They have been married for eighteen years. Still, Patricia can't relax until Dagmar disembarks at the picture framer's.

Silently they proceed to Admiral Dirk's. Patricia watches the flat landscape, considering how like the ocean it feels—empty and endless and bare. Dad is captain of his ship as he has never been at sea; Dagmar is his trusty first mate. He hasn't retired so much as gone to heaven.

Admiral Dirk is a few years older than her father, a tall New Englander cut from a richer crust than the Lesters, but rank disappears as the men inspect the new birds. The cages are smelly, crowded and dusty. The two friends consult about incubating times and pen temperatures. Patricia is drawn away to the high-pitched squawk of a peacock in the far pen. As she approaches, he turns his back, raising his feathers; a fire of iridescent greens and blues. Patricia aches to see him in the sunlight.

"I call that one 'King Walter,' in honour of your dad." Admiral Dirk comes up behind her. "Likes to show off before the ladies. Best feathers in town."

"Don't listen to this old coot." Her father slaps his friend on the back. "We really call that one Emperor Dirk."

She watches the two men laughing and wonders how anyone can be so easy with her father.

"Promised Dagmar I wouldn't bring anything home," he chuckles. "She sent this one as watchdog."

"OK, Walt, see you soon. Happy new year. To you, too, miss."

◆

Dagmar is waiting outside the frame shop, slapping her hands together against the cold.

She hops in and blows fog on the windshield.

"Whadya waiting in the cold like a dummy for? You'll get pneumonia."

"I was just trying to make it easier on you." Dagmar shakes her head and turns to Patricia. "He's something, isn't he? You do him a favour and he complains. Hey, Walt, where are you going?"

"Home."

"You forgot that I have to pick up the pattern for Mrs. MacLeod. And the basket of fruit for Hunter."

"God damned church people. You're always running around doing things for them. And here we have our own family visiting."

"He's such a gentle soul." Dagmar winks at Patricia. "I've got an idea. You two take a ride around town while I run errands. It will only be twenty-five minutes. You'll hardly notice. Here, pull over just here, will you, Walt?"

He checks his watch. "Ten-thirty, sharp. But wait inside Nedley's Grocery, don't stand out in the cold. You'll catch your death."

He rips away from the curb and Patricia thinks how her brother Art was grounded a whole month for making the family car screech like that.

"Well, I guess I can show you the new residential park. Can't for the life of me figure why people come to the edge of nowhere and live in a housing tract."

As they drive, she tries not to be frightened. He's with her now. They're together for a while. And this time she'll be the one to leave —to return to her own apartment in Boston.

"Dagmar has these friends who like to eat out. Now I enjoy a good meal, but there's only one decent restaurant here—a Wop place over on the south highway. Anyway, her friends like to eat at 'Sitting Pretty,' ridiculous name for a restaurant. And the food is like frozen dinners, not always thawed. Or they like the Chink place down the street. Not bad for a Chink place, but they put in so much MSG you can't see straight for three days."

"You all compromised on the Italian restaurant?" Patricia asks.

"Naw, we don't go out with that couple at all no more. Dagmar said I let off my big mouth once too often. We used to go out with the Wops, themselves. They're bigshots in the church. Dagmar met the wife at some knitting thing. But him and me got into a fight about the mob and we don't see them no more. Here, I'll show you where they live in the housing estate—see that pink palace up there, lording it over all the other ticky tackys. That's them, the Antonellis. If that don't sound like a mob name, I don't know what does."

"Remember Father Antonelli at St. John's?"

"Yeah, well, a big family."

◆

The following day he drives them to the taxidermy studio in Silverton. Patricia sits in the backseat, next to a carefully wrapped pheasant. The bird has keeled over suddenly, a perfect specimen. Well, she has wanted to know her father's life. Still, she hasn't bargained for Dagmar's constant chatter. Poor woman, Patricia tells herself, she's lonely. She is doing her best to adapt with the painting and the church activities and the social life Dad keeps ruining. Still, Patricia is beginning to feel like a kidnapped ear.

". . . So what do you think about that, Patricia?" Dagmar asks.

"About what? Sorry, I was looking at the scenery." She regrets speaking brusquely, then feels mad at Dagmar for making her mad with herself. As always, Dad seems out of anger's range.

"Leave her alone, Motor Mouth. Let her enjoy the country. She has to get back to that damn city soon enough."

"I didn't mean . . ." Patricia rubs her right shoulder, for she can feel the migraine ticking. "Sorry, what did you ask?"

"It's OK." Dagmar sits straighter and peers across the flat scrub as if scouting for the Strategic Air Command. "Let's just enjoy the world around us for a while."

Patricia tries to stretch away the tension, her hand falling on the dead bird's head. She shivers and stares out the window, counting cactus.

◆

Murphy's Taxidermy Ltd. is an inconspicuous enterprise in a green Quonset hut on the edge of town. One could easily miss it. Her father is clearly a frequent patron.

Dad grows enthusiastic as they make their way through the dimly lit, vacant waiting-room. "Come on back. They all work here."

Dave Murphy, a big man wearing casual clothes and a baseball cap, raises one hand in salute. He continues to stitch with the other hand. Nell Murphy turns and rushes to Dagmar. A skinny young man, probably their son, is eating a McDonald's hamburger at a sawhorse in the middle of the room.

"Like you to meet my daughter," her father calls to Dave.

Dave nods. "Welcome."

Patricia reads "Dodgers" on his cap and wonders if the bus has made it to Los Angeles.

"Brought up that pheasant," her father says nervously.

"Get right to it, after this squirrel. One of Leonard's pets—you know the two he fed in the front yard? Just expired."

"Could have been the cold," her father says.

"Yep." Dave concentrates on the small, neat stitches. "Speaking of which, help yourselves to coffee over there. And Skip, hey Skip, offer the visitors some of them fries. Wouldn't mind a couple myself."

"Sure, Pop." The boy unfolds himself and stands about seven feet tall. Even if Patricia had been hungry in the midst of all the carnage, she wouldn't consider taking potatoes from this rake of a lad. Her father grabs a handful and pours her and himself coffee.

She accepts the cup and walks around the cold room. She has never visited a taxidermist or a mortician before. The chill reminds her of church. She stops at one trophy, then the next and the next, hanging at evenly spaced intervals from the wall, like stations of the cross. An elk shot in its prime. A raccoon growing threadbare. Two pheasants. A quail. A blue jay. Suddenly she is exhausted, almost faint. How long are they going to stay here anyway? She notices Dagmar and Nell Murphy sitting at a table of feathers, laughing. Dave and her father are arguing football as Dave sews. Skip is munching his Big Mac. They can't have been here long, she tells herself, if he is still eating the hamburger. Yet she has had enough of the gallery and wanders into the waiting-room.

How had she thought the room was vacant? A grizzly bear feigns menace from the corner. You have to look close in the desert, Dagmar said. A defeated moose hangs his head from the wall over the clock. A coyote prances on top of the wide-screen television. *Dad brought her dolls from Japan and fabric from Brazil. She always wanted to say, forget the presents and stay awhile. But she had to avoid his answer, which would have been a lie.* Patricia sinks down into the Naugahyde couch and picks up a copy of *Taxidermy Today.*

An hour later—she has consulted the clock every five minutes— Dagmar and her father come looking for her.

"Always reading," he turns to his wife. "Always that way as a kid. She didn't get it from me."

"How about lunch?" Dagmar enquires.

"Sure," he says. "There's a great steak house on Main Street. You feel like steak, Patricia?"

"To tell you the truth," she says, "I feel like a little air. Why don't I just walk around town while you and Dagmar have lunch."

"What's wrong with you anyway? You used to like to eat. You trying to turn yourself into one of them Twiggies?"

"No, I'm just not hungry. And I wouldn't mind some exercise."

"Let her do as she likes, Walt."

He begins to protest, then his attention is caught by the grizzly. "Ralph Foster got that one, on his last trip to Alaska."

"Why didn't he take it home?"

"Well, it was a tie. I mean Ralph didn't last much longer than it took to fly back to El Paso. Heart attack. His wife knew he'd want the bear stuffed, but then she couldn't bring herself to put it in the house."

"So what's it doing here?" Patricia is appalled by her morbid curiosity.

"For the grandchildren," explains Dagmar. "The Murphys are saving it for Ralph's grandchildren."

◆

They drive through Silverton in silence, stopping at the Carousel Steak House.

"Sure you're not hungry?" he asks. "They have a salad bar with garbanzo and kidney beans."

She smiles, touched that he remembers her favourite beans. "No, no thanks. I'll just wander around the shops. Maybe I'll join you for coffee."

An hour later Patricia enters the loud, smoky restaurant, feeling revived by her solitude. "Hi!" She waves, glad to see them. "Hey, I got a surprise for dessert. A lottery ticket for each of us."

"Oh, let me see," Dagmar says. "We need coins to rub off the markings. No, no, I didn't win a thing. How about you, Walt?"

"No, two of a kind, but not three."

"No," Patricia shakes her head, "I didn't win either."

◆

She rises early the next morning in the hope that she will get some time alone with him. Maybe they can feed the birds together. She pours coffee from the thermos and pulls on her coat. Walking along the pens, she is amazed how quickly the chickens skitter, seemingly oblivious to the cold. Her father has explained the elaborate heating system and now she understands how complicated it must be. Sweet that he would go to such lengths for the birds. It is begging the question to ask why he couldn't nurture his own children.

Turning a corner by the pheasants' pens, she sees him, bent over, digging seeds from his bag; his white hair swirling around red earmuffs; his cheeks ruddy; his eyes almost bulging from the strain of stooping so low. Suddenly she notices his hands—small and thick—the fingers more like the dried, cracked legs of a turtle than digits of a man. She has always wondered where she got her tiny hands, for Mother's are large and competent. She is at once repelled and relieved. She had thought there was a mutant gene.

"Shhhh." He turns, as if he had seen her all along. "Come this way, the Prince of Hearts is displaying this morning."

She tiptoes over the sawdust and straw, inhaling the pungent birdshit and taking a step back upon seeing the peacock, even more glorious than the one two days before. The sun is bright now, a crisp, unfiltered morning sun that ignites the peacock's colours, his feathers like rainbows rippling across a lake. He moves the radiant tail slowly, bestowing his gift.

"Beautiful," she says, regretting she doesn't sound more intelligent, "beautiful."

Her father winks.

Her breath catches at his boyishness, at the clarity of the morning, at the power of forgiveness.

"Here," he hands her the bag with a plastic scoop. "You feed him. I'll take care of the bantams."

The Prince scrutinizes her. He waits until she finishes pouring his food. Carefully he tucks away his glory and walks, as if in stiletto heels, to the dish. He stares at her. She steps back. He begins to eat.

"Good," her father calls. "He never lets anyone watch him eat. You made a friend."

She looks up and smiles.

"How about a ride to Mexico? Just the two of us. Dagmar said we should spend some time alone. I've got a couple of errands. Things are ten times cheaper there, you know."

"Sure," she says, but she is reluctant to leave the bird.

—◆—

Over breakfast he checks his shopping list. The dogs are barking to join them. "No," he shouts back, "can't take you to Mexico."

Dagmar counts the cash from a canister. "Be careful," she says.

Patricia excuses herself to the living-room while they complete their transactions. Fog still shrouds the mountains. It does seem strange weather for the desert. Maybe it will clear tomorrow before she leaves.

"Be careful," Dagmar hugs her. "They pretend they don't speak English and cheat you every opportunity."

"She speaks Spanish," her father explains, with pride or irritation, Patricia can't tell.

"Then take care of him." Dagmar remains anxious.

"We'll be fine," he calls gruffly. "Back about three o'clock."

The ride is flat and white and peaceful. They are silent. He never said much when she was a child. She wonders how he can stand Dagmar's chatter, but she doesn't know him well enough to ask. Maybe next time. Yes, perhaps she will come back. It hasn't been a bad trip. They have been close, on and off. He has made a great effort baking cakes and cookies, loaning her handbook to the dentist, driving up to Silverton and now down to Mexico. So he is still loud and cranky and destroying himself with too much food. She is no longer a child; how can this affect her so? His grammar and lack of sophistication—which used to embarrass her—now seem almost the hallmark of his success in the world. After all, he immigrated with nothing at the age of seventeen. And here he is, owner of a ranch house, friend of Admiral Dirk, caretaker of the Prince of Hearts and father of someone who has been published. Yes, she is gratified that he would count her book among his trophies.

The car is slowing down. Ahead the sign reads, "Mexico. *Bienvenido!*"

"Just wait in the car. With the doors locked. I'm going to change some money." He points to a row of wooden huts. "Be right back."

"Be . . ." she begins, almost repeating Dagmar's warning.

"I'll be fine; don't worry."

He returns promptly. The tyres squeal as he speeds towards the border gate. The air in the car is moist and she tries to ignore his heavy dose of cologne, which is making her stomach turn.

"*Buenos días,*" the guard greets them.

"No speak Spanish," her father says, as if he were refusing an exchange of pornographic jokes.

The guard straightens slightly. "Good day. Do you have anything to declare . . . ?"

She wants to speak up, to temper her father's rudeness, but she knows that neither man would appreciate the intrusion.

Mother cried for a month after he filed for divorce. Patricia had tried to hold them together, had tried to explain one to the other. She couldn't comfort Mother because for years Mother had comforted her, promising that he would return, that one day he would return for good. And she was wrong.

They are admitted to Mexico.

Los Altos is a small, poor town of tarpaper shacks and muddy roads, made almost impassable by the weather.

"Snow in Mexico; this is ridiculous," her father sniffs as he tries to pull the truck out of a rut.

"We've only driven twenty miles," she snaps in spite of herself. "Did you expect the equator?"

"If they maintained the damn roads, it would be all right. How do they plan to do trade when you can't get in and out of their damn . . ." The engine goes whizz-whizz and suddenly they are out of the rut, almost running over a little boy playing nearby.

"*Madre mía!*" the boy's father shouts, shaking his fist.

Her father shakes his fist back, then proceeds gingerly over the corrugated road.

"Damn Mexicans, letting their kids play in the street."

She closes her eyes, knowing not to provoke him for they will wind up in jail if he gets any angrier. *She remembers him sitting in his undershirt and boxer shorts drinking beer in front of the TV and yelling at the umpire, at Edward R. Murrow, at Sergeant Bilko. After a while her girlfriends stopped visiting when he was on leave. She didn't know if it was the yelling or the boxer shorts which kept them away.*

"Here we are," he said abruptly. "*Señora* Garcia. The only honest woman in town."

They walk into a shop lined with bottles of liquor; boxes of detergent; cans of car oil: an extraordinary assortment of American goods. As Patricia's eyes adjust to the light she finds a white-haired woman knitting behind the counter. An orange cat sits on the empty shelf behind.

"*Buenos días,*" he has suddenly become a linguist.

The old woman nods, without recognition.

"Nearsighted," he whispers to Patricia.

"*Señora* Garcia," he says more loudly, moving closer.

"*Sí,*" she says, still apparently without recognition.

"She'll remember me. Dagmar sent a box of clothes for her daughter last month. And once I gave them a fan."

The old woman stands up and asks if she can help.

"*No Español,*" he says gently, with a touch of pique. He turns to his daughter. "She speaks perfect English."

"Mr. Lester," he explains. "From America."

The woman nods. "Welcome," she says finally.

He smiles triumphantly at Patricia. "See. Now what do you drink? We'll send you back to Boston with something to see you through winter."

"Oh, I don't know." She is suddenly embarrassed. "I don't drink much."

"Don't give me that bull." He is offended. "You've had a drink with me and Dagmar every night since you been here. Whiskey, I know." He turns to the counter. "What's your best Irish?"

She frowns.

"Ah, never mind. I see some Bushmills. No, Jameson. We'll send you back with a big Jameson."

"Dad, really."

Señora Garcia is climbing a step-ladder, reaching for the bottle.

"See, I told you they speak English when they want to."

Patricia can feel the headache rising up the side of her neck.

"And we'll take two Beefeaters. Two Bacardis. One big Johnnie Walker Red."

Silently the woman places bottles in a box. She writes down the price on a scrap of brown paper bag.

"No way," he explodes. "No way; that's eight hundred pesos too much!"

The woman shrugs, remaining steadfast about the amount.

"You're not gonna rip me off just 'cause you gone mute," he shouts.

Señora Garcia returns to her stool and watches him.

"Eight hundred pesos too much!" he declares.

Patricia hears a giggle and turns to find five children grinning in the doorway.

"Dad," she whispers. "Eight hundred pesos is less than a dollar."

He glowers at her. She remembers years of vengeful silence at home and can't stand this anymore. "Perhaps if I translated."

"Translation isn't the problem."

"Well, somebody doesn't understand something," she tries.

"It's a question of principle. It's not the dollar. These people will rob you blind in a flash. She knows the price. I buy here all the time."

Her father puts both hands on the counter and stares at the old woman like a belligerent teenager. The woman has retreated behind heavy eyelids. The cat purrs.

Patricia looks from one person to the other in dismay. They could stand here all day. For the rest of their lives. Maybe they should call in Skip Murphy to stuff them and create a diorama for twenty-first-century tourists.

Patricia has an inspiration. Turning to the children, she asks, *"Tu Abuela?"*

A little girl steps forward, saying yes, she is the old woman's granddaughter. Patricia walks to the doorsill and hands the child two dollars. *"Por tu. Por tu Abuela. Por Navidad."* The child's face lights up.

"Hey, hey," her father calls. "Don't play with those kids, they'll wring every last penny from you. They always want pennies. Pennies add up."

Patricia knows he knows what she has done.

Señora Garcia, who has followed the exchange from behind closed eyelids, glances at Patricia neutrally.

Patricia stares at her feet.

The woman stands up to the counter.

"So you've decided to be honest," her father barks, his voice betraying his relief.

She ignores him and crosses out the first sum, noting down the amount he has demanded.

He pays her, picks up the box and leaves, tugging on Patricia's sweater.

Patricia looks back with a mixture of shame and resignation. As a child she knew everything would work out perfectly. It had taken years to develop her dubious talent for compromise.

They cross the American border at the far gate, manned by a friend of her father's. They ride back to Murdoch in strained, not companionable, silence.

Dinner is his famous meatballs and spaghetti. With lots of red wine. And Jameson afterwards. He is sweating as they take their drinks to the living-room. She knows he is worn out, creating the perfect farewell.

◆

The snow is heavy as they drive to the Greyhound depot. Dagmar has stayed home so Patricia can have a last private moment with her father. And Fritzie.

"I would of drove you to El Paso," he begins.

"No chains," she says.

"Yeah." He is nervous. "But you'll be fine. Those buses are equipped."

"Yes." She stares at the fog.

"I seen worse snow. Once in Jersey, when I was taking a ship out. Why the bus just crawled along the turnpike. I thought I'd never make it. Hell, forget the ship. I thought I'd never make it to the dock. But it was fine. The bus was fine."

"Yes," she says, patting the dog. "Don't worry."

As they pull up, the Greyhound driver is loading bags.

"Well, this is it, honey. Thanks for coming." He stands stiffly, holding the dog by a leash.

"Thanks for having me." She reaches up and hugs him, resisting the mad impulse to pull him on the bus with her. She used to imagine him carrying her onto his ship just before the gangplank was lifted.

"For the trip." He pulls a brown sack from his pocket. "Meatball sandwich and some cookies."

"Thanks," she says, unable to speak more for fear of crying. She can't hold herself this tightly for long and she is grateful when the driver opens the door.

"Hey, don't forget the booze." Her father hands her a shopping bag. The passengers surge forward. She wishes he would let go of it, so she can get on the bus. She is having a hard time breathing.

"OK." She pulls on the bag and just at that moment someone knocks into her from behind. She teeters to keep her balance. Turning, she sees a large Black woman and for a second wonders if this is the lady returning from Los Angeles.

"Shit," her father shouts.

She hears a crash.

"Damn hippopotamus, can't watch her step." He is shouting at the woman, who has the good sense to ignore him and claim her seat on the bus.

"No, Dad, it's good luck, really."

Patricia rushes to save the situation. "Sort of like christening a ship as it's launched."

He stares at her for a second, his jaw clenched, his brows knit and then he shakes his head. "Yeah." He is almost smiling. "Good luck."

They walk to the bus door and he waves her a kiss as she hands the driver her ticket.

"You'll be fine." He is talking to the bus driver. "Once I took a bus down the Jersey Turnpike, snow so thick you couldn't see a foot in front. You'll make it fine."

At age thirty-nine, Chase quit his job as a professor of paleontology at an old New England university, came back home to Lost River, Idaho, and bought a run-down Texaco station. He's been there since, running the station from a stool tilted against one of the walls. Around the stool is a layer of beer cans and Bull Durham wrappers, a layer beneath which his past has been carefully buried.

But when he first came back he was asked to speak to the Lost River Rotarians about local geology. He gave a lecture explaining why the landscape around Lost River is frozen lava flows and cinders and dark river canyons that cut deep into the South Idaho Plain. He showed them the fossilized vertebra of a camel that had grazed locally four million years earlier. By means of a time line that compressed the earth's whole history into one year, he showed them that the moments of their lives were inconsequential and few.

The Rotarians didn't care for the message. There were among his audience fundamentalist Christians who regarded the piece of camel as a lie invented by Satan. Others—the car dealers with new models under wraps in their showrooms, or merchants with new fashions in their shop windows—were upset by a vision of history not marked by continuous happy progress. Because Chase, after describing the cycles within cycles of earth's past, had ended by describing the biggest cycle of all. Earth, he told them, would someday be devoured by a fat and dying sun. Convertibles and polyester suits and even the rocks upon which churches had been built—would melt.

The rest of them were horrified by Chase's descriptions of lava fields red and flowing, poisonous gas drifting from cracks in the desert, and the thin green of riverbanks aflame.

It was only MacShane, the Lost River mortician, who liked Chase's talk. MacShane was cheered by the perennial sequence of birth, life, and death that gave his profession a dignity it lacked in the daylit world of Lost River commerce. He looked at Chase's camel fragment and saw a vision of the earth as a vast graveyard, of dear departed creatures preserved in a huge sedimentary cemetery, all of them giving eloquent silent testimony to the embalming skill of God the Undertaker. MacShane asked Chase where he could get himself a fossil to show his kids. Chase gave him the camel vertebra.

"Fossils are everywhere," he told MacShane and the rest of the Rotary Club. He smiled, as if this were wonderful news. Sullen businessmen studied their watches.

A week later MacShane came to the Texaco station.

"I can't sleep," said the mortician. "I see it in my head, all ten billion years of it. You know how many things can die in ten billion years?"

Chase didn't answer. Morticians shouldn't have a fantasy life, he thought.

"Since the human race began," said MacShane, "over seventy billion of us have passed over to the Great Beyond. That many dear departeds would require a cemetery half again as big as Texas. Seventy billion top-of-the-line airtight aluminum caskets."

MacShane borrowed paleontology books from Chase. He gazed with wonder at illustrations of horn corals, trilobites, brontosauri, giant sloths, and woolly mammoths. He pronounced new names—Eocene, Mesozoic, Silurian—as if he were learning a language of love. If he spoke the name of an extinct species, it came out like a song.

"They all lived," said MacShane, holding one of Chase's books and pointing to a color plate of a large dinosaur munching on a small one. "And then they all departed."

"Died," said Chase.

"Died," sang MacShane.

MacShane began drinking. Chase heard he had shown up at several funerals drunk. A rival funeral home had begun to pick up some of the families who had been MacShane's steady customers. His wife was threatening to leave him. His children were demanding that he drop them off two blocks from Lost River High School.

MacShane brought Chase a newspaper clipping detailing how the body of a miner buried in a Peruvian copper mine had been discovered ten years later not as decaying flesh but as a statue of copper sulfate. The straining muscles of the man, the weave of his clothes, his hair, and even his dying grin had been replaced by blue crystal.

"He's a fossil," said MacShane.

"Technically, no," said Chase. "He's supposed to be twenty-five thousand years old if he's going to be a fossil. But as long as nobody leaves him out in the rain, he'll last that long. Give him time. He'll be a fossil."

"Time," said MacShane, "there is plenty of. Give him his time. I declare him fossilized."

MacShane began to bring a jug with him on his visits to the station. He would sit in a chair he tilted against the wall beside Chase's stool. He would pass the jug to Chase, and Chase would pass it back. When both of them were drunk, MacShane would curse time.

"You say the last eruption was two thousand years ago?" asked MacShane, pointing to one of the several black cinder cones that marked the city limits of Lost River. "I piss on two thousand years."

MacShane had begun to see the world from the standpoint of its immense history. He claimed he could look at any man and see in him a long line of departed organisms all the way back to an original departed proto-DNA molecule.

"My wife," said MacShane. "She's de-evolving. Last week when I looked at her I saw a reptile. Today she's an amphibian."

MacShane's wife did leave him. She moved to Boise with the kids and filed for divorce.

The next time MacShane came to the station he did not pull up a chair beside Chase's stool. He stood in front of Chase, swaying back and forth, and stared down at him.

"I've found some fossils," he said.

Chase looked at MacShane with an immense weariness. His mind went back to a huge, dusty warehouse at his university, one filled with cabinets that were filled with drawers that were filled with hard bits of dead plants and animals.

MacShane began digging in his pockets. He finally found something and extended his hand toward Chase. In MacShane's palm were a half-dozen small white objects.

Human teeth.

"Fossils," said MacShane.

"Where did you get these?" Chase looked at MacShane. The man just stood there, emanating the odors of fresh alcohol and nervous sweat.

"If nobody leaves them out in the rain," said MacShane, "they should last practically forever."

Chase pointed. "Where did you get these?" he asked again. A crafty smile began flitting about MacShane's mouth like a small, spastic fly.

"Oh, no," he said. "It's not that easy. I'm not going to tell you just because you asked me where I got these. It's just not that easy. You should know better."

MacShane nodded knowingly, turned, staggered to the door, swiveled his head around, gave Chase an unfocused glare, and left.

Chase watched MacShane weave down the sidewalk and lurch out of sight around a corner. He should have seen the signs before. MacShane, alienated from his fellow Rotarians by his dark profession, had finally reached escape velocity, had become twisted and wacko.

Chase felt a sudden guilt at having delivered the lecture at the Rotary Meeting. He had supplied MacShane with that truth that subsumed all hope. The infinite geologic timescape, with its visions of island gardens rising out of the oceans and sinking again, of quiet forests being buried by volcanoes, of trillions of odd, discontinued animals hopping and jumping and slithering about—here was MacShane's defense against people who smelled death on him. MacShane could smell death back. If old age makes fools of us all, Chase thought, how much greater fools we are, viewed against the ages.

Chase shuddered. Morticians should not show up with human teeth.

But MacShane appeared the next day, sober, and apologized for leaving so abruptly.

"I've decided I want you to be my friend," said MacShane.

"Oboy," said Chase.

"I'm going to show you where I got the teeth," said MacShane, smiling. "Get in the hearse." MacShane pointed toward the black four-wheel-drive smoke-windowed Subaru station wagon he used for unpaved departures.

The smile made Chase worry. If he takes me to the cemetery, he thought, I'm going to call the sheriff.

"I'm going to win a Nobel Prize for this," said MacShane.

"They don't give Nobel Prizes to fossil collectors," said Chase.

"I'm not a fossil collector," said MacShane. "I'm a paleontologist. Like you. Maybe you think you have to have a Ph.D. to be a paleontologist. All you have to have is a fossil."

"I'm not a paleontologist," said Chase, thinking of the tenured position he had resigned and its endless committee meetings and its burden of murderous university politics. And turf battles. Once a colleague had told him to stay out of the Cretaceous. "I sell gas," he said.

"Maybe when you see what I'm going to show you you'll want to quit selling gas. Hop in." MacShane giggled. "You don't even have to ride in the back."

He's going to kill me, thought Chase. He's going to take me out in the middle of the sagebrush and dump me in a collapsed lava bubble. Chase closed his eyes and saw, imprinted on his eyelids, an image of his own body, dead, crumpled, unembalmed, staring up at a sky rimmed by black rock. He felt a curious peace.

He got into the Subaru.

MacShane, whistling as he drove, took them past the cemetery and onto a dirt road that led out into the desert.

So if you're nuts and you're a paleontologist, Chase thought, you don't want another paleontologist around. If he finds the jawbone you're searching for, he's the one who gets on the cover of *Time*. He's the one who gets to heft that bone and imagine what it must have been to live on the other side of a million-year-high wall. Could you murder a man for holding bones in his hand and inventing a whole world?

And then Chase thought of an endless clear sky under which small bands of laughing people gathered fruit from trees and snared small animals and sat close around fires night after night and sang and told stories. You could kill somebody for a ticket to that place, Chase thought.

Chase looked around for a weapon, spotted the heavy chromed club of a flashlight clipped to the underside of the dash in front of him. It made him feel a little better.

A few minutes later, MacShane drove up to the rim of a canyon. Like most of the canyons around Lost River, its walls were vertical. The old lava flows had cracked into columns when they cooled, in a process analogous to mud cracking in a drying lakebed. When water cut through these columns, it toppled them and dissolved them away, leaving canyons that were narrow and deep, with pillared sides.

Chase watched as MacShane got out, pulled a shovel from the back of the Subaru, and walked to the edge. He wavered there for a moment, and Chase half expected him to turn and smile and then step off into short and blissful flight.

Instead, MacShane reached down at his feet and picked up a

rope that had been tied to a large sagebrush growing out of the rimrock. "Come on," he said, turning toward Chase and gesturing with the shovel. Then he grasped the rope, stepped backward, and disappeared.

Chase stared for a few moments through the windshield, watching the sagebrush shake and bend with the tension on the rope. Then the bush snapped upright and the rope went slack. Chase got out and hurried to the edge, dropped to his knees, and peered over.

And looked down, down, down through four hundred feet of the thinnest, most transparent air, to where a short talus slope lay tumbled between the wall and the river. Junked cars, victims of final pilotless joyrides, lay crumpled and shattered and small amid great black stones. The ripples of the river were so far away it no longer looked wet. It looked like smooth green silk lining the bottom of the canyon.

MacShane was nowhere to be seen. Chase searched the rocks below for a broken, doll-like body. Then MacShane's face and arm suddenly popped out of the wall thirty feet below him, where the far end of the rope fluttered in the wind.

MacShane waved something at him. A bone.

Even from where he was, Chase could see that it was a human femur.

He's discovered an Indian grave, thought Chase. He thinks he's found human fossils. He shook his head, smiling at his notion that he was about to be murdered.

I could still die, thought Chase. He stared down at MacShane's disembodied head, its mouth open and moving.

Bones in a lava cave, thought Chase. He smiled at the irony of some poor Indian being dug up by a mortician. He wondered how MacShane would take the news he was only being an archaeologist, that, geologically speaking, he and the bones he was digging up lived at virtually the same moment in time.

But still, there was something—what was it? A memory, perhaps, in that femur, of people on a wide continent, living free lives, hunting pine nuts and seed, fishing for salmon, living under buffalo skin, moving when they felt like it. Land was free then. You could drink from the rivers. You could get old happily. People would make a place for you around the fire because you could tell them about the old days.

Chase picked up the rope, tested the sagebrush it was tied to, turned away from the canyon, and then stepped back into it. He felt a sudden giddy tickling on the bottoms of his feet as they moved out over nothing—a lot of it.

It wasn't as bad as he had expected. By looking down as far as his feet and no farther, he discovered cracks, holes in the wall, small ledges, all places where he could put a hand or foot. Of course, if the sagebrush pulled out of the rock above, he would die. Depart, as MacShane would say, on a four-hundred-foot journey, at the end of which he would join his gathered ancestors.

Then he stepped on a slanted ledge and a loose rock under his foot kicked out into the canyon and he was flying, slowed only by his burning palms as they wrapped hard around the rope. He yelled in pain and had half thought a picture of rope end when he felt himself swing forward a bit, into an empty space in the wall. His feet hit flat rock and his momentum slammed him forward to his knees.

Chase looked first at his rope-blistered hands and then around him. He had landed on a narrow ledge that protruded from a cave mouth. It wasn't a real lava cave, though, like the long caverns made when lava empties out from under a hardened crust. This cave had been formed when a river had deposited a thick bed of gravel and sand atop a lava flow. Then another flow had boiled away the river and locked its sediments in molten rock. In a later, cooler time, when the river had cut down through the lava again, the gravel had fallen out into the canyon. Where it had been was the cave he was in. Its roof was too low to make standing comfortable, but it was deep enough that shadows deepened to darkness at its back.

MacShane, apparently unimpressed by the suddenness of Chase's arrival, was on his hands and knees, digging furiously, scraping away the sand and rock from around a rib cage. The femur was beside him on the cave floor.

Chase picked up the femur. It was heavy. It was not bone. It was opalized quartz shaped like a human bone. It was old—far older, he thought, than any Indian. It was one thing for replacement to go on in a highly mineralizing environment, as in a copper mine. It was another for enough silica to leach out of the lava to turn bones into opal. Millions of years were involved.

He hefted the femur, and watched its pale iridescence against the black cave walls. That iridescence came from tiny spherical droplets of quartz, formed in wet darkness over years so many as to make a human life into a quick snap of divine fingers. And during those years, as far as any paleontologist knew, humans had not walked the earth. This bone—this thing—should not exist, he thought.

He wondered about the original owner of the bone, who must have used it to walk over a land alive with herds of horses and camels and elephants. Did he walk hand in hand with another of his kind? Did he point at the spring-dancing animals? What words did he say to the sun in the morning? Thank you, Chase thought. It's what I would have said.

He saw then, in that cave, a gateway. All you had to do was find the right shadow in the back, step into it, and people would be there, people with two million or more years of bright future ahead of them, living where the weather was gentle, the trees laden with fruit, the rivers full of fish. And they'd greet you with open arms.

"Look at this," said MacShane. He held an object between his hands as though it were a chalice. It was a skull. Like the femur, it had been opalized. Sand, in small, hard chunks, trickled out of its eye sockets. It was human. The cranium was large, Chase thought, as large as any of those tottering along the streets of Boise atop more modern spinal columns. The jaws and remaining teeth—the ones not in MacShane's pockets—were small, delicate, only a little predatory. He wondered what kind of mind had been matched with them. Maybe one that could live for a hundred thousand generations without betraying the earth with its presence.

Chase gently took the skull from MacShane's outstretched hands.

"You're going to be famous," said MacShane to the skull. "You're going to be Idaho Man."

Looking up from the skull's eye sockets into MacShane's eyes, Chase had a sudden sympathy with the man. The bones MacShane had found, the beautiful bits of a creature unknowable and long dead, had seduced MacShane irrevocably. Never again would he be able to see time measured by anything less than lifetimes.

But by staring into the eye sockets of the skull, Chase thought, MacShane might also have seen a gateway—to where he didn't know, but he had an idea it was to some sanctuary aeons away, where you didn't have to embalm bodies and smile for a living.

Then Chase thought of the people who would flock to a discovery of this importance, the experts and theoreticians and paleontological prima donnas, and finally, the philosophers who would come forward to speak as members of a newly ancient species. MacShane's fossils would be taken from him. His bones would be given to those who could say what his bones meant.

Chase thought of Lost River, and of his own recent return to it, and about being a paleontologist who returned to a place where fossils didn't mean much, where no one much cared about whether a rock had once been alive or not.

"What will you say to them?" he asked MacShane. "What will you do when they pull you back from that sanctuary, back into the here and now?"

MacShane didn't know what he was talking about. But he turned away from Chase and looked across at the far canyon wall.

"You can see all layers over there," MacShane said, pointing. "Lava flows on top of lava flows. And they're all on top of a seabed. The earth is old, Chase," he said, and these words, too, sounded like a song.

"I know," said Chase. And then he took a step back into the cave, placed his foot on the small of MacShane's back, and pushed with all his strength. MacShane shot forward, into open air. His arms and legs waved for a second, reaching for something solid. Chase heard him hit the talus a few seconds later.

Chase placed the skull and femur gently, almost reverently, in the center of the bones MacShane had been excavating. Then he began the delicate task of burying them again, shoveling fine, drifted-in cave dust around them until they were well covered, then covering them with coarser gravel and slabs of lava. When he was done, there was only a steep slope of rock against one side of the cave, with no indication anything lay under it.

He ran the shovel through his belt and with burning and weeping hands grasped the rope. He climbed slowly back up to the canyon rim. This time he made no mistakes, and when he reached the sagebrush he untied the rope and coiled it. He looped the coils over his shoulder, picked up the shovel, and began the long trek back into Lost River, staying off the road so his tracks wouldn't be noticed. Halfway there he tossed shovel and rope into a lava tube. They rattled down into the earth for a few moments. Then there was silence.

MacShane was found a week later, after an air search discovered his car. He was declared a suicide. No one thought to examine the canyon wall thirty feet below his parking spot, because no one thought MacShane would climb down thirty feet to ensure a softer landing. Even suicides are given credit for common sense.

Chase remains at the Texaco station, pumping gas for an occasional car, cleaning the bugs off an occasional windshield, but mostly sitting on the stool against the wall and contributing to the sediment around it.

He has not been back to the cave. There is plenty of time for that, he thinks. Plenty of time to call in teams of bright young paleoanthropologists eager to become famous. Plenty of time to scour the floor of a cave for pieces of stone that could change what it means to be human, here and now in Lost River. And best of all, he thinks, there is plenty of time to sing in dreams with all the dead who drift beneath the South Idaho Plain, one of whom was named MacShane.

SLAUGHTERHOUSE

I was fourteen. Thirteen maybe. I was worried I couldn't shoot. I mean take care of business once I got there. That's all us guys talked about. And I had a girl who would've let me. Her name was Caroline. A Indian just come to town and winds up in The Hole. Eyes pretty as nighttime sky in the country. Believe me, fine. And she's looking at me like I'm something, even I'm a Indian, but a half-breed. But I'm scared about this taking-care-of-business stuff. Then luck gives out on me and I win a trip inside that slaughterhouse barn and know I'm a man no matter what.

The slaughterhouse barn was down Santa Rosa Avenue, where folks had animals and stuff. Chickens in the yard, cows. But the houses didn't look like anything, no better than ours. Small and needing paint. Stuff like refrigerators and washing machines here and there where you could see them if you looked. Around the sides of houses, on back porches and in garages, like folks didn't think stuff that didn't work wouldn't stand out. Either that or they wanted you to see the stuff, like it was something, which everyone knowed was nothing. Falling ragged barbed wire fences surrounded the places, except for the slaughterhouse where there was thick plank boards. Along the street, plyboard was nailed to the planks so you couldn't see the horses. On the plyboard you seen advertisements for things in town. Coca-Cola. Cherri's Chinese Kitchen. Hamburger Dee-Lux. The freeway wasn't finished yet, so folks coming north drove through town, up Santa Rosa Avenue.

It was two barns at the slaughterhouse. One was in the middle of the corral. Its roofline sagged like the swayed back of one of them horses. It's where the hay was, where the horses fed. From there we watched the goings-on in the other barn, which was across the way. It was three stories high and painted. I say watched the goings-on, but we couldn't see nothing. Just trucks carrying in horses and carrying out pet food. But it was no secret what happened in that place at night. Smoke and Indian Princess Sally Did sold girls.

Smoke had eyes the yellow color of his straw hat. The eyes looked out from his black face just like they was set in a dark wall. Folks said they was goat eyes, square in the iris. I wondered if the white people who came about the horses seen his eyes that way. Smoke looked like the devil. Indian Princess Sally Did was worse. She was the one who went around talking to folks. She had balled up black hair with a white stripe down the middle. She never took off her sunglasses and she dressed in a purple getup and high heels. Thing is she thought she looked like she was society. I remember seeing her in the market on Grand Avenue. I thought she couldn't see I was looking because she didn't pay attention to anything that wasn't of use to her. She was reaching for a can of coffee when I seen it on her leg, just above her knee—a tattoo, which said 1946. Whatever that year was to her. "What you looking at, smelly Indian scoundrel?" she snapped, scaring me half to death. Made you feel she had something personal against you.

Anyway, it was out of Sally's Cadillac we stole the girlie magazine, one showing everything on a body. Me. Buster Copaz, who was the oldest and the leader of our gang. Micky Toms, another Indian, like me and Buster. Victor James, who was black. And the angel face Navarro twins, Jesus and Ignacio, who we called Nate. I seen the car parked in our neighborhood, and it was Buster who spotted the magazine and told Micky to reach in the open window and take it. There was paper and stuff like phone numbers which flew out the magazine as we tore down the street and made our way to the barn. "Good thing," Buster said, "because if we get caught with this there's no proving our connection to it. Like it could be anybody's." It was summer and we was too young for the cannery and too old for our mothers. We was fourteen or so, like I said. So we messed up like this.

Up in the hay Buster started looking at the pictures. From where I was I seen the curves of naked women, soft-like and the pale color of a half-cooked hotcake. Micky, who don't have much of a neck to stretch, sat next to Buster. The rest of us looked from where we sat, even if what we seen was upside down.

"Turn it so we can see," Victor said to Buster, who hogged the pictures on his lap. But I knowed what was next.

"Just picture it like it's real," Buster said.

See, Buster couldn't control himself. He made it like if we didn't follow we wasn't cool. We had ourselves a hideaway in that barn, a fort made by moving hay bales around so we couldn't get seen. Just then it looked like Buster was going to share the pictures because he put the magazine in the middle of our circle. But it was only so he could get his drawers down and have us look at the pictures and do the same. So he wouldn't be alone not controlling himself.

"Close your eyes," Buster said.

By this time we was exposed, too. Or partway. The closing-eyes part I went along with. You know how guys check each other out, and no one compared to Buster then. Least of all me and the Navarro twins. Which caused the shooting worries. But I seen Buster's eyes closed but not closed, all glassy, like hard murky marbles over them pictures. He was gone already. Then I closed my eyes completely. I tried to keep seeing the picture which showed a woman in black stockings. Never mind the hay poking my ass and the back of my legs, I was starting to feel pretty good, like things was working, when what I seen was Caroline. It was her come to my mind, and I kept on.

I thought first it was them stray cats, which had a way of coming out of nowhere in that barn and scaring the hell out of us. Things got still and at the same time voices. I heard Buster jump, then the others. I opened my eyes. Buster and them wasn't there, but moved, over the side of the hay looking down on the mangers. I blinked a few times to catch what just happened. Then I pulled up my pants and joined the others. Buster turned and put his finger to his lips for us to shut up. I moved between Micky and Victor and seen what Buster was looking at. It was Smoke and some black girl talking.

"You just shut up and never mind," Smoke was saying. He chewed her out like nobody's business.

"Well, I—" she started to say with her hand on her hip.

"Well, you nothing," he said. "You jealous 'cause you old whore. Let me and Sally run things. And tonight we doing a run and it ain't just you."

It was like he said something all of a sudden took the air out of her. Her hand fell from her hip, like she wilted. She stood there looking foolish even to me just then. Standing in that short black skirt two shades darker than her skin. Standing in high heels sunk flat in the dusty horse shit. I could see the black where her orange hair growed out.

"Now you just get," Smoke said. "And you go through the fence there. Go up the railroad tracks and don't be coming round here in broad daylight. You look worse than you is."

The black girl disappeared. Smoke lifted his straw hat like to cool his head. He was dressed in overalls, like someone who just works with horses. After a minute, he left, too. Only he went through the gate to the other barn.

"We're going in there tonight," Buster said like he'd been thinking it over the past two days. We sat back in our spots and Buster closed the magazine and stuffed it between two bales of hay.

It was Smoke saying tonight that hung in our ears and then grew inside our brains. Like tonight was a star just now so close we might touch it.

"We can't all go in," Victor said, "because there's a big pit in there full of dead horses and we could all fall in."

Pit or no pit, that wasn't the point. Nobody knowed for sure what was in that other building. Sure they killed horses in there and folks talked about a hole where they ground up the meat. But Victor was just talking covering over what we was feeling. It was dark, scary. The only way to get in that place besides the front was to sneak up the chute in back where they took the horses to kill them. No one wanted to go through that to see what tonight was all about. No one had the guts.

Buster acted a smartass. "We all die," he said. But he had things figured out. He played on what Victor was saying. "If we're dead then there's no way anybody knows what's going on in there. So one of us is going to stand near that chute and the rest is going to watch outside the fence . . ." He stopped for a second, breaking up his line of words like he was in a movie. A cool guy. ". . . Oh, and in case you all forgot, *one* of us *is* going inside."

He grabbed six pieces of straw and started arranging them in his hand, like he couldn't see what he was doing. "There's one short one," he said.

Victor's eyes popped out of his head. He must've been picturing himself drowning in a hundred feet of molding horse intestines. He had a sister who rode off with Smoke one night, at least somebody said that, and when one of us, I forgot who, asked him about it, his eyes got big like now and he looked over his shoulder like his mother or somebody was listening. He was quiet as a cat walking, and just turning his head to see behind him.

"Think of the girls," Buster said. "Girls."

I must've looked scared as Victor. Thinking of girls in that barn didn't help none. Thinking just then couldn't have changed what happened. I picked the short straw.

"Micky, you stand by the chute. Me and everybody else stand guard." Now Buster was a commander of the troops making his strategy, all business. He looked at each of us. Then stopped on me. "Frankie, if you don't show up . . ." He stopped and spit and looked at me again. "Get some points, Frankie."

◆

The plan was to meet at nine o'clock, when it was dark. I was standing outside the market on Grand, just about home, and I seen on the store clock it was only three. Six hours, I thought, and I'm superstitious. Six ain't a good number. Buster and them split, went home. I couldn't just sit. I went back to the slaughterhouse, probably just to see where I was going.

Nothing seemed the same in that haybarn. I thumbed through the magazine, but without the guys there I felt like a pervert or something. I seen the cobwebs on the old roofboards and the way the main beam swayed under the weight of the roof. Like them endless spiders had eyes and was seeing me in my secrets. The beam would snap, coming down, keeping me forever with the whole world to see with them pictures in my hand. I thought of Mom or Sis finding me like that. And Dad: Can't you get the real thing, boy? That's okay to study, but don't be no fool. Remember what I tell you. I heard that drunk talk of his with me and my friends about what you're supposed to do with a woman to make her happy.

I put the pictures back between the hay bales and crawled to where I could look to the other barn. It was quiet over there and I seen Sally's gold Cadillac like it was resting. It looked small, miniature-sized against that large white barn growing up all around it. In the corral just below me them horses stood swatting flies like they had a million tomorrows. I couldn't sit still.

I went out, behind the barn, and made my way along the railroad tracks. Lots of times us guys followed the tracks, which cut right through town, from the slaughterhouse north to the station on lower Fourth, where there's bars and poolhalls. The tracks pass back of that white place. Which is where you can see the chute they take the horses up to meet the gun, which is where I was supposed to go in a matter of hours. I came to the fence and saw the burlap hanging from the top of the chute, covering half the gaping black hole that led inside. All at once a old white cat appeared. Scared me on account I was just starting to picture myself up the chute. It stopped and looked at me, then came down the ramp like I was nothing. In the sunlight it was old and matted, white hair gray and dusty-looking. It moved slow, stiff-legged. What that cat must know, I thought, watching it cross the corral to the other barn.

It was then I decided I needed luck.

Do a good thing, Grandma says. I thought of her cousin, Old Julia. They didn't talk much, even though Julia just lived around the corner. Something about something Julia did a long time ago, which had Indians mad at her. Something about who she married, some white man. I don't know. Folks don't talk. Point is she had no friends and lived alone. When I got to Old Julia's, I seen her front door was open and I walked up and tried seeing through the screen.

"Auntie Julia," I called.

She came through the kitchen into the front room and I seen her face all pushed up, set hard. Like she was going to talk back to someone, mad-like. Or not talk at all, refuse to answer up to all the things folks accused her of. Then she let down, and her eyes came out big and watery. "Frankie," she said, pushing open the screen.

"Auntie," I said, "them weeds out back of your house, they going to catch fire and burn you down."

She giggled and covered her mouth with her hand, like a young girl. "Oh, gee," she said, and you'd think I told her her slip was showing. I seen lots of old Indian ladies do this. Grandma does it, and it's her way of covering how she's thinking in the situation. And Old Julia, I should've figured the range of her thinking after I'd just found her face hard as the porch I was standing on.

"Now come in," she said, shaking the screen door she held open.

Inside Old Julia's place you'd think time stopped. The world hadn't touched her. Not a speck of dust. Not a scratch. Not a dent or sign anyone sat on the puffy couch or rested their elbows on the pressed white doilies over the armrests. The purple and pinkish blooms of her African violets in the windows looked fake, cloth-like. It looked like she'd just put the pictures of her one daughter and grandson in new frames and placed them perfect on the walls that morning.

In the bright yellow kitchen her redbud and sedge roots for basketmaking sat on the table in neat coils wrapped and tied with strips of yellow cloth. Like my grandma, Old Julia was what they call a famous Pomo basketmaker. But there were no signs except her roots, no peelings on the floor or wet hairy sedges drying on newspapers. No signs of her weaving. She poured me a glass of milk, placed it in front of me on a napkin, then stood by the counter, like she was waiting for what I wanted next. I sat down. I felt like she'd been waiting and hoping all day for me to come. Like she had that milk just for me and the house perfect the way she thought I liked it.

"I don't have much to do today, Auntie, so I thought I'd take care of your weeds out back and side of the house." It felt good telling her this, seeing how she was. I sipped my milk.

She shifted on one foot. "Oh, dig them out? That's too much work." Her voice was steady but tired-like.

"Someone could throw a match, Auntie, and that's it."

"True," she said, shifting again. She looked old. She wore a red scarf, and wisps of white hair stuck out bright against her sagged brown face. Her slip showed below her faded print housedress. It was like she didn't belong in that house. Her eyes was still big and watery. "That would be nice," she said finally.

She offered me a plate of cookies, but I wanted to start on the weeds. I couldn't sit still. I went out the front door and started pulling the tall oat grass that lined the sides of her house and filled her garden. I seen a couple of her window screens was rusted out. Really, her place was like anybody else's, only she had no junk, refrigerators and stuff, sitting around. In-town-reservation-living we called it. I was at the oat grass half a minute when I realized I couldn't pull it out. It was summer, like I said, too far in summer, and the tops of them dried oat stalks just busted in my hands. I should dig them, I thought, turn over the soil. But that would take too long, too hard. The earth was dry clay packed tight as stone. A small plot was all I could do.

I thought on this.

Then I seen the scythe. It was leaning upright against the fence. The scythe's wooden handle growed out of the grass like something looking at me just then. I walked over and seen the blade was rusty, but it cut. Not good, but it cut. I'd do the whole place, surprise Old Julia. I swung that scythe like crazy, and in a hour or so I'd hit everywhere, alongside the house, in front by the rose hedge, the whole back.

I was standing catching my breath and admiring the territory I covered when Julia stepped out on the back porch. I started to gesture with my free hand, as if to say look, when I seen she was chuckling to herself.

"Oh, gee," she said. She was looking down where I butchered her small roses by the porch, not just those but the ones beneath the back window.

I seen the chipped paint now and the rusted-out screens and I seen Old Julia's hanging slip. But there was nothing sorry about her. Her whole body started shaking, the slip and housedress jumping up and down, and she done nothing now to cover that laugh sounding like a crow calling and shrinking me to the size of a pea. I looked away and seen the yard like a blond kid with a bad haircut. I wanted to apologize about the roses, but she was laughing so loud and hard I couldn't get her attention to say a thing. She stopped a split second and her face changed hard. She looked at the chopped oat grass, then at me, and before she busted up worse than ever, I seen what her squinting bird's eyes said: Throw a match and that's it.

◄━━

I went home and sat in the shed back of our house. Just plopped myself on a prune crate in the dark. I seen my luck like it was a movie in a theater. The short straw. Old Julia's cursing laugh. She'd seen what would happen the minute she found me on her porch, and she let me fall in. She tricked me. Tricked me into entering that strange, clean-like house where nobody lived because Old Julia wasn't a person. Tricked me with them watery eyes like she done that first time at the grocery store so I would carry her groceries. Hooey about some white man, whoever she married. The old folks knowed. Old Julia was a witch, a poisoner. Why else would Grandma and them keep away from her? Not because of a white man. Indians around here got secrets. Don't want people knowing certain things. Make us forget, not think of stuff. But they wasn't hiding nothing from me. Old Julia seen where that straw torn me wide open. She seen the hole and hooked herself there, and then like she had that straw in her hand, she tickled me with it for no reason except to laugh at me and feed her evilness.

I had to turn things around.

I went to Caroline.

That movie was still going in my mind. I wanted a different

picture, and it was Caroline I thought of because no matter how low I was I felt high as the tallest tree around her. And none of the guys was around to make fun of me and her. I'm not lying, she was fine. But she was different.

"She's weird," Buster said. "Stinky virgin."

That was on the first day I really noticed her. Buster and me and Micky was sitting on the bike racks in front of the market and she come walking up the street. Looked like a schoolgirl, white bobby socks and tennis shoes, pants rolled up at the cuff, plain white blouse. She tossed her silky black hair around to keep it out of her face, and the way she walked she could've been anywhere, going down the hall at school, at the fair. Like she wasn't paying attention to nothing. Maybe that's what caught my eye, because to me just then there was something woman about her, no schoolgirl.

"Hah! She's your cousin," Micky said, laying one into Buster.

"Shit, I don't know them drunks from Graton. Stinky Indians," Buster said.

I knowed she was Buster's cousin first day in history when the teacher called her name—Caroline Copaz. That and she was some relation to that lady Grandma knowed in Graton with the same name. But it wasn't till just then on the street I seen her potential, like I said.

Anyway, that same afternoon I went to the Hole, where she lived, and played like I was visiting old man Toms, Micky's Grandpa. The Hole is in our corner of town, which is called South Park. Only it's in the worst part of South Park, south end of Grand Avenue. It's two lines of brown army barracks separated by a potted dirt road. All kinds of Indians end up there. Blacks, too. Micky's Grandpa lived in a place at the end, just across from Caroline. I found him sitting on his ripped-apart piss-stained-looking couch halfway in the middle of the road. Like him and that couch was a roadblock at the end. He sat all day like that, watching folks and sucking his empty pipe. I greeted him and sat on the wobbly armrest. He asked how Grandma and Old Uncle was and then laughed showing a long yellow tooth, his big belly with his pants pulled up quaking up and down causing his half-un-done zipper to come open more and more.

"*Mata*," he said, which means woman, and I seen Caroline come out her door.

I seen the old man's Stetson hat on the couch and I picked it up and made like I just took it off my head for Caroline. Like a dude of high class. "Good day, lady," I said.

It stopped her short. She studied me like. Her eyes focused and then I seen her face changed like she knowed me half her life and just then remembered. "Good day, sir," she said in the same kind of voice I used.

That's how I got to know Caroline. And how I knowed she was different.

I struck a lucky note. Caroline loved games. We played we was different people. Used accents and that stuff. Sometimes we'd be married and discuss our children. Oh, Peter has such a problem with his homework. And what is it, my dear husband, that keeps our Allison brooding? Mostly Caroline. She'd start like out of nowhere. We're just walking along or sitting back of the fairgrounds and she'd start into something. I couldn't keep up with her, all that different kind of language. She lost me. I felt funny or something.

"You read too many books," I told her.

It was me started the Romeo thing one day. Except she thought it was a damsel-in-distress story. Point is Juliet wanted same as Romeo, which Caroline hadn't figured. We was in our spot under the cypress trees back of the fairgrounds. I helped her down where she could sit.

"Thank you, kind sir," she said. "I narrowly escaped."

I kissed her, started pressing on her, too. I moved up her skin, under her blouse. She pushed up and hunched over kind of. She was that girl again, the one I didn't look at in history class. Only I seen her now, and when she turned to look at me I was something cool, the toughest guy on earth.

She looked away and let out a sigh like she was tired. But she was already somewheres else. "Peter got another note," she said, disgusted-like.

◄━━►

It was almost six when I knocked on her door. It was bright outside still. Old man Toms was watching from under the Stetson hat that shaded his face, and his big belly started heaving again, but I turned away. I was about to leave when the door pulled open, then closed just as fast. Like a window shade popping up, then down. Now you see, now you don't. Then the door opened a couple inches, then slowly a couple inches more until Caroline's mother was there. Only her face and fingers on the door. The face just appeared, come into the light, and wasn't attached to nothing. It was a mask, painted orange lips the same color as the nails on the door, pencil brows and false eyelashes, one of the lashes drooping over her eye like on a busted doll. She moved so slow and strange and stared with that drooping eye like she was looking at something beyond me.

"Carol, your nigger boy's here," she said without putting expression in that puppet face.

Her voice swerved and bumped, like a car out of control. It told everything you couldn't see past the mask. She was drunk, as usual. The booze smell coming from that brown painted-up head enough to knock old man Toms off his couch. I knowed what she meant saying "nigger boy." My father and uncle them's all Portuguese. Part black, folks say. But this woman's thing was something with my dad. I don't know. It didn't bother me none. I didn't say nothing, not then, or even before, when she first showed her face. I just waited. She said something again about me being a nigger, then Caroline came out and the door closed behind her.

She was bright-looking, clean with her white blouse and tennis shoes and socks, her pants rolled up just so. Only thing, she didn't give me them eyes. No princess look. Not the wife, either. Nothing. Like she didn't even look at me. She brushed past me. "Come on," she said. Old man Toms was laughing so loud I wanted to kick him one in that fat, unzipped gut.

I figured Caroline was mad on account I hadn't come by for a while. She was stepping fast and big, like she knowed where she was going. I trailed behind her and kept asking over her shoulder what was the matter. I thought it might be her mom being drunk and all that. After all, it was just Caroline and her mom in that place. Living with that foul-smelling puppet head was no pleasure. But it wasn't her mom. It was me, what I first suspected.

She led me to the cypress trees and then sat down. I caught her eyes once, but she looked away.

"You're just a dumb boy," she said.

Her voice was different. Nothing I recognized. None of the voices I knowed from her. Caught me off guard, but it went along with her being pissed like. She had her face in her hands, the long fingers up her cheeks, and she was looking back down the street, toward Grand. The sun showed her eyes, but I couldn't see her straight on.

"I been looking for a job," I said.

"You lie, Frankie. You can't get no job." She wasn't moving.

"I want to do something. Not just sit around here all day like a nobody bum."

"You're a nobody."

Her voice was ten miles away same time it was right there. I wasn't stupid. She was mad on account I kept reaching for more than she wanted to give and then stopped showing up to see her. Which was the truth. She pushed me to it.

Then I put my arm around her. I felt good. But she was hard as a rock, unmoving yet.

"I never went to the park with Buster to see them other girls."

The soft sell. I figured I'd play it from her point of view. I was telling the truth, even if the truth was them girls around the park moved too fast. But nothing seemed to matter to Caroline. I had to approach it different.

"Me and Buster's going to do something tonight. I'm—"

"Probably you are," she said, "because you're a nobody."

It was like she talked all of a sudden. Cut me off without thinking about it. Like her voice come out of the sky and then was gone so you didn't know if you heard it or not. It was strange. Sounded something like a disgusted mother, but it went too fast for me to say for sure. She went with her voice, farther away. It wasn't what I wanted. I heard my own words about tonight, me and Buster, and I remembered why I was sitting there just then. Where I'd started to feel good with Caroline, now I was sinking. The stakes was high. I had to win. Even if she just looked at me in that certain way said I was something cool. I held on to her like she was a card I could will into an ace. Time was all I had. I knowed if I just held, and I would've held till dark, she'd give in. And I was right.

The sun dropped two fingers' worth in the sky. That's how I was measuring time, with my free fingers against the sun. I first seen her kicking at the dirt, just a little with one foot, then she adjusted her shoulders. I started moving, too, but not where she could see. The tide turned, the ace came up and got me moving. I leaned over and kissed her. Her eyes was open and holding that sun in little dots of light, and if I hadn't closed my eyes just then and kept looking I would've seen the mountain range, everything in her eyes clear to the

ocean and back. She put her arms around me like never before. I felt
her hands back of my shoulder holding on. I leaned her against the
tree. Then, all at once, she twisted and bolted upright, and when she
pulled away, my hand was caught in her blouse, which pulled her
toward me and made her pull back again so we was caught together,
and when she jerked free she flew against the tree and hit with a
thud.

I jumped to her, then coiled back. Her eyes shot through that
tangled mess of hair at me like I was the devil himself. She pushed
herself upright with her elbows, still glaring at me, then faced the sun
and started clearing the hair out of her face.

"It's no use," she said, "you're like all the rest. It's all the same.
Mama's right."

I didn't follow her. Everything changed so fast. She arched her
back, stiff. The wife, I thought. I worked my throat so my voice would
be the husband. Caroline's lips started, but nothing came out, no
words. Then she wilted, folded up into her lap, and I could tell what
she said before she said it.

"It's no use," she said into her hands.

She crossed the line. She was on the other side, gone. I felt we
wouldn't be friends after that. I cramped up, felt sorry, because just
then I also knowed I liked her special. I found out too late. I cramped
up, felt sorry and mad at the same time.

She braced herself, hands on knees, like she propped herself up,
then she was on her feet. I seen the sun glistening down one side of
her face. Then she was running. She'd gone halfway down the block
before I could move. I chased her far as Grand, then quit.

I was just plain mad. Mad at her, Buster, everybody. Mad at
myself. Damn this sex business anyway. Damned if I did, damned if I
didn't.

I went home.

◆

The house was noisy and stuffy-smelling. Kids everywhere. The
TV. Mom cooking. Dad and his brother, Uncle Angelo, and their six-
packs of beer at the kitchen table. Mom over the stove with the pink
plastic curlers in her hair from morning. Grandma and Old Uncle in
their spots next to the stove, two old Indians, sitting like they was in
the park or on the front porch, just watching.

"Frankie, you want some beans here?" Mom asked without turning to look at me standing behind her. She's like that. Got a sixth sense where she knows each of her eight kids without looking.

She dished a bowl of chili from the big pot she was stirring. "Get yourself a spoon," she said and then dropped a spoon in the bowl she handed me. I looked for a place to sit. The chairs and couch was filled in the front room, so I sat at the table across from Dad and Uncle Angelo. Which I didn't want to do on account of their getting drunk and loud. Mom handed me a warm tort in a paper towel. "Where you been?" she asked, turning back to the stove.

Just then Uncle Angelo's fists hit the table, causing my plate of beans to jump half a inch. "Son of a bitch, the bastard was in his car already," Uncle Angelo said.

It was something about somebody Uncle Angelo wanted to beat up at work. Him and Dad always talked like that when they was drinking. Fighting and women. They was more drunk than I first figured. Both of them cussed up a storm. They looked the same, curly black hair, lightish skin, tight faces that opened and cracked in lines when they laughed. And when they was drinking, their eyes got small, black beads like rats' eyes, so you couldn't tell what they was thinking and what was coming next. I looked to Grandma in the room with all that talk. She seen me and she giggled, lifting her hand to her mouth. Mom lifted the pot of beans to the sink. At least I got interrupted and didn't have to think of an answer for her about where I'd been. I could thank Uncle Angelo's fists for that.

Most of the time I wanted Dad and Uncle Angelo to leave, get on with their routine, which was drinking, then out on the town to the bars and poolhalls on lower Fourth. They picked on everybody. Old Uncle about never being married. Me if I got a piece of ass yet. But just then, watching for what come next out of them, I didn't have to dwell on the fact I was sunk worse than a brick in a fish pond. I did start thinking about the scene, though, Sally Did and Smoke. I thought of asking Uncle Angelo about Sally on account his wife was related to Sally, sister or something, which is how we knowed Sally was just another Indian from around here and not a princess from some faraway tribe, like she was claiming. See, I was thinking if I could find out something about Sally and the goings-on in that slaughterhouse I wouldn't have to go all the way inside. Just fake it, go in a little, then tell the guys a story.

But I wouldn't get a chance to ask Uncle Angelo nothing.

Everything got quiet. Just the TV and Mom taking plates from the cupboard. I kept my eyes on my food. I kept eating. I felt Dad and Uncle Angelo move past me, behind me. They was going to tweak my ear, pinch my chest. I could hear even what they was going to say. "You get your whistle wet, boy? All that stuff. I just kept my head down, chewing my beans, and because the longest time went by, I figured the worst possible thing would happen. Like they'd hit me a good one upside the head and then I'd have to sit there watching them laugh at me. Like I was supposed to be quicker and outsmart them. What could I do? Then from the corner of my eye I seen Mom picking up the empty beer cans. And I seen Dad and Uncle Angelo was gone, not anywhere. I turned clear around until I seen the open front door.

Mom put plates of beans on the table for Grandma and Old Uncle. The two of them sat down with me. But I didn't look at them any more than I looked at Dad and Uncle Angelo. I seen only the open front door and the streetlight shining beyond. It was my time to go, too.

I started seeing my life movie again. Not like I turned it on, but like it turned itself on, the whole day's events running past my eyes. And this time Caroline added in. I had nothing to take out that door with me. No luck, only a empty barrel. I looked at my sisters and brothers in the front room and then at Grandma and Old Uncle. I was alone all of a sudden. I started to shake like. I thought of Buster and them out back of that slaughterhouse. They'd be waiting for me. Points. Points. Points. I had no points. I was washed up, broke. Sunk. Then something come to me, not in my head, but in my shaking. Like something just give up in me and let me go. I seen my movie still going and it wasn't just Buster and them. It was the whole thing. And me. Me. What was I holding on to, anyway? Nothing. What did I have to lose? What I had was one more chance not to lose, to turn the whole picture around. The short straw, Old Julia, Caroline. Everything. It was my only chance. So I got up and left.

◆

It was cool, clear. The night opened itself for me. I slipped down Grand and up Santa Rosa Avenue like a eel in water. Nothing stopped me until the slaughterhouse fence. Turns out I was the only one there. Seemed like forever, but Victor and Micky finally showed.

Buster didn't turn up for another half hour, it seemed. The Navarro twins didn't show at all.

"Okay," Buster said, "it's just us." He looked at me and then started explaining how I just walk up the chute. He talked like it was some technical maneuver, as if I couldn't figure out how to walk up a ramp and hadn't thought way beyond that the whole time I was waiting for him. But he was going through the motions, saying stuff so he could still play Buster. He didn't know what to do after going up that chute. He couldn't say if he had to and he knowed it. Nobody could. It was a big deal. "All clear," Buster said, but I was already through the fence.

The chute had crossboards like steps so the horses wouldn't slip back or fall. That struck me funny. Like to make sure the horses would go in and not hurt themselves and miss out on dying. But soon as I was under that burlap and in the dark I had to pay attention. I couldn't see a damn thing. And the horse gut pit and all that come to mind. But funny thing, it never crossed my mind to lie just then, like I planned at home. I never thought of stopping and hiding in the dark. I already done more than Buster or any of them.

I followed a fence railing. I walked sideways, like a crab, never letting go of that railing. I was thinking. Like I said, that hole of horse guts was on my mind, and I took little steps, holding on to the railing and testing with each step to make sure I had solid ground. I looked back to the light from the chute hole every once in a while. Then something happened. I couldn't see anything. Frontward or backward. My way out was gone. I couldn't see the chute hole. I must've rounded a corner. Things shifted. The railing stopped, and I was clinging to a flat wall. I froze up, spread-eagled on the wall. I was completely lost.

I thought of tearing out of there, making a mad dash for the chute hole. The place had no windows, so I couldn't think of that. There was no way out but the chute and the front door, and I was a far ways from the front door. I was on the second floor somewheres, and the front door was on the first. I almost panicked. But I had enough reason left to tell me that tearing off in that darkness was likely to land me in the horse pit or something worse. I stood there awhile, my palms flat against the wall. I was spread-eagled, like I said, facing the wall like I was caught and waiting for cops to frisk me. Then I started moving real slow, going sideways with the toes of my tennis shoes and my palms holding to the wall. I'd gone about five feet when I heard it. Actually, I felt it, a vibrating sound in the wall, like a bass pounding through the wood. I stopped, then moved a little backward, then forward. Forward it was stronger. I followed and it got stronger, louder so that it was music I was hearing. A clear beat, a drumbeat for some rock and roll song or something. Still I took small steps, testing that I had solid ground beneath me. I kept moving sideways. And for reason. I started smelling something like meat, a thick, copper-like smell that was warm and damp. It choked me. I felt like I was moving between flesh. Like it was hanging on either side of me, all around. But I kept going, a little forward, then stopping, then on again. Like that I kept moving. I was following the music, and then just as fast as that meat smell come, it disappeared and I was standing on a landing looking down a flight of stairs to light below.

It was the Supremes singing "Got Him Back in My Arms Again." The way was clear, just down the steps. But I was more scared than ever. Like down those steps I would see the goings-on firsthand. I could hear people moving and talking. What if it was nothing, just some folks partying? What if it was something and I got caught? Like I seen something illegal and they killed me so I wouldn't tell. It was this last thing pushed me on. Fear, it was what I knowed best. Not Buster and them. They was so far behind me now. I was alone and scared to death, and if I stopped I might've lost my fear. I went down one step at a time. The boards creaked but by now the music was so loud nobody below could hear. Two steps from the bottom I stopped, and when I peeked around the corner, bracing myself against the wall, it all come into plain view, the room with Smoke, Sally, and the girls.

I moved down one step and situated myself so I could watch. It wasn't really a room but a clearing of cardboard boxes stacked nearly high as the ceiling. That was three walls, and Sally's gold Cadillac made the fourth. Like it was a movable wall and it was in place now. A big transistor radio sat on the hood of the car, and a black girl in a short dress that looked like a pink flowered towel around her body played with the dials, trying to find another song. The rest of them was in the middle of the room. But they hadn't stopped. They was still moving like the music was still playing. They wasn't dancing really, but walking in a pack slowly around the room, going in a circle. Like in some ceremony. Smoke out in front a little with a wine jug in a brown paper sack, his straw hat on and overalls. Sally was in the middle, her skunk-striped hair showing in the small crowd. They turned so that they had their backs to me, and when they turned again, coming in my direction, I see a smaller girl in the middle, between Sally and the orange-haired black girl, and Sally and the orange hair was holding on to her arm in arm, walking her along. Sally yelled for the pink-dress one by her car to hurry and find some music. The girl Sally was holding on to wore a dark shawl, and when a song came on booming into the room, I seen the fringes of the shawl start shaking, dangling. I must've had my eyes fixed on that shawl because I didn't see if any of them started moving faster or not. I didn't see that the girl had stepped out of the crowd, not until the shawl dropped on the floor, and when I looked up I seen the girl was Caroline. She was still moving, taking little steps, one at a time by herself, wobbling some, like she was just learning how to walk or had too much of Smoke's wine. Caroline with lipstick and done-up hair, and even in that tight red dress that would never let me see the color red again in peace, she looked to me like a butterfly just out of its cocoon. Nothing I had known before. And she was looking right at me, her eyes in mine and mine in hers, and not knowing it. Then she looked up, like she was looking to heaven, and she couldn't have seen any more than I did, which was that blasted naked light bulb over everything. "Over here," Smoke said, and I seen he was next to the Cadillac, holding the door wide open.

I pushed myself back up the stairs to the landing. Somehow I had sense enough to know if I stood there any longer I'd likely fall forward out of the stairwell in front of all those people. Somehow, even when you're dead inside, you think how to live. Something takes over. I should've just collapsed there, letting Caroline and everyone else see how small and dumb I was. But, like I said, something takes over. A million things raced through my mind. I thought of rescuing Caroline. I pictured myself charging down the stairs and whisking her out the front door and us running along Santa Rosa Avenue to safety. I must've been standing there awhile like that because I heard Sally's car start. I thought of Caroline. But it was no use. Things was bigger than me.

I groped in the dark and found the railing. Going out was easier. I came up under the burlap and stood on top of the chute. You'd think I was a king or something by the looks on the guys' faces. I had a long view of the empty railroad tracks leading into town. I didn't want to move, but I was already going down the chute.

"What'd you see in there?" Micky asked.

"Nothing," I said, crawling through the fence.

Victor stood with his eyes popped out of his head. I looked to Buster, who was quiet. He knowed like the rest I'd seen something. Must've been on my face.

"Just some people dancing around. That black whore with orange hair. There's no horse gut hole or nothing," I said and spit. My voice scared me. Like it was telling what I just won was nothing to wear a crown about.

"Man, you *did it*," Micky said.

"Shit," Buster said. "It ain't no big deal." He spit like to outdo me. But he didn't believe himself, and nobody else believed him, either.

I looked back at the burlap hanging over the top of the black hole.

"Shit, let's go to the park and get us some chicks." Buster was still at it. He turned up his T-shirt sleeves to show his muscles.

We started making our way back to Santa Rosa Avenue.

"Frankie, you smell like meat or something," Victor said, first time opening his mouth. "You better go change your clothes."

"Yeah," I said, and looked up, and there was nothing in the sky.

CAROLYN SEE

◆

WHITNEY
AND TRACIE

Maui, June 26

Because the plane was overbooked, they got bumped up to first class. A stewardess came by with a tray of free champagne. And they weren't even off the ground yet!

A few other travelers, who had just taken in the fact that they would be crossing the vast Pacific in a dangerous DC-10, turned their heads to train disapproving stares on these two giddy teenagers. "Are they old enough to drink?" one woman asked her husband.

Her husband was staring as well. These girls! How long had it been since he'd traveled with girls who wore shorts? Those *legs*. He could, if he closed his eyes for a few delicious seconds, feel either pair of those legs locked around his neck. . . .

He opened his eyes. The two girls were still bursting with laughter. His wife wore a tailored white silk blouse and loose yellow silk slacks. Her waist was bound by a belt with bright stones. He knew about the two sets of scars behind her ears from her two full face-lifts. And yes, her thighs were strong, from tennis. But when he tried to remember when she'd last laughed like those girls, he couldn't. When he tried to remember when last he'd been around girls who laughed so heedlessly at nothing, he couldn't.

"Don't worry about it," he said briskly to his wife. On impulse, he kissed the fine skin stretched across her cheekbone. She turned from him, in habit and exasperation.

"Oh," Tracie groaned, "I can't stand it! Can you *believe this*?" Two days before, they had received their tickets and reservations at the old Sheraton Maui on Kaanapali Beach; instructions to bring bathing suits, party dresses, and to "go easy on the makeup," because José Cuervo's whole thrust was to appeal to "an upscale, wholesome market." Tucked into their press kits (along with pictures of the Mexi-

can town of Tequila and photocopies of cactus fields) were designer
sketches of how they should look during working hours: Hawaiian
outfits with wide sashes saying *Miss José Cuervo! Miss Gusano!*

"You have lived a long and varied life," Tracie remarked. "You
have lived so long that you have become Miss Gusano."

"Miss Worm, right?"

"Yes. It's a grave responsibility, let me tell you."

The plane coughed underneath them. The stewardess came by
with a second swipe of champagne.

The plane taxied toward the runway. "I don't want to go," Tracie
said, her face suddenly sallow with fear. "I think I should have passed
on this assignment."

The plane took off. It's like the incline, Whitney thought, like
driving up the California Incline, up from the beach along the cliffs,
going home. It's not so bad. If I look out the window, I see the ocean
slipping away, just like on the incline. It's not so bad, I could almost
like it. I could almost love it. When the plane banked sharply left, she
thought, *So?* It's just like turning left or right on Ocean Avenue, no
biggee! The plane, after a few shudders and rumbles, hacking coughs,
finally decided to go ahead and fly. The men got up to go to the
bathroom.

"I forgot to say," Tracie whispered weakly, "that I usually try to
pack an extra airplane. Just in *case*, you know?" She put her palm on
Whitney's arm, removed it, and pointed to the wet palmprint she had
left. "Look at that. That's *pathetic.*"

"Look at that lady," Whitney whispered, to get her mind off it.
"Would you say she's had a few *lifts?*"

Up here the sky was electric blue and the sun shone like a mil-
lion-watt bulb. The ocean looked like bright ink and little boats sailed
right under them. They were still close enough to the airport that the
white sails must be traffic from the marina. *Traffic from the marina!*

Full of happiness, Whitney chose a mushroom omelet, with sau-
sage on the side. Tracie asked for French toast. "It's nice, isn't it? Up
here in first class?"

Five hours later, they stepped from the plane and felt, for the
first time, the trade winds, the flowery, soft air, dampening their hair.
Two men waited for them at the foot of the salt-warped stairs.

"Welcome to Maui," one of them said, "the island of romance.
Remember us?" He was chubby, and thin blond hair fell on his
round, tan face. He wore a short-sleeved khaki jacket with fake epau-

lets. "I'm Hal," he said. "This is my buddy, Steve. I'm José Cuervo, he's Gusano. I keep telling him he hasn't got a chance. How can you sell something with a worm out here? José Cuervo, *that's* the only one!"

Steve wore a clean white baggy shirt and overly stylish baggy black cotton pants. Standing next to Tracie, he came out about three inches short. The island spirit seemed not to have caught up with him. He shook their hands and, walking with them to the luggage hangar, explained what was what. "This thing goes for three days. We're coming in late for the first day. I'll be frank with you kids, nobody out here wants to buy tequila. It's rum with them all the way, because of the sugarcane. And when you put a margarita up against a daiquiri, they don't see the advantage. They don't want any *salt.*"

"Well," Tracie said, "Here's the deal on those rum drinks. Two daiquiris and you're blotto. . . ."

Whitney burst into giggles. Tracie shot her a severe look. "With margaritas, you can dance all night."

"Good point," Steve said. "The trouble is, though, with all this drug business and all this lead-a-clean-life-for-Jesus stuff, I hope I'm not stepping on any toes, but people don't want to drink anymore at all. We should be in the mineral water business, the Orange Crush business."

"*You* in the Orange Crush business? Excuse *me!*" Hal kept his hands jammed in his pockets and let Steve handle the luggage.

"We had some time to kill, so we ducked in here and found you something to wear."

Here, by the cab stand, next to a souvenir store that sold Hula Girl floor lamps, was an expensive last-chance tourist trap that sold Hawaiian shirts and garish sarongs.

"I don't *think* so!" Tracie blurted, but Hal was already pushing them inside, where a saleswoman in a muumuu waited.

"Here they are, honey," Hal said. "Do your best."

"You lucky girls! Neither one of you can be more than a size six. Am I right?"

Something about the way Whitney clutched her arm sent Tracie around the bend. "Why *not?* Have you got a grass *skirt? We'll* go for it. Why *not?* Do we have to wear a top? I certainly hope not!"

The woman quickly chose them matching outfits with matching patterns. Skimpy halter tops and wraparound skirts that scooped up on the left side to show plenty of thigh. Whitney's came in vivid persimmon stamped with large white gardenias; Tracie's was a knock-out in morning glory blue. They thrust their narrow feet into white sandals. Hal excused himself and came back with an armful of leis, which he carefully put over the girls' heads. White carnations mostly, and on top several circles of pink and lavender baby orchids.

Tracie and Whitney went back into the dressing room to take a look. *"Spectacular,"* Tracie said. "And if I'm not mistaken, we've been getting paid ten dollars an hour since the plane took off this morning?"

Before they went to the hotel, Hal and Steve decided they all needed lunch. "Don't worry," Steve said. "We're not hitting on you girls. You're minors. We could go to jail for that, or at least have to change our temp agency. We've all got lunch coming to us. We can't sell tequila with low blood sugar."

They drove in a rented convertible to the Sunrise Café, a pretty place on the beach, on the leeward side of the island. Islanders greeted them politely and showed them to a table by the water's edge. It was shady here, under a blanket of palms. Whitney couldn't get over the feel of the air on her skin, the sweetness of the feel of the air. The ocean's waves didn't crash here. They rolled and rolled and rolled, then slapped on the sand like a series of love pats. Each wave, as it crested, was perfectly clear.

"Hal and I have known each other for years," Steve volunteered after they'd ordered. "We served together in the army reserve, up in Newfoundland. We're new to liquor, but we've sold all sorts of things. We started out in New England. We were in fish for a while. . . ." He looked over at Hal, who smiled.

"Cod," Hal said mildly. "We turned over plenty of cod."

"But cod tastes like cotton balls, and that's on a *good* day. On a bad day it tastes like cat food."

"Ends up cat food, a lot of the time."

"We went into furniture. Nobody ever buys furniture. Americans only buy mattresses every seven years. We both got divorces—we thought, life is *short!* We're salesmen, we're old friends. . . ."

Their orders came. Barbecue jumbo shrimp for the men, shrimp salad for the girls, four foaming margaritas. The time was going on to three, but Steve said not to worry. "We decided to sell something that people would want forever, and that they'd have to keep on buying. We really couldn't get behind food. We'd had that cod experience. We thought—booze."

Hal spoke up. "Not the brown stuff."

"No. We thought, Go for the vodka. Tequila. Even gin. Things you can see through. We've done pretty well."

"We have a very clean route," Hal said. "San Francisco, Denver, L.A., Hawaii, and once a year a tour of the factories in Mexico. We're supposed to widen our markets. Bora Bora. Because honeymooners need margaritas. Singapore. They tell us we're supposed to get those guys to make their slings with tequila. Will that be the day or *what?* Melbourne, Sydney . . ."

"My stepfather works out there," Whitney said. It was the first time she'd opened her mouth in a while and her throat felt grainy and unused. "He works in developing hotels. Industrial complexes. Resorts. Things like that. He's a financier?"

Steve and Hal exchanged glances. This was good news! Then Hal put his arm across the back of her chair. "I guess we'll have to wine and dine you, then, Whitney. Steve and I are going to turn into ravening beasts. It's our duty to the company. You don't mind, do you?"

Whitney turned her wicker chair directly to the ocean. "This is a strange world," she said. "What would you ever guess would be the odds on the four of us being together in a place like this? The odds would be long, like a . . . long shot?"

No one took the trouble to answer. The only sounds were the winds in palm fronds, the smack of orderly waves climbing up along the smooth beach. Whitney looked at Tracie who, in the last minutes, had begun to fool with her hair, absently making a few braids, so that they crept like little snakes through the mountain of her light blond frizz. Two hours ago, she and Tracie had been in a plane. Two hours from now, they'd be, like, in a hotel. Somewhere. Here was just this gorgeous moment. Six months ago everybody had been telling her that she was "lucky to be alive." She hadn't believed it.

"Robin," Tracie said. She, too, had turned her chair to the sea. Her head tilted all the way back to catch the sun. "He'd like this."

"Sure would." But she didn't feel sad.

"'Kay, girls. We've got to get going. Think tequila."

They drove with the top down. They saw that the island came in layers: the sea, the sand, banana palm, coconut palm jungle; then dark green sinister patches that Hal said he thought were coffee plantations. Then up, up into steep peaks as bright as ice cream, and those peaks topped off by gray and white clouds.

Steve pulled into the parking lot of the Sheraton Maui. "Why they picked this place for a liquor convention beats me entirely. You need a regular clientele that fits the market. Everybody at this hotel outside of the convention is pushing eighty. You feed them tequila, it might work like Drāno on their poor old bodies."

Tracie kept quiet. Whitney knew she had something on her mind. When the girls walked into the liquor convention, it was true, the action seemed to center over at the Bacardi booth, where they'd hired hula girls and invested in some flashing pink lights. But Tracie, after shaking hands with the pale, disheartened tequila salesmen in gabardine suits who'd worked the morning shift, went rummaging behind the table to see how they were making up their margaritas.

"What are you guys using for mix? Damiana instead of Cointreau? Radical. Steve! Want to sell some *drinks* here? Want to take some orders?"

They stared.

Tracie jabbered as she cut up limes, fresh and green, on a white china plate. "Go find waiters, borrow a couple of white jackets. Find if this place has a doctor. Get a stethoscope. Whitney! Find a felt pen. We're going to have some fun here!" With a pen she scribbled on the back of a sign: *Tequila, para la vida! Damiana, for immortality!* Then, while the men gaped, she stepped out from behind the table into the crowded aisle.

"*Don't* go over there," she ordered every passerby within hearing. "That stuff'll *kill* you! Don't you know rum is bad for your liver? I want to tell you something. Do you know that Aztecs routinely lived to be over a hundred years old? Don't you want to know why? The margarita is the culmination of over forty thousand years of experimentation. Lime to prevent scurvy. Salt for warm weather. Tequila as disinfectant. Drāno for your intestines. But the secret ingredient here is the *damiana!* Because, you want to know why? Damiana is a herb that grows *only* in Baja California. It has the same properties as gotu-kola, borage tops, yellow dock root. It cures impotence—not that you'd have to worry—it does away with female trouble, it prevents cancer *and* the common cold. How do those Indians live down in Baja California, where there's nothing but stone and rock and hardly any fresh water at all? Tequila, distilled from the inside of the cactus, lime—*if* they can get it—and a tonic made from damiana, the true wonder drug of the Aztecs!"

By now Tracie was getting excited. "*Ice* is a modern invention.

There's no value to it. Egg white is awful. They just put that in to keep the bubbles stiff, but it gets in the way of the total purpose of the margarita, which is to straighten out your heartbeat, clean out your liver. I'm telling you the truth now. My mother at home in California goes to some fancy Beverly Hills doctor who charges her a hundred and sixty dollars an hour. You know what he gives her? Borage! Boldo root! *Damiana!* So *I* say, Save the hundred and sixty dollars. Spend six on two margaritas! Wake up in the morning glad to be alive! *Here!* Taste this!"

Tracie held up a new margarita, thickly rimmed with salt. "Take a lick! Then take a swallow. *Now.* Tell me you don't feel better! And over there behind the counter, see that Gusano? The worm at the bottom means a hundred years of life!"

At Golden Oaks, during a seminar on guided imagery, some guy had come in and told them about energy fields. *Never let an obstacle get between you and your projected goal!* Whitney joined her friend in the aisle, working differently, *being* instead of doing. Being a blonde out for fun. She carried a bottle in one hand, salt, lime and a shot glass in the other. Every man there—she knew it, she willed it— was going to halt in front of her, look at her breasts and her long blond hair and her bottle of José Cuervo and ask, as though he was the only man on earth and she the only woman, "What you got there?"

And she would take his hand and hold it for a minute, then show him how to hold the shot glass, hold the lime, and in the fleshy folds between thumb and forefinger pour some coarse grains of kosher salt, and pour that first heartening shot into him. *Wow!* Then it was time to taste the new batch of margaritas. Hal and Steve, without being told, had shrugged into white waiters' jackets. Steve wore a stethoscope. Tequila for life! The men had the sense to confine their advice to a simple injunction to go easy on the salt in cold climates, and to be sure not to drive after three of these, because too much of any tonic was bound to make you feel dizzy. Mostly they stayed busy writing up orders.

Some elderly tourists sneaked in to explore the convention. Tracie and Whitney grabbed them, gave them one shot each, then sent them back out to the bar, where, incredibly, orders came in for extra fifths of José Cuervo, a couple of bottles of Gusano. Around seven, some of the other booths began to close for the night. The men from Jack Daniel's came by, submitted to Tracie's harangue, and refreshed themselves with a frothy margarita. The Seagram's men slunk off without a word. Hal and Steve ran out of invoice pads and had to borrow some from Gilbey's gin. By seven-thirty the hula girls, dead on their feet, had come over for a free sample. "You know where that damn dance gets you?" one of them asked Tracie. "Right here." She poked at where the joint of her leg joined her hip, her hand disappearing into fresh, dry grass.

Whitney didn't say much. It wasn't her way. That's why, she thought, some people got the wrong idea that she was aloof. She tried to express this to one of the hula girls, whose skin glowed with eight hours' exertion. "You were beautiful," Whitney said. "I've been watching you all afternoon. I'd do anything to be able to do what you do. I'm too shy, I guess."

"No, man, it's *easy!* I've been giving hula lessons my whole *life,* it's easier than standing still!" Soon the girls were teaching Whitney and Tracie some of the rudimentary steps, but Whitney had trouble with the arm movements. "I was in a car accident a few months back," she said, and a Hawaiian girl answered, "Then you got to do it with your knees and your head."

Steve finished writing up the orders. "Three hundred and seventy cases since four this afternoon. And we're back-ordered on damiana for a hundred years. We've got to buy up some Cointreau and decant it into the damiana bottles for tomorrow. No yard sales this year, Hal. Thank Christ!"

Hal nodded, watching the girls and seven or eight salesmen dancing in the aisle. Last year, no, the year before that, had been so bad for him that he'd spent the summer in New England in his dead mother's old family house. His wife returned aluminum cans for pay. On weekends she took a selection of whatever she found around the house and set it out on the lawn to sell for food money. They'd been up against it. He went along with her, because what else was he supposed to do? There wouldn't be any other money coming in until he went on the road in the fall, and they couldn't go on welfare because they knew everyone in town.

One afternoon in August he woke up from a nap in the backyard, heavy and sweaty and insect-bitten. He heard, down the driveway, hushed voices. "Can you believe?" a woman's voice said. "She *gave* them to us?"

He roused himself and shambled out to the front lawn, where his wife, pale and tired, was folding away two bills into her coin purse.

On a blanket, spread out on the lawn, kitchen and dining items made a forlorn display.

"Did you just sell something?" Mosquitoes buzzed around his head. His son's pale body hung in the loop of an old rubber tire from the elm in the front yard.

"Salt and pepper shakers. They gave me five dollars apiece."

"The silver ones?"

"Were they silver?"

He remembered the antique salt and pepper shakers and the castor set and the silver candlesticks and all the other silver that used to sit on the dining room sideboard, that he hadn't noticed in years and years. He went back inside, looked at the sideboard, completely bare now, tried to remember the marks on all that stuff, things that had gone back to before the Revolutionary War. He came back outside where his wife stood, staring at the blanket.

He must have been so unpleasant that he lost his wife that day. (And gave her the house, since he didn't want it and didn't have anything else to give her.) He wrote his son once a month or so, and the kid generally wrote back, but he'd lost his son, too, over those salt and pepper shakers. Which he would still have now, along with his family, if he'd had these girls on a Hawaiian island two, three years ago.

So he stood and watched, and didn't join in the dancing, although every time Whitney moved quietly by him with a shot of tequila, he downed it. The girls were right. There was something about the lime. Something about the salt. Since the breakup—which he could never say broke his heart, although thinking about it depressed him—he tried to keep his world within the confines of what his eyes could see. The less you thought, so to say, the less you thought.

He followed the quiet blonde with his eyes because she was so restful, so easy on the eyes. He thought he saw flashes of alternating ease and melancholy that she gave off like a faulty electric light. Hadn't he heard her say she'd been in a car crash? So . . . maybe she saw what he did. That all it took was one brush with the cosmic drum brush, one blast of the cosmic drum cymbals, what did they call those things? The cosmic *high hat!*

"Time to close up. No more customers. And we've sold out. Totally."

The last thing they all needed was another drink. But Steve and Hal pointed out to the girls that what they had bought to wear under their flowered skirts and might even have dismissed as so mundane a thing as underwear were actually the bottoms of bikinis. After they closed the booth, the four of them, bone-tired but elated, headed for the smallest of the resort's four pools. Here in an artificial grotto hidden from the ocean and hotel rooms alike, a partly submerged bar with a bored bartender waited for their business. Under tiki lamps, the bar stools were placed so that if you were tall, the water might come up to your chest, and if you were short, the water lapped your chin.

Now they could peel off their long skirts, half wade, half swim over to the bar and sit up at it, underwater, the tepid wavelets washing away sweat, hard work, plane fear. The Hawaiian behind the bar gave them each a gardenia for their hair and a new orchid lei. Why, there were plenty of flowers around here! You could never use them up!

Steve and Hal excused themselves and returned by the time the girls had taken sips of their first drinks—something with fruit juice and pineapple and paper umbrellas.

Here they were again, Steve and Hal, old guys in their late thirties, who, it was pretty well established, were going to be coming on to these young girls. Their appearance in bathing suits was going to be crucial. "Are we going to be embarrassed by this?" Tracie muttered. "Are we going to *die* from this upcoming moment?"

The old guys handled it pretty well. Steve, who, Whitney decided, looked a little like Dean Stockwell, had a nice brown hairy chest, and baggy black and white trunks that came almost to his knees. *I'm harmless!* his whole body said. *Don't worry about me! You've got nothing to worry about!* Hal, taller, chunky, had that light, buttery tan. His shorts were innocuous khaki, almost part of him. Pool lights caught his sandy hair. And the lines in his face.

They had three rounds of drinks at this quiet bar, but there was no question of the men trying to get them drunk. They spent two whole hours, from eight until almost ten, very quietly sipping, talking, leaning into the water. Steve was making Tracie laugh, and Whitney thought there was no better sound in the whole world than her friend's reckless, insistent laughter. She had Tracie to her left, Hal to her right. He turned on his stool, facing her. Whitney could see, from where she sat, blankets of greenery behind Hal's head. He told her a little about losing his wife, his child, his house. About how his wife had been as good as she could be under the circumstances, until she just couldn't do it anymore. That he tried not to think about his son, because it made him feel bad. "There were things I could have done, I guess, but I couldn't think of them then, when they might have made some difference. So I try not to think about them now."

Whitney put her head down on the bar. "I know. I know exactly. Because when I was in that car crash six months ago, it was very bad. A boy I knew made a right turn and a truck slammed into him. He got slammed. But I didn't know that because I went unconscious. When I woke up I looked over, and I knew he was dead. His head was tilted back against the seat, and the steering wheel had gone into his chest, but I didn't see that then. His mouth was closed and his eyes were closed but blood was coming out of his eyes like he was crying blood, and I . . . drifted down. I drifted down for a minute as far as I could go. I thought, Please God, take these last five minutes back. Let us be turning out onto Santa Monica, laughing and talking. Let Robin be alive. Please let him be alive! But he wasn't alive. And you couldn't get those five minutes back, no matter what. So I came back up. I'd lost a bunch of teeth. They were still in my mouth so I moved my right arm, my left arm was broken, and fished around and found my teeth and balled them up in my cheek, because they always say you can put them back in, and I didn't want to be stuck with false teeth for the rest of my life. And I concentrated on remembering my stepfather's last name, and our telephone number, and my Social Security number, and the name of our insurance company, and even who the president was, but I couldn't remember. Because I knew those were the questions they ask you when they come with the ambulance. I even had the sense to reach over with my right hand and turn the ignition key off so we wouldn't have a fire. I didn't look at Robin anymore. When I got out of the hospital, he'd already been buried for two weeks."

Hal took Whitney's shoulders and turned her around so that she saw, past Tracie and Steve, to the other side of the grotto.

"Take a look," he said.

At first she set her shoulders impatiently. He hadn't been listening to her—well, who ever did? What was she supposed to be looking at, the *view?* What was the big deal, some *plants?* But as she gazed, the landscape began to move and breathe for her. She saw vines curling and clinging to trees; she saw leaves breathing good stuff back into the air. She saw hanging flowers and blossoms, and from the way she perceived them, she knew that they effortlessly existed simply as a way to ornament the universe. She reached with her injured arm to touch her lei, and got the message from all around her neck: *still an orchid, still being an orchid.* She tensed to turn to the liquor salesman to say *wow!* But his fingertips on her shoulders told her to stay the way she was. *What more was there to see?* Then she saw natives who had been there all the time. Half-naked brown-skinned men and women moved soberly in a clearing that seemed far away, but not so far that she couldn't see the men clustered together, painting their cheeks with fine lines of white paint, and tying up their loincloths. She flicked her eyes to the girls, so beautiful! Their long hair fell over their shoulders and across their haltered breasts, their legs moved under full grass skirts. Their bare feet gleamed like dark coral in the dust. Seriously and carefully they plucked flowers from the vines around them and put them in each other's hair.

Once again, Whitney barely began to move her shoulders, to turn to her companion. Once again, her companion kept her steady, turned away from him. "Wait," he whispered, and with that whisper, his breath in her ear, she became aware of all the sounds that went with all the sights. It was fierce! Not just the steady thump of waves on the beach, but the whine of mosquitoes, the hum of some kind of gnats that she saw now, floating around them, since someone had turned on the pool's underwater lights and tinted the water and the air just above the water an iridescent turquoise. She heard the skid of Tracie's straw as it poked around through crushed ice for a last taste. She heard the light slap of water against the sides of the pool. To her right, out of sight in the dark trees, she became aware of human murmuring. There must be a bunch of other people over there! And they were getting louder, hitting a yearning, greedy note. The brown-skinned kids heard it, too. They sped up their gestures, flicked out their skirts. A few boys jogged in place. One of them handed around a bottle of baby oil which some of them took and some of them didn't, spreading it on their chests, their muscular arms.

It was almost too dark to see! But one of the boys turned on what looked like a faucet by the side of a rickety building that Whitney just then saw—if you went on looking like this, what else could you see, like, *if you went on like this?* A boy struck a match under the faucet, which squirted out a yellow flame. He turned the flame down. The girls retreated to one side of the clearing, keeping their skirts out of the way. The boys, one by one, picked up poles which had been propped up against the side of the wooden building. As each boy passed the end of his pole under the faucet of flame, the pole, which had a cup of something at its end, caught fire. Brilliant yellow fire lit up the clearing. There was a ramshackle balcony along the upper story of the building. Across the top of the balcony, laundry hung every which way on hand-strung lines. Some of the most vivid flowers weren't real at all, but part of the patterns that huge dark women were wearing as muumuus. A hand-lettered sign flapped in the soft leeward wind: EMPLOYEES ONLY.

The girls fluffed their hair and sorted themselves out in pairs. One snatched off a wristwatch at the last minute and handed it to a big woman in a muumuu. Two men picked up drums. Then, off to the right, lurid red and blue lights lit up the manicured tropical forest that surrounded an outdoor restaurant. Under these lights, Whitney saw, as through a scrim, the sad faces of several hundred Americans, all very old. Their faces stretched with longing. A record, very scratchy, came on over the speaker, the Hawaiian war chant.

The boys shook out their arms for looseness as it came their turn to run. Carrying their torches they trotted, chanting, out into the center of the restaurant, bowed to the customers, then ranged themselves around the sides. One man pulled out a conch shell, and blew. The music changed, to "Sweet Leilani." *Sweet leilani, heavenly flower!* The girls waited in the clearing until their cues came. Then, in pairs, they lifted their arms in hula position and undulated out onto the restaurant floor. The applause increased. In the clearing, lit now by the single gas jet, the older women watched, critical and proud, like mothers anywhere.

Hal's right index finger tapped her shoulder. "OK," he said, in an almost normal voice. Whitney turned to see Tracie and Steve watching, too, their elbows set back on the bar, pool water curling around them. Tracie was pretty drunk. "Not *every* day! You don't see that every day." Hal smiled off at the clearing. It seemed a shame to stop looking.

They decided it was time to order something to eat, and sitting out of the water now, up at a table, high and dry by the side of the pool, they ate great plates of spareribs and fresh pineapple. The girls finished everything on their plates, and most of what the men left. From where they were sitting they could catch most of the floor show, which got cornier and cornier. By the time it ended, all four of them were back in the water, doing laps. Whitney thought, With every stroke I shed the past. With every stroke I shed the past.

Hal was the first to quit, and a few minutes later she swam over to the side to be with him, while in the pool the competition got heavy, and Tracie shouted out, "*Another* one, you bastard? Not *another* one!" Their strokes got more erratic, but finally Tracie rested and Steve did two more laps, triumphant. When he swam over to them he ducked his head over to sleek his black hair back, then said, "We could go over to the ocean. See what *that* looks like."

No later than eleven-thirty, maybe midnight. Still eighty degrees. Why not? The bartender made them up double daiquiris in green coconuts. "That way you don't mess up the beach!" The four of them ambled down a set of stepping stones that took them past outbuildings of this old, pretty hotel. Just before they got to the beach, the men stopped at a deck where hundreds of palm mats were rolled and stacked for hotel customers, and picked up a few. Then the path ended. They picked their way through rocks and outcroppings onto a sheltered beach no bigger than a living room. The ocean thumped and foamed, and the sand was creamy as a carpet.

Whitney's eyes filled with tears and for a second or two she went back down that long black slide. Robin will never see this. He will never get to see this. Then she remembered the English lady out in Simi Valley. "He doesn't even know he's dead! Be honest!" If you're here, Robin, take a look.

The men unrolled the palm mats in overlapping patterns, while the girls held all their drinks. The four of them lay down in a row. And it wasn't as if Whitney's mind hadn't been working, ticking, all along. It was. It had been. This is all a come-on. This is what they do all the time. Take a look at how they put those *mats* down! Don't you think the two of them have done that a thousand times before? But the moon registered a kind of whimsical *So?* So *what?* And the waves thudded, so *what?* Tracie, quiet now, registered, under her lashes, so *what?* You've got to do it sometime, why not now? Because, for one reason or another, Whitney had never gotten around to doing it.

Still, she thought she might not do it, because wasn't this a silly way to do it? Shouldn't she wait for something, someone, more significant? But the moon, once she lay back on the warm mats and sand, loomed over her as big as a bicycle wheel. More significant than *this?* Get serious! *Robin?* Are you here or not? Hal, as quiet as she had been, leaned over to kiss her. She'd reserved judgment until then, she really had. Her bathing suit came off, she shut her eyes and let her body feel pleasure, pleasure instead of pain. What a zinger. What a buzz! Notice that, Robin? Hal tapped her at one point to get her to open her eyes, smiled down at her, opened the palm of his hand. What is that, a medal of some kind? A quarter, maybe? She saw it was a condom, neatly rolled. Shut her eyes again. And one way or another in the hours that followed got rid of her virginity, felt pleasure, more than she would have ever guessed, and a couple of times lost herself completely, as any sounds the four of them made were swallowed up by the thuds and wheezes of the waves. Once, her hand, carelessly flung out, caught Tracie's arm, carelessly flung out. They took each other's hands and held on tight, cheating the gods.

CHARLOTTE WATSON SHERMAN

EMERALD CITY: THIRD & PIKE

This is Oya's corner. The pin-striped young executives and sleek-pumped clerk-typists, the lacquered-hair punk boys and bleached blondes with safety pins dangling from multi-holed earlobes, the frantic-eyed woman on the corner shouting obscenities, and the old-timers rambling past new high-rise fantasy hotels—all belong to Oya even though she's the only one who knows it.

Oya sits on this corner 365 days of the year, in front of the new McDonald's, with everything she needs bundled inside two plastic bags by her side. Most people pretend they don't even see Oya sitting there like a Buddha under that old green Salvation Army blanket.

Sometimes Oya's eyes look red and wild, but she won't say anything to anybody. Other times her eyes are flat, black and still as midnight outside the mission, and she talks up a furious wind.

She tells them about her family—her uncle who was a cowboy, her grandfather who fought in the Civil War, her mother who sang dirges and blues songs on the Chitlin Circuit, and her daddy who wouldn't "take no stuff from nobody," which is why they say some people got together and broke his back.

"Oh yeah, Oya be tellin' them folks an earful if they'd ever stop to listen, but she don't pay 'em no mind. Just keeps right on talkin', keeps right on tellin' it."

One day when Oya's eyes were flat and black and she was in a preaching mood, I walked down Third & Pike, passed her as if I didn't know her. Actually I didn't. But Oya turned her eyes on me and I could feel her looking at me and I knew I couldn't just walk past this woman without saying something. So I said, "Hello."

Oya looked at me with those flat black eyes and motioned for me to take a seat by her.

Now, usually I'm afraid of folks who sit on the sidewalks down-town and look as if they've never held a job or have no place to go, but something about her eyes made me sit.

I felt foolish. I felt my face growing warm and wondered what people walking by must think of me sitting on the street next to this woman who looked as if she had nowhere to go. But after sitting there for a few minutes, it seemed as if they didn't think more or less of me than when I was walking down the street. No one paid any attention to us. That bothered me. What if I really needed help or something? What if I couldn't talk, could only sit on that street?

"Don't pay them fools no mind, daughter. They wouldn't know Moses if he walked down Pike Street and split the Nordstrom Build-ing right down the middle. You from round here?"

I nodded my head.

"I thought so. You look like one of them folks what's been up here all they lives, kinda soft-lookin' like you ain't never knowed no hard work."

I immediately took offense because I could feel the inevitable speech coming on: "There ain't no real black people in Seattle."

"Calm down, daughter, I don't mean to hurt your feelings. It's just a fact, that's all. You folks up here too cushy, too soft. Can't help it. It's the rainwater does it to you, all that water can't help but make a body soggy and spineless."

I made a move to get up.

"Now wait a minute, just wait a minute. Let me show you some-thin'."

She reached in her pocket and pulled out a crumpled newspaper clipping. It held a picture of a grim-faced young woman and a caption that read: "DOMESTIC TO SERVE TIME IN PRISON FOR NEAR-MURDER."

"That's me in that picture. Now ain't that somethin'?"

Sure is, I thought and wondered how in the world I would get away from this woman before she hurt me.

"Them fools put me in the jail for protectin' my dreams. Humph, they the only dreams I got, so naturally I'm gonna protect em. No-body else gonna do it for me, is they?"

"But how could somebody put you in jail for protectin' your dreams? That paper said you almost killed somebody."

I didn't want to seem combative but I didn't know exactly what this lady was talking about and I was feeling pretty uneasy after she'd almost insulted me then showed me evidence she'd been in jail for near-murder, no less.

"Now, I know you folks up here don't know much bout the importance of a body's dreams, but where I come from dreams was all we had. Seemed like a body got holt of a dream or a dream got holt of a body and wouldn't turn you loose. My dreams what got me through so many days of nothin', 'specially when it seemed like the only thing the future had to give was more of the same nothin', day after day."

She stopped abruptly and stared into space. I kept wondering what kind of dream would have forced her to try to kill somebody.

"Ain't nothin' wrong with cleanin' other folks' homes to make a livin'. Nothin' wrong with it at all. My mama had to do it and her mama had to do it at one time or nuther, so it didn't bother me none when it turned out I was gonna hafta do it, too, least for a while. But my dream told me I wasn't gonna wash and scrub and shine behind other folks the rest of my life. Jobs like that was just temporary, you know what I mean?"

I nodded my head.

"Look at my hands. You never woulda knowed I danced in one of them fancy colored nightclubs and wore silk evenin' gloves. Was in a sorority. Went to Xavier University."

As she reminisced, I looked at her hands. They looked rough and wide, like hands that had seen hard labor. I wondered if prison had caused them to look that way.

Oya's eyes pierced into mine. She seemed to know what I was thinking. She cackled.

"Daughter, they'd hafta put more than a prison on me to break my spirit. Don't you know it takes more than bars and beefy guards to break a fightin' woman's spirit?"

She cackled some more.

"Un un. Wouldn't never break me, and they damn sure tried. I spent fifteen years in that hellhole. Fifteen years of my precious life, all for a dreamkiller."

I looked at her and asked, "But what did you do? What did they try to do to your dreams?"

Oya leaned over to me and whispered, "I was gonna get into the space program. I was gonna be a astronaut and fly out into the universe, past all them stars. I was gonna meet up with some folks none of us never seen before, and be ambassador of goodwill; not like the fools bein' sent out there now thinkin' they own the universe. I was gonna be a real ambassador of goodwill and then that woman I scrubbed floors for had the nerve to tell me no black maid was ever gonna be no astronaut. Well, I could feel all the broken dreams of my mama and my grandmama and her mama swell up and start pulsin' in my blood memory. I hauled off and beat that fool over the head with the mop I had in my hands till I couldn't raise up my arms no more. The chantin' of my people's broken dreams died down and I looked and there was that dreamkiller in a mess of blood all over the clean floor I'd just scrubbed. And they turned round and put me in jail and never did say nothin' bout that old dreamkiller. Just like my dreams never mattered. Like I didn't have no dreams. Like all I could ever think bout doin was cleanin up after nasty white folks for the rest of my life.

"Humph!" She snorted, and I almost eased to my feet so I could run if I had the cause to.

"You got any dreams, daughter?" Oya asked with a gleam in her eye.

I knew I better tell her yes, so I did.

"Well I don't care if you is from up here, you better fight for your dreams!"

Slowly, I reached out and held one of her rough hands. Then I asked, "But was your dream worth going to prison for all them years?"

Oya looked at me for a long, long time.

"I'm still gonna make it past all them stars," she said as she freed her hand and motioned for me to get to getting.

"Right now, this street b'longs to me and don't *nobody* mess with me or my dreams!" She was still shouting as I walked toward Pine Street.

IT'S COME TO THIS

No horses. That's how it always starts. I am coming down the meadow, the first snow of September whipping around my boots, and there are no horses to greet me. The first thing I did after Caleb died was get rid of the horses.

"I don't care how much," I told the auctioneer at the Missoula Livestock Company. He looked at me slant-eyed from under his Stetson. "Just don't let the canneries take them." Then I walked away.

What I did not tell him was I couldn't stand the sight of those horses on our meadow, so heedless, grown fat and untended. They reminded me of days when Montana seemed open as the sky.

Now that the horses are gone I am more desolate than ever. If you add one loss to another, what you have is double zip. I am wet to the waist, water sloshing ankle-deep inside my irrigating boots. My toes are numb, my chapped hands are burning from the cold, and down by the gate my dogs are barking at a strange man in a red log truck.

That's how I meet Frank. He is hauling logs down from the Champion timberlands above my place, across the right-of-way I sold to the company after my husband's death. The taxes were piling up. I sold the right-of-way because I would not sell my land. Kids will grow up and leave you, but land is something a woman can hold on to.

I don't like those log trucks rumbling by my house, scattering chickens, tempting my dogs to chase behind their wheels, kicking clouds of dust so thick the grass looks brown and dead. There's nothing I like about logging. It breaks my heart to walk among newly cut limbs, to be enveloped in the sharp odor of sap running like blood. After twenty years on this place, I still cringe at the snap and crash of five-hundred-year-old pines and the far-off screaming of saws.

Anyway, Frank pulls his gyppo logging rig to a stop just past my house in order to open the blue metal gate that separates our out-buildings from the pasture, and while he is at it, he adjusts the chains holding his load. My three mutts take after him as if they are real watchdogs and he stands at the door of the battered red cab holding his hands to his face and pretending to be scared.

"I would surely appreciate it if you'd call off them dogs," says Frank, as if those puppies weren't wagging their tails and jumping up to be patted.

He can see I am shivering and soaked. And I am mad. If I had a gun, I might shoot him.

"You ought to be ashamed . . . a man like you."

"Frank Bowman," he says, grinning and holding out his large thick hand. "From Bowman Corners." Bowman Corners is just down the road.

"What happened to you?" he grins. "Take a shower in your boots?"

How can you stay mad at that man? A man who looks at you and makes you look at yourself. I should have known better. I should have waited for my boys to come home from football practice and help me lift the heavy wet boards in our diversion dam. But my old wooden flume was running full and I was determined to do what had to be done before dark, to be a true country woman like the pioneers I read about as a daydreaming child in Chicago, so long ago it seems another person's life.

"I had to shut off the water," I say. "Before it freezes." Frank nods, as if this explanation explains everything.

Months later I would tell him about Caleb. How he took care of the wooden flume, which was built almost one hundred years ago by his Swedish ancestors. The snaking plank trough crawls up and around a steep slope of igneous rock. It has been patched and rebuilt by generations of hard-handed, blue-eyed Petersons until it reached its present state of tenuous mortality. We open the floodgate in June when Bear Creek is high with snow melt, and the flume runs full all summer, irrigating our hay meadow of timothy and wild mountain grasses. Each fall, before the first hard freeze, we close the diversion gates and the creek flows in its natural bed down to the Big Blackfoot River.

That's why I'd been standing in the icy creek, hefting six-foot two-by-twelves into the slotted brace that forms the dam. The bottom board was waterlogged and coated with green slime. It slipped in my bare hands and I sat down with a splash, the plank in my lap and the creek surging around me.

"Goddamn it to fucking hell!" I yelled. I was astonished to find tears streaming down my face, for I have always prided myself on my ability to bear hardship. Here is a lesson I've learned. There is no glory in pure back-breaking labor.

Frank would agree. He is wide like his log truck and thick-skinned as a yellow pine, and believes neighbors should be friendly. At five o'clock sharp each workday, on his last run, he would stop at my blue gate and yell, "Call off your beasts," and I would stop whatever I was doing and go down for our friendly chat.

"How can you stand it?" I'd say, referring to the cutting of trees.

"It's a pinprick on the skin of the earth," replies Frank. "God doesn't know the difference."

"Well, I'm not God," I say. "Not on my place. Never."

So Frank would switch to safer topics such as new people moving in like knapweed, or where to find morels, or how the junior-high basketball team was doing. One day in October, when red-tails screamed and hoarfrost tipped the meadow grass, the world gone crystal and glowing, he asked could I use some firewood.

"A person can always use firewood," I snapped.

The next day, when I came home from teaching, there was a pickup load by the woodshed—larch and fir, cut to stove size and split.

"Taking care of the widow," Frank grinned when I tried to thank him. I laughed, but that is exactly what he was up to. In this part of the country, a man still takes pains.

◆

When I first came to Montana I was slim as a fashion model and my hair was black and curly. I had met my husband, Caleb, at the University of Chicago, where a city girl and a raw ranch boy could be equally enthralled by Gothic halls, the great libraries, and gray old Nobel laureates who gathered in the Faculty Club, where no student dared enter.

But after our first two sons were born, after the disillusionments of Vietnam and the cloistered grind of academic life, we decided to break away from Chicago and a life of mind preeminent, and we came to live on the quarter section of land Caleb had inherited from his Swedish grandmother. We would make a new start by raising purebred quarter horses.

For Caleb it was coming home. He had grown up in Sunset, forty miles northeast of Missoula, on his family's homestead ranch. For me it was romance. Caleb had carried the romance of the West for me in the way he walked on high-heeled cowboy boots, and the world he told stories about. It was a world I had imagined from books and movies, a paradise of the shining mountains, clean rivers, and running horses.

I loved the idea of horses. In grade school, I sketched black stallions, white mares, rainbow-spotted appaloosas. My bedroom was hung with horses running, horses jumping, horses rolling in clover. At thirteen I hung around the stables in Lincoln Park and flirted with the stable boys, hoping to charm them into riding lessons my mother could not afford. Sometimes it worked, and I would bounce down the bridle path, free as a princess, never thinking of the payoff that would come at dusk. Pimply-faced boys. Groping and French kisses behind the dark barn that reeked of manure.

For Caleb horses meant honorable outdoor work and a way to make money, work being the prime factor. Horses were history to be reclaimed, identity. It was my turn to bring in the monthly check, so I began teaching at the Sunset school as a stopgap measure to keep our family solvent until the horse-business dream paid off. I am still filling that gap.

We rebuilt the log barn and the corrals, and cross-fenced our one hundred acres of cleared meadowland. I loved my upland meadow from the first day. As I walked through tall grasses heavy with seed, they moved to the wind, and the undulations were not like water. Now, when I look down from our cliffs, I see the meadow as a hand-made thing—a rolling swatch of green hemmed with a stitchery of rocks and trees. The old Swedes who were Caleb's ancestors cleared that meadow with axes and crosscut saws, and I still trip over sawed-off stumps of virgin larch, sawed level to the ground, too large to pull out with a team of horses—decaying, but not yet dirt.

We knew land was a way to save your life. Leave the city and city ambitions, and get back to basics. Roots and dirt and horse pucky (Caleb's word for horseshit). Bob Dylan and the rest were all singing about the land, and every stoned, long-haired mother's child was heading for country.

My poor mother, with her Hungarian dreams and Hebrew up-bringing, would turn in her grave to know I'm still teaching in a three-room school with no library or gymnasium, Caleb ten years dead, our youngest boy packed off to the state university, the ranch not even paying its taxes, and me, her only child, keeping company with a two-hundred-and-thirty-pound logger who lives in a trailer.

"Marry a doctor," she used to say, "or better, a concert pianist," and she was not joking. She invented middle-class stories for me from our walk-up flat on the South Side of Chicago: I would live in a white house in the suburbs like she had always wanted; my neighbors would be rich and cultured; the air itself, fragrant with lilacs in May and heady with burning oak leaves in October, could lift us out of the city's grime right into her American dream. My mother would smile with secret intentions. "You will send your children to Harvard."

◆

Frank's been married twice. "Twice-burned" is how he names it, and there are Bowman kids scattered up and down the Blackfoot Valley. Some of them are his. I met his first wife, Fay Dell, before I ever met Frank. That was eighteen years ago. It was Easter vacation, and I had taken two hundred dollars out of our meager savings to buy a horse for our brand-new herd. I remember the day clear as any picture. I remember mud and Blackfoot clay.

Fay Dell is standing in a pasture above Monture Creek. She wears faded brown Carhartt coveralls, as they do up here in the winters, and her irrigating boots are crusted with yellow mud. March runoff has every patch of bare ground spitting streams, trickles, and puddles of brackish water. Two dozen horses circle around her. Their ears are laid back and they eye me, ready for flight. She calls them by name, her voice low, sugary as the carrots she holds in her rough hands.

"Take your pick," she says.

I stroke the velvet muzzle of a two-year-old sorrel, a purebred quarter horse with a white blaze on her forehead.

"Sweet Baby," she says. "You got an eye for the good ones."

"How much?"

"Sorry. That baby is promised."

I walk over to a long-legged bay. There's a smile on Fay Dell's lips, but her eyes give another message.

"Marigold," she says, rubbing the mare's swollen belly. "She's in foal. Can't sell my brood mare."

So I try my luck on a pint-sized roan with a high-flying tail. A good kids' horse. A dandy.

"You can't have Lollipop neither. I'm breaking her for my own little gal."

I can see we're not getting anywhere when she heads me in the direction of a pair of wild-eyed geldings.

"Twins," says Fay Dell proudly. "Ruckus and Buckus."

You can tell by the name of a thing if it's any good. These two were out of the question, coming four and never halter broke.

"Come on back in May." We walk toward the ranch house and a hot cup of coffee. "I'll have 'em tamed good as any sheepdog. Two for the price of one. Can't say that ain't a bargain!"

Her two-story frame house sat high above the creek, some Iowa farmer's dream of the West. The ground, brown with stubble of last year's grass, was littered with old tennis shoes, broken windshields, rusting cars, shards of aluminum siding. Cast-iron tractor parts emerged like mushrooms from soot-crusted heaps of melting snow. I wondered why Fay Dell had posted that ad on the Sunset school bulletin board: "Good horses for sale. Real cheap." Why did she bother with such make-believe?

Eighteen years later I am sleeping with her ex-husband, and the question is answered.

"All my wages gone for hay," says Frank. "The kids in hand-me-downs . . . the house a goddamn mess. I'll tell you I had a bellyfull!"

Frank had issued an ultimatum on Easter Sunday, determined never to be ashamed again of his bedraggled wife and children among the slicked-up families in the Blackfoot Community Church.

"Get rid of them two-year-olds," he warned, "or . . ."

No wonder it took Fay Dell so long to tell me no. What she was doing that runoff afternoon, seesawing back and forth, was making a choice between her horses and her husband. If Fay Dell had confessed to me that day, I would not have believed such choices are possible. Horses, no matter how well you loved them, seemed mere animal possessions to be bought and sold. I was so young then, a city girl with no roots at all, and I had grown up Jewish, where family seemed the only choice.

"Horse poor," Frank says. "That woman wouldn't get rid of her horses. Not for God Himself."

March in Montana is a desperate season. You have to know what you want, and hang on.

◆

Frank's second wife was tall, blond, and young. He won't talk about her much, just shakes his head when her name comes up and says, "Guess she couldn't stand the winters." I heard she ran away to San Luis Obispo with a long-haired carpenter named Ralph.

"Cleaned me out," Frank says, referring to his brand-new stereo and the golden retriever. She left the double-wide empty, and the only evidence she had been there at all was the white picket fence Frank built to make her feel safe. And a heap of green tomatoes in the weed thicket he calls a garden.

"I told her," he says with a wistful look, "I told that woman you can't grow red tomatoes in this climate."

As for me, I love winter. Maybe that's why Frank and I can stand each other. Maybe that's how come we've been keeping company for five years and marriage is a subject that has never crossed our lips except once. He's got his place near the highway, and I've got mine at the end of the dirt road, where the sign reads, "County maintenance ends here." To all eyes but our own, we have always been a queer, mismatched pair.

After we began neighboring, I would ask Frank in for a cup of coffee. Before long, it was a beer or two. Soon my boys were taking the old McCulloch chain saw to Frank's to be sharpened, or he was teaching them how to tune up Caleb's ancient Case tractor. We kept our distance until one thirty-below evening in January, when my Blazer wouldn't start, even though its oil-pan heater was plugged in. Frank came up to jump it.

The index finger on my right hand was frostbit from trying to turn the metal ignition key bare-handed. Frostbite is like getting burned, extreme cold acting like fire, and my finger was swollen along the third joint, just below its tip, growing the biggest blister I had ever seen.

"Dumb," Frank says, holding my hand between his large mitts and blowing on the blister. "Don't you have gloves?"

"Couldn't feel the key to turn it with gloves on."

He lifts my egg-size finger to his face and bows down, like a chevalier, to kiss it. I learn the meaning of dumbfounded. I feel the warmth of his lips tracing from my hand down through my privates. I like it. A widow begins to forget how good a man's warmth can be.

"I would like to take you dancing," says Frank.

"It's too damn cold."

"Tomorrow," he says, "the Big Sky Boys are playing at the Awful Burger Bar."

I suck at my finger.

"You're a fine dancer."

"How in God's name would you know?"

"Easy," Frank smiles. "I been watching your moves."

I admit I was scared. I felt like the little girl I had been, so long ago. A thumb-sucker. If I said yes, I knew there would be no saying no.

◆

The Awful Burger Bar is like the Red Cross, you can go there for first aid. It is as great an institution as the Sunset school. The white bungalow sits alone just off the two-lane on a jack-pine flat facing south across irrigated hay meadows to where what's left of the town of Sunset clusters around the school. Friday evenings after Caleb passed away, when I felt too weary to cook and too jumpy to stand the silence of another Blackfoot night, I'd haul the boys up those five miles of asphalt and we'd eat Molly Fry's awful burgers, stacked high with Bermuda onions, lettuce and tomato, hot jo-jos on the side, Millers for me, root beer for them. That's how those kids came to be experts at shooting pool.

The ranching and logging families in this valley had no difficulty understanding why their schoolteacher hung out in a bar and passed the time with hired hands and old-timers. We were all alike in this one thing. Each was drawn from starvation farms in the rock and clay foothills or grassland ranches on the floodplain, down some winding dirt road to the red neon and yellow lights glowing at the dark edge of chance. You could call it home, as they do in the country-and-western songs on the jukebox.

I came to know those songs like a second language. Most, it seemed, written just for me. I longed to sing them out loud, but God or genes or whatever determines what you can be never gave me a singing voice. In my second life I will be a white Billie Holiday with a gardenia stuck behind my ear, belting out songs to make you dance and cry at the same time.

My husband, Caleb, could sing like the choir boy he had been before he went off to Chicago on a scholarship and lost his religion. He taught himself to play harmonica and wrote songs about lost lives. There's one I can't forget:

> Scattered pieces, scattered pieces,
> Come apart for all the world to see.
>
> Scattered pieces, lonely pieces,
> That's how yours truly came to be.

When he sang that song, my eyes filled with tears.

"How can you feel that way, and never tell me except in a song?"

"There's lots I don't tell you," he said.

We didn't go to bars much, Caleb and me. First of all we were poor. Then too busy building our log house, taking care of the boys, tending horses. And finally, when the angina pains struck, and the shortness of breath, and we knew that at the age of thirty-seven Caleb had come down with an inherited disease that would choke his arteries and starve his heart, it was too sad, you know, having to sit out the jitterbugs and dance only to slow music. But even then, in those worst of bad times, when the Big Sky Boys came through, we'd hire a sitter and put on our good boots and head for the Awful Burger.

There was one Fourth of July. All the regulars were there, and families from the valley. Frank says he was there, but I didn't know him. Kids were running in and out like they do in Montana, where a country bar is your local community center. Firecrackers exploded in the gravel parking lot. Show-off college students from town were dancing cowboy boogie as if they knew what they were doing, and sunburned tourists exuding auras of camp fires and native cutthroat trout kept coming in from motor homes. This was a far way from Connecticut.

We were sitting up close to the band. Caleb was showing our boys how he could juggle peanuts in time to the music. The boys tried to copy him, and peanuts fell like confetti to be crunched under the boots of sweating dancers. The sun streamed in through open doors

Lyrics from "Scattered Pieces" by David J. Smith, 1973.

and windows, even though it was nine at night, and we were flushed from too many beers, too much sun and music.

"Stand up, Caleb. Stand up so's the rest of us can see."

That was our neighbor, Melvin Godfrey, calling from the next table. Then his wife, Stella, takes up the chant.

"Come on, Caleb. Give us the old one-two-three."

The next thing, Molly Fry is passing lemons from the kitchen where she cooks the awful burgers, and Caleb is standing in front of the Big Sky Boys, the dancers all stopped and watching. Caleb is juggling those lemons to the tune of "Mommas Don't Let Your Babies Grow Up to Be Cowboys," and he does not miss a beat.

It is a picture in my mind—framed in gold leaf—Caleb on that bandstand, legs straddled, deep-set eyes looking out at no one or nothing, the tip of his tongue between clenched teeth in some kind of frozen smile, his faded blue shirt stained in half moons under the arms, and three bright yellow lemons rising and falling in perfect synchronicity. I see the picture in stop-action, like the end of a movie. Two shiny lemons in midair, the third in his palm. Caleb juggling.

—◆—

It's been a long time coming, the crying. You think there's no pity left, but the sadness is waiting, like a barrel gathering rain, until one sunny day, out of the blue, it just boils over and you've got a flood on your hands. That's what happened one Saturday last January, when Frank took me to celebrate the fifth anniversary of our first night together. The Big Sky Boys were back, and we were at the Awful Burger Bar.

"Look," I say, first thing. "The lead guitar has lost his hair. Those boys are boys no longer."

Frank laughs and points to the bass man. Damned if he isn't wearing a corset to hold his beer belly inside those slick red-satin cowboy shirts the boys have worn all these years.

And Indian Willie is gone. He played steel guitar so blue it broke your heart. Gone back to Oklahoma.

"Heard Willie found Jesus in Tulsa," says Melvin Godfrey, who has joined us at the bar.

"They've replaced him with a child," I say, referring to the pimply, long-legged kid who must be someone's son. "He hits all the right keys, but he'll never break your heart."

We're sitting on high stools, and I'm all dressed up in the long burgundy skirt Frank gave me for Christmas. My frizzy gray hair is swept back in a chignon, and Mother's amethyst earrings catch the light from the revolving Budweiser clock. It is a new me, matronly and going to fat, a stranger I turn away from in the mirror above the bar.

When the band played "Waltz Across Texas" early in the night, Frank led me to the dance floor and we waltzed through to the end, swaying and dipping, laughing in each other's ears. But now he is downing his third Beam ditch and pays no attention to my tapping feet.

I watch the young people boogie. A plain fat girl with long red hair is dressed in worn denim overalls, but she moves like a queen among frogs. In the dim, multicolored light, she is delicate, delicious.

"Who is that girl?" I ask Frank.

"What girl?"

"The redhead."

"How should I know?" he says. "Besides, she's fat."

"Want to dance?"

Frank looks at me as if I was crazy. "You know I can't dance to this fast stuff. I'm too old to jump around and make a fool of myself. You want to dance, you got to find yourself another cowboy."

The attractive men have girls of their own or are looking to nab some hot young dish. Melvin is dancing with Stella, "showing off," as Frank would say, but to me they are a fine-tuned duo who know each move before they take it, like a team of matched circus ponies, or those fancy ice skaters in the Olympics. They dance only with each other, and they dance all night long.

I'm getting bored, tired of whiskey and talk about cows and spotted owls and who's gone broke this week. I can hear all that on the five o'clock news. I'm beginning to feel like a wallflower at a high-school sock hop (feelings I don't relish reliving). I'm making plans about going home when a tall, narrow-hipped old geezer in a flowered rayon cowboy shirt taps me on the shoulder.

"May I have this dance, ma'am?"

I look over to Frank, who is deep in conversation with Ed Snow, a logger from Seeley Lake.

"If your husband objects . . ."

"He's not my husband."

The old man is clearly drunk, but he has the courtly manner of an old-time cowboy, and he is a live and willing body.

"Sure," I say. As we head for the dance floor, I see Frank turn his head. He is watching me with a bemused and superior smile. "I'll show that bastard," I say to myself.

The loudspeaker crackles as the lead guitarist announces a medley—"A tribute to our old buddy, Ernest Tubb." The Big Sky Boys launch into "I'm Walking the Floor over You," and the old man grabs me around the waist.

Our hands meet for the first time. I could die on the spot. If I hadn't been so mad, I would have run back to Frank because that old man's left hand was not a hand, but a claw—all shriveled up from a stroke or some birth defect, the bones dry and brittle, frozen half shut, the skin white, flaky, and surprisingly soft, like a baby's.

His good right arm is around my waist, guiding me light but firm, and I respond as if it doesn't matter who's in the saddle. But my mind is on that hand. It twirls me and pulls me. We glide. We swing. He draws me close, and I come willingly. His whiskey breath tickles at my ear in a gasping wheeze. We spin one last time, and dip. I wonder if he will die on the spot, like Caleb. Die in midmotion, alive one minute, dead the next.

I see Caleb in the kitchen that sunstruck evening in May, come in from irrigating the east meadow and washing his hands at the kitchen sink. Stew simmers on the stove, the littlest boys play with English toy soldiers, Mozart on the stereo, a soft breeze blowing through open windows, Caleb turns to me. I will always see him turning. A shadow crosses his face. "Oh dear," he says. And Caleb falls to the maple floor, in one motion a tree cut down. He does not put out his hands to break his fall. Gone. Blood dribbles from his broken nose.

◆

There is no going back now. We dance two numbers, the old cowboy and me, each step smoother and more carefree. We are breathing hard, beginning to sweat. The claw-hand holds me in fear and love. This high-stepping old boy is surely alive. He asks my name.

"Mady."

"Bob," he says. "Bob Beamer. They call me Old Beam." He

laughs like this is a good joke. "Never knowed a Mady before. That's a new one on me."

"Hungarian," I say, wishing the subject had not come up, not mentioning the Jewish part for fear of complications. And I talk to Mother, as I do when feelings get too deep.

"Are you watching me now?" I say to the ghost of her. "It's come to this, Momushka. Are you watching me now?"

It's odd how you can talk to the ghost of someone more casually and honestly than you ever communicated when they were alive. When I talk to Caleb's ghost it is usually about work or the boys or a glimpse of beauty in nature or books. I'll spot a bluebird hovering, or young elk playing tag where our meadow joins the woods, or horses running (I always talk to Caleb about any experience I have with horses), and the words leap from my mouth, simple as pie. But when I think of my deep ecology, as the environmentalists describe it, I speak only to Mother.

I never converse with my father. He is a faded memory of heavy eyebrows, Chesterfield straights, whiskery kisses. He was a sculptor and died when I was six. Mother was five-feet-one, compact and full of energy as a firecracker. Every morning, in our Chicago apartment lined with books, she wove my tangled bush of black hair into French braids that pulled so tight my eyes seemed slanted. Every morning she tried to yank me into shape, and every morning I screamed so loud Mother was embarrassed to look our downstairs neighbors in the eyes.

"Be quiet," she commanded. "They will think I am a Nazi."

And there was Grandma, who lived with us and wouldn't learn English because it was a barbaric language. She would polish our upright Steinway until the piano shone like ebony. I remember endless piano lessons, Bach and Liszt. "A woman of culture," Mother said, sure of this one thing. "You will have everything."

"You sure dance American," the old cowboy says, and we are waltzing to the last dance, a song even older than my memories.

"I was in that war," he says. "Old Tubb must of been on the same troopship. We was steaming into New York and it was raining in front of us and full moon behind and I saw a rainbow at midnight like the song says, 'Out on the ocean blue!'"

Frank has moved to the edge of the floor. I see him out the corner of my eye. We should be dancing this last one, I think, me and Frank and Old Beam. I close my eyes and all of us are dancing, like in the end of a Fellini movie—Stella and Marvin, the slick young men and blue-eyed girls, the fat redhead in her overalls, Mother, Caleb. Like Indians in a circle. Like Swede farmers, Hungarian Gypsies.

Tears gather behind my closed lids. I open my eyes and rain is falling. The song goes on, sentimental and pointless. But the tears don't stop.

"It's not your fault," I say, trying to smile, choking and sputtering, laughing at the confounded way both these men are looking at me. "Thank you for a very nice dance."

<hr />

I cried for months, off and on. The school board made me take sick leave and see a psychiatrist in Missoula. He gave me drugs. The pills put me to sleep and I could not think straight, just walked around like a zombie. I told the shrink I'd rather cry. "It's good for you," I said. "Cleans out the system."

I would think the spell was done and over, and then I'd see the first red-winged blackbird in February or snow melting off the meadow, or a silly tulip coming up before its time, and the water level in my head would rise, and I'd be at it again.

"Runoff fever" is what Frank calls it. The junk of your life is laid bare, locked in ice and muck, just where you left it before the first blizzard buried the whole damned mess under three feet of pure white. I can't tell you why the crying ended, but I can tell you precisely when. Perhaps one grief replaces another and the second grief is something you can fix. Or maybe it's just a change of internal weather.

Frank and I are walking along Bear Creek on a fine breezy day in April, grass coming green and thousands of the yellow glacier lilies we call dog-tooth violets lighting the woods. I am picking a bouquet and bend to smell the flowers. Their scent is elusive, not sweet as roses or rank as marigolds, but a fine freshness you might want to drink. I breathe in the pleasure and suddenly I am weeping. A flash flood of tears.

Frank looks at me bewildered. He reaches for my hand. I pull away blindly, walking as fast as I can. He grabs my elbow.

"What the hell?" he says. I don't look at him.

"Would you like to get married?" He is almost shouting. "Is that what you want? Would that cure this goddamned crying?"

What can I say? I am amazed. Unaccountably frightened. "No," I blurt, shaking free of his grasp and preparing to run. "It's not you." I am sobbing now, gasping for breath.

Then he has hold of both my arms and is shaking me—a good-sized woman—as if I were a child. And that is how I feel, like a naughty girl. The yellow lilies fly from my hands.

"Stop it!" he yells. "Stop that damned bawling!"

Frank's eyes are wild. This is no proposal. I see my fear in his eyes and I am ashamed. Shame always makes me angry. I try to slap his face. He catches my hand and pulls me to his belly. It is warm. Big enough for the both of us. The anger has stopped my tears. The warmth has stopped my anger. When I raise my head to kiss Frank's mouth, I see his eyes brimming with salt.

I don't know why, but I am beginning to laugh through my tears. Laughing at last at myself.

"Will you marry me?" I stutter. "Will that cure you?"

Frank lets go of my arms. He is breathing hard and his face is flushed a deep red. He sits down on a log and wipes his eyes with the back of his sleeve. I rub at my arms.

"They're going to be black and blue."

"Sorry," he says.

I go over to Frank's log and sit at his feet, my head against his knees. He strokes my undone hair. "What about you?" he replies, question for question. "Do you want to do it?"

We are back to a form of discourse we both understand.

"I'm not sure."

"Me neither."

◆

May has come to Montana with a high-intensity green so rich you can't believe it is natural. I've burned the trash pile and I am done with crying. I'm back with my fifth-graders and struggling through aerobics classes three nights a week. I stand in the locker room naked and exhausted, my hips splayed wide and belly sagging as if to proclaim, Yes, I've borne four children.

A pubescent girl, thin as a knife, studies me as if I were a creature from another planet, but I don't care because one of these winters Frank and I are going to Hawaii. When I step out on those white beaches I want to look good in my bathing suit.

Fay Dell still lives up on Monture Creek. I see her out in her horse pasture winter and summer as I drive over the pass to Great Falls for a teachers' meeting or ride the school bus to basketball games in the one-room school in Ovando. Her ranch house is gone to hell, unpainted, weathered gray, patched with tar paper. Her second husband left her, and the daughter she broke horses for is a beauty operator in Spokane. Still, there's over a dozen horses in the meadow and Fay Dell gone thin and unkempt in coveralls, tossing hay in February or fixing fence in May or just standing in the herd.

I imagine her low, sugary voice as if I were standing right by her. She is calling those horses by name. Names a child might invent.

"Sweet Baby."

"Marigold."

"Lollipop."

I want my meadow to be running with horses, as it was in the beginning—horses rolling in new grass, tails swatting at summer flies, huddled into a blizzard. I don't have to ride them. I just want their pea-brained beauty around me. I'm in the market for a quarter horse stallion and a couple of mares. I'll need to repair my fences and build a new corral with poles cut from the woods.

My stallion will be named Rainbow at Midnight. Frank laughs and says I should name him Beam, after my cowboy. For a minute I don't know what he's talking about, and then I remember the old man in the Awful Burger Bar. I think of Fay Dell and say, "Maybe I'll name him Frank."

Frank thinks Fay Dell is crazy as a loon. But Fay Dell knows our lives are delicate. Grief will come. Fay Dell knows you don't have to give in. Life is motion. Choose love. A person can fall in love with horses.

TOM SPANBAUER

SEA ANIMALS

I asked her to show me what was wrong with him. It was still winter when I asked, sometime within the first ten days of his one hundred days, after he got home from the hospital, before the time when she thought she had smothered him, before the time when the pigs got out, before he died in the spring, after the chores were done, and after school and before supper. I asked her to show me in the late afternoon what was wrong with him, when it was not day and not night, when the shadows were long and running in together and when the chickens flew up to roost, to sit, and to listen to the world.

On the porch, before I went in, before I asked her, I could smell her bathing him. I took off my coat, my cap, my mittens, pried off my overshoes on the top step, and all the while, in there, in the kitchen, I could smell her: the Ivory soap, the steaming water in the porcelain pan, the baby oil, and the clean diapers. All of those were her smell, and his.

These were my chores: to water and feed the hens, to gather the eggs, to water and feed the baby chicks under the brood lamp, and to slop the kitchen garbage to the pigs.

They were Barbara's chores, too, but most of the time I liked to surprise Barbara when she came home from the third grade at the St. Joseph's School and tell her that everything was done and that we were free to do things, to play if Russell wasn't crying; free, for instance, to make cocoa and sit in the kitchen, and free for Barbara to try to show me how to write in longhand the way she could do, and sometimes Mom would come and have some cocoa, too, if Russell was sleeping and wasn't crying.

Another part of my chores was making sure that the doors were locked and that the windows were shut up tight in the coop for the hens, and especially for the chicks. Dad said that if an owl or a hawk or some kind of varmint got in there we'd lose all of the chicks for sure, because the ones who weren't killed right off would suffocate in a heap trying to get away. I want you to know that Dad gave this chore to me especially, not to Barbara, and I was always careful to lock the doors, and I always checked the windows, even though they were too high for me to reach, and sometimes at night I would wake up and think I had forgotten to lock the doors and to check the windows.

◆

Before Russell was born, the new word that everybody said was *brood lamp.* After he was born, they were *incubator, disease,* and *cripple.* That's what I heard the doctor tell Mom, that she had a cripple, and because of his disease, he had to be in an incubator. I heard those words all the time and thought about them all the time, even when I did my chores. I asked Barbara to write them out for me in longhand. I thought about them even more after Russell came home, after they let him out of the incubator and he came home. But he looked just like a baby to me. After all that talk, after all those words so many times, my brother looked like a baby to me.

◆

When I asked her, she did something that she hadn't done in a long time. She picked me up. She leaned her body so that her hip held me. Her arm was around me, the flesh of her arm against my arm, the smell from her armpit under the red housedress. She showed me Russell's head and said, "You see how his head is so much larger than the rest of him is?" And then she showed me his foot. It went over to the side, and she moved it up so that it was straight, and then she let it go, and the foot went crooked again. "That's his foot," she said, and then she sat me on the table. She took Russell's hands in hers. "They will not open," she said. "I have to open them for him and put powder in there for him."

She pried open his right hand and told me to put my finger in there. I didn't want to do it because his palm looked like a terrible blossom to me, or like an egg that the rooster had got to.

She said, "Come on, you wanted to know."

So I put my finger in there and my brother grasped my finger.

◆

Before Russell came home, I don't remember much. There are some photos of me and Barbara, and sometimes of Mom, standing and squinting into the sun that I think I remember living in. But it's hard to say which came first, the photo of me and the experience of living it from it, or the living of it reminded by the photo.

I do remember six things: I remember when our dog Toby died. He came over to me and stood next to me for a while and then did the same thing with Barbara, and then he went into the barn and died on the hay.

I remember Mom saying that animals do that, that they say good-bye before they die.

I remember a lightning storm that blew one of the poplars in front of the house over. The sky was black and it was day and we prayed the rosary loud and lit a candle and Dad wasn't home.

I remember Mom taking the paring knife out of where the silverware was in the kitchen and going outside and sitting on the patch of lawn she had planted and digging dandelions out of the grass with the paring knife.

I remember the Door of the Dead. It was a game that Barbara and I played, and the way you played it was you would go into a room, into the room which Barbara and I had together, and we'd close the door and then you'd say that the closed door was the Door of the Dead, and then we'd get scared, or I should say that I would get scared, and then after saying "The Door of the Dead, the Door of the Dead" over and over again, we'd make scary sounds and then Barbara would open the door, and it was always the same thing, I always was the one who ended up yelling, no matter how many times I told myself I wouldn't yell this time.

I remember that everybody said *brood lamp*.

Before Russell came home, that's it: six memories. But after Russell came home and before he died, those one hundred days, are not just a memory, not just some things I am recalling, and it has always been that way for me.

◆

The house was warm all winter, that winter, and there was steam on the windows that I was not allowed to swipe through, which was ice in the morning and blue, and orange when the sun was up. Dad carried in wood and stacked it high by the stove and on the porch. Sometimes I helped.

Russell cried all the time and never slept, although I know that's not the truth. There were times that he was not crying, times when I stood by his crib and he wasn't crying and he was sleeping. I wasn't allowed near him because he had a lot of mucus and I had a lot of childhood diseases in me like measles and mumps that he could catch and make him more sick, but I still snuck in a lot and looked at his head and his foot, but mostly I looked at his hands, to see if they had opened up yet. Sometimes Russell was awake and not crying and he just lay there quiet, his eyes rolled back up a little, as if he was looking at his head, too, as if he was wondering what to do with all the mucus I could hear up there, wondering when the egg would hatch, as if it was a problem and he was planning a solution, a way to make it go away, and he was trying so hard that it made his hands fists.

I woke up once.

It was spring I think by then, the river was high, and Russell was crying and I was surprised that he was crying just the same way that I had been surprised by his crying when he first got home in the winter, and then I wondered if my brother had always been crying and if I just didn't hear him anymore or if he had stopped for a while, for days, for weeks, and then started up again. My brother's cries were like the sound the pipes made when you turned on the water in the bathtub, that sound, and then the sound like the pipes were singing high, off tune. Sometimes the pipes didn't make that sound, but mostly they did, and sometimes I didn't hear them when they did, and only remembered that they had made that sound when it was over.

◆

That afternoon she ran out of the bedroom and walked around the house, inside, near the walls. I was making incubators with my Tinkertoys on the floor of the front room, Barbara wasn't back from school, and Dad wasn't home. I could hear my mother crying and walking around and around. I thought she might run out into the field and that Dad would have to go bring her back again and he wasn't even home like the last time. I didn't know what to do when she cried but cry, and I didn't know at all what to do if she ran out into the field. And then she said, "Tommy, you have to be a grown-up now. I'll make us some coffee and we'll put the cloth tablecloth on the table and we'll have a cigarette. I've got something I've got to tell you, but you must be a grown-up for it to work, and then you must never tell anybody ever. Do you promise?"

"Yes," I promised.

She took out the tablecloth as she spoke to me, and floated it down onto the table. I had seen her do that with Russell, float his blanket up in the air like that, like a fan, and then let it settle on him, and then flip it up again and then let it settle again. Russell liked that. I think I could see him almost smile whenever she floated the blanket down on him like that, floated it onto him, so soft, like a big bird flying.

I was watching her when she took out the tablecloth, and I wanted to be lying on the table and let it come down on top of me; that clean wave of air, her smell, the slow, graceful descent.

She put four tablespoons of coffee into the percolator and plugged it in. She went to the bathroom and pulled the bobby pins from her hair and fluffed it out, and put lipstick onto her lips, and blotted her lips with a square of toilet paper, and let the square float from her hand into the air onto the floor by her high heels with no toes in them. She had put on her high heels and her nylons with the seams in them and her brown dress with the orchid all the way down the front. I wet my hair and parted it, and put the clip-on tie on my white shirt on the collar, and polished my shoes the way I would do if I was going to church. She poured us coffee in the cups that matched the saucers and she smoked. I smoked, too, French-inhaling, my hair slick, me in my tie with her, with her having coffee in the afternoon.

But it's not the truth.

I didn't smoke.

There was her lipstick on her Lucky Strike, and there was her lipstick on her cup.

"Just now, when I was sleeping with Russell," she said, "I woke up and I was laying on top of him. I thought I had smothered him. I thought he was dead. Tommy, you know what that means, don't you? Dead?"

"Yes," I lied. I didn't know.

I knew the Door of the Dead. I knew that my dog Toby said good-bye first.

"I thought I had killed him," she said. "And this is the part where you have to be a grown-up and never tell, Tommy. Thomas? I was glad," my mother said.

◆

It was spring when the pigs got out. Sometime within the last ten days of his one hundred days, and this day, the day that started out with the pigs getting out, is the most important of all of the one hundred of those days.

Mom had bought a window fan for the window in her bedroom for Russell with her S&H Green Stamps. The June grass was already going dry and the river was back down. Dad had built a pen out of wire fencing and old doors in the corral behind the barn, with part of the pen in the river so that the pigs could lay around in the water and the mud.

Those pigs were in that water all the time. Dad called them the bathing beauties. The brood sow he called Esther. Esther Williams, he called the brood sow.

That day when they all got out was a Saturday, because school was still on and Barbara was home and wasn't sick, and it wasn't Sunday, because we didn't have our Sunday clothes on and didn't go to church. Dad was usually home on Sundays, because there wasn't supposed to be any servile work on Sundays and he wasn't there that day, and so that was the day when Barbara and I walked out the back door of the barn and there were the pigs, out of their pen, squealing around the corral.

"Pigs are out! Pigs are out!" Barbara yelled, and then I yelled it, too.

◆

Mom flipped her fingers the way she always did when she was nervous when she heard anything about the pigs, and went into the bedroom and looked at Russell, who was sleeping. Barbara and I looked in after her. The room was dark and the fan was on. My mother turned to us and put her finger to her lips and motioned for us to get out of there, so we went into the kitchen. We weren't in there long before suddenly a streak of red shot past us. It was Mom.

"Last one to the corral gate is a cow's tail!" my mother yelled, already down the steps of the back porch, opening the screen door, stretching out the screen-door spring and going into the bright large flat dusty world; we followed her, first past the little green square of lawn with no dandelions in it, then past the rose hanging on to the back fence, then past the gas pump, then past the Buick, then onto the graveled yard that stretched out acres between us and the corral gate, Mom ahead, the skirt of her red housedress flying up above her knees, Barbara right behind her, my sister's hair blowing like her mother's, her legs like her mother's—those females.

I stopped running.

I stopped running and stood and watched them running.

Mom cleared the three poles of the fence like a bird flying, like something wild leaping, and Barbara never hesitated. My sister dived under the bottom pole and rolled and stood up next to her mother. They smiled at each other. I stood there and watched, and my mother and my sister smiled at each other. A flock of sparrows flew over the ridgepole of the barn then, between me and the sun, and I was there watching things. The barn, the house, the pole fence, the gate, the pigs out, Mom and Barbara, everything different, everything different and bright, nothing the same, and I felt as if I had never even been anything before.

"Come on! Come on, cow's tail!" my sister yelled at me, waving her arm. "We have to get these pigs in before they get to the river!"

"Sooo-eeee! Soooo-eeee!" Mom yelled.

"Sooo-eeee! Soooo-eeee!" Barbara yelled, and so did I.

We circled the pigs. Mom got between them and the river, Barbara got in the middle and me on the other side, and we herded them slowly back into the pen, our arms out to make us wider.

"Sooo-eeee!" we all yelled.

One of the doors of the pen was down, the closest one to the barn, so we had a corner to herd them into. We were doing pretty well until Barbara pointed to the door lying on the ground, to the door that was part of the pigpen, which the pigs had knocked over, which was lying there like a door into the ground, underneath the dry cow manure. My sister pointed to that door and said, just only so I could hear, "The Door of the Dead."

I was almost standing on it.

I was almost standing on the Door of the Dead.

I jumped right out of there and yelled with all my might, which spooked the pigs, and they ran back out into the corral, through the place where I was supposed to be standing, and went straight to the river, Esther Williams in the lead, and the rest of them after her, the rest of the bathing beauties running after Esther Williams.

◄►

When that fat sow dived off the riverbank, the same way I think a ballerina would dive, poised in the air, and then, when she hit the water, gliding like a seal, gliding as I thought Esther Williams would glide, through the current toward the small island of brambles and scrub elms some feet off from the bank, when that pig just went like that, I stopped and looked again, looked as I had looked before, stopped and looked at what the world looked like. It was a world that was suddenly full of things, mysterious things, things that weren't me.

I could see my mother and my sister doing everything they could do to keep those pigs out of the drink. They were screaming and waving their arms and putting their bodies in front of the pigs, but it was no use. Mom was able to grab one pig by a hind leg and drag it away, but the pig kicked and squealed and Mom didn't have enough energy to pull it any farther, so there they stood, Mom and the pig in the middle of the corral, a standoff, the pig kicking and my mother jerking with every kick. Finally she just had to let go. The pig ran and dived, just like the others, and swam, just like the others, to the island, to where Esther Williams was with the rest of the bathing beauties.

It got quiet then.

Mom just sat down right there in the manure.

They were gone.

All the pigs got wild, got crazy on us, and swam away, dived the way they weren't supposed to, got out of there, swam like other animals, like sea animals, not like pigs, swimming, dumb farm animals diving, swimming, escaping, showing off.

It was then that I saw the owl in the tree on the other side of the river, just above the bank, just a little ways past the island where the pigs were, in shallow water you could wade through right to the tree where the owl was. If you moved your eyes a little, the owl would disappear like magic, but then, if you knew how to look, it would appear again, out of the leaves and out of the twigs, there were its eyes.

"Sons of bitches!" Mom yelled.

She picked herself up off the ground and picked up a hard horse turd and threw it at Esther Williams. And then she picked up a rock. She spun in circles, around and around, winding up for the pitch, twirling, a dust devil, her arms in the air, her skirt riding up, a dance, and hurled the rock with a sound from her inside and deep, a grunt, and the rock sailed through the air and went through the window of the chicken coop, the side where the baby chicks were. There was a little sound, a slight shattering in the sunny afternoon, and that was all.

"Sons of bitches!" my mother cried, her fists, like Russell's, aimed at the sky. "Damned sows, damned sows sons of bitches!"

I didn't tell Dad about the broken window in the coop, because Russell died the next day. No, actually, it was Monday that Russell died, because the next day, the day after the pigs got out, was Sunday, and on that day Dad got the pigs back in with the horse, had to lasso each pig and bring it across one at a time, even though it was a Sunday, but it was an emergency and not that servile.

I was picking up my Lincoln Logs off the floor of the front room, or Tinkertoys; Barbara hadn't been home long, and I had done the chores. I had leaned a board in front of the broken window and was going to tell Dad about it at supper. We were going to make cocoa, because Russell wasn't crying. Mom was sitting in her special chair, she and Russell's special chair, holding him the way she always did, rocking, when she said, "Go get your father—Russell's dead."

◆

This part is not as clear as the other parts.

What happened next are these things: Monsignor Cody was there, and so were Aunt Marguerite and Uncle Pat, and more people. I was supposed to stay in my room and so was Barbara. In the kitchen, on the table, was the cloth tablecloth and the percolator and the cups with matching saucers, a chocolate cake and red Jell-O with fruit cocktail in it and bananas. They put Russell in his bassinet in the bedroom. I wasn't supposed to go in there, but I went in there when nobody was in there, even though there were people everywhere, some of them crying. The fan was off and there were candles all around him and everything was white: the blankets, the bassinet, his nightie.

It smelled like him in there, like her.

He was just lying in there the same way I had seen him so many times, his eyes closed, the covers pulled around him. I touched him a little on the shoulder, through his nightie, and he was no different. But then I pulled the cover back and saw his hands. They were open, palms up, sunny-side.

◆

On the day of the funeral it rained. Barbara says it was sunny, but I remember that there were umbrellas and that we all stood under umbrellas, and that I was wearing my overshoes. I stood to the right of the monsignor and the altar boys. I got to smell the incense. My grandmother was behind me. Barbara stood by me on the side, and then Aunt Marie, Aunt Zita, Aunt Alma, Aunt Marguerite, and then Mom here on the other. Dad had bought her a new coat. It was navy-blue, with big buttons. Behind Dad stood my other grandma and Great-aunt Monica.

When they lowered the casket, I thought about the Door of the Dead in the corral on the ground that day the pigs got out and that Russell was still alive, but this is what is most important about what happened that day and the thing that I remember most of anything, in those days, those one hundred days. It's that Dad started crying so hard that they had to wipe the rain off the folding chair so he could sit down. As soon as I saw him sit down like that, I was on my way to him, and I was halfway there, just past Aunt Alma and almost to Aunt Marguerite, before Grandma, the one behind me, got ahold of my arm and pulled me back, past the flowers, past the Door of the Dead, and put me back in my place; in my place in front of her, back in my place, seven females from my father.

◆

There was a reception at St. Joseph's Hall.

Barbara showed me her classroom, although we weren't supposed to go upstairs. I heard Aunt Zita say that it was a blessing, because there was so much wrong with him. Afterward, we went home. Mom drove, and when we got home I changed my clothes and did my chores. The board was down from the window of the coop and all the chicks were dead. It looked to me that those who weren't killed right off by the owl had smothered in the corner, in a heap, trying to get away.

KATHERYN STAVRAKIS

◆

THE ROOM

Helen emerges from the runway ramp, her jacket over her shoulders and her purse locked in her arm, and looks past the row of expectant faces lined up at the railing, across the hallway to the windows, and out the other side to the blue runway lights. At the periphery of her vision she is aware of Bill standing back from the others. And though she knows the boy, Wayne, is there too, Helen does not really see him until she leans across the railing and he throws his arms around her.

She pats Wayne lightly on the back and pulls away to circle the railing, and then they are both before her, watching; uncertain. She kisses Bill quickly and says, "I guess we'd better go get my bags."

Helen and Bill walk side by side and the boy first hangs back, then makes a few running leaps ahead of them, then back again, all the way down the hallway of the airline terminal.

"How was your flight?" Bill asks.

"Fine," she answers. "Fine."

He tries to tease her. "Bet you had a drink on the plane, thinking about us."

"No," Helen says, and she thinks, *I must say something to the boy. I have said nothing to the boy.* He is ahead of them now, leaping from one foot to another.

"Did you watch the plane come in?" she says to his back.

"No," he says without turning around.

"Yes, he did," Bill adds quickly. "He was so excited he was glued to the window, watching for your plane."

◆

The dim lights in the pickup don't work so Bill uses the high beams. On the other side of the road, approaching cars flick their headlights in annoyance. Light illumines them for an instant, then fades just as quickly. They are all three sitting in the cab of the pickup, Helen in the middle, her knees pulled up over the hump, her purse pulled tightly into her lap.

Rain spatters the windshield—heaped mounds of snow melt in the rain. Along the road, trees stand jagged, their fallen branches littering the snow.

"I want it to snow, Dad. Do you think it'll snow again?"

"Don't think so, fella," Bill answers across her. "That was pretty unusual for Oregon." He inclines his head toward her. "Quite a storm we had. Ice, snow, power lines down. But I guess you heard about it on the news."

"But Dad." The boy leans across Helen and peers anxiously out into the rain. "I want it to snow, why won't it?"

"Would you just sit back and relax? I'm trying to talk to Helen." He half turns to her again. "Didn't you?"

"Didn't I what?"

"Hear about the storm on the news?"

"Dad—"

"SIT BACK AND BE QUIET."

The boy throws himself back against the seat, his chin dropped to his chest. They pass through a small town—doors stand open. Helen sees a large hall with a few pool tables; a handful of people are scattered about, indolent in the vast, smoky interior. They pull up to a traffic light. At the intersection, a tight band of teenagers stands before the ragged pasteboard advertisements of a movie theater—rain from the gutter lining the roof shoots in a heavy stream over their heads and into the street, but they seem not to notice. For a moment, the traffic light casts a reddish glow over Bill's face.

Helen pulls in her elbows around her purse. "Where are we?"

"Lents. Part of Portland. Not the best part." Bill smiles and shakes his head. "After all the times I've told you how Oregon is God's country, the first thing you see now is Lents in the rain."

The boy jumps forward. "Oh wow, did you see that pile of snow, Dad? That wasn't even a pile, that was a mountain!" Then, just as suddenly, "Are you guys married?"

"No," Bill says with a hint of annoyance. "You know we're not." There is a pause.

"Are you going to get married?"

"Maybe."

Wayne considers this, then leans close to Helen and tilts his head, squinting at her. "Are you going to sleep in bed with my dad?"

"Yes."

"How come?"

Helen maintains a silence until Bill says, "Because we love each other. When two people love each other they like to sleep together."

Wayne wrinkles his nose and fixes a stare on Helen. Then he purses his lips and starts to make loud kissing noises. "Oh sweetie, sweetie . . . I love you . . . sweetie. . . ."

"That'll be enough." Bill's arm shoots out across Helen. "I told you to sit back. It's late. Lay your head back and close your eyes till we get home. Dad and Helen haven't seen each other for several months, and we want to talk without being interrupted."

As he sinks backward again, Helen catches his smirking look.

The wipers groan across the windshield. It is as though, now that there is quiet, they can think of nothing more to say. Helen turns her head slightly to watch the boy's profile. His brows are drawn into a perpetually worried frown, as if he were always figuring a puzzle that is too hard for him. She can see the glistening of his upper lip where his nose is running. His mouth hangs open. He does not seem ten years old, she thinks. And Helen feels a deep, sudden pain, a longing for what is missing. She does not love the boy. She doesn't even know if she can like him.

Of course she knew about Wayne before this. They'd even stopped to see her in Maryland and she'd taken him to the zoo and bought him presents. Bill had explained how the boy came into his life. He'd been visiting relatives when he heard an odd sound coming from another room. Bill asked about it, and they told him the story of Wayne, a child of alcoholic parents; a child with scars where his hands were pressed against a hot stove. When state workers found him in the middle of winter in an unheated cabin, they also discovered his baby brother stuck to a mattress, frozen in his own urine.

Wayne was in foster care, but soon would be sent to another home, the nineteenth in his four years of life. He was too difficult, the relatives had said. Life was too short.

Bill had excused himself. The voice, thin, high and animal-like, mesmerized him, and he followed it to its source. At first he saw no one in the bedroom, but as he adjusted to the light, Bill spotted the boy huddled on a bed. His eyes, deep shadows under a ragged fringe of black hair, hardly focused. He couldn't speak, but continued his soft moaning. He was so slight, such an insignificant shape under the blanket, that it seemed to Bill as if God had barely finished the job of creating a body to house this fragile soul. And at that moment, he knew he would take the child.

In the pickup, Wayne has fallen asleep and slumps against Helen. She watches his distorted image wavering in the windshield and tries to understand what makes him so different. It was in the way he held his hands, his long thin arms; always in awkward positions as though he were trying to imitate the people around him with no success. It was his thinness, no matter how much he ate, that gave his head a skull-like appearance, and made it seem oddly large. And in that continually puzzled look, as though he had just been rebuked for something he didn't understand.

Helen stares ahead into the rain-washed road, lined with gas stations and burger restaurants. A red neon horseshoe imprinted with the name "Sirloin Stockade" passes into her vision, then out again. A flush of defiance rises to her face. *What do you expect of me? I'm not a saint,* she thinks, challenging the dark sky that surrounds them as they huddle, all three, in the cab of the pickup.

For six years she had lived with her own brother's illness and slow death from multiple sclerosis. Helen can see it now, the room with a hospital-sized bed pushed up against the blue wallpaper and a urine bag attached to it, and by it a nightstand with the perpetual bottles and tissues, water glasses and pills. And on the wall, blue and red ribbons from the athletics he loved so much, the poster board on which they were pinned now yellowed.

The road seems to be quickly falling away from them, and Helen has the sensation that they are running after it, but can never seem to catch up. A marquee before a large chain supermarket with a name Helen doesn't recognize advertises:

MIRACLE WHIP   98¢
APPLESAUCE
PORK CHOPS

Yes, Helen thinks. She had put in her time in antiseptic waiting rooms, leafing through magazines while he went to physical therapy. And worked with him, trying to coax his lips into forming words, when his speech was going. Fed him, while food dripped from the sides of his mouth and down his plastic bib. And hadn't they sat together, he slumped in his chair, she across from him reading aloud when his eyes could no longer focus, the two of them confined in a circle of lamplight?

She had listened to his moaning late at night, in the room next to hers—a moaning she could not muffle or mute, even with a pillow covering her head, and that took the form of her own name, *He-lenn, He-lenn*. She could hear him against the wall, and imagined him shifting and tossing in the dark. And still the moaning, low but persistent, which she could not stop except by going to him and staying there in the darkened room, leaning against the bed railing, trying not to touch the catheter tube for fear of pulling it out. Remembering the lullaby her mother had used to soothe their childish fears, she would sing:

> *Guten Abend, gute Nacht*
> *Mit Rosen bedacht*
> *Mit Näglein besteckt*
> *Schlupf unter die Deck'*
> *Morgen früh, wenn Gott will*
> *Wirst du wieder geweckt*
> *Morgen früh, wenn Gott will*
> *Wirst du wieder geweckt.*

In the small fluorescent light from the alarm clock, she would see his face and the glimmer of recognition there, and she would keep singing as he gradually grew quieter. She had entered that room with its peculiar heavy smell that no amount of disinfectant could, it seemed, scrub away—in that room she would purposely take shallow breaths, as though she could avoid what it held simply by refusing to breathe the air.

Now Helen is keenly aware of the pungent burned air, the same as she remembers it from her last visit. It is a smell that pervades everything within several miles of the paper mill, seeping even through the thin crack in the closed car window.

Etched in her mind Helen sees, as she has over and over again, the image of her mother on that last day, holding him as he vomited blood on the front of her print dress. And as she imagines it, the details of the scene blur and fade until all that remains is an outline in bold strokes, like a painting, and the powerful image of a mother, every mother, not hers alone. Every mother who has ever looked into the face of her dying child.

No, Helen thinks. *I can't save anyone. I'm just human, nothing more.*

They have left the business area and are following a long dark road alongside a river—and then, up ahead in a brilliant orange haze of light and smoke, the long towers and pipes of the paper mill come into view. The eerie glow in the night creates a striking effect, transforming the usual drabness of the mill. The smell has grown, it seems to Helen, even stronger.

"I hate it," Helen says aloud.

"What?"

"I hate that smell."

She has apparently spoken more sharply than she intended, for Wayne, beside her, stirs out of his sleep.

◆

"You haven't had a good word to say since you got here." An hour later, Helen is lying in a hot tub trying to soak away a headache. Bill leans against the bathroom wall.

"What is there to say?" She pushes the hot water spigot with her foot. "I can't deal with him. I can't imagine living with him all the time."

"Maybe my mother can take him weekends. Or we can get a sitter."

Helen reaches for the soap. "You said yourself how hard it is to get sitters for him. He's so demanding, wanting attention all the time."

"All children want attention."

"You refuse to face reality." She sits up straight and speaks slowly, emphasizing each word. "He is not like other children. He's strange. The way he jumps around and doesn't listen when people talk to him. Like a wild animal."

Bill pauses. Finally, he says, "Just give it some time. With a good school, with a real home . . ."

"I don't think good intentions are enough." Helen shakes her head and says, almost to herself, "What makes you want to rush in and save someone, anyway? My god, what makes you think you *can?*"

"Helen." He steps closer. "You knew the situation before you came out. You have a choice."

"Some choice."

"Well, what the hell am I supposed to do?" The words come stronger than Bill intends and seem to hang in the air. Helen and Bill stare across the space between them.

Finally, Bill takes off his glasses and rubs his eyes. "Look, I'll be in the bedroom." His shoulders, always a bit stooped, seem more so than usual.

When he goes out, Helen climbs out of the tub and wraps herself in a clean towel that Bill has left for her. In the hallway, she sees that the door to Wayne's room is ajar. It is decorated with his school picture—Wayne sitting behind a desk in a new cowboy shirt and smiling, with only a trace of the usual suspicion narrowing his eyes. Tacked beneath the photo is an award with a blue ribbon that says, "For Wayne Johnson—A Good Workweek—Nice Job!" Helen turns her back and quietly pushes open the opposite door, to the other bedroom.

Bill is seated on the edge of the bed in his boxer shorts and socks, staring ahead of him at the floor. When he looks up, she turns away, as if to see the room.

It is small and sparse. There is the double bed, its sheets pulled crookedly across it. *He never could make a bed,* she thinks, and smiles. One bureau and a gun cabinet, his prized possession, which now stands empty, for the safety of the child. There are no piles of dirty clothes—Helen realizes that he has cleaned up for her arrival.

She crosses to the window, where whitish curtains hang limply from a metal rod, and pulls one back. A ragged field stretches to a dark patch of trees. She lets it fall again. On the bureau beside her are Bill's dress shoes, carefully placed side-by-side, hardly worn. And above the bed, the museum poster she had sent him from her trip to New York stands out against the nondescript wall. Even with the windows closed tight, she can still smell the paper mill.

He is pale, drained of color by the yellow light overhead, his dark eyes darker than usual; waiting. She crosses to stand in front of him. She touches his hair, then gently lifts off his glasses, and smiles as he begins to blink. He takes the glasses from her hand and places them with great care on the plastic seat of the folding chair, next to the alarm clock.

It is at this moment that, for the first time, Helen becomes fully aware of the noise—a noise that has been gradually becoming more insistent. It is a thin, high sound, like that of an animal whining.

She drops her hand. "What is that?"

"Wayne. He's singing."

"Why does he do that?" She is unable to hide the trace of irritation.

"He has trouble getting to sleep. So he sings to himself."

"Well, how long does this go on?"

"Sometimes for hours."

For a moment longer, Helen stands there. Then she goes to her suitcase, slips on her flannel nightgown, and climbs into the opposite side of the bed, her back to Bill. The mattress creaks as he rises. She senses the room darken as he turns out the light, then feels him come and lie pressed against her back.

"Helen."

She doesn't answer.

"You are what I need. But I can't give him up unless I'm sure."

She opens her eyes to stare at the wall.

"Helen. Tell me what you want."

She lies awake in the dark listening to the soft, high hum gradually grow fainter.

◆

Helen awakes in the night, unsure how much time has passed, unable to remember when she fell asleep. Even before she becomes fully conscious, she knows it was a dream that awoke her—she dreamed there was something burning. She half sits up in bed, taking deep breaths and growing accustomed to the dark. Yes, she still smells it. Carefully, she slips to the foot of the bed and pushes up the window a crack. It creaks with age, but Bill does not awake. *He must be so tired,* she thinks.

And then, yes, she remembers—it comes to her. The paper mill —she is in Oregon City and the mill is operating. Helen leans against the window and thinks how at that very moment, while they sleep, there are people in that mill, working. In the dark of the field, she sees again the haze of smoke and somewhere within it, the people— incredible that they survive; impossible. She sees their forms wavering in the intense heat amid the towers and the brilliant smoke rising into the night as if it were all part of some vast explosion. As she is brooding on this, Helen realizes that she hears it again—the singing; the thin, high voice.

It can't be, she thinks. *It is too late. No, I am dreaming. I am still asleep.* And she quickly pushes down the window and curls up in bed, closing her eyes.

It is still there.

Helen pulls the pillow over her head and presses it with her fist against her ear. The singing, thin as a cry, goes on.

Helen lies there with the pillow pressed against her ear, for a moment, or longer; she can't tell how long, but there is no sign that it will stop. Bill does not awake.

Carefully, she slips out of the blankets and trembles as her feet touch the cold floor. She feels her way around the bed and into the hallway, and stands there, listening.

It is a high, tuneless song, a jumble of words—a song that seems to come from some inner place, as when one wakes from a deep sleep, and speaks, but the words hold no meaning that anyone else can grasp.

Helen pushes open the door. At first she can't see him, but sees only the outline of his bed. Then she begins to make out his form, so slight that it barely shows under the huddle of covers. He doesn't stop; doesn't even seem aware of her. He is lying on his back, singing into the dark. She comes up to the edge of the bed. He is small, so thin, his dark eyes vivid in his face. He is still singing, though more softly than before, and he is watching Helen.

"You can't sleep," she says.

He shrugs.

The nightlight casts a small circle on the floor by her feet. "How about if I sing to you and you think about sleep?"

He is still watching her, the singing now down to an uncertain hum.

She sits on the edge of the bed, very carefully, for he seems so fragile. "You know, I had a brother once, and when he was worried in the night or had bad dreams, I would sing to him."

PRAGMATISTS

I don't pretend to understand the forces that push our lives in the directions they follow, but the summer I was twelve years old I saw enough to make me wonder at them. My mother moved us to eastern Oregon early that spring, to Court Rock and the farm she'd inherited from my grandparents. They'd sold a few of the parcels closest to town to a developer who put up tract houses. My mother swore never to sell another inch of land when she saw those houses.

"There's nothing here," my brother Wayne said as we drove into Court Rock.

"There's plenty here," my mother said, "and part of it is ours."

I tried to see the land as my mother described it, and to imagine her being a young girl in this place. The sloping hillsides were covered with juniper and brush, and layered by abrupt rimrocks. Looking at them rising up from the Two Cabin River left me with a weightless feeling, like the three of us would have a new chance here, and who we'd been no longer mattered.

Wayne was against the move. He wanted to be an architect, and planned on going to the University of Oregon when he graduated. He drew perfect, straight lines without a ruler, and his handwriting was the same way, all precise angles and straight edges.

The farm was run down; the ground had lain fallow for over ten years. We didn't have money or equipment to tackle the forty acres in a big way, so my mother decided we'd reclaim it a piece at a time, in blocks small enough that hand labor could make a difference. Early in May, we planted an acre and a half of corn, tomatoes, potatoes, and peppers. We didn't get any frosts after the plants came up, so my mother said we were off to a good start. But the weeds were off to a better start. All those dormant seeds came to life and sprouted with water and cultivation.

My mother found work at the grocery store in town, so she gave Wayne and me the job of weeding. Wayne was to get the money from produce we sold for college. He didn't like the arrangement. Wayne was seventeen and wanted to be working on one of the big alfalfa farms on the river. It was a constant source of irritation between him and my mother.

She said the land was ours, and she wanted to work it rather than line someone else's pockets. "I've worked for other people long enough," she said. "Now we have this place and I want us to know what it's like to do for ourselves."

School ended the weekend before Memorial Day, and Wayne and I started weeding. We'd worked at it evenings after school but hadn't gained any. My mother made us breakfast and left for work at seven; then Wayne and I headed for the garden, or the fields, as my mother called it. At first it was hard to see where the weeds stopped and the plants started, but within two weeks Wayne and I had the rows hoed out, and started pulling the weeds closest to the plants. We worked every day until two o'clock. I enjoyed working out there with Wayne, and if he didn't enjoy it, he at least accepted that it was going to be his summer job. But that all changed when Brady started coming around again.

Brady lived with us for most of the last two years we were in Springfield. He was a man my mother enjoyed being with and at times even loved, despite her best efforts. I was young, and I liked Brady; having him there was as easy for me as not. But Wayne was old enough that Brady's presence changed his role with our mother, and not in a way he liked.

Brady played the guitar and cards. He'd been injured in a logging accident up in Alaska years ago, and between his settlement and what he won at poker, he got by. He played country and folk music; a lot of Woody Guthrie tunes. He sang songs like "Tom Joad" and "This Land Is Your Land," with all the verses you never learn in school. Then he'd tell us about how Woody was a voice for the working man.

Things were always prickly between Brady and Wayne. The garden was the one issue they agreed on. As soon as Brady showed up, he said we should have planted just enough to feed ourselves. "If people in this country want farm-fresh produce, they'll grow it," he said.

The bottom line was that Brady thought Mom should sell most of the farm and keep just the house and a few acres around it. One night, when they were sitting out on the porch, I heard them from my bedroom window.

"When those zoning laws come in, you'll either have to sell all of it or nothing," Brady said.

"That's fine," my mother said. "I don't plan on selling any of it."

"There's no way a small farm can make money," he said. "Look down the river, all the places making a go of it are big outfits."

I heard the metal patio chair creak as Brady stood, then his boot heels thumped up and down the porch. "Dammit, Kay, I just want to see you and the boys have something."

"What about your man Woody Guthrie?" my mother said. "Wasn't he all for the small farmer?"

"Yeah, he was," Brady said. "But remember 'Roll on Columbia'? Woody was working for BPA when he wrote that. Who do you think dammed the river?"

"What in the hell does that have to do with this?" my mother said.

"I'm just saying sometimes it pays to be a little pragmatic about the situation. A great song came out of doing what it takes to get by. Sometimes you do what you have to and look at the bigger picture."

I heard my mother's softer footsteps cross the porch and the screen door slammed.

As the weather turned hotter, Brady was gone more. He made trips to Bend, or Boise, and sometimes Portland. Usually he came home from these trips broke, but once in a while he returned flush with cash, and when he did, he was generous. That meant Black Hills Gold jewelry for my mother and fishing rods for Wayne and me. One time, Brady brought Wayne a copy of *Architectural Digest*. Wayne's English teacher gave him her old copies, and he saved all of them.

"No more looking at them dog-eared old things, sport," Brady said as he tossed the magazine to Wayne. "Four bucks for a bunch of advertisements, but here you go."

◄━━◆━━►

Later, while we were hoeing, Wayne told me about an adobe house in the magazine. "The whole thing is basically made of dried mud," he said.

"It'll fall apart when it rains," I said.

"No, I don't think so. This house is in New Mexico, but I bet it would work here, too. This is almost like desert."

Wayne and I hoed up and down the rows and the dirt sifted into my tennis shoes and gritted between my toes. A fine film of dust covered us and ran in dirty, brown streaks from our sweat. I looked over where we'd weeded yesterday and saw damp spots where the sun drew water up from cut stems. One evening I'd brought my mother out here and shown her those spots.

"They're beautiful, Charlie," she'd said, and hugged me tight. "Look at all that water those weeds suck up, and just think of all the nutrients. Now all that will go to the corn and potatoes. I think we're doing fine, Charlie."

Walking down those rows with my mother, I thought we were doing fine, too. With the sun down and the soil still warm, the garden seemed like a different place. And I'd wished that Brady and Wayne were there to see it.

It was almost noon when Wayne and I heard a car come up the driveway. There were willows between us and the house, so we could see dust boiling up but couldn't see the car. "Maybe it's Brady," I said. He'd been gone for almost a week.

"Didn't sound like his pickup to me," Wayne said, and kept on hoeing.

"Shouldn't we go see?"

"If they want something they'll come out here or leave us a note. It's probably some salesman."

The car didn't leave, and no one walked out to the garden. I chopped at weeds halfheartedly and kept looking toward the house, trying to see through the willows. Finally Wayne quit hoeing and walked to the edge of the garden. "Let's go see who it is," he said. "It's lunchtime anyway."

We walked toward the house, stomping our legs to shake off loose dirt. I realize now that Wayne probably knew a lot more about Brady than I did, so he might have had an idea that the car involved him in some way.

When we were through the willows and could see the yard, there was a man sitting in one of the chairs at the end of the porch. He held a straw hat in his hands and wore a white shirt with the sleeves rolled up. He had on snakeskin cowboy boots and a big silver and turquoise belt buckle. "Hello, boys," he said as we crossed the yard. "Looks like you been rolling in the dirt."

"No, we've been hoeing weeds," I said.

"I can see that from those blister sticks you're packing," he said.

"What can we do for you?" Wayne said.

"A man in town told me I might find a friend of mine here. A guy by the name of Brady Wilson."

"He's not here," Wayne said, crossing the yard and leaning his hoe on the porch.

"Well, that's too bad," the man said. "Can you tell me when he might be back?"

"We don't know when, or if he's coming back," Wayne said.

"I kind of thought you might say that," the man said, picking up his straw hat and twirling it on his finger. "But I'll tell you what, if you don't mind, I might just sit here in the shade awhile and wait."

I looked at the man sitting there, and that turquoise and silver reminded me of Wayne's adobe house, and I wondered if this was a man who would live in a house like that.

"I told you we don't know if he's coming back," Wayne said.

"And you told me you didn't know when he was coming back," the man cut in. "Now, what if I took off, and not five minutes later old Brady drove up that road. Wouldn't that be a stupid thing for me to do?"

Wayne sat down on the porch and I went over and leaned my hoe beside his, then sat down. The direct noonday sun beat down and bleached the dry yard of color. I could hear the sound of grasshoppers rattling their wings from the perimeter of the yard. When I walked to town with my mother and heard them in the bushes, I thought they were rattlesnakes. "Don't worry," she said. "When you hear a rattler you'll know it." And she was right. Wayne and I were hiking on the back side of the place a few days later when a rattlesnake buzzed from under a rockjack. I didn't have to wonder, I jumped straight up before I had a chance to register the sound. And I felt that way about this man in our yard. I knew the turquoise and silver on his belt buckle were real. By watching him and from the way Wayne acted, I knew he was genuine.

Wayne sat on the porch with his hands on his knees and seemed to be measuring something, calculating things I could only guess at.

"You fellas look hot and tired," the man said. "Is there anything in the house we might drink while we wait?"

"There might be some lemonade," Wayne said.

"Lemonade, lemonade," the man said. "To hell with lemonade. A couple big boys like you coming in from the fields, I'd think you'd have a cold beer."

"There isn't any beer," Wayne said.

"No beer in the house, huh? What's Brady going to drink when he gets home?"

"I don't know, and I don't care," Wayne said, standing up. "Why don't you just leave. We told you we don't know anything about Brady."

"Sit down, you little shitheel," the man snapped. "Now, you look here; Brady Wilson owes me five hundred and fifty dollars, and he's damned sure going to cover it. You got that?"

"I got that, I got that all right," Wayne said. "But that's between you and Brady. Don't bring us into it."

"Well, you are into it. See that car out there?" the man said, pointing to a big silver car in the driveway. "That's a Lincoln Continental, and I didn't get it by letting assholes like Brady Wilson run back to hick towns and hide behind kids."

"How did you get it?" I asked.

"Shut up, Charlie," Wayne said.

"No, that's a good question," the man said. "Deserves an answer. I got that car by moving money around. Moving it from people too dumb to keep it to people that wanted it, needed it. Hell, money isn't any good for some people, only causes them trouble. The sooner they're rid of it, the better. Now go in the house and get us some of that lemonade."

I didn't know which one of us he was talking to. I started to stand, but Wayne put his hand on my shoulder and stood up. The man watched him go into the house. I sat there on the porch and started wishing Brady would come. He could handle this, I thought, he got along with people.

Wayne pushed the screen door with his shoulder and walked out with a glass of lemonade in each hand. He gave me one, then took the other to the man.

"Thanks," the man said. "We'll get along okay, no reason not to. You just get ahold of Brady and tell him to come home and we'll work this out."

I took a sip of my lemonade. It was cold and tart. My mother had mixed it before she left for work. Wayne went back in the house to get some lemonade for himself. I thought about asking the man to tell me about moving this money around, but I decided to wait until

Wayne came back. I took another drink and watched the man over the rim of my glass. I heard the screen door fly open, and a look of surprise shadowed his face for an instant, then vanished. I looked up and saw Wayne pointing my grandfather's bolt-action Winchester .22 at the man's forehead.

The man took a drink of lemonade and crunched an ice cube with his teeth. "What in the hell do you think you're going to do with that?" he said through the ice.

"You finish that lemonade, then leave," Wayne said, holding the gun level.

I looked back and forth between the muzzle of the gun and the man's forehead, and I could see the exact spot where the bullet would enter. I'd watched Wayne shoot ground squirrels from fifty yards with that gun, and I knew he wouldn't miss.

The man set the glass between his legs and put his hands on the arms of the lawn chair. "I'll tell you something," he said. "If I was of a mind to, I'd walk over there and kick your ass, then take that gun for part of what Brady owes me."

"You'd never make it out of the chair," Wayne said.

The total lack of emotion in Wayne's voice and the way he held that Winchester convinced me that the man wouldn't make it out of the chair. Whether it was something that had been there all along, or had just sprung up, I knew Wayne was someone real, too. I could tell from the man's expression that he'd decided Wayne might actually shoot him. He didn't look worried or nervous, though. He put the sweaty glass to his temple and held it there, and now he was doing the measuring. I knew he was checking distance between him and Wayne, and him and me. I could feel the man's eyes on me, calculating actions and reactions, and I moved back toward Wayne.

That was when I knew this was something I was going to see concluded. I knew that either the man was going to leave, or Wayne was going to shoot him. I felt almost relieved. Everything had seemed open-ended since we'd come to Court Rock. Brady came and went, my mother worked in the store and wanted to be farming, and Wayne put in his time before he left for college. But I knew there wasn't going to be any gray area about this. It was something that was going to be settled.

The man swallowed the last of his lemonade. "I'll tell you what," he said. "I'm standing up, and I'm leaving, for now."

"If you have a gun in your car, don't try it," Wayne said. "If you don't get in and turn that thing right around, I'll start shooting."

The man opened his mouth to say something, but he didn't. Then he stood up and walked slowly to his car. When he reached it, he pulled up the door handle and watched us. Wayne kept the .22 pointed at his head, but I could no longer determine the exact spot where the bullet would hit.

The man smiled and opened the door. He climbed in, started the car, and backed up. When he turned around the wheels spun, and dust and gravel rooster-tailed into the air. I saw the car disappear into dust, and only then, when it was completely gone, did Wayne lower the gun.

"He's not going to come back," I said.

"I don't think so," Wayne said.

"He didn't bluff us, did he, Wayne?" I said. "Wait until we tell Brady how you backed him down."

"Brady's an asshole," Wayne said. "Don't you tell him anything."

Brady came back about a week later, but only long enough to pick up his things. He'd heard what happened and said he sure hadn't meant to bring any trouble on us. Looking back now, I believe he was sincere. Other things changed, too, but not in ways so sudden or tangible. My mother resigned herself to a long stint at the grocery store, and Wayne quit drawing building plans and became sullen. He put his *Architectural Digests* in a box and never looked at them. My mother said it was his way of distancing himself so it would be easier to leave, but I knew it ran deeper.

Wayne quit talking about the University of Oregon and its School of Architecture altogether. Two weeks after Labor Day he enlisted in the navy. He wrote me letters for the first few years. The last one was from Norfolk, Virginia. It was written in a flowing cursive that I couldn't connect to Wayne. He said he liked the navy and the sense of control in his life.

For a long time I thought about Brady and I thought about Wayne, but never together or at the same time. And then one day I was thinking about Wayne moving all over the country to different naval bases, and I remembered Brady traveling through the West with his guitar and pickup. That was when I decided that Wayne and Brady were pragmatists in the same way. I realized that neither of them wanted responsibility for my mother and me, and neither of them was interested in the commitment to a person or a place to the point of taking whatever came with it.

Brady had been that way for as long as I'd known him. As for Wayne, I'm not sure. I wondered if maybe that day on the porch had just overwhelmed him. If maybe he'd been forced to face down his whole life at once, and he'd had to turn away.

I stayed in Court Rock, and I'm not saying that was wrong or right. I'm thirty-five years old now and still live in that farmhouse with my mother. I planted our farmland into alfalfa and drive a school bus route for a steady income. Sometimes on January mornings when I'm warming up that yellow bus, and watching the exhaust float up into the frozen dawn, I feel pragmatic myself. I used to think about leaving every year. But when I'm out in the field during the summer, and I watch a thunderstorm build over those high, basalt rimrocks, and see the rain coming down in streaks, I know I'll never leave. The wind sweeps down, and brings with it the smell of rain on the dry soil, mixed with pungent sage and juniper, and I take the air in gulps.

The music I listen to is still that spare, open sound of men and guitars. When I play a Woody Guthrie or Dylan album, I picture all that distance in our lives, and how it's up to each of us to fill it the best way we can.

ELIZABETH TALLENT

◆

MIGRANTS

◇◇◇◇◇◇◇

S issy isn't a small-town girl at heart—only through a steady refusal of circumstances, luck and love, to align themselves her way. Two years ago, Sissy's mother left Iowa with her boyfriend for L.A.; now they manage a trailer park of unpaved lanes and old palms whose lowest branches are dead, dry fans. Sissy's father sells the big Rain Cats, irrigation sprinklers that pivot around fields cut circular to accommodate them, the air above the pipes stunned with heat, the winter wheat below abruptly glistening, so that a long shadow seems towed by the sprinklers across a solid light-tan plane. Immediately below the pipes is the dividing line, drawn slowly forward, between drenched and parched, with the crossed wheat darkening in a sharp stretch and throwing off a thin, prismatic spume, or entire moving rainbows no bigger than birds' wings. Someday, Rafer says in his sales pitch, all of this will be run by computers, and in a far field the linked arms of Rain Cats will spring to life whether anyone is there to see them or not.

Just after Sissy's junior year of high school, Rain Cat relocated Rafer to Wheaton, Colorado, and paid for the Mayflower van. Sissy left a boyfriend Rafer didn't know about; Rafer left a bowling-alley waitress Sissy did. His new territory is vast and marginal, dusty fields of wheat, alfalfa, soybeans, and sugar beets worked by wetbacks and owned by farmers who are barely making it and already have too much capital tied up in obsolete heavy equipment—the kind of men, Rafer says, who shyly tap toothpicks from the plastic dispenser beside the cash register when they finally pay for the cup of coffee they nursed all morning long, and whose own fathers were so poor they cut the eyes from potatoes, planted the eyes, and boiled the potatoes to feed their families. All spring in Wheaton, where she knows no one and nobody seems to be under forty anyway, Sissy has been lonely; all spring Rafer has been on the road. Once when she thought she was cracking up, he warned her long-distance, "Sissy, it's a good thing I'm gone. If I wasn't gone, would I be making sales?" More gently, "Don't you know I go through this all week because I want a future for you?" Gentlest of all, "You're not going to grow up into one of those women who think the world owes them a living."

"Daddy, don't talk like that." Because she knew he meant her mother.

"We're in this together, aren't we? You just want to keep your head. I know that I can count on you."

Rafer says she shouldn't live for the weekends, but on Saturday nights they eat steak in a restaurant and he tells her about his week. Sunday mornings they take Joe, Rafer's dog, and his old .22, and drive out to one of the arroyos where a million shattered bottles lie, and Rafer steadies her arm while she shoots chips of glass, and sometimes dimes, from the eroded wall. She likes the way the dust floats up and smokes away. When they come home her hair is always lighter, her shoulders sunburned, and she cooks dinner for them both. Joe licks Rafer's face to wake him up, weekend mornings, and Rafer lifts Joe's floppy ear and sings into it as if it's a microphone, until Joe growls.

◆

Sissy stops her bicycle at a windmill far out in the grasslands—stops as if windmill water, scummed with algae the dead landlocked green of pool-table felt, has some faint connection to clear Rain Cat water; stops as if Rafer, wherever he is, can feel her stopping. Though there seems to be no wind, the windmill blades keep turning, and blades of shadow switch with light on Sissy's face. The heat pausing on her cheek is pleasant, though she's almost sure the part in her hair is burning, her forehead and nose flecking with more ugly, sharp freckles. Now that she's resting, the gloss of sweat, absent throughout the long bike ride, pricks her shaved armpits—a feeling like the beginning of a rash. A mourning dove lands on the holding tank's rim, peers at Sissy, fails to see her, and flutters to the ground, which is rutted by thousands of sunbaked cattle tracks, hoping to find a track that still cradles an inch of sour water. It used to puzzle her that the birds wouldn't bathe in the holding tank, but then she figured it out—it is impossible for a dove to drown in a cattle track.

She tips her bicycle up and walks it back to the highway, studying low bluffs that fade backward into a line of identically eroded, shades-paler bluffs; under the shadows of small moving clouds, the bluffs seem to be folding and unfolding. Between her and them lie a hundred miles that are nothing but empty. After that a thousand miles, and after that, L.A. Ah, she hates it here. *Hates* it. From dry weeds drawn into the bicycle spokes, a hail of grasshoppers patters against her bare legs. When their wings flick open, oval dapples form glaring eyes precise down to the honey iris and darker pupil. The eyes wink out as the grasshoppers fasten again onto trembling grass, and Sissy looks behind her at the bicycle's snaking track. All that way for what? For nothing.

But the highway radiates a tarry heat different from the heat of the grass, and exchanging one for the other is a relief. For an hour, by the watch loose on her sweating right wrist, she is the only moving thing in that landscape. Stranded on the horizon is a peaked farmhouse gray with weather, its frame sides narrow as shutters closed against noon. This farmhouse has always depressed Sissy. She shakes her head, the bicycle wobbles dangerously, and from behind there is a blare of sound, rusty but convincing. Astonished, she looks over her shoulder to find a Gypsy line of junk cars, moving probably at thirty miles an hour, so that, as they very gradually gain on her, she can drink it in: the candied sweetness of hot car paint, a whiff of burning engine oil and the cigarette smoke of the drivers, who are all young Spanish men; the charred doors wired shut with coat hangers, windshields that are cobwebs of fracture sealed by graffiti of yellowed tape; other windows ballooning with wet shirts or hung with ragtag, brilliant bits of underwear; grandmothers sleeping in the improvised shade of diapers flapping as they dry. Sissy loves them for having appeared behind her, out of nowhere. The dusty dashes hold groves of plastic saints, and rosaries wag from the rearview mirrors. A child sucking on its fist pushes aside a pair of fluttering pantyhose and gazes out at her. Another child pushes up beside the first, yawns widely, peels up a damp T-shirt, and shyly scratches a scarred chest. Sissy, too, feels shy. She is so exposed on the bicycle. They're migrants, she knows, up from Mexico for the summer. That, too, is cause for shyness, because the migrants who camp and work in the fields around Wheaton are shunned by the Anglos. Rafer has told her some cruel things he's seen.

The grown women all seem to be sleeping, many with children sprawled across their laps. Sleeping children look so much hotter than sleeping adults, Sissy thinks. They look as if they've fainted, their hands loose and their hair stuck to their foreheads. She laughs when a passing car shows the soles of two tiny bare feet resting flat against a window rolled halfway up. The heels are black. Gusts of real heat hit Sissy between the cars. She feels she belongs with them now, and resists falling behind. She chooses a Cadillac with scorched fins and burnt-out taillights, and tires herself in keeping alongside it; she wonders whether the driver, who never once glances sideways, has speeded up a little to lose her, and then she wonders at the enraged alarm she feels, knowing that he has. It is a brief battle. The Cadillac noses gently, very gently, into her lane, and she is forced to slow onto the shoulder. She feels flat amazement: Why did he do that? The Cadillac eases back into line, and the cars are gone. The highway's two lanes go desolate, the silence extremely definite. She sees a Coke bottle someone threw from a window. The bottle is rolling down the yellow line above its own delicately coasting shadow, to a hollow tone that seems to come from far away.

◆

In Wheaton's post office there is a clerk, nearsighted Mr. Cox, who loves twiggy young trees fresh from the nursery, and Sissy likes him for that, though he is old and often cranky. Sprinklers fret across the dozen new dogwoods staked along the sidewalks, their slim trunks bandaged in gauze like the legs of colts. "Good for you, Coxy," Sissy says to herself. In fact, according to Rafer, Mr. Cox is less hostile to wetbacks than post-office clerks in the surrounding small towns are, and on Saturdays the migrants can be found, in from the fields, patiently waiting for Mr. Cox to hand them the money orders necessary to convey their entire paychecks home to Mexico. The ruined cars that passed Sissy three weeks ago in the grasslands are lined up now along the yellow curb in front of the post office. She glances into an ancient Chevrolet with a corroded hood; an empty baby bottle is nested upright in a child's torn sneaker. She shoulders open the glass door, and the men inside, scarcely turning, make way for her so subtly that she sees only their shaven napes, sunburned even through the darkness of the skin, and the backs of thin white shirts showing the ghosts of undershirts. There is a good, sharp barbershop smell. She stands, biting her lower lip, while the line dissolves away from her, the men gravitating toward a wall of wanted posters, making it seem that there is something irresistible and natural in their attraction to this wall.

Mr. Cox, squinting up from his scales, sees her standing alone. "Well, Sissy," he says. "This is a pleasure. Come on up."

"I can't, Mr. Cox," she says. "I was last in line."

He aims around himself a mole's assessing squint, suddenly exposed to light. "No line left, Sissy."

"But there was."

He assents, "I guess there was. You may as well take advantage."

"That's exactly it, Mr. Cox."

"What's exactly what?"

"If I came to you, I'd be taking advantage." She nods to the wall of wanted posters, but she means the men, and he knows she means the men.

Mr. Cox looks moleishly amused. "Did you see my trees, Sissy?"

"They're great trees. I like dogwoods. You did all of that?"

"Nobody else was about to," he says sourly. She has offended him. With Mr. Cox it always happens so fast. Where she has offended, Sissy has always felt an instant need to appease, and this, though nothing else would have, gets her to the counter, where she must hand over her letter to her mother, aware, suddenly, that she is being watched. She examines the backs of the silent men from the corner of her eye. One is leaning against the counter, not having removed himself as far as the others from her exchange with Mr. Cox. Rafer said that one of the migrants speaks a wary but quite good English, and stays by the counter all day, using the post-office pen on its chain of chrome beads to fill in the money-order forms for the others, who speak only Spanish. Rafer guessed that in Mexico he had been a teacher. Now, though she is not absolutely sure she is right about who he is, she smiles, the smile divided lightly between Mr. Cox and the young migrant and falling on no one. Mr. Cox, unbemused, gives an economic lick to her stamp, and strikes it onto the letter's corner with his fist. "In here all day," he says, leaving off the *I've been* because he knows she knows that, "I forget what English is supposed to sound like. This all you came in for, Sissy? *One* stamp? We have these with wildflowers on 'em. I got the first sheets and thought of you."

She shakes her head.

"I thought you'd like 'em," he complains. "See?"

"You're busy," she says, to remind him of the migrants' silence.

"Always am, Sissy," he says. "Don't let it fool you that there's usually nobody in here. Nice to see you. Did you like those trees of mine?"

"Very much," she says.

"*Bueno hay,*" he says to the young teacherlike migrant. "Let's get this damn operation under way again, *qué no?*"

The migrant fingers the glossy pen at the end of its chain and pulls a fresh set of papers near. "O.K.," he says politely. Mr. Cox squints at the migrant and the pen with moleish rue, his mouth shut grimly. Sissy senses he dislikes this day-long appropriation, by the young teacher, of U.S. Postal Service property.

◀━━━▶

Dead, the jackrabbit lies with its legs stretched out behind it and its chin pillowed on the leaf of a wild gourd, halting the trembling of that one wide, insect-frayed leaf, though the other leaves still rock along the rabbit's back and past its outflung heels, showing here and there, within the pointed shadows the leaves cast against each other, the hot yellow trumpet of a flower. A bloody cowlick is hardening at the base of the rabbit's skull, and a stray ant searches the pads of its extended forefoot, where the claws indent the coarse fur in snug stitches, each claw a pale husk with a curved marrow of compacted dust grains. Joe shudders beside Sissy with the intensity of the effort required to *stay;* he yawns and begins to pant. Tears fall from his tongue straight to the ground, where the dust pops into craters quick as those holes that percolate in wave-wetted sand. His ears are laid back, his eyes anxiously narrowed in the guilty look of a dog who is waiting for a human to perform some minor but necessary task. She whistles, willing Joe to glance at her, but he continues to stare at the rabbit in the leaves. His sense of what is right is as severe and un-swerving as his gaze: She cannot shoot something and leave it to the crows.

She squats to draw the rabbit out by its hind legs, the smudged leaf, as the rabbit's head slides from it, springing up with an injured jack-in-the-box wobble. She tears a leaf away and wipes the ants from the rabbit's fur, trying to get them all, because they're red ants and can sting. For some reason, she is being gentle.

"All right, Joe." She stands, and bends for the .22. "Is that what you wanted?" He only yawns foxily and trots away, looking back just often enough to make sure they're still a pair, that he doesn't get so far ahead that she feels abandoned: she is a responsibility Rafer has left with him. They are roughly a mile from the pickup, which she left on the highway's shoulder, and to get there they will cross a pair of irrigation ditches separated by an expanse of eroded furrows and wild grass dyed a starchy, faintly pink tan by the summer. Joe leaps the first irrigation ditch with several feet to spare, then circles back and wades into the massed reflections of the cattails on the bank. He drinks noisily, water striders skating between his legs, and once he snaps at a dragonfly. Sissy crosses above him on a bridge that is a single rocking plank. She lays the rabbit on the far end, puts the gun down, and takes off her sneakers. The dark water folds itself around her ankles and her reflection melts downstream in idle zebra stripes. The wind makes all of the reeds on the bank bend together, into each other, with a sound like slapping. She arches her feet and spreads her toes as wide as they will go. She examines her freckled arms for fleas from the rabbit. She shot it out of the worst sort of boredom, because it sat up in the field in front of her when Joe wasn't in the way, and she is sorry for it now. The rabbit's eye made a neat brown marble of a target, smaller than a chip of glass in the arroyo wall. This is Sunday, and Rafer was supposed to have been home last night; so it is almost sure he will be coming in tonight, and she can beg pearly garden potatoes and carrots from her neighbor, and slice them for a stew.

When she lifts her feet out, they feel silky, as if with algae, though they're quite clean. Joe looks up, water running from his jaws and chest. She picks up the gun, lifts the rabbit, and hastily changes her grip: its legs have stiffened, and the hocks resist her grasp in knuckly points, like a pair of dice. Joe is out of the water and far ahead, not even troubling to look over his shoulder this time, and she doesn't even try to keep up. The rabbit's head swings, upside down, past the arched tips of dry grasses.

Cautiously, she avoids a prickly pear that has occupied the peeling basin of an ancient tractor tire; some of the prickly pear's pads are engraved with zigzags of tire tread. In front, Joe gives two short, sharp barks—of warning—as she moves into the deep cattails of the second ditch's bank. She comes out beside Joe, who is sitting quite still on the steep bank, and together they look down at the young migrant who has been bathing there. The man cups his genitals in his hands and stares up at her, amazed and wild. Only after a shocked silence does she remember the gun in her hand and the rabbit she holds by its heels. She lets the rabbit slide slowly into the reeds, which close over it, and then kneels in studied slow motion, still facing the migrant, to lay the gun behind her, within reach but on the ground. She stays like that, very nearly kneeling, very nearly at eye level with the man in the stream.

His eyes are large, his lips drawn away from his teeth in a fear so extreme it seems unreal to her. She tries to think whether she has ever really frightened, really terrified anyone in her life before, and knows that she hasn't—not like this, and not even close. A thin white shirt is pinned like a kite in the cattails behind him. He had wanted to keep it dry, or air his sweat from the cloth, and this is a revelation of his fastidiousness, of something as private as his nakedness. She loves the half-floating, half-sagging shirt. She shakes her head softly, meaning it as an apology to him. She wants to apologize for coming so suddenly through the reeds, for forgetting the gun, for the way Joe is watching him, a strict surveillance. For everything. He must have understood what she wanted, because he says—oddly, perhaps even ironically, but with a certain sweetness—*"Mil gracias."* It is a phrase she has always liked. A thousand is so many, so generous.

Then, startled at seeing what—distracted by his nakedness—she hadn't seen before, she is sure that she knows him, that he is the schoolteacher from the post office. It is so quiet that she can hear the water running between his thighs. *"De nada,"* she says. It is nothing.

It isn't nothing. She has seen in his face how scared he was, and she watches the significance of this dawn on him. He bends forward until the water laps across his flat belly. It is a clumsy position, but his body to the chest is hidden from her. He is still cupping himself, under the water. She can see his hands dimly.

"Do you speak any English?" she says.

His hair is dripping into his eyes, and he no longer wishes to look at her; it is as if he has an answer, and is deliberately withholding it. She likes the clean line of his cheekbone, the gravely downcast glance, but there is something mocking and set about his dark upper lip, where the mustache is a feathery trace. He looks over his shoulder to his shirt. She understands that this means she should now back away; she should let him get his shirt. She almost wants, so silently instructed, to do so, yet she wants—it is so exquisitely clear what she wants that she can't, for the fraction of an instant, condemn herself for wanting it—to watch him rise from the water.

Joe releases them from the game of statues. He laps noisily from the ditch and sniffs at the young migrant, who holds out his hand shyly. Joe ignores the hand. It is tipped up slightly, the fingers curled and at ease, the palm a grid of old cuts, some healed, others healing. The man begins to make coaxing noises, musical little whimpers. Coins of light reflected from the current float over his dark shoulders like minute spotlights. His chest, when he extends his arm, is adazzle. He smiles to himself at the dog's stubbornness. She knows that he will never, if he can help it, look at her again. He knows something is wrong with her from the way she is just standing there, but he doesn't know what it is, or how to free himself of her.

"You could talk to me if you wanted," she says. "Please? *Por favor?* You don't understand. I've heard you talk. I know you."

She tries to think if there is anything else she can say. There isn't. There simply isn't. She doesn't know any more Spanish. The man in the stream whines gently, like a dog.

◆

That night, to make up for having been gone longer than he'd warned her he would be, and for whatever else it is that is wrong (something is), Rafer drives her the forty miles north to Cheyenne for a movie. She watches the taillights of the car before them blink and elide into the corner of his eye like a tear swept sideways by the wind. Then the red light vanishes and his eye is clear and dark until another set of taillights appears in it. She wonders where, in the unlit fields stretching away from the highway, the young migrant is, and what his life will be like after this. Rafer takes her hand in the dusk of the theater before the movie begins, rubs their two sets of knuckles along the armrest, and whispers, "This was a long way to come for a movie. You ought to feel properly grateful," and though for a moment she is, she does feel that, she whispers back, "Daddy, I want a bus ticket to L.A."

My daughter wanted to go to China for her second honeymoon, but now she is afraid.

"What if I blend in so well they think I'm one of them?" Waverly asked me. "What if they don't let me come back to the United States?"

"When you go to China," I told her, "you don't even need to open your mouth. They already know you are an outsider."

"What are you talking about?" she asked. My daughter likes to speak back. She likes to question what I say.

"Aii-ya," I said. "Even if you put on their clothes, even if you take off your makeup and hide your fancy jewelry, they know. They know just watching the way you walk, the way you carry your face. They know you do not belong."

My daughter did not look pleased when I told her this, that she didn't look Chinese. She had a sour American look on her face. Oh, maybe ten years ago she would have clapped her hands—hurray!—as if this were good news. But now she wants to be Chinese, it is so fashionable. And I know it is too late. All those years I tried to teach her! She followed my Chinese ways only until she learned how to walk out the door by herself and go to school. So now the only Chinese words she can say are *sh-sh, houche, chr fan,* and *gwan deng shweijyau.* How can she talk to people in China with these words? Pee-pee, choo-choo train, eat, close light sleep. How can she think she can blend in? Only her skin and her hair are Chinese. Inside—she is all American-made.

It's my fault she is this way. I wanted my children to have the best combination: American circumstances and Chinese character. How could I know these two things do not mix?

I taught her how American circumstances work. If you are born poor here, it's no lasting shame. You are first in line for a scholarship. If the roof crashes on your head, no need to cry over this bad luck. You can sue anybody, make the landlord fix it. You do not have to sit like a Buddha under a tree letting pigeons drop their dirty business on your head. You can buy an umbrella. Or go inside a Catholic church. In America, nobody says you have to keep the circumstances somebody else gives you.

She learned these things, but I couldn't teach her about Chinese character. How to obey parents and listen to your mother's mind. How not to show your own thoughts, to put your feelings behind your face so you can take advantage of hidden opportunities. Why easy things are not worth pursuing. How to know your own worth and polish it, never flashing it around like a cheap ring. Why Chinese thinking is best.

No, this kind of thinking didn't stick to her. She was too busy chewing gum, blowing bubbles bigger than her cheeks. Only that kind of thinking stuck.

"Finish your coffee," I told her yesterday. "Don't throw your blessings away."

"Don't be so old-fashioned, Ma," she told me, finishing her coffee down the sink. "I'm my own person."

And I think, How can she be her own person? When did I give her up?

◆

My daughter is getting married a second time. So she asked me to go to her beauty parlor, her famous Mr. Rory. I know her meaning. She is ashamed of my looks. What will her husband's parents and his important lawyer friends think of this backward old Chinese woman?

"Auntie An-mei can cut me," I say.

"Rory is famous," says my daughter, as if she had no ears. "He does fabulous work."

So I sit in Mr. Rory's chair. He pumps me up and down until I am the right height. Then my daughter criticizes me as if I were not there. "See how it's flat on one side," she accuses my head. "She needs a cut and a perm. And this purple tint in her hair, she's been doing it at home. She's never had anything professionally done."

She is looking at Mr. Rory in the mirror. He is looking at me in the mirror. I have seen this professional look before. Americans don't really look at one another when talking. They talk to their reflections. They look at others or themselves only when they think nobody is watching. So they never see how they really look. They see themselves smiling without their mouth open, or turned to the side where they cannot see their faults.

"How does she want it?" asked Mr. Rory. He thinks I do not understand English. He is floating his fingers through my hair. He is showing how his magic can make my hair thicker and longer.

"Ma, how do you want it?" Why does my daughter think she is translating English for me? Before I can even speak, she explains my thoughts: "She wants a soft wave. We probably shouldn't cut it too short. Otherwise it'll be too tight for the wedding. She doesn't want it to look kinky or weird."

And now she says to me in a loud voice, as if I had lost my hearing, "Isn't that right, Ma? Not too tight?"

I smile. I use my American face. That's the face Americans think is Chinese, the one they cannot understand. But inside I am becoming ashamed. I am ashamed she is ashamed. Because she is my daughter and I am proud of her, and I am her mother but she is not proud of me.

Mr. Rory pats my hair more. He looks at me. He looks at my daughter. Then he says something to my daughter that really displeases her: "It's uncanny how much you two look alike!"

I smile, this time with my Chinese face. But my daughter's eyes and her smile become very narrow, the way a cat pulls itself small just before it bites. Now Mr. Rory goes away so we can think about this. I hear him snap his fingers, "Wash! Mrs. Jong is next!"

So my daughter and I are alone in this crowded beauty parlor. She is frowning at herself in the mirror. She sees me looking at her.

"The same cheeks," she says. She points to mine and then pokes her cheeks. She sucks them outside in to look like a starved person. She puts her face next to mine, side by side, and we look at each other in the mirror.

"You can see your character in your face," I say to my daughter without thinking. "You can see your future."

"What do you mean?" she says.

And now I have to fight back my feelings. These two faces, I think, so much the same! The same happiness, the same sadness, the same good fortune, the same faults.

I am seeing myself and my mother, back in China, when I was a young girl.

◆

My mother—your grandmother—once told me my fortune, how my character could lead to good and bad circumstances. She was sitting at her table with the big mirror. I was standing behind her, my chin resting on her shoulder. The next day was the start of the new year. I would be ten years by my Chinese age, so it was an important birthday for me. For this reason maybe she did not criticize me too much. She was looking at my face.

She touched my ear. "You are lucky," she said. "You have my ears, a big thick lobe, lots of meat at the bottom, full of blessings. Some people are born so poor. Their ears are so thin, so close to their head, they can never hear luck calling to them. You have the right ears, but you must listen to your opportunities."

She ran her thin finger down my nose. "You have my nose. The hole is not too big, so your money will not be running out. The nose is straight and smooth, a good sign. A girl with a crooked nose is bound for misfortune. She is always following the wrong things, the wrong people, the worst luck."

She tapped my chin and then hers. "Not too short, not too long. Our longevity will be adequate, not cut off too soon, not so long we become a burden."

She pushed my hair away from my forehead. "We are the same," concluded my mother. "Perhaps your forehead is wider, so you will be even more clever. And your hair is thick, the hairline is low on your forehead. This means you will have some hardships in your early life. This happened to me. But look at my hairline now. High! Such a blessing for my old age. Later you will learn to worry and lose your hair, too."

She took my chin in her hand. She turned my face toward her, eyes facing eyes. She moved my face to one side, then the other. "The eyes are honest, eager," she said. "They follow me and show respect. They do not look down in shame. They do not resist and turn the opposite way. You will be a good wife, mother, and daughter-in-law."

When my mother told me these things, I was still so young. And even though she said we looked the same, I wanted to look more same. If her eye went up and looked surprised, I wanted my eye to do the same. If her mouth fell down and was unhappy, I, too, wanted to feel unhappy.

I was so much like my mother. This was before our circumstances separated us: a flood that caused my family to leave me behind, my first marriage to a family that did not want me, a war from all sides, and later, an ocean that took me to a new country. She did not see how my face changed over the years. How my mouth began to droop. How I began to worry but still did not lose my hair. How my eyes began to follow the American way. She did not see that I twisted my nose bouncing forward on a crowded bus in San Francisco. Your father and I, we were on our way to church to give many thanks to God for all our blessings, but I had to subtract some for my nose.

—

It's hard to keep your Chinese face in America. At the beginning, before I even arrived, I had to hide my true self. I paid an American-raised Chinese girl in Peking to show me how.

"In America," she said, "you cannot say you want to live there forever. If you are Chinese, you must say you admire their schools, their ways of thinking. You must say you want to be a scholar and come back to teach Chinese people what you have learned."

"What should I say I want to learn?" I asked. "If they ask me questions, if I cannot answer . . ."

"Religion, you must say you want to study religion," said this smart girl. "Americans all have different ideas about religion, so there are no right and wrong answers. Say to them, I'm going for God's sake, and they will respect you."

For another sum of money, this girl gave me a form filled out with English words. I had to copy these words over and over again as if they were English words formed from my own head. Next to the word NAME, I wrote *Lindo Sun*. Next to the word BIRTHDATE, I wrote *May 11, 1918*, which this girl insisted was the same as three months after the Chinese lunar new year. Next to the word BIRTHPLACE, I put down *Taiyuan, China*. And next to the word OCCUPATION, I wrote *student of theology*.

I gave the girl even more money for a list of addresses in San Francisco, people with big connections. And finally, this girl gave me, free of charge, instructions for changing my circumstances. "First," she said, "you must find a husband. An American citizen is best."

She saw my surprise and quickly added, "Chinese! Of course, he must be Chinese. 'Citizen' does not mean Caucasian. But if he is not a citizen, you should immediately do number two. See here, you should have a baby. Boy or girl, it doesn't matter in the United States. Neither will take care of you in your old age, isn't that true?" And we both laughed.

"Be careful, though," she said. "The authorities there will ask you if you have children now or if you are thinking of having some. You must say no. You should look sincere and say you are not married, you are religious, you know it is wrong to have a baby."

I must have looked puzzled, because she explained further: "Look here now, how can an unborn baby know what it is not sup- posed to do? And once it has arrived, it is an American citizen and can do anything it wants. It can ask its mother to stay. Isn't that true?"

But that is not the reason I was puzzled. I wondered why she said I should look sincere. How could I look any other way when telling the truth?

See how truthful my face still looks. Why didn't I give this look to you? Why do you always tell your friends that I arrived in the United States on a slow boat from China? This is not true. I was not that poor. I took a plane. I had saved the money my first husband's family gave me when they sent me away. And I had saved money from my twelve years' work as a telephone operator. But it is true I did not take the fastest plane. The plane took three weeks. It stopped every- where: Hong Kong, Vietnam, the Philippines, Hawaii. So by the time I arrived, I did not look sincerely glad to be here.

Why do you always tell people that I met your father in the Cathay House, that I broke open a fortune cookie and it said I would marry a dark, handsome stranger, and that when I looked up, there he was, the waiter, your father? Why do you make this joke? This is not sincere. This was not true! Your father was not a waiter, I never ate in that restaurant. The Cathay House had a sign that said "Chi- nese Food," so only Americans went there before it was torn down. Now it is a McDonald's restaurant with a big Chinese sign that says *mai dong lou*—"wheat," "east," "building." All nonsense. Why are you attracted only to Chinese nonsense? You must understand my real circumstances, how I arrived, how I married, how I lost my Chinese face, why you are the way you are.

When I arrived, nobody asked me questions. The authorities looked at my papers and stamped me in. I decided to go first to a San Francisco address given to me by this girl in Peking. The bus put me down on a wide street with cable cars. This was California Street. I walked up this hill and then I saw a tall building. This was Old St. Mary's. Under the church sign, in handwritten Chinese characters, someone had added: "A Chinese Ceremony to Save Ghosts from Spiritual Unrest 7 A.M. and 8:30 A.M." I memorized this information in case the authorities asked me where I worshipped my religion. And then I saw another sign across the street. It was painted on the outside of a short building: "Save Today for Tomorrow, at Bank of America." And I thought to myself, This is where American people worship. See, even then I was not so dumb! Today that church is the same size, but where that short bank used to be, now there is a tall building, fifty stories high, where you and your husband-to-be work and look down on everybody.

My daughter laughed when I said this. Her mother can make a good joke.

So I kept walking up this hill. I saw two pagodas, one on each side of the street, as though they were the entrance to a great Buddha temple. But when I looked carefully, I saw the pagoda was really just a building topped with stacks of tile roofs, no walls, nothing else under its head. I was surprised how they tried to make everything look like an old imperial city or an emperor's tomb. But if you looked on either side of these pretend pagodas, you could see the streets became narrow and crowded, dark, and dirty. I thought to myself, Why did they choose only the worst Chinese parts for the inside? Why didn't they build gardens and ponds instead? Oh, here and there was the look of a famous ancient cave or a Chinese opera. But inside it was always the same cheap stuff.

So by the time I found the address the girl in Peking gave me, I knew not to expect too much. The address was a large green building, so noisy, children running up and down the outside stairs and hallways. Inside number 402, I found an old woman who told me right away she had wasted her time waiting for me all week. She quickly wrote down some addresses and gave them to me, keeping her hand out after I took the paper. So I gave her an American dollar and she looked at it and said, *"Syaujye"*—Miss—"we are in America now. Even a beggar can starve on this dollar." So I gave her another dollar and she said, "Aii, you think it is so easy getting this information?" So I gave her another and she closed her hand and her mouth.

With the addresses this old woman gave me, I found a cheap apartment on Washington Street. It was like all the other places, sitting on top of a little store. And through this three-dollar list, I found a terrible job paying me seventy-five cents an hour. Oh, I tried to get a job as a salesgirl, but you had to know English for that. I tried for another job as a Chinese hostess, but they also wanted me to rub my hands up and down foreign men, and I knew right away this was as bad as fourth-class prostitutes in China! So I rubbed that address out with black ink. And some of the other jobs required you to have a special relationship. They were jobs held by families from Canton and Toishan and the Four Districts, southern people who had come many years ago to make their fortune and were still holding on to them with the hands of their great-grandchildren.

So my mother was right about my hardships. This job in the cookie factory was one of the worst. Big black machines worked all day and night pouring little pancakes onto moving round griddles. The other women and I sat on high stools, and as the little pancakes went by, we had to grab them off the hot griddle just as they turned golden. We would put a strip of paper in the center, then fold the cookie in half and bend its arms back just as it turned hard. If you grabbed the pancake too soon, you would burn your fingers on the hot, wet dough. But if you grabbed too late, the cookie would harden before you could even complete the first bend. And then you had to throw these mistakes in a barrel, which counted against you because the owner could sell those only as scraps.

After the first day, I suffered ten red fingers. This was not a job for a stupid person. You had to learn fast or your fingers would turn into fried sausages. So the next day only my eyes burned, from never taking them off the pancakes. And the day after that, my arms ached from holding them out ready to catch the pancakes at just the right moment. But by the end of my first week, it became mindless work and I could relax enough to notice who else was working on each side of me. One was an older woman who never smiled and spoke to herself in Cantonese when she was angry. She talked like a crazy person. On my other side was a woman around my age. Her barrel contained very few mistakes. But I suspected she ate them. She was quite plump.

"Eh, *Syaujye*," she called to me over the loud noise of the machines. I was grateful to hear her voice, to discover we both spoke Mandarin, although her dialect was coarse-sounding. "Did you ever think you would be so powerful you could determine someone else's fortune?" she asked.

I didn't understand what she meant. So she picked up one of the strips of paper and read it aloud, first in English: "Do not fight and air your dirty laundry in public. To the victor go the soils." Then she translated in Chinese: "You shouldn't fight and do your laundry at the same time. If you win, your clothes will get dirty."

I still did not know what she meant. So she picked up another one and read in English: "Money is the root of all evil. Look around you and dig deep." And then in Chinese: "Money is a bad influence. You become restless and rob graves."

"What is this nonsense?" I asked her, putting the strips of paper in my pocket, thinking I should study these classical American sayings.

"They are fortunes," she explained. "American people think Chinese people write these sayings."

"But we never say such things!" I said. "These things don't make sense. These are not fortunes, they are bad instructions."

"No, miss," she said, laughing, "it is our bad fortune to be here making these and somebody else's bad fortune to pay to get them."

◆

So that is how I met An-mei Hsu. Yes, yes, Auntie An-mei, now so old-fashioned. An-mei and I still laugh over those bad fortunes and how they later became quite useful in helping me catch a husband.

"Eh, Lindo," An-mei said to me one day at our workplace. "Come to my church this Sunday. My husband has a friend who is looking for a good Chinese wife. He is not a citizen, but I'm sure he knows how to make one." So that is how I first heard about Tin Jong, your father. It was not like my first marriage, where everything was arranged. I had a choice. I could choose to marry your father, or I could choose not to marry him and go back to China.

I knew something was not right when I saw him: He was Cantonese! How could An-mei think I could marry such a person? But she just said: "We are not in China anymore. You don't have to marry the village boy. Here everybody is now from the same village even if they come from different parts of China." See how changed Auntie An-mei is from those old days.

So we were shy at first, your father and I, neither of us able to speak to each other in our Chinese dialects. We went to English class together, speaking to each other in those new words and sometimes taking out a piece of paper to write a Chinese character to show what we meant. At least we had that, a piece of paper to hold us together. But it's hard to tell someone's marriage intentions when you can't say things aloud. All those little signs—the teasing, the bossy, scolding words—that's how you know if it is serious. But we could talk only in the manner of our English teacher. I see cat. I see rat. I see hat.

But I saw soon enough how much your father liked me. He would pretend he was in a Chinese play to show me what he meant. He ran back and forth, jumped up and down, pulling his fingers through his hair, so I knew—*mangjile!*—what a busy, exciting place this Pacific Telephone was, this place where he worked. You didn't know this about your father—that he could be such a good actor? You didn't know your father had so much hair?

Oh, I found out later his job was not the way he described it. It was not so good. Even today, now that I can speak Cantonese to your father, I always ask him why he doesn't find a better situation. But he acts as if we were in those old days, when he couldn't understand anything I said.

Sometimes I wonder why I wanted to catch a marriage with your father. I think An-mei put the thought in my mind. She said, "In the movies, boys and girls are always passing notes in class. That's how they fall into trouble. You need to start trouble to get this man to realize his intentions. Otherwise, you will be an old lady before it comes to his mind."

That evening An-mei and I went to work and searched through strips of fortune cookie papers, trying to find the right instructions to give to your father. An-mei read them aloud, putting aside ones that might work: "Diamonds are a girl's best friend. Don't ever settle for a pal." "If such thoughts are in your head, it's time to be wed." "Confucius say a woman is worth a thousand words. Tell your wife she's used up her total."

We laughed over those. But I knew the right one when I read it. It said: "A house is not home when a spouse is not at home." I did not laugh. I wrapped up this saying in a pancake, bending the cookie with all my heart.

After school the next afternoon, I put my hand in my purse and then made a look as if a mouse had bitten my hand. "What's this?" I cried. Then I pulled out the cookie and handed it to your father. "Eh! So many cookies, just to see them makes me sick. You take this cookie."

I knew even then he had a nature that did not waste anything. He opened the cookie and he crunched it in his mouth, and then read the piece of paper.

"What does it say?" I asked. I tried to act as if it did not matter. And when he still did not speak, I said, "Translate, please."

We were walking in Portsmouth Square and already the fog had blown in and I was very cold in my thin coat. So I hoped your father would hurry and ask me to marry him. But instead, he kept his serious look and said, "I don't know this word 'spouse.' Tonight I will look in my dictionary. Then I can tell you the meaning tomorrow."

The next day he asked me in English, "Lindo, can you spouse me?" And I laughed at him and said he used that word incorrectly. So he came back and made a Confucius joke, that if the words were wrong, then his intentions must also be wrong. We scolded and joked with each other all day long like this, and that is how we decided to get married.

One month later we had a ceremony in the First Chinese Baptist Church, where we met. And nine months later your father and I had our proof of citizenship, a baby boy, your big brother Winston. I named him Winston because I liked the meaning of those two words "wins ton." I wanted to raise a son who would win many things, praise, money, a good life. Back then, I thought to myself, At last I have everything I wanted. I was so happy, I didn't see we were poor. I saw only what we had. How did I know Winston would die later in a car accident? So young! Only sixteen!

Two years after Winston was born, I had your other brother, Vincent. I named him Vincent, which sounds like "win cent," the sound of making money, because I was beginning to think we did not have enough. And then I bumped my nose riding on the bus. Soon after that you were born.

I don't know what caused me to change. Maybe it was my crooked nose that damaged my thinking. Maybe it was seeing you as a baby, how you looked so much like me, and this made me dissatisfied with my life. I wanted everything for you to be better. I wanted you to have the best circumstances, the best character. I didn't want you to regret anything. And that's why I named you Waverly. It was the name of the street we lived on. And I wanted you to think, This is where I belong. But I also knew if I named you after this street, soon you would grow up, leave this place, and take a piece of me with you.

◆

Mr. Rory is brushing my hair. Everything is soft. Everything is black.

"You look great, Ma," says my daughter. "Everyone at the wedding will think you're my sister."

I look at my face in the beauty parlor mirror. I see my reflection. I cannot see my faults, but I know they are there. I gave my daughter these faults. The same eyes, the same cheeks, the same chin. Her character, it came from my circumstances. I look at my daughter and now it is the first time I have seen it.

"Ai-ya! What happened to your nose?"

She looks in the mirror. She sees nothing wrong. "What do you mean? Nothing happened," she says. "It's just the same nose."

"But how did you get it crooked?" I ask. One side of her nose is bending lower, dragging her cheek with it.

"What do you mean?" she asks. "It's your nose. You gave me this nose."

"How can that be? It's drooping. You must get plastic surgery and correct it."

But my daughter has no ears for my words. She puts her smiling face next to my worried one. "Don't be silly. Our nose isn't so bad," she says. "It makes us look devious." She looks pleased.

"What is this word, 'devious'?" I ask.

"It means we're looking one way while following another. We're for one side and also the other. We mean what we say, but our intentions are different."

"People can see this in our face?"

My daughter laughs. "Well, not everything that we're thinking. They just know we're two-faced."

"This is good?"

"This is good if you get what you want."

I think about our two faces. I think about my intentions. Which one is American? Which one is Chinese? Which one is better? If you show one, you must always sacrifice the other.

It is like what happened when I went back to China last year, after I had not been there for almost forty years. I had taken off my fancy jewelry. I did not wear loud colors. I spoke their language. I used their local money. But still, they knew. They knew my face was not one hundred percent Chinese. They still charged me high foreign prices.

So now I think, What did I lose? What did I get back in return? I will ask my daughter what she thinks.

◆◆◆◆◆◆◆

JOYCE THOMPSON

◆━◆

BOAT
PEOPLE

◆◆◆◆◆◆◆

When my mother calls them "boat people," I have to bite my tongue to keep from reminding her her own none-too-distant relations reached American soil by the same means of transport. The stories she likes best to tell feature my Swedish grandmother in her lady phase, straight-spined, her white gloves spotless, every tortoiseshell hairpin in its place beneath a flowered straw hat, at home among the silver-plated splendors of Frederick and Nelson's tearoom when visiting the city, the woman rural neighbors applied to in time of want or sickness, when babies needed assistance entering this world or elders were ready to depart it. About the sixteen-year-old girl who landed all by herself at Ellis Island and somehow made it to Montana with little money and less English, my mother keeps resounding silence, whether from ignorance or through discretion, I do not know.

My mother calls Medicare with a question, hangs up without an answer. She splutters, then shrugs. "I got a boat person."

My mother goes to the neighborhood market, wanting artichoke hearts, and comes home empty-handed. "Boat people," she says.

New graffiti blossoms in black and red on the brick walls of Rainier Valley buildings, spray-paint calligraphy, a chaos of Chinese characters my mother can't understand. She is sure the message is hostile, that the pictographs speak of her, unkindly.

My mother detested Douglas MacArthur and his imperialism; in 1961, she joined the NAACP; she wrote her congressman to protest the bombing of Hanoi. Now lithe bronze teenage boys with stiff black buzz cuts and slanted almond eyes skateboard through her neighborhood. On hot summer nights, throngs of black-haired barefoot children play tag in the dusty blacktop parking lots of cheap two-story apartment buildings, their cries incomprehensible to her, and the local Safeway carries bok choy and ginger root, tofu and wonton wrappers, six different brands of soy sauce.

"Too much," my mother says. "I want to move."

Part of me wants to correct her myopia, part to excuse it. "Most Southeast Asians came by plane," I say, or else remind her that the *Mayflower* was originally a boat and not a fleet of eighteen-wheelers. "We're all immigrants," I say, "except the Indians," realizing even as I do how sanctimonious that sounds. When my mother was born, people lighted their houses with kerosene and cooked with wood, they rode in buggies. Seventy-five years of changes have eclipsed her tolerance for change.

◆

At nineteen, I wanted to be president. I would have fired Henry Kissinger, I would have stopped the war, mandated free, fair public elections in a unified Vietnam, elections I had no doubt that Ho Chi Minh would win. One night in 1968 I flew the red-eye from Seattle to New York. I was the only female on the plane except the stewardesses, the only civilian. The rest of the passengers were soldiers, on the third leg of a drunken journey home. At first a corporal from Vermont sat down beside me but his sergeant ordered him to move and took the seat himself. He was drinking Jack Daniel's, straight. The sergeant was burly and half bald, his tan face seamed with a cheek-long scar. After the third shot of Jack, he pulled a skinning knife from the sheath on his belt and caressed the blade with the callused pad of his thumb.

"Feel this," he said. "Feel how sharp." His voice was deep and hoarse, as damaged as his dried-kelp skin. I pretended to be asleep. He thrust the knife in front of my face, just inches from my nose. "Feel it, I said."

I opened my eyes and told him I didn't want to.

The knife moved closer to my nose. "Feel it."

Being young and righteous, I was more angry than afraid. "I'm not in the army," I said. "I don't take orders."

"You're one of those protesters, aren't you? One of those snot-nose smartass rich kids."

The whites of his eyes were yellow, webbed with red. The irises looked furry at the edges. "Yes," I said.

His fingers were stubby, I remember, fleshed with something that looked tougher than human skin, strong when they bit into my shoulder. The knife approached my throat. He held it steady, two inches from the skin. "I use this knife to scalp gooks," he said. His words came clothed in the commingled smell of alcohol and rotting teeth. "Thirty-seven gooks," he said. "There's something real satisfying in the first cut. It makes a noise, not like anything else you ever heard."

"I wish you'd put your knife away," I said. I spoke slowly, with no inflection.

"You think I'm crazy," the sergeant said. "Don't you?"

When I didn't answer, his fingers tightened on my shoulder. "Don't you?"

"Yes," I said.

He laughed. "You're right. War makes you crazy. Especially war with gooks." Laughed again, a gust of stink. "I love this war."

I knew he was telling the truth. The steel blade of the skinning knife touched my throat, whispered when he flicked it against the skin. How calm I was surprised me. It was my lesson in the difference between fear and terror. "Would you please turn on my reading light?" I asked him. "I want to see your knife."

The request surprised him. He squinted at the overhead panel, and I felt his grip slacken a little on my shoulder.

"The red button," I said.

He hesitated. "You want to see my knife?"

"Please."

With his right hand, he kept the knife poised at my throat, but his left released my shoulder. He used his middle finger to stab the red button. No light came on. He jabbed again.

"It must be broken," I said.

"Tough luck," he said. "Now I'm going to show you how to skin a gook." The sergeant inched forward on his seat, swiveled to face me, so the breath-stench came full strength. His left hand pinned my shoulder to the seat back. The blade edge teased my throat, not breaking skin. We were like that when the stewardess came.

She wasn't much older than I was. I watched her eyes, shocked, then opaque. "You start right under the hairline," he told me. "Sometimes I cut the ears off first. When they dry up, they look like prunes," he said.

"Excuse me, Captain," the stewardess said. She was blond, with a long, high-tied ponytail.

Without releasing me, he looked up at her. "Forget the glasses," he told her. "Just bring the bottle."

"The young lady needs to go to the bathroom," the stewardess said. Her voice was admirably level.

"I'm not done," he said. "I'm teaching her about war."

"I really do need to go to the bathroom," I said. "Bad."

Confusion softened his face, slacking the scar seam. The stewardess said, "Just put your knife away and let her get out of her seat."

The sergeant looked from her to me, from her to me, from her to me. I imagined I could hear the slow grind of his synapses.

"No more drinks for you," the stewardess said, "until you let her go."

"I want the bottle," he said.

"Let her go."

Slowly he lowered the knife.

"Put it away," she said.

Slowly, he did.

"Now let her stand up."

Slowly, his hand retreated from my shoulder.

Slowly, I stood. The stewardess stepped back to let me out into the aisle. My legs had no feeling in them, and I wondered if I remembered how to walk. She gave me a gentle shove, propelling me toward the rear of the airplane. When we got to the galley, we hugged each other. "Thank you," I said. It was as much as I saw of that war.

◆

A new job maps new routes. First day, almost late, I wheel-squeal into the tiny parking lot of a neighborhood market still bravely withstanding the offensive of the namebrand chains. Inside, it does what it can to mimic a 7-Eleven: coffee urn here, slushies and donuts there, sad zap-fried chicken slowly drying in a lighted display case. My mind's already at the office, befriending the secretary, calculating the relative merits of claiming my dependents, all or none, on yet another W-2. The coffee smells promising and is not too translucent in its white cup. I lid it and join the line to pay. If I'm lucky, my new boss will oversleep today.

"Two packs of Merits, please."

They appear on the counter before me. The four bills I push forward return as assorted coins. It's not until I ask for matches, too, please, that I look up. The most evident thing about the woman behind the counter is how much she doesn't want to be there, the second, how beautiful she is. Used but lovely, her skin the color of fine brass lightly tarnished, the eyes surprising, round as olives and as black. They study me closely, taking stock of my hair, my dress, without revealing how they judge. Her lips are full, pouting, and painted siren red. The fingernails match, two broken ones with ragged white edges, the rest perfectly soignée. She wears a silk blouse, narrow stripes of black and dulled gold, cut low for evening, safety-pinned chaste by day.

I thank her for the matches.

A thin worried man in a white shirt appears beside her, scolding in Vietnamese. She does not answer him, but lifts her head until it blooms alert, queenly, on her slim brass stem of neck, and she raises her eyes to mine. A smile both utterly mechanical and wholly charming lifts her red lips from their pout.

"You have nice day now." The syllables taste sour, I can tell; defiance abrades a melodious voice. Beside her, the worrier nags on. Because I have no right to tell him to back off, I hold her gaze, trying to invest particularity in the ritual reply. "Thanks. You, too."

On the freeway, I speed toward work, but my new boss fades into a cartoon shadow. Portland dissolves and with it, twenty years. It is Saigon, a humid night. The bar is dim and blinking neon reddens the resinous haze. Music, raw male guffaws, the sibilant giggles of girls. The woman from the market wears a black silk sheath and the heat of the night polishes her brass skin shiny. The chirp of cracking ice cubes amuses her. Her smile is real.

◆

What did it cost me personally, that war? A couple of friends, pieces of more, boys I drank beer with, kissed on summer nights but never would have married. It was, be honest, a conflict that institutionalized class. Our leaders were willing to sacrifice a quantity of young Americans, but the draft was a winnow. The sons of the successful, the professional, the rich were safe unless they kamikazied out of the safety net themselves.

The friends I lost: a full-blooded Suquamish Indian named Jim, whose father was a commercial fisherman; Ray, who stocked shelves at Thriftway; Bill, who hated school and wanted war—he was a helicopter pilot, re-upped three times himself. Doug lost his hearing in the upper ranges when a bomb went off too close; he dresses like Rambo but holds a steady job. A grenade blew off half of Carl's left leg; he is a college professor now and skis one-legged. Flat feet and good grades kept my cousins home.

When the boy I loved in 1970 drew number nine in the draft lottery, he went out to his father's garage on Sunday afternoon and chainsawed off two fingers. He wanted to be a doctor, so expatriation and jail were not choices. Lacking the manual dexterity to practice surgery, he became a psychiatrist instead.

The war cost me any lingering illusions about American righteousness, but having grown up left, there wasn't much to lose. Protests curtailed my college classes three springs running, so that I'm left with odd gaps in my knowledge of esoteric things, but that was a small price to pay for the self-righteous exhilaration of protesting. It opened a dossier I hope by now is fat and made me wish, for the first and only time in my life, I was a man, so that my choices would be hard and meaningful. I have always believed that I would have gone to jail, but that conviction remains necessarily untested.

The price of dissent, my penance for self-righteousness has been exacted late and in a strange way. I am a writer and teach writing. I do this in the West. Starting ten years ago, the manuscripts began arriving in my life, the stories of the men who went, bad novels, mostly, too poorly structured and crudely written for me to coach or counsel them into public acts, yet each one an absolute necessity, each one, no matter how artless or awkward, an utterly authentic human act. These men find me in community college classes, at writing conferences, sometimes through friends of friends of friends, they give me their nightmares in cardboard boxes.

I never refuse them. Our part of the country is vast, much uninhabited. The ratio of published writers to square western miles overwhelmingly favors the land. If a story finds me, I embrace it. The need to tell is a healthy impulse. Telling can shrive, can save, and story wants an audience. Sometimes I am the only one. I read, every word and every page of every book. I cherish the illusion, before I read, that the definitive novel of my generation's war has just passed into my hands, that it will fall to me to recognize genius and speed it on its way. At the same time, I know it doesn't matter.

Stan came from a big family in a small coastal Oregon town. Geographical placement and his own good grades won him a four-year free ride at Yale and a solid gold exemption from the draft, but it didn't seem right to him that the system should value him above the guys he played football with at Seaside High School. Besides, it was *his* war, and he didn't want to miss it. As soon as he graduated from college, he joined the Marines. In Vietnam, he was a lieutenant. He spent two years in combat, five years writing about it. Except for their names, he and his protagonist are the same man.

This man went to war to test his mettle. He wanted to learn firsthand about adrenaline, about courage and cowardice, to know how men act and what they feel when what's at stake is life. One day, under enemy fire on a mountaintop, his troops were charged with holding, against great odds and to no particular strategic purpose, in his eagerness to be a hero, he shot and killed his best friend. It was an accident of timing, the miscalculation of a few seconds and a few inches, it was a small mistake and a gigantic crime. Stan never told anyone and he never forgave himself until he handed me his thousand-page confession.

Reading Stan's book, I cried. My son, a baby then, was playing on the floor at my feet. I gathered him in my lap and held him close, swore on his soft spot I would die before I let my government send my son to war. Later, when we met to talk, Stan cried. He had needed to cry for a long time.

——◆——

Every day now, I stop at the Thurman Market for my morning coffee and cigarettes. The thin worried man has a thin worried wife. They dress alike in white shirts, black trousers, tennis shoes. My beauty is someone's sister, hers, I think. She has a second silk blouse, white flowers parading on a navy field, which she wears on alternating days. Those times she is out from behind the counter, stacking soup cans on the shelves or rearranging Popsicles, I can see her black stockings with their straight seams, her short straight skirt and high spike heels. The man and his wife are fond of correcting and directing her. She absorbs their criticisms without expression. They expect her to be grateful, I think.

Slowly, my morning visits build familiarity, shrinking her wide

performance smile to one of friendly shyness. She produces my cigarettes, then asks, "Merit, please, they are strong?"

"Medium, I guess. Not the strongest, not the weakest."

"I smoke Merit, too," she tells me.

It becomes a bond between us, thin but durable. One morning
she's alone in the store and looks upset when I come in. She reaches
across the counter to touch my arm with one red nail. "You help me?"

"Sure."

She hands me an open copy of the *National Enquirer*, points to a
picture in the lower left-hand corner of the page. "Please, what is the
matter with her?"

The photograph shows a disheveled blonde, eyes wide with fear
or loathing, face streaked with grime. The caption tells me she is
Leigh Taylor-Hunt, a star of *Knotts Landing*, shown here in her role
as an Australian miner's daughter, in a soon-to-be-released film.

"She's okay. She's an actress, playing a part."

Concern persists, depressing her eyebrows.

"It's a movie. It's pretend. She'll get paid a lot of money for
pretending."

"A movie? Oh." With the oh, her face clears, then brightens.
Nodding, she takes the paper from my hands. "A movie." Now she
laughs, a sound that has the random, happy clarity of wind chimes, or
a small stream rising over small stones.

She is about my age, I think, about forty. I want to know everything that has happened in her life.

◆

My own stories are small, domestic, civilian; their politics is the
politics of the heart. When human hardships were divided up by sex,
women got childbirth, men got war, one cataclysm each. Sometimes,
when my universe seems too small, I make up new worlds, new be-
ings. Writing of war, I would feel illegitimate. Besides, I'm superstitious, half believing the admonition "Beware what you imagine, lest
imagination make it so."

I write as a woman, but I dream of war. I have been in the jungle
so long the flesh of my feet turned soft and gray. My arms and legs
have been covered with leeches and I have seen the work of tigers,
men with their throats ripped open and their bowels spilling out. I
have been in the paddies when the bombs rained down. I know what

it smells like when napalm melts human flesh. I have been ordered to burn villages and to shoot children. I have been so frightened I shat and pissed my pants, so homesick it gnawed like hunger, so angry I thought I would go mad. I have patrolled dark trails on moonless nights, afraid of every sound. I have machine-gunned the wind in the leaves. My radio has crapped out on me. I have waited dying on the bald tops of mountains for the helicopters to come save me. I have screwed black-haired black-eyed Vietnamese teenage whores despite the stories of syphilis and how they keep razor blades deep up inside them. I have smoked the best hash and shot the best heroin. I hate my sergeant and my president. I have knifed old men in the back. I have thought it would never stop raining. I have killed my best friend.

So much horror, so much pain. Perhaps if I were trained as psychiatrist or priest I would know how to hold it lightly, how to touch the flame without burning, but the men who bring me their stories have turned not to counseling nor to religion for absolution, but to art itself. Art arises from life and then transforms it. I am made into a warrior, grieving for my dead comrades, sick with my sins.

The definitive novel of the Vietnam war will most likely be authored by a man who stayed home and studied writing. This seems unfair.

◆

It is a Saturday morning, and my son comes with me to the Thurman Market. He browses the bins of candy, seeking the treat I've promised, thoughtfully examining each box and bar before he finally chooses a grape lollipop. My arms are loaded with weekend needs—paper towels, milk, a loaf of bread. I drop my purchases on the counter and call to my son, "It's time to pay now."

The counter is tall and my son is short. He stands on tiptoe to add his treat to the pile. When my beauty, waiting, sees him there, her whole face blossoms. She points at my son. "Is yours?"

"Yes." I claim him, smiling.

"Mommy," my son says, "I can't see."

I lift him up to sit on the counter and he watches the woman push cash register buttons, tallying our bill.

"How old?" she asks me. "Four?"

My son says, "You're right. I'm four."

The woman reaches out to touch his short gold hair. My son, who has always appreciated beautiful women, beams back at her. He says, "Do you have any little boys?"

"You wait," she tells him, and ducks down behind the counter, retrieves a patent leather purse, takes out a wallet of red leather, from this extracts a battered snapshot. Our three heads almost touching, we study the photograph of a black-haired, big-eyed boy about the same age as mine. "My son," she says. "His father is American."

"Can I play with him sometime?" my own son asks.

The woman tucks the photograph back in its plastic sleeve. "He would be a teenager now," she says. "But he is dead."

My son did not expect this. It takes him a moment to process the information. I know he is reviewing all he knows of death. At last he says, "My grandpa's dead, too. I miss him." He runs the palm of his hand across his close-cropped hair. "What did he die of?" he asks.

"In the war," she says. Her big black eyes take refuge in the numbers on the cash register. "Eight sixty-five, please."

To say I'm sorry is to say nothing. I hand her a ten-dollar bill. The woman counts out my change.

◆

"Strange music, strange writing, strange food," my mother says. "I've lived in this neighborhood for twenty-five years. Now it feels like a foreign country."

My mother blames the boat people. Myself, I don't know whom to blame.

TALKING TO
THE DEAD

W e spoke of her in whispers as Aunty Talking to the Dead, the
half-Hawaiian kahuna lady. But whenever there was a death in
the village, she was the first to be sent for—the priest came
second. For it was she who understood the wholeness of things
—the significance of directions and colors. Prayers to appease the
hungry ghosts. Elixirs for grief. Most times, she'd be out on her front
porch, already waiting—her boy, Clinton, standing behind with her
basket of spells—when the messenger arrived. People said she could
smell a death from clear on the other side of the island, even as the
dying person breathed his last. And if she fixed her eyes on you and
named a day, you were already as good as six feet under.

I went to work as her apprentice when I was eighteen. That was
in '48—the year Clinton graduated from mortician school on the G.I.
Bill. It was the talk for weeks—how he returned to open the Paradise
Mortuary in the very heart of the village and brought the scientific
spirit of free enterprise to the doorstep of the hereafter. I remember
the advertisements for the Grand Opening—promising to modernize
the funeral trade with Lifelike Artistic Techniques and Stringent
Standards of Sanitation. The old woman, who had waited out the war
for her son's return, stoically took his defection in stride and began
looking for someone else to help out with her business.

At the time, I didn't have many prospects—more schooling didn't
interest me, and my mother's attempts at marrying me off inevitably
failed when I stood to shake hands with a prospective bridegroom and
ended up towering a foot above him. "It's bad enough she has the
face of a horse," I heard one of them complain.

My mother dressed me in navy blue, on the theory that dark
colors make everything look smaller: "Yuri, sit down," she'd hiss, tug-

ging at my skirt as the decisive moment approached. I'd nod, sip my tea, smile through the introductions and small talk, till the time came for sealing the bargain with handshakes all around. Then, nothing on earth could keep me from getting to my feet. The go-between finally suggested that I consider taking up a trade. "After all, marriage isn't for everyone," she said. My mother said that that was a fact which remained to be proven, but meanwhile, it wouldn't hurt if I took in sewing or learned to cut hair. I made up my mind to apprentice myself to Aunty Talking to the Dead.

◆

The old woman's house was on the hill behind the village, just off the road to Chicken Fight Camp. She lived in an old plantation worker's bungalow with peeling green and white paint and a large, well-tended garden out front—mostly of flowering bushes and strong-smelling herbs.

"Aren't you a big one," a voice behind me said.

I started, then turned. It was the first time I had ever seen the old woman up close.

"Hello, uh, Mrs., Mrs., Dead," I stammered.

She was little—way under five feet—and wrinkled, and everything about her seemed the same color—her skin, her lips, her dress —everything just a slightly different shade of the same brown-grey, except her hair, which was absolutely white, and her tiny eyes, which glinted like metal. For a minute, those eyes looked me up and down.

"Here," she said finally, thrusting an empty rice sack into my hands. "For collecting salt." And she started down the road to the beach.

◆

In the next few months, we walked every inch of the hills and beaches around the village.

"This is *a'ali'i* to bring sleep—it must be dried in the shade on a hot day." Aunty was always three steps ahead, chanting, while I struggled behind, laden with strips of bark and leafy twigs, my head buzzing with names.

"This is *awa* for every kind of grief, and *uhaloa* with the deep roots—if you are like that, death cannot easily take you." Her voice came from the stones, the trees, and the earth.

"This is where you gather salt to preserve a corpse," I hear her still. "This is where you cut to insert the salt," her words have marked the places on my body, one by one.

◆

That whole first year, not a single day passed when I didn't think of quitting. I tried to figure out a way of moving back home without making it seem like I was admitting anything.

"You know what people are saying, don't you?" my mother said, lifting the lid of the bamboo steamer and setting a tray of freshly steamed meat buns on the already crowded table before me. It was one of my few visits home since my apprenticeship—though I'd never been more than a couple of miles away—and she had stayed up the whole night before, cooking. She'd prepared a canned ham with yellow sweet potatoes, wing beans with pork, sweet and sour mustard cabbage, fresh raw yellow-fin, pickled eggplant, and rice with red beans. I had not seen so much food since the night she'd tried to persuade her younger brother, my Uncle Mongoose, not to volunteer for the army. He'd gone anyway, and on the last day of training, just before he was shipped to Italy, he shot himself in the head when he was cleaning his gun. "I always knew that boy would come to no good," was all Mama said when she heard the news.

"What do you mean you can't eat another bite," she fussed now. "Look at you, nothing but a bag of bones."

I allowed myself to be persuaded to another helping, though I'd lost my appetite.

The truth was, there didn't seem to be much of a future in my apprenticeship. In eleven and a half months, I had memorized most of the minor rituals of mourning and learned to identify a couple of dozen herbs and all their medicinal uses, but I had not seen—much less gotten to practice on—a single honest-to-goodness corpse.

"People live longer these days," Aunty claimed.

But I knew it was because everyone—even from villages across the bay—had begun taking their business to the Paradise Mortuary. The single event which had established Clinton's monopoly once and for all had been the untimely death of old Mrs. Pomadour, the plantation owner's mother-in-law, who'd choked on a fishbone during a fundraising luncheon of the Famine Relief Society. Clinton had been chosen to be in charge of the funeral. He'd taken to wearing three-piece suits—even during the humid Kona season—as a symbol of his new respectability, and had recently been nominated as a Republican candidate to run for the village council.

"So, what are people saying, Mama?" I asked, finally pushing my plate away.

This was the cue she had been waiting for. "They're saying that That Woman has gotten herself a new donkey"; she paused dramatically.

I began remembering things about being in my mother's house. The navy blue dresses. The humiliating weekly tea ceremony lessons at the Buddhist Temple.

"Give up this foolishness," she wheedled. "Mrs. Koyama tells me the Barber Shop Lady is looking for help."

"I think I'll stay right where I am," I said.

My mother drew herself up. "Here, have another meat bun," she said, jabbing one through the center with her serving fork and lifting it onto my plate.

◆

A few weeks later, Aunty and I were called just outside the village to perform a laying-out. It was early afternoon when Sheriff Kanoi came by to tell us that the body of Mustard Hayashi, the eldest of the Hayashi boys, had just been pulled from an irrigation ditch by a team of field workers. He had apparently fallen in the night before, stone drunk, on his way home from Hula Rose's Dance Emporium.

I began hurrying around, assembling Aunty's tools and bottles of potions, and checking that everything was in working order, but the old woman didn't turn a hair; she just sat calmly rocking back and forth and puffing on her skinny, long-stemmed pipe.

"Yuri, you stop that rattling around back there!" she snapped, then turned to the sheriff. "My son Clinton could probably handle this. Why don't you ask him?"

Sheriff Kanoi hesitated. "This looks like a tough case that's going to need some real expertise."

"Mmmm." The old woman stopped rocking. "It's true, it was a bad death," she mused.

"Very bad," the sheriff agreed.

"The spirit is going to require some talking to."

"Besides, the family asked special for you," he said.

No doubt because they didn't have any other choice, I thought. That morning, I'd run into Chinky Malloy, the assistant mortician at the Paradise, so I happened to know that Clinton was at a morticians' conference in the city and wouldn't be back for several days. But I didn't say a word.

◆

Mustard's remains had been laid out on a green Formica table in the kitchen. It was the only room in the house with a door that faced north. Aunty claimed that you should always choose a north-facing room for a laying-out so the spirit could find its way home to the land of the dead without getting lost.

Mustard's mother was leaning over his corpse, wailing, and her husband stood behind her, looking white-faced, and absently patting her on the back. The tiny kitchen was jammed with sobbing, nose-blowing relatives and neighbors. The air was thick with the smells of grief—perspiration, ladies' cologne, last night's cooking, and the faintest whiff of putrefying flesh. Aunty gripped me by the wrist and pushed her way to the front. The air pressed close—like someone's hot, wet breath on my face. My head reeled, and the room broke apart into dots of color. From far away I heard somebody say, "It's Aunty Talking to the Dead."

"Make room, make room," another voice called.

I looked down at Mustard, lying on the table in front of me—his eyes half open in that swollen, purple face. The smell was much stronger close up, and there were flies everywhere.

"We're going to have to get rid of some of this bloat," Aunty said, thrusting a metal object into my hand.

People were leaving the room.

She went around to the other side of the table. "I'll start here," she said. "You work over there. Do just like I told you."

I nodded. This was the long-awaited moment. My moment. But it was already the beginning of the end. My knees buckled and every-thing went dark.

◆

Aunty performed the laying-out alone and never mentioned the episode again. But it was the talk of the village for weeks—how Yuri Shimabukuro, assistant to Aunty Talking to the Dead, passed out under the Hayashis' kitchen table and had to be tended by the grief-stricken mother of the dead boy.

My mother took to catching the bus to the plantation store three villages away whenever she needed to stock up on necessaries. "You're my daughter—how could I *not* be on your side?" was the way she put it, but the air buzzed with her unspoken recriminations. And whenever I went into the village, I was aware of the sly laughter behind my back, and Chinky Malloy smirking at me from behind the shutters of the Paradise Mortuary.

"She's giving the business a bad name," Clinton said, carefully removing his jacket and draping it across the back of the rickety wooden chair. He dusted the seat, looked at his hand with distaste before wiping it off on his handkerchief, then drew up the legs of his trousers, and sat.

Aunty picked up her pipe from the smoking tray next to her rocker and filled the tiny brass bowl from a pouch of Bull Durham. "I'm glad you found time to drop by," she said. "You still going out with that skinny white girl?"

"You mean Marsha?" Clinton sounded defensive. "Sure, I see her sometimes. But I didn't come here to talk about that." He glanced over at where I was sitting on the sofa. "You think we could have some privacy?"

Aunty lit her pipe and puffed. "There's nobody here but us. . . . Yuri's my right hand. Couldn't do without her."

"The Hayashis probably have their own opinion about that."

Aunty waved her hand in dismissal. "There's no pleasing some people. Yuri's just young; she'll learn." She reached over and patted me on the knee, then looked him straight in the face. "Like we all did."

Clinton turned red. "Damn it, Mama! You're making yourself a laughingstock!" His voice became soft, persuasive. "Look, you've worked hard all your life, but now, I've got my business—it'll be a while before I'm really on my feet—but you don't have to do this," he gestured around the room. "I'll help you out. You'll see. I'm only thinking about you."

"About the election to village council, you mean!" I burst out.

Aunty was unperturbed. "You considering going into politics, son?"

"Mama, wake up!" Clinton hollered, like he'd wanted to all along. "The old spirits have had it. We're part of progress now, and the world is going to roll right over us and keep on rolling, unless we get out there and grab our share."

His words rained down like stones, shattering the air around us.

For a long time after he left, Aunty sat in her rocking chair next to the window, rocking and smoking, without saying a word, just rocking and smoking, as the afternoon shadows flickered beneath the trees and turned to night.

Then, she began to sing—quietly, at first, but very sure. She sang the naming chants and the healing chants. She sang the stones, and trees, and stars back into their rightful places. Louder and louder she sang—making whole what had been broken.

◆

Everything changed for me after Clinton's visit. I stopped going into the village and began spending all my time with Aunty Talking to the Dead. I followed her everywhere, carried her loads without complaint, memorized remedies and mixed potions. I wanted to know what *she* knew; I wanted to make what had happened at the Hayashis' go away. Not just in other people's minds. Not just because I'd become a laughingstock, like Clinton said. But because I knew that I *had* to redeem myself for that one thing, or my moment—the single instant of glory for which I had lived my entire life—would be snatched beyond my reach forever.

Meanwhile, there were other layings-out. The kitemaker who hung himself. The crippled boy from Chicken Fight Camp. The Vagrant. The Blindman. The Blindman's dog.

"Do like I told you," Aunty would say before each one. Then, "Give it time," when it was done.

◆

But it was like living the same nightmare over and over—just one look at a body and I was done for. For twenty-five years, people in the village joked about my "indisposition." Last year, when my mother died, her funeral was held at the Paradise Mortuary. I stood outside on the cement walk for a long time, but never made it through the door. Little by little, I had given up hope that my moment would ever arrive.

Then, one week ago, Aunty caught a chill after spending all morning out in the rain, gathering *awa* from the garden. The chill developed into a fever, and for the first time since I'd known her, she took to her bed. I nursed her with the remedies she'd taught me—sweat baths; eucalyptus steam; tea made from *ko'oko'olau*—but the fever worsened. Her breathing became labored, and she grew weaker. My few hours of sleep were filled with bad dreams. In desperation, aware of my betrayal, I finally walked to a house up the road and telephoned for an ambulance.

"I'm sorry, Aunty," I kept saying, as the flashing red light swept across the porch. The attendants had her on a stretcher and were carrying her out the front door.

She reached up and grasped my arm, her grip still strong. "You'll do okay, Yuri," the old woman whispered hoarsely, and squeezed. "Clinton used to get so scared, he messed his pants." She chuckled, then began to cough. One of the attendants put an oxygen mask over her face. "Hush," he said. "There'll be plenty of time for talking later."

◆

The day of Aunty's wake, workmen were repaving the front walk and had blocked off the main entrance to the Paradise Mortuary. They had dug up the old concrete tiles and carted them away. They'd left a mound of gravel on the grass, stacked some bags of concrete next to it, and covered them with black tarps. There was an empty wheelbarrow parked on the other side of the gravel mound. The entire front lawn was roped off and a sign put up which said, "Please use the back entrance. We are making improvements in Paradise. The Management."

My stomach was beginning to play tricks, and I was feeling a little dizzy. The old panic was mingled with an uneasiness which had not left me ever since I had decided to call the ambulance. I kept thinking maybe I shouldn't have called it since she had gone and died anyway. Or maybe I should have called it sooner. I almost turned back, but I thought of what Aunty had told me about Clinton and pressed ahead. Numbly, I followed the two women in front of me through the garden along the side of the building, around to the back.

"So, old Aunty Talking to the Dead has finally passed on," one of them, whom I recognized as the Dancing School Teacher, said. She was with Pearlie Mukai, an old classmate of mine from high school.

Pearlie had gone years ago to live in the city, but still returned to the village to visit her mother.

I was having difficulty seeing—it was getting dark, and my head was spinning so.

"How old do you suppose she was?" Pearlie asked.

"Gosh, even when we were kids it seemed like she was at least a hundred."

" 'The Undead,' my brother used to call her."

Pearlie laughed. "When we misbehaved," the dancing teacher said, "my mother used to threaten to send us to Aunty Talking to the Dead. She'd be giving us the licking of our lives and hollering, 'This is gonna seem like nothing, then!' "

Aunty had been laid out in one of the rooms along the side of the house. The heavy, wine-colored drapes had been drawn across the windows, and all the wall lamps turned very low, so it was darker in the room than it had been outside.

Pearlie and the Dancing School Teacher moved off into the front row. I headed for the back.

There were about thirty of us at the wake, mostly from the old days—those who had grown up on stories about Aunty, or who remembered her from before the Paradise Mortuary.

People were getting up and filing past the casket. For a moment, I felt faint again, but I remembered about Clinton (how self-assured and prosperous he looked standing at the door, accepting condolences!), and I got into line. The Dancing School Teacher and Pearlie slipped in front of me.

I drew nearer and nearer to the casket. I hugged my sweater close. The room was air conditioned and smelled of floor disinfectant and roses. Soft music came from speakers mounted on the walls.

Now there were just four people ahead. Now three. I looked down on the floor, and I thought I would faint.

Then Pearlie Mukai shrieked, "Her eyes!"

People behind me began to murmur.

"What, whose eyes?" the Dancing School Teacher demanded.

Pearlie pointed to the body in the casket.

The Dancing School Teacher peered down and cried, "My God, they're open!"

My heart turned to ice.

"What?" voices behind me were asking. "What about her eyes?"

"She said they're open," someone said.

"Aunty Talking to the Dead's eyes are open," someone else said. Now Clinton was hurrying over.

"That's because she's not dead," still another voice put in.

Clinton looked into the coffin, and his face turned white. He turned quickly around again, and waved to his assistants across the room.

"I've heard about cases like this," someone was saying. "It's because she's looking for someone."

"I've heard that, too! The old woman is trying to tell us something."

I was the only one there who knew. Aunty was talking to *me*. I clasped my hands together, hard, but they wouldn't stop shaking.

People began leaving the line. Others pressed in, trying to get a better look at the body, but a couple of Clinton's assistants had stationed themselves in front of the coffin, preventing anyone from getting too close. They had shut the lid, and Chinky Malloy was directing people out of the room.

"I'd like to take this opportunity to thank you all for coming here this evening," Clinton was saying. "I hope you will join us at the reception down the hall."

◆

While everyone was eating, I stole back into the parlor and quietly—ever so quietly—went up to the casket, lifted the lid, and looked in.

At first, I thought they had switched bodies on me and exchanged Aunty for some powdered and painted old grandmother, all pink and white, in a pink dress, and clutching a white rose to her chest. But the pennies had fallen from her eyes—and there they were. Open. Aunty's eyes staring up at me.

Then I knew. In that instant, I stopped trembling. This was *it*: My moment had arrived. Aunty Talking to the Dead had come awake to bear me witness.

I walked through the deserted front rooms of the mortuary and out the front door. It was night. I got the wheelbarrow, loaded it with one of the tarps covering the bags of cement, and wheeled it back to the room where Aunty was. It squeaked terribly, and I stopped often to make sure no one had heard me. From the back of the building came the clink of glassware and the buzz of voices. I had to work quickly—people would be leaving soon.

But this was the hardest part. Small as she was, it was very hard to lift her out of the coffin. She was horribly heavy, and unyielding as a bag of cement. It seemed like hours, but I finally got her out and wrapped her in the tarp. I loaded her in the tray of the wheelbarrow —most of her, anyway; there was nothing I could do about her feet sticking out the front end. Then, I wheeled her through the silent rooms of the mortuary, down the front lawn, across the village square, and up the road, home.

◆

Now, in the dark, the old woman is singing.

I have washed her with my own hands and worked the salt into the hollows of her body. I have dressed her in white and laid her in flowers.

Aunty, here are the beads you like to wear. Your favorite cakes. A quilt to keep away the chill. Here is *noni* for the heart and *awa* for every kind of grief.

Down the road a dog howls, and the sound of hammering echoes through the still air. "Looks like a burying tomorrow," the sleepers murmur, turning in their warm beds.

I bind the sandals to her feet and put the torch to the pyre.

The sky turns to light. The smoke climbs. Her ashes scatter, filling the wind.

And she sings, she sings, she sings.

≈≈≈≈≈≈≈≈

JAMES WELCH

◆

THE
INDIAN
LAWYER

≈≈≈≈≈≈≈≈

J ack Harwood first heard the sound of urgency—the quiet footsteps on the concrete floor, the hesitation, the silent preparation
—then he heard the click and hum, the blowing, the loud voice on
the loudspeaker rousting the unit. He pulled on his khakis just as
the door banged open. The light flicked on, blinding him for a moment.

"C'mon, Harwood, we haven't got all day."

He could hear the running footsteps on the concrete, no attempt
now to hide the urgency. He heard more doors being opened and the
guards yelling to the inmates inside their houses.

"What time is it?" Harwood padded in his bare feet to the door.

"Just stand there outside the door. You know the drill."

"What are you looking for?" It was too early in the morning to be
a standard toss. He looked down the hall and saw other inmates
standing outside their doors. Beyond, the window at the end of the
corridor was black with night. He heard the guard ripping the blanket
and sheet off his bed.

"Maybe you could tell me what you're looking for—I could tell
you if it's there or not."

"Shut the fuck up, Jack."

The sound of the guard sliding his hands under the mattress
made Jack uncomfortable. Did he have anything in there? They were
looking for contraband—booze, drugs, pornographic Polaroids of
wives or girlfriends, weapons. Jack looked down the hall toward the
guard station. An officer stood on a stepladder, unscrewing a ventila-
tor screen.

"Hey, what's going on, Duds?" Jack peered around the corner.

Dudley was looking at a picture taped above Jack's desk. "She's some looker, Jack. When are you going to straighten up and fly right? Jesus, if I had a squeeze like that I'd be out selling Bibles." Dudley was puffing from his efforts. Like a lot of the guards he was big, his beer belly straining the buttons on the thin white shirt.

"Get me out of here and I'll sell you anything you want."

"Don't talk like that, Jack. It makes you sound like one of these white-collar boys we've got on Lower C."

"What's the problem?"

"Aw, we got word that someone in your cube is packing iron. The source is very reliable, but I'm getting too old for this shit."

"Visitor?"

"That's enough, Jack. Just to answer your next question, if we don't find it your cube is locked down until we do." Dudley brushed past him and entered the next house.

Down the hall Jack saw Peter Quinn standing outside his door with another inmate, a stocky little guy. Mutt and Jeff, their nicknames. Both were wearing Jockey shorts and T-shirts and looking forlorn. They were double-bunked because of the overcrowding of the prison. Jack knew the little guy was being shaken down for his canteen money. It wouldn't be long before the Indians had him sending home for protection money. A couple of years ago Jack might have tried to help him out—but not anymore. Jack didn't need trouble because he had a plan, and that plan did not call for trouble with anyone. Especially the Indians.

Shit. If they were locked down he couldn't call Patti. It had been two weeks since his last call to her. He couldn't tell if he had really made his point. She had sounded like she was terrified for him. He had made it, all right, he had done a good job. Throwing a metal chair against the wall during their last conversation had shaken her up. The unknown. He had become a master of psychology, a real terrorist.

The next step was going to be the hardest and he didn't know if he had the heart for it. If he did, things with Patti would be changed forever, even when he got out. If he didn't, he might wind up dead or broken. He had seen too many guys just give up after a while. They might be rejected for parole or brought back on a parole violation—or they might simply tire of the struggle after their fifth, sixth felony. Jack would rather be out on the streets or dead.

The trouble was, the Indians still thought he had the money. He had made the major mistake of telling Bill Shanley one day in the library that the judge had thrown the book at him because he thought that Harwood had ratholed the nine thousand that nobody could find. He had laughed about it. But when the Indians started bulldogging Shanley, he had told them about Jack and the money. Jack didn't blame Shanley. He might have done the same thing in his place. Besides, Hardass Hartpence had rolled over on him before Shanley. Trouble was, the Indians believed Shanley. The games were serious in the joint.

One morning on the way to the chow hall, two of the biggest—Walker and Old Bull—caught up with him. He glanced at them and his heartbeat fluttered in his throat. They were smiling. Walker, the taller of the two, had short hair and a strong, lean face. He was from Great Falls, part of a family of strong-arm robbers who always had at least one member in prison.

"Hey, Harwood, slow down. We want to talk to you." Walker put a large hand on Jack's shoulder and pressed him close. Jack glanced at the hand and saw a long red welt that ran from the middle knuckle to the bottom of the thumb.

Old Bull stepped to the other side of Jack. He was short and stout. He wore mirrored glasses and a red bandanna around his long hair.

"We were going over to the weight room this afternoon and we wanted to know if you wanted to come along. You're looking a little white, Jack." Walker squeezed him tighter.

Jack knew better than to resist the pressure. "I have to work today. Why don't you come to the library and read a book?"

"You got any good fuck books over there? I'm getting a little horny just holding you, Jack. I ain't nothin', though. You ought to see Leonard there when he gets worked up for some white meat. He gets a little rambunctious, to say the least." Walker laughed and slapped Jack on the side of his head. It wasn't a hard slap, but the fingers were strong and Jack felt it. He glanced at Old Bull but Old Bull stared straight ahead, no expression on his face.

"By the way, we were talking with your pal Shanley the other day. It was quite interesting. It's nice to get to know your fellow students, don't you think?" When Jack didn't answer, Walker laughed and pointed to a building identical to theirs—a concrete block in the shape of an X. There was heavy iron mesh over the windows. "See that unit, Jack? That's for crazies and sex fiends. Lot of old perverts in

there, creeps who roll their shit in little balls, child molesters. That's
the kind of place that is. Then you got your max, your death row—"

"I've been here before."

"That's right! No shit, you been down before. You know how the
game is played. Okay, Harwood, let me see if I've got it right—the
strong preys on the weak, just like in nature. The fish eats the worm,
the eagle eats the fish, I don't know who eats the eagle, but you get
the idea."

They were at the end of the line. Suddenly Old Bull darted
ahead, then turned. Jack had to stop quickly to keep from bumping
into him. As it was, the part in Old Bull's long hair was less than a foot
from Jack's eyes. He smelled after-shave or hair tonic. He could see
his own eyes in the mirrored sunglasses.

"The thing is, Harwood, we know you've got nine thousand buck-
eroos stashed somewhere. We want it." Walker was whispering, his
lips four inches from Jack's ear. "Nothing's going to happen to you
out here. We're going to give you the day to think about it. Then
we're going to come looking for you. No big deal, you just tell us
where it is and you've got our protection for the rest of your stay."

"What if I don't have it?" Jack tried to see through the mirrored
sunglasses. "I don't have it."

Old Bull raised his face and smiled. Three teeth were missing
from the left side of his smile.

"I think Leonard almost wishes you didn't have it." Walker tou-
sled Jack's hair, as though they had been playing. "See you tonight,
Harwood. Try to get some religion before then, okay?"

They beat him up twice after that, once that night and then a
week later. Neither beating was very serious—they didn't crush his
skull or run a broom handle up his ass. They were quick and efficient.
Both Walker and Old Bull had done a lot of boxing and they used
their fists all over Jack's body, never in the face. Jack told them he
didn't have the money. Even after the second beating, as he lay gasping for breath on the bathroom floor, he managed to tell them he had
never had the money, it didn't do any good to beat him up. Walker
knelt down and patted Jack on the cheek; then he and Old Bull
disappeared.

The next day Jack made up his mind to tell the officer at the
library what was going on. It took him a long time to walk across the
yard to the building which housed the library and counselors' offices.
He changed his mind several times during his walk. He tried to imag-

ine what would happen, and it wasn't hard. The officer would ask him if he wanted Administrative Segregation, which was a fancy phrase for Protective Custody, which meant a shift in max. If he took up the offer he would carry a jacket—a pussy, a snitch, a bellycrawler—which would follow him when he returned to population, if he ever could. His escape made it impossible to transfer to one of the letter units on the low side. But he couldn't stay in Close II with the Indians. The beatings would continue. And when he finally convinced them he couldn't produce the money, he'd probably get stuck or get his head caved in with a hunk of pipe—a message to the rest of the population. There were not enough officers to keep the heavy shit from coming in. Already Jack had seen the shanks made out of spoons, forks, angle iron. Walker had shown him his "little tomahawk"—a razor blade embedded in a toothbrush handle. The periodic shakedowns of Close II produced a few weapons but not all. It only took one.

By the time Jack reached the library he was determined to tell the officer on duty what had happened. He could serve out his shift and discharge from max, if necessary. Maybe he could parole out of there. Maybe he could rejoin population in a couple of months and nothing would happen. Maybe a lot of things. But the officer was Beasley, and Jack knew he didn't have a chance. Beasley would ridicule Jack in front of the other inmates and he would be dead for sure. He thought about sending in a kite to talk to one of the counselors that day or getting near the warden or associate warden, but nothing seemed enough. The only way he could get help was by rolling over on Walker and Old Bull and the others and blowing their whole operation. He knew several inmates in the close units who were being bulldogged, beaten, raped. Walker's old lady on the outside was sitting on a ton of money that parents and wives were sending every month to keep their boys safe. Jack could name names and tell the warden and his staff exactly how it worked. He could be the trap, he could spring it and get out. Montana had an agreement with Oregon, Nevada, Minnesota to exchange prisoners. He could get a transfer to another state.

But as Jack looked at Beasley, his heart sank. It could take a month or two to get transferred and even max would not be safe. Besides, they could get him in another state if they wanted—it only took one inmate, one letter, one Beasley to alert the bad boys in another prison. Nobody loves a snitch.

Jack worked his shift that day and nothing happened that night. In fact, nothing happened for two months. Jack healed up. He even took up jogging. He stayed away from the unit as much as possible. He avoided the weight room and the gym. He bought a shank from one of the inmates who was discharging and he slept with it under his mattress just about level with his chest. At night he would practice reaching for it until he became good at grasping it, rolling onto his back, and sticking the air. He knew it wouldn't be enough but he was determined to stick at least one of them before they got him.

Then one late afternoon he was pushing a rolling cart full of books back into the stacks. Putting the books back on the shelves was his last task of the day. He enjoyed it because the library was quiet. The inmates were back in their units or at chow, the yard was quiet, and he could think of any number of things that were always on the back burner. That day he was thinking of the night he and Patti celebrated the news of her first pregnancy with him. It was just like in the movies, a candlelit dinner, the clinking of wineglasses. He looked at her through the burgundy glass and smiled and felt the sharp sting of the shank as it entered his lower back near the kidney. He turned quickly and saw the heavy body of Old Bull disappear around the front of the stacks. He heard the door open, then the slow whoosh of its closing.

He held his handkerchief hard against the sting and felt it get wet, but he made it to the rolling metal gate, and the guard in the sally port who activated the gate saw him fall to his knees.

The blade had nicked the kidney, and he bled a lot. They kept him in the infirmary for nine days while they tried to figure out what to do with him. They couldn't send him back to his unit and there were no prisoners in the other state prisons to be swapped just then. Nevada had one, but he was testifying in a lengthy trial and a deal might be worked out to get him back on the street. The warden told Jack he had cashed in a lot of chips to get Jack down there. For what it was worth, Nevada could fuck itself next time they wanted a favor.

So Jack was sent to max for three months. It wasn't too bad. He read a lot of books, watched some TV. He had an hour each day of yard time and he took up jogging again, although the circles were a little tighter in max. He eventually became the swamper on his unit and he had the cleanest floor on max. Above all, he had peace of mind. There were fewer games—most of the cons stuck by themselves. It was kind of a badge of honor to do your own time, not ask for favors, not run games. The guards were tough but they left you alone if you left them alone. So Jack spent a peaceful three months basically by himself. But he managed to make a couple of friends there, guys who had gotten tired of the cheapshit stuff out in population and had elected to get sent to max and serve their shift there. Both were near the end of their sentences, both had served full sentences, no parole, no sentence review, no good time. One of them, Woody Peters, was a bank robber who took up jogging with Jack. The other, Robert Fitzgerald, was a breed from eastern Washington. He had stabbed a bouncer in the parking lot outside a club in Missoula. They were both about the same age as Jack, middle thirties, and admired him for his education and thought he was a dumbass to spend his life in the joint.

They discharged within a week of each other. Both were going to Helena, Woody Peters to work for his brother-in-law as a drywaller and Fitzgerald to enter a chemical dependency program. He wanted to get straight with the booze but not necessarily give up the life of crime. Peters gave Jack his sister's address and phone number—if he ever needed anything, or wanted to buddy up for some action on the outside—then both were gone. Three weeks later, Jack returned to Close II.

And now here he was, standing in his jeans out in the corridor, his feet freezing on the concrete floor. He had been back nine months and nobody had bothered him. He still watched his back but he was beginning to think that the Indians now believed that he didn't have the money.

Suddenly he heard a loud crash, the sound of broken glass followed by the pop of a small explosion. He heard a guard yell and then three others were running past him. Duds puffed after them. "Get back in your houses! Stay there, goddammit!" He swung a waist chain and bracelets over his head like a calf roper. Jack saw inmates ducking in their haste to get into their houses. Then he was inside and he heard the bolt shoot. The commotion at the far end of the hall was muffled. Jack stood looking out his window into the corridor for several long moments. His feet were no longer cold but his hands were shaking. Then he saw three guards half leading, half carrying Old Bull past his window. Old Bull was in his shorts, trying to keep up, but the ankle bracelets were too short and his feet were dancing and dragging. His face was bloody and his eyes were puffed up, almost closed. It took a moment to register that Jack had never seen him without the mirrored sunglasses, and even in that flash he still hadn't seen Old Bull's eyes.

Jack turned away, then turned back as something else flashed by. It was Duds, his shirttail out and the buttons ripped off the thin shirt. His white belly preceded him. He was holding a revolver by the butt with two fingers, holding it away from his body as if he had a putrid cat by the tail.

Jack walked over to his bed and lay down. He crossed his arms, his hands in each armpit. He stared at the ceiling and watched it lighten as the gray dawn entered his world.

BURIED
POEMS

There is a man in Boulder, Utah, who buries poems in the desert. He is an archaeologist who knows through his profession that eventually his words will be excavated, that although they may not be understood now by his community, at a later date his poetry will be held as an artifact, mulled over by minds that will follow his.

This man is alone, walled in by the wilderness he loves and neighbors who don't understand him. They say he spends too much time with the dead, that his loyalties are to bones, that the land could be better used for the planting of corn than the digging of corpses. They say he talks too little and thinks too much for a town like Boulder.

He has lived among the locals for decades, but he is still an outsider. It is the Anasazi who keep him here. They are his neighbors, the ones who court his imagination. It is their echoes reverberating through the canyons that hold him.

He listens and he studies. He pores over the artifacts that come into the museum where he works. When no one is around, he pulls out his glasses, slips on his white cotton gloves, and carefully turns the objects over and over as though some wisdom might speak to him from a sandal or basket or cradle board.

Occasionally, a local or two drop in. He invites them outdoors and encourages them to sit between sage. He takes his hand and sweeps it across the valley and tells them this site was once occupied by over two hundred individuals, continuously from A.D. 1050 to 1200, that this is twice the population living in Boulder today. He tells them the Anasazi were born farmers, and hunters and gatherers—planting beans, squash, and corn as they supplemented their diet with big game and rodents. He tries to convince them that the Anasazi, through their technology of manos, metates, pinched pots, and atlatls, were remarkable people well adapted to an inhospitable environment. And then he stops himself, realizing how carried away he has become. He lets the visitors wander among the ruins.

On another day, some neighbors ask, "Are you finding anything good out there?"

"It's all good," the archaeologist replies, "corn cobs, charcoal, and chipping debris. . . ."

The neighbors are unimpressed. He gives in.

"But one time, we were excavating in a particular site and uncovered three ollas—corrugated vessels used for carrying water. Next to these pots were two large balls of clay that had been kneaded. You could still see palm marks from the anonymous hands that had made them. Beneath the pots and clay balls was a burial, the delicate placement of female bones."

He pauses as he rubs his hand over the soil. "I honestly believe she was a potter. We have found no reference to anything like it in the literature. It is most unusual."

The locals look at him, puzzled, and shake their heads. It doesn't register. He sees it in their eyes. They ask him for evidence and he says they buried it for another generation to uncover. They look at the dry land and they look at him, and they walk away.

The man leaves the museum for the day, locks the door behind him, and retreats to his spot in the rocks. He pulls out his pencil and spiral notebook from a front pocket of his cowboy shirt and begins writing. Poems come to him like wild horses to water. He writes a few lines, tears the paper, and burns the edges with his lighter. He writes another verse, tears it from his notebook, antiques it with fire, and places it in a pile that he holds down with his boot. By the end of the afternoon, he has a dozen or more poems. On his way home, he buries them.

The man knows the ways of these people. They ranch and they farm. They know the contours of the land, and if a white triangle of paper is sprouting where corn should be, they'll pull it up. Or if the cows are out grazing and happen to kick a sheet of paper into the air, it'll get read by the wranglers. And when women are planting borders of zinnias around their homes and uncover a poem with their trowel, they'll call their neighbors just to pass the words along.

Which is exactly what happened. Within a matter of days, the whole town of Boulder was reading each other poetry.

Some think they are love poems written by an Indian. Others guess they are clues to a buried treasure left by John Wesley Powell or Father Escalante. And still others believe they are personal messages left especially for them by a deceased family member, which is how they became known as "the ghost poems."

The archaeologist listens. He walks about town with his hands in his pockets. People are talking across fences, over melon stands, and inside their automobiles. Some individuals are even offering to buy them from their friends. But the finders of the poems won't sell. The man who buries the poems quietly slips into the convenience store and buys another notebook and lighter and returns to his place in the rocks.

His poems become shorter, more cryptic, until, finally, they are a series of pictographs—the pictographs found in Calf Creek Canyon, Coyote Gulch and Mimi's Grotto.

The town eventually seeks him out, asking if he knows what these picture poems might mean. He refers them to different canyons, invites them to his slide shows, and tells them stories about the Anasazi who once lived where they do now. He explains how these drawings on canyon walls are a reflection of Anasazi culture, of rituals, and all that mattered in their lives. Now, he tells them, we can only speculate. The townsfolk are listening. He sees it in their eyes.

A local hands him a poem and says, "Read this. My boy found it buried near the overhang behind our ranch."

The archaeologist reads the poem out loud.

SOUNDS

The ruin clings to the cliff
Under the arching sandstone.
It is quiet now.
No longer do you hear the laughter,
The everyday sounds:
Women making pottery—the slap, slap of clay,
People cooking,
Men returning from the hunt,
The builders,
Children playing,
The cries of sorrow when a loved one passes on.
They are gone now—
The Anasazi.

The survivors.
The adaptors.
The only sounds now
Are those of the wind
The raucous sound of the raven, and
The descending sound of the canyon wren.
The guardians.

Poem by Larry Davis, an archaeologist in Boulder, Utah.

By now, the town of Boulder has hundreds of these poems in its possession. They hang in the schoolhouse, where the children are taking up the mystery. The community still wonders who is responsible for these writings, questioning just how long they will continue to be found. But poems keep appearing in the strangest places: in milk cans, on tractor seats, church pews, and irrigation ditches. And rumor has it, the canyons are filled with them. It just may be that the man who buries poems in the desert has turned the whole damned town into archaeologists. The next thing we'll hear is that the locals want to preserve the wilderness for its poetry.

AUTHOR BIOGRAPHIES

Kathleen Alcalá

Kathleen Alcalá is a Seattle writer and editor, with degrees from Stanford and the University of Washington. She is assistant editor of *The Seattle Review,* and was guest editor of a special *Science Fiction* issue in 1986 and of a multicultural *Science Fiction* issue in 1990. She edited the "Diverse Views" feature for the Seattle Arts Commission newsletter in 1990. She is coeditor of the multicultural magazine *The Raven Chronicles,* a 1991 Bumbershoot Bookfair award winner. Her collection of short stories, *Mrs. Vargas and the Dead Naturalist,* was published by Calyx Books in 1992.

Rudolfo A. Anaya

Rudolfo A. Anaya lives in New Mexico and is a professor of English at the University of New Mexico. He received his bachelor's and master's degrees in literature from the University of New Mexico. His fiction and nonfiction have been published in numerous books, journals, and anthologies. He has been awarded a Rockefeller Foundation Residency in Bellagio, Italy, and a fellowship from the National Endowment for the Arts. He has been named New Mexico Eminent Scholar, has received an Honorary Doctorate of Humane Letters from Marycrest College in Iowa, and was awarded the Premio Quinto Sol, a national literary award, for his novel *Bless Me Ultima.* He is currently working on another novel.

Rick Bass

Rick Bass lives in northern Montana. He has recently published *Winter: Notes from Montana, The Watch,* and *The Ninenile Wolves,* Clark City Press. He is now working on a novel, *Where the Sea Used to Be.*

Mary Clearman Blew

Mary Clearman Blew grew up on a ranch in Montana on the site of her great-grandfather's homestead. She attended the University of Montana and received her Ph.D. in English literature at the University of Missouri. She now teaches fiction writing and Renaissance literature at Lewis-Clark State College in Idaho. Her short fiction has appeared in *The North American Review* and *The Georgia Review* and has been anthologized in the *O. Henry Prize Collection* and *Best American Short Stories.* She has published two collections of short fiction, *Lambing Out* and *Runaway.* Her collection of essays, *All But the Waltz,* has just been released by Viking Press.

Ron Carlson

Ron Carlson lives in Arizona, where he is director of the creative writing program at Arizona State University. He is the author of a collection of short stories, *The News of the World,* and of two novels, *Betrayed by F. Scott Fitzgerald* and *Truants.* He has written for various publications, including *Playboy, The New Yorker, Harper's,* and *The New York Times.* His stories appear in several anthologies, such as *Sudden Fiction, Best of the West,* and *Best American Stories 1987.* His monologues have been produced by several companies, and he was awarded a National Endowment for the Arts fellowship in fiction in 1985. His collection of short stories, *Plan B,* was published by W. W. Norton in 1992.

Rick DeMarinis

Rick DeMarinis teaches creative writing at the University of Texas, El Paso. He is the author of six novels, including *The Year of the Zinc Penny,* cited by *The New York Times Book Review* as a notable work of fiction of 1989, as well as two story collections, including *Under the Wheat,* winner of the Drue Heinz Literature Prize. In 1990 he received a Literature Award from the American Academy and Institute of Arts and Letters. His stories have appeared in *Harper's Magazine, Antaeas, Story,* and many other periodicals.

Ivan Doig

Ivan Doig was born in Montana and grew up along the Rocky Mountain front, which is the setting for his trilogy of novels, *Dancing at the Rascal Fair, English Creek,* and *Ride With Me, Mariah Montana.* His memoir, *This House of Sky,* was a finalist for the National Book Award. Five of his books have been read on "The Radio Reader" on National Public Radio; his nonfiction book *Winter Brothers* was adapted for television by KCTS/Seattle; and his novel *The Sea Runners* has been bought by a film company.

David James Duncan

David James Duncan, a lifelong Oregon resident, is the author of two novels, *The River Why* and *The Brothers K.* He lives in Portland with his wife, the sculptor Adrian Arleo, and their family.

Percival Everett

Percival Everett, a professor of English at the University of Notre Dame, lives in both Indiana and Colorado. He has taught at the University of Kentucky and in the Department of American Studies at the University of Wyoming. He is the author of five novels, a collection of short stories, and a children's book. He has served on the National Endowment for the Arts fiction panel and as a judge for the Pen/Faulkner Award.

Richard Ford

Richard Ford lives in both Montana and the South. He has written many essays, four novels, and a book of short stories. He wrote the screenplay for the movie "Bright Angel," which was released in summer 1991.

Tess Gallagher

Tess Gallagher lives in Washington State and has recently published two new books of poetry, *Moon Crossing Bridge* with Graywolf Press and *Portable Kisses* with Capra Press. Her work has appeared in *The New Yorker, American Poetry Review, The Atlantic,* and *The Paris Review.* Her first collection of short stories is *The Lover of Horses.* She has written introductions for a book of photographs from Scribner's entitled *Carver Country* on her late husband Raymond Carver's work as well as an introduction to the uncollected works of Raymond Carver, Volumes I and II. She is currently at work on a novel.

Molly Gloss

Molly Gloss is a fourth-generation Oregonian and has been a teacher, freight clerk, housewife, and full-time writer. She is the author of *Outside the Gates,* a fantasy novel for young adults, and of numerous short stories that have been published in *Calyx, Northwest, The Magazine of Fantasy and Science Fiction,* and *Isaac Asimov's Science Fiction.* Her most recent novel, *The Jump-off Creek,* is the winner of the 1989 Pacific Northwest Booksellers Award and the winner of the 1990 H. L. Davis Book Award for Fiction. She currently is at work on a novel.

Ron Hansen

Ron Hansen lives in California, where he is an associate professor and director of the creative writing program at the University of California, Santa Cruz. His works include the novels *Desperadoes, The Assassination of Jesse James by the Coward Robert Ford,* and *Mariette in Ecstasy,* as well as a short story collection, *Nebraska,* for which he received the 1989 Award for Literature from the American Academy and Institute of Arts and Letters.

Linda Hogan

Linda Hogan lives in Colorado and is an associate professor at the University of Colorado. She is a novelist, essayist, and the author of several books of poetry and a collection of short fiction. Her book

Seeing Through the Sun received an American Book Award from The Before Columbus Foundation. Her most recent book, *Mean Spirit,* was published by Atheneum. She is the recipient of a National Endowment for the Arts grant, a Minnesota Arts Board grant, and a Colorado Writer's fellowship, as well as the Five Civilized Tribes Museum playwriting award. She has served on the National Endowment for the Arts poetry panel for two years and is involved as a volunteer in wildlife rehabilitation.

James D. Houston

James D. Houston lives with his wife, Jeanne Wakatsuki Houston, in California, where he is a visiting professor in literature at the University of California. He is the author of five novels, including *Gig, Love Life,* and *Continental Drift,* the last of which was completed with a grant from the National Endowment for the Arts. Among his nonfiction works is *Californians: Searching for the Golden State,* which received an American Book Award from The Before Columbus Foundation. His shorter works have appeared in *The New Yorker, The New York Times, Rolling Stone,* and *Best of the West.*

Jeanne Wakatsuki Houston

Jeanne Wakatsuki Houston lives in California with her husband, James D. Houston. She is the coauthor of the book and screenplay *Farewell to Manzanar,* which is based upon her family's experience during and after the Second World War internment of Japanese Americans in California. She has a degree from San Jose State University and has pursued graduate work at San Francisco State University and The Sorbonne. She has received the Wonder Woman Award, honoring women over 40 who have made outstanding achievements in "the pursuit of truth and positive social change." She received a U.S.-Japan creative arts exchange fellowship to spend six months in Japan to complete her first novel.

Lawson Fusao Inada

Lawson Fusao Inada lives in Oregon. He has taught in universities for twenty-five years and is now a professor of English at Southern Oregon State College. He is the author of *Before the War,* the first volume of poetry by an Asian American to be published by a major American publisher. He is also the editor of *AIIIEEEEE!*, published by Doubleday, and *The Big AIIIEEEEE!*, published by New American Library. His work has appeared in various anthologies and was the subject of the documentary film "I Told You So," sponsored by the U.S. Department of Education. In 1980, he was invited to read at the White House for "A Salute to Poetry and American Poets." He has received two creative writing fellowships from the National Endowment for the Arts, has served on its literature panel, and is the former chairperson of the Coordinating Council of Literary Magazines. He is currently serving on the National Council of Teachers Commission on Racism and Bias in Education.

Karen Karbo

Karen Karbo lives in Oregon and is the author of two novels, *The Diamond Lane* and *Trespassers Welcome Here*, for which she received the General Electric Younger Writers Award. Her short stories and journalism have appeared in *Esquire*, *The Village Voice Literary Supplement*, *The Massachusetts Review*, *Zyzzyva*, and *Other Voices*.

John Keeble

John Keeble lives in Washington State. Educated at the University of Redlands, the University of Iowa, and at Brown University, he has taught at Grinnell College and Eastern Washington College. He is the author of five books, including the novels *Yellowfish* and *Broken Ground* and a work of nonfiction, *Out of the Channel: The Exxon Valdez Oil Spill in Prince William Sound*, published by HarperCollins. He has been a writer for a public television documentary on Raymond Carver and was the recipient of a Guggenheim fellowship. He is now at work on book projects in fiction and nonfiction.

Barbara Kingsolver

Barbara Kingsolver lives in Arizona. She is the author of *Homeland and Other Stories*, *The Bean Trees*, and *Animal Dreams*. Her poetry and fiction have been published widely in anthologies and journals, including *Redbook* and *The Virginia Quarterly Review*. She has contributed articles and reviews to *The New York Times* and many other publications.

William Kittredge

William Kittedge grew up in Oregon and now lives in Montana. He studied at the Writers Workshop at the University of Iowa and is now a professor of English and creative writing at the University of Montana. He has been published in magazines such as *The Atlantic, Harper's Magazine,* and *The Paris Review.* The author of numerous Western novels and a collection of short fiction, he has held a Stegner fellowship at Stanford, received two writing fellowships from the National Endowment for the Arts, and two Pacific Northwest Booksellers Awards for Excellence. He was the cowinner of the Montana Committee for the Humanities Award for Humanist of the Year and the winner of the Montana Governor's Award for the Arts. His memoir, *A Hole in the Sky,* was published by Knopf in 1992.

David Kranes

David Kranes lives in Utah and teaches in the creative writing program at the University of Utah. He has written five novels and many short stories and plays, including radio plays for production both in the United States and Europe. He is the artistic director of the Playwrights Lab at Robert Redford's Sundance Institute.

Alex Kuo

Alex Kuo lives in Idaho. His fiction has most recently appeared in *Blue Mesa Review, Caliban, Chicago Review, New Orleans Review,* and *The Redneck Review of Literature.* His most recent book is *Changing the River,* a collection of poems. A recipient of a National Endowment for the Arts fiction fellowship, he went to China in 1991– 1992 as a Fulbright Scholar, where in four winter months he completed the novels *Cold War* and *Point Blank.*

Ursula K. LeGuin

Ursula K. LeGuin lives in Oregon. She has degrees from Radcliffe College and Columbia University. She has written numerous novels for both adults and children, over sixty short stories, poetry, criticism, and screenplays. In 1991 she was honored by the American Academy and Institute of Arts and Letters with the Harold D. Vursell Memorial Award. Her short story collection *Searoad: Chronicles of Klatsand* received the Oregon Institute of Literary Arts Fiction Award in 1992.

Craig Lesley

Craig Lesley lives in Oregon with his wife, Katheryn Stavrakis. He is the author of two novels, *Winterkill* and *River Song*, and the editor of *Talking Leaves: Contemporary Native American Short Stories*. He has received the Western Writers of America Golden Spur Award for Best Novel of the Year, the Medicine Pipe Bearer's Award for Best First Novel, and two Pacific Northwest Bookseller's Association awards. His short stories have appeared in publications such as *Massachusetts Review, Northwest Review,* and *Seattle Review.* He has been the recipient of a National Endowment for the Arts fellowship as well as two National Endowment for the Humanities fellowships to study Native American literature. He has been fiction editor of *Writers' Forum* for the eight past years and has taught English and creative writing at the college level for fifteen years.

Barry Lopez

Barry Lopez lives in Oregon. His books include *Arctic Dreams,* which received the National Book Award; *Of Wolves and Men;* a collection of essays, *Crossing Open Ground;* and *Crow and Weasel,* an illustrated fable. His essays and short stories often appear in *Harper's Magazine* and *The North American Review.* He is a recipient of the Award in Literature from the American Academy and Institute of Arts and Letters, the Lannan Foundation Award in Nonfiction, and other honors. He is at work on a book about geography, for which he has been traveling worldwide.

Colleen McElroy

Colleen McElroy lives in Washington State, where she is a professor of English at the University of Washington. She has written six books of poetry, a textbook on speech and language development, and two collections of short stories, and she has written for stage and television. Her two latest books are *Driving Under the Cardboard Pines* and *What Madness Brought Me Here: New and Selected Poems.* Winner of The Before Columbus American Book Award, she also has received two creative writing fellowships from the National Endowment for the Arts, a Fulbright creative writing fellowship, and a Rockefeller fellowship to Bellagio, Italy. Her work has been translated into Russian, Italian, German, Malay, and Serbo-Croatian.

Valerie Miner

Valerie Miner is from Arizona. She is associate professor of English at the University of Minnesota, Twin Cities. She is the author of six books of fiction about the lives of western Americans. Her latest book is *Rumors From the Caldron: Selected Essays, Review and Reportage,* published by the University of Michigan Press.

John Rember

John Rember lives in Idaho. He is the author of *Coyote in the Mountains.*

Greg Sarris

Greg Sarris lives in California, where he is an assistant professor of English at UCLA. His articles and essays have appeared in numerous journals and magazines, including *MELUS, College English, National Women's Studies Association Journal, American Indian Quarterly, Studies in American Indian Literature, Decolonizing The Subject: Race and Gender in Women's Autobiography, The Ethnography of Reading,* and *Stanford Magazine.* He is currently completing the story of his life with Pomo basketweaver and medicine woman Mabel McKay in a book entitled *Prayer Basket.* He received his Ph.D. in modern thought and literature from Stanford University.

Carolyn See

Carolyn See lives in California, where she is a professor of English at UCLA and a book reviewer for *The Los Angeles Times.* She has written numerous works of nonfiction and fiction, including the novel *Making History.* She has received a grant from the National Endowment for the Arts, a Bread and Roses award, and a Guggenheim fellowship in fiction.

Charlotte Watson Sherman

Charlotte Watson Sherman lives in Washington State. She is the author of the short story collection *Killing Color* and the novel *One Dark Body.* She has received the King County Arts Commission Publication Award and the Great Lakes College Association Award.

Annick Smith

Annick Smith lives in Montana and is a freelance writer and filmmaker. She was coeditor of *The Last Best Place: A Montana Anthology.* Her stories have appeared in numerous journals, including *Outside, Story, Modern Maturity,* and *Travel and Leisure.* She was executive producer of the prize-winning film *Heartland* and an associate producer of *A River Runs Through It.*

Tom Spanbauer

Tom Spanbauer lives in Oregon. He is the author of two novels, *Faraway Places* and *The Man Who Fell in Love with the Moon.* His work has received national acclaim and a Pacific Northwest Booksellers Association Award.

Katheryn Stavrakis

Katheryn Stavrakis lives in Oregon with her husband, Craig Lesley. She received her M.F.A. in creative writing at the University of Massachusetts, where she also received a Harvey Swados Award. Her short fiction has appeared in many literary magazines, including *Writers' Forum* and *Grover.* Of Russian and Greek extraction, she is a first-generation American and specializes in teaching English as a second language and in teaching creative writing. She currently is completing a novel.

Robert Stubblefield

Robert Stubblefield lives in Oregon. He is pursuing his master's degree in creative writing. He was the recipient of a Fishtrap fellowship in 1991. He recently had his work published in *Rhapsody* and *Left Bank #1,* and currently is working on a collection of short fiction.

Elizabeth Tallent

Elizabeth Tallent lives in California. She is the author of the novel *Museum Pieces* and the story collections *In Constant Flight* and *Time with Children.* Her stories have appeared in *The New Yorker* and numerous anthologies.

Amy Tan

Amy Tan lives in California, where she is working on her third novel, *The Year of No Flood.* She received degrees in English and linguistics from San Jose State University and her master's in linguistics from UC Santa Cruz and UC Berkeley. Her first novel, *The Joy Luck Club,* received the Bay Area Book Reviewers' award for fiction and the Commonwealth Club Gold Award and is being made into a television and film screenplay. Her stories have appeared in *The Atlantic, Grand Street, Lear's,* and other magazines. Her essay "Mother Tongue" was published in *Threepenny Review* and was recently selected for the 1991 edition of *Best American Essays.* Her second book, *The Kitchen God's Wife,* was published in 1991, and she has recently completed a children's book, *The Moon Lady.*

Joyce Thompson

Joyce Thompson lives in Washington State. She has published five novels, including *Bones* and *Merry-Go-Round.* An earlier collection of stories, *Thirty-Five Cent Thrills,* was a selection of the Small Press Book Club. In addition to fiction and poetry, she has written several screenplays and is a member of the Writers' Guild of America. She has taught fiction workshops at universities and writing conferences throughout the West and counts several of the region's finest new writers among her former students. She was one of twelve writers invited by the Washington State and Oregon Arts Commissions to pilot Across the River: A Northwest Reading Series. She is currently at work on her sixth novel.

Sylvia A. Watanabe

Sylvia Watanabe lives in Michigan. She is the recipient of a Japanese American Citizens League National Literary Award and a fellowship from the National Endowment for the Arts and was a 1991 O. Henry Award winner. Her work has appeared in various publications.

James Welch

James Welch lives in Montana. He is the author of four novels, *Winter in the Blood, The Death of Jim Loney, Fools Crow,* and *The Indian Lawyer,* as well as the poetry collection *Riding the Earthboy 40. Fools Crow* received *The Los Angeles Times* award for Best Novel.

Terry Tempest Williams

Terry Tempest Williams lives in Utah. She is the naturalist-in-residence at the Utah Museum of Natural History in Salt Lake City. She has written two novels and two children's books. Her first novel, *Pieces of White Shell: A Journey to Navajoland,* received the 1984 Southwest Book Award. Her most recent book is *Refuge.*